10/87

Jim,

Thanks for your interest... This is for when your hands get tired.

Sincerely,

Patrick

BLOOD BROTHERS

Patrick DeVine

EF

THE
ENGLISH
FACTORY

Phoenix, Arizona
1987

Printed in the United States of America.

Cover Design: Michael Sidorak, Tempe, Arizona

ISBN: 0-911349-01-4

Dedication

The author wishes to acknowledge his debt to the many fine men and women with whom he served in the United States military and law enforcement. Their daily commitment of their lives and individual safety insures the protection and continuation of our way of life.

Acknowledgements

The author wishes to acknowledge his sincere appreciation to Susan, Rosemary, Ken, his parents, and especially, Cheryl. Without their assistance and support, this project would never have been completed.

About the Author

Patrick DeVine is a native of Detroit. An honor graduate of Wayne State University, he is a Marine veteran, and a former Detroit Police Officer. After 15 years in law enforcement in metropolitan Detroit, he presently lives and works in Phoenix, Arizona.

Blood Brothers is his first published novel.

Preface

Blood Brothers is a totally fictional account, and all characters and events are either imaginary or based on events in the public record, but viewed through the author's imagination, combined with personal experience of similar events. Any connection between the characters in this book and actual persons, living or dead, is purely coincidental.

The story is set in two primary locations: the battlefields of Vietnam and metropolitan Detroit. Language used in dialogue is based on the author's own military experience and time on Detroit's streets. It has been edited for acceptable usage, wherever possible. To aid readers, a brief glossary is appended at the end of the book, which concentrates on the highly-specialized language and jargon of the two locales.

Considerable effort has been made to be as detailed and authentic as possible. However, the author was required in some areas to sacrifice chronological accuracy and sequences in order to develop a flowing story line and to aid the reader's comprehension.

Patrick DeVine
Phoenix, Arizona

1

March, 1948—August, 1967

MARCH, 1948
DETROIT, MICHIGAN

The cold Winter wind blew a bone-chilling draft through the old flat. Tyrone Hackett turned up the small gas oven and left its door open in an attempt to warm the place. The aged building's system had stopped properly heating the cold-water flats a decade before, and the owner had not spent a dollar since to repair the brick four-story in the center of the city's Black Bottom ghetto.

Tyrone Hackett's common-law wife, Margaret Johnson, was seated on a tattered couch, biting her lip from the labor pains that grew closer and closer.

Tyrone had called a cab, but with the severe snow storm, the dispatcher made no promises. Tyrone went back down the hall to the pay phone and called the Detroit Fire Department for a ride to the city hospital.

Just before Margaret gave birth in the cluttered living room, the Fire Department rescue van arrived. Four gentle, patient firemen helped Margaret deliver her first child. They placed the newborn on Margaret's stomach and wrapped them both against the weather as they placed her on a stretcher. They laughed and congratulated Margaret, Tyrone, and each other for the successful delivery of the baby boy. They had delivered a total of 22 babies among the four veteran firemen. They were all charter members of the department's "Stork Club."

They gently placed Margaret's stretcher in the van and drove her to the hospital.

Tyrone stood in the cold living room and watched the van drive off into the blowing snow. He took a long swallow of whiskey. "Damn", he thought, "I'm a daddy now. I guess I better go out and find me a job."

The city hospital cared for those who could not pay or who had no insurance. Margaret and infant son were admitted. Both were healthy. Margaret named her first born Tyler Lee Johnson. She prayed that Tyrone would decide to marry her now and give their child a proper name with proper parents.

In an upper-middle class suburb on Detroit's Eastside, the late winter storm seemed less threatening. The streets were plowed and the walks shoveled. Grosse Pointe's Bon Secor Hospital faced Cadieux Road, and the maintenance crew worked through the night to keep the emergency entrance clear.

At 4:05 a.m., the first born of Dennis and Maureen Cavanagh arrived on schedule and Sean Dennis Cavanagh was an even eight pounds at birth. Mother and child were doing fine.

The hall, with a viewing window to the nursery, was empty at that hour. Twenty-five-year-old Dennis Cavanagh stood alone, peering through the glass, watching his son for the first time. The child was sleeping peacefully.

Dennis and Maureen Kelly Cavanagh were from proud Irish Catholic families. Generations of both families had been born and raised on Detroit's Eastside and the eastern suburbs. Shortly after Dennis and Maureen were married, Dennis had entered the Marine Corps and fought in two Pacific Island battles during World War II. When he returned from the war, his father helped him start his own auto parts machine shop and plastic parts business. Dennis and Maureen had decided to get a solid financial base before starting a family. His small businesses were successful at once, however, and they were able to start their family sooner than they had expected.

Dennis had purchased a new two-story brick home on Detroit's far Eastside on Nottingham Street. The home was within sight of the Detroit city limits. It was one of Detroit's last undeveloped areas for new growth at the end of the 1940s.

He now leaned against the glass and watched his son, absentmindedly rubbing his left knee. The ache there always seemed worse when the weather was damp. A Japanese rifle bullet had nearly taken off his knee cap at Okinawa.

Dennis realized he was rubbing his knee and stood upright. He considered all that had happened to him since he had been wounded in 1945. In less than three years, he had started a successful business with two small factories. He and Maureen had found a beautiful new home and had purchased a new car. And now, now he could hardly make himself believe he was looking at his own healthy new son.

Dennis crossed himself. He said a private prayer asking God that his son be spared the life and death violence, spared the terror and agony of war and combat. He remembered his own father, who had been a veteran of World War I, telling him that they believed that they had fought the war to end all wars. Surely, after World War II, and the massive new destructive power of the Atom Bomb, the nations would be forced to coexist in peace.

Young Sean Dennis Cavanagh was not born rich, but he did have some of the silver spoon. As the first grandchild, he was showered with gifts and attention from grandparents, aunts, and uncles.

After Sean had been christened, Dennis and Maureen sat in front of the fire. Dennis cautiously held his infant son's frail body in his strong arms. Sean slept soundly in his father's grasp, and Dennis and Maureen talked well into the early morning. They talked of many things. The primary topic was that they would do whatever was necessary to offer their new son every advantage possible to build a happy, successful life.

After Easter, the weather broke and metro-Detroit was treated to its first taste of the promise of Spring. Maureen carefully dressed her new son and gave him his first lengthy encounter with the out-of-doors during a long baby carriage ride up to Morang Street on Nottingham's new sidewalk.

In Detroit's Black Bottom, no one would have described the break in the Winter weather as a promise of Spring. There was little promise of anything positive in the old Detroit ghetto.

Margaret Johnson held her new son close to her chest. Tyler was a good baby. She was thankful the child almost never cried. Tyrone's moods had seemed to worsen after the child had arrived. He drank more and more. He complained about not finding work but often did not get out of bed until afternoon.

Margaret was forced to apply for Aid to Dependent Children in addition to welfare to feed the child. She was a proud young woman, but she would need help until her son was old enough for her to go to work.

Margaret Johnson was not surprised the afternoon she came home and discovered that Tyrone had taken his few things and left without a good-bye. She and her son were alone. She rocked the sleeping child in her arms and stared at the cluttered street below through the dirty, cracked window of her flat.

No promise of Spring for Margaret Johnson that April afternoon. The only hope she held was that she would be able to keep her child fed and keep a roof over his head.

"Poor chil ', ain't got nothin'. I'm sorry, baby, but I's afraid life ain't ever gonna be easy for you. You gonna hafta struggle for anything you get."

SEPTEMBER, 1957
DETROIT, MICHIGAN

The brisk, overcast Saturday afternoon was custom made for a football game. The cool snap in the air mixed with a faint odor of burning leaves.

Dennis Cavanagh sipped at hot chocolate as he sat on the top rung of the bleachers. He rubbed his stiff knee and wished to himself that he had brought a blanket. He was there to watch Sean's first little league football game. He spotted his son wearing number 22, the same as his hero, Bobby Layne. The Cannon Tars played their home games at Cannon Field at Cadieux and East Warren. Dennis smiled to himself. Thirty youngsters dressed in their maroon and gold uniforms and he could still pick out Sean, even without knowing his number.

After the team's warmup, the boys trotted to their bench. Sean spotted his dad and waved. His mother was always supportive, but she had wisely decided that watching her oldest son being knocked all over a football field was not the best way to spend an afternoon. Besides, now there were three more Cavanagh children to care for, and the baby was still too small to take to an outdoor event in the cold of a Michigan Fall afternoon.

Sean was average-sized for nine years old, but football seemed to come naturally for him. His throwing arm was much better than average, and even at nine he seemed to know the team's offense as well as the coach.

They played the Oakwood Blue Jackets, from the city's Westside, and won easily.

After the game, Sean ran to his dad's side. Dennis congratulated him on his performance and the victory. He smiled at the beaming nine year old, now a football veteran. "Well son, since you seem to enjoy this stuff, I suppose we should decide some way to celebrate after the games. I think that a hot fudge sundae at Sanders would be appropriate."

Sean couldn't keep the grin from his face. "That's great, Dad, whatever you think. Did I play alright? Did I do O.K.?"

"You played just fine, Son. I was proud of you. I bet if Bobby Layne had been watching, he'd be proud you were wearing his number."

"You think Mom will come next week?"

"Son, after seeing you get tackled out there today, I'm not certain you'd want your mother here. She's a brave woman, Sean, but I don't think she'd enjoy herself, especially after you were knocked down a time or two. You'd feel pretty silly if she ran out on the field to see if you were alright after every tackle."

"You're right, Dad. No use her going to the trouble to find someone to watch the kids, especially if she'd just come out and worry. Besides, football really is a man's sport."

His father looked down at the little nine year old in full gear, not yet 100 pounds. "Right son, but if you ever say that in front of your mother, make certain you're wearing that helmet."

———————————

Tyler "T.J." Johnson was riding his new bicycle through the neighborhood. He had just received the bike from his step-father. His mother had married an older man when T.J. was three and he now had two half-brothers and a new half-sister. They lived in a small three-bedroom house at the edge of the old Black Bottom area, but still in the midst of the Black ghetto.

T.J.'s step-father still frightened him. He was a huge man who always seemed angry. He struck T.J. and his brothers often, but even at nine years old, T.J. was grateful the man never struck his mother.

T.J.'s step-father, Ben Winston, was 45 and worked as a laborer at a Chrysler plant. Ben was a stern, serious man. He met Margaret Johnson after he returned from several years in the Army. He had considered the Army as a career, but felt as though he had no future. He got out just weeks before the war in South Korea. Ben Winston tried to treat T.J. as one of his own children, but he could never seem to forgive the boy for being another man's son.

Ben was very frustrated. He worked hard at his job. Despite the effort, he could do little more than pay for the aging house in a bad neighborhood and keep the 1954 Ford running so he could get to work.

Ben Winston was a man that would never ask for anything. Ben had a hatred for the white man. He had hated whites before joining the Army in World War II. Nothing in his Army experience helped to dilute that hate. Part of Ben's frustration was that no matter how hard he worked, the white man worked even harder to keep him down. Ben felt the white man kept him and his family in the ghetto, living from payday to payday.

T.J. saw a crowd gathered in front of the local poolhall on Mt. Elliot Street. He rode the bike up to the crowd. He saw a well-dressed young Black man slumped in a huge pool of blood on the sidewalk. He recognized the man as the neighborhood small-time gambler and novice pimp. The blood already had started to flow across the sidewalk and down the littered gutter toward the sewer. Finally someone spoke in the crowd.

"Somebody better call the po-lice. This man gonna die."

The poolhall owner strolled out from the front door of his business.

"I called. Anybody that don't wanna see the po-lice better get. They's on the way."

T.J. decided to ride home at once and tell his mother and step-father what he had seen.

When T.J. reached the alley of his block, he was roughly pulled to a stop by two Black teen-agers. "Say boy, where'd you get this here bike?"

"My step-daddy bought it for me last month."

"Don't lie to me, you little mother fucker. This bike is too nice for a little nigger boy. I bet you stole it from some rich little white boy."

"Naw man, I didn't never steal nothin'. Like I said, my step-daddy done bought this wiff his own money."

"You got any money on you, so we can see you tellin' the truth?"

"Like I tole you, my step-daddy bought it. I ain't got no money."

The larger of the two teens moved closer to T.J. He suddenly punched T.J. squarely in the face with his fist. The blow knocked him off of his bike and onto the sidewalk. "Since this here bike already be stolen, it'll be alright we jus' up an' take it from you."

T.J. attempted to get to his feet. The teen kicked him hard in the groin. Both teens got on T.J.'s bike and rode off laughing. T.J. rolled on the cold sidewalk holding his testicles and gagging.

T.J. never once cried. He limped to his house and let himself in the side door. His step-father had seen him come home on foot. His lip bled freely and he still held his groin.

"Where's your new bicycle?"

"Daddy, two big boys took it from me. They was way older, teen-agers."

The big man backhanded T.J. across his face with his open hand, "White boys do this?"

"No, Daddy, they was colored."

"You jus' let some boys take your brand new bicycle. I spend good money 'cause your mama say you was needing a bike. Then you let some punks take it? Well boy, you won't get another one. I won't buy you another, and that's for certain. Now, get cleaned up and ready for supper. You get blood on your jacket and I'll whip you for true."

Two weeks later, T.J. had another bicycle. His step-father had kept his word, he would never buy him another. T.J. had gone to another neighborhood and stolen an even better bicycle. His step-father never asked where he got the bike. T.J. never offered to tell him.

Even at nine years old, T.J. knew that nothing came his way the easy route. Maybe nothing would be easy, but he would make do. T.J. would be a survivor.

OCTOBER, 1965
DETROIT, MICHIGAN

The Friday afternoon was unseasonably warm for Detroit in mid-October. The sky was cloudless, and the sun had pushed the mercury in excess of 85 degrees in the shade. The high humidity made the air muggy, so it seemed even warmer. The weeks since Labor Day had been cool and wet, and Detroiters had been adjusting to the Fall and preparing for a long Winter. The Indian Summer heat seemed to catch everyone unprepared.

Class "A" high school football was still a major event in metro-Detroit during the 1960s. On Detroit's far Eastside, Denby High School had been a football powerhouse for decades. The school name and football were synonymous. The Denby Tars were 3-0 on the season and well on their way toward another run at the state championship.

That afternoon, they traveled to the small inner-city home field of the Northeastern High School Falcons. Northeastern was a Class "A" school with a nearly all Black student body while Denby was one of the few remainng white public city schools. Although in the same division, Denby had not played Northeastern in several seasons. Each school's season schedule rotated for an attempt to have an even game distribution.

Northeastern's home field was nearly a mile from the school building, hidden in the midst of a residential neighborhood on E. Warren Street, just west of Gratiot Avenue.

The Northeastern Falcons were in gold and green. The 27-member squad was 0-2-1 on the season. Denby was a heavy favorite with everyone but the Northeastern players. Denby was their only game against a white team scheduled for that season. The previous year, they had played a suburban team in a non-league game and beaten them soundly.

The Falcon players were confident of upsetting the famous boys from Denby High. They expected that, like the white suburban boys of the year before, Denby would learn a lesson about how real football was played in the inner-city. What they didn't know was that most of Denby's regular season opponents were inner-city school teams. The Black verbal jive and attempts to intimidate the Denby players would be fruitless.

T.J. was starting defensive at left cornerback. At 17, T.J. was 6'1" and weighed 185 pounds. He was a defensive captain and already had three pass interceptions that season.

T.J. was fast and liked to tackle. He enjoyed football more than basketball because he could vent his frustration with the violence that was a part of the game.

No one from T.J.'s family had ever seen him play during his three varsity seasons. His step-father worked on Friday afternoons, and his mother was occupied watching a house full of brothers and sisters.

T.J. and the Falcons warmed up with pre-game drills. He saw his girl, Shanna, sitting with the few dozen other students who had come to watch their game. Charles Davis, the Falcon's right defensive corner-back began to play catch with T.J.

"We gonna hafta play some heads up football today, Brother. I hear this Denby team is tough. They done a real number on everybody they played so far."

Ben Winston's hate for whites had been easily passed to his serious step-son. T.J. smacked his fist in his open palm.

"We gonna show these honkies how real men plays football. The way we like to stick people, they ain't seen nothing like our defense."

Three city buses rolled into the small park through the open gate. At the sight of the Denby team and student buses, the Falcons began their loud, insulting verbal rap for the benefit of their guests. They suddenly fell silent as 40 perfectly-uniformed players quietly filed from the team bus and began their well-organized warmup drills. Denby's players were trained to ignore an opponent prior to the game. Their navy blue helmets had gold and white stripes and their anchor logo on the sides. Not even the previous season's suburban team "looked" so good. In their dark navy blue football jerseys, the Denby team looked as big as a college team to the Falcon players.

Sean Cavanagh loosened his throwing arm in a passing drill with his receivers. At 17, Sean was 5'11" and weighed 170 pounds. He spent his first two years of varsity football being beaten up all week by the first-string defense and riding the bench on game day. He was Denby's starting quarterback, but not satisfied with his own performance in the first three games. If he was going to lead his team to the city and state championship, his play would have to improve.

A very talented junior quarterback was improving each week, and Sean felt that he could not wait much longer for a big game or he'd spend the rest of his senior year where he had started his high school career, on the bench. The damp heat of the afternoon seemed to cover him like a thick blanket. He was not sharp in pre-game drills, and that did nothing for his already shaken confidence.

Across the field, T.J. felt an anger building inside. In addition to the two bus loads of Denby students, at least 100 or 200 more Denby supporters were arriving at the field by car. It was a Northeastern home game, yet Denby would have several times as many supporters in attendance.

Charles Davis took off his helmet and wiped the sweat from his head with a towel.

"Take a look at them boys. Shit, I never seen a team that big 'cept on the T.V."

"Lookin' don't mean shit, Charles. I bet they is all show and no go. What counts is what they do between the chalk lines, not how pretty or big they are."

Denby's coach, Roger Palmer, briefly discussed the game plan with his quarterback. Palmer was one of the most successful coaches in Detroit's history. He knew his players and how to get the most from each of them. He had an All-State tailback and an All-City fullback and wingback. He knew Sean was capable of much better performance and merely needed the confidence to go with his natural ability and good football sense. With the season in full swing, Palmer intended to concentrate on making Oct. 15 a day Sean would long remember; the day he came of age as a football player and a team leader.

The Denby band struggled through the National Anthem. Sean stood next to Coach Palmer, helmet in hand. He felt the same pressure to turn in a good game as if this were for the championship. Another flat game would be his last as a starter.

He looked across the field at the Northeastern Falcons, standing on the sideline. They glared across the field, hate in their eyes. To beat the white boys from ol' Denby High would make their season, even if they didn't win another game.

To the kids from Denby, football was their school world. All else revolved around their senior season. The games were serious and played with 100 percent of their teen-age emotions. But there was no hate in their hearts for each week's opponents. They came from middle- and working-class, white, ethnic homes. Their prejudice had been taught secondhand at the dinner table. Except for Friday afternoons in the Fall, the boys from Denby had no firsthand contact with their Black counterparts.

It was different for the ghetto kids from Northeastern. They had nearly all been socialized to blame and mistrust white people. The 40-member, well-equipped Denby team and their hundreds of supporters represented everything they recognized as unfair in their world. They had four quarters of football to help them even the score.

Sean could feel their hate. To him it was a game. Very important, but still a game. To the Falcons, it was far more than a game. It was a social statement. In some arena, they could be superior to the white boys if only given the chance to prove it.

Denby won the pre-game toss of the coin and chose to receive. As Coach Palmer encouraged the knot of psyched Denby players, Sean got to one knee, said a brief prayer, and crossed himself.

It was all so natural, so routine. The pre-game activity had been nearly the same in the seasons he had played since he was nine; whistles, refs moving and waving, the crowds cheering, the coach tense and watching the effectiveness of the return specialists. Denby took possession on their own 27. The first running play had been determined on the bus ride. Sean had a last word with Coach Palmer and trotted to the huddle to call the play.

He moved past the Falcon defensive huddle and their chorus of threats and insults. He noticed the hate in the face of number 40, a tall, solid defensive back. He pretended to ignore the verbal barrage. He saw number 40 move from their huddle. "Hey, Number 7. You're dead meat, Honkie. You're mine, Chuck. You'll never finish the game. Your win streak ends right here, today."

The huddle was silent, waiting for Sean's direction.

"O.K. gang, let's keep possession and move down the field. Ram, 'I' right. Gunner power at four. On two, break."

The perfect huddle broke and moved up on the ball like a well trained dance troupe. Sean moved behind the center. He waited for his people to get set. The Falcon defense increased their volume of threats and personal insults. Sean barked out the signals over the verbal abuse. He took the ball and smoothly moved to deliver a perfect hand-off to the deep running back in the "I". The big running back rumbled for 6 yards before the Falcons could bring him down. It was second and 4.

The offensive tackles alternated and brought in plays from Coach Palmer to Sean. The next two plays were passes. Sean was as tight as a cheap watch. He overthrew two open receivers on two consecutive plays. The second overthrow even caused a collective moan from the Denby supporters. As the punting unit came onto the field, Sean trotted to Coach Palmer's side.

"Coach, I know my receivers were in the open. There was no rush, I just screwed up. Sorry."

Coach Palmer grabbed Sean's face mask and pulled him close.

"Cav, these boys don't belong on the same field with our team. You loosen up and play the way I know you can, and it'll be a cakewalk. Now, go sit down and get a drink. We've got a whole ball game ahead of us."

Sean went to the bench and found a plastic water bottle. He really felt the heat, and the squirt of water settled his nervous stomach. The wing back, Jim Potter, mentioned that the flat was open.

Sean spotted his dad near the stands, smiling and giving Sean the thumbs-up sign. He saw his childhood friend, Terri Murphy, with his dad, and wondered why she had decided to come to the game. She attended Grosse Pointe High School and was not known as a football fan. Sean's father had never missed one of his games since '57. Sean hoped he had not come that day, with pretty Terri Murphy, to see him benched.

He had only rinsed his mouth when he saw the Falcon punt returner fumble the ball. Denby recovered at mid-field. Without a word, Sean had his helmet back on and stood next to Coach Palmer, waiting for his play selection.

"Run a Gunner sweep right from a Ram, 100." Sean trotted onto the field. He would rephrase the coach's selection to the correct play call.

The Falcon defensive huddle was in absolute confusion. T.J. struggled to redo his chin strap. He could not remember being hit so hard, so often, so early in a game. While the middle linebacker attempted to call defensive formations, T.J. leaned in to help calm the Falcon defense, "Shit, let's just stay in a 4-3 and hope their Q.B. keeps on choking and throwing the ball away."

The Falcon defense was in position when Denby broke out of their huddle and came out over the ball. The All-State halfback swept right end and picked up almost 7 yards. The Denby huddle formed with precision, and Sean waited for the alternating tackle to deliver the next play from Coach Palmer on the sideline. "Cav, Coach Palmer says same formation, only run the keeper round left end."

Sean called the play by the correct designation and briskly broke the offense from the huddle. He was surprised by the play selection. There were three superior running backs in their back field and two second-string backs that were better runners than Sean. In their three previous games, the coach had never selected a play where Sean was *intended* to run. Sean was not reluctant to carry the ball, but he worried about the motive behind the play selection. He glanced to the bench almost expecting his backup to be warming up his arm. He wasn't. He briefly caught sight of Coach Palmer intently working over a wad of chewing gum and looking from the field to his clipboard.

Denby's big fullback told Sean to follow his block, under his breath, as Sean passed him on the way to the center.

He began to call out the signals over the renewed verbal taunts from the Falcon defense. Sean received the snap and rolled to his left behind the fullback. There was a large opening at the line of scrimmage and Sean sharply cut up field behind the fullback's crushing block on a linebacker. Sean cut to the inside, against the defensive flow, then back to the outside when the defenders reacted. Sean's second directional change gave T.J. and the other defenders the opportunity to overtake the quick Denby quarterback.

At the Falcon 27-yard line, Tyler "T.J." Johnson and Sean Cavanagh were formally and violently acquainted for the first time. T.J. drove his gold helmet into Sean's side, and the two young men slammed to the warm turf in a chorus of curses and grunts.

"How'd you like that stick, White Meat?"

Sean quickly stood and tossed the ball to the nearest referee.

"Hey man, you're scaring me to death. If that was your best shot, you're going to have a long afternoon." Sean's back ached from the rough tackle.

Sean waited for the next play from Coach Palmer, standing near the perfectly-formed huddle.

"Coach says to do the same thing the other way from the opposite formation."

Sean quickly thanked the line and backs for their blocking. He could have driven a truck through the hole they had made for him at the line of scrimmage. The chain markers and down box had been moved into position, and the ref signaled to Sean to resume play. Sean looked back to his coach. He had not changed expression or his position. Sean's backup was still seated on the bench. Sean fought to catch his breath in the muggy afternoon heat. He did not understand the coach's play call. Had he spotted a weakness in the Falcon defense, or did he want to show Sean that it would be easier to throw for yardage, rather than run for it?

Sean stood behind his center, calmly calling signals. The Falcon defensive backs moved back and forth, faking a blitz. T.J. ran at Sean, stopping just short of the line of scrimmage. "Come on chump, come this a way, we waitin' on you. They gonna hafta call you an ambulance."

Sean took the snap and rolled behind his blockers, around the right end. Once past the line of scrimmage, he cut to the outside and made it to the sideline. T.J. shook off a solid down field block and managed to force Sean out of bounds just inside the 10. He had delivered another hard hit.

"How'd you like that one, Honkie? How's it feel to have your bell rung twice in a row?"

"Hey man, you're killing me. I only gained 15 yards on that play."

"Your ass is mine, mother fucker. They gonna hafta carry you off the field before this game is over."

Sean got to his feet and handed the ball to the nearest referee. He started back to his huddle. T.J. was overcome with anger and frustration. As Sean passed, T.J. roughly shoved him off the field of play with both hands. Two referees threw their yellow penalty flags at T.J.

"Half the distance to the goal line. You do that again, young man, and you're out of the game."

T.J. stormed into the defensive huddle. No one spoke to him. Their co-captain was in a rage. They knew T.J. to be an intense player, but they had never seen him as emotional. "That lilly-white pecker-wood, I'm gonna take Number 7's head off. Come on you guys, what's the matter with you all? These guys ain't shit. Let's kick some ass and stick somebody."

Charles Davis rubbed his bruised ribs, "You say these guys ain't shit, man? Are you playin' in the same game we are?"

In the Denby huddle, Sean again thanked his blockers and struggled to catch his breath as they patted his back for the two healthy gains.

At the 5-yard line, everyone in the park figured Coach Palmer would call for Sean to carry it in. Palmer knew the Falcon defense would be after his signal caller. He called a play that looked just like the previous two runs, but instead of keeping the ball, Sean rolled a little deeper and passed to his tight end.

Sean brought his team up on the ball. The Falcons anticipated the run and were poised for a blitz. Sean took the snap and rolled to his right. The Denby blockers picked up most of the blitz, but Sean had to evade one rusher. He set himself briefly and as he threw, the Falcon blitz buried him. The crushing tackle came a second too late for the Falcons. Sean had thrown a perfect pass to his tight end for a touchdown.

T.J. had been part of the rough gang tackle. In the pile of players, T.J. punched Sean in the back with his fist. "How you like that, White Boy?"

Sean pointed to the referee in the end zone, his arms skyward, signaling a touchdown. "How do you like that, buddy?"

"I ain't your mother-fuckin' buddy, Honkie."

Sean's sarcastic grin nearly sent T.J. over the edge. He was pulled back to the huddle by his teammates.

With Denby's regular place-kicker nursing a twisted ankle, they would attempt the conversion the tough way, from the 3-yard line. Coach Palmer expected Northeastern to utilize their goal line defense, and they did. Sean executed a perfect play fake and threw a bullet to his split end, who stood alone in the corner of the end zone. T.J. got to Sean after the throw, but could only push him with a referee standing 5 yards away watching him.

"It's gonna be a long day," T.J. said.

"Man, I don't know what your problem is, but you're going to have to show me much more than what I've seen so far. I've been hearin' a lot, but I haven't seen shit." Sean turned and trotted to his bench. Charles Davis dragged T.J. away from following Sean.

Just minutes into the game, Denby led 7-0. As the Denby offense reached their bench, everyone at the small park that afternoon knew the Denby Tars had only started. Their machine was just beginning to roll, and on that hot Detroit afternoon, it would roll over the Falcons from Northeastern High.

Coach Palmer greeted his offense with words of encouragement, clapping his hands. "Come here, Cav."

Sean trotted over to his coach.

"Good drive, Cav. Get a drink and sit down. I have a feeling that this is your day."

"Thanks Coach. The blocking is great. I think we can run and pass all day on these guys. If we do some play action and misdirection, the only thing to stop the ball carrier will be all the dropped jocks."

"Just protect yourself from the cheap shots. These are tough ghetto kids. I know their coach, Nate Washington. He's a gentleman, but he can't control 22 street kids at the same time. You stay on your toes."

Sean walked to the bench through a barrage of back pounding and hand slaps from teammates. He took a long drink from the plastic water bottle, and spotted his dad and Terri Murphy. He smiled and waved. Maybe Terri brought him the luck of the Irish. Sean had never felt as confident as he did now. He realized why Coach Palmer had called for his running plays. He had seen that Sean was wound up too tight. Build up the confidence, get rid of the jitters. The man sure as hell knew his players, and he knew football.

Denby's defense stopped the Falcons in three downs. Their punt took a good roll, and Denby had the ball back on their own 27-yard line again. The Denby offense then moved down field with play book perfection. Behind excellent protection, Sean completed four passes, and after a mixture of runs, Denby had the ball on the Falcon 15, with a first down.

T.J. was in a painful daze. He was taking a physical beating like nothing he had ever experienced playing football. On every play, he was either belted by a solid downfield block or physically punished when he attempted to tackle the big Denby backs and ends. The fact that all the hits were clean and legal did nothing to ease the discomfort. In his third varsity season, T.J. had never experienced a game as punishing as this.

The fact that his opponents were white, along with the temperature, fed his anger and frustration. His step-father had taught him that even though it was a white man's world, given the chance to be one on one, he would always be superior. T.J., like Ben Winston, set out to prove his superiority at every opportunity. He clenched his fists and yelled at his teammates. It was a white man's world, and now whitey was giving him a beating that could only be matched with what he had received in the tough city streets while growing up.

Sean brought the Denby offense up over the ball. To T.J., Denby's number 7, Sean Cavanaugh, came to represent all that was unfair in his world.

"Pretty little white boy, in his perfect uniform, got the world by the ass," T.J. thought. He intended to make him pay for it that afternoon.

As Sean began to shout the signals, his eyes met T.J.'s hateful glare. "What you lookin' at, Honkie? You better hope yo' mama got your in-surance all paid up."

Sean took the snap and rolled right. T.J.'s responsibility was the second receiver out. Denby's All-City wing back put a move on T.J. that caught him flat footed. He cut hard for the sideline, leaving T.J. 5 yards behind him.

Sean led the receiver perfectly with the pass so he didn't need to break stride. He cut up the field and into the end zone. T.J.'s diving attempt at the receiver was in vain. He didn't even touch him.

T.J. lay face down on the turf for a few seconds. With the heat and frustration, he was afraid he was about to lose control.

Denby lined up for the extra point attempt from the 3-yard line. This time the Falcon's deployed their regular 4-3 defense and spread their defensive backs out, expecting a pass. Sean gave the ball to the fullback, off tackle, and the solid back bulled into the end zone. T.J. had crashed through the line with one purpose, to destroy number 7. He was partially blocked but still managed to knock Sean off his feet. Concealed by the fallen linemen, T.J. punched Sean in the side with his fist. "How you like this, Honkie?"

Sean got to his feet. As a quarterback, he was used to late hits and cheap shots, but this defender seemed obsessed. Sean was getting tired of it.

"Was that it, was that your best shot? Come on, motor-mouth, I'm waiting. Let's see what you've got. You've got no trouble running your mouth, but you've got a lot of trouble playing your position. I keep hearing you, let's see it."

"Fuck you, Honkie."

"That was very good. Did you think of that all by yourself? Why don't you grow up, and we'll just play some football."

Sean turned and headed toward his bench. T.J. started after him again but was brought to his bench by his teammates. "You're dead, Number 7. Hear me, White Meat? You are dead."

On the Denby sideline, Sean rinsed out his mouth and wiped his sweating face with a clean towel. Denby's All-American guard, Doug Hooper, shared the water bottle with Sean.

"Hey Cav, I see you've made a real friend. That number 40 has really taken to you."

"Damn Hoop, I have no idea what his problem is. I never said a word to him, until he started punching and getting up in my face with the threats and insults. I know they like to intimidate, but he's got a wild hair up his ass about something."

"Maybe he just doesn't appreciate that cute quarterback baby face like we do?"

"Yea? Well, screw him. We've got a game to win. I'm not going to worry about one skinny defensive back."

"Listen Cav, I've seen dudes like him before. He's got a screw loose. He'll keep coming after you until he hurts you, or they toss his Black ass out of the game. You keep alert. We've got an entire season to play yet."

Across the field, Nate Washington grabbed T.J. by his face mask.

"What's the damn deal between you and their quarterback? Is he baitin' you? I watched him in game films, and I've never seen him act a fool. And in three seasons, I've never seen you carry on this way. What's the real deal?"

T.J. looked down and kicked at the chalk line.

"Square business, Coach. We been havin' words but he didn't start it. He ain't baitin' me or jerkin' me around. Only time he says anything is when I jump in his shit."

Coach Washington let go of T.J.'s face mask. T.J. was a tough street kid, but he didn't lie to those he respected. Washington liked that. "What's the problem then?"

"The chump jus' got under my skin. Pretty white boy quarterback candy ass, dressed up all pretty with new uniforms and sweat bands and grease pencil under his eyes to help with the glare. They come rollin' in here like they own the place. Well, I'm gonna take Number 7's head off and show him how a ghetto boy can play football."

Coach Washington put his massive hand on T.J.'s shoulder.

"Then start playin' football and quit acting like you're back on the block. You settle down, T.J., or I swear I'll pull you out and you can watch the rest of the game with me on the sidelines."

The second quarter was a carbon copy of the first. Denby's defense stopped Northeastern's every possession and the offense seemed to move down field at will, adding two more touchdowns. After the last score of the half, the backup place-kicker got a chance for a point after. The attempt was wide, and the half ended with Denby in complete control, 27-0.

Denby held their halftime discussion near the team bus. They had to wear their helmets throughout the halftime break because neighborhood youngsters pelted them with rocks from the houses that faced the small field.

Coach Palmer had little to say. With the exception of their first possession, Denby had scored every time they got the ball, with time-consuming, well-executed drives. The defense had shut down the Northeastern offense. Northeastern's punter had managed to at least force Denby to start their drives from deep in their own territory.

Palmer allowed the players to rest from the heat and talk together. The first-stringers knew that they'd be pulled after one or two more scores. For the state's ratings, they needed a solid win, but Coach Palmer would not let his team embarrass Northeastern with any more than five unanswered scores.

On the Northeastern side of the field, Coach Washington cursed out loud as he watched neighborhood youths throwing rocks at the Denby team. Some of his players seated in front of him laughed and cheered encouragement to the rock throwers.

"You all damn well better shut up. You like that do you? They come to this field as our guests and the punks that ain't got the guts to go on the field with them hide between the houses and throw rocks at them. And then some of you fools laugh and encourage them. If I hear another word like that, you can go join them 'cause I don't want you here. They already know they comin' to a rough neighborhood. So what happens? Those fools gotta act like niggers. Tell you what, boys. This shit keeps up every week, we either won't be allowed no more home games or they'll just boot us out of the league altogether.

"On second thought, some of you should go over and join in on the rock throwing. So they're whippin' your ass out on the field where it counts. You got nothin' to be ashamed of if you act like men. Hell, they're a much better team. Quit all the rap about how they look and all that racial jive. If you want, I'll invite them to a street fight after the game.

"But I'll tell you something, those white boys across the way ain't a bunch of rich sissies. They look sharp 'cause their school has got an excellent football program. They might also surprise you all in a street fight. Them boys are from workin' families. I don't believe you boys today. You all get pissed when someone is prejudiced 'cause you're Black. You are always bitchin' about this white man's world. Look at yourselves.

"When these boys come here, you were the ones that were prejudiced. First, you figured they was gonna be a push-over 'cause they were white and ain't got no ghetto Soul. Then, when they start blowin' you off the field, you blame it on the fact they are bigger and got more advantages. If you play your best and get beat by a better team, you can still walk off the field proud. If you play the game like some jive nigger, with cheap shots and insults and running your mouths, and they still whip your ass, when that final gun goes off it's gonna be a long walk to the bus.

"Nobody gonna even start to treat you like men until you start actin' like men. I won't stand for the type of unsportsmanlike play I saw in the first half. Now let's go out there and just do our best."

T.J. listened carefully to his coach. He respected Coach Washington. But T.J. was still determined to destroy the Denby quarterback. The fact that nothing T.J. had said or done to number 7 in the first half had any adverse effect on him only magnified the frustration.

Denby kicked off to Northeastern to start the second half. Once again, the Denby defense stopped the Falcons, and after the punt, Denby took possession on their own 24-yard line.

Sean had been able to wash his face at halftime, and the student trainer had placed fresh grease pencil under his eyes. He no longer felt the heat. With the kind of a game he was having, he had become oblivious to the weather.

Sean called the play and brought the Denby offense to the line of scrimmage. He looked over the Falcon defense. T.J. was still wired. "Hey, Number 7, what's that black shit under your eyes? You tryin' to look less white, or you tryin' to look like a ra-coon."

Sean considered several racially motivated verbal comebacks to T.J.'s comment but decided he didn't need all 11 Falcon defenders out to kill him over a smart-ass racial slur. Sean took the snap and pitched to his big fullback, who swept the right end for a first down.

At midfield, Coach Palmer could smell an all-out Falcon blitz. He called for a screen pass over the center. Sean would drop deep and straight back. Then, the wing back would move behind the center and the rushing Falcons.

Sean began to call signals. He looked over the Falcon secondary. The linebackers and defensive backs were dancing about, yelling and taunting, working themselves into a frenzy. By that point of the game, Sean could recognize T.J.'s voice in the chorus of shouts and yelling.

Sean took the snap and dropped straight back. The defenders had anticipated the snap well, and were only a half a step from Sean. When he was about 10 yards deep, he managed to flip a quick pass over the heads of the blitzing Falcons to his wing back. As he released the ball, the rushers reached him and collectively slammed him to the ground. The weight of the gang tackle knocked the wind out of him, and the several players still laying on top of him did not help his attempt to catch his breath. He felt a couple of concealed punches and then suddenly his right calf seemed to get a sharp, severe cramp.

He realized that somehow, one of the Falcons had moved his helmet enough to clear his face mask so that he could bite Sean's leg. The referee finally unpiled the players. Sean was about to complain but thought better of it. He could see the teeth marks on his navy blue football sock. But the wing back had gained 20 yards, and since the referree obviously didn't see the bite, it was a moot point.

Two plays later, Denby was faced with a third and 13 from the Falcon 33-yard line. Sean ran a bootleg pass to the right. He gave a good fake to his halfback that allowed the pulling guard to neutralize the defensive end. Sean reached the right flat. The Falcon secondary had double covered his primary and secondary receivers, but that left no one to cover Sean. He tucked the ball under his arm and headed up field. He was nearly to the 20 before the defensive backs could respond. Sean sprinted up the right sideline at full speed. Only T.J. was positioned between Sean and his first touchdown of the season.

The lean Falcon defensive back planned to do more to number 7 than merely tackle him out of bounds. He ran at Sean determined to destroy Denby's quarterback. Their paths intersected at the 15-yard line. Everyone watching the game, especially T.J., anticipated that Sean would step out of bounds just prior to contact. Quarterbacks are instructed to avoid head-on, open-field tackles whenever possible.

T.J. began to position his body to unload on the unsuspecting number 7, the moment he crossed the sideline. It was T.J. that was most surprised by what happened. Sean lowered his head and cut away from the sideline, driving his helmet and shoulder into T.J.'s chest. T.J. didn't get the chance to move to protect himself and took the full impact of the full speed, head-on collision with the exposed front of his body. The impact could be heard over the collective moans of everyone watching the game. Sean's momentum and better angle knocked T.J. back and both young men fell hard to the turf tangled together.

No one who had witnessed the collision would have been the least surprised if neither player got back up. But both young men hid their discomfort and quickly got to their feet.

T.J. was dazed. Sean's whole body ached, but he had become fed up with T.J.'s constant abuse during the game. Sean handed the ball to the referee, who spotted it at the Falcon 13. T.J. slowly turned and walked toward his huddle. Sean trotted back to his.

The ref was aware of the ongoing verbal abuse Sean had endured all day. He turned away as Sean called back at T.J.

"Hey, Big Mouth, is that the best you've got? Is that what you've been warning me about all game? Guess what, slick? I've been hit harder in scrimmage with our J.V."

"Game ain't over yet, Honkie."

"It is for you, man."

In the Falcon defensive huddle, T.J. merely glared at his teammates. No one spoke to him about the play. It was a defensive back's nightmare. He managed to tackle the Denby signal caller, the player he had abused and harassed throughout the game. But he fully realized that the smaller quarterback had just knocked him on his ass.

In the Denby huddle, Sean shook his head in an attempt to clear his vision. "Damn, that spook is as hard as rocks. That was like running into a telephone pole at full speed." The alternating offensive tackle brought in the next play and a message from the side line.

"Hey Cav, Coach says if you ever do that again when we have a four touchdown lead, he'll boot your butt all the way back to Kelly Road."

Sean called for a power sweep, with the guard pulling. Hooper leaned into the huddle. "Ya know, that number 40 is starting to piss me off. I respect intense play, but enough is enough. I think I'll ruin Shadow's day. I'm going to knock him up into the cheap seats."

T.J. was still dazed as the entire Denby offense seemed to come his way. He didn't see Denby's 220-pound guard until the moment Hooper slammed into him with a powerful double-forearm shiver. The crushing block lifted T.J. off of his feet and knocked him back 2 yards. The halfback was stopped at the Falcon 5-yard line.

T.J. managed to stumble back to his huddle. The vicious hits on two consecutive plays had him in the ozone. Denby Coach Palmer knew that T.J. was in no condition to cover any receiver and called a pass play in his direction. T.J.'s coach also could see the condition T.J. was in. Coach Washington decided T.J. needed to stay in the game at least until the end of that series. He needed to stay for his self-pride. And Washington felt he needed to be taught a tough lesson about life in general.

He quietly said to himself, "What goes around, comes around, boy. You spend all afternoon makin' them boys mad with you, now you pay the price. Ain't no different than bein' on the street. You go talkin' all that shit, you better be able to back it up."

Sean rolled to his right. He fired a perfect pass to the receiver T.J. was attempting to cover. He was not even close to the wing back, who caught Sean's third touchdown pass of the day.

Coach Palmer called a pass play for the conversion attempt. The play broke down, and Sean was forced to scramble. He headed for the right corner of the end zone.

At the goal line, Sean and T.J. had their last contact for a while. The two tired, determined young men hit head on. The impact was less dramatic than the previous collision for those watching, but it was just as uncomfortable for the participants. T.J. had called upon every fiber of reserve strength to stop Sean's advance. Sean was on an adrenaline high and moving at nearly full speed. Sean lacked T.J.'s natural strength and overall toughness, but when they both finally fell to the turf, the football was well within the end zone. Denby led 34-0. Sean made a final attempt to end their strange personal feud. "Nice stick, man. You really hit hard."

T.J.'s head was spinning as he struggled to his feet. His entire body hurt. "Screw you, chump. I'll see you again, Honkie."

Sean tossed the ball to the ref in the end zone. He had tried with the Falcon defense back. "I doubt it, slick, not unless you buy a ticket to get in to watch the game."

"You ain't shit, man."

"Maybe not, but 34 to zip is some real shit, and that's what really counts."

The game was over for them both. Denby's coach put in the second teams and Coach Washington pulled out T.J. and put an ice pack on his head.

Sean and Hooper sat on the Denby bench enjoying the natural high of their win and the Indian Summer afternoon that had cooled enough to be pleasant. Sean took a long drink from the plastic water bottle while Hooper buried his face into a large half slice of an orange. "Hey Cav, look across the way. Your favorite spook, number 40, is sitting on their bench with an ice pack on his hard head."

"I've got to tell you, Hoop, he was one tough dude. He sure had a motor-mouth, but he was tough as nails. Like I had said before, it was like running into a telephone pole. I'd never seen the guy and I could see the hate he had for me in his eyes."

"He probably just hates all pretty white quarterbacks, unless you've been datin' his sister or somethin'."

"I don't think so. I've dated a lot of girls since I've been driving, but I think I would have remembered his sister."

"Shit, Cav, I didn't know you were prejudiced."

"A couple more games like today and I could learn to be."

The Denby team's ride back to their school was pure male teenage insanity. The players let themselves go that late afternoon. They were half way to the championship and everyone on the bus fully believed that now the whole team was in gear. Nothing could keep them from the championship. There was singing and horseplay and cheering which created a team bond that they had been too cautious to embrace until that warm afternoon.

An hour later, the players filed out of the team locker room in small groups. Sean was walking out with Hooper when he caught sight of Terri Murphy, waiting outside with the other players' friends and family.

"Nice game, Sean. You really did well. Your dad dropped me off here. My folks are at your house for dinner. I thought I'd wait and bum a ride."

"Sure, Squirt, I'd be glad to. Thanks for coming to the game. I think you brought me some of our combined Irish luck. With a Murphy and a Cavanagh rooting for me, I had to do well."

"Sean, I know you've called me Squirt since we were kids, but I am 17 now and . . ."

"Terri, I'm sorry. You know I call my sister the same thing, and she's going to be a nun in a couple of years. Can you imagine if I called her Sister Squirt? No disrespect intended. Old habit and all that, you know."

"Sean Dennis Cavanagh, don't play coy with me. We've known each other our whole lives. I didn't start coming to your games because I'm a diehard football fan."

"Alright, Miss Upfront Terri Murphy, why did you start coming to my games?"

"Because I think I've become a Sean Cavanagh fan."

"Oh, I see. This could be serious."

"I certainly hope so."

They drove to Sean's house in his Triumph, excused themselves and went to dinner and a movie. After the good-night kiss at Terri's side door, Sean would never need to be reminded again not to call Terri Murphy by her nickname.

———————

The Cavanagh and Murphy families had been business and social friends for three generations. Grampa Cavanagh and Tim Murphy became business associates and good friends shortly after World War I. In 1944, their sons, Dennis Cavanagh and Danny Murphy, joined the Marine Corps together and both served in the Pacific in combat units. Right after the war, Danny joined his father's business, and he and wife Mary had Danny Jr. early in 1947. Four more children followed, including Terri in October of 1948.

The Murphys lived in the Eastside suburb of Grosse Pointe Woods, and Dennis and Danny Sr.'s families seemed to grow up together. Despite seeing each other about once a month since childhood, it had become obvious that Sean and Terri did not feel as though they were merely cousins.

Terri attended Grosse Pointe High School. The petite 17-year-old may have looked like an Irish pixie, but she had the spirit of a Dublin rugby team. Like Sean, she had dark brown hair and blue eyes. She was far from fair complected, and with Winter visits to Grampa Tim Murphy's Florida home, she looked tanned all year.

If one could stereotype an upper-class, Grosse Pointe preppie, Terri would fit the mold. She drove the new Mustang that had been her sixteenth birthday present. She had more clothes than her closet would hold. Except for maintaining her "A" average, she did not have a care in the world. Terri had been born into the "good life," and she knew how to make the most of it.

———————

The Northeastern Falcons finished the year without a victory. Only their single tie game prevented them from the worst record in school history.

T.J. had performed well despite their poor record. He was named defensive player of the year by his teammates. But in spite of his good speed and size, he did not receive so much as a look from a college scout. The only Falcon game that was seriously watched by college scouts had been against Denby, T.J.'s least impressive game of the year.

The Denby Tars went on to win the Eastside and Public School League championships. The night of Nov. 19, they met Notre Dame High's Fighting Irish at Tiger Stadium for the city championship and the number one slot in the state poll. In a football game that would long be remembered by the participants, the two powerful high school teams battled to a frustrating 14-14 tie.

Sean's parting comment to T.J. during their game in October had been correct. In order for T.J. to see Sean again, it required an admission ticket. Coach Washington had obtained courtesy tickets so his team could attend the championship game at Tiger Stadium, where the Detroit Lions and Tigers played their home games.

T.J. had driven to the stadium with a car load of teammates and girls. They drank cheap wine and found themselves cheering for Denby, the team that had punished them the month before. The wine had taken the edge off of their prejudice, and while they didn't necessarily like the white boys from Denby, at least they lived in Detroit. Even T.J. found himself on his feet, cheering for his former personal enemy, Denby's number 7.

After the game, the Falcon players discussed the game while their car was stuck in the massive traffic jam.

Charles Davis took a long swallow from his wine bottle and said, "Man, that was one hell of a game. I ain't never seen as much hard hittin' in one high school game. If them Denby boys woulda done us like they did tonight, it woulda been 34-0 at the first quarter."

T.J. looked pensively at the half-empty bottle of Thunderbird. "Shit, don't mean a damn thing. All that hittin' and pain, still end up a 14-14 tie. Damn, like our tie, ain't as bad as losing, but it's close. Damn them ties, a tie be 'bout as satisfying as kissin' yo' own sister."

The girl under T.J.'s arm pulled him close. "Come here Sugar. Tell me if this is like kissin' your sister."

Sean lay motionless, stretched out on the floor of the Murphy home in front of the fire in the fireplace. He took a silent inventory and could not locate any part of his body that was not still very sore from the pounding he had taken from the Notre Dame defense.

Terri came out of the kitchen with a bottle of beer for both of them.

"Maybe if you'd have told them you are a nice Irish Catholic boy, they would have been nicer to you."

Sean winced as he sat up to take the beer. "I doubt it. They would have probably killed me as a traitor."

"Sean, I didn't mention it before because I forgot at the party after the game. I'm home alone for the weekend. Mom and Dad took everyone up North to close up the cabin and Danny Jr. is away at school."

"I don't want your folks upset with us because we're here alone. If you'd like, we can go to my house. I'm sure everyone is in bed by now."

"No, it's O.K. They trust us."

There was a long moment of silence as the young couple looked into each other's eyes. They both broke into a wide grin at the same time.

That night, the two life-long friends became lovers and that cold, damp November night changed their lives.

———

The Spring of 1966 brought high school graduation for Sean and T.J. Their worlds were much further apart than the few city miles which separated them.

In June, Sean and Terri attended each other's senior prom. Grosse Pointe's prom was at the lake front Grosse Pointe War Memorial. Denby's prom was a few miles out of the city at the Hillcrest Country Club.

By June, Sean and Terri were convinced that they shared a love unique in its passion and intensity. Their attraction for one another pleased and amused their families.

There was no prom for T.J. No prom, no job, no football scholarship. T.J. hit the streets — he found odd jobs when he could, but as Summer's heat approached, he had little to look forward to.

Sean accepted a football scholarship at Eastern Michigan University in Ypsilanti. Terri would attend U of M in nearby Ann Arbor. Even though they would again attend different schools, they were close to each other, and the short distance wouldn't interfere with their intense relationship.

After Sean's graduation, the Cavanagh family moved to a larger, nicer home on Birch Lane in Grosse Pointe Woods. The handsome, two-story brick colonial had served the family well, but Dennis decided the home in Detroit would never be worth more so he would move their family to their "dream house" while the children were still at home to enjoy it. He waited two years so Sean could finish high school at Denby and have the chance to play on a championship football team and to improve his chances for college football.

The other four Cavanagh children would either transfer to Grosse Pointe schools or to local Catholic schools. The move to the locally-famous suburb put them within a mile of both sets of grandparents and the Murphy home.

During the Summer, Sean worked a couple of days a week at his dad's office. His spare time was spent with Terri. They'd drive to Metro-Beach to swim and lay in the sun. On weekends they'd drive over to Pointe Pelee, Canada, over the bridge, or go to the Cavanagh family lake-front cottage on Lake Huron.

Terri would never be recruited as a magazine centerfold, but she was never without a great deal of male attention while in her two-piece bathing suit. Even Terri knew she had somehow been blessed. She could eat as much as her older brother, never exercise, and never gain an ounce.

Sean lifted weights and ran every day . He threw the football daily to Danny Jr. or his own brothers. He knew he'd have to be in shape even before he reported to Eastern Michigan in August.

On Labor Day weekend, Sean returned home for the holiday and to take the remainder of his personal items to school with him. He spoke candidly with his dad about the football team. After weeks of two-a-day practice, Sean was less than encouraged by his status on the team or with the freshman coach. It had been obvious to Sean that long before the first day of practice he had been positioned as the team's second-string Q.B. A talented, tall, lean quarterback from a local Ypsi high school had obviously been chosen as the starter before the first drill was run. No deed or overall steady performance displayed by Sean in practice during August seemed to have the slightest effect on his initial pre-season decision. Sean's dad felt a new concern. He knew Sean had never complained about sitting the bench to wait his turn, or pay his dues, or if he was not performing well. Sean had never accused any coach of being unfair before.

After Labor Day, Terri and Sean drove to their schools in their own cars. They had decided that despite the relatively short drive to either campus, the couple would not return home until the Thanksgiving break. That would give them time to adjust to the new lifestyle, and by then Sean's football season would be complete.

When possible, Sean's dad drove up to Ypsi for Sean's home games. He'd sit in the stands with Terri. But their combined Irish luck seemed to have faded. Most of what they saw was Sean pacing the sidelines with a clipboard and wearing a headset connected to the spotter in the stadium booth. When Sean did get to play, the game was out of reach in either direction.

At the close of the long season, Sean had thrown two touchdowns and scrambled for another. He knew unless he grew four inches taller within the next year, his next three seasons at Eastern Michigan would be spent holding a clipboard, not a football.

Having Terri with him helped ease the total frustration of his football season. They were college freshmen and in love, and made the most of the situation.

Terri easily maintained her 4.0 average at U of M. Sean's grades did not suffer from football, romance, or his social life, but he was becoming increasingly troubled by the mixed signals he received about the draft and war in Vietnam. He had always been concerned about world events and was keenly aware of the world around him. He seemed to become more and more aware and serious, while Terri was very content with their private little world, with no thought of what took place on the "outside."

While at home during Thanksgiving break, Sean and his dad spoke for hours concerning alternate plans as they related to school and his college football career. Sean had no illusions of ever playing in the N.F.L., but his dad knew Canadian team owners, and with the right coaching and experience, he might be good enough to play in the Canadian League. Sean loved the game. He had learned to use all of his talents to their fullest, despite his size and lack of superior skills. They agreed to make a decision in the Spring. Terri didn't even want to think of Sean not going to Eastern Michigan. She wanted them to remain near one another.

The Murphy family had their own concerns of a more serious nature. Danny Jr. was flunking out of U of M. His dad quickly got him enrolled in a local junior college full time to maintain his 2-S draft status. Danny Jr. had made it clear to his family, and anyone else who could listen, that he would run off to Canada before he would fight in an immoral war. The words made Danny Sr. wince. The proud World War II Marine would still rather have his son "avoid" the draft in college than to run off to Canada like a coward.

Back at school, Terri continued to excel in the natural sciences. Her life was school and her love for Sean, who spent every free moment trying to become politically educated. He studied political science and social science and began to feel torn by the dramatic contrasts of the views of the strange dirty little war in the place called Vietnam.

Sean loved Terri more with each passing week, but at times, Terri's apathy toward the things that did not directly affect her irritated him. He didn't understand how anyone so bright, so intelligent, could be satisfied to remain so unaware and seemingly uncaring about the world around her.

Things seemed better for a while after Christmas break, but as Spring approached, the campus at U of M and at Eastern Michigan became alive with political activity. The lectures in the halls did not always conform with the 6 o'clock news or the news magazines. The confusion and frustration seemed to worsen.

Terri offered Sean much comfort and pleasure, but she could not ease his growing consternation over the Vietnam issue. Nearing the Easter break, Sean was afraid that not football nor school nor even Terri could offset his personal concerns.

T.J. worked at a car wash on Mt. Elliot St. He made some extra pocket money at the pool hall and had little hope that Chrysler would call him for a job, even though he had put his name on the list right after graduation. He had been arrested for being in a stolen car, but charges were dropped, and they only prosecuted the driver for the theft.

T.J. was becoming more street wise by the day, but even he knew inside that he was living on borrowed time if he didn't get a job soon. He'd either end up shot, in prison, or both. "Washing cars," he thought to himself out loud, "Gotta be something I can do be better than this."

EASTER, 1967
GROSSE POINTE WOODS

Dennis and Maureen knew there was something wrong when Sean didn't suggest going to Florida during spring break. Sean arrived home just after 11 a.m. on Good Friday, hugged his mother, brothers, and sisters, and then went to his room to put away the things in his suitcase. Sean's mother commented to his sister, Irene, that Sean was probably the only male college student that didn't visit home with two suitcases of dirty laundry.

Sean still felt like a visitor in his parent's new home. He had spent countless hours in his bedroom in their home in Detroit. He had spent 18 years in that room.

His old bedroom had changed and matured with him. His dad had repapered the room four times. In 18 years, the room had gone from a nursery to his private young adult haven. It had been his space where he was secure in the knowledge that he could conceal his *Playboy* magazines and an occasional bottle of beer.

His mother would only enter his room to change the linen once a week. His clean clothes were merely placed on his bed for him to put away. His room was his private sanctuary. In a family of five children, it was his birthright as the eldest son to have his own room in their four-bedroom home. Now that they had moved to Birch Lane in Grosse Pointe Woods, his new bedroom felt less his own than the dorm room he shared at Eastern University.

Sean's mother looked forward to this Easter more than usual. Her children were beginning to go their own way; Sean at college, Irene at the convent, their own parents were getting old. Maureen knew there would be very few future Easters that they would all be together.

Sean was pensive, and his mother sensed that he was troubled. Normally verbose, Sean was quiet. He politely answered questions, but he lacked enthusiasm in his voice. He lacked his usual spirit.

He went to the kitchen and got himself a Pepsi. He sat in the kitchen, where his mother was making tuna salad for lunch, and sipped at the soft drink. He sat staring at the bottle and did not speak. Sean's dad came in the side door. He always closed his business at noon on Good Friday.

Sean greeted his dad with a masculine hug and lots of back slapping. Dennis was unsettled by his son's greeting. It had only been a month since they had been together, and he immediately sensed that his eldest son was deeply troubled.

That evening, the entire family gathered in the large family room and watched their new color television together. Sean and Brian had built a fine fire in the massive fieldstone fireplace. In Michigan, early April was still cold and damp, and the fire seemed to warm everyone's spirit.

By design, Sean remained in the family room with his parents after the others had retired, one at a time. Sean's dad went to the wet bar in the family room and retrieved three brandy snifters. He found his best bottle of brandy, still unopened, broke the seal, and poured three generous portions. He balanced the glasses and carefully handed one to Sean's mother, the other to Sean. He turned off the television as he passed, and took his seat in his large leather recliner.

They sat in silence for a few moments staring at the fire. Sean's dad raised his glass in a toast, "To good health." Sean and his mother gestured with their glasses, and each took a swallow of brandy.

The liquid warmed Sean's insides to the pit of his nervous stomach. It calmed him.

Sean smiled to himself. "Ol' Dad" never went to college, but he knew more about the psychology of people than his Psyc. 101 prof ever dreamed of knowing. Give the kid a shot of brandy, loosen the tongue, relax the restraints. Give the kid a drink and treat him like a man.

Sean positioned himself so he could look at both of his parents as he spoke.

"I appreciate the time and space you've all given me today. I guess I wear my emotions on my shirt sleeve. I'll return the gesture of your understanding by getting straight to the point. I don't want to be a disappointment to either of you, but I don't want to go back to school in the Fall.

"I'm just not ready for this now, or not this way. At Christmas, we thought it was maybe the disappointment with the football team that had me turned off. I swear, it's way more than that. The whole thing just seems so fruitless and trite with the way things are in the world. It's all just phoney crap, frat parties and keggers and anti-everything rallies, with a bunch of unaware kids who grew up like this and complain how terrible the country is.

"With the draft hanging over my head, waiting for me to stop being a student, I believe I have two choices. I can stay in school for the next 10 years, or go get it out of the way." Sean's mother winced, but the expression of concern was concealed by her glass.

"Would you like to try a school around here for a year?" his father asked. "U of D maybe. See if an urban university might be better?"

"No, Dad. I've given it a great deal of thought. At first, I was just going to volunteer for the draft at the end of this semester, but I did some checking. The Marine Corps has a two-year enlistment program, probably because of Vietnam, so they won't have to use the draft. I'll finish this school year, hang out here for a couple of weeks, then join the Marines for two years and leave in the Summer. I can come back when I'm done and decide what to do with my life, without the Sword of Damocles hanging over my head."

Sean's mother put down her glass. "Son, you know about Vietnam. Do you believe that now is the best time to go?"

"Mom, there is nothing to indicate that we are not going to be there for a very long time, probably longer than we were in Korea. I don't want to go to war, I just want to get this draft thing off my shoulders. Maybe I won't go to Vietnam. Army, Marines, either way it's a crapshoot. If I've got to go, I'd rather go as a Marine."

Sean's dad ached inside. He remembered when the solid, bright young man that sat in front of him was the size of the new television screen. He remembered how he thought he had helped end all wars. Then, when Maureen's kid brother, Bobby, was badly wounded at the Chosen, in Korea, he realized that probably his own sons would not be safe from war's terrible sting. Dennis felt a terrible, knowing, personal fear for his eldest son and absentmindedly rubbed his aching knee.

He couldn't help but feel proud of the young man he had raised. Sean couldn't know what he was about to get into, but he was certain Sean had no visions of being a hero. At least the boy had some sense of duty, of honor, of tradition. So Sean would be a Marine, like his father and uncles and grandfather and great-uncles. Dennis was afraid, but he was proud. He blushed when he realized he'd rather have his boy run off to Canada than come back in one of those cold, flag-draped military coffins. He washed away both thoughts with a large swallow of brandy.

"Son, this is no football team you are thinking of joining. Boot camp alone is tougher than anything you've ever experienced. And if you went to Vietnam, it would be one of life's worst experiences. Your Uncle Bobby and I have talked to you and told you enough that you've got some idea. You are a sensitive, bright young man, Son. But if you go to Vietnam, you won't come home the same, no matter how strong you are."

Sean stared down at his glass of brandy. "Dad, I'm really confused. I don't know what is right anymore. I don't want to go to war, but I don't want to stay in school just to avoid being drafted. I've heard so much crap at school about the Vietnam thing that I don't have any idea of what the truth is. I just know what I feel I have to do. I've got to get this thing over with, or I'll go batty."

AUGUST, 1967
SAN DIEGO

"Get off that God damn bus, maggots!"

Sean hung his head and spoke quietly to himself under his breath from the rear of the crowded vehicle. "Welcome to sunny San Diego and Marine Boot Camp."

The scores of frightened, bewildered, young men scrambled from the Olive Drab bus and began to pile into each other in a panic in front of a poster-perfect Marine drill instructor.

"Don't just stand there, you stupid fucking herd. Get on the yellow footprints."

There, painted on the black asphalt, were rows of yellow footprints in long rows and positioned at the correct 45 degree angle, the proper angle for the position of attention. As the frightened recruits scrambled for their own set of footprints, the handful of Marine D.I.s roved through the group. They were all screaming at the recruits. "Get on the yellow footprints! Get on the yellow footprints!"

Sean located an unoccupied set of prints and carefully placed his penny loafers within them. Other recruits were pushing and shoving one another as they arrived at a set of footprints simultaneously. The screaming drill instructors were making everyone frantic.

The raw Marine recruits were being exposed to the first of countless boot camp paradoxes. The D.I.s ordered and threatened each recruit to get on a set of footprints; there were four more recruits than there were sets of footprints. The unfortunate leftovers were set upon by the hovering drill instructors. They began to shove, slap and punch the recruits. The unlucky four were led away by the tallest D.I. Sean and the other recruits on the footprints never saw them again.

Sean stood at his best untrained version of the position of attention. He was attempting to maintain emotional control with the insanity taking place around him. He had heard all the Marine Boot Camp horror stories from relatives and friends. He tried to mentally prepare himself for the extreme culture shock, but nothing could have prepared him for this. He thought for a moment about the young men around him. They were mostly street kids and small town or rural hard asses. They had enlisted for three or four years. They enlisted to become fighting men and win the war.

Sean had enlisted for two years as an alternative to the draft and the Army. He didn't want to fight in a war, and wished the Marine Corps still had a college-level football team. The hard truth was that most of the teen-agers on the yellow footprints would be fighting for their lives in Vietnam in five months. The group of drill instructors apparently had their own ideas about how to prepare them for the conflict in their future.

They were left standing there for more than half an hour. Sean had managed to stand still, with only his eyes moving from side-to-side, watching the action around him. The helpless recruits stood at attention, and the D.I.'s abused them verbally and physically.

Suddenly, Sean realized that it was his turn. He was in trouble. A short, Black drill instructor was screaming in his right ear. "You are suppose' to be at the position of attention, maggot. You interested in buying some real estate here in San Diego?"

"No, Sir."

"Then how come you eye-fucking the area?" The stiff brim of the D.I.'s Smokey-the-Bear hat hit hard against the side of Sean's head.

"No reason, Sir. I'm sorry, Sir."

The drill instructor removed his hat. "You right 'bout that, puke. You're 'bout the sorriest mother fucker I ever seen."

Without warning, the D.I. bit Sean's right ear lobe until the pain brought tears to his eyes. The drill instructor released his toothy grip on his ear and replaced his hat. "You better keep your head and eyes forward, worm. You hear me, boy?"

"Yes, Sir."

"I can't hear you, lady!"

Sean wanted to grab the D.I. by the throat. He was no fighter, but no one had ever bitten him on the ear before. He thought again of moving against the D.I. He decided that if he had wanted to commit suicide, he could have jumped out of the plane. It would have been quicker. Sean fought off his anger and answered louder. "Yes, Sir."

"I can't hear you, crazy!"

"Yes, Sir."

"I can't hear you!"

Sean screamed at full voice, it served as a release for his emotions. "Yes, Sir!"

Just as quickly as he had pounced on Sean, the D.I. was screaming at a recruit near him. "What kind of long hair faggot are you, boy? You gotta be a Communist. I think the Kremlin sent you here to fuck up my Marine Corps."

The tall D.I. walked amidst the group of recruits. "I see by your records that most of you scumbags are from that bad-ass De-troit city. Now, I want you little hoods to put all the shives, zip guns and other shit in this here box. You ladies won't need them here."

The D.I. made his rounds through the group. He left the room shouting out insults. He had collected a small pocket knife, two finger-nail clippers and a ballpoint pen.

An hour later, the group of recruits had been moved through the room where their heads were shaved. Bald, the young men could not recognize the new friends they had made during their trip to California, especially after they had loaded their civilian clothes for shipment back home and they all stood naked. Sean had spent enough time in locker rooms to know that the Constitution had said all men were created equal, but God had not made them that way. The sight amused Sean. Bald, wide-eyed, frightened, nude young men filling out address labels.

The new recruits were pushed into a large shower room. They had to take an ice cold shower. Standing in the cold water, Sean thought his testicles would not come back down where they belonged for a month. It was a morbid thought, but Sean would not have been surprised if gas pellets had dropped from the shower room ceiling.

After standing at attention in a large room, still cold, bald and naked, they were issued their initial uniform. It was not the famous dress blue look or even the familiar combat look. The unstarched utility hats fell down over their bald heads and rested on their ears. Their O.D. green utility trousers touched the floor. They wore bright yellow sweat shirts with a large red Marine logo on front. Instead of boots, they wore white, high-top tennis shoes.

Sean was thankful no one he really knew could see him now. They looked much more like a Special Olympics team than a platoon of new

Marine recruits. They would receive the remainder of their uniform issue needed for boot camp in the week called the Receiving phase of their 11 weeks at the Marine Corps Recruit Depot.

"Line up and stand at attention, you worthless herd."

Sean watched the D.I. that had bit him on the ear, standing in front of him. He looked at him and thought, "God, maybe I should have just let myself get drafted into the Army."

Sean got two weeks leave at Thanksgiving. His M.O.S. was 0311, a basic infantryman, a Grunt. He had been selected as his boot camp series honor man. His athletic ability helped him excel throughout the rigorous training. His education and I.Q. placed him head and shoulders above his peers. Sean had learned to get along with other Marines from all backgrounds. They had approached Sean to go to Officer Candidate School but he would have to increase his enlistment to do so. In the Fall of 1967, there were not many upper-middle class preppies filling the enlisted ranks of the Marine Corps.

The Cavanagh family knew where Sean would be sent before Christmas, even though he had not received his official orders. The war in Vietnam was reaching a turning point. America had more than half a million men in Vietnam in late 1967. Sean was soon to become one of them.

2

December, 1967—January, 1968

DECEMBER, 1967
VIETNAM

By December, 1967, Marine replacements needed for duty in Vietnam were flown directly from El Toro Marine Corps Air Station in California. The journey was made by commercial jet and took many hours.

The stewardesses prepared the plane load of restless, weary young men for final approach to the Da Nang airfield. It had been the most uncomfortable trip Sean had ever experienced. Every seat on the plane was occupied, there was always a line to use the head, the cabin seemed too warm, the food was bad, and even the soft drinks were lukewarm: they had run out of ice in mid-flight. The flight seemed endless. Sean concentrated on attempting to sit still. He had used everything he knew to pass the boring hours by writing letters, reading, and taking a series of restless cat naps. He had a window seat. The young Black Marine seated next to him seemed to be able to sleep for almost the entire trip. Sean envied his ability to sleep on the way to war, but it certainly eliminated the opportunity for any conversation.

The pilot's voice came over the plane's P.A. system, "We'll be landing at Da Nang, Vietnam in a couple of minutes. The tower reports the temperature is 94 degrees. Tower also reports ground fire as light to moderate. Welcome to Vietnam, men, and good luck."

The big plane smoothly touched down. There was no ground fire. From the plane window, Da Nang's airfield looked like any other.

Sean thought about the pilot's comment, and it angered him. The pilot was a smart ass. The stewardesses were even more testy than the Marines.

The Marine next to Sean finally said, "Don't know why they're actin' so bitchy. They're leavin'. We're the ones got to stay in this here mother for the next 13 months. If I was flyin' back to the world in a couple hours, I'd be grinnin' like a fat cat."

Sean reached the door of the plane and stepped outside. He would never forget his first breath of Vietnam. The hot, stale, humid air seemed too thick to breathe. The collection of foul odors seemed to suck the air from his lungs. The sensation of being breathless startled him, and he gasped briefly for air. By the time he walked down the steps to the runway surface, his starched utilities were soaked with sweat, but at least he could breathe.

"Alright, people, let's get your head and ass wired together. I want every swinging dick over to hanger three to the Admin desk so you can check in, on the double."

The First Sergeant was dressed in starched jungle utilities. He looked squared away despite the wet heat, but the tough, weathered skin on his face made him look like an old man to the collection of 18- and 19-year-old replacements.

As if in the same theme as the plane ride, everyone the replacements encountered at Da Nang took a verbal shot at breaking their spirit. The base personnel treated them much more like recruits than trained Marines who were about to join combat units. It was no surprise when the quality of the chow at the mess hall fit the mood — foul.

The replacements were broken up into small groups, depending on their destination. Some men left by truck that night. The rest would leave the following morning via helicopters or C-130 transport planes.

Sean's small group found an empty tent with stripped canvas cots. The tent stood in an area near where they were instructed to wait. It was only 2300 hours.

Everyone in the small group knew they wouldn't move out until the next morning. The empty tent, with its cots, seemed a much better place to spend the night than a concrete corner of the busy airfield.

Sean stretched out on a cot and tried to sleep. He couldn't get the odors of the place out of his mind. He had tasted it in the food. Now the smell of mildew from the canvas tent and cots had been added. The odor kept him awake, as did the sound of planes taking off and landing all night.

Just before dawn, a large figure appeared at the tent doorway, "What the hell you people doin' in here? Nobody told you to use this tent. Get your lazy F.N.G. asses out of here, on the double. You'd better not leave no mess. Police the area real good or you'll be one sorry bunch."

The small handful of drowsy Marines grumbled to themselves and gathered up their gear. They filed past the overweight sergeant dressed in starched jungle utilities, who stood next to the door with his hands on his hips.

The short, Black Marine spoke to the angry N.C.O., as he walked past him, "Take it easy, Sarge, we didn't mess up nothin'. We was just lookin' for a place to crap out overnight."

"I don't want none of your lip, Marine. You people better learn to stay where you are told."

Sean stopped in front of the glaring man, "Is there something in the water here in Da Nang, Sergeant? Everyone we've encountered at your lovely base seems to have a royal case of the ass. We're on our way to the boonies to get our butts shot at, and you people treat us like we're back in boot camp."

"Lance Corporal, you're breaking my heart. I'll check and see if the chaplain is awake yet so he can punch your tough-shit card. We hurt your feelings being rude and talking rough? Wait until you join your units, the V.C. and N.V.A. gonna hurt your feelings more than any police sergeant."

Sean moved away from the angry N.C.O. The Black Marine turned around to ask Sean a question, loud enough to be heard. "Hey Cavanagh, he the police sergeant? That like in military police?"

"Nope, that's like in trash police."

The stout sergeant stormed after Sean, grabbed him by the arm and spun him around.

"Watch that mouth, smart ass. You F.N.G.s got lots of smart talk until you hit the bush. You think you're dealing with some rear echelon poques? Almost everybody here is on their second tour. This ain't the bush, cherry, but there ain't no secure place in this whole damn country. I got scars on my legs that say I got the right to be here my second tour. I earned it. If you're still alive in four months, come on back and tell me about it. For now, get your sorry asses over to the field desk set up in front of hanger three. The major there will give you your orders. Put a zipper on that mouth, or you'll be cleaning heads until your transportation leaves."

"Better do as the po-lice sergeant say, Cavanagh. Else wise, they cut off your hair and send you to Vietnam."

Sean shook his head and slowly walked to the field desk across the runway.

"I don't think I'm going to like it here. Where do I go to resign my lance corporalship?"

"You clowns won't be so funny in a week or two."

"Hey Sarge, don't catch a cold at the air-conditioned N.C.O. club."

"Fuck you, F.N.G."

"That must be how you make sergeant. You've got to be articulate and creative with your comebacks."

The Marine major behind the O.D. field desk had an annoyed expression on his face. Sean was not surprised. He handed the officer his personnel folder.

"Sir, L/Cpl. Cavanagh, S.D., 2341174."

The major looked at his roster of names, then up at Sean.

"Cavanagh. Let's see, you're going to join the 1/1. Those CH46 Sea

Knight choppers over there are going to resupply the firebase from which your battalion operates. Be on one of them. They'll leave in a half hour. The 1/1 is a good unit, Marine. They've been chasing the Gooks all over I Corps since '65. Be thankful you're not going with the 26th Marines to Khe Sanh. Khe Sanh is too close to the trail and the D.M.Z. to suit me. Here's your papers. Good luck, Marine."

Sean came to attention and saluted the major, "Thank you, Sir."

"Remember not to do that in the bush, son. You salute an officer in the field, he'll kick your ass, if Charlie don't waste him first."

Working parties were busy loading five CH46 choppers through the rear ramps. Sean approached a young man in a flight suit. The man was changing barrels on an M-60 machine gun on the port side of one of the choppers.

"Excuse me . . . are you headed for the firebase for the 1/1?"

"*Excuse me ?* Where you think you are, kid? On a field trip?"

"No, I've met so many fucking clowns since I've been here I think I'm at the circus. Are you going to the 1/1 or not?"

The crew member looked at a clipboard. "Don't get your tail in a knot, pal. We're going to the 1/1. Go ahead and get aboard. We'll be takin' off in about 15 minutes."

Within five minutes, Sean was joined by three other fresh replacements. He watched out the round porthole of the chopper as a C-130 took off. He guessed it contained the remaining replacements who were headed for Khe Sanh, wherever the hell that was.

The inside of the chopper was filled with rifle ammunition, grenades, C-rations and other assorted supplies.

Sean overheard the door gunner talking with the co-pilot, "Appears that 1/1 is getting some fresh meat along with its supplies. They must have stepped in some shit. Everybody's been going to the 26th Marines at Khe Sanh. Sorry about that."

The helicopter lifted from the runway and Sean made himself as comfortable as possible on the web seat. He stared out of the chopper port hole. The drastic contrast of colors in the passing landscape engrossed him in deep thought. He lost track of time. The flat areas seemed to be a greenish yellow. The brown of the rice paddies had light green centers and edges. The mountains were such a deep green they took on a bluish hue. When Sean felt the chopper descend, he could not even guess how long they'd been airborne. Except for the scars of war, it was a beautiful country from the air.

The flat red dust helipad of the firebase was a stark contrast to the concrete runways of Da Nang. The rotors of the landing choppers created a huge, thick cloud of choking red dust. The moment the choppers touched down, their ramps were lowered. Dust covered

Marines in helmets and flak jackets scrambled aboard to unload the supplies. Sean and the other three replacements each grabbed a crate and carried it with them out of the chopper. They stacked their crate with the others and stood with the half dozen new men from the other choppers.

The moment the choppers were empty of supplies, another group carried stretchers with wounded onto two of the choppers. Body bags were loaded into the third, and soon the choppers were airborne and disappearing in the southern skyline. It was as if the entire process had not taken two full minutes.

The men of the working party began to load the crates onto small jeeps and mules. They moved around the knot of new men as if they were not there.

"Where the hell do you people think you are, Disneyland?" A huge Black Marine in helmet and flak jacket stood with his hands on his hips. He reminded Sean of Detroit Lion defensive tackle Roger Brown. "You new people adjust your brain housing group. Take your sorry asses to that tent down there at the base of the hill. Battalion X.O. will assign you to your outfits. You all better start realizin' where you at and get your heads outa yo' butts or you gonna have a real short tour. You all get my drift?"

The Marine firebase was a flurry of activity. It seemed to be on the only high ground within sight. There were rows of tents, a few sand-bagged bunkers, 106mm recoiless rifles, 81mm mortar gun pits, and a row of 105mm cannons on the hilltop. There was an assortment of vehicles, including jeeps, mechanical mules, six-by trucks, armored personnel carriers armed with .50 caliber machine guns, and at least four M-48 tanks. The whole base sat on a bluff of red clay that became red dust at the merest touch. It was surrounded by a maze of barbed wire. The gate faced west. Just outside the gate was a wide, shallow, brown river.

Sean stood frozen on the helipad looking over the activity of the firebase. He realized that when he wasn't in the bush, this would be his home for the next 13 months.

The red dust seemed to cling to everything and everyone. He wondered what happened to the red clay when it rained.

"You waitin' for an engraved invite, Marine? I done tol' you, get your butt to the X.O.'s tent. You got 13 months to eyeball this place. Now move out."

At the battalion tent, Sean received his company assignment and directions to the company C.O.'s location. He was ordered to the supply tent to draw his combat gear. The supply clerk issued him the equipment, and he walked to meet his new company commander.

Due to the clouds of dust, Sean's new flak jacket and trousers were dust covered by the time he found his company C.O.'s tent. He wondered how he would ever keep his M-16 clean.

He knocked on the wooden tent pole of the company C.O.'s tent. The company clerk, a frowning, red-haired lance corporal, told him to enter. The clerk smirked as he gave Sean the visual once-over, as if he knew a joke not to be shared. He handed Sean's personnel folder to the captain behind the field desk. Capt. Kincade was in his early thirties. His head was shaved, and he was wearing aviator sunglasses even though the inside of the tent was dark in the shadows compared to the bright sun outside of the green canvas roof.

Sean came to attention, his M-16 at order arms, "Sir, L/Cpl. Cavanagh reporting as ordered."

Capt. Kincade's eyes darted from Sean to the contents of his folder.

"Cavanagh, you've got a year of college, real good test scores, Bootcamp Series Honorman, made E-3 in training. How come you didn't go to Officers Candidate School, Marine?"

"I enlisted for two years, Sir, to fulfill my military obligation. I couldn't go to O.C.S. without extending. At 19, I'm not certain I could lead a platoon in combat. Sir, I just want to do my tour and get on with my life."

Capt. Kincade slowly removed his glasses in disgust. "I'm surprised they made you an Honorman with that attitude. It takes a hell of a lot more conviction and confidence than that to be a Marine officer. Listen real hard boy, we're only a 105-round distance from the D.M.Z. If you do exactly what you're told, maybe, just maybe you'll live long enough to fulfill that obligation and get on with your life. You'll see very soon whether you have what it takes to be a regular Grunt, much less an officer. You are in the first platoon. Go down that row of tents to the last one. Report to Lt. Fox."

"Aye, aye, Sir." Sean turned and stepped back into the choking dust. "Charming guy," he thought. "The civilians think you're a madman for joining the Corps, and the Marine officers jerk you around if you don't extend. Can't fucking win."

Sitting on the step of the last tent in the row was a slim, 24-year-old second lieutenant from Long Island, New York. Lt. James Fox hummed to himself as he scrubbed at his .45 caliber pistol with a tooth brush. He was 6'1" with short, curly black hair and light brown eyes.

Sean stood in front of Fox and identified himself. Fox merely looked up and nodded, "Where you from, Cavanagh?"

"I still live with my folks in Grosse Pointe, Michigan. It's a suburb of Detroit."

"Yea, I heard of it. All the auto execs live there, don't they?"

"Yes, Sir. A lot of them still do."

"What you do in the world, Cavanagh?" Lt. Fox moved his head from Sean to his disassembled .45.

"I went to Eastern Michigan University for a year. I didn't like the draft hanging over my head, so I joined for two to get my obligation over with."

"You tell the Captain that?"

"Yes, Sir. That motive went over like a whore in church."

"Yea. Skipper can be a real hard ass. Kincade eats, sleeps, and breathes the Corps. It is his whole life. He can't relate to the fact some of us would join the Marines to fulfill our military obligation instead of being drafted in the Army. I've heard him say that all non-career Marines should have gone in the Army. I got news for you, Cavanagh, if it wasn't for guys like us, they could hold the battalion muster in a phone booth. Some of the biggest shit birds I've encountered in this big green machine were lifers. Most are so damn set in their ways, and all that old Corps bullshit. That crap doesn't mean a thing over here. The old Corps is a thing of the past. We are merely a mixed bag of guys—different races, different backgrounds, from a thousand different places. We pull together because it increases our chances of staying alive. What was your major in college?"

"Sports. I majored in football and baseball. I hadn't decided whether I was going to get a business degree or try and be a teacher."

"Football and baseball. You any good?"

"If I was any good, Sir, I wouldn't be here."

Lt. Fox smiled. "I got my B.A. in business. While I fiddle-dicked around deciding on a grad school, I got my draft notice. Like you, I chose the Corps over the Army. I believed all that recruiting hype about serving with the best. I still believe it."

"I'm from a Marine family, three generations. If I've got to be here, it might as well be as a Marine."

"Detroit had a hell of a race riot last summer. You got a hangup about Black Marines, Cavanagh?"

"No, Sir. That was no race riot, but it doesn't matter. I grew up in an all-white Detroit neighborhood. But if the guy is good, I don't give a damn if he's purple. The best of my D.I.s was a Black E-5. He was a Nam Vet, taught us a lot about ourselves."

"Glad to hear you talk like that. Lots of middle-class white college boys look down their noses at these street wise Black N.C.O.s. You don't need to speak Queen's English or hold a degree to be good in the bush. Some of these ex-street kids are the best Marines in the company. I'm going to put you in the first squad. A tall, skinny Soul Brother named T.J. will be your squad leader. He's from some shit-hole ghetto, Philly,

Chicago, maybe even Detroit. Don't let his street talk and jive fool you. He knows how to keep his people alive. Best squad leader in the battalion. I swear the guy can smell Gooks. T.J. is his nickname. Everyone gets a nickname. I'm sure you'll have one before tonight. We go back in the bush in a couple days. Cavanagh, you seem like a bright kid. Do what they tell you and keep your mouth shut for a few weeks. Did you get leave at Thanksgiving?"

"Yes, Sir. I was home for 10 days, then went to Staging Battalion before being shipped out."

"What kind of shape you in?"

"Michigan in November, home cooking, the good life. All considered, pretty good."

"A day or two in the bush and you'll be back in shape. Be glad you got here in December. Except for the friggin' rain of the monsoons, it beats the hell out of the heat of the Summer. July in this place really sucks. Go find T.J. and report to him. His squad is in those two tents over there by the trenches. If things get out of hand, come see me. You'll be alright."

Sean slung the M-16 on his shoulder and headed for where he was to find his new squad leader. Lt. Fox was a refreshing change from everyone else he had encountered since leaving California. He felt comfortable with Fox. He sensed the young lieutenant cared about his platoon. He reminded himself to stay clear of Kincade.

He saw the tall, lean Black Marine talking and laughing with a small group of Marines. He wore an O.D. undershirt, undershorts, boots, and a bush hat. There were two other Black Marines and two white Marines involved in the loud discussion. A portable radio blared R&B music through the tent area.

Sean walked up to the group and stood silently, waiting for their discussion to end. Finally, the center of the discussion quieted. The tall Black Marine pushed his bush hat back on his head, "What you standin' there for, Boy? You lose somethin'?"

"Lt. Fox sent me to report to T.J. I've been assigned to the first squad. I'm a new replacement."

There was a collection of moans from the small group.

"Just exactly what we need, an F.N.G., like we need Gook sores or hemorrhoids." The group laughed and moaned again at Sean's expense.

"You a lance corporal, Boy? You straight from the world or you piss somebody off an' get transferred?"

"Straight from training. I made E-3 in B.I.T.S. training. Two days ago, I was in California. Now, I'm here enjoying the climate and scenery."

T.J. pulled the brim of his bush hat down even with his dark brown eyes, "You tryin' to be funny or are you just some kind of a smart ass?"

"Probably a little of both?"

"O.K. smart ass, what's your name?"

"Cavanagh."

T.J. paused for a long moment and grinned. "Got a first name, Boy?"

Sean suddenly felt embarrassed. They were really testing him. "Sean, Sean Cavanagh."

"Sean? Sean? What kinda name is Sean for a man?"

Sean took a step toward T.J. "It's a fucking Irish name. It was good enough, and man enough, for my grandfather, who fought in the Corps in World War I. It's been in my family for generations."

"Cool your jets, Dude. Just only heard of one Sean back in De-troit City. That James Bond actor, ain't his for-real name Sean? Wait a minute, where you from, boy?"

"Detroit."

"No shit, I'll be go to hell. I've done met you. You went to Denby High School, didn't you?"

Sean was caught off guard. He was certain they'd never met before. His anger was gone. He was speechless, unusual for him.

"Two years ago, you peckerwood. Remember bumping heads with a defensive back on the Northeastern Falcons, football season of '65?"

Sean broke into a wide grin, "Bad ass Number 40, was that you? Damn, did you hit hard. I heard bells for two weeks."

"Tell you what, son. I've had a lot more fun than I did that afternoon. Gentlemen, this boy threw three T.D. passes against my team, an' me and him 'bout beat each other to death. Sean Cavanagh, I'll be damned. You related to the mayor of De-troit?"

"No, different family altogether. He even spells it different. I wouldn't be here if I was related."

"No matter, Sean ain't no name for no Grunt. You were runnin' off at the mouth about it bein' a proud Irish name. Well, that'll be your new name, 'Irish.' So dig this, from now on, you answer up to Irish."

"Thanks, T.J. I know I could do a lot worse than Irish for a nickname."

T.J. patted Sean hard on the back and grinned. "Besides, after watching you boys tie Notre Dame High School in the championship game, it's kind of fittin'. What they called, the Fighting Irish?"

"I should have known there was a catch."

"These white dudes is Yance and Logs. Logs will be your fireteam leader. Brothers here are Bad Ass and Mr. Cool. Mr. Cool is our M-79 man."

Each man nodded with T.J.'s introduction.

"Suppose Lu-tenant tol' you. We're headed back in the bush in a couple days. N.V.A. got somethin' up their sneaky sleeves. You bound to get your cherry your first ops."

The five men resumed their conversation. Sean sat next to them but said nothing. He was still an outsider, new, untested, untrusted. He couldn't remember when he had ever felt so out of place, so alone.

"Hey, Irish, why didn't you go to college and play football?"

"I did, T.J. I went to Eastern Michigan for a year and rode the pine."

"Well, son, you gonna get plenty a chances to get in the game over here."

Before dark, Logs helped Sean find a cot in the squad's tent. He made certain that Sean had drawn all the proper gear.

"Listen, Irish, first few nights take some getting use to. Don't be ashamed to wear your flak jacket after lights are out. Most of us did it for a while, some still do. We're safer here than the bush, but we are only a Gook rocket distance from the D.M.Z. There are sandbagged shelters at the end of this row of tents. If we take incoming, you grab your gear and haul ass for the hole. This firebase hasn't been hit in a while, but that don't mean squat. Just stay close to me, and don't freak if we catch some shit."

After lights out, Sean returned from the head. He kept on his boots and flak jacket and tilted his helmet so he could rest his head inside it. He put his M-16 on the cot next to him. The chorus of snores from his new tent mates did more to comfort than annoy him. If they could sleep so soundly, the danger must be minimal.

The concussion from the first incoming rocket explosion knocked Sean's cot over.

"Incoming! Incoming! Get your asses in gear and head for the bunkers."

Sean stumbled to find his rifle and get to his feet. Logs grabbed his arm. "Damn, Irish, you hit?"

"No, Logs. Concussion blew my ass out of the rack. I'm alright."

"Come on, man. We gotta make some serious tracks to those bunkers. Stay close."

At the end of the tent area, was a group of six-foot deep pits, rimmed with sandbags, but open at the top. Logs and Sean dove in.

"If one of those 120mms or big Gook mortars lands in this hole, they can send home our remains in an envelope and save the body bag and military coffin. But it's a whole lot safer here below ground than up there."

The firebase continued to be pounded by heavy rocket and mortar fire. A shell landed near their bunker and showered them with dirt. Sean ducked his head down so his helmet touched his flak jacket. He had a white knuckle grasp on his M-16. The grinding, tearing roars of

the incoming rounds terrified him. He felt helpless in the open hole. He
could sense the size and power of the incoming blasts.

He imagined a letter to his parents from the Defense Department,
"Dear Mr. and Mrs. Cavanagh, The remains of your son are contained in
this sponge. Notice that it fits nicely in a cigar box for easy disposal in
your back yard, next to the pet canary."

The concussion of a rocket bounced him off the Marine crouched
next to him. Sean noticed it was T.J. His new squad leader had an
expression of apathy on his face. It was as though the vicious rocket and
mortar attack merely annoyed him, because it had interrupted his
sleep. T.J.'s attitude calmed him somewhat.

T.J. sensed the extreme fear in Sean. He realized that it was his very
first contact. It was tough enough on the seasoned grunts to sit in a
hole, helpless, and simply pray that it's not your time. T.J. decided
conversation with his new man might help him keep his mind off the
instant, violent death that was at ground level.

"Say, Irish, was you still in De-troit during the riot last Summer?"

"Yea, I went to M.C.R.D. in San Diego in early August."

"Was it as bad as they said? You see any of the shit firsthand?"

"My dad's got a warehouse near the Eastern Market. We went down
and checked on it. Saw some fires, some looting, tanks and the National
Guard. The warehouse is in the middle of nowhere. They didn't touch
it."

"They, you mean the niggers?"

"No, I mean the rioters."

"You mean the nigger rioters?"

"Hey, T.J., I don't know what you heard. That was no race riot like in
'43. There were some isolated incidents, but this was a poor people's
riot. I saw film of Black and white people helping each other carry the
shit they were looting. Most of the rioters were Black, more poor Black
people in the city. It was poor folks against the establishment. Lots of
stories about Black neighborhoods protecting the businesses of white
people that treat them right. It was different. There's a lot of racial fear
and mistrust now. But, it was no race riot, not Black against white."

"You say your folks moved to Grosse Pointe? Your daddy owns a
couple of factories and warehouses? Kind of makes him part of that
establishment, don't it?"

"Bullshit, T.J.! My dad nearly had a Jap bullet take off his kneecap in
the Pacific. I'm not saying he didn't have a break or two, but he earned
everything he has, and he treats people fair. My granddad fought in
France; he paid his dues too. We come from a poor, shanty Irish
background, and they made good. If we were part of the establishment,

T.J., I wouldn't be sittin' next to you in this stinkin' hole waiting to get my white ass blown up."

"I don't need no social studies lesson from some cherry honkie. You 'bout breakin' my heart with that poor Irish boy bullshit. You get outa here in 13 months and go work for your daddy's business, or maybe you just go back to college and live like a fat cat. Sundays, you and daddy go to your fancy Grosse Pointe Country Club and play a little golf. Your biggest worry will be keepin' your score under 90. I go back to nothin', man. Just another nigger, in a city with a whole lot a niggers. Talk your poor Irish shit to somebody else. It ain't like being Black in a white world."

"O.K., T.J., I know it's not the same. I'm not saying it's equal for you and me. I was born with the silver spoon, I know that. I could be in college right now, if I wanted to ride on my student deferment. I know I've got the world by the butt, if I make it out of here. Look, I was just saying that back in my family, people busted ass to get what they have, paid their dues. I joined this green machine so I could do my thing and get on with my life. The bottom line, T.J., is that tonight we're both hiding in this hole."

Another large rocket round hit close to their hole, and they were again showered with dirt from the explosion. T.J. brushed the loose dirt from his shoulders.

"Irish, I'm here 'cause some hard ass De-troit judge give me a choice of four years in the Corps or going to prison. The damn recruiter was in the court room with the papers, grinnin' like a big dog. You got a point, though. If your daddy was part of that establishment we talkin' about, you sure as hell wouldn't be sittin in here as an E-3, waitin' for some Gook rocket to cancel your ticket. Ask me, you got oatmeal for brains bein' here instead of college, gettin' all the trim you could. But I respect you not likin' the draft hangin' over your head, waitin' on your ass. Could be like Lt. Fox. He finished college, then pow, they drafted his young ass. Now, he's humpin' the bush as a brown bar at 24."

T.J. slipped a plastic canteen from his belt. He selected the canteen with Kool-Aid in it. The sweet flavored powder helped make the foul-tasting, lukewarm water more drinkable. T.J. took a long swallow.

Sean's mouth was so dry it upset his stomach. He had to struggle to gather enough saliva to keep from gagging. T.J. offered his canteen. Sean took it, nodded in a gesture of appreciation and put the plastic canteen to his lips. He took a large mouthful. Nothing had ever tasted so good, had been so refreshing. He closed his eyes and smacked his lips. He handed the canteen back to T.J.

"Thanks. I needed that. My mouth felt like the inside of an old gym shoe. I guess the fear's showing. Hands wet, mouth so dry I could puke."

T.J. gave Sean a piece of C-ration chewing gum from his flak jacket pocket. "Here, when the shit hits the fan, chew some gum. It helps keep your mouth moist. It helps keep your stomach settled."

T.J. rested his head against the bunker wall, as the incoming rounds continued to pound the Marine firebase. They could hear the sound of jets and prop planes overhead. T.J. sported a large grin on his face that seemed out of place.

"I know I'm not going to get a chance to use my dick for a long time, but what you grinning at? What you do, put salt peter in your canteen?"

"Naw, man, it's cool. Irish, no shit, you the first Chuck dude that I gave a drink to that didn't wipe off the top of the canteen before he'd take a drink."

"Sorry, T.J. I never even thought about it."

T.J. —still grinning—slapped Sean's hand. "No, man, that's cool, that's what I'm sayin'. You didn't even think about wiping off the nigger's lip prints. Other dudes wipe the top like they afraid of gettin' some kind of nigger germs, or maybe they get something and they turn black. You drank from my canteen as if it were given to you by another white guy."

Sean didn't understand the importance of his unintentional gesture. He shrugged his shoulders and wildly chewed the flavor from the C-ration gum. T.J. slapped Sean on the helmet.

"Irish, you may be a white, upper-class honkie, but damn, son, you *are* from Mo-town. If you can fight, you ain't gonna have no problems getting along with me. Shit, if you fight like you played football, you gonna really help this squad."

The incoming had stopped. T.J. was out of the bunker and on his way back to his rack without another word. Sean slowly walked back to the tent. Logs gave him a "thumbs-up" signal. He pondered the blind luck on his passing T.J.'s personal acid test for white Marines. A friendship established on a drink from a canteen; the foundation was on very solid ground.

The following day, T.J. and his squad were assigned a number of "make work" tasks and working parties. They unloaded supplies from a half dozen CH46 helicopter arrivals. They filled sandbags and policed the area around their tents. They were all surprised at the lack of obvious damage to the firebase from the previous night's attack.

After evening chow, the squad members gathered outside an empty tent. They talked about home and their favorite topic, girls. Some shared stories of sexual conquests. To admit to the group that you were a virgin would be a fate worse than cowardice in combat. Those young Marines that had never been with a woman either borrowed someone else's story or portrayed their favorite fantasy as fact. Sean was still content with sitting with his new squad, but keeping to himself.

The conversation made him think of Terri. He missed her, and he was troubled with the thought of her at U of M, while he was 12,000 miles away. When he thought of the time they had spent together when he was home on leave at Thanksgiving, it warmed his insides. He fought the physical excitement he began to feel when he thought of their young passion. Sean was certain that T.J. had not put salt peter in the Kool-Aid.

He ached when he thought that he was several months away from R&R and possibly meeting Terri in Hawaii for a week the following Summer. He wrote Terri a brief letter, telling her he was well. He also wrote a brief letter to his parents. He wanted them to know he was in the First Regiment, like his dad and Uncle Bobby before him.

The rocket and mortar attack the night before had been the only time the base had been hit in December. T.J. said it was just the N.V.A's welcome to Vietnam for Sean. Everyone figured that there would not be another rocket attack for a while. The jets and "Puff" had done a real number on the foothills around the firebase.

The sides of the tents were left rolled up. The quiet firebase smelled fresh without the choking dust, upwind from the row of plywood heads. Sean was tired from the work parties, jet lag and the extreme change of cultures, Nam from California in only one day. He fell asleep before the tent filled with its chorus of snoring and groans.

The first volley of incoming rockets fell on the empty chopper pad. Everyone was on their feet and headed for the bunkers. Logs gave Sean a slight nudge from behind.

"Here we go again. Come on, Irish, we gotta haul ass to those holes. If the Gooners found their mark last night and drop the next volley in these tents, we're dead meat."

Sean and Logs ran with the others about 30 yards to the line of open bunkers. They found an empty one and dove inside. Sean laced up his boots and closed his flak jacket. He readied his M-16 and found a piece of gum. Even he could tell that the rocket and mortar attack was more severe and intense than the night before. Logs put a full magazine in his M-16 rifle.

"I don't like this, Irish. Two nights in a row. Gooks got something up their sleeves. I think we stepped in some shit and never left the firebase."

"Swell, what the hell do we do now?"

Logs just looked at his loaded rifle, "Nothing for now. If this is just another rocket and mortar number, we sit here and ride it out like last night. If Charlie decides to follow with an all-out ground assault, you will get your cherry tonight. Those sandbag bunkers all around the base have M-60 crews in them. Stand down platoons and H&S company guys man the bunkers each night. If the Gook sappers blow the wire and enough of those little fuckers get inside the firebase, they'll organize Reaction Forces. That will mean us."

"What about more rounds and grenades and . . ."

Logs put his hand on Sean's helmet to show support. "No sweat. If they need us, they'll give us all the hardware we need. You may not always get fed in the Corps, but you'll always have enough ordinance."

A full 120mm mortar volley tore into a row of tents about 50 yards away. Logs carefully lifted his eyes to ground level after the explosions. "Shit, if the Gooners had dropped their first volley there, ol' Bravo Company would be in the hurt locker. Sorry about that, you Gook bastards."

Sean crouched closer to the ground and covered his head. "So much for air strikes knocking out the N.V.A. rockets and mortars."

Logs gave Sean a half grin. "Hell, Irish, this close to the D.M.Z., this could be an entirely different bunch. The N.V.A. could bring a whole damn Gook regiment down in one day."

"Then why haven't they brought a whole division down and taken this firebase at will?"

"Nothing the Brass would like better than for the Gooks to mass a whole division in one box on a map. We'd bring enough fire power to make a parking lot out of the whole D.M.Z. Nope, Gooks are smarter than to mass more than just enough people to do their mission. If they really wanted this firebase, they'd have to wait until real bad weather. Then, they'd pay too much for it.

"From what I hear, those guys over by the trail, the 26th Marines, at a big base called Khe Sanh got more to worry about. Gooks hold the high ground, and the cover on the mountains is so thick it could hide a couple Gook divisions with heavy guns."

A moment later, the roar of incoming explosions was joined by an assorted collection of new sounds. There was outgoing fire from Marine 105mm cannons, 81mm mortars, 106 recoiless rifles, automatic weapons, and rifle fire. Most of the small arms fire seemed to come from the area of the firebase nearest the river and from the front gate.

Logs pushed live rounds into an empty magazine, "Shit, those sounds mean the Gooks are doing a ground assault. Listen hard, Irish, you'll hear the satchel charges of their sappers in the wire. Then, our primary defense positions will get hit. I wouldn't want to be in one of those M-60 bunkers near the wire tonight."

They heard the distinctive sound of the sappers' satchel explosions. The volume of fire incoming and outgoing became very intense.

Logs was sure all his rifle magazines were ready. "We're in for a shit storm tonight. Damn, you sure didn't bring any of our Irish luck with you. Your first night we get shelled; your second, the Gooks do their first ground assault in almost nine months. By the sound of things, you're going to get your cherry tonight, son. If those Gooners are getting in through the wire, we're going to get a chance to get into the game."

Seconds later, T.J. and the stocky, Black platoon sergeant jumped into their open bunker. T.J. gave Logs and Sean a bandoleer each of live M-16 rounds and two M-26 frag grenades.

As T.J. handed out the gear, he said calmly, "Logs, take yo' fireteam and hook up with Yance and his people. Me and Mr. Cool will join you over near the command post. Lieutenant and I will get the skinny and pick you up there. It sounds bad. It sounds like a bunch of Gooks made it through the wire. Logs, you know how those little turds can get around. Be on your toes from now on."

Logs gathered the other two fireteam members, and the squad assembled in an open bunker near the well-built covered command bunkers. The fierce fire fight continued in the area of the firebase, near the main gate.

Sean had never been more frightened in his young life. Despite the conscious fear, it all seemed to be unreal, like a terrible dream. The maddening noise, the strange combination of lights from explosions, flares and tracers. The Marine Corps had conditioned him well. In spite of his fear, he automatically, almost mechanically, followed orders.

T.J. reappeared with Lt. Fox and grabbed Sean by the shoulder, "You doin' alright, Irish?" Sean nodded, and T.J. quickly looked over his and Sean's equipment. He made certain Sean had bent the spoons on his grenades, so they weren't lost the first time he hit the deck. "You stay close to me and Mr. Cool," he said. "I ain't gonna jive you, we got problems."

Lt. Fox spoke loud enough to be heard by the entire squad. Sean slipped more gum into his mouth, attempting to settle his stomach. Already, a lesson learned from a Vet.

"I got the word from the Skipper. The Gooks have blown the wire and poured in. Our 81s and 105s neutralized their additional threat from the main force. Gooks took the M-60 bunker nearest the wire and the 106 gun pit nearest the wire. From those two positions, they are kicking ass through the entire firebase. If that 106 is still functional, and they turn it around, they'll shit all over us. Our own 81s can't get in that close with their rounds.

"We've got to take back the 106 gun pit, then the bunker. They're bringing up a tank to back us up. If the Gooks do turn that 106 around, that tank is history. Alright, stay low, let's get as close as we can. Move out, on the double."

The squad all chambered live rounds as they ran. "Lock and load, this time for real."

Heavy rocket and mortar fire continued to fall throughout the firebase. But it was answered by increased fire from Marine cannons and mortars. The squad was joined by a lean Texan with a M-60 machine gun and his assistant gunner. They were from the weapons platoon and saw Fox and the squad head for the wire. They asked to join the team and were welcomed. The small Reaction Force got within 60 yards of the overrun 106 position and came under savage crossfire from the 106 pit and the overrun sandbag bunker to their right flank. No one was hit, but they were pinned down.

Fox crawled over to Mr. Cool, who was sighting his M-79 grenade launcher. "Mr. Cool, can you drop a round in that 106 pit with your blooper?"

"No can do, Lu-tenant. Too close to get any arc."

"Damn. I hear those little suckers movin' that 106 into position. We're too far away to throw a frag. If we don't take them out, they'll take us out with one fleshette round."

T.J. fired at the muzzle flashes. He stopped and rubbed his chin in thought.

Sean sighted his M-16 at the muzzle flashes in the 106 gun pit and fired five well-aimed rounds. The slight recoil of the M-16 was almost comforting. The risk was greatly increased, but this all out contact was less frustrating than just sitting in a hole waiting for a rocket to join them.

"Say, Lu-tenant," T.J. said. "I got an idea. The M-60 and the squad lay down some heavy fire. We keep the little suckers' heads down. Mr. Cool, he drops some M-79 frags on the bunker to our right flank. Then, Irish belly his way another 10 or 15 yards and throw a frag in on top of them in the 106 gun pit."

Sean looked back at T.J. as if he expected Sean to sprout wings and fly over the firebase.

"T.J., that would be a hell of a throw under perfect conditions. We've got a brand new man, under heavy fire."

"It be alright, Lu-tenant. I know it's a hell of a throw, but Irish got a hell of a throwing arm, for a white boy."

Fox encouraged the squad to put out more fire, then looked to Sean. "What say, Irish? Can you do it?"

"I can give it a try, Sir."

T.J. tossed Sean one of his hand grenades, "Boy, in Nam, you don't just try. You either do or you don't do. We don't grade on effort, only results. Tryin' don't mean shit here."

Sean began to crawl toward the 106 position held by the sappers.

"You ain't gonna get more than one or maybe two chances, Irish." T.J. said. "Once they see what you tryin' to do, they gonna bring all their fire on your young ass. Show these boys how we do it in Mo-town. Throw them Gooks in the 106 position one of your famous T.D. passes." T.J. fired his M-16 and grinned at Sean.

The squad's rate of fire increased. Most of the enemy return fire was directed at the squad. Sean's advance had gone unnoticed by the Communists in the 106 position, and the bunker.

Sean decided to stop just behind a slight mound. He was still about 45 yards from the 106 gun pit. A slight raise in the earth offered some protection. He sat his M-16 on the ground and readied two hand grenades. He looked again toward the gun pit and saw the AK47 muzzle blasts. His target.

He clutched the hand grenade in his right hand, the spoon firmly in the center of his palm. He positioned himself so he faced his intended target directly. Someone in the 106 gun pit had spotted him. The ground near him made a thudding sound with the impact of rifle rounds. Sean pulled the grenade's ring and removed the safety pin. He quickly raised to his knees and threw the 1½ pound grenade with all the combined athletic skill of 10 years of organized sports. The O.D. green sphere arced through the night air, as if in slow motion.

The instant after he threw, Sean dove back down and hugged the ground. The firing stopped for an instant. Sean heard the metal grenade strike the tripod of the big 106mm recoilless rifle inside the gun pit. An instant after the strange metallic ping of the grenade's contact, it exploded. A huge secondary explosion lit up and shook the entire firebase.

The grenade had set off at least one of the N.V.A. sapper's satchel charges and also set off two of the powerful 106mm high-explosive, anti-personnel rounds. Had the explosions been at ground level, instead of in the gun pit, Sean would have surely been killed. The large barrel of the big gun fell within 10 yards of Sean's position.

Sean lay dazed by the tremendous explosion's concussion. The N.V.A. soldiers at the overrun bunker, to their right flank, spotted Sean and turned their fire toward him. Fox directed all of the Reaction Force's fire on the bunker. Most of the N.V.A. fire was surpressed.

T.J. began to crawl toward Sean, "Hey, Irish, you alright, Man?"

Sean shook his head in an attempt to focus his vision. His ears were ringing so loudly he could barely hear T.J.'s voice.

"Think so, T.J. What the hell do I do now?"

"Just lay chilly. The tank's comin' up and help us take the bunker. Get your rifle and watch the 106 pit. Make sure no more Gooks get in there."

Sean shouldered his rifle. His own squad was doing a good job keeping the Gooks at the overrun bunker from putting out accurate fire.

The M-48 tank approached the front gate from the center road of the firebase. It rumbled to within 50 yards of the enemy-occupied bunker. The tank's 90mm cannon barrel moved into position and erupted in an orange-red flash. It fired a cannister round at the rear entrance of the bunker. Thousands of small darts tore into the sandbags and the ground around the bunker. A moment later, enemy fire resumed.

Lt. Fox called for his radio man, "Stupid shits. Why did they fire a fleshette round at a damn bunker?" Fox attempted to raise the firebase command post on the radio.

A few seconds later, the tank's 90mm cannon fired again, this time a high explosive round. The round slammed into the rear of the bunker and the explosion drove the Reaction Team even closer to the ground. T.J. changed magazines in his M-16. "Get some, tank, get some."

The cannon round had demolished the rear of the sandbag bunker.

Sean had crawled another 10 yards closer to the 106 gun pit. He could see the front side of the sandbag bunker, hidden from the line of sight of the tank and his squad. He saw half a dozen figures hiding up against the front of the bunker wall.

Sean pulled the pin from another hand grenade, once again lifted himself to his knees and threw the grenade with all of his strength, this time for distance. The grenade disappeared into the shadows of the bunker front.

Sean warned the squad, "Look out, there's Gooks hiding in front of . . ."

The hand grenade exploded. Four N.V.A. soldiers broke and ran, two in either direction from their place of concealment in front of the captured bunker. The two who ran to the right disappeared in the explosion from another of the tank's 90mm rounds. The other two ran toward the squad and were cut to pieces in mid-stride.

Sean stayed on his belly, crawling another 10 yards closer to the bunker. He reached into his trouser pocket, took out another grenade and threw it toward the front of the bunker. After the explosion, the squad rushed the smoking pile of sandbags. The bunker was silent. There was no return fire.

Sean saw a Marine squad approaching the gate from the other 106 gun pits. They secured the gun pit that had been overrun, then continued toward the main gate. Rifle fire and grenade blasts were still heard throughout the firebase.

Sean joined his squad at the retaken bunker. Lt. Fox reported by radio that the area was secured. Fox turned to T.J. "Check the inside of the bunker. We'll set up here tonight, in case they try us again."

T.J. took out a grenade, "Logs, you and Irish cover me." He threw the grenade in the destroyed bunker's opening and shouted, "Fire in the hole."

After the explosion, he entered the bunker with Logs and Sean behind him. As the smoke began to clear, they could make out the ghostly figures of four N.V.A. soldiers. T.J. put his M-16 on automatic and sprayed the bodies of the enemy soldiers with rifle fire. The lifeless bodies of three Marines lay in the far corner of the bunker with their destroyed M-6O.

Sean heard Yance from outside the bunker, "Hey, Irish, get your butt up here and check this out."

Sean was glad to get out of the choking smoke and cordite of the bunker. He found Yance standing in front of the bunker. There was the body of a badly mauled N.V.A. soldier. Two R.P.G.s lay beneath him.

Lt. Fox walked over and put his hand on Sean's shoulder. "Good thing you spotted these assholes. Looks like they were going to lay chilly until our tank got close, then R.P.G. its big green ass. Outstanding. Damn outstanding."

Sean was still in a daze. He looked at the gore of the dead bodies but didn't really see it.

A Marine from the tank approached on foot, still wearing his tanker's helmet, "Who's in charge here?" Lt. Fox identified himself. Fox told the tank crewman about the R.P.G.s. The crewman walked up to Sean and extended his hand. Sean looked at him for a second, then shook his hand.

"I'm Sgt. Denten. Anytime we're in the firebase, you got all the beer you want. Just come down and ask for me. We all knew what it meant for you to take out that 1O6 position before the Gooks could use it on us. A couple R.P.G.s at close range could have ruined our whole day. Thanks, Man." Sgt. Denten disappeared into the darkness toward his tank.

The night sky seemed to be filled with jets and chopper gunships. The area across the ugly little river was being blasted with bombs, rockets, and napalm. The 1O5s and 81s from the firebase continued to pour rounds into suspected enemy positions outside the firebase.

Lt. Fox instructed the squad to spread out in a line near the bunker. They would hold the position until daylight because of the large hole in the wire near the front gate.

Another squad set up in and around the 1O6 gun pit that had been previously overrun. The powerful explosions had left no trace of the Marines in the pit when it was overrun, or the N.V.A. sappers. The big 1O6mm recoilless rifle had been destroyed.

Minutes later, there was no more rifle fire from inside the firebase.

The 105s continued to pound the nearby hills, and jets continued their bomb runs, but it was quiet inside the firebase. The cries of the wounded had stopped. The corpmen had moved them to the aid station.

Sean carried a half dozen loose sandbags and made a protective position for the remainder of the night. He lay alone, watching the gate and the river. Only dead N.V.A. bodies littered the ground. The 81mm mortar crews kept the firebase lit in the dancing blue-white light of their parachute flares. He added another piece of gum to the collection already in his mouth.

His thoughts wandered from the stark horror of reality to a dreamlike peaceful daze. His mind had been violated that night, as if it were a victim of a rape. He may have been trained, conditioned to merely respond, but nothing in life had prepared him for the horror of combat. Torn, shredded bodies. Death and destruction. He thought of his dad, 12,000 miles away. He wondered if his dad would sense that Sean had experienced his first contact with the enemy.

He also realized that the fear and terror had been matched with an adrenaline high such as he had never experienced. Part of him was terrified by every shadow outside the wire. Yet, there was another part of him that reminded him of an old John Wayne movie. "Come on you little bastards, you want some more?"

He wondered if taking human lives would start to bother him as he came down from the adrenaline buzz. He had known he could kill if he had to. He didn't know how he would feel about it afterward. He never expected the lack of feeling he experienced that night. There were no tears, no remorse. He cared a great deal about the 12 dead Marines that filled the body bags near the helipad. He cared about the wounded Marines in the aid station and those being medevaced out by chopper. He winced when he realized he had more confirmed kills of N.V.A. soldiers than he had days in-country.

The grey light of dawn was a welcome sight. Lt. Fox went to the firebase Command Post. He returned after the sun had appeared above the ridge line to the east. "Good news, men," he said. "Bravo Company drew the duty to check the bush across the river for the body count. Base personnel are going to police up the dead Gooks. We can shower, get some chow and some sack time. We're headed for the bush on an operation tomorrow so we skate today. Skipper said you people did an outstanding job.

"Irish, you really must have pissed him off the other day. He was going to write up the Marine that had secured the captured 106 position until he found out it was you. He said it might be bad for company morale to write up a man in his first contact."

T.J. stood up and began to brush the dust from himself. "Screw it, Irish, don't mean nothin'. That tank crew and us know you did a hell of a job. Unless you gonna be a lifer, that's all that matters."

Sean felt exhausted and a little weak. A Bronze Star was on the bottom of his priority list that morning.

T.J. placed his big hand on Sean's shoulder and smiled. "Guess what, Lu-tenant? Skipper may not want our new boy to get a Bronze Star, but I'm afraid he can't stop him from gettin' a Heart. You better lay down for a minute, Irish."

Sean was confused. He did what T.J. told him, but didn't understand why T.J. had instructed him to lay in the dirt.

"Corpman, corpman up. Irish, my boy, you took some shrapnel in the back of your neck, just above the flak jacket. Your back is peppered, but looks like the jacket took almost all of it."

"I thought that was sweat running down my back." Sean put his hand to his neck and saw his own blood. "Ah, shit. I'm bleeding."

"Logs, why don't you take our new hero to the aid station. He's lookin' a little green around the gills."

"Sure, T.J. We did such an outstanding job last night, we wouldn't want him falling down and embarrassing us in front of the Captain."

As Logs led Sean away from the group, T.J. spoke to Fox. "Boy's gonna be alright, Lu-tenant. He does exactly as he's told, he's got good instincts and he's got enough balls."

Lt. Fox watched Sean stagger up the hill. "I hope he gets a little more lucky. The kid's in-country 36 hours and gets wounded. It could be a tough 13 months for that boy."

In the aid station, the corpman gave Sean a healthy hit of morphine. Because the wounds in the back of Sean's neck were not serious, he was treated at the firebase aid station. The Navy doctor there removed three shrapnel splinters from the back of his neck and put in a total of 15 small sutures. That same evening, Sean was released and joined the squad for evening chow. He was placed on light duty until they could remove the sutures, in 10 to 14 days. He couldn't carry the equipment needed on an operation in the bush, so he watched his platoon leave the firebase the following morning. Logs told Sean he was still half a cherry, despite his actions and wounds during the firebase attack, because he hadn't been out in the bush yet.

"Boy, you ain't a real Marine until we get you out in the bush."

On Christmas Eve, the corpman removed Sean's sutures. The platoon was back from their operation and would be at the firebase for Christmas. Sean and the others wrote letters and talked about home even more than usual. A Marine in another squad had a tape with Christmas music, but so many men asked him not to play it that he replaced it with a Rolling Stones tape. The Christmas music was a form of torture.

Sean sat in a tent with Logs and the two other members of their fireteam. Stoney was from a steel town in eastern Ohio, and Little Joe was from Galveston, Texas. Little Joe was so named because his real name was the same as the actor who played the character, Little Joe, on *Bonanza*. Logs, Stoney, and Little Joe had all been in Vietnam since the early fall of 1967. Sean tried not to let himself think about the fact that he would still be in Vietnam the next Christmas. If he survived.

T.J. joined them. He and Sean told the others how Detroit's main street, Woodward Avenue, was decorated for the holiday with a huge tree of lights on the J.L. Hudson's building. Logs was a Boston Irish Catholic whose family owned an Irish pub in the heart of an Irish neighborhood. He had gone to junior college for a year. Then, like Sean, joined the Corps for two years.

Little Joe was a handsome 18-year-old who had joined for three years right after high school. He had become disenchanted when he failed to receive any large college scholarships. He had managed to get his 17-year-old girlfriend pregnant during his two weeks home on leave before being shipped out. He didn't know if they'd be waiting for him with open arms, a shotgun, or an arrest warrant when he finally got back to Galveston. Stoney wanted out of his hometown, and the Corps seemed as good a vehicle as any.

Different cities, different backgrounds, but united by a common ache to be home for Christmas.

They flew in a Navy chaplain by chopper on Christmas Day, with special chow. Sean, Logs, Yance, and Stoney went to Catholic mass together. Logs whispered to Sean during mass, "Chaplain says we can take communion even if we missed confession. Good thing, with this bunch he'd be hearin' 'em until next Christmas."

That night, half an hour after lights out, the firebase was rocketed by the N.V.A. in the hills for 15 minutes. They wanted to wish the Marines a Merry Christmas—in their own special way.

Two days after Christmas, their platoon readied itself for another operation in the bush. This time, sutures removed, Sean would join his squad.

I Corps Intelligence reported heavy N.V.A. concentrations and movement much farther east than just the activity around the 26th Marines at Khe Sanh.

Each man in the platoon was loaded with approximately 60 additional pounds of equipment. In addition to rifle and ammunition, they carried hand grenades, a LAW rocket, belts of M-60 machine gun ammo, and two 60mm mortar rounds. That was in addition to four full canteens, flak jacket, helmet, and pack.

By the time Sean had stumbled through the shallow stream bed of the river just outside the firebase gate, he fully realized how physically uncomfortable the next 12½ months promised to be.

The platoon turned north. By mid-day, the terrain changed, and they started up and down a series of steep hills. The thick growth and tall grass cut paper thin slices in their exposed flesh. They doused themselves in bug juice. Like the old salts, Sean carried bug juice in the thick black rubber band he wore on his helmet cover. The bands were cut in strips from tire inner tubes and became as much a trademark of the combat Marine in Vietnam as the bush hat, flak jacket, and jungle boots.

Sean carefully watched the members of his squad and tried to emulate their postures and movements in the bush. Yance reminded him of a high school friend he had hunted game birds with in Michigan. He seemed to glide through the bush, eyes constantly moving. Mr. Cool seemed to be T.J.'s shadow. His M-79 grenade launcher was always at the ready. He could instantly respond to a mere gesture by his squad leader, T.J., his real life hero. T.J. seemed like a natural. For a city kid, T.J. had adapted to the bush and moved carefully, but with confidence. He gave the impression he had done nothing else his entire life.

Sean attempted to ration his water. He used T.J.'s tip about the chewing gum to help keep his throat moist. He had already requested that everyone at home send him chewing gum with each letter.

By 1500 hours, Sean and the others were soaked in sweat. The sky threatened rain. Their squad was walking point. Suddenly, T.J. raised his open hand above his head.

Everyone stopped at once. When he dropped his hand quickly, everyone dropped to the ground where they stood. Not a word had been spoken.

Sean leaned next to a tree and brought his rifle up. T.J. began to crawl back to where Lt. Fox and the radio man were positioned in the column.

Sean spoke to T.J. as he moved past him. "What's the deal, T.J.?"

"Just lay chilly. Point man thinks he seen some N.V.A. in the open on the next ridge. Say' it looks like a row of Gook bunkers. Could be a trap, or coulda caught them with their pants down for once. I'm goin' back an' tell the lu-tenant. Keep your head down, son."

He watched T.J. crawl to where Fox was. Sean took out a canteen. The gum wasn't going to be enough if he had to sit there and wait for a fire fight. Bunkers. He could only pray that the Marine assault on the N.V.A. bunkers would be more successful than the N.V.A. assault had been on the Marine bunkers three weeks prior.

T.J. crawled back toward his original position near the front of the column. As he passed Sean on the way back, he said, "Lu-tenant gonna have the 105s and some air strikes drop in on the Gooks first, case it's a trap. Belly up to that tree and stay down 'til the show's over. All that fire power don't always soften them up, but it never hurts."

Sean looked back at Fox, who was talking on the radio and carefully studying at his map. Within a minute, they heard the 105mm cannon shells passing overhead on the way to the N.V.A. positions. The ground vibrated from the shells' impact. The vegetation shook. The rumbling of the exploding rounds made each man wince.

The shelling stopped as two F-4 Phantom jet fighters made several passes, dropping 500 pound bombs on the slope where they saw the N.V.A. troops. As the jets finished and headed south, the 105s began again.

T.J. crawled back to Sean. "When this shit lifts, we're goin' in. Stick close to Logs an' do exactly as he say. Won't jive you Irish, if they got decent bunkers built, they'll be waitin' on us."

"Between you and me, T.J., I'm so damn scared, I could freak."

"Listen, you Mo-town honkie, I know you got what it takes. You proved it back at the firebase. We're all scared. You embarrass me, I'll boot your white preppie ass all the way back to Grosse Pointe. Now be cool, dude. You'll be alright." T.J. moved down the line.

Logs slid next to Sean. He put an ear to the explosions. "Get some, Arty. In fact, get them all. The more Arty gets, less that can mess with us.

"Listen, Irish, we're point squad, so we'll do a frontal assault as soon as the 105 barrage lifts. Try to keep moving. Keep behind any cover you can find and put out some rounds. We let them sit there and aim in, they'll shoot us to pieces."

The shelling stopped. T.J. was on his feet. "Come on, herd. You all know the drill. Keep your proper interval. Double time. Move out."

The squad ran down to the base of the hill, then started up the gradual slope of the next. They had formed an irregular wavey line. T.J. continued to encourage the squad, reminding them to maintain their proper interval and get ready. If the bunkers existed, shit would hit the fan any second.

The hillside was badly scarred by the air strike and the lengthy 105 barrage. Trees had been literally torn from the ground. From halfway up the slope to the ridge line lay only shredded tree trunks and freshly plowed earth. At the same time, several different hidden positions near the ridge line opened up on the advancing Marines with automatic weapon and rifle fire.

The Marines hit the deck behind any available cover. The return fire was meek at first. With vigorous coaching from T.J. and Lt. Fox, the Marine's return fire was soon as intense as the N.V.A.'s, but the N.V.A. held the high ground and fired from concealed bunkers. Sean hid behind a fallen tree and returned fire from the cover of the upturned roots. He watched for the red muzzle blasts of the AK47s to locate his target and squeezed off well-aimed shots.

Two more Marine squads were moved into the frontal assault. Numerous Marine LAW rockets were fired at the N.V.A. bunker positions. Sean heard a chorus of calls for the corpman.

T.J. fired his LAW rocket and threw aside the empty tube. "Logs, take your fireteam out to the right flank and move on the bunker protecting their flank. We'll give you as much cover fire as we can with our LAWs and M-60s. The Lu-tenant has asked weapons platoon for a couple of 3.5 rocket teams. We can't just sit here. They'll chew us up."

Logs got eye contact with his three other fireteam members. "Come on, boys, they just called our play."

The four men darted from one portion of cover to another. Sean had left his LAW rocket for T.J. to use to cover their advance. N.V.A. rounds smacked the loose soil and fallen trees all around the advancing fireteam. The cover fire was distracting the N.V.A. enough to keep them alive as they sprinted up the hill to the right flank. When they reached the right flank of the line of bunkers, the fireteam split up. Logs and Sean went to the first bunker, Little Joe and Stoney to the second bunker.

Out of breath, Sean fell against the dirt mound roof of the N.V.A. bunker, struggling to get his wind. Two N.V.A. soldiers emerged from the rear entrance, 10 yards behind Sean. The first one out fired at Sean. The rounds tore up the loose dirt near Sean's head. Logs cut down the North Vietnamese soldier with a short burst from his M-16. The second N.V.A. soldier turned to go back in the bunker. He was downed at the mouth of the bunker by fire from Sean and Logs. They both quickly changed magazines in their rifles. Logs dove next to Sean. Both young men waited for further threat from the concealed entrance to their backs. "Damn Gooks sure can make bunkers," Logs said. "They got tunnels everywhere. Nothing like ours."

Sean took out a grenade, "Logs, watch my back. I'm going to crawl over this mound and drop this frag through the gun port."

"It's our only chance, Irish. We try to follow them through that rear entrance and we're dead meat."

Sean lay flat on his belly and inched his way toward the front gun port. As he was about to pull the grenade's pin, a Marine 3.5 rocket slammed into the front of the bunker. Sean was not hit by any shrapnel, but the concussion lifted him up and tossed him roughly to the ground, next to

Logs. The explosion deafened him for a moment. The concussion gave him a bloody nose.

Logs moved to Sean's side, while still watching their rear. "Stupid S.O.B.s! Don't those dip shits know we're up here? Damn, where the hell is T.J. or the Lieutenant? They send us up here, then don't maintain fire discipline. Christ's sake. Irish, you hurt bad?"

Sean leaned his helmet against the soft soil of the mound that was the bunker's roof.

"I don't know yet, Logs. Stay with me a minute, buddy. I'm helpless, Logs. I can't see. Can't hardly hear. Can't move."

Stoney and Little Joe were having no better luck with the second bunker. Stoney missed the gun port opening with his grenade and took some of his own shrapnel in the upper leg. Little Joe applied a combat bandage and covered the bunker entrance.

Logs sat close to Sean. Sean felt all of his senses returning. He wiped the blood from his face with his sleeve.

"Damn, Irish, you never let go of the grenade. If you'd have pulled the pin before you got knocked over here, you'd have fragged us both."

"No sweat, Logs. Look, I've still got a good hold of the spoon. Now that's a trained quarterback, son. Blind-sided and still no fumble."

Sean wiped the blood again with his sleeve. "Aw, shit, I started it, I'll finish. I'm still dizzy, but now I'm pissed. If our own people don't blow me away, I'll take out the little fucks."

Sean again inched over the mound. He got within reach, pulled the pin, tossed in the grenade and buried his face in the dirt. The explosion inside the bunker lifted him up from the ground an inch, then he plopped back down. The N.V.A. bunker's guns went silent.

Logs and Sean moved to help Little Joe quiet the second bunker. Logs' fireteam saw most of their platoon advancing up the hill from the new safety of the right flank. Little Joe crawled over the top of the bunker. Sean moved to where they could just see the gun port. He fired five rapid shots into the side of the narrow opening to move the occupants back. The moment he stopped firing, Little Joe lobbed in a grenade. Little Joe lunged away from the opening and covered his head as the grenade exploded.

Sean plopped down on his seat. He was still dizzy from the concussion, and his nose was still bleeding. Logs knelt at his side. "You want me to get you a corpman, Irish?"

"Naw. Just let me sit for a minute, I'll be alright. I just got my bell rung."

The approaching squads moved along the ridge line and neutralized the entire bunker complex. Half an hour later, a team of Marine engineers was destroying the bunkers with large charges of plastic C-4 explosive.

Stoney and several other Marines waited in a small group to be medevaced as soon as a small landing zone could be cleared by another team of engineers.

A corpman had given Sean the once over. He washed the dry blood from Sean's face, and Sean rested on his back with a wet cloth across his eyes. He was still a little dizzy, but was determined to stay with the platoon.

Two HUEY choppers took turns landing on the small, crude L.Z. The first brought food and supplies, then took out the wounded. The second brought water cans and ammo, then took out the body bag containing the one Marine killed in the fight.

With darkness approaching, no one was surprised by the order to dig in for the night. T.J.'s squad was placed in the center of the platoon's night defensive position along the ridge line.

While it was still light, the men hurriedly dug their two-man fighting holes so they could heat their C-rations and smoke before it got dark and strict light discipline went into effect. Logs let Sean continue to recover and dug their home for the night by himself. It was easy work in the soft soil of the hillside.

The squad, minus Stoney, sat around their fighting holes and ate their C-rations. Sean opened a can of fruit cocktail. It amazed him how the simple pleasure of drawing a good C-ration selection could bring such enjoyment. The juice was sweet, the fruit refreshing. It seemed to rejuvenate him.

T.J. lit a cigarette and took a long, thoughtful drag. "You boys did a damn righteous job on them bunkers. Tell you what, though, we is lucky as hell. If the point man hadn't seen them Gooks running around this slope, we'd have been torn a new asshole strolling up this hill. Lu-tenant says ol' Capt. Kincade ready to cream his jeans. We got a confirmed 22 N.V.A. dead, a whole bunker complex, weapons, food, even some medical supplies."

Logs bummed a smoke from T.J. and added "Glad to hear the Skipper's got a stiff dick. How bad we get hurt?"

T.J. mixed a can of beans and didn't look up at Logs. "One K.I.A., new kid from second platoon. Came here same day as Irish. Only one serious medevac, half dozen walkin' wounded, including Stoney. They'll all be back, 'cept the K.I.A., I mean."

"That's a bitch. Boy's here for only a couple of weeks and gets zapped."

Sean leaned over and joined the conversation, "If the Lord decides I'm gonna get wasted here, I'd rather buy it my first month than my last month."

T.J. shook his head but still did not look up. "Yea, I dig that."

Logs looked at his cigarette as if it tasted foul. "T.J., you know I'm not a cry baby, but what the hell are we doing out here? That kid got zapped, Stoney and a half dozen others got hurt and medevaced. Irish was nearly wasted by friendly fire, and for what? I tell you for what, for some fucking box on some fucking map back at Regiment. Today, we take the box on the map. Tonight, we sleep on the box on the map. In a day or two, we'll move out and the Gooks will be right back on this box on the map. Then, next month, we'll come back, the Gooners will have fixed their bunkers and we can do the whole thing over again."

T.J. carefully held his hot can of beans and taste-tested a single bean from his spoon. "Logs, if I didn't know you better, I'd say you startin' to sound like one of them anti-war hippie assholes. I'm startin' to get the idea that you don't like it here."

"I'm serious, T.J. If this stinking hill is so important, then let's hold onto it. If the N.V.A. want to fight a war, then let's drive the little bastards back across the D.M.Z. and all the way to Hanoi, instead of all this wasteful dicking around."

Sean located his canteen Kool-Aid and washed down the last of a C-ration chocolate bar. "Say T.J., how come I nearly got waxed by friendly fire? The whole platoon knew you sent us up there. Did some numbnuts get excited to use his LAW?"

"Man, sorry 'bout that Irish. The Lu-tenant tole the 3.5 teams from weapons platoon the situation, but this big dude, Spike, he got a mind of his own, what little mind he's got."

Sean sat up on the edge of his fighting hole. "Spike? Spike? You've got to be shittin' me. What kind of a name is Spike?"

Suddenly, out of nowhere, a very large, very ugly Marine stood towering over Sean. Sean remained seated on the rim of his fighting hole in the midst of his squad.

"It's a man's name, you sorry little F.N.G. You don't like it? You wanna say something to my face?"

Sean replaced his canteen. He reached up and moved his helmet back on his head. He slowly looked up at the big man standing over him.

"Yea, Sure Shot. I really don't care what your nickname is. I'm more concerned that another Marine nearly killed me today."

"You're breakin' my heart, cherry. I got more time on R&R than you got in-country. I don't owe you an explanation for nothin'."

"I'm not asking you to explain anything to a mere mortal. I did think, John Wayne, since we're both Marines in the same company, and you almost killed me because you had your head up your ass, that you might apologize."

"The F.N.G. wants an apology? I'm sorry about that. I'm sorry I missed you and did't blow off that smart ass of yours." He kicked Sean solidly in the buttocks.

Sean sprang to his feet. He knocked down the Marine before anyone could even move to prevent it. He had caught the giant man by complete surprise. He was kneeling in the man's chest, punching him squarely in the face with both fists. Logs and Little Joe pulled him off Spike. T.J., Yance, and the others restrained the big man from instant retaliation.

Spike was screaming at the top of his voice. "Let go of me. I'll kill that little sucker-punching cocksucker. Let me go."

T.J. took out his Ka-bar knife, "You ain't killin' nobody, Spike. Man, you were way outa line sayin' you should have offed him, then bootin' him in the ass. You don't care you almost killed a good Marine? That's your business. But you ain't gonna come down here an' mess with my people."

Spike turned his screams and anger to T.J. "Put the big knife away nigger, and let go of me. I'll kick his ass and yours."

Lt. Fox appeared, standing with his hands on his hips. "What in the hell is this? Didn't you people have enough fighting for one day? Maybe I can arrange a night ambush or a L.P. for you people. Spike, if you want to kick some ass, go to the perimeter and beat up on the bodies of the dead N.V.A. If you mess with any of my people again, or I ever hear you say nigger again, I'll have you digging heads for the rest of your tour. The only reason I didn't write you up for that shot on the bunker today was because I thought it was an honest mistake. You've always been a good man in a fight. Now, go back to your platoon. The Gooks might decide they want this mound of dirt back and try to take it tonight."

Spike picked up his 3.5 rocket launcher and stomped along the hill slope. "You're dead meat when we get back to the firebase, you F.N.G.," he said to Sean. "I'll catch you alone and you . . ."

The first incoming N.V.A. 82mm mortar round seemed to land directly on the angry big Marine. Spike's form was initially concealed by the explosion, then blown to pieces.

"Incoming!" The platoon was below ground level within a second of the first explosion. Five rounds fell on the hill. Spike was the only casualty. The short, deadly barrage appeared to be from only one concealed N.V.A. mortar.

Sean looked in the direction where Spike had been hit. "I'm sorry, Lieutenant. He nearly killed me today and then when he started to jerk me off and say he was sorry he'd missed me, I lost my poise. I'm really sorry, Sir. It won't happen again."

Fox scanned the area for any trace of the man. "It sure as hell won't happen with him again, Irish. We've lost enough people today. Let's stay sharp."

The N.V.A.'s counterattack to retake their bunker complex never materialized. The platoon spent a restless night on 50 percent watch and waited for dawn. They remained on the hill the next day and improved their fighting holes and fields of fire. That night, they were once again placed on 50 percent watch, but everyone slept better.

The following morning, after the company ate their rations, they left the hillside and continued their sweep back toward the firebase. The battalion C.O. wanted everyone back before the Tet truce that had been arranged with the Communists. The operation had taken almost three weeks. Sean had ushered in 1968 sleeping in the bottom of a two-man fighting hole on a nameless hill.

The company filed back to the firebase through the main gate. Some cursed as they tripped on the stoney river bottom and fell into the ugly brown water. The red dust of the firebase clung to their wet gear. They were all already filthy from the bush. They were bone tired and their mood was foul. They only wanted to wash off the crud and have their first hot chow in three weeks.

T.J.'s squad reached the center of the firebase, which was on a slight rise, then turned toward their tent area.

A few yards away, three 105mm Marine cannons opened fire at a distant, unseen target. A couple of the platoon members, including Sean, threw themselves to the ground at the startling sound of the loud cannon fire. Everyone else flinched or ducked their head in an involuntary response.

Rusty Robbins, the homely, red-haired, freckled, battalion clerk was passing T.J.'s squad in his clean jungle utilities and new flak jacket. "Boy, you sure can spot an F.N.G. Dumb shits can't tell the difference between outgoing rounds and incoming."

Sean got to his feet and glared at the clerk's toothy grin. He felt the anger from the insult swell but he reminded himself of his loss of control with Spike a couple weeks prior. As he began to turn, Logs grabbed his arm and spun him out of the way. Logs moved very close to L/Cpl. Robbin's face with his own.

"What the hell would you know about it, asshole? These boys have just seen more action in their first operation than you've seen the eight months of your tour. You are one of those in-the-rear-with-the-gear big mouth poques who's going to live to make it back home and tell 'em how tough it was over here. You've got the balls to call these Grunts F.N.G.s? You're just a sissy Remington Raider. Major give you a Purple Heart for cutting your index finger on a typewriter ribbon?"

"At least I know the difference between the sound of incoming and outgoing rounds."

"So would these boys, if they spent their entire tour jerking off at a safe firebase, instead of humpin' in the bush. I tell you what, Poque. Come out in the bush with us next operation. When you get back to this safe little place you have here, you'll hit the deck if someone passes air loud enough to hear. That's how we Grunts manage to stay alive."

Robbins rolled his eyes and smirked in Logs' face. "Man, you're breakin' my heart, Logsdin. You Grunts . . ."

Logs tossed his rifle to Sean, who caught it in mid-air. He roughly grabbed Robbins by the front of the flak jacket and shook him, "So I'm breaking your heart? How about I break some of your teeth?"

T.J. grabbed Logs firmly on the left shoulder, "Let go of the poque, buddy. He ain't worth gettin' busted over."

Logs released his grip on Robbins, "Yea, T.J. You're probably right. If I give this brown noser a fat lip, he won't be able to kiss the major's ass for a week or so. The major would get real angry and probably send us right back in the bush."

Robbins took two steps back, out of Logs' reach, "Hard ass Grunts. All you guys think you're so bad."

T.J. moved closer to the clerk. His release from Logs' grip had obviously given him new bravado. T.J. reached out and put his arm around Robbins shoulder, "Son, we know we're bad. We prove how bad we are 'bout every day in the bush. Then, when we're here on stand down, we gotta protect your candy ass if the firebase gets hit."

"Listen, Cpl. Johnson, we get incoming here on a regular basis, couple times a month, at least."

There was a loud chorus of sarcastic moans from the squad. Robbins balled up his fists, "Hey, well then fuck you guys."

T.J. pulled Robbins close to him and spoke clearly into his ear under his new helmet cover, "Boy, you better shut that big mouth and be on your way. I already saved yo' ass from one whipping. If you stand there running that mouth at my squad, one of them crazy Grunts you see there gonna take your fat ass out where you stand."

"You threatening me, Corporal?"

"Get outa my face, Robbins. Threatening you? Boy, I wouldn't threaten you, I'd just zap you. Now listen up, Turd. I don't care if you are the major's kiss ass clerk. If you mess with any of my people again, they'll have to fly us both to Da Nang to get my boot out your ass."

Robbins stormed away, cursing under his breath at the Grunts. He sat down at his field desk. He comforted himself with the knowledge that they were nothing more than crude, uneducated bullies. And he fully knew L/Cpl. "Logs" had been correct when he said Robbins stood a much better chance of survival than Grunts who were always out in the bush.

T.J. led the squad to their assigned tents, "Let's get us a shower and some chow A.S.A.P. Never know about them sneaky Gooks. They want a Tet cease fire. Probably so they can attack this here firebase and we can get our butts shot up protecting Robbins and them other poques."

Sean gave Logs back his M-16, "Everyone is talking about the Tet cease fire. What the hell is Tet?"

Two squad members looked at Sean as if he'd asked where babies came from.

"Irish, Tet is the Gooks' New Year. We lay chilly at Christmas. They ask to do the same for their New Year. Ask me, it's just an excuse for them to regroup. Cease fires —just a bunch a bullshit."

Sean was showering the filth of the bush from his body. He stood next to Logs, who covered his short hair and face with soap lather, "Thanks for stickin' up for me with that jerk Robbins. That guy could piss off the Pope. I was already embarrased by falling to the deck. He sure didn't help."

Logs rinsed his short hair and lathered again. "Forget it, Irish. I get fed up with some of these guys going on and on with all that F.N.G. crap. I figure, a Grunt is an F.N.G. until he gets his cherry and proves himself. Once that happens, we're all equal. Some guys may have shorter tours left than others, but we're equal. The only guys that continue to rap that F.N.G. shit are either piss-poor Grunts that only have their time in-country to talk about or in-the-rear poques, like Robbins. That's the only thing Robbins has on a good Marine like you, more time in-country. That's why he jerked you off. He's jealous."

Sean felt confident as he dressed in a set of clean jungle utilities. First T.J. then Logs had said he was a "good" Marine. With only six weeks with the unit, he felt as if he was fully accepted as a dues-paying member. They could keep their medals and citations. If the men that fought beside him respected him, they could put all their ribbons where the sun didn't shine. He had all the recognition he needed. If he would ever see his home again, it would be with their help.

The squad laughed and talked loudly together as they ate their first hot meal in over a week. The battery of 105mm Marine cannons fired another unannounced volley. This time, Sean merely tucked his head down against his shoulders at the sound. He looked across the wooden table at Logs, who was concentrating on the tough piece of beef on his mess tray. "Hey, Logs, for an F.N.G. I'm improving. I didn't hit the deck that time, I only flinched."

"You did good, Irish. Keep up the good work and maybe you could become the battalion clerk some day."

T.J. could hardly be understood with his mouth crammed full of instant mashed potatoes. "Shit, I'd rather have my sister in the whore-house than my brother be the battalion clerk."

At that moment, Rusty Robbins entered the mess tent, unaware of the squad's conversation or presence. He stood in the center of the tent, wondering why all of the tent's occupants were laughing at his mere arrival, and obviously at his expense. He decided to see his friend, the mess sergeant, later that evening for something to eat. He was glad that at least some of the guys assigned to the firebase stuck together like the Grunts did. Rusty Robbins pushed his hands deep into the side pockets of his utility trousers and walked back to the battalion tent.

"Stupid Grunts," he muttered. "They don't realize how hard we all work back here. Vietnam is different than other wars; it's not safe anywhere. Grunts talk like the firebase is like some damn fancy country club. I sure don't know any country club that gets rocketed every week."

After lights out, the squad sat around the steps of the tent and talked. By now, every letter and package Sean received from home contained at least two pieces of chewing gum. He reread a letter from Terri and pressed the letter to his nose. He closed his eyes and pictured her in his arms as he gathered in the scent of the perfume she had sprinkled on the paper. Logs had received two large blocks of solid chocolate and shared the candy with his squad mates. Yance savored every bit and cupped his hand around his cigarette to conceal the red glow of the burning end.

"Hey, T.J., did you and Irish really play football against each other in high school in Detroit?"

"No lie, Yance. Ol' Irish come to our field with his Denby Tars. Forty of the biggest, baddest white dudes I ever seen. We figure they is all show and no go, we gonna teach these honkies how to play some football, ghetto style, for real."

"What happened?"

"Son, they knocked our dicks in the dirt. I see this pretty boy, Number 7, their quarterback. Right off, I don't like the peckerwood. I give him some hard sticks, and a couple cheap shots. You know, a man's got to do what a man's got to do."

Mr. Cool was engrossed by the details of the sports story. "Yea, Brother, you do him up right?"

"Shhhit, Bro. Honkie threw three touchdowns and hit me so hard when I tired to tackle him I heard bells for a week."

Mr. Cool's disappointment was obvious. Yance took a long drag from his smoke. "And may we assume that Number 7 was our newest squad member?"

Sean had stayed in the shadows, somewhat embarrassed by T.J.'s account of their game. "Yea Yance, I was Number 7. Truth is, that T.J. kicked my ass the whole game, and he's not the only one that heard bells for a week."

Mr. Cool was less upset. At least the white boy who had gotten the better of his hero in high school was Sean. "What was the final score, T.J.?"

"Don't remember. Thirty to somethin'."

Sean broke into a shy grin and moved to T.J. "It was thirty-four zip. October 15, 1965."

T.J. pretended to throw a stone at Sean and smiled. "Irish, you honkie peckerwood. You actin' all modest an' shit like you don't remember. You even remember the date."

Logs nudged Sean, "Hey, Slick, the Denby Tars? What the hell is a Tar?"

There was a slight defensive tone in Sean's voice. "It's an old term for a sailor."

Yance threw down his cigarette and shook his head. "A friggin' swabby? You guys had a swabby as a nickname and still had a good team?"

"Wait a minute, Yance. T.J.'s school was the Falcons. Would you rather be a sailor or a bird?"

Yance rubbed his chin and lit another cigarette. "Let me think on it. I'll get back to you."

Just before Sean fell asleep that night, he thought again of Terri. Not a day passed that he didn't miss her. Or write her, if he could. January was nearly over. A year to go and he'd be home, holding her and loving her again.

3

February, 1968

FEBRUARY, 1968
VIETNAM, HUE CITY

Just as nothing in life's experience can fully prepare a young man for combat, none of their combined combat experience prepared the men of the First Marine Regiment for the battle to retake the city of Hue.

In the midst of the Tet truce, the Communists launched a massive assault on the populated areas of South Vietnam. As many as 12,000 regular N.V.A. troops and additional local V.C. managed to capture and hold the entire city of Hue. The old Imperial City was locked in the grasp of the Communists for a full day before Marine and A.R.V.N. units could regroup and begin their attempt to retake the city.

On the morning of Jan. 31, 1968, a two-company-sized force of Marines fought their way up Route One into Hue City. They managed to relieve a group of Army M.A.C.V. personnel trapped south of the Perfume River. As Marines crossed the river to relieve an A.R.V.N. command post near the large walled fortress of the Citadel, they were pushed back south of the river.

The Marine Corps had created an obscene term for a condition which may be unique to the extreme violence of intense combat. When the mind is violated with too much horror, it seems to create its own defense system. The man takes on the famous "50-mission stare" and begins to function without thinking. The term is known as a "mind fuck." It was a condition that seemed to exist among most of the platoon after only a few days in Hue.

Sean's company had been taken from their stand down at Phu Bai and fought into Hue on most of Jan. 31st. That night, the company had slept in the rubble and smoke near the Perfume River in the M.A.C.V. compound.

Lt. Fox informed the platoon that luckily the Fifth Marines had been called in to assist, along with additional A.R.V.N. units. The First Battalion was to clear the portion of the city south of the river. Every man in the platoon knew that someone was going to get his ass kicked attempting to take the Citadel that loomed on the river's north bank. Each man privately prayed it wouldn't be him. Most hoped the job would go to the A.R.V.N.

T.J.'s squad had taken shelter for the night in the walled-in yard of a large church cemetery. It was raining and the men found what cover they could from the steady, light downpour. They had been in Hue a week.

T.J. called to his people to eat their rations and be prepared to move out.

Sean and Logs sat close together and shared a poncho liner as a cover from the rain. They were both in a daze from the terrible fighting of the days before. Their platoon was in decent shape, but they knew their company had been badly beaten up in their first days of combat in the city.

Lt. Fox sat next to T.J. "Your squad did a hell of a job this week. Pass the word, Skipper's pleased. Tell them to stay on their toes. This place is lousy with Gooks and they've got good equipment. This is not the type of combat we've been trained for."

T.J. smiled at his lieutenant and lit a C-ration cigarette. "Maybe not you, Lu-tenant. Some of us been city-fightin' our whole lives. It'll be good to be out of the bush for a spell, if it would stop raining and warm up a bit."

Fox folded up his map of Hue City in absolute disgust. "T.J., let your people know that Charlie's got his shit packed tight. This is going to be one ass kicking operation. This will be the fight of our lives. Don't let them get spooked and sky out. After another day or two in this living hell, you'll pay to be back in the bush."

The row of small houses across the narrow street from their yard erupted in massive, ear-splitting explosions. T.J. ran for the stone wall. "Incoming, incoming. Big shit. Get your asses to huggin' the deck or kiss them good-bye." The second barrage of 120mm Communist rockets fell in the street just outside the courtyard. Sean had wedged himself between a palm tree and the four-foot wall. He concentrated on making himself as flat as humanly possible and prayed to himself. He had a terrible feeling he couldn't explain, a feeling of impending doom. He had reached inside his flak jacket and clutched the St. Christopher medal attached to his dog tag chain. He turned his head so he could see the center of the walled-in courtyard. He saw Tiny from Yance's fireteam. Tiny was curled in the standard, and now familiar, "fetal incoming position". They had all entered the world from that position. Sean briefly wondered how many thousands of men left it the same way.

Sean saw one of the large rockets explode on the small space that had been occupied by Tiny's cowering body. The ground shook violently from the horrible, grinding crunch of the explosion. Thick smoke hung for a moment in the light rain. As it slowly thinned, Sean saw that Tiny was gone. The young Marine had disappeared, vaporized by the large rocket's explosion. Large pieces of hot shrapnel had ripped into the palm tree trunk and the wall, inches above his helmet. Sean held his St. Christopher's medal with his praying hands, "Holy Mary, Mother of God, pray for . . ."

Another large rocket tore into the two-story house, showering the yard with plaster and other flying debris. There were several calls for the corpman. Sean heard Logs being sick behind him. He could only hope it was from fear and not wounds. Sean could not safely lift his head to check. Sean cried. " . . . now, and in the hour of our death, Amen."

A rocket barrage fell several dozen yards outside the wall. Then, the rocket attack stopped.

Members of the squad moved to help the corpman attend to the wounded. Logs was not hurt and only slightly embarrassed. Only Sean knew he had been sick, and he said nothing. The two of them slowly walked to the deep circular hole that had been dug in the muddy yard by the rocket hit on Tiny's position. Tiny was gone from the site, but Sean spotted one shredded jungle boot up against the corner of the house. There was a portion of bloody flesh still inside. Sean fought back the need to gag, quickly took a swallow from his canteen, and pretended he never saw Tiny's boot.

The wounded and dead were moved toward the old school, where battalion had set up shop. T.J. gathered the rest of the squad. Lt. Fox pointed down the ugly street, and T.J.'s squad had the point. It started out like every day in Hue. Lt. Fox needed his best squad up front, on point. It was a difficult dichotomy for the young officer. He was forced to expose his best, and personal favorite, squad to the most extreme danger for the sake of the entire platoon. A combat Marine's reward for being dependable and proficient seemed to be to increase his chance of being killed.

T.J. arranged his people so they would be as effective as possible. "Logs, you boys got point first. Irish, make sure you got a couple extra frags. Speedy, you throw like a girl, give Irish your frags. We got a M-60 team and a 3.5 crew right behind us for when we step in some shit. Mr. Cool, stay with me, Bro. Remember, people: little Gook bastards are everywhere, behind every wall, rock, bush, tree, window. They're everywhere."

Sean adjusted the M-26 grenades on his gear. "T.J., if they think there's a few thousand Gooners in this friggin' city, why don't we pull out and let the Air Force merely erase this place?"

"Can't. This ol' town is a special place to the Vietnamese, Imperial

City and all that. Besides, they say there's still thousands of civilians trapped here."

"Screw em . Gooks are Gooks. I say call in the Air Force and let God sort them out."

"Irish, that's no way for a nice Catholic boy from a nice family to talk about your fellow man."

"Oh yea? Well, I nearly got my nice Catholic ass blown all over that courtyard back there. Now I get to walk point down a street we all know is lousy with Gooks."

"Irish, quit your bitchin'. You and Logs were sayin' you were gettin' tired of just fightin' for some box on a map. Well boys, here's a whole city we can fight for. And if we win it back, we can keep it. Now, move out."

They moved out in a well-spaced, staggered column. The narrow street was heavily littered with assorted debris. There was some evidence of a brief battle by the A.R.V.N. troops when the city was captured. Most seemed to be from the rapid, panic evacuation of the majority of the civilian population.

The platoon continued up the narrow street. Some of the houses had large iron gates near the street. Others were surrounded by walls instead of fences. Every door, window, wall and corner could be concealing Communist troops.

At mid-block, T.J.'s point squad came under intensive cross fire from rifles and automatic weapons. The ambush fire was coming from a church directly in front and a row of small one-story houses to their right.

T.J.'s entire squad and their support people were pinned down. They could hear T.J. yelling from midway in the long column of men.

"Logs, keep your people down. The Gook's volume of fire sounds like we walked into a whole N.V.A. platoon. Put out some fire, boys. I'll get some more help. We better surpress some of that fire of theirs or they'll cut us to pieces."

Yance crawled along the stone street to the motionless body of the newest member of his fireteam.

"You need a corpman, Yance?"

"Don't bother, T.J. The kid is deader than shit."

Most of the squad members merely raised their M-16's up over their cover and fired in the direction of the N.V.A. with one hand. The poorly-aimed Marine return fire did little to slow the deadly N.V.A. fire.

Lt. Fox was busy on the radio as he studied his map, "Yankee X-Ray, requesting immediate 81mm fire mission...request A.S.A.P. . . . stand-by for coordinates . . ."

There was a brief silence on the radio.

"Shot's out. Fire mission on the way, Yankee X-Ray. Stand-by for impact."

The first volley of 81mm fire fell short of the target, and fell only 30 yards in front of T.J.'s squad. Lt. Fox was screaming into the radio handset, "Add 50 and watch those short rounds. You nearly dropped that volley on our own people."

"Affirm, Yankee X-Ray. It is raining, you know? The mortar increments get wet and . . ."

"I don't give a flyin' fuck about your wet increments. I'll come over there and stuff your increments up your ass. I've got a whole squad getting torn up by the Gooks. I won't have anyone hurt by friendly fire."

The radio was silent again.

"Roger, Yankee X-Ray. Shot's out."

A moment later, several 81mm mortar rounds fell on the N.V.A. positions.

Lt. Fox gathered up the remainder of his platoon. He quickly organized a well-armed Reaction Force. The platoon carefully advanced up the cluttered street to join T.J.'s squad. Fox wanted to move on the N.V.A. positions before they could recover from the mortar barrage.

T.J.'s squad began to use fire discipline, and their fire improved in accuracy. The M-60 crew began to put out fire. The 3.5 rocket gunner fired two well-aimed rounds into the church.

Sean and Logs concentrated their fire on the row of small houses to their right flank. Logs sprayed the one-story buildings with a full magazine of M-16 fire. Sean positioned himself, then threw a hand grenade through the open door of one of the small houses. The explosion seemed to take the small house right off its foundation. They were encouraged by the sight of Lt. Fox leading the rest of their platoon up the street at a dead run. Fox suddenly wheeled around and fell hard to the street. An AK-47 round had torn into the right side of the young officer's chest.

T.J. saw Fox fall. He knew Fox was shot. He didn't know if Fox was still alive. He called to Sean. "Irish, throw another for cover, then give me a hand. Lu-tenant's been shot bad. We gotta get him to cover."

Sean took another frag grenade from a trouser pocket. Logs again sprayed the hooches with M-16 fire as Sean set and threw the round hand grenade. After it exploded, Sean and T.J. sprinted to Fox's unconscious body.

The two young men dragged the limp body of their lieutenant to the cover of a stone wall. Sean tore open a combat bandage as T.J. opened Fox's flak jacket and jungle jacket. "Shit, been chest shot, he's got him a sucking chest wound. I can see some little bubbles in the blood."

Sean handed T.J. the battle dressing. Sean looked up and down the busy street for an available corpman. Sean was frantic. "Shit T.J., we can't let the lieutenant die. Damn this, Goddamn this. We need some more help. Corpman, corpman, we need a corpman here, damn it."

T.J. skillfully placed the back of the combat bandage on the wound to create an air-tight seal. "Don't you freak on me, Irish. The lu-tenant is one tough dude. He'll pull through."

The busy corpman ran from one wounded Marine to another. As a corpman ran near them, he saw the expression on Sean's face and dove to the street next to Fox. The skinny, acne-faced Texan sat his heavy equipment bag next to the lieutenant's head. "You all can go back to doin' yo' thang. I'll take good care of yo' buddy here."

T.J. grabbed the corpman by the upper arm. "He's got a suckin' chest wound, not a through and through."

Sean changed magazines and knelt close to his lieutenant, "Take good care of him Doc. They don't make 'em any better."

Lt. Fox briefly regained consciousness and attempted to sit up, despite the pain. The corpman and T.J. gently held him down against the road. "Lay still, Lu-tenant. You got yourself shot, but you be back in no time. You're one skating S.O.B. You gonna sky out on us and leave us to chase all these Gooks from Hue City without you."

Fox looked down at his bandage, "I can't believe this. Damn. I'm sorry you guys. T.J., you and Irish take care of the platoon and yourselves. I'll be back. We'll all be together again, I promise."

"No sweat, Lu-tenant. We gotta catch up to the platoon. Doc here will take care of you. We'll be seeing you, Sir. Take care."

T.J. and Sean sprinted to catch up with their platoon, a full city block away. "Was hell of an officer, Irish. Damn, he apologized for gettin' shot. We gonna miss him."

Sean wiped the tears from his eyes, "Yea, sucking chest wound. It figures, though. The wind doesn't blow in this place, it sucks."

An hour later, Fox was on an operating table at a Navy hospital at Da Nang. The skillful Navy doctors and nurses struggled to keep young Lt. Fox alive. On a rubble-strewn street in Hue, the platoon was pinned down again. T.J., Sean, Logs, and the others struggled to keep themselves alive.

The days seemed to blend, one into the other. The smoke, fog, rain, and haze helped the mind view the horror of the battle as a confused, terrible dream. Time seemed to be measured in casualties rather than days of the week. No one spoke of Tuesday or Wednesday, but rather the day Ski, Tiny, or Lt. Fox was hit.

The company continued its savage fight to clear the area south of the

Perfume River. The fighting was house to house, street to street. They were often cut off, as N.V.A. and V.C. troops moved around behind them, taking hours to evacuate the wounded.

T.J.'s squad looked for a dry place to take a break. T.J. found a one-story hooch with an undamaged section of roof that could provide cover from the near-constant drizzle. The men leaned against the wall, broke out their C-rations and the letters from home that had finally caught up with them.

Sean reread the latest letter from Terri. He pressed the perfumed paper to his nose. It still held a trace of her perfume, although kept in the wet pocket of his flak jacket. She wrote about their families and the harsh Michigan Winter. Terri did not once mention Vietnam or the war. The content and mood of her letters seemed to Sean more appropriate if he was away in Europe for a year on a school exchange. He counted on her letters to keep him going, but he wished that at least once she would acknowledge where the hell he was. She always ended her letters with a suggestive sentence that caused him to recall the lust of their relationship.

Yance sat next to Sean, also reading a letter from home. He began to laugh out loud and finally fell over onto Sean in laughter.

T.J. tossed an empty ration can in his direction, "Hush fool. We finally find a place to crap out and you'll alert every lifer and brown bar in Hue City that we're in here."

"Can't help it, T.J., listen to this. I got a letter from my dad. He says my whole family is grateful I'm not with the 26th Marines in Khe Sanh. He read that the 26th is really seeing the action. Get this, my grandmother and mom stopped at church and lit a candle in a prayer of thanks that I'm not at Khe Sanh."

Sean frowned as he looked down at his can of ham and lima beans.

"Yance, better tell them to blow out the candle before it's too late. The 26th stepped in some deep shit in Khe Sanh. They have their problems, but your dad should know we're not having any fun here either. Hell, N.V.A. took this city a week ago, and we're no closer to securing this toilet than we were then."

Yance turned to his box of C-rations, "Naw, don't mean nothin', Irish. The less they know, the less they worry."

"Don't you want them to know what the hell we're really doing here?"

"What for, Irish? Do you think it will mean a flyin' fuck if my folks know we're gettin' torn a new ass-hole? Is it going to help end the war? Will it get you home for your 20th birthday?"

Sean became frustrated and fumbled with the can. "My dad was with the First Division in the Pacific. I want him to know we're out here fighting a real war, not in some air-conditioned hooch in Da Nang jerking off."

"So show him your Purple Heart and scars when you get home. Maybe your dad cares, but I'm tellin' you, Buddy, nobody back in the world gives a shit for this war. You've said yourself that your girl has never even admitted that you are here. Irish, it's like the man says, don't ask the question if you don't want the answer. Fuck em'. They don't want to know."

Logs sat down next to Sean and put his hand on his shoulder, "Irish, this isn't a college campus. In Nam, life's a bitch. You're wrapped too tight for the mind trip of this war. You spend a few more months here and you'll understand what Yance is saying. Even *"Stars and Stripes"* reports on the war like it was a damn ballgame. They talk about losses as light and moderate. Ask the dude that got wasted how light he thought the losses were. We do body counts instead of ground gained, like other wars. I picture the war stats on the back of the sports page. 'At the end of the third quarter: Marines 125, N.V.A. 55.' "

Sean's expression of frustration and disgust was obvious. "I need more than that to go back out there to get my ass shot off."

Logs pulled Sean close and spoke in his ear. "No you don't. None of us do. We do what we're told, and we do the best we can. That's why we're here instead of Canada, or college, or prison. Irish, you're doing your thing so you can go back to your little red TR6 and ride down that Lake Shore Drive you're always telling us about with your girl. If you need somebody to pat you on the back and say, 'Thanks Marine for risking your life for freedom,' you're gonna stay an angry young man."

Sean winced as he bit into a large, dry lima bean, "None of this seems to make any sense."

T.J. took a long swallow from his canteen, "Irish, the day any of this crazy shit starts to make sense, I'm skying outa here, on the double. They can go fuck themselves with all that fallen domino jive. First *this* country be Communist, then the next. That's all talk an' politics. Irish, the Nam is for real."

Logs helped Sean fill his pockets and gear with several M-26 hand grenades. They prepared to move out with what was left of their platoon.

"Hey Logs, we been down this street before?"

Logs carefully peeked around a stone pillar, "Don't think so, Irish. They all look alike, but there's not enough damage on the walls to look like we've been here."

Little Joe and Stoney worked as one segment of the fireteam, Logs and Sean the other. They had become skilled and well-coordinated in their method of securing the individual houses. Stoney covered the rear, Little Joe the front, Sean and Logs took turns kicking in the doors and entering. Often, Sean preceded their entry with a hand grenade. They seemed to be in near constant contact with the enemy.

The fireteam sprinted into the yard of a battered, two-story brick house. Logs got a glimpse of a N.V.A. soldier darting past a blown-out window. "Little Joe, Stoney, cover the rear. There's Gooners in the house."

Logs took cover behind a gutted car in the center of the yard. Sean moved behind a large palm tree near the main gate and took a hand grenade from his gear. He set his M-16 against the tree, pulled the pin, stepped away from the tree, and accurately threw the grenade into the house through the open window. A moment later, the first floor was lit up with an orange flash, then filled with grey smoke. Suddenly, N.V.A. soldiers began to pour out the front door, wildly firing their AK47 rifles. Logs shouldered his M-16 and began to fire. "Holy shit, that place is lousy with Gooks."

Sean had already prepared to throw a second grenade. The sight of the N.V.A. soldiers startled him for an instant, and he froze. An AK47 round slammed into the palm tree next to him. The sight reminded Sean, in that instant, of the cliché of rats leaving a sinking ship.

He reset himself and threw the hand grenade at the doorway of the house. The 1½ pound metal ball struck one of the N.V.A. soldiers in the head as he emerged in the doorway. Both he and the grenade fell back inside the house. The grenade's explosion ended the mass exodus from the house.

There were still four N.V.A. soldiers in the courtyard, sprinting toward the gate, firing at Sean and Logs. Little Joe moved in response to the fire and shot down two of them. Logs and Sean each shot one. The yard was still for a moment.

Then, without warning, two more Communist soldiers emerged from the front door. The first one out was obviously badly wounded by the grenades, and he staggered toward Little Joe. Little Joe fired once and the man fell. The other man had moved the bayonet of his AK47 forward into the attack position. He ran directly for Logs.

Logs was on one knee, changing magazines in his M-16. Sean raised his rifle to fire, but the N.V.A. soldier moved in front of Logs before he could get off a shot. The N.V.A. soldier lunged the rifle and bayonet at Logs. Logs managed to move back against the car and batted away the first bayonet thrust with his own empty rifle.

Sean bolted the few yards between their positions. As the Communist soldier poised himself to thrust at Logs again, Sean hit him just below his pith helmet with a savage stroke from his rifle butt. Despite the fact the M-16 stock was plastic, the hard hit of the rifle butt knocked the man against the old car. Sean lowered the barrel and fired a full burst into the small man. His lifeless body crumbled to the ground near Logs, who was unharmed.

T.J. and the rest of the squad arrived in response to the heavy fire. Mr. Cool began to fire M-79 grenades into the house. An M-60 machine gun crew poured fire into the door and windows.

Logs jammed a full magazine into his M-16. He stumbled to his feet, looking at the body of the man who had tried to bayonet him. His expression was of total disbelief. He fired three rounds into the body and kicked the dead man in the side of the head.

"You wanna fight, you little bastard? God, I'm so sick of this shit! Come on outa there you little S.O.B.s. Come on, let's fight some more." He sprayed the big house with the remainder of the rounds in his magazine.

An M-48 tank rumbled up to the gate. T.J. looked into a hatch and said, "Hey, Dudes. That two-story hooch is lousy with Gooks. We fragged the place and they come pourin' out. How 'bout givin' the place the zippo so I don't lose none of my people going inside?"

The barrel of the tank slowly moved to aim at the house. There was a "wooshing" sound, as a line of napalm streamed from the tank barrel into the house. There were several secondary explosions as the house was engulfed in flames.

Logs had again changed magazines. He aimed intently at the burning house. They heard a scream from inside. Sean saw a grin on his friend's face he did not recognize. "Get some tank. Get some. Out-fucking-standing."

Sean knelt next to his friend. Logs' expression was frightening. "You alright, Logs? Did that Gook stick you?"

"Naw Irish, I'm cool. Real close. If you hadn't bipped him on the melon when you did, he would have got me next try. Thanks Irish, you saved my aching Irish ass. I'm beginning to wonder what for, but thanks."

T.J. moved the entire squad to a secured courtyard a block from the current fighting. The smoke from the burning house hung close to the ground with the fog and mixed with the steady rain.

Sean filled empty M-16 magazines using the charger guides and rounds from his bandoleer. He looked out over the squad in the courtyard. It was as though he was viewing the world through frosted glasses at the unique sights and smells that the veterans of Hue would never forget, but could not seem to adequately describe.

Lt. Remmick, Fox's replacement, entered the courtyard with the remainder of the platoon.

"You men did an outstanding job. It appears you walked up on one of their command posts. They must have got themselves cut off without realizing it. They had radios, food, the works. Too bad we burned it. We might have recovered some key intelligence."

"No offense, Lu-tenant. If we'd a tried to take that big ol' house full a' Gooks, we'd have got some people hurt. My man Irish, he fragged the first floor twice and they was still comin' at us."

The new officer put his fist to his lips to cover a nervous cough, "Certainly, Corporal. I didn't mean to sound as if I was second-guessing. I just . . ."

Logs stood quickly, "Well then, don't, Lieutenant. Next time we'll wait for you. Then you can lead us in to gather the key intelligence. You are real tight, Lieutenant."

Logs stormed out of the courtyard. The new lieutenant looked puzzled, "Now what's the matter with him?"

Sean got up and went after Logs. "I don't think he likes it here anymore," he said.

Two nights later, the squad spent a windy, rainy night huddled together in the dry shelter of a small Catholic church. The windows had been blown out during the fighting, and there was a hole in the roof. In spite of battle damage, the church had fared well compared to the other structures in the area.

T.J. returned from a platoon briefing. "You all better chow down. We gonna be movin' out in a few minutes. Seems that battalion found a whole new sector fo' us to secure."

Sean ate peanut butter and crackers from his C-ration unit. He wiped the grime from the white plastic spoon on his pant leg, then carefully spread the dry, canned peanut butter on the brittle, canned, tasteless cracker. He winced and washed down his breakfast with a gulp of lukewarm grape Kool-Aid.

Sean had felt a strange sensation when T.J. returned from the briefing. He felt that something was very wrong. He couldn't clearly identify or explain the sense of impending disaster. He chose to ignore it. "Hell," he thought. "The whole battalion has been shot to shit. Why shouldn't I have a feeling of impending doom?" He was still unsettled.

Logs was seated next to him, near a partially-destroyed confessional. He opened his pack and took out the cardboard C-ration box he had drawn the night before in the dark.

"Oh no, not ham and mother-fuckers. We get one or two rations a day and I go and grab ham and mothers. I bet the jerks that invented these culinary delights have never even eaten them." He opened the large

O.D. green can and looked in disgust at the contents. Small balls of white grease floated on top of chunks of salty, fatty ham and large, dry lima beans.

"Man, I'm so hungry that I could eat the south end of a north-bound skunk. But there's no way I'm going to eat this shit." He threw the full can across the church. It splattered against the opposite wall.

Sean cleaned the last of the peanut butter off his plastic spoon with his mouth and replaced it in his flak jacket.   "Haven't you heard, Logs? Shouldn't waste food, there's people starving in China. You say you could eat skunk butt, but you can't do ham and limas? I thought they taught you about fine food in Boston."

"Irish, when we get back to the world, I'll show you some fine food. We'll go to Fenway Park to watch the Red Sox. We'll eat red hots while Yaz chases baseballs off the Green Monster. Then we'll go to my folks' pub. We'll eat fresh clams and get shit-faced on Guinness Stout. Then, we cross the bridge to Cambridge and pick up a couple ladies. We cruise down near the Charles River and get our brains screwed out by moonlight. You smart-ass Motor City Mick, after a day like that you'll know why I can't eat ham and limas. Oh, Holy Mary, what I wouldn't give for a tray of fresh clams and a Guinness, right now."

T.J. tossed Logs an unopened can of "ham and eggs - chopped". Not good, but much less offensive than ham and limas at O5OO hours.

"You honkies is a strange breed. You confuse this simple Black boy from the Motor City. Logs talk all that shit about seeing a ballgame and drinkin' and gettin' some trim in the moonlight. Then, he wanna sell his soul for eatin' some fish and a warm dark beer. Tell you what dude, while you eatin' the fish and drinkin' that bad beer, I'll take your place with the lady on the blanket down by the river."

Logs took out his can opener again. "T.J., clams aren't fish."

"Man, like I give a shit what a clam is. I know what screwin' is, and I'd rather screw than eat clams any day."

"T.J., you've got to imagine the day as a multifaceted event. The game at Fenway, the food and drink at the pub, the girl in the moonlight. Oh, like you died and went straight to heaven."

T.J. merely shook his head in disbelief. "If you wanna eat at all this morning, better get to it. We're movin' out soon."

T.J. finished checking over his gear. He spoke briefly with one of the new replacements. He put the new man in Yance's fireteam. He was still down to two members. Most squads were in much worse shape. T.J. was only two men short overall with only two fireteams. He looked at Sean, Logs, and Yance talking together near the confessional. T.J. walked over and stood in front of them.

"You know, something been buggin' me for a month now. Everybody says that all us Soul Brothers look alike. Well, you three look like you was cut outa the same mold. You all the same size, age, you all talk alike, 'cept Logs. **Sometimes he sounds like President Kennedy. If I didn't know you all so well, I wouldn't be able to tell you apart.**"

The three of them looked at each other. Yance stood up and began to look over his own gear, "You've got a point, T.J. The only difference between us is that Irish is a rich preppie and we suspect Logs is a virgin."

Logs laughed with a mouth full of cold "ham and eggs - chopped." "You're dreamin' Yance. Shit, I bet I've screwed more than you've beat off."

Yance slapped Sean across the helmet, "What you got to say for yourself, rich preppie?"

Sean readjusted his helmet. "T.J. has always been someone I've respected. But if he thinks I look like you two, I may have to reconsider my opinion. As for this sexual thing, I'm saving myself for marriage." The sound of the young men's laughter inside the small church seemed out of place in the center of the rubble. But it served to comfort all that heard it. Laughter was very rare in Hue City during those weeks.

The bad weather, foul smell, and savage fighting the Marines encountered each day wore every man to his own personal emotional and physical limit. Exchanges of meaningless conversation about things and places they had previously enjoyed, either real or imagined, helped to keep a slight grasp on their sanity. Any humor served as mental medicine. A squad member that could initiate a laugh was appreciated nearly as much as if he'd have performed an act of bravery. In a way, he had.

The squad moved into a different portion of the city, south of the river, near the canals. T.J. stopped at the end of a short block of residential one- and two-story brick houses with yards. The squad broke into two fireteams. Logs' team moved up the left side. T.J. and Yance's team moved up the right side. They all knew they were headed for trouble when a battered M-48 tank rumbled up to cover their advance up the small street.

Sean put a piece of gum in his mouth. "Shit, that tank's presence isn't doing a thing for this bad feeling I've got. They didn't send us a tank as back-up 'cause they like us."

Logs, Sean, Stoney, and Little Joe had worked their way to mid-block, using their well-developed technique. They had not had any contact with enemy troops yet. Across the street, T.J. and the others kept pace, also without contact.

Logs directed his team into the yard of a neat, one-story house. The pleasant-looking home seemed nearly untouched by the battle. Stoney ran to cover the back. Little Joe positioned himself behind a short stone fence to cover the house's front. Sean and Logs slowly stepped up on to the porch, one on either side of the front door. Sean removed a grenade and prepared to throw it through the front glass window.

Logs seemed to be elsewhere. "Hey Irish, when you come to Boston, we better not go to a Tiger game. Those crazy Sox fans hear you cheering for the Tigers and we'd have to fight our way out of there too. We'll go see the Yankees. Nobody likes them."

Sean smiled but he was concentrating on the small house. "Hang tight a minute, Logs. Let me frag the inside of this hooch before we go strolling in. Something's not right. I've got a feeling."

"Irish, you'd frag the whole damn city given half a chance. Save your grenades for later. Looks like the Gooks skyed out of this entire street. They probably weren't ready for the tank. My bet is that they're regrouping at that little park at the end of the block to give that tank of ours a little welcome. Those damn RPGs of theirs kick the shit out of Grunts. But I hear they really do a number on a tank or an Ontos crew."

Logs readied his M-16 and took his familiar pre-entry position. "Irish, I swear, you'll love old Fenway Park. When I was a kid I use to watch ol' Ted Williams blast the horse hides into the cheap seats."

Sean held a grenade in his right hand, "Let me frag it Logs, I got a feeling..."

"Just cover my entry, Irish. You and your feelings. Hell, you're almost as bad as the damn Doggies. If we did it your way, it would take us all day to do this one block. Let's just do it."

Sean replaced his grenade and readied his M-16. Logs looked over to Sean who was frowning, but nodded that he was set.

"Relax, Irish. Trust me. Have I ever lied to you? Here we go."

Logs moved in front of the wooden door and kicked it open with one solid thrust of his jungle boot. Logs stood for a second in the open doorway, his eyes adjusting to the absence of light inside the small house. Sean moved a step closer but could not advance into the doorway because Logs was still standing in the entrance. Logs managed a brief, terrifying glimpse of a N.V.A. soldier, hiding in the interior shadows. Logs identified in his conscious mind what he was seeing the instant before the little man fired a full automatic rifle burst into Logs' torso.

Logs' body heaved violently and was roughly pushed all the way back to the iron entrance gate to the house's courtyard. His body was lifeless before it fell to the stone walkway. Seven AK47 rifle rounds had found their mark in the young Marine's 19-year-old body.

Sean's M-16 selector was on full automatic. He wheeled into the doorway a millisecond after Logs had been shot. Sean's immediate presence actually startled the young Vietnamese. He expected more

Marines to attack the house, but not that suddenly. The half second of hesitation, caused by his surprise, was fatal. Sean's eyes met those of the frightened N.V.A. soldier whose last vision was a flash of hate and fury from Sean's eyes. Sean's rifle was waist-high. He opened fire just an instant before the soldier could respond. The long burst of M-16 fire hit the N.V.A. soldier in the chest and throat. The body was flung over backwards, crashing into a small table. The table and dead soldier toppled to the house's stone floor.

Sean walked into the small house and glanced quickly for any other N.V.A. soldiers. There were none. He shouldered his rifle and emptied his magazine into the dead soldier's body. He changed magazines. He knew the mangled corpse of the dead, uniformed N.V.A. soldier posed no further threat. Little Joe reached the doorway in time to watch Sean fire a second full magazine into the dead man. When Little Joe saw Sean change magazines again, he ran to get T.J. Sean's fire had nearly shot the body in half.

"Come on you Gook bastard, get up!" he was shouting. "Get up you S.O.B.! Hiding in the dark, hiding in ambush, day after day. Come on, you little bastard. Let's fight some more." He shouldered his rifle again.

He felt T.J.'s solid hand grab him firmly on the shoulder. "O.K., Irish. Let's move out. You killed that Gook enough. He's dead, boy. He's real dead."

Sean ignored T.J. and his words and set to fire. "Get your fucking hands off of me. He killed Logs.   I'm not finished."

T.J. spun Sean around, "Irish, you been nothin' but outstandin' since you joined the unit. But ain't none of my people gonna talk to me that way. None of my people gonna waste good ammo shooting up dead Gooks. We're in the middle of the worst battle of the war. Damn if you gonna waste that shit when there's a thousand live Gooners out there waitin' on us."

"God damn you, T.J. I just watched Logs get wasted. If it had been me, he'd do something for me. He wouldn't just move on without doing more about it. He'd do something."

"Irish, you go back out in the street and say good-bye to your friend before they take him to the rear. I'll do something for Logs that you will be satisfied with. We can't bring him back, but we'll say good-bye in a most righteous fashion."

Sean lowered his M-16 and walked back out in to the rain. He passed Stoney and Little Joe without a word. He walked slowly, his head hung.

An overweight corpman, new to the platoon, had made certain Logs was dead and covered his body from the rain with a poncho liner. The fullfaced corpman had been nicknamed the Padre. He had wanted to be a priest and often prayed over dead Catholic Marines with his rosary, when conditions permitted.

Sean knelt down next to Doc Padre, over the covered body of his dead friend. The corpman completed his prayer, crossed himself, then left Sean to be alone with Logs for a moment. The only sounds were assorted distant gunfire, the shuffle of Marines walking in the yard, and the rain falling on the poncho liner that covered L/Cpl. B.T. Logsdin's lifeless body.

Little Joe went out into the street and recovered Logs' helmet. Sean pulled the poncho liner off his friend. He could see that Doc Padre had opened Logs' flak jacket to inspect his wounds. The enemy rifle fire had destroyed his chest up to the throat. Logs' face was pale and wore the expression of sudden, violent death. His eyes were still open, but the witty blue sparkle was gone.

Sean gently forced the eye lids shut. He lifted Logs' body and held Logs' head against his own chest. He softly stroked Logs' wet, matted hair and rocked back and forth as he hugged his dead buddy. Sean could not conceal his emotions. He wept as he held Logs' body in his arms, and he didn't care who saw him.

"You stupid Beantown Mick. You had to be in such a damn big hurry. Couldn't let me frag the hooch first. You promised me, damn you. Fenway, the clams at the pub, the girls at the Charles River. Damn you, getting yourself killed, you promised. We had things to do in the world. I love you, you son-of-a-bitch. Look what you've gone and done. Oh, God, why?"

T.J. knelt down next to Sean. "Come on Irish, let Doc Padre take care of Logs. He'll cover him back up against the weather and stay with him until they move him to the rear."

T.J. lifted Logs' body out of Sean's arms and gently laid him back on the wet, stone walkway. T.J. and Little Joe each took Sean by an arm and lifted him to his feet. Little Joe handed him his M-16. He seemed to be in a daze. At T.J.'s direction, Little Joe led Sean to a secure courtyard nearby.

The M-48 tank had moved to mid-block during the brief fire fight. T.J. sat up on the tank and spoke with the Black tank commander.

"Say, Brother, you'd be doing us Grunts a big favor if you'd put a Willie Peter round in that hooch over there, in the one where my man got zapped."

The tank commander rubbed his chin and shook his head, "Sorry, Blood. No can do. You got no hostile fire, nobody in danger. We got absolute orders. No rounds fired unless necessary."

"Brother, I got a platoon of Grunts that believe you doin' that hooch is most necessary. If you do that house, you'll have a platoon that will protect your tank as if it were their old lady. Grunts may not seem real smart, but they are one loyal bunch."

The young tank commander surveyed the entire block. "If I put a Willie Peter round in that hooch, probably the whole street will burn. We could really hear some shit about burning a whole city block."

"What they gonna do, cut our hair and send us to Nam? We lost a hell of a good man. Burning a block won't bring him back, but it will help those that's still alive. If anybody gives you any stuff over this, I'll take the heat. I'll say we were pinned down. Dig it Brother, like it won't be my first lie."

"Ah shit, you won't have to explain nothin'. It's still my fuckin' tank. If the Gooners killed your buddy from that hooch, we'll raze the mother. We'll raze the whole damn block. Get your people in the clear, shot on the way. Fuck it, we'll raze the whole damn city."

"You won't be sorry, Brother."

"Bro, I'm only sorry I'm here at all. And we're sorry your man got wasted. This city is bad news."

The barrel of the tank moved toward the small house. It stopped, and a moment later the 90mm cannon belched a giant red muzzle blast. The Willie Peter round ripped into the small house. Whatever wasn't destroyed by the initial explosion was set on fire. As the tank commander had predicted, soon the entire side of the street was set ablaze. Yance put his hand on Sean's shoulder. "Get some, tank. Get some for Logs. Burn this entire fucking city to the ground."

Sean moved to where T.J. was loading his empty rifle magazines. He looked over at the burning house that still held the remains of the North Vietnamese soldier that had killed his friend from Boston. "Burn you rotten Gook bastard. Burn."

Sean went to the box and drew a few fresh bandoleers of M-16 rifle rounds. He came back and stood over T.J., "You did good for Logs, T.J. He'd groove on it, you did real outstanding, T.J."

T.J. looked up and stared hard at Sean. "You better get yo' head outa yo' ass and back on straight, Irish. All that show, Willie Peter round, fire, it's all bullshit. It won't bring Logs back. You gotta suck up your guts or you'll end up just like Logs. Dead. You're a damn good Marine, Irish. You gotta let it go, my man. You let it go, elsewise it will eat you up until it kills you, one way or another."

Sean moved close to T.J. so no one else could hear. "Logs was my friend, T.J. I loved him like I love my brothers. He's been dead for 10 minutes. What do you want from me? You want light talk and jokes? Fuck you, fuck the squad, fuck the platoon, fuck the whole damn Corps."

"Listen up, ass-hole. We all cared for Logs. He was a friend to Yance and me and Mr. Cool. But Irish, it don't mean nothin'. You go ahead and miss him. We'll all miss him, like we miss Lt. Fox and all the others.

Point is, you can't let it get in the way of you stayin' alive. All any of us got left is each other. But that won't mean nothin' if you get dead too. When you alive, you're a buddy, a friend, dig? When you dead, you become nothing but a memory."

"Give me some time, T.J. You've always been fair, just give me some time."

"Normally Irish, you'd have some time. We ain't got that luxury here in Hue. I talked to Little Joe and Stoney. You're the new fireteam leader. Neither of them want it and both say you're the best man for the job. You'll probably get some turd from H&S company as a replacement."

"T.J., I can't take Logs' place. I can't be the fireteam leader in his..."

"Damn you Irish. We all lost friends in Nam. You know you the best man to take over the team. Them boys is only 18. We need you. Do it for me, or you, or Little Joe and Stoney, or even for Logs. But take over the team."

Sean rubbed at his tear-filled eyes and winced. "Give me the word, T.J., we'll be ready."

It had been three days since Logs had been killed. Even T.J. was surprised with the natural ease Sean had in taking over the position of fireteam leader.

The platoon received another group of wide-eyed, frightened replacements. Some were fresh from the world, others were battalion support personnel pressed into combat by the unit's heavy losses, most members of H&S company's administration and motor-pool platoons.

T.J. approached Yance and Sean, who were leaning up against a wall, while they cleaned off their M-16s with tooth brushes.

"Well boys, we got the last of the replacements until this here battle for Hue City is over. The Skipper says the well is dry now. We've gotta make do. The Fifth Marines is all chewed to pieces too. A.R.V.N.s is all shot to hell. But who really knows about them dudes? Far as I'm concerned, they ain't never held their own. They worse than Marines. They judge their success by how many of them gets killed. Anyway, whole mess of Army boys from the Army's 1st Air Cavalry are fighting the Gooks west of the city. Now that the Army is in the fight, we'll see lots more choppers. Normally, Marines would bitch about havin' to be helped by the Army, but here in this damn Hue City, they can call in the Boy Scouts 'fore I give a shit. Yance, you got a new boy. Name's Cowboy. Grew up on some ranch some place out West. Irish, I got a nice surprise for you. Seems the Brass is puttin' every swinging dick up on the line. You got your old buddy, Rusty Robbins, the clerk, in your fireteam."

"Ah no T.J., my aching ass. I'd rather fight short then have a poque getting in the way."

The tone in T.J.'s voice became stern. "You'll take him and be glad you got him. I got the feeling that by the time we finish taking this city, we'll be able to hold a platoon muster in a wall locker."

Sean attempted to make light of the situation. "How about givin' Robbins to the A.R.V.N.s?"

"Come on Irish. Of all these crazy Grunts, I figured you'd be the most understanding. It's only been two months since you were a cherry yo' self."

"Two months, already? Damn does time fly when you're havin' fun." Sean went to find the other members of his fireteam, Little Joe and Stoney, and tell them the news about their replacement.

T.J. sat down next to Yance after Sean left. "Well, Yance, how's our boy Irish doin', for true?"

Yance put his rifle cleaning gear away and lit a smoke. "Hard to figure, T.J. You've seen him during contact. He already knows his shit, and there's not a better man in a fire fight. But inside, I think he's a time bomb waiting to go off. He's really trying to get over Logs' death. But we've always said that Irish might be wrapped too tight for all this madness. It's a coin toss, buddy. He'll either keep a cap on it, or lose his cool."

"Yea, I see the same thing, Yance. You an' I know him best, now that Logs is gone. Keep an eye on him. Let me know if you think he's gonna freak."

Sean was stretched out on the floor of a small, partially-destroyed house. Little Joe and Stoney sat near him, talking and smoking C-ration cigarettes. L/Cpl. Rusty Robbins stood over Sean for a full minute without speaking. "Excuse me, Cavanagh, I was told to report to you."

Sean had considered the way he would treat Robbins since T.J. informed him of the new assignment. Sean slowly got to his feet and looked over the replacement's equipment. It was clean and new, and also appeared to be complete. Sean pointed at Robbins' M-16. "Can you use that thing?" he asked.

Robbins automatically held his rifle at the position of port arms. "I shot Sharpshooter in boot camp. I've fired it a couple times when the firebase was attacked. I can break it down and keep it clean."

"O.K. Rusty, for a day or two, stay close to me and do exactly what I tell you. Just don't shoot one of us by mistake. We use Grunt names here, not clerk names. I'm Irish. That's Little Joe, Stoney, and you better call Johnson T.J., instead of Johnson, or you'll be wearing your helmet around your waist. Rusty may be a nice nickname, but it's no Grunt name. As long as you're with us, you're name is Red. Rusty sounds more like the name for an Irish Setter."

Robbins looked down at his boots and shuffled his feet, "Irish, sorry about that F.N.G. crap back at the firebase last month. I was out of line. Goes to show, what goes around comes around."

Sean gave Red a friendly slap on the side of the helmet. "Don't mean nothin', Red. Let's just concentrate on keeping each other alive."

T.J. called to the squad to move out. They walked about three blocks to where the fighting began.

"O.K. boys, you know the drill. Yance, take your fireteam down the right side. Mr. Cool will go with you. I'll go with Irish's team, and we'll do the left side. Yance, make certain we all advance up the street together. That way we cover each other's back."

Sean moved next to T.J. as they began to advance on the first house on the block. "T.J., our new man has a new name. Red is going to stick close to me until he gets the feel of things here."

T.J. could not hide his grin of satisfaction. "That's cool. Go ahead, Irish, do your thing. I'm just along for the ride, so to speak."

They entered the yard of a large, two-story brick house. A tall iron fence encircled the old building.

Sean called out instructions as if he was still a quarterback in school. "Red, you and Stoney go around the rear and cover the back. Find some cover and make sure that if there's any Gooks in there, they don't sky out on us. Little Joe, you and I will go in the front. T.J., if you will, cover our butts once we're inside. Damn, big house like that could hold an N.V.A. platoon."

The fireteam crouched, then sprinted to their positions. Sean, T.J., and Little Joe ran onto the long covered porch. They carefully stayed out of the line of sight of the house's windows and front door. Sean ducked under an open window and moved toward the front door. As he passed under the window, he heard a sound of moving furniture from inside. Little Joe was on the other side of the door. T.J. was still on the other side of the open window. Sean pulled a grenade from his gear and shouted inside, "Come on, you sneaky little bastards. Come out of there. Lai Day, DiDi, or I'm going to frag your Gook ass."

T.J. crawled up next to Sean. "What you got, Irish?"

"Inside, I heard someone moving around."

All three young men called inside, in very poor Vietnamese, for the occupants to come out. There was no response from the interior. Sean pulled the pin from the grenade, but held on to the spoon, "Come on out, you little prick."

T.J. shouldered his M-16 and pointed it at the open window. He nodded at Sean. Sean threw the grenade through the open window very hard, so it would bounce around the room until it exploded. That made it nearly impossible for someone to pick it up and throw it back out. A second later, the house's interior roared with the explosion. Sean threw in a second grenade. The house was large and he was taking no chances. The second grenade exploded.

Sean moved in front of the door. "Little Joe, cover our backs. T.J., you follow me in. Little Joe, wait until I call you."

Sean kicked the wooden door open. He darted inside and moved to the right. T.J. was directly behind him and moved out of the open doorway to his left. The large first floor was filled with thick, choking, grey smoke from the hand grenades. Sean's rifle was on automatic.

As the smoke began to thin, he saw a prone figure near the stairs leading to the second floor. All he could identify was that the body was dressed in black. He fired a short burst into the motionless figure. As the smoke continued to clear from the room, Sean felt sick when he began to see the body clearly. He wished he could have called back the M-16 rounds and the grenades. The clearer air revealed that the body was smaller than a soldier's. T.J. scanned the room for any threat and covered the stairway, as Sean slowly approached the body. He nearly gagged when he realized he had shot a small Vietnamese girl, about 11 or 12 years old. She was taller than normal, but not yet a young woman. She wore the traditional black pajamas, normally seen in the rural villages. They had not seen such clothing worn by civilians in the city.

Sean stood over the body, staring over the little girl. "Dear God, what have I done?"

T.J. pushed past him and got close to the child's corpse. "Damn. Irish, you couldn't have known. We all called out for her. You heard a noise, it could have been a Gook waitin' on us, like the one that did Logs. These folks know the rules. We called first."

"Maybe she was injured or too afraid to come out. Maybe she had..."

"Fuck your maybes. Maybe if frogs had wings they wouldn't have to hop."

"I swear to God, T.J. I didn't know."

T.J. moved to walk around the child's corpse. "We better check upstairs and make sure some Gook ain't up there waitin' with his AK47 to do us while we're cryin' over this child here. Could be another Gook trick, using the dead kid to get our attention."

Sean moved toward the little girl. T.J. grabbed his arm firmly and stopped his advance. "Where you think you're going?"

"I've got to inspect her wounds. I've got to know if I really killed her or if she was already dead."

"Let it go, boy. Look how pale she is. I bet she's been dead since yesterday. She hardly even bled from the wounds. Let it go, I tell you."

"Don't you understand, T.J.? I've got to know if I killed her. I've got a sister that age."

T.J. shook his arm firmly as he clenched his teeth. "Why you gotta know, asshole? So you feel even worse, an' go around cryin' and feelin' sorry for yourself? Poor little Grosse Pointe boy. What Goddamn good will it do? Will it bring her back? Will it bring Logs back?"

T.J. put his M-16 on automatic and fired a full magazine into the dead child's body, nearly shredding it. Little Joe appeared at the doorway, "What the hell you guys got in here?"

T.J. snapped at him, "Get yo' ass back where you were told, until we call you."

"Why, T.J.?" Sean asked.

"I say the child was dead before we got here. She certainly ain't any more dead than when we come inside the room. Now, you ain't never going to know when she died. You may never know you didn't kill her by mistake. But, you'll never know for sure if you did."

They checked the second floor. It was vacant. T.J. instructed Sean to say nothing about what took place in the house. T.J. would tell them they had killed a local V.C. who had been wounded by the grenades.

Sean was sick to his stomach. He walked, without speaking, back into the courtyard. T.J. took out his Zippo lighter and with the oil from a lamp, set the house interior on fire.

Little Joe walked up to his squad leader. "What went down in there, T.J.?"

"Add one V.C. for the Skipper's body count."

Red joined the fireteam. "Lots of shootin' for one V.C."

T.J. grabbed Red by the front of his flak vest. "Listen, asswipe, next hooch you be the first one in. Then tell me how many rounds need to be fired, if you're still alive."

"Look, T.J., the place is on fire, really burning to beat hell."

"Yea, we must have hit an oil lamp. Them old houses burn like a mother."

Red watched the flames dance out of the open window. "Shouldn't we do something?"

"Look around you, you stupid shit. What you want to do, call the fire department?"

The squad cleared the remainder of the block without incident.

While the squad was taking five in a small Catholic cemetery, T.J. called for Sean and they walked behind a tall stone wall, out of the view of the other squad members. Sean hung his head.

T.J. struck like a cat. He grabbed Sean by the front of his flak jacket, at the throat. With the other hand, he slapped Sean across the head hard enough to knock off his helmet.

"Listen up, you sorry-ass son-of-a-bitch. You're one hell of a nice guy.

Maybe you're just too damn nice. You're a good man in a fight, but all this emotional shit gonna fuck you up. You gonna have to decide to suck up your guts and be a Marine or be some slimy Grosse Pointe cry baby that ain't worth squat. If you flip out on me, Irish, I swear I'll off you myself. I ain't gonna let you get some people killed 'cause you got your head up your ass 'cause of Logs and some dead Vietnamese kid. You gotta stop thinkin' that everything that happens has only happened to you. Do you think you're the only man ever lost his buddy? You think you the only Marine that offed a civilian? Son, up near the D.M.Z., in the bush, some dudes just do Gook civilians 'cause they get bored, or frustrated, or just plain crazy."

Sean's eyes filled with tears despite his efforts to maintain his poise in front of the squad leader and friend. "I'm sorry if I've let you down, T.J, I . . ."

"Stop bein' sorry. Be as good as I know you can be. We got new people. We still got a hell of a battle to fight. You stay here for a few minutes and get yourself together. Then Irish, let go of all of this excess mental bullshit for now."

T.J. placed his wide hand on the side of Sean's head for a moment. Then he turned and walked back to the squad at the small cemetary, leaving Sean alone.

Sean kneeled down to pick up his helmet from the ground. As he reached his knees, he lost control and began to weep. He wept so hard that he fought audible sobs, as his chest heaved with accumulated grief and fear. He fell onto all fours and lost his C-ration lunch in the bushes.

It seemed to the Marines that since the Army had arrived, there was continuous fighting somewhere in the city.

T.J.'s squad rested in the small yard of the house being used as the Company C.P. T.J. and Sean often talked about their senior football season. The conversation would always include some play-by-play of their game against each other.

Lt. Remmick ran out of the house, yelling, "T.J., get your people. The second platoon stepped in some deep shit and they're pinned down. We got some people from the weapons platoon to make a Reaction Force. We got to try and reestablish contact. They're cut off and can't get their wounded out."

T.J. slowly uncurled and got to his feet. "Come on boys. You heard the Lu-tenant. Let's get our asses in gear and save the second herd."

The section of the city they were operating in had been reduced to rubble. The re-enforced squad ran toward the sounds of a vicious fire fight.

Lt. Remmick called out to his best squad leader. "T.J., take your people down that block and try to work your way around behind the N.V.A. in those houses."

The squad followed T.J. at a full sprint for about 100 yards. Suddenly, both sides of the street erupted with rifle and machine-gun fire. Stoney went down hard. Sean and Little Joe were able to drag him to cover. Little Joe began to call for a corpman as Sean opened Stoney's flak jacket. Stoney was still conscious and screaming from pain and fear. Sean couldn't believe he was still alive, much less conscious. He was hit in both lungs and near the heart. He began to choke on the blood he was coughing up. He died in Sean's arms. Little Joe was still calling for a corpman, knowing it wouldn't help. T.J. was yelling to the squad to return fire.

Little Joe grabbed Sean's forearm tightly. "Irish, I saw the Gooks that did Stoney. I saw the muzzle flash, light machine gun, that little white hooch there across the street."

Sean gently lay Stoney back down onto the street. "Little Joe, the fire is thick enough out there to walk back to Phu Bai on."

Little Joe looked at Sean as if in complete disbelief. "Irish, Stoney was my buddy. Either help me do those Gooks in the hooch, or I'll do it alone. You can save your orders bullshit. I respect you, but nobody could order me not to do the Gooks that killed Stoney."

Sean readied a hand grenade, "Screw it, we might as well do something. We're not doing anyone any good laying here."

Sean rose to his knees and threw the grenade at the front of the small one-story house Little Joe had pointed out. They advanced with the cover of the explosion at the front of the house. Sean was then close enough to throw a grenade into the front window. The next explosion roared inside the house.

Sean and Little Joe sprinted across the small yard toward the house. A round from a AK47 tore into Little Joe's right shoulder. As he fell, another smashed his other collar bone. The support 3.5 rocket team saw the sniper and fired a round into his position.

Sean kicked open the door and sprayed the two-man N.V.A. machine-gun crew with M-16 fire. He ran back out into the yard and began to place combat bandages on Little Joe's wounds. The sounds of the fierce fire fight roared around them.

Little Joe looked up at Sean with an expression of pain. "How's it look, Irish?"

"You'll make it, Little Joe. But you're outa this toilet for a while. You can skate for a while in a Navy hospital."

The volume of enemy fire decreased drastically. It appeared that the N.V.A. were satisfied with the damage their ambush had done. As soon as they began to take losses, they pulled out.

Sean knew that the only real threat to Little Joe would be his bleeding to death, or shock, while waiting to be medevaced. Sean lifted Little Joe on his back, using the fireman's carry, and headed for the Company C.P. T.J. yelled to Sean, "Irish, Little Joe hurt that bad?"

"Bad enough not to wait for some chopper pilot to decide the L.Z. is safe enough for a medevac. I'll take him back to the C.P. That area is secure enough."

T.J. waved, then had a second thought. "What about Stoney?"

"Just have somebody cover him up. I'll be right back."

Sean stumbled past Red under the uneven weight of Little Joe's body.

"Red, go join up with Yance until I get back." He could see the complete terror in the ex-clerk's face. "Hang tough Red, you'll be alright."

An hour later, Sean located the remainder of his squad. They were eating their evening rations. He sat down next to T.J. and Yance. He waved at Red.

"Doc Padre says Little Joe will make it. He'll probably be back to finish his tour. How bad we get it other than Little Joe and Stoney?"

T.J. cut at a piece of timber with his bayonet. "Lu-tenant was killed. Head shot by a sniper. Yance lost the new man, Cowboy. A dude from weapons platoon was also K.I.A."

Yance rested his head in his hands. "Man, they sure set us up that time. They pin down a platoon as bait, and ambush the Reaction Force that they know will come."

T.J. turned and spoke firmly to Sean. "Irish, I told the squad to return fire, not to attack."

Sean took out his evening C-ration meal. "Little Joe knew that was the hooch that the Gooks that killed Stoney were in. I either went with him or he'd have got zapped alone. Besides, right after we wasted those two bastards, the rest decided to sky out. They didn't mind the ambush, but they didn't want to fight."

"Screw it, ain't gonna second-guess you. 'Sides, can't argue with success."

Sean attempted to cover himself with rubble, as the heavy incoming rocket and mortar barrage fell on the street they occupied. When the deadly barrage finally lifted, the Marines tentatively raised up from their hasty positions of cover.

T.J. brushed dust and small pieces of debris from his flak jacket and trousers, "Damn. How can it be so dusty when it ain't done nothin' but rain since we got here?"

There were calls for a corpman. Yance trotted up the short street looking for Sean. Like T.J., Sean attempted to brush some of the city's debris off his clothing.

Yance found Sean and grabbed him by the arm. "Irish, you better check with Doc Padre down by the end of the street. Red has been hit. Looks real bad."

T.J. wiped his face with a small O.D. green towel as Sean sprinted to Red's location. T.J. called to Sean, "It's just like my man Slim Jim usta say when we did ops near the D.M.Z. Sometimes you counts the meat, sometimes the meat counts you."

Sean knelt next to Doc Padre, who was busy working on Red. The corpman was busy putting a large bandage on Red's face. He looked at Sean and shrugged his shoulders in a sign that Red's chances of survival were even unknown to the experienced corpman.

Sean leaned all the way over to speak to his new man. "Don't even try to talk, Red. Doc Padre says you're going to be fine. We'll miss you, Red. You were a damn fine Grunt, for a clerk."

The badly-injured Marine held up his hand. Sean held it and felt Red squeeze it firmly, letting him know he understood, saying good-bye.

Sean went looking for T.J. after they evacuated Red from the street. He found his friend smoking a C-ration cigarette, seated against a topless palm tree. Sean dropped down next to him.

"T.J., the Gook New Year, Year of the Monkey. Happy fucking New Year. This must really be the year of the ass-hole. It sure is starting out shitty. Gooks have a unique way of celebrating a holiday."

"Irish, you gotta know by now, Gooks got a unique way of doing everything. They been spendin' three weeks trying to do us."

Sean unwrapped a C-ration candy bar. "T.J., I've been fighting the thought, but we're never going to get out of here alive. They'll keep us jerking around in this hell hole until we all get wasted."

T.J. took a long drag from his cigarette. He brushed away some loose debris so he could stretch out his long legs. "Irish, quit your bitchin'. The Corps is doing us a favor by sending us here. If we were back in good ol' Mo-town, we'd just be gettin' into trouble. You'd be playin' stink finger with some sweet young thing in the bucket seats of your TR6, gettin' her daddy all pissed off at you. Me, I'd be rippin' off the man an' making my mama sorry for the day I was born. We oughta be thankful. By sending us here, they're keeping us out of trouble."

They paused a moment, and looked at the total ruin and destruction around them.

"Yea T.J., never thought of it that way. I don't know how I'll ever be able to thank them."

They both laughed out loud and patted each other on the back.

The Battalion finally secured the area south of the Perfume River. Three weeks of intense combat had taken every fiber of emotional and physical strength from those that survived. There was little left in the personality that allowed a young man to laugh or cry.

Hue created its own kind of living dead. Their total concern was reduced to survival from minute to minute. For those who fought in Hue, there was no next month, next week, or even tomorrow. Life consisted only of the agony of the present.

The platoon was reduced to little more than a reinforced squad. There was no platoon commander after the loss of two in three weeks. The only original squad members not killed, or badly wounded, were T.J., Sean, Yance, and Mr. Cool.

At the direction of Regiment, Capt. Kincade was ordered to send one complete platoon-sized unit to join the 1/5 in their final, all-out assault on the Citadel, across the Perfume River. The career Marine officer protested bitterly. He felt his people had already been through hell. He didn't like the idea of his people going to a different company, much less a different regiment. But the 1/5 had also been chewed up. The Marine commanders realized they'd need every man they could muster to retake the old Imperial fortress.

Weeks before, they might have underestimated the N.V.A. strength in the city. *Life* magazine had reported 2,000 N.V.A. troops in Hue. Later they'd estimate more than 12,000 with more than 6,000 enemy killed. Not a single Marine underestimated the cost in life and suffering that would have to be paid to secure the Citadel.

T.J.'s squad was selected as part of the newly organized platoon that would join the company from the 1/5. T.J. was made a fireteam leader; his fireteam was Sean, Yance, and Mr. Cool. Lt. Pollock was placed in charge of the makeshift unit.

Before they crossed the river, Lt. Pollock found a hooch for them to spend the night. Marines from the 1/5 brought them C-rations, water, ammo, grenades, LAW rockets, and other supplies.

One of the N.C.O.s from the 1/5 told the platoon, "We're really glad to see you guys. We know we'll need all the help we can get. This is going to be one hell of a shit-kicking contest."

T.J. lit one of his C-ration smokes. "Sure glad he told us that. I figured the Gooks had enough, and they'd just let us take the Citadel without a fight."

The men tried to eat some of their rations. There was the same nervous energy that one experiences in the locker room before the championship game. They loaded their M-16 magazines and loaded themselves down with grenades and as much extra ammo as they could carry, yet still sprint.

T.J. adjusted his position several times in an attempt to get comfortable, loaded with all the gear.

"Irish, we sure been through a lot together the last few weeks. Man, just think of it, two and a half years ago we were messing with each other on a football field back in De-troit. Now, I'd say we've saved each other's life 'bout half dozen times, at least.

"Boy, you done a damn fine job since you joined the squad. You did an outstanding job taking Logs' place, being so new in-country. You are by far the whitest, preppie dude I ever known. But you make me proud that we both from Mo-town. And for what it's worth, you're the only white guy I'd ever really call my friend."

Sean was writing his dad a letter. He had been very pensive.

"Being your friend is the best compliment I could have now, T.J. I got one of those damn feelings. Like before Logs got waxed. If I buy the farm tomorrow, make sure my dad gets this letter. Then, promise me you'll go to my house and tell my dad what happened here. The friggin' reporters must be writing their articles from Da Nang. Our squad has wasted more Gooks than the people home think are defending the whole city. And let him know that you thought I was a good Marine."

T.J. slid his helmet onto the back of his head.

"Don't go talkin' the fool. Ain't nothing going to happen to you, Irish. You're my main man. You, me, Yance, and Mr. Cool will take care of each other tomorrow.   Besides, I couldn't go to your house. Hell, if I went strollin' up to your dad's house in Grosse Pointe, like I was datin' one of your sisters or something, they'd kick him out of the country club."

All Sean had left was part of his sense of humor, "I thought about that, T.J. Just tell them you're there to do the lawn."

T.J. grinned and he and Sean exchanged a firm "Brother" hand shake.

"Tell you what, Irish. You gonna be alright, but I will make you a deal. If something did happen to you, I give my word I'll see your folks. You make me the same promise. If I buy it, you see my mama and tell her I got my shit together over here. Lord knows, I never give the woman nothin' but grief. She deserves to be proud of me least once, even if I gotta be dead to have that happen."

Sean showed his friend a sarcastic smirk.

"She must have been proud of you when you played football. You were a real decent defensive back."

"You ain't never gonna let up about that damn game, are you?"

Sean pretended to look puzzled. "What game? Oh yea, Oct. 15, 1965, Denby and Northeastern, 34-O."

T.J. merely shook his head and grinned.

"You peckerwood. I bet you remember every single play of that game. Well, superstar, do you remember getting your calf bit in the middle of a gang tackle?"

Sean sat up straight and set down his rifle.

"I'll be go to hell! That was you? I knew it all along. You finally admit that you're the one that bit me. I'll be damned."

T.J. broke into a broad, toothy grin.

"You still whipped our butts. But it seemed like the right thing to do at the time."

Sean decided to press the issue for a final time. "So, how did I taste?"

T.J. offered up the palm of his hand for a hand slap. "Man, you know I don't like white meat."

The two young men from Detroit shared Sean's last C-ration candy bar and talked together through the night. Detroit was a very different city for each of them. But 12,000 miles from the Motor City, they brought great pleasure to each other, speaking of places they had seen. Despite their different worlds, they had shared common places: the Downtown Loop, the riverfront, Belle Isle Park, Tiger Stadium, the small football field where they played football on a warm October afternoon nearly two-and-a-half years before.

Near dawn, Lt. Pollock entered the room.

"Saddle up, people. The day is finally here for us to chase the N.V.A. out of this city for good. They've had it three weeks. Today we take it all back."

Sean checked over his gear for the last time. "Hey, Lieutenant. Since the N.V.A. want that damn Citadel so bad, why don't we let them stay there and just charge them rent?"

"Don't be a smart ass, Cavanagh. Let's go. We're moving out."

T.J. gently slapped Sean across the back of his helmet, "Yea, boy, watch your mouth. You piss off the Lu-tenant, they'll cut off your hair and send you to Nam."

The fighting at the Citadel was savage. Accounts of that struggle reported that the Marines suffered a casualty for every meter of the Citadel they retook.

T.J. moved his fireteam skillfully into the rubble of the large, walled fortress. They were pinned down by two N.V.A. light machine guns. Yance crawled over to Sean, who was hiding behind a pile of bricks.

"Irish, try to drop a frag into that machine gun position to the right. I'll lay down some fire."

Sean took out a grenade and got into position. He nodded to Yance, raised to his knees and threw the grenade. Yance raised, and fired his M-16. While the grenade was in route, the machine gun opened up on Yance. Four rounds hit him in the left leg, nearly tearing it off. The grenade's explosion silenced the machine gun. Mr. Cool fired an M-79 grenade into the other machine gun position and killed the N.V.A. crew.

Sean crawled to Yance.

"Irish, I really went and did it this time. I'm screwed, buddy. Even if I don't lose my leg, they shot my knee cap right off."

Sean tied off Yance's leg and moved forward with T.J. and Mr. Cool, after the corpman arrived. Sean couldn't hide the tears in his eyes as he held Yance's hand and said a quick good-bye. "Irish, I'll be O.K. You guys take care. Stay alive, buddy, please."

Sean fell next to T.J. and Mr. Cool.

"Yance will probably lose his leg. Corpman says he'll make it if they can get him . . ." Sean put his eyes against his sleeve and cried.

T.J. put his hand on his shoulder. "Come on, Irish, we gotta keep moving."

An hour and 50 yards later, they were once again pinned down. Mr. Cool had found a full bandoleer of M-79 rounds on a wounded Marine. He was crouched behind a brick wall, pouring out a steady stream of the 40mm grenades. He raised to fire again, when an N.V.A. rocket propelled grenade exploded next to him. The blast blew part of his upper body away, killing him instantly.

Sean had taken cover behind a partially-destroyed inner wall. He didn't see Mr. Cool get hit. He tried to catch his breath in the choking smoke and dust. Changing magazines, he carefully lifted his head so he could see over his cover. He watched T.J. struggle to his feet and sprint to change positions. T.J. was shot in the upper left leg as he ran. He toppled into a deep bomb crater.

Sean yelled at the top of his voice, "T.J., you hurt bad?"

"Irish? Irish, fetch me a corpman. Damn if I didn't go and get myself shot in the leg."

Sean called for a corpman. Those who hadn't been hit were already occupied with the many wounded. The crater was about 30 yards to Sean's left. T.J. was fully concealed, but Sean could hear his voice from inside.

"Lay chilly, Buddy," Sean called. "I'll get you a corpman A.S.A.P."

"Not to worry, Irish, I ain't going no place."

Suddenly, three N.V.A. soldiers emerged from their hiding places and rushed the crater where T.J. lay wounded. Sean got to his feet, put his M-16 on full automatic, and ran toward the crater.

"T.J., the Gooks are rushing your position. Get your shit ready. Come and get some, you rotten bastards."

Sean fired as he ran. The advancing N.V.A. soldiers had not seen him. Sean's rifle fire cut down the first two. The third returned fire from his AK47 rifle. It felt to Sean as though he had run full speed into a tree. His left shoulder was ripped by a bullet, and he fell hard on the loose brick rubble. T.J. had managed to crawl to the lip of the bomb crater. He nearly cut the last N.V.A. soldier in half with a long burst from his M-16.

Sean was laying in the open, exposed to enemy fire. He was stunned, and he had fallen on his rifle. He rolled onto his back, to free the rifle, and grabbed it by the hand grip with his right hand. His entire upper left side was nearly paralyzed with blinding pain.

"Where you hit, Irish?"

Sean struggled not to pass out. "Shoulder, T.J. I think it's a through-and-through. It feels like it tore the shit out of me."

"Well, get your dumb ass over in this crater, or you'll be dead meat."

It took all of Sean's strength to even speak.

"T.J., I feel as though I can't move."

Two more N.V.A. soldiers changed their positions, about 40 yards in front. They fired at Sean as they ran. The rounds smacked the rubble all around Sean's body. Sean raised his M-16 with one hand and returned fire with the remainder of the rounds in his magazine. One of the soldiers tumbled to the ground in a flash of red and a jerking motion.

T.J. extended his rifle toward Sean. "Grab hold of the barrel with your good hand and I'll pull you in."

Sean put the sling of his own rifle over his shoulder and clutched T.J.'s rifle. After some groaning, and terrible pain, Sean slid on the rubble to the outer rim of the crater.

An enemy R.P.G. hit a pile of rubble just a few yards away. The blast knocked T.J. back down into the crater. It lifted Sean off the ground and tossed him to the crater bottom. Shrapnel from the rocket ripped into Sean's buttocks and the back of his legs. T.J. was peppered across the back of his arms and neck.

There were several inches of rain water on the crater bottom. Sean had been knocked unconscious by the rocket blast. He lay on his back in the cool water and mud until he regained consciousness in a wave of screaming pain. T.J. had slid down the muddy crater slope and sat next to Sean in the muddy puddle. He tied off his own leg. The light brown crater water was turning red from the severe blood loss from both men's wounds.

T.J. shook the body of his friend. "Irish, you awake, boy?"

"Oh God, T.J., I think I'm really fucked up. Whatever the AK47 didn't do, the shrapnel did."

T.J. changed magazines in both of their rifles.

"No time to feel sorry for yourself now, Irish. For some reason, the Gooners seem intent on takin' us out. They seem to want us 'cause we're wounded, and a bit more helpless. We gotta get back up to the rim and protect ourselves when they rush us again."

Sean shook his head to clear his vision. He looked up at T.J. through the blur of terrible pain. He took his M-16 from T.J. and crawled up the side of the crater, in absolute agony. T.J. crawled up next to him.

Both men carefully looked out from the relative safety of the crater. A fierce fire fight raged around them. Sean saw the back of T.J.'s jacket was soaked with blood, as were his trousers. He felt light-headed when he realized that most of the wetness he felt under his flak jacket and trousers was from blood, not the crater's puddle.

"Damn, Irish, I don't believe it. All that shit an' you never lost your helmet. Man, you got that thing glued on?"

Sean rested his dizzy head on the muddy slope. "It's just a matter of style, T.J."

Sean looked back down at the puddle at the crater bottom. He saw that it was red with blood. "Look at that water, T.J. That's our blood mixing, buddy. That makes us blood brothers. That's tight."

T.J. slowly shook his head and pulled a hunk of mud from his short afro hair.

"Ain't this a bitch. Now I gotta call a honkie Brother." Another R.P.G. round struck the ground in front of them, driving their faces into the mud.

"Does this mean you call me Blood, and I'll want to eat greens and ribs and that Soul food shit?"

"Oh sure. Get you a subscription to *Ebony* magazine and . . . Oh shit, Irish, here come three more."

The three N.V.A. soldiers charged, firing as they ran. Sean and T.J. opened up with poorly-aimed fire. They hit one. The other two were killed by a relief Reaction Force, sent to rescue T.J. and Sean. T.J. changed their magazines again. Sean took out a grenade. "Irish, you can't throw, all shot up like that."

"I know, but if we get overrun, I'm taking some of those little bastards with us."

T.J. gave Sean his rifle back. He called to the Marines he heard advancing to their rear.

"Corpman up! Sure could use a corpman in here."

Sean heard someone approaching their bomb crater from the rear. He painfully rolled onto his back, and aimed his M-16 toward the approaching sound with one hand. Doc Padre dove head first into their crater.

"Don't shoot, Irish! Damn, son, you call for a corpman, then almost shoot me when I come."

Machine-gun and rifle fire split the air over their heads. Doc Padre began to look over Sean.

"There must be a Gook reward on you two. They act like they're mad at just you two."

Sean lay back into the puddle at the crater bottom. "Hey, Doc Padre, reach in and get out my St. Chris medal on my dog tag chain, will you.? Then take care of T.J. He's all chewed up."

T.J. was still at the crater rim.

"No way, Doc. Take care of Irish, you can see he's goin' into shock."

Doc Padre took out his rosary and snapped at both young men.

"If you two don't mind, I'll decide how best to do my job. T.J., stay up there for a minute, and make sure no Gooks decide to drop in on us. It interferes with my concentration."

Sean began to protest, but the second hit of morphine quieted him. Doc Padre gently placed battle dressings on his shoulder. He rolled Sean onto his side and put two more bandages on the most severe of the shrapnel wounds. Sean rested his head in the mud. Some water poured into his helmet, but none got near his nose or mouth. The morphine seemed to separate his mind from his body. He felt himself floating away in the morphine euphoria.

"T.J., Brother, you saved my ass again. If you get wasted, I'll never forgive you."

"Be cool, little white Blood. You saved my bacon too, son. We'll skate now, some hospital with clean beds and hot chow. We got it made in the shade now. Just don't die."

Sean closed his eyes. He heard the constant roar of the on-going battle for the Citadel. He heard the voices of T.J. and Doc Padre, but could no longer understand them.

He saw Terri's face. She was smiling. They were floating in a small boat, in the middle of some peaceful, Michigan lake. It all disappeared in a rolling thick fog. The drug-induced fog lasted two full days. Not yet 20 years old, Sean spent 48 hours much closer to death than to life.

4

February, 1968 — December, 1968

FEBRUARY, 1968
VIETNAM

At first, all Sean felt was severe pain in his left shoulder. Then he realized the other pain at the back of his legs and buttocks.

His eyes were still closed, and as his feelings sharpened, he realized he was finally regaining consciousness. He didn't recognize the sounds around him. He could tell he was inside a large building. As he was able to organize his senses, he further realized that he was in a real bed.

He opened his eyes. At first his vision was very poor. He could only identify moving, white forms. As his vision cleared, he saw that he was in a hospital ward. Doctors, nurses, and corpmen moved among the double rows of hospital beds, attending to the wounded.

Sean turned and saw his left arm in a large heavy cast, from the shoulder to the wrist. The plaster cast held his arm up in the air, bent in front of him. His other arm was strapped to a board and had an I.V. attached. He felt the strange pulling sensation on his backside that he identified as numerous sutures. His mouth was dry. All he could remember since the bomb crater were brief moments of movement and horrible pain. Then someone would give him an injection and he would again drift away.

He lay on his back for a few minutes, watching the activity around him, organizing his thoughts as best he could. He only had the pain to convince himself he was still alive.

A Navy nurse appeared at the foot of his bed and grabbed his chart. She walked next to him and checked his pulse.

"Well, good afternoon, Marine. Welcome back to the land of the conscious. Are you in a great deal of pain?"

"My shoulder really hurts. My backside is just uncomfortable."

The nurse was obviously exhausted. Her lab coat was splattered with blood. She sat on the edge of his bed and took his blood pressure.

"I'll get you something, but try to tough it out as much as possible. This damn war is creating more junkies than any big city drug pusher.

After another day or two, I'd suggest you only take a pain killer to sleep."

"Excuse me, Ma'am. Since I was hit, I've been in the twilight zone. I have no idea where I am or even what day it is."

The nurse stuck a thermometer under his tongue and read his chart.

"Says you were brought in here the evening of 23 Feb. *Here* is lovely downtown Da Nang, at a Navy hospital. You were shot in the left shoulder, through and through, broke your clavicle. You have multiple shrapnel wounds to your buttocks and upper portions of the backs of both legs. You were in deep shock and suffered from severe loss of blood. Thanks to the wonders of modern medicine, and the invention of the helicopter, they got you here still breathing. We gave you some blood, sewed up your butt, put your arm in a cast, and put you in a warm, clean bed. Today is the 25th."

She removed the thermometer. "Also says you are going to be fine. The prognosis is for a full recovery. The good news is that in a couple months you'll be good as new. The bad news is you'll go back and finish your tour."

"Ma'am, how can I find out about my buddies and let my family know I'm alright?"

"Tomorrow morning. A Red Cross rep will come by and help you track down your friends and get you scheduled to call home. I'll get you some ice water for now. I'd bet you're real thirsty. Go easy on dinner tonight. Your body has been through hell the past few days, so don't make yourself sick.

"Marine, you say a prayer tonight. If you'd have been hit like that in the middle of the Tet battle, you'd have died at the aid station. There were a bunch of you people hurt taking that damn Citadel, but we were prepared for it. Not like that first week."

Sean turned his head to scratch his nose on his shoulder. "Did we retake the Citadel?"

"Oh yea. You all paid for it, but you took it. A.R.V.N.s raised their flag the next morning. Listen, Marine, take some advice. I know you lost friends, but for your own sake, don't be in too much of a hurry to get back. I hear the same shit from you kids every day. Buddies left behind, scores to settle, more Gooks to kill, all gung-ho, macho, John Wayne, Marine bullshit. Believe me, it's like you guys in the field always say, it don't mean nothing. Let your body heal. Let the days of your tour pass getting better, instead of getting shot at. You're still 19 years old. Don't be in a big fucking hurry to go back and die."

Tears filled Sean's eyes and he began to cry. The tears rolled down onto the pillow.

"Sorry, Ma'am, I don't know what's wrong with me. I guess I'm finally aware that I'm still alive."

"You go ahead and have a good cry, Marine. God knows you deserve it. And cry for me. I lost the ability about a month ago."

The bland dinner was his first solid food in days and first hot food in weeks. He ate slowly and only about half. He was glad he had taken her advice. The dinner gave him cramps, but he managed to keep it down. At lights out, he received a pain killer injection from a corpman. He fell into a dream-filled, drug-induced sleep.

The next morning, he met Mrs. Anna Webster, the Red Cross representative. She was the widow of a career Navy officer and had asked to be sent to Vietnam to do her part. She got Sean on the telephone schedule and took down the names of the friends Sean thought had been wounded, in an attempt to locate them.

The following day, Sean painfully moved into a wheelchair. Mrs. Webster wheeled him to the telephone room at the hospital. The voice in the telephone receiver did not sound 12,000 miles away. Sean forced back a sob when he heard his dad answer the phone.

The operator asked, "Will you accept a long distance call from Mr. Sean Cavanagh in Da Nang, Vietnam?"

Sean had never heard that tone in his dad's voice. "Oh my God, yes. Yes, operator, of course."

Sean cleared his throat and spoke clearly as possible, "Dad?"

In the kitchen of his home in Grosse Pointe Woods, Dennis Cavanagh wiped the tears from his eyes and also forced back a sob as he looked out of the window at the falling snow.

"Son, are you alright? Officers were here. They said you were wounded and were expected to pull through, but no details. We've all been praying."

"I've only got a couple minutes, Dad. I'm in a hospital in Da Nang. They say I'll be back 100 percent in a few months. I'll write you as soon as I can."

Sean spoke briefly to his mother, brothers, and sisters. His mother said she'd call Terri up at U of M that very night and fill her in. By the end of the conversation, there wasn't a dry eye on either end of the 12,000 mile phone connection, including Mrs. Webster's. She wiped her eyes with her hankie. She looked at the 19-year-old boy, still pale from the blood loss, hindered by a heavy, plaster cast on his entire left arm, painfully seated on over 100 sutures, and wished she had asked for a stateside assignment. Back in the world, she could promote blood drives and hand out doughnuts to firemen at big fires. There, she wouldn't suffer from this emotional stress, that was beginning to give her acute stomach problems and had turned the middle-aged woman into an after-work alcoholic.

After the call, Mrs. Webster wheeled Sean back to his bed. The only name she could locate from Sean's friends was that of Cpl. Tyler Lee Johnson. He was in the same hospital, but in a different ward. She promised to wheel him to visit his friend the next day.

———————

Mrs. Webster rolled Sean's wheelchair next to the bed. She said she would be back in a half hour to take him back. His I.V. was attached to the wheelchair, and his arm stuck out in the cast.

T.J. was soundly sleeping. His lips were dry and cracked. He was also hooked to an I.V., and a catheter snaked from under the bedding to a large glass bottle on the floor. T.J.'s left leg was in traction and in a full cast.

Despite the drug-induced sleep, T.J. opened one eye quickly. After a year in the bush, he sensed someone was watching him. He opened the other eye and focused his vision on Sean's figure seated next to him.

"Damn, if I ever thought I'd be glad to see a white boy. What it is, little white Brother?"

"Well, my ass end looks like a zipper display, I got so many stitches. My shoulder still hurts like hell. The doctors have said I'll be 100 percent in a couple months. Then it's back to Nam. What's the skinny on you, buddy?"

T.J. sat up slightly and pointed down to his cast.

"As you can see, my leg is fucked up for real. They say I got way better than 50-50 chance for full use. They took enough Gook shrapnel out of my neck and arms to build a transistor radio. I'll have over two-and-a-half years to go in my enlistment. They'll probably send my Black ass back for a whole 'nother tour, after a year in the world. Next tour I won't have the squad lookin' out for me."

Sean shook his head. "Oh yea, you look like we took care of you. Speaking of the squad, you know anything about our people?"

Sean helped T.J. take a sip of ice water and loaned him his chapstick to relieve his cracked lips.

T.J. leaned his head back against his pillow and stared up at the ceiling.

"There's a Soul Brother corpman from De-troit here. He did some checkin' for me. I knew you was here and alright, but I can't get up yet.

"Yance is in Japan. They had to take his leg. They'll fly him back to the world in a couple of weeks. Mr. Cool, little Brother, died at the Citadel. Man, probably 'bout same time you and me got hit."

T.J.'s eyes filled with tears. "Ol' Doc Padre an' me lay chilly in that fuckin' crater until they finally secured the area for a medevac. Man, you were lookin' bad. Another half hour, Padre say you'd been dead. He scared the piss outa me. He start sayin' all them Catholic prayers over you.

"The thing that frosted my balls was what happened after the Citadel was secured. I hear the A.R.V.N.s raised up their flag the next morning, as if they took it alone. Irish, I got no use for those A.R.V.N. turds. Far as I'm concerned, lots of good Marines got wasted 'cause the A.R.V.N.s didn't hold up their own and we ended up doing their job too. You know how much I hate the N.V.A. and V.C. But I shit you not, in an ass-kicking contest, I'd rather be on the same team with the N.V.A. than any A.R.V.N. I seen. Tell you what, Bro, A.R.V.N.s won't last three years without us fighting their war."

"Hell, T.J. I thought this was our war too. What the hell we doing here, if it's their war?"

"Son, if it was our war, we'd have raised our flag over the Citadel instead of their rag for the fuckin' media."

Sean rubbed his burning eyes.

"Well, T.J., ol' Hue City sure closed the book on our squad. Lt. Fox, Logs, Yance, Stoney, Little Joe, Mr. Cool, you and I; 100 percent wiped out taking that place so the A.R.V.N.s could raise their flag."

T.J. shook his head in disgust. "What a bitch, Irish. I ain't ever got 100 percent in anything before in my life."

The events of April 1968 would have a profound and lasting effect on each young man, for very different reasons.

There would be scars that would influence their personal and emotional lives for a very long time.

Sean and T.J. were watching the television in the hospital rec room when the word was announced. Both were still in casts and wheelchairs.

The emotional television announcer reported that Dr. Martin Luther King had been assassinated in Memphis.

Patients and hospital staff crowded around the televisions and radios. Some wept openly at the news. Some hid their tears of sadness. Others pounded their fists in violent displays of grief and frustration.

There were a few ugly, racial incidents in the wards, but most recognized that it was a collective loss, and an interracial sorrow for the death of a great man.

Like John Kennedy in 1963, Dr. King's murder seemed to say that to be loved in America meant terrible risk. He was like a friend to the Black Marines, and his death seemed to have the same emotional impact as the loss of a buddy in the field. The collective grief hung over the hospital like the death haze that had clung to Hue City during the battle.

The day after the news report, Sean went to see T.J. He rolled next to T.J.'s bed. The Black Marine in the bed next to T.J. stared coldly at Sean.

"Why don't you go back to your own ward, Chuck? I don't need to hear no honkie runnin' his mouth today."

T.J. was staring out at nothing. His eyes were still red from countless tears of grief. T.J. softly spoke to the Black Marine in the next bed.

"Be cool, Brother. My man here is number one. We is tight, dig?"

"Bullshit, man. I don't need to look at no white meat today."

T.J. was in no mood to verbally joust with anyone. "Then close your curtain, chump. This man is my friend, so lighten up."

Sean began to turn to leave, "Hey T.J., never mind, I understand. I . . ."

"Irish, stay man. I mean it. If the Brother don't want to see you, he can turn around. You an' me is friends, and I really need my friend right now."

The angry Black Marine jerked the curtain between the beds, blocking his view.

T.J. and Sean shook hands with a "Brother" handshake.

"Don't mean nothin' personal, Irish. All the Soul Brothers be messed up for a few days." Tears began to roll freely down his face. "I jus' don't understand how this world works, Irish. Don't make no sense. A fine boy like Logs gotta be killed at 19. But Logs was a Grunt, fighting in a war. The Dr. King, he never hurt no one. He only spoke of peace and non-violence and justice. Other Brothers, Eldridge Cleaver, Huey Newton, they preachin' to kill white people, kill the po-lice. Doctor King say love yo' neighbor, turn the other cheek. Then some gutless slime hides a block away with a rifle and takes the man's head off. Bastard worse than any Gook. What the hell is I doin' here? What we fightin' for when they kill a man like Dr. King? Man, all I can say is that it ain't right."

T.J. began to cry. Sean put his uninjured arm around his friend and muffled T.J.'s sobs in the cloth of his hospital robe.

"It's a crazy world, Brother, Sean said. "But please, try to remember that one hateful, bigoted, madman killed Dr. King. The same kind of a son-of-a-bitch that killed Kennedy. The fact Oswald was white doesn't bring Kennedy back, or reduce the hurt and loss."

A nurse silently appeared at the foot of T.J.'s bed. She came to tell Sean it was curfew, that he had to go back to his own ward. She quietly watched for a moment, understanding Sean's sincere attempt to offer some masculine support to his emotional friend. The simple scene of the two young men touched her more than any of the terrible pain and suffering she had witnessed the previous six months. Tears began to stream down her face and she decided to get very, very drunk that night after her shift and have a joint or two. She turned and walked away without speaking.

By the end of April, there had been a great deal of healing. The focus of the hospital conversation had turned from Dr. King's death to President Johnson's decision not to run for re-election. There was excitement about the anti-war, peace candidates, Eugene McCarthy and Bobby Kennedy. Sean's arm remained in the cast, but he could walk around on his own. T.J.'s leg also remained in a cast, but he was out of traction and in a wheelchair.

Sean had become obsessed with his relationship with Terri. He now received only one letter a week, and they seemed to contain all the warmth of a newspaper article.

Sean spoke to her while she was home on Easter break. The phone connection was poor, and Terri sounded very cool and distant. He had felt so close to her when he was home on leave at Thanksgiving. Like millions of couples before them, they had assured each other that their love could endure the separation caused by his 13 months at war.

But Sean had sensed a change in Terri after he had been wounded in February. It was subtle at first, little things he noticed in her letters. The number of letters and cards he received began to decrease, and their warmth diminished with their frequency. He privately knew what was happening.

Sean lay on his hospital bed, staring at the ceiling. He couldn't sleep or eat, and he had become less than pleasant company. He closed his eyes and pictured her image. He ached inside as he thought of her gentle embrace, her firm young body. The way she moved when he touched her that made him feel as though her skin beckoned his touch. He could almost hear her soft, sensual moans, almost feel the warmth of her kisses.

His mind drifted to a vision of he and Terri riding along Lakeshore Drive on a warm Spring afternoon. He could feel the fresh, crisp breeze off Lake St. Clair. He smelled the freshly-cut grass and the blossoms of the mansion gardens.

Then, the all-too-familiar pattern began. Two weeks passed without any letter at all from Terri. T.J. attempted to comfort his friend by insulting the mail service. Since Sean received letters from other family members, the effort was in vain.

The day the letter arrived, Sean knew the contents without opening it. "Shit, real personal touch. She even typed the fucking thing."

The neatly typed, one-page letter was not unlike the thousands of other "Dear John" letters received by thousands of other service men during countless wars. His time away had caused her to reconsider their relationship. There was a new love interest. This was better for all involved. Etc., etc. She signed off with "Sincerely."

T.J. struggled into his wheelchair and decided to go looking for Sean, who had not arrived for his daily visit. He found Sean sitting in the ward's small recreation room. He held his head in his right hand, his left arm still extended by the heavy cast. It appeared as though Sean was merely looking at the letter in his lap, not reading it. Just staring at the paper. T.J. wheeled himself in the rec room and stopped next to Sean's chair. "Bad news from home, Irish?"

Sean handed the letter to T.J. "I've known the girl my whole life. We've been lovers since high school. We talked about getting married after college. Lovers for three years. I don't see her for five months and she gives me a 'Dear John.' I must have been a great lover. I sure made a hell of an impression on the girl: she lasted five whole months."

T.J. repositioned himself in his wheelchair.

"Hey, asshole. We're friends, and I know you is feelin' bad, but I ain't gonna listen to none of that kinda rap. You over here doin' nothin' more than trying to stay alive. You write her almost every day, even from Hue City. The bitch drops you and you gonna blame yo'self?"

Sean continued to stare down at the letter. "I should have known, T.J. I should have known she wouldn't be strong enough to cope with this."

"You and this lady got all them things together, and she don't wait more than five mother fuckin' months before she starts screwin' around? You don't want to hear it now, Brother, but seems like you better off you know about her now. You marry the girl, you for sure be the one with the problem then. She's at school entertaining all them boys with the 2-S draft status while you're here keeping your thing in your pants 'cause you can't even draw off base liberty."

"But damn it, T.J., you know after all this time that I love her."

"Love? Love? What the fuck you know about love, boy? You just turned 20 years old. Some sweet young girl makes your dick hard and you talkin' you in love. Irish, you ain't dipped your wick enough to know about women. You done fell in love with your first piece of ass.

"Son, loving is nothing more then needing. Trouble is, with you in Nam and her at school, you need her a whole lot more than she needs you. Nice looking lady like her, she always gonna find some swinging dick willing to take care of her needs. So, she ain't got no needs. You over here, she's all you got, even if she is 12,000 miles away.

"You gotta learn about women, boy. There always gonna be some dude come along with a bigger car, better looks, more bread, bigger lump in his shorts, something. Unless the lady needs you like you need her, ain't never gonna last. Dig this, Irish, like when the squad was in combat, we had something special, something that was for real. We really needed each other. When I needed you, man, you was there. There's some folks go through a whole lifetime never needing or being needed. You, me, Yance, Mr. Cool, Logs, that's for true, not like back in the world. The world's just full of cheatin' women, phony friends, asshole relatives, and users, man. What you need is for us to get some off-base liberty. I'll find you some local lady to suck all that poison out of your body."

Sean crumbled up the letter in his fist. "I still love her, T.J."

"Yea. But you can't let it eat you up, little white Brother. Truth is, ain't a damn thing you can do about it while you here. Like we say in the bush, 'fuck it. Don't mean nothing'."

In early July, Sean was released from the hospital and assigned to a small military-police unit at the Da Nang airfield until he was fit for full-field duty. T.J. was flown back to California. After he was fully recovered, he would get leave and go home to Detroit for two weeks. He would then to return to Camp Pendleton and train troops as a troop handler with an I.T.R. company at Camp Horno, in California.

Their last night together at the hospital, T.J.'s friend, the corpman from Detroit, sneaked him in a bottle of Old Crow. The three young men hid in a storage closet and talked the night away, getting very drunk. The next morning, Sean was thankful he was merely a short jeep ride from his destination at the Da Nang airfield. The thought of an air flight made him green. T.J. was too glad to be leaving Vietnam to be ill.

Sean reported in at the small M.P. office at the airfield. It had been attacked during Tet, then again in May, but it was light duty compared to being with his outfit. They assured Sean he would rejoin what was left of his own unit when he returned to full duty in a couple of weeks.

Except for an occasional rocket attack, Sean's brief tour of duty at the Da Nang airfield seemed little different than stateside duty. The airfield was very busy. In his off-duty hours, he could go to a movie, get a burger at the air-conditioned E.M. club, eat hot chow, shower, sleep in a real bed. Along with the creature comforts came the strict uniform standards, inspections, lots of saluting, and the usual "chicken shit" attitude encountered in the rear. Sean watched the Marines headed home in the "Freedom Birds," laughing and cheering as they boarded the planes. He saw the frightened faces of the hundreds of replacements that arrived every week. He saw the countless plane loads of badly wounded being flown to places with better, or more comprehensive, medical care.

Sean also watched then load stacks of silver caskets on to the ramps of C-130 cargo planes for their trip to a U.S. cemetery.

Sean opened a letter from T.J. about his leave in Detroit. He went on and on about the Tigers and how he just knew it was to be their year. He told him how pitcher Denny McLain was leading both leagues in wins and had set a record-breaking pace. He was certain that Boston, Baltimore, and New York would not catch them this year. T.J. knew that 1968 was the year for the Tigers. Sean folded his letter and put it back in his pocket.

"The year for the Tigers? Lord knows it hasn't been our year. I hope it really is the Tigers' season."

It was hotter in Vietnam in July than anything Sean had ever experienced. After dark, Sean began a daily running schedule. He knew the bush would be much different in July than the previous Winter. He had to force himself back into shape or he wouldn't last a day on an operation.

In the last week of July, Sean received a medical release and his orders to return to his company. The First Regiment H.Q. was moved to Gio Linh, but his Battalion's combat base was at the same I Corps location. Since he knew his stay with the Da Nang M.P.s was to be a short one, he made no real friends, though he got along well with them.

The morning Sean was to fly to the combat base, he was summoned to the M.P. office. Still armed with the issued .45 pistol, Sean kept his cover on and rendered the M.P. C.O. behind the desk a salty Marine salute.

"Sir, L/Cpl. Cavanagh, reporting as ordered."

The captain stood and walked over to the far end of the office where two other officers were standing.

"At ease, Cavanagh. Cavanagh, this is Col. Royce from Regiment, and Maj. Jesseps. They want to speak with you before you rejoin your outfit."

The tall, slim, middle-aged Marine colonel approached Sean, who again snapped to attention. The colonel began to read from a paper but put it down. "Cavanagh, S.D.?"

"Yes Sir, L/Cpl. Cavanagh."

"Cavanagh, I'm sorry we can't present these things in a proper ceremony, but time and this damn war don't permit it. 'For heroism in combat during the battle to retake Hue from Communist forces on 13 Feb. 1968, you have been awarded a Bronze Star. For wounds suffered 23 Feb. 1968, you have been awarded the Purple Heart. For leadership

qualities displayed in combat that meet the highest tradition of the
Marine Corps, you've received a Meritorious promotion to Corporal,
effective as of 20 July 1968. Finally, although a little delayed, for your
heroism in combat the night of 15 Dec. 1967, at combat firebase Stop
Gap, you are awarded a Bronze Star.'

"Seems your C.O. got delayed in writing up the paperwork. Congratulations Cavanagh. Good luck back at your unit. We need good N.C.O.s
in the field. As you know, the Marine N.C.O. is the backbone of the
Corps."

Sean saluted, "Yes Sir. Thank you, Sir."

"Dismissed. Get ready to ship out."

Sean did an about-face and briskly marched out of the office.

The colonel walked over to the file cabinet and poured himself a cup
of coffee.

"You see the face on that kid, Frank? Damn, he looks like he's 16.
Baby-face kids fightin' this stinkin' war. Did you see his file? He's been
here since December. He has two Purple Hearts. Now we send him
back to the bush so he can get killed. He lost his whole squad in Hue,
almost the whole platoon.

"God damn war. No parade. No band. Just come into the office, boy,
we got something for you: two Bronze Stars, a Purple Heart, and a
promotion. Hell of a ceremony. The kid and three officers he'll never
see again.

"I don't care if it is only 1000 hours. Let's go to the club. I need a
drink. After three wars, I'm tired of patting these kids on the back and
then sending them back out to die."

———————————

The long, O.D. green CH46 Sea Knight helicopter lifted from the Da
Nang landing pad. Sean looked at the other occupants and the crates of
supplies piled on the deck. It was much like his first chopper ride in
appearance, but not in emotions. He peered out of the round porthole
along the bulkhead. The landscape was browner. It seemed even more
pockmarked with shell holes and bomb craters.

The chopper headed north, toward the D.M.Z. and the firebase that
would be his home again. Sean sensed a change in himself since Terri's
letter. He couldn't put his finger on it. It was as though his senses were
numbed and he had turned almost all of his emotions inward.

Minutes later, the chopper hovered over the firebase landing pad. He
looked down at the busy, dusty combat base and just shook his head.

The chopper landed and the rear ramp lowered. Sean picked up a
box of C-rations and briskly walked past the knot of bewildered new

replacements that gathered between the choppers and the small working party that was busy unloading the crates and supplies.

He walked past the N.C.O. who was yelling at and insulting the small group of new Marines. Sean went directly to the Admin tent to report in and locate his company's area. The X.O. gave him directions and briefly welcomed him back.

As Sean slowly walked up the narrow, dust-clogged path of the combat base, he was pulled apart by a strange ambivalence. He was frightened again, only this time he didn't have Logs or Yance or T.J. looking after him. He truly hated combat, the terrible waste in human life and suffering. But he knew that he had left too much undone to leave Vietnam and go home.

Sean had lost so much in such a short time. Logs, Stoney, Mr. Cool, so many others were dead. Yance, Little Joe, Lt. Fox, T.J., badly wounded. He had even lost Terri, indirectly.

He was afraid, but he secretly knew he was not quite ready to leave the contact. He needed to go back or the terrible frustration would haunt him the rest of his life. The paradox was simple. Returning to settle things might cost him his life.

He entered the shade of the company C.O.'s tent. A new, uninterested clerk took his folder. He called to the man at the cot in the tent. "Skipper, we got a man rejoining the unit."

At the rear of the tent, Sean recognized Capt. Kincade stretched out on the cot. Kincade wore his aviator sunglasses and a bush hat.

"Well hot damn," thought Sean. "At least the hard-ass Skipper has survived. He was a damn good C.O. during Hue."

Kincade sat up and seemed to be straining to see through his sunglasses. He pulled them off with a swift motion. He sprang to his feet and approached Sean.

"Cavanagh. Damn, Man, it's good to see you. I was told you were K.I.A. with the 1/5 taking the Citadel. None of the people I sent to the 1/5 that day ever came back to us. We were told your whole squad bought it."

Sean wiped the building sweat from his forehead. "Mr. Cool was killed. Yance lost a leg. T.J. got tore up but is fine now. He's stateside. I stepped in some deep shit, but all those Navy doctors in Da Nang say I'm ready for duty."

"You look good, Cavanagh. You feeling strong enough to go out on an ops and get me some Gooks? This isn't Hue, but the N.V.A. are all over I Corps." Capt. Kincade carefully read the additions to Sean's personnel folder.

Sean felt the humid heat sweep over him. "I know I'm still out of shape, Sir, but a couple days in the bush will whip my butt back into condition."

Capt. Kincade looked up from the folder to look at Sean.

"Says you were shot in the shoulder. Did it hurt your throwing arm?" Kincade turned to the clerk. "Cavanagh here can throw a frag better than any Marine I've seen in two tours."

Sean automatically rubbed the healing bullet wound.

"I was hit in the left shoulder. I played some ball while at Da Nang. I'm still a little stiff, but with a little practice, I should be fine."

Kincade flipped through the pages in his folder.

"Good, they gave you both Bronze Stars, and made you a corporal. That's damn outstanding. It's what this company needs the most right now, some seasoned, veteran N.C.O.s. You give any more thought to O.C.S.?"

Sean remembered too well Kincade's scorn during their first meeting.

"Sir, I've only been thinking about getting better and getting back with my company. There will be time for me to evaluate my future when this tour is up."

"You keep it in mind, Cavanagh. The Corps can use good men like you. Say the word, and you're on the way to O.C.S. in a week. You'd be back here when you finished, but as an officer."

"I'll give it serious thought, Captain."

Kincade wiped the moisture from his face and head with a small O.D. towel.

"Cavanagh, you Marines did a damn outstanding job in Hue. We lost most of a damn fine company in those three, lousy, stinking, raining, bloody weeks. I'll always be proud I served with such a fine bunch of young men. Go on now, find your platoon commander. He's crapped out in his tent, end of that row. They just got in from the bush. You'll be standin' down a day or two. Welcome back, Cavanagh. I'm damn glad you're back with us."

Sean went to the supply area and drew a full complement of gear. In the short distance from the supply tent to his new platoon commander's tent, he was soaked with sweat and covered with the familiar red dust. He was amazed at the change in Capt. Kincade's attitude. The living hell of retaking Hue had convinced the career Marine that the men of the New Corps weren't so bad, after all.

Sean quietly entered his platoon commander's tent. A lone man lay sleeping on an empty cot. A towel protected his face from the light and dust.

Sean recognized the man at once. It was Lt. Fox. He couldn't make himself believe it. Fox had received a sucking chest wound the second week in Hue, and yet he had preceeded Sean back to the field.

Sean sat next to Fox and said loudly, "Hey Brown Bar, is this where the lifers billot?"

Fox slowly lifted his right arm from his chest and carefully removed the towel from his face. He was in no mood to be jerked around by some smart ass, no matter what his rank. When Fox's eyes focused in the shadows for him to recognize Sean, he vaulted to his feet and briskly shook Sean's hand. "I'll be a son-of-a-bitch. Irish, they said you were killed at the Citadel."

"I know, Lieutenant, I heard. Like Mark Twain said, 'Rumors about my death have been greatly exaggerated.' Hell, I see you've got your first lieutenant bars. Nice shade of silver. No more Mr. Brown Bar."

"Irish, I can't tell you how glad I am to see you. Shit, this calls for a celebration of major proportions. I've got a personal friend in supply that owes me a big favor. I'll get us a couple of cool beers and we can catch each other up on the true skinny."

Minutes later, Fox returned with a canvas backpack containing six cans of beer and crushed ice. They sat in the shade of the large tent, the flaps rolled up to catch any breeze, and sipped the cool beer.

They shared grim tales of what had happened to their platoon, after Fox was hit the second week in Hue. Fox would mention a name and Sean would either tell the story of the man's demise or report the man's status in a few words. Sean offered a brief rundown of his own squad without being asked. It was quicker and less painful.

Fox emptied his beer can, crushed it and tossed it outside.

"Damn, Irish. Sorry about Logs. I'm damn glad T.J. made it back. He may have been a jive-ass, street slick in Detroit, but he was an outstanding squad leader."

Sean thought of T.J. and couldn't help but smile. "He was acting P.C. half the time in Hue. He saved a lot of people in the city."

Fox opened another beer and took a long sip.

"Irish, I won't shit you. We've got a good bunch of kids, but after Hue, most of the platoon is new kids. Your buddy, Little Joe, is back. I've made him a fireteam leader. I think you'll like them. They know they don't have all the answers, and they listen."

"I've got to tell you, Lieutenant, it's going to take me some time getting use to being in the field without T.J. and the rest."

"I understand, Irish. Look, I'm giving you the first squad. Little Joe will be one of your fireteam leaders, the rest are all new. Before we go on another operation, I'll give you the scoop on each man so you'll know what to expect."

"You think I'm ready for a squad, Sir?"

"Irish, I think you're ready. Besides, you are the senior N.C.O., other than the platoon sergeant, S/Sgt. Ware. You've got more combat experience than anyone in the platoon except Little Joe. He's still a lance corporal. He'll be ready for a squad in a month or two."

Sean took a sip of beer and shook his head. "Won't the present squad leader get pissed about being bumped?"

Fox rubbed his tired red eyes and paused. "He won't mind, Irish. He was filling one of the body bags you passed at the base L.Z. He was K.I.A. last night. They decided not to do an evac until daylight. No hurry."

"Shit, I'm sorry Lieutenant."

"You need to be more than sorry, Irish. Be damn good, like T.J. was. Help me to keep these kids alive the next few months, so we can all get out of this hell hole together in one piece."

Sean spent the next two days getting to know his new squad. At night, he and Little Joe told them of the ground attack on the firebase in December and the horrible ghost stories of Hue.

The night before the platoon was to go on another operation in the bush, P.F.C. Charles Flagstone approached Little Joe. "Hey Little Joe, give me the straight dope on this new squad leader. You were with him. Is he worth a shit?"

"Listen, Flag Day, you wouldn't make a pimple on his ass on your best day. If that man says jump, you better only ask how high."

Pvt. Flagstone was still not totally convinced. "Dude looks young."

"He's a year older than you, slick. And you'll never see a more vicious dude in a fire fight. Don't ever let that baby face of his fool you. He'll tear off your arm and serve it to you for lunch."

"He a lifer? He seems kind of quiet and serious."

"No fuckin' way. He's no career man. In fact, he's only got a two-year enlistment. He's just probably uptight because he watched his whole platoon get hit in three weeks. He lost a buddy and others got hit real bad. He doesn't have to run his mouth. He's got nothin' to prove to you. Do what he says in a fire fight. He'll help keep you from going home in a body bag."

———

The long days turned into weeks. The strenuous life of the foot soldier, the Marine Grunt, seemed to drain every ounce of Sean's physical and emotional strength.

The extremes faced by the combat Marine made adaptation impossible. The adrenaline rush of contact, flashes of fear and excitement were in deep contrast to the boredom of long marches in the bush and work details while back at the firebase.

Fox could not have been more pleased with the way Sean handled his squad. T.J. had taught him well. Fox and S/Sgt. Ware sat together beside the trail. The platoon was taking a break during the tough, hot force march to their preassigned destination.

S/Sgt. Ware was newly promoted. He was doing his second tour in

Vietnam. The fit, Black 22-year-old looked like a middleweight boxer. Ware had grown up in a tough ghetto and had never been treated as well as he had while in the Corps, despite two Nam tours. He intended to make the Marine Corps his career. But S/Sgt. Ware was also street wise. He knew he'd get much more from the men if he didn't act like a lifer. S/Sgt. Ware enjoyed a long drink from a canteen.

"Say Lu-tenant, you say Irish was with you before he got wounded?"

"Yea. The kid got a Purple Heart his second night in-country. He was with me when I was hit. The boy is a natural, Staff. I swear, they must make natural-born Grunts in Detroit. His buddy T.J., a Soul Brother from Detroit, was an outstanding squad leader. Irish seemed to just pick up where T.J. left off. You're the best platoon sergeant I've ever worked with. Are . . .?"

"No Lu-tenant, I'm from Oakland, long ways from De-troit. Maybe the city boys from tough towns been fightin' their whole lives, so it seems to come natural."

"I might have thought so, but Irish is from an upper-class family, living in the suburbs. The only thing they had in common was that they came from the same city. T.J. was a ex-jive-ass, street punk. Irish is an ex-college boy preppie."

"Well, for a preppie, he's a damn good Grunt. He seems like kind of a cold dude, though. He's O.K. with Little Joe. I see lighten up with you, and he's cooperative and respectful to me, but otherwise don't nobody get close to that boy."

"That's a change I've seen in him, Staff. Hell, before Tet, Irish was tight with the whole platoon. Since Hue, he's cautious and holding back. He got a 'Dear John' while in the hospital. I think that's still eating him up."

S/Sgt. Ware took a drink from his canteen. "One thing for certain, Lu-tenant, the lad can throw a frag. Last week I saw him toss one on a Gook machine gun position at about 50 yards. Damn if it didn't hit the fuckin' gun, before it exploded. It's as if he looks for chances to frag Gooks. He'll drop one on them, then get a look on his face like he just threw a T.D. pass. Kind of spooky."

Fox patted S/Sgt. Ware on the shoulder. "Like having another M-79 grenade launcher in the platoon."

"Yes, Sir, got that right. I lost my lady with a 'Dear John' my first tour. Maybe some night me an' him can rap a while. Maybe get out some of that shit he got built up inside."

———————

The file of exhausted Marines snaked over the soft slopes of the gentle hills. The cover was moderate, only the heat made the trek so uncomfortable.

Sean's squad was walking point. Tree was the point man. Flag Day had become Sean's M-79 man. He stayed close to Sean. Flag Day had grown to deeply admire his new squad leader in their weeks together.

Sean called to Little Joe, who was several yards in front of him, "Little Joe, tell Tree to watch his ass, I've got a . . ."

The explosion from the mine literally blew off both of Tree's legs. The tree line to their right flank erupted with rifle and light machine-gun fire. Tree was the only casualty from the mine. A corpman crawled along the trail to Tree's location.

Sean began to shout at his squad and others, "Put out some fire, damn it." Sean and Flag Day moved up the trail, "Come on, people. They can't hit you if they've got their heads down." Sean pointed to the area he wanted Flag Day to concentrate his M-79 grenade launcher rounds. "O.K. Pal, see that clump of trees? I can see the muzzle flashes. Mix some frags and some Willie Peter. I don't think Charlie much likes Willie Peter."

Sean continued to encourage his squad to increase their volume of return fire. He crawled to where Little Joe was positioned.

"Sorry about Tree, Little Joe. Sounds like it is a squad size ambush. I figure as soon as they know we've got the whole company with us, they'll sky out. As soon as second squad starts to lay down some heavy fire, what say we advance on their position before they can get away clean?"

Little Joe looked at the corpman working over Tree's body up the trail, then at the tree line where the enemy fire was coming from. "Damn Irish, if they do know we're a whole company, they could be using us as bait."

"Remember when Stoney got wasted? That could have been a trap, too.

"I don't think so. They would have never passed up the chance to take out our whole squad. They would have waited for the meat of the company to reach the ambush site."

"Shit, I hear second squad has moved up. They got an M-60 with them. O.K., Irish, let's go. Fireteam up. Follow me, boys."

Sean called back to his grenadier, "Flag Day, stay there and keep pouring in the rounds. Watch our advance. Don't frag any Marines."

Sean, and the three remaining members of Little Joe's fireteam spread out and quickly advanced on the tree line. Sean reached a point where he was close enough to reach the tree line with hand grenades and took cover behind a tree. He threw two grenades into the thick growth of the tree line, then resumed his advance. The enemy fire had stopped. As the Marines reached the tree line, the platoon's support fire stopped. They found three dead V.C. bodies, two blood trails and four AK47 rifles.

Little Joe surveyed their confiscation. "Damn Irish, local V.C. We haven't had any contact with V.C. since before Tet."

Sean kicked one of the bodies to make certain the man was dead. "Yea. Maybe if it had been N.V.A., they'd have put us in the hurt locker. Probably live in that ville a couple clicks over the hill to our flank. We should call an air strike and win some hearts and minds with 500-pound bombs."

When they reached the trail they saw the corpmen wrapping Tree's body in two poncho liners. He had died from wounds from the mine. Sean turned over the rifles to Fox and Ware and reported what they found in the tree line. He gave Fox all the papers and articles found on the V.C. bodies. He and Little Joe walked back to their position in the front of their long colume.

"Little Joe, ol' Logs was right about this war. It's nothing more than a stupid fucking game. Today's score: Marines 5, V.C. 1."

———————

As the months passed, Sean forced himself to write his folks once a week. He tried to write his grandparents at least once a month. He had started to write Terri a dozen times. He kept in contact with T.J., who was now based at Camp Pendelton.

Sean developed a reputation. It was not uncommon in combat units for members to be known for specific talents or events. Some were considered fearless, others lucky or charmed. A few were known for being cruel to civilians or wounded enemy. Sean's reputation stemmed from his accuracy with the hand grenade. Every man in the company believed that Sean could "drop a frag grenade into a Gook's back pocket at 50 yards".

In mid-November, the company returned to the firebase for a well-earned break after a long operation in the bush. Sean made certain that his squad got a hot shower, hot chow, and clean jungle utilities and that they were all crapped out on their cots before he went looking for his lieutenant. When he found him, Fox had several cans of beer in the special backpack, stuffed with ice. They were joined that night by Ware. None of them spoke while they rapidly downed their first beer.

"Damn, I needed that Lu-tenant," Ware said. "Got to say, I'd rather have me a lady, but for sure it's the next best thing."

Sean covered a beer belch with his hand.

"Hey, Lieutenant. I got a letter from T.J. He says Detroit went nuts after the Tigers won the Series. Crazy shits, in '67 they were killing each other; in '68, they're dancing in the streets together. T.J. likes his job as an I.T.R. troop handler. He says every liberty, he goes down to San Diego and comforts all those lonely swabbie wives. T.J., that horny bastard. He says he'd never do no Marine's wife. Hell, he'd screw the crack of dawn."

S/Sgt. Ware finished his second beer, and they just rapped for a while. Sean always learned something new when he spoke to Ware for any length of time. He knew T.J. would groove on Ware. He was another street-wise kid who got his shit together in the Corps.

S/Sgt. Ware began to rib Sean. "Hey Irish, you talkin' 'bout your man T.J. chasin' women, you gonna say a pretty boy like you ain't got all kinds of women?" Ware gave a knowing wink to Fox.

"Staff, I had a girl friend when I left home. We were real serious. I got a 'Dear John' while in the hospital at Da Nang."

"Same thing happened to me first tour. You ever want to rap about it with somebody, let me know. I been there. What you gonna do back in the world, be a priest?"

Sean was mid-swallow with his beer and he nearly choked.

"Staff, I haven't been with a girl since last Thanksgiving. I'm going to spend the rest of my life trying to make up for all the screws I've missed already."

The three young men laughed out loud and opened another beer.

Fox let out a long, loud belch. "Yes indeed, an officer and a gentle-men. Men, you may wonder why I called this meeting. I got good news, and I got good news. First, S/Sgt. Ware, I got word tonight. Effective as of 1 December, you are Gy/Sgt. Ware." Fox raised his beer can in a toast. "To the best platoon sergeant in this big green machine."

Sean raised his beer can, "Here, here, about time Staff Sergeant, out-fucking-standing. Congratulations Staff, hell you'll be a mustanger in another year at this rate."

"I've gotta live long enough to see it, Irish."

Fox put his half-drunken hand on Ware's shoulder and said, "Our platoon has suffered the fewest losses in the company. You're a big part of that, Ware. Irish, you only lost one man since you got back in July. You've got to continue the good work because good news part two is that my tour is up. I'm outa this toilet tomorrow morning and on a Freedom Bird no later than the following day. Hell, I could be eatin' Thanksgiving dinner on Long Island with my family, if all goes well."

Sean and Ware moaned loadly and Ware pretended to fall over backward.

"Don't get us wrong, Lu-tenant. We're happy for you. But the thought of breakin' in a new brown bar, oh my aching ass. Ain't like we jealous of you going home to real food, comfortable beds, hot showers, clothes that ain't green, no Gooks tryin' to waste your ass every day and all them women, but to make us break in a new brown bar, that's damn cruel, Sir."

Sean put his arm around his Lieutenant's shoulder. "Couldn't you extend for just a few months and stay with your friends?" Sean looked over the Spartan, darkened firebase, "How could you just pack up and leave all this?"

Fox put his arm around Sean in jest. "How could I? It'll be real easy, my Irish friend. Just be up at 0 dark 30 hours tomorrow morning and you can watch me."

Ware struggled to open another beer can. "With all due respect, Lu-tenant, I request we get properly shit-faced to celebrate my promotion and your rotation."

Fox rendered the Marine salty salute, "Damn capital idea, Staff. So be it. I'll fetch us some additional liquid refreshments."

Fox walked off to find them more beer and ice. Sean sipped at his beer and looked pensively out over the shadows of the dark combat base.

"Staff, this is your second tour. I've got this feeling that I'm never going back to the world. I'm not saying that I have a death premonition or anything like that. We all figured we'd buy the farm in Hue.

"Out here, it's bad, but you see guys like the Lieutenant walk out back to the world, go on R&R, it's different. I can't make my mind believe that there will ever be anything other than this. Maybe I won't let myself think about going home, or I'd go nuts. But I can't think any farther than our next operation in the bush."

The young staff sergeant finished off his beer, and his face took on a thoughtful expression.

"Never happened to me my first tour, but the war was way different then. Hell, we still had M-14s and stayed within 50 miles of Da Nang, chasing around some poorly-armed, raggedy ass V.C.

"I remember at boot camp, though, I had the same kind of feeling there. I figured I'd spend the rest of my life in boot camp. I didn't think I'd die, just couldn't imagine nothing else. I suspect it's just your mind doing one of them defense things, you know. Too painful to walk through the bush thinkin' of being home, so you don't.

"It's like you, since you got back from gettin' wounded. The Lieutenant says you keep to yourself more, ain't as friendly. I figure you lost so many buddies in Hue, you won't get close to many folks this time. Even tougher as a squad leader. Ain't easy telling a buddy to move on a Gook position, then maybe he get wasted."

"Staff Ware, if you ever get out of the Corps, you should go into psychology. You see right through all the bullshit. I'm damn glad for the whole platoon you made Gunny."

"Ain't really bullshit, Irish. It's just a matter of gettin' by."

Lt. Fox returned with the canvas field pack refilled with beer and ice. "Would you believe me if I told you I'm gonna miss you guys?"

Sean helped himself to another cold beer. "Yes, as long as you qualify it with a time limit, like until you step off the plane in New York."

Ware opened another beer. "Or, when he sees one of them pretty stewardesses on the Freedom Bird."

Fox took a beer can. "Oh, ye of little faith."

Ware said, "Ain't got nothin' to do with faith, got to do with your dick. You can't be thinkin' 'bout your buddies here and what you'd like to do with the stewardess at the same time."

Their collective laughter abruptly stopped with the crunching impact of a 120mm enemy rocket in the center of the base. "Incoming, damn it to hell. Gooks got no respect for a man's going-away party."

Sean and Ware were on their feet. "It's just the N.V.A.'s special way of saying farewell, Lieutenant."

Rocket and mortar explosions ripped through the base. By the extreme incoming concentration, even the new men knew to expect a ground attack. Men ran for bunkers and to their defensive positions.

Fox got to his feet and followed Sean and Ware. "Shit, used to be people got a parade when they went home."

Sean headed for his people and looked back. "In this war, Lieutenant, a full scale N.V.A. ground assault is the closest thing to a parade you can get."

Fox ran to the C.P. for instructions. Ware and Sean ran to find and prepare their platoon. The incoming was the worst Sean had seen since Hue. He thought that tonight might be the night the N.V.A. decided they wanted to overrun the Marine firebase, "Come and get some, mother fuckers," he yelled.

The heavy rocket and mortar barrage continued. Ware and Sean had made up a React Force with two re-enforced squads. They waited in the open bunkers near the base command bunker. The 105mm cannons and 81mm mortars from the base returned fire at the unseen enemy positions. But the intense inbound ordinance hampered their volume of fire. Enemy rounds tore through the firebase, turning neat rows of tents into smoking debris and pounding the empty chopper L.Z.

Lt. Fox dove into the bunker with Ware and Sean. "No doubt the Gooks will hit us when this lifts. Irish, you remember last time, in December. They've dug some fighting holes and trenches by the 106 position and M-60 bunker nearest the main gate. Take your people down there. If N.V.A. get through the wire, we can't let them take either of those positions, or we'll have a lot of people hurt. If they're intent on overrunning the base, they'll have to take those two positions first. O.K., move out."

Sean led the React Force to the area near the M-60 machine gun bunker, nearest the main gate, and jumped into the chest-deep trench. He had a clear field of fire of the gate and the 106mm recoiless position, nearest the gate, the same position that had been taken during the enemy attack in December.

Kansas, the newest member of the squad, was next to Sean in the trench. He had replaced Tree. The 18-year-old had even more of a baby face than Sean.

Kansas had been in the choir in high school. The frail youngster was very fair, with pale blue eyes and a head of light curly hair. Now, he had a look of terror on his face. Sweat poured from under his helmet. He repeatedly muffled a nervous cough, and looked as though he would be ill at any moment.

Sean put an additional stick of gum in his mouth. He took out another and said, "Here, kid. Chew some gum. It helps your mouth not get too dry, and it'll settle your stomach. If you're gonna barf, you change positions. If you puke in here, I'll kick your ass."

Kansas stuffed a piece of gum in his dry mouth. "Thanks Irish. Oh man, this is some serious shit. I heard a guy from the other squad say there are a couple thousand Gooks on the other side of the river, waitin' to attack this base."

Sean readied two hand grenades. His grenadier, Flag Day, readied his M-79 at the far end of the trench. Sean checked over Kansas' gear, "No way, kid, we'd never be so lucky."

The new replacement looked at Sean as though he was insane.

"Listen hard, Kansas. When ol' Luke the Gook comes storming across that piss-ant river there, we're going to shit on him so hard that they won't have enough live bodies left to carry away their dead bodies. Boy, we've got tanks, 105s, 81s, 106s, Ontos, and Dusters. By now, the C.P. has called for air support, so there will be Puff, jets, and chopper gunships. If they're dumb enough to mass that many people together in good weather, I'll kiss your ass at noon in front of the C.P. Hell, we can get Navy ship 14-inch fire if we needed it."

Kansas already looked better. The look of terror was gone. He wildly chewed the gum and didn't look sick.

"Kansas, what the hell is a nice choir boy like you doing in the Marine Corps? You should be in the Air Force singing in some base men's choir."

"Well Irish, I had this girl friend in high school and I, well, in my town . . ."

' "Never mind kid, I understand. Now listen, lock and load. Take your time and squeeze them off. This won't be like the bush. They'll be in the open and the flares will light 'em up. Make your shots count. They may send a bunch, but keep your poise, and we'll knock their dicks in the dirt."

Sean looked over his shoulder and saw a volley of Communist rockets roar into a row of plywood heads. For some unknown reason, the sight struck him as being funny. "I've heard of the shit hitting the fan, but I guess this time the fan hit the shit."

Almost unbelievably, the savage rocket and mortar barrage had little effect on the defensive ability of the combat base. Tents, plywood heads, the officer's mess tent, a C-ration supply tent and one Ontos had been destroyed by the attack. The N.V.A. commander, across the river, had watched the red-orange explosions fall throughout the Marine base for several minutes through his field glasses. He badly miscalculated the barrage's effect, and ordered the preplanned ground assault to proceed.

First, the sappers sprinted across the shallow river. Sean knew they were intent on overrunning the firebase when the Communist rocket and mortar barrage continued, even after the sappers were at the wire. Some were killed by their own rockets. The N.V.A. commanders were willing to sacrifice a sapper platoon to continue the barrage, which reduced the effectiveness of the Marine's defensive fire.

The brave suicide sappers accomplished their mission. They opened a 10-foot-wide hole in the protective firebase wire, near the front gate. The moment the Communist rocket and mortar barrage lifted, the primary N.V.A. attack force poured across the shallow river from their hiding places on the other side. The Marine response was massive and deadly. The air support, now overhead, and large guns pounded the N.V.A. staging area across the river. The 105s, tanks, mortars, 106s, and small arms from the firebase concentrated on the advancing N.V.A. soldiers. Those that made it to the breach in the wire were destroyed by Sean's React Force and M-60 fire from the bunker. Sean's unit laid down well-coordinated fire and used good fire discipline. Sean and the new Gy/Sgt. Ware shouted encouragement to their people. Sean directed Flag Day's M-79 fire.

Four N.V.A. soldiers advanced on their trench, firing as they ran. Flag Day was reloading and Kansas was changing magazines. Sean grabbed a grenade and tossed it. The grenade's explosion dropped three of them and Sean downed the fourth with his M-16.

Sean changed magazines quickly and saw Kansas was crouched at the bottom of the trench. "Come on, Kansas. That was close, but we're alright. Don't sky out on me kid, you're doing fine. We're not done yet."

He grabbed the young Marine by the back collar of the flak jacket and jerked him up. The strange blue-white light from the flares lit the area like a ballpark. The dancing light revealed that Kansas had taken a hit in the side of his head with an AK47 round. A portion of his skull had been shot away. Sean's hand was wet with blood and brain matter.

Sean released his grasp as if he were holding a ghost. The body fell to the bottom of the trench. "Holy Mary . . . ." Sean fought off a gag.

He added another stick of gum to his mouth and took the grenades and loaded rifle magazines from the body. Flag Day looked to Sean for additional instructions and a report on the condition of young Kansas.

"The kid bought it. Keep dropping them at the hole in the wire. The fewer that get inside, the better for us."

Despite the deadly Marine fire, several N.V.A. had made it into the base. Sean saw Lt. Fox lead another React Force toward the 106 position nearest the wire, to reenforce its security. The 106 position was about 50 yards to Sean's left flank.

A squad of N.V.A. attackers had made it inside the wire to a position between two 106 pit positions, behind two mounds of dirt. Another half dozen N.V.A. soldiers lay unhurt near the mouth of the bunker. They had fallen to remain undetected among the dead and wounded.

As Fox's team reached the 106 position, both N.V.A. units opened up on them with automatic AK47 fire. The small React Force was cut to pieces in the brief but savage cross fire. About half of the dozen React Force members made it safely to the 106mm gun pit. The others, including Lt. Fox, fell to the dusty earth, still exposed to enemy fire.

Sean picked up a hand grenade and turned to Flag Day. "Did you see those sneaky bastards near the bunker open up on them? They're not hurt, just layin' chilly. I'm going to throw a frag in the middle of them to spot them for you. Follow it with a Willie Peter. Then get a frag ready to cover our evac of those wounded out in the open."

Flag Day nodded. Sean readied a hand grenade. He called to Little Joe to get ready to have some people get the wounded to cover, after they eliminated the Gooks near the bunker. Sean threw the grenade in the center of the area where he had seen the muzzle flashes from the prone N.V.A. soldiers, "Want to play dead, you sneaky Gook bastards?"

The horrible grinding sound of the grenade's explosion on the hard ground was followed by a scream. The Willie Peter round from Flag Day's M-79 stopped the scream. The M-60 machine gun in the bunker sprayed the group of N.V.A. soldiers with deadly fire.

Sean instructed Flag Day to stay at his position and continue to drop M-79 grenades into the opening in the wire. He called to Little Joe to follow him to recover the wounded. Sean, Little Joe, and two others ran toward the 106 pit, and the six Marine bodies lying near it.

The N.V.A. squad still hidden near the wire was determined to overrun the 106 position and kill the Marine survivors inside. Their rifles opened up on Sean and those helping the Marines still in the open.

Ware directed cover fire from the positions around the M-60 bunker. The men quickly checked the downed Marines. Two were obviously dead. Lt. Fox and the others were dragged into the 106 pit, with the assistance of the men from Fox's team that had made it through the cross fire. The rescue took place amidst heavy fire from the N.V.A. squad near the wire and three more Marines were wounded during the effort.

The bottom of the 106 gun pit was littered with dead or badly-wounded Marines. Sean struggled to catch his breath as he raised his eyes slowly over the lip of the sandbag-rimmed gun pit, to see the muzzle flashes from the enemy squad inside the wire. Only Sean, Little Joe, and three others were not wounded.

Sean automatically took control.

"Little Joe, you and those two cover the gate side of the pit. The Gooks are still coming in, we don't need them dropping in on us while we're busy with the back door. You, Marine. Put out some fire at that group by the wire or they'll overrun us before we can respond."

N.V.A. hand grenades fell short of the 106 position. Little Joe called cross the gun pit to Sean, "I'm sure glad the Gooks don't play baseball. Lucky for us most of them throw like girls."

"Little bastards, all that fish heads and rice makes them sneaky but doesn't do squat for your throwing arm."

Two more Marines in the 106 pit were badly wounded by enemy rifle fire. Suddenly S/Sgt. Ware dove into the 106 gun pit.

"You boys have stepped in some shit this time. Looks like the attack at the wire is about over. Them Gooks inside the base want this position awful bad. Comin' to get it is gonna cost them. Irish, you coordinate fire, I'll start to check on the wounded. Where's the Lu-tenant?"

"He's got a sucking chest wound, same as before. He's hurt bad, Staff, we need a corpman. Corpman up, corpman up, damn it."

Ware calmly opened a battle dressing. "Irish, don't get too pissed off. You won't do us or the Lu-tenant no good. You keep them Gooks off our backs. We'll get some help soon and evac these boys to the aid station. The corpmen are real busy tonight. We ain't gonna get one to make a house call this close to the wire until we can secure it enough for him to get here."

Ware gently opened the lieutenant's flak jacket and placed the band-age on the wound like a skilled doctor. He carefully turned Fox's body onto his injured side. Sean wondered to himself if Ware and T.J. had gone to the same secret ghetto medical school.

Ware looked down at his lieutenant and grinned.

"Well, least ways he been hit in the same lung. You hold on, Lu-tenant, you short-timer son-of-a-bitch. Me and these boys get you evacuated in a couple minutes. I figure you'll be chasing the nurses before Christmas."

Sean's collective anger and frustration was at the surface. He screamed toward the N.V.A. squad as he fired his M-16 on full automatic.

"Come on you little bastards. Come and take us. Just like when T.J. and I were all screwed up in the bomb crater. You like to attack the wounded and helpless. Little shits never want to go one-on-one unless we're all chewed up. Come on you little bastards, I got something for you."

After nearly a year of frustration, Sean was close to losing control, and Ware sensed it. "Hold fire, Irish. Sounds like they're layin' chilly. They're either waitin' for us to try and evac these folks so they can zap our asses or they'll try to sneak back out the hole in the wire."

Sean sat his M-16 against the wall of the gun pit and pulled out a hand grenade.

"I heard of the reputation I have. In a Gook's back pocket at 50 yards. Isn't that what they say? Well, let's just see. Where exactly are those little turds? Let's see if I can motivate them to move to a new location so we can get these wounded out of here."

A Black Marine from another squad moved close to Sean. He nervously bobbed his head as he spoke.

"Dig this, man. See that little mound of dirt and debris, just in front of the wire? I seen some muzzle flashes from there. Some movin' too."

Sean patted the new Marine on his helmet. "Thanks Slim. Get ready. If any of them move after the frag, waste them."

"I can dig it, Man. If we don't e-liminate them A.S.A.P., they gonna do the bunch of us."

Sean set and threw the grenade. Fifty yards away, an N.V.A. sergeant was discussing the squad's best course of action. One of his people was slowly attempting to cut them an escape route in the wire. He could not decide whether to move to the large break in the wire or sacrifice the squad in a full assault on the Marine 106 position.

Sean's grenade hit the hard earth in front of him. The strange sound briefly startled him. The explosion killed him just before he realized what had made the noise. There was a scream and the sight of running figures. The Marines opened fire, and the running figures disappeared.

Sean heard Lt. Fox from the bottom of the 106 gun pit, "That's my man Irish. Get some."

Slim changed magazines and moved back next to Sean. "I seen 'em drag a couple. There's some behind that little mound, 'bout 20 yards to the right."

Sean took out another hand grenade. "One more time men, get set."

The hand grenade landed in the center of the stunned N.V.A. squad survivors. The explosion killed all but two. Confused, they stood and ran toward the hole in the wire. Marine rifle fire dropped both in less than 10 yards.

One of the attackers had staggered back into the barbed wire after being badly wounded by a grenade. He became tangled and looked like a rag doll. The more he struggled, the more entangled his body became. He called for help in Vietnamese. In his condition, he didn't care who helped him, or even how they helped him. Anything had to be better than being tangled in a death grip of thick, razor-sharp barbed wire, bleeding to death.

Ware shouldered his rifle. "Poor Gook done got himself all hung up in the wire. Say good night, Dick."

The N.V.A. soldier seemed to bounce in the wire, his arms and legs held outward in strange positions, lit by the dancing light of the numerous parachute flares. Slim grabbed Ware's arm, "Naw Sarge, let him be. Them little bastards wanted in here so bad, let him hang there and enjoy the view."

Sean clutched his last hand grenade, "This is all bullshit. No one is risking their ass to go out and get the asshole, and I wouldn't let a dog suffer like that."

The small group of Marines in the gun pit watched Sean's grenade arch through the blue-white light and land at the feet of the enemy soldier hung up in the wire. The little man turned toward the sound of it hitting the ground and said something in Vietnamese the second before it exploded.

"Get some, Irish." Sean felt a wave of embarrassment. He instantly realized that every man in the gun pit knew he had killed the N.V.A. sapper out of rage, not as a humanitarian act. Sean also sensed that none of them cared about his motive or thought less of him as a man because of the cold, violent act.

Sean held his rifle stock close to his face. The plastic felt cool against his flushed skin. "Get some Irish". They didn't care if Ware shot him or Sean fragged him. "Seemed like the proper thing to do at the time. Fuck it. Don't mean nothing."

Except for occasional rifle fire, the attack appeared to be over. Sean helped Ware secure the bandage on the lieutenant's chest wound. They carefully lifted him onto a poncho liner, lifted him out of the 106 gun pit and began to carry him to the aid station. The other uninjured Marines began to move the injured to the protection and care of the busy, well-protected aid-station bunker.

A platoon-sized React Force passed them. They were on their way to resecure the hole in the wire and mop up on any sappers en route.

Over the combined noise of the madness around them, Sean detected the muffled, "tunk" sound of an M-79 grenade launcher firing. It sounded as though it had been fired from the river outside the wire, not by a Marine inside the wire. Sean struggled to hold the dead weight of Fox in the poncho liner and his M-16. Suddenly, he had a frightening realization of what the sound he heard could mean to those headed for the aid station with the wounded.

Sean had barely uttered "Son-of-a-bitch!" when the ugly red-orange explosion erupted. The grenade's explosion blew him over backward, filling the front of his legs and left side with hot shrapnel. Because of their angle of approach during the impact, Sean absorbed most of the shrapnel. Ware was not seriously peppered, and Fox escaped further injury. Sean, Fox, and Ware lay together in a bloody pile, stunned or unconscious. Members from another React Force got them to the aid station.

Artillery and air strikes continued to pound the area around the firebase. They called for choppers to medevac the most serious wounded, now that the base L.Z. was considered to be secure.

At the aid station, the Navy doctor took one look at Fox and tagged him for evac. Sean was losing blood from the numerous frag wounds and was in shock. He was ordered out with Fox. They were given I.V.s, placed on stretchers, and taken to the L.Z. to wait for the choppers, now en route from Da Nang.

Sean slowly regained consciousness and realized he was screaming. A corpman quickly knelt at his side. "O.K., Marine, you're gonna be fine. Chopper evac is en route."

Sean was dizzy and nauseous. He saw Lt. Fox on the stretcher next to him. He felt the searing pain in his legs and left side. There was also pain in the general area of his genitals. He layed his helmet back down on the stretcher and felt as though he was going to pass out. "Oh Holy Mary, not again. Please, not again."

He reached down to his groin. All he felt were bandages and blood-soaked trousers.

The corpman pulled his hand away and said, "I swear to God, Marine. You still got all your equipment. The family jewels are intact. I give you my word. Frags came close, but you'll be fine."

Tears of relief rolled from his eyes. "Still got my helmet on. T.J. will groove on it. He thought it was magic how I'd never lose my helmet, even when we stepped in some shit."

The corpman gave Sean a mouthful of water. "How you feelin', Buddy?"

"I'm hurtin', Doc. I'm in pain, and I feel dizzy and nauseous."

The corpman gave Sean a healthy hit of morphine.

"That will help you relax. It should settle your stomach. Them chopper crews don't like when you puke in their birds. Go ahead and chew some more gum. But spit it out if you feel like you gonna sleep. Don't want you sick but can't have you choke. Gonna keep your flak jacket on until you're on the chopper and outa here."

Sean could see two corpman attending to Lt. Fox, on the stretcher next to him. He saw Ware walk up to him. Ware had been watching over Fox. Ware knelt down and took Sean's hand. He wiped dry blood from Sean's hand with a towel. "You're gonna be just fine, Irish."

"How about you, Staff?"

"I took a little shrapnel. Doc at the aid station took it out. I got a few stitches. You and my flak jacket caught the most of it."

"Hell, Staff, least I can do. Ain't this a bitch, all that reputation B.S. about me fraggin' the Gooks, and they end up fragging me."

"Don't really count as a frag, Irish. I figure it was a stolen Gook M-79. For certain, ain't no Gook threw that mother. You may be gettin' medevaced, but you're still a legend in your own time in this platoon."

"Shit, Staff, more like a legend in my own mind."

Capt. Kincade appeared at the L.Z. as the faint thud of approaching choppers became audible in the distance.

Sean could see that Fox was conscious. Capt. Kincade stood between their stretchers and looked down at them. "You men did a damn outstanding job tonight. You plugged that hole in the wire and reduced our losses. God damn men, we're going to miss you two. I wanted to come up and say good-bye personally."

Sean raised up from his stretcher. "I'll be back, Skipper. I'm not hit that bad. The Doc at the aid station said . . ."

"I know, Irish, you'll be fine in a few weeks. But you won't be back, Son. The Corps' three-Heart rule, remember? You're done here, Marine. You men make me proud I'm a Marine. You may just be passing through, but you people give your best while you're here." Kincade quickly turned and disappeared as the medevac choppers hovered for landing position.

Sean rested his spinning head back down on the stretcher. He closed his eyes. It was what he and Ware had spoken of that very night. He never let himself consider going home. For some time, the only way he could imagine being home before January, 1969, was being shipped in a body bag.

He looked up at Ware, half concealed in the dust from the chopper rotor's wash. "You relax, Irish. The Lu-tenant gonna be O.K. Boy, I seen that look you had when you fragged that Gook in the wire before. Let it go, Irish. You ain't never gonna be able to undo what's been done here. Don't go through life all pissed off. Be cool, my man. You the best squad leader I seen in two tours, square business. Now go work at your old man's company and let all this bullshit go. Just fucking forget it."

Ware helped put Sean in the chopper. They exchanged salutes, and a brief moment later the chopper was airborne, en route to Da Nang.

Sean spent the next day in and out of consciousness. He remembered arriving at the hospital, being placed on the operating table, a brief moment in the recovery room, and being lifted into his own bed on the ward. He heard bits of conversation around him that had nothing to do with his wild, drug-induced dreams.

Fox was flown to Japan. He was expected to make a full recovery, then go back to the States.

Sean's shrapnel wounds were not large, but there were many in his upper legs and left side. He took over 100 sutures. Two weeks later, the Navy doctors removed the sutures. He was on "light-duty" status, but had little problem walking. He convinced the doctor to allow him to go back to the world on a Freedom Bird with the other Marines who finished their tours, rather than on a hospital plane.

By the first week in December, Sean had tracked down his seabag and caught a jeep ride to the airbase at Da Nang.

Sean passively limped from one location at the busy airbase to another. He checked in, showed his orders, checked out, showed his orders, ate chow, showed his orders.

An Admin Sergeant told him that a commercial jet was due at any time. After the replacements aboard were off loaded and the plane was readied and picked up a new crew, it would take him back to the States.

Sean saw the big 707 land and taxi toward where he was waiting. He moved away so he could not see the new replacements deplane. He felt as though it would be bad luck, somehow, actually seeing the men that would take his place.

Two hours later, he limped up the big jet's forward gangway. He found a window seat forward and stared out the plane's window as darkness fell over Da Nang. The plane filled with over 100 other Marines who had finished their tour, one fashion or another, and were also on their way back to the world.

Moments later, the well-lit, easily defined coast line of the Republic of Vietnam passed from their view. The plane was still silent. Sean leaned to look back at the coast.

"So long, you nasty green mother fucker."

5

December, 1968—January, 1969

DECEMBER, 1968
CALIFORNIA

Sean's dad had arranged for his early release from active duty. At the height of the Vietnam Conflict, the Marine Corps was geared to fight the war. There were very few positions for Marines who had served in Vietnam with less than a year remaining in their enlistment, so Sean was granted an early-out to return to college.

His dad had called in some favors to have him out so soon. He was only requested to sign a waiver that he was not physically permanently disabled by his wounds. To avoid months of boring stateside duty at Camp Pendleton, Sean would have signed anything but a re-enlistment form.

As his orders were being processed and he prepared for separation from active service, he was assigned to a light-duty billet at Main-side, Camp Pendleton.

The officer assigned to be in charge of the personnel in transit was a two-tour Nam vet. Capt. Smuthers was 30 going on 60. He wore an ugly scar across the bridge of his nose that traveled up his forehead.

Sean reported to the stout captain and handed him his folder. The officer read the contents carefully. Sean was still wearing the starched jungle utilities from the flight from Vietnam.

"Cavanagh, have you got any of your uniform ready to wear?"

"I don't understand, Sir."

"Marine, you can't wear that type of utilities or jungle boots State-side. How about your class A?"

"Sir, everything I own has been packed in the bottom of my seabag. My dress uniform doesn't have the correct rank, much less the correct ribbons."

"Go to the Main P.X. and buy some civilian clothes to get you into town." He gave Sean the address of a cleaner-tailor in Oceanside.

"Go see this guy A.S.A.P. He'll fix you up. Tomorrow come back and see me. I'll keep you out of the way until you go home next week. You still in pain?"

Sean was caught off guard and embarrassed by the question. "No, Sir, but still tender as hell. The stitches have only been out a few days."

The captain gave Sean a visual once-over. "You stop by the Main-side hospital at least once before I'll cut your final orders. I won't have you signing away a disability if you rate one, just to get an early-out. You'll be home for Christmas either way. Now, go get your uniform squared away."

"Aye, aye, Sir."

A week later, Sean stood at attention in his pressed Class A uniform in front of Capt. Smuther's desk. Smuthers gave Sean the once over and grinned. A little over a year in the Corps and the kid was an N.C.O. with three rows of battle ribbons.

"What time is your flight home, Cavanagh?"

"Tonight, Sir, from L.A.X. I'll take a bus from Oceanside. It leaves in an hour."

"No you won't. I got you a jeep ride to L.A.X. That gives you time to ride over to Camp Horno and see that buddy of yours that's an I.T.R. Instructor for a couple hours."

Sean broke into a wide grin. "Thank you, Sir. For everything. Good luck, Captain."

The officer stood and firmly shook Sean's hand. "My own enlistment is over in three months, kid. I don't need much luck now. Good luck yourself, Marine, back in the world."

Sean and T.J. were able to talk for only an hour. They finally tracked the I.T.R. company down at a live fire rifle range. T.J. jived Sean about his ribbons and they made plans to meet in Detroit during T.J.'s next leave.

Just before Sean left, the I.T.R. company was gathered on the roadway. T.J. addressed the company,

"Listen up. The corporal jus' back from Nam. He's got something to say to you."

The entire company was silent, waiting for Sean's combat advice. He looked over the collection of intent, young faces.

"I'd only suggest that you listen to everything Cpl. Johnson tells you. We served together earlier this year. I'm going home today, for good, standing up, because I listened to him."

T.J. had the company come to Present Arms in a gesture of respect. Sean returned the gesture with a crisp salute. Sean got back in the jeep.

"Take care, T.J. What I told those kids was the straight skinny. Even after you were here, what you had taught me kept my squad and me alive."

"We'll be together again, white Brother. Have a good trip home. De-troit never looked better."

The cool, rainy, California night seemed appropriate for the conclusion of his last day as an active duty Marine. It would be three hours before his lengthy, non-stop jet flight. He walked alone through the crowded terminal. There was a vast assortment of business and holiday travelers filling the waiting areas.

Sean strolled in to the lounge and bought a cola. He was still too young for a legal drink. He sipped the Coke and nervously watched the schedule board to make certain his plane was leaving on time, despite the weather. They had told him Detroit was being clobbered by a snow storm.

The damp weather made his shoulder ache. The newest wounds to the front of his legs were still healing and were very uncomfortable.

Sean thumbed through a *Time* magazine. He silently watched the people pass. He felt like a stranger in his own country. He tried to absorb what had happened. One week at Pendleton, two weeks at Da Nang. Only three weeks since combat. It was the first time he had been with civilians since Thanksgiving of 1967.

He tried to make himself believe he would be in Detroit for bedtime. In little more than a few hours, he would be with his parents. He would be at home sleeping in his own bed.

Sean was getting restless. He finished his Coke and decided to wait the remainder of the time at the plane gate. He walked down the terminal hallway. He walked slowly in an attempt to conceal the limp. His legs were killing him.

He walked past a group of hippies, with a couple of children sprawled up against the wall seated on the floor. They were poorly-groomed and spoke to each other loudly. The young men were bearded with long hair, and covered with beads and assorted patches. The young women had dirty straight hair and wore buckskin. The loudest member of the group wore a military type field jacket. It had an American flag sewn up-side-down on the back.

As Sean approached, he moved to the opposite side of the hallway and was careful not to make eye contact with anyone in the group.

The young man with the flag on his jacket stopped his conversation and turned toward Sean, as he slowly walked past. "Hey, hero . . . ," he called.

Sean ignored his taunt. "Hey, hero Marine. I'm talking to you."

Sean stopped and slowly turned to the young man yelling at him. "Are you addressing me?"

Sean's tormentor looked to his friends and mocked him. "Shit, a well-spoken killer. Tell us, hero: how many babies did you kill in Vietnam?"

Sean could not have been in a less tolerant mood for the insult. He was still much too near to his dead and maimed friends to accept that, especially while he still wore a Marine uniform. Certainly not from a low-life like the youth on the floor before him. "I killed a few," he said. "Hand me that little bastard there, and I'll kill it too."

The entire group was stunned for a moment. After the initial shock wore off, four of the young men stood up, their fists clenched at their sides. "How'd you like us to stomp your ass, tough hero Marine?"

"Well, I figure it will take all four of you long-haired fucks to do it. Come on, assholes. Go for it. You all feeling froggy? Then leap on over here and let's get to it."

The four young men paused for a moment, then began to spread out and move toward Sean.

The thought shot through Sean's mind that his last official act in a Marine uniform would be to have his ass stomped by four draft-dodging hippies. He sensed someone standing on his left, a step to his rear. A quick glance allowed him to identify the large man dressed in an Army uniform. A second look revealed a 6'3", Green Beret captain. He was in full dress green uniform, complete with spit-shined jump boots, cords, badges, patches and several rows of ribbons. He had his hands on his hips.

"You boys gonna play, are you? Excuse me, Marine, do you mind if I join in on the fun? It must be the kid in me. I really enjoy mixing it up. Which two can I have?"

The four young men took a step back. The group's spokesman began to gather up their belongings. "Hey man, forget this bullshit. You two tough war heros can brutalize some defenseless villagers or something. We're leaving."

The Captain's voice changed in tone. "Watch your big mouth, punk, or I'll send you directly to your dentist."

The group got to their feet and walked together, away from the plane gate. The one young man called back, "Fuck both of you Nazis."

The Green Beret Captain grinned at Sean. "Nice lads. Hope they're all 1-A."

Sean picked up his bag from the floor and put on his Garrison cap.

"I don't know how to thank you, Captain. I wasn't looking for trouble, but I let my alligator mouth overload my tadpole ass. On my best day, the four of them would beat my ass, and I'm still not 100 percent."

The Army Captain glanced at Sean's ribbons. "Christ, Marine: three Hearts. How many tours were you in Nam?"

"Less than one, about nine months in the field."

"I did two tours in I Corps. Twenty-four months in-country and got two Hearts, one each tour. I missed Tet — I was in the hospital."

"I didn't, Captain. That's why I've got all this shit, for all the good it will do me."

"Can't hurt your chance for promotion, an impressive service record like yours."

Sean smiled and again checked on his boarding pass. "I'm all done, Sir. I've got my separation papers. I'm on my way home to Detroit. This is my last day as an active duty Marine."

Sean figured the captain to be in his mid- to late-twenties. The Captain's face broadened with a wide grin.

"Well, that's outstanding. I'm on my way home too. I live in Lansing. I'm going to finish law school and go into practice with my dad and uncle. I didn't want to say anything if you were just going home on leave."

"Thanks for being sensitive, but I'm outa here. No, Sir, as per my orders, tomorrow I'm a civilian."

"Well, Marine, we've got to count our blessings. I can tell you're still limping. My body is scarred as hell, but we're going home in one piece, alive. I'm certain we've both left buddies and other damn fine people there. I'm sure we've both lost more than one friend. They can take their war and stick it up the new President's ass. I've had a belly full. I'm all done with that stinkin' war and with the Army."

Sean rendered the Green Beret Captain his best, salty, Marine hand salute. The captain matched the Marine's salute style. "Thanks again, Captain, for saving my butt back there."

"Damn proud to have the chance, Corporal. Shit, A-Teams and Marines have bailed each other out a hundred times in I Corps, why not in L.A.X.?"

Sean would always remember that four-hour flight as his favorite. He'd never forget some very special service from an attractive stewardess. She had overheard that the wounded veteran was going home for good. She thought of her own brother at college in L.A. She was very attracted to Sean and privately wished that the young Marine was 27, instead of 20. She served him vodka tonics and the best in-flight steak on board.

The pilot announced initial approach to Detroit Metro Airport. It was still snowing, but the pilot assured them that their flight would land on schedule. The plane's air speed decreased and they slowly descended into the weather.

The vodka had a calming effect on Sean. He tugged to tighten his seat belt as the jet made its final approach. As they neared the ground, Sean could see the snow falling past the visible lights. The 7O7 touched down and taxied to the terminal. On the ground, the passengers could see that the snow storm was severe. The pilot's skill helped the landing seem as though it had been perfect weather. As the plane stopped, and the tunnel walkway was extended to the front hatch, Sean could see a crowd of people waiting inside the terminal, looking out at their plane.

As Sean approached the door to the terminal, he felt strong, in control. He walked out of the tunnel and saw the small knot of people watching the faces that were leaving the plane. His parents, brothers, sisters, and grandparents waited nervously. His mother spotted him and began to wave. At first, he controlled his emotions. He hugged his family members and comforted his mother who had been crying since she had first spotted him. He felt the lump building in his throat and the tears in his eyes. Sean was surrounded with family members, most of whom were in tears.

Sean's father stood on the fringe of the group, as though waiting his turn to greet his son. He met his father's eyes. He moved through the other family members and embraced his father in a double armed bear hug. He held his father tightly and began to cry. He buried his face against his father's solid shoulder and wept. His father put his arms around Sean and gently patted him on the back.

The remainder of the family grew silent. They seemed to move around father and son, held in each other's arms, both openly crying. Sean felt the warm moisture of his father's tears against his face. He spoke softly so that only his father could hear. "Dad, you were right about war. Nothing will ever seem the same again."

Sean's father placed his hand gently on the back of Sean's head.

"It's over for you now, Sean. Time is a wonderful healer, and although it won't all go away, it will slowly get better. The doing part is over. The coping part lasts the rest of your life. We're proud of you, Sean. But this is an strange, ugly war. You won't know there is a war still going on unless you watch the news on television. No flag waving. No parades. No one will even ask about it. Just remember that what matters is how your family feels about you. Thank God you're home safe. Welcome home, Marine."

The ride to Grosse Pointe Woods from Metro Airport, in a blinding snow storm, was much longer than usual. Sean sat in the front seat of his dad's Olds 98, next to his mother. He was very tired.

He stared out the car window at the passing landscape. Even in the snowstorm, everything looked familiar, comfortable, friendly.

He closed his eyes and thought of the confrontation with the hippies at L.A.X. He reached across his body and gently ran his finger across the rows of ribbons on his chest. They were the outward symbols of the inner changes that made him feel like a stranger in this once-familiar scene.

Sean slowly awakened. He opened his eyes, and for a brief, terrible instant did not know where he was. He smiled as his eyes focused and he realized that he was actually in his own bed. For an instant, he was afraid he had been dreaming about home.

He sat up and pulled up the window shade. It was still snowing and he could hear the sound of snow shovels scraping against sidewalks and driveways. He could smell the bacon cooking. He could hear other family members talking and walking through the house. He lay in bed just looking around his own bedroom. He thought that if he tried to reorient himself a little at a time, he might reduce the culture shock.

He got up and searched through his closet until he found his winter robe. He had slept in just his skivvy shorts; one of a hundred subtle changes since pre-Marine days. He had always worn pajamas to bed while growing up. He wondered how much he had really changed. Wearing his underwear to bed would go unnoticed, but he worried that some of his behavior changes may have made him a different person.

Sean studied the group of photos hung on the wall. There were team pictures and action shots of his high school football senior year. It seemed a hundred years ago. He ran his fingers over the cloth Detroit Tiger penant and looked carefully at the collection of trophies on the top of the chest of drawers. He glanced over at the dresser and night stand. He smiled to himself; his mother had removed the half dozen photos of Miss Terri Murphy that had decorated his room. He felt at home, but still somewhat out of place. It was as though he had gone through a time warp. He had returned a scarred young man, sleeping in the room of an innocent teenager.

Sean joined his family in the kitchen. His mother was busy cooking breakfast and his sisters, Irene and Colleen, were helping. Sean's father had taken the day off from work to spend time with Sean. He sat at the head of the table, reading the morning *Free Press*. Brothers Robert and Brian had already eaten and left the table to get ready for school.

Sean poured himself a cup of coffee and took great enjoyment from simply being in the same room with his family. Brian hugged Sean on his way out the door. Robert said good-bye with a firm handshake, an important difference between grade school and high school boys.

Sean's mother set a huge plate of food in front of him. "Mom, you know I'm not a breakfast person. It looks wonderful, but there's enough food here to feed a squad."

"So just eat what you can. You're too thin. You're not used to this cold weather. We need to keep you well fed and healthy. You'll heal faster."

Irene and Colleen gave him a good-morning kiss on their way to their places at the table. The remainder of the family made small talk over breakfast. Sean cleaned his plate and thanked his mother, as she cleared off the table. She just smiled when she picked up his empty plate. "Yea, Mom, I know. It must be that I missed your home cooking."

"If you are up to it, Sean, we'd like to have the entire family over Sunday, before Christmas, to have a welcome-home dinner. That gives you a few days to relax and get used to being home first."

"That's fine, Mom. It really feels strange. I'm sure I'll come around in a couple of days."

Sean's father folded up the *Free Press*. "Well, Son, what would you like to do today?"

"Mostly lay on my butt and recharge my batteries. But if it stops snowing, I'd really like to go to Sanders for a hot fudge sundae. Dad, I can't tell you how many times I thought of how you and I always went for a hot fudge sundae after my ballgames. I've been craving one of those for over a year."

"Sounds fine, you know I've never been one to turn down a Sanders hot fudge sundae. And since you made it home in one piece, my treat."

"I know this will sound strange from the kid who was voted the boy who most hated chores, but I want to shovel the snow from the driveway and walk." He smiled at the expression on his parents' faces. "Don't look at me as though I have battle fatigue. I haven't seen snow in almost two years. Let me get sick of it all at once."

Sean went to his room. He took off his robe and stood in front of the full-length mirror on his closet door. The Marine cliché had been correct. They had made a new man out of him. He still had a trace of a farmer's tan on his face, neck and arms. There was a circular pink scar at his left shoulder. His legs and buttocks had more zipper scars than a motorcycle jacket. But he still felt lucky. He was alive. He was whole. Everything still worked, and soon the tenderness of the latest wounds would be gone.

There was a quiet knock at the door. Sean quickly put on his robe. "Come in." Sean's father closed the door behind him and sat down on the bed.

"Well, Dad, I remember when I was growing up, I asked to see your battle scar about a dozen times. I suppose you, more than anyone, have the same right."

"Son, if you'd rather not. You're my boy and I deeply care what happened to you."

Sean dropped his robe. He admired his father's ability not to show emotion.

"The scars from my first Heart are almost all covered by the hair on the back of my neck. This beauty on my left shoulder is from the AK47 rifle round through and through that broke my collar bone. That and the scars on the back of my legs I got in Hue, in February. These fresh ones in front are from last month. If it's all the same to you, Dad, I won't show you the ones on my rump."

"That's fine, Son, no need to drop your drawers. I'm your dad, I've seen it. Can't look that much different with a few scars."

"Navy docs guarantee I'll be 100 percent before Spring. They say that I can play football again, if I choose to."

"Yea, well, I'd like you to get a complete physical after the New Year from Dr. Fleming. You signed the waiver to get your early-out, but if there is something that's going to bother you for life, we'll go after the V.A. Sean, how about tonight if Grampa Cavanagh, Uncle Bobby, you and I sit around the fireplace and get stinko while we swap war stories? First step in getting over all that is to talk about it with those that can relate to combat's madness. You won't find many friends or people that want to hear what you've got to say. We three old Jar Heads will match you tale for tale and tell you what it was like in the old Corps."

"Yea, I'd really like that, Dad. You know, my mind is still spinning, but it sure is good to be home."

"Son, believe me, I understand exactly what you're feeling, and I had three months to adjust from combat to State-side."

Sean was still full from dinner. He couldn't remember when he had eaten so much in one day. He opened the sliding glass door in the family room and stepped out into the back yard, closing the door behind him. He wore no jacket, and it only took a minute for the bitter cold to penetrate his navy blue crew neck sweater.

It had stopped snowing, but the strong wind blew the powder and it stung his face and flushed his cheeks. He took a deep breath of the cold, clear Winter air. It smelled fresh, no odor of cordite, mildewed canvas, rot, urine or the other foul smells that were a part of the Vietnam experience. There was no choking red dust. What he enjoyed, as never before, was the smell of a cold, Michigan, Winter night. Nothing seemed as different, or more distant from the thick, hot, damp air that was Vietnam.

Sean re-entered the family room and took a seat nearest the raging fire in the large field stone fireplace. Grampa Cavanagh sat in the recliner, Uncle Bobby was on the couch, and his dad was at the wet bar.

"What you drinking, Son?"

"Vodka tonic, Dad. They sure didn't do any harm on the plane ride home."

"How about you, Pop? The usual?"

Sean's grandfather filled the bowl of his favorite pipe. "Dennis, I've been drinking the same thing for nearly 50 years, there's no use changing now. Damn, Son, if it hasn't killed me yet, it's not likely to."

Sean's father brought Bobby and himself a bottle of local Stroh's and sat down on the couch next to Bobby.

Grampa Cavanagh raised his shot glass full of Seven Roses whiskey toward Sean as if in a toast and quickly swallowed the contents. He took a sip of his beer chaser. He smacked his lips twice and leaned back in the big chair.

"By God, Sean, it's good to have you home safe. From your letters and what your dad has told me, things sure are different than when I fought the Hun back in 1917. For one thing, it took us nearly a full month to get to Europe by troop ship. I was seasick almost the whole trip. Thought I'd die.

"Now, you boys are half way around the world in a day. Took your dad four days to get home from California by train. You got here in four hours. But all those damned new weapons are what amaze an old war horse like me. I saw some pictures, and I see on the T.V. the new power a platoon has at its disposal these days. Back in '17, in the Belleau Woods, we only had our rifles and bayonets."

"Gramps, all the weapons and uniforms have changed but the most important part of combat is still the same — the individual Marine with his rifle. It still boils down to man against man. When we retook the city of Hue from the Communists last February, we had fire power unmatched in any ground combat to date. The combined fire power from land, sea, and air ordinance turned parts of that city into a big parking lot. But the Marine rifleman still had to retake every stinking foot of ground.

"You and dad fought in great world wars. Bobby and I fought in small, unofficial political wars. Fifty years between our combat, Gramps, yet we've all killed men to stay alive. We all lost friends. We all suffered from wounds. Germans, Japs, North Koreans, Chinese, North Vietnamese, Viet Cong. The enemy changed. Your .03, dad's M-1 garand, Uncle Bobby's B.A.R., my M-16, the weapons have surely developed. But in those 50 years, our four different wars, I maintain there's still more that's the same about our combat than different."

The four men drank and talked late into the night. They shared stories and a unique common bond. On other nights, the men had spoken of the Devil Dogs at Belleau Woods, Okinawa, Inchon. That night, new words were added to the family history: Hue, the D.M.Z. and I Corps.

By midnight, the four men were drunk enough that they began to display their scars and the telling of the complete details of how they were received.

The three senior men made an honest attempt, but they could not comprehend the tactics of the Vietnam war. They fully understood the cost of taking a hill or a box on a map. But to move on and leave the objective after paying the price in human life and suffering was beyond them. They knew of the madness of war, but that seemed too senseless.

Grampa Cavanagh downed another shot of Seven Roses. It was followed by the standard double smack of his lips. "Well, Lad, we know we're killing a whole bunch of those little bastards, but are we winning over there or not?"

"Gramps, we're not fighting to win. We're fighting for a tie. It's a holding action, a war to wear down the Communists so they'll give up and go home, north of the D.M.Z., like they finally did in Korea. The main problem is that this isn't Korea. There are nearly as many Communists, Viet Cong, who live in South Vietnam. If every N.V.A. soldier went home tomorrow, the war would continue. We are not losing by any means, but we sure as heck are not winning."

"If you got orders to go back there, would you go?"

"If they said we were going to fight a different kind of war, fight to win, I'd go to O.C.S. If they'd send a couple of U.S. divisions across the D.M.Z. to invade the North, or stage a massive amphibious assault like at Inchon, I'd be in the point platoon. If they'd want me to go back to the same kind of waste, I'm sure I'd do what my orders told me to do, but I'd be very bitter."

By 2 a.m., Grampa Cavanagh was sleeping soundly in the leather recliner; Uncle Bobby was stretched out asleep on the coach. Sean and his father sipped brandy on the rug near the fireplace. Father and son were well on their way to becoming intoxicated. Sean focused his stare on the logs burning in the fireplace. He watched a sheet of fire consume the large piece of dry firewood. He spoke to his father, but his eyes never left the fireplace.

"Did you ever kill any civilians, Dad?"

His father sipped his brandy and thoughtfully pondered the question. "Didn't see any at Peleliu. Damn hell hole, just crazy Japs and coral. By the time what was left of my outfit reached Okinawa, we really had it in for those bastards. Some Jap civilians got killed. When you fight in towns and villages, it just happens."

Sean's eyes teared but they did not leave the fire. "Both sides killed a lot of civilians in Hue. I know of at least one I killed, but not on purpose. Damn, all that contact, the world was upsidedown, Dad. In Hue, the whole city was a free-fire zone."

"Son, you can't judge the terrible insanity that happens in combat by the standards of regular life. If you try to compare apples with oranges, you'll lose your mind. The U.S. purposely killed thousands of civilians in World War II. We fire bombed Dresden and Tokyo. We A-bombed two Jap cities off the map. The media acts like this is the first war that civilians ever suffered. Shit, a hundred years ago, Gen. Sherman burned Atlanta to the ground. The way I see it, Sean, is that you do what you feel you need to do to survive and still be true to yourself. Then, the hell with what anybody else thinks."

Sean sat in the center of his bedroom floor, the contents of his seabag spilled out in front of him. The melancholy tune of his Simon and Garfunkel album filled the room.

He found the O.D. towel and slowly unwrapped it. It contained his medals in their presentation boxes. He put them aside. He took out the empty antique jewelry box his mother had found for him in the attic and took off his dogtag chain. With the two I.D. tags was his St. Christopher Medal and his "John Wayne" C-ration can opener. They were the first items to go in the antique wooden box.

Other items to follow were small reminders of his life during the past year: empty M-16 rifle brass, hand grenade safety pins and pull rings, photos protected from the moisture by plastic, a "bug juice" bottle containing water from the Perfume River, and his prize possession, the metal circular N.V.A. emblem from an officer's pith helmet, taken in Hue.

By most standards, they were small, insignificant souvenirs. But to Sean, each item held a personal importance greater than captured rifles or swords. He found a large piece of military map from the Hue battle, and one small piece of an N.V.A. battle flag that the squad had ripped up and shared.

He sat staring at the contents of the box for several minutes, closed the lid and began to clean up. Some scars, a few souvenirs and some medals. That's what he had to show for his year at war. But it was what he had seen and learned about life and death that could not be measured by photos, medals, or souvenirs.

His head pounded from his hangover. His father had taught him well: no Cavanagh ever complained of a hangover. He took two aspirin and explained to his mother that his shoulder ached a bit from the Winter dampness. She just smiled and said nothing when he only had coffee for breakfast.

Sean's grandfather, Uncle Bobby, and his dad all managed to make it

into work. Sean was thankful that his only task for the day was to clean
out his seabag.

His mother knocked softly on his closed bedroom door and said
there was someone in the living room to see him. He slowly got up from
the floor. His legs were very sore and he leaned against the wall for a
moment until he felt he could walk without an obvious limp. Sean
walked out into the living room.

There, in the center of the room, stood Miss Terri Murphy. His
mother had taken her coat. In a becoming skirt and sweater outfit, she
was never more attractive. Her hair was longer and straighter than he
remembered. Her face was slightly flushed from the cold, and he could
still see the sparkle in her blue eyes.

Terri was obviously uncomfortable. She shifted her weight from one
foot to the other and nervously folded her hands in front of her. Sean's
mother had left the room.

He didn't know what to say. Since the previous Spring, a day had not
passed that he didn't imagine venting the anger and frustration on the
young woman he had loved. He thought he had grown to hate her, yet
the sight of her standing before him stirred him. He had experienced
every human experience while in Vietnam: fear, hate, pain, love, so
many others. The only thing he felt he had not been able to work with
was betrayal. His only contact with betrayal had come from a distance
of 12,000 miles. He had seen cowardice, selfishness, and every cruelty,
but the only betrayal was from home, from Miss Terri Murphy.

"Hello Terri. You look nice, kiddo. I've got to give you credit, I never
expected that you'd have the courage to stop by."

"I didn't have the courage not to. I'm really glad you made it home
safely. Look, Sean, I know I must have hurt you, and I'm really very sorry.
I just . . ."

"No, Terri, you don't have any idea how you hurt me. You see, I really
loved you. You had become my reason for putting one foot in front of
the other, the reason to try and stay alive. Hey, couples break up every
day. You were 19, at college, I expected too much. I should have seen it
coming. Hell, Terri, no one knew you better than I did. You were not
ready to commit to that degree. It was nice you stopped by. Thanks.
Take care of yourself."

"Wait, Sean. I'd like to sit down and talk with you. We've known each
other our whole lives. I'd like to explain to you everything that happened. We've always been friends. Maybe we could manage to salvage
that part of our relationship."

Sean feared his legs would give out from under him. He plopped
down in an over stuffed reading chair.

"First of all, I don't believe ex-lovers can ever be just good friends.

Too many ghosts get in the way. Secondly, I'm still really angry at you. I'm so angry and hurt, I don't know if I want to be your friend."

"I know it doesn't matter, but I haven't even seen that other guy I was with for a few months. I miss you more than I deserve to. I give you my word, I'm not seeing anyone now. I'd like to maybe go out to dinner and just talk. Then, we can close the book, one way or the other."

Sean stared at Terri for a moment. If their worlds were different when he left, they were a million miles apart now. But he also wanted to close the book on his anger. He wondered whether he was about to close the book or open himself up to be hurt again. "You have plans for tomorrow night?"

Terri looked relieved, "I'm home from school until after New Year's. I don't have any plans."

"Fine. I'll pick you up for dinner at 7. We'll see if our favorite Italian restaurant is still open."

After she retrieved her coat, he walked her to the front door. She turned quickly and kissed his cheek, her eyes filled with tears. "Thank God you're home safe."

Sean watched her drive away. The months of hate and anger seemed very distant, almost as distant as Vietnam itself. Sean felt void of emotion. Even at the sight of her tears, he was cool and detached. He'd take her to dinner, listen to what she had to say, but he would not berate her as he had imagined.

Sean went back into his room and sat down again, amidst the contents of his seabag. Uniforms, souvenirs, medals, an old piece of a military map, a piece of an enemy flag spread around him. He thought that he should have shown Terri his souvenirs. He closed his eyes and pictured her standing before him, tears in her eyes. "What goes around, comes around," he thought. "Don't mean nothing."

Sean's mother stuck her head around the door.

"Mom, I'm going to take Terri to dinner tomorrow night."

"You be careful, Son. You know how vulnerable you are."

"Thanks, Mom, but trust me on this one. Miss Terri Murphy will not hurt me again. Once, shame on her. Twice, shame on me."

Sean felt as though he had to reprogram himself to do even the simplest of things taken for granted in civilian life. He felt strange behind the wheel of his father's plush Olds 98. Driving was, of course, familiar, but it somehow felt different after a year. He felt a keen awareness of the small comforts and pleasures of normal life. He realized that his appreciation of every minor experience would fade quickly with time back in the world. But for now, he felt like a blind man who had suddenly been gifted with sight and was actually seeing things for the first time.

There was no traffic, but he just sat at the stop sign for a full minute. The Olds smelled clean and had the unique odor of a new car interior. The radio filled the vehicle with traditional Christmas music. He stared at the snow-covered lawns and the large, attractive homes decorated with colored lights.

Sean finally drove the few blocks to the Murphy home. His date with Terri was at 7 and there was one thing that hadn't changed in a year. He was on time. He pulled in the drive and walked to the front door. The cold night air smelled fresh and was blowing in off of Lake St. Clair, a quarter of a mile away. He could detect just a hint of burning logs in the crisp air. He stopped on the porch steps for a moment.

He filled his lungs again, and wondered if there was any other smell in the world that could be more different than the collective smell of Vietnam. God, how good it felt to have a chill from the cold, dry Winter wind. He could feel the new snow under his shoes and hear the crunching sound of each step. He could see the steam of each breath and it was as though the cold night was making him stronger. There were no wet tropical monsoons in Michigan, and certainly not in December.

Terri answered the door. She still dressed like the preppie poster girl. Her burgandy crew neck sweater had her monogram at the neck. He was speechless for a moment, and they seemed frozen in time as they stared into each other's eyes.

"Come in, Sean. The family is all down in Florida for the holidays. I bought some steaks and made a salad. I thought that since we have so much to talk about, we'd have much more privacy if we ate here. Is that alright?"

Sean entered the Murphy home and surrendered his coat. "Thank you, Terri, that's fine with me. How about we sit down and get all this baggage we've carried since April out of the way? I'm not going to enjoy dinner with that waiting over our heads."

Terri poured them both a glass of wine and they sat facing each other next to the raging fire in the family room fireplace.

Terri took a swallow of wine. "Well Sean, I don't know exactly where to start."

"How about last year at Thanksgiving, when you were going to wait for me, and we talked about getting married when I got out?"

"Things started to change around the time you got shot in February. Sean, Danny Jr. flunked out of junior college. When he got his draft notice, he ran off to Canada. It broke my dad's heart and ruined his lifelong friendship with your dad. No matter how hard your dad tried, it always got in the way; Danny Jr. a long-haired draft-dodging hippie, and you were nearly getting killed and winning medals for your country. You were the example of the Cavanagh and Murphy tradition.

"I've got no excuse for what I did to you. But at least try and understand all that was involved. I loved you, part of me always will. It was our first real love with all the passion and the romance. But I was not as mature and strong as you were. I told you I understood what your going off to war really meant to us as a couple. I knew nothing of the sort.

"There was all the anti-war stuff and school. You nearly being killed, Danny running away, I was being torn apart. I met this guy at school who became my vehicle to escape the conflicts in my life. He was an absolute, total clown. To him, life was nothing but a continuous joke, a mere game. Nothing was ever serious with him.

"What probably attracted me to him is that no one I've ever known was more unlike you. Your pain was too real for me, so I just checked out of life for a couple of months. I did a lot of grass but managed to maintain my G.P.A.

"By the Summer break, I came back to earth. I quit feeling sorry for myself and grew up a lot. I worked all Summer for my dad, and I honestly believe I went back to school in the Fall as a young adult and not a sheltered, naive kid.

"The clown I had been seeing became a complete burn-out. He started to drop acid, and it fried his brain. He dropped out of school before the Summer break, and moved back to New York. I haven't even talked to him since last May. I'm not telling you this because I expect anything to be as it was. I never wrote after the letter in April because I wanted to explain in person, and I was afraid I would insult you if the letter wasn't worded correctly."

Sean sipped his wine and stared at Terri as she sat at the edge of her chair and spoke. He remembered the countless nights in Vietnam when he ached inside from the thought of her being with someone else. His emotions had alternated from jealous rage to self-pity. He felt his pulse rise when he remembered his violent fantasy of fragging both Terri and her new lover. He was still very close to the sadness of the lonely nights of self-pity that often brought tears.

The minute of silence after Terri's explanation seemed appropriate, rather than uncomfortable. He had imagined their first conversation after the Dear John letter many times. He had dreams of shouting at her in righteous indignation. But now, face to face, Terri had been more direct and shown more courage than he thought she would ever be capable of. If she had been this strong the year before, the Dear John incident would probably have never happened.

He felt somewhat ambivalent. He felt certain that she was explaining the circumstances as her sincere apology, not making excuses. But the betrayal of the previous April had left a scar deeper than the one from the enemy AK47 bullet. He reached out his glass so she could refill it with red wine.

"Terri, I respect you for facing me one-on-one with this. You no longer owe me an explanation or anything else. Kiddo, I knew you better than anyone. I shouldn't have set my expectations so high. When I left you at Thanksgiving, I realized you were totally unaware and probably vulnerable.

"In your letters, you wouldn't let yourself even admit I was away fighting a war. I don't expect you to understand. When a guy is over there, the only thing that keeps him alive is what's back here. Life in combat is so uncomfortable that you pick a person or thing to motivate you to keep on living. When any love affair breaks up, someone gets hurt, even under regular conditions. When you Dear John a guy in combat, it's magnified about one hundred times.

"Don't misunderstand me. I'm thankful you didn't lie to me for a year then let me hear it from someone else, or now. As your friend, I understand your turmoil and intellectually understand what happened to you. Terri, I won't lie to you and suggest that I can ever forgive you. I can only ask you to comprehend the impact your betrayal had on me in that insane environment. It would have been tough to accept back here. You caused me more emotional pain and suffering than I experienced being physically wounded three times.

"Terri, I always thought I had my head screwed on straight. If they would have sent me home after I received that letter, I'm not certain what I might have done. Considering what I had just experienced, I might have been capable of anything.

"You were my first love. You will always be very special to me, but it will never be the same. When we made love for the first time, it changed our lives. Well, with this betrayal, I will never forget what you did to me, no matter how hard I try or how mature I attempt to be."

"I think I understand as much as I can, without really knowing what you've been through. The $64,000 question is, what do we do now?"

Sean glanced at the fire. "I guess the only thing we can do is to try to start a new and different relationship. If we can't turn the clock back a year, we've got to start from scratch."

Terri filled her own wine glass. "Sounds easier than it will be. How do we start from scratch, when I've known you my whole life?"

Sean reached out and took her hand. "Well, let's see, how did we start? If you still have coloring books and crayons, we could color for a while!"

Terri leaned forward and softly kissed the palm of Sean's hand. "Let's not go back quite so far. After dinner and some more wine by the fire, let's go to bed."

"You'd rather go to bed with a scarred veteran than color?"

"I'll take my chances with the scarred veteran. I never could stand coloring with you as a kid. You were the only boy who could color better than me, and it drove me crazy. It wasn't enough that you were bigger, faster, and could throw farther, you even had nicer handwriting. I've got a better chance in bed."

After their pleasant steak dinner and lengthy fireside, wine-induced chat, Sean called home. He talked to his dad and told him he was at Terri's, would be late and not to be concerned. He was not on the road.

On Birch Lane, Sean's father turned off the television and went to bed. He understood his son's phone message. He appreciated his oldest son's gesture so he would not worry. He wondered how safe Sean was emotionally from the attractive Terri Murphy. He cursed Danny Murphy Jr., hiding in some draft evader's commune in Canada, and he thanked God his own boy was home, scarred, hurt, but whole. He was never more proud of his son, Sean Dennis Cavanagh, than at that private moment.

Sean requested the room be totally dark before he could undress and relax. He was very self-conscious of the numerous scars on his body that had not existed when Terri had last seen him undressed. She did everything she could to try to convince him he need not be embarrassed with her, but to no avail.

They made love late into the night. As with other areas of Sean's life, their love-making was satisfying and passionate, but somehow different. The year had changed them both. Sean determined that the element gone from their sexual relationship was its previous innocence. The young couple fell to sleep just after 4 a.m.

Sean slowly opened his eyes. Terri's bedroom was flooded by bright morning sunshine. He focused his eyes on the figure sitting next to him. Terri sat with her legs crossed, still nude, staring down at him. She had been watching him sleep.

The sunlight had revealed some of his scars. Her eyes were filled with tears. "Good morning, Marine. Would you like some breakfast?"

Sean wiped one of her tears away with a soft touch of his hand. "Now, do you understand why I insisted on it being dark? I don't think your tears would have helped my libido, if you get my drift. Just some coffee would be great, Terri."

"Sean, it was really wonderful. I've missed you so. I've dreamed of the time when . . ."

"You were right, Terri, it sure beat the hell out of coloring. You always were brighter than me. I had the better handwriting, but you had the 'A' average."

"I'm sorry, Sean. Your scars don't turn me off. They just make me realize how you must have suffered, and it makes me so sad. We'll put coconut oil on them and with a little tan, no one will notice. I swear, they are no turn-off. They're not as bad as a tatoo."

"Well, I've got several Vietnam tatoos, courtesy of the N.V.A."

"I wasn't snooping. You were still sleeping and uncovered."

"How about I save the backside view for if we decide to do this again? You'll have to help me to adjust gradually to the new version of my body."

"Thank God you are still in one piece and everything still works."

"Yea, I'm really lucky compared to some. Come over here and give me a hug. Let's see if everything still works in the daylight."

On Birch Lane, Dennis Cavanagh sipped his morning coffee and glanced over the sports section. His wife stormed around the kitchen in a huff. She slammed down the silverware.

"Alright, Maureen, what in the world is bothering you?"

She tossed her dishtowel down on the sink. "Dennis, you know full well what's bothering me. Sean staying out all night like some damn alley cat. I know that he's been through a lot, but that does not give him the right to act that way while living under our roof."

"Maureen, you know I love and respect you, but you do not have the beginning of an idea of what he has been through, even with your mother's instinct. That boy has been in hell for the past year. He has seen and done things you don't know even exist in this world, despite your sensitive nature and knowledge. Listen to me. After all he's been through, he called so we'd not worry. Maureen, he's nearly 21 years old. He surely didn't do anything last night he hadn't already done at college or while in the Marines."

"Dennis Cavanagh, you would never, ever tolerate such behavior from any of the other children, certainly not one of your daughters."

"No, you're wrong, you miss the whole point. That boy has been in combat for a year. Remember when I came home from the war in the Pacific? Do you remember how you and I behaved my first few weeks home?"

"That's different, Dennis. We were married."

"Yes, dear, it's different. This is 1968, not 1945. Search your heart, my love. Do you truely believe we would have acted any differently if we weren't already married?"

"Dennis, as long as he lives under this roof, he will behave like a gentleman and live by our rules."

"This is not an issue for debate, Maureen. Sean has been to hell, and spent a year there. He has witnessed life at its very worst. His mind and body have been violated.Don't even suggest to that boy that his behavior is immoral. Spending the night with a pretty young girl he has known his entire life, may be something you cannot condone. But, Maureen, as God is my witness, I know where he is mentally right now. If you push him on this issue, you'll lose him. We must force ourselves to be thankful that he is sensitive enough to call, so we know he is safe, and not with some street girl, or crawling into a bottle. Sean spent a year of his life killing other human beings, and you welcomed him home with joyful tears. Keep that in mind when you pass judgement on him for spending the night with a girl he has loved most of his life."

"How long do you intend to excuse everything that boy does?"

"A hell of a lot longer than three days."

———————————

Sean went with his entire family to Christmas Eve Mass. His dad had invited Terry to join them for the evening, and for dinner Christmas Day, since she was alone for the holiday.

The old wooden pews of St. Paul's Church were filled with holiday worshipers. The huge church organ filled the air with wonderfully familiar Christmas hymns.

As a personal Christmas gift to his mother, Sean had gone to church that afternoon and struggled through a half-hour confession with a local parish priest. Doing so allowed him to join his family in taking communion. Sean and his other Catholic friends compared their church rule of no confession, no communion with the cliché "no tickie, no washie."

Sean could feel the low notes from the church organ in his chest. They created the same vibration in his sternum as the near-by ordinance explosions in Vietnam.

Sean became privately angry and bitter during the beautiful Christmas Mass. He looked around the large crowded church. Not even one young man was in uniform. St. Paul's was located in the heart of metro-Detroit's old money suburb, Grosse Pointe. He wondered about the working-class neighborhoods, or T.J.'s church. He wondered about the number of kids home on Christmas leave, home for their last Christmas. The priest spoke of peace on earth, good will toward men. The heavy organ music of *Oh Holy Night* seemed to engulf him. The tears began to roll down his face. He moved to the kneeler and buried his face in his praying hands. He fought back a sob.

He thought as he cried, "Peace on Earth. Not where I was, Pal. All those boys dead or maimed, and you wouldn't even know that it was going on this very second."

Sean wondered if as he prayed safe and warm in the beautiful old church, some bunker full of Grunts were huddled together riding out a Gook rocket attack. He swore to himself at that moment, that no matter how much he hurt, no matter how angry or frustrated, that Christmas Eve cry would be his last. "Fuck your peace on Earth."

T.J. took a long pull on the bottle of cheap wine he and Hawk had bought in a liquor store near the Pike, in Long Beach, California.

"Shit, second Christmas in a row I ain't at home. Last year I was in Nam. This year I already used up all my leave time when I got back. Lord knows, these fools gonna send me back for another Nam tour. I might as well save two weeks to see my mama 'fore I go back to that hell hole."

Hawk, a tough Chicago street kid before the Corps, took the wine bottle. "Be cool, Blood. Maybe you go to the East Coast an' be with them Fleet Marines. You know, the dudes that goes to the Middle East wiff the Navy."

"You some kinda fool? I'm a nigger, and an N.C.O. and a Nam vet-ter-an, my man. That means the Corps really needs my young Black ass back over in the Nam, baby sittin' all those cherries we've been training for the past six months."

Hawk took another long swallow of their wine. "They gonna start pullin' out troops, Man. I heard it."

"Dude, listen here. They got a half a million swinging dicks over there, most of this whole green machine. You think they gonna pull out overnight? Son, there's gonna be several tours to be done, by many young mother's sons, 'fore we hat outa there entirely. A.R.V.N. won't last three years without us fightin' their war."

The racial friction in the Marine Corps was steadily increasing. It made T.J. very uneasy. He'd seen very little racial tension during his first two years in the Marines. He knew that men needed each other to survive in combat, and the tension unsettled him.

After the Christmas liberty in Long Beach, they returned to their training duties at Pendleton.

T.J. liked his I.T.R. troop-handler assignment. He felt he had a great deal of experience to share with the troops who spent a month with him and the other instructors before they moved on to B.I.T.S., then Staging Battalion, then Vietnam. He could help them to help themselves stay alive when they reached Vietnam. He added hard-earned tips he'd learned in the bush and in the combat of Hue.

T.J. was not well-spoken in front of a group. He did not sound educated. But the men in his company sensed that the tall, lean corporal from Motown knew what he was talking about, and most of them listened, and listened well.

He grooved on the last day I.T.R. ceremony. He could wear his greens and show his double row of battle ribbons. That day, any doubtors who remained after a month, disappeared. They all recognized the Nam ribbon, the Bronze Star, and maybe the one that meant the most in their morbid curiosity, the Purple Heart.

T.J. looked sharp in his uniform. He was a Grunt at heart, an ex-street slick from the Motor City. But, T.J. was also a Marine N.C.O. and he could really dress the part.

It was 1969, the last year of one ass-kicking decade. T.J. looked out over a company of new men. They had been through bootcamp, and were returning from Christmas leave. He looked at the sea of faces. All those boys, boys from all over America; boys from every racial and ethnic group in the nation; boys who could all be in Vietnam fighting to stay alive in 10 weeks. T.J. ached inside when he realized that he could probably be sent back for his second tour in Vietnam about the time their tour was half completed. "Sweet Jesus", he thought. "I might be fightin' with some of these boys."

T.J. moved to front center of the assembled I.T.R. company.

"You boys been home for two weeks enjoyin' the good life. You been gettin' fat offa yo' mama's home cookin' and gettin' lazy laying around watchin' cartoons an' shit. Well, I got some news fo' you all. Me and the other troop handlers gonna whip yo' butts back into shape an' get you ready as possible fo' where you all know you goin'. You better get yo' head out of yo' ass and become mo-ta-va-ted. 'Cause if you slack off, it's gonna be your butt they carry back home. This ain't no pep talk, boys. It's the way it is."

The Winter quarter at Wayne State University started classes early in January, 1969. With his brother's assistance, Sean managed to get registered for four classes. He was considered a transfer student from Eastern Michigan University, and started at Wayne State as a sophomore.

Sean's dad had not been completely correct about the awareness of a war being limited to the 6 o'clock news. On campus, the signs and speeches were a constant reminder, but a view far different from Sean's experience.

He was set upon when he walked out of the Student's V.A. office by other alleged Nam Vets, attempting to recruit him to join the small Nam Vets Against The War group on campus. He took all of their hand-outs and said he'd read it over and get back with them. Once out of sight, he tossed the literature in the nearest trash container.

Wayne State was a commuter college. Most students lived at home, many held part-time employment. Sean didn't expect the closed university atmosphere he enjoyed at Eastern Michigan, but he didn't expect the angry mood he felt at Wayne State. These kids lived at home, in nice neighborhoods. The university was in the heart of the city, but the student body was mostly from the white fringe and local suburbs.

It got so that Sean would not read his own school's weekly paper. Its articles were so far to the left, they neared revolutionary. Each passing day at Wayne troubled Sean. He had quit school to join the service because he felt he was too aware, and didn't fit in with the idealistic lifestyle at Eastern University. Now, back from hell, he felt like a complete stranger in his own city. He knew he could not fit into Wayne State's atmosphere. He was not ready to sign up for another Nam tour, but he was not ready to carry a N.V.A. flag in protest.

No one wanted to listen about Vietnam, they wanted to debate every Vietnam issue.

No one really noticed his shorter than average hair. He wore his navy blue ski parka and went to class alone. He spoke to no one unless approached, or to answer a question from an instructor.

Sean could bury his thoughts in the two urban social science and psychology classes. His political science class was like going to the dentist. The well-educated, idealistic, bearded professor bombarded the students with his personal views for 50 minutes at a time. A minor birth defect caused one of Prof. Linderman's legs to be shorter than the other. The defect gave him a slight limp and a 4-F draft status, which gave him the ability to openly oppose everything from Vietnam to the many ills of Capitalism.

Prof. Linderman was nearly 30 and still lived with his parents in their large home in Southfield, a northern suburb. His adult life experience consisted of being at a college. He went from student to instructor; never leaving the ivy walls of Old Main or the comfort of his parents' home.

Sean listened to Linderman start off again on the American involvement in an immoral war. His thoughts wandered from the lecture to the sloppy wet snow falling outside. Sean thought of what he had been doing exactly one year ago that day. His squad had probably been up near the D.M.Z., chasing some N.V.A. battalion all over their sector of I Corps, still a couple weeks before the nightmare of Tet and Hue City.

He tried to listen to Linderman, but his mind wandered again. He absentmindedly rubbed his left shoulder. It still bothered him when it was damp. The most recent wounds on his legs were still healing and increased his physical discomfort.

But the physical pain could not compare with the emotional discomfort he felt from the lecture. Linderman insisted it was each student's duty to oppose the draft and the war at all costs. No one in the class had any idea Sean was a Vet.

Sean raised his hand, and Prof. Linderman pointed to him. "Excuse me, Professor, I want to make certain I fully understand. You say we must resist the war at all costs. If I lost my 2-S status, and get my notice, what should I do?"

Prof. Linderman stood straight. "I'm saying it is your moral duty to resist in every way."

Sean glanced at the wall clock and closed his notebook. "You mean go to Canada, or maybe even to prison."

"I'm saying whatever is necessary."

Sean sat up straight in his seat. "What's your draft classification, Professor?"

"That's not the issue here . . ."

"Excuse me, Sir, but it most certainly is. You're telling us to go to Canada, or jail, if we lose our 2-S. What's your status?" The classroom buzzed with pro and con comments on Sean's question.

"I happen to be 4-F due to a physical problem, but that has . . ."

Sean raised his voice, "Professor, you are full of shit."

Prof. Linderman looked at the wall clock. "Class is over for today." The students quickly left the room. Some looked back at Sean as if he were a monster with horns and a tail. Sean remained seated.

"What's your name? You're out of here, Pal. No one talks to me that way."

Sean slowly stood. The lean professor was no physical match for Sean. "I understand. I believe that you are full of shit, but this is your class and I had no right to talk to you that way in front of the other students. I respectfully request full refund for this class drop."

The professor seemed to become braver when he saw Sean was not going to impose a physical threat. "Like hell. We're too far along into the quarter for a full refund."

"Listen hard, Linderman. My dad did not pay tuition money for you to preach revolution and revolt for 50 minutes a session. You want to tell us how fucked up this country is, and how immoral the war is, fine. When you instruct us openly and directly to disobey the law, you're out of line. You talk like a man with a paper asshole, Linderman. Go to Canada. Go to prison. How you've got the nerve to stand up there and influence these kids, while you hide behind your 4-F status is what's immoral. I get a full refund for this drop, or my dad and the V.A. will be on you like white on rice."

"The V.A. That's it. Trained killer. You don't have a 2-S. You're one of those heroes that went over to kill babies and interfere in a civil war."

"Listen, you skinny cocksucker. I apologized for name-calling in front of your class. I was out of line. But now it's just you and me. If you believe for a moment I'm going to stand here while you insult me, you are going to get a terrible surprise. I said I was sorry for what I said in class. Give me your word that I will get a full refund on the class and I'm out of here. Verbally joust with me or call me names and it will get personal. If it gets personal, you will have more than a slight limp to keep you safe from the draft."

"Are you threatening me?"

"I won't play semantics with you, Professor. Warning, advising, instructing, threatening, I'll settle for threatening."

"You have my word on full refund. Now get the hell out of my classroom, before I call the campus police."

"It's too damn bad, Prof. Linderman. You're very intelligent, well-spoken, and still so damn one-sided and naive. You have no life experience. You hear only one side, so you believe only one side."

Linderman lowered his voice. "And only you who have been there deserve an opinion?"

"No, Sir. We may be the only ones that know what it's like to be there. We do not have an exclusive on the multifaceted aspects of the politics of the war. But damn it to hell, Linderman, neither do you."

Sean walked out of Old Main. His shoes were soaked from the wet snow before he reached Warren Avenue. Life was less than perfect, and he felt depressed as he walked with his head down, eyes watching the slush on the sidewalk. With Terri back at school he spent his non-school hours with homework and getting back into condition with his brothers and dad at a local Vic Tanny's Health Club. He went to the student center to wait for his psych class to begin. He bought a cup of foul-tasting vending-machine coffee and found an empty table. He thought of young Prof. Linderman, "Man, would my boot camp D.I.s have done a head case on that skinny Commie creep."

Sean became aware of someone standing next to him. "Hey, Cavanagh! Cav, is that really you?"

Sean looked up to his high school friend and football teammate, Mark Polowski, standing next to him. "Yep, it's me, Mark. Despite this clever disguise as a college student, it appears you have recognized me."

Mark explained he was a junior at Wayne State and the football team's tight end.

"Damn, Sean, when did you start here at Wayne State?"

"This quarter."

Mark bought himself a coffee and sat at Sean's small table. "We sort of lost touch with you when your folks moved out to Grosse Pointe. You had a free ride at Eastern Michigan. What happened? We heard different shit. Some said you dropped out to work for your dad. Even heard you had married that cute Grosse Pointe girl you were dating our senior year."

"Nope, I dropped out after my freshman year. They had a freshman signal caller from Ypsi they thought walked on water. I was destined for four seasons of playing sideline and clipboard. I went and got my military thing out of the way, and here I am."

"You go in the Guard or Reserves?"

"Neither. Joined the Marines for two years. I got hurt, so they gave me an early-out to come back to school. I joined the Marines for two years as an alternative to the Army draft."

The expression on Mark's face became very serious. "What do you mean you got hurt?"

Sean stared at the cardboard coffee cup in front of him. "I got wounded, Mark."

Mark's mouth hung open and he seemed to give Sean the visual once-over to see if he was missing any equipment. "Cav, you were in Vietnam?"

Sean took a sip of coffee and watched an attractive co-ed walk past and smile. "Yes, Mark, I was in Vietnam."

"Wow, Cav. Vietnam. That's a heavy trip."

Sean considered throwing the remainder of his coffee on his friend. Since Mark was 100 percent healthy and weighed about 215 pounds, he thought better of it. He looked at Mark, his mouth still hanging open. Sean was too frustrated to speak.

"A heavy trip, you naive numb nuts. You and all the rest of these candy-ass college jerks. You bet your ass it was a heavy trip," he thought. Sean broke the silence by crushing his empty coffee cup and tossing it in a nearby waste basket.

Mark finally closed his mouth. "Did you get hurt too bad to play ball again?"

Sean smiled for the first time in their meeting and thought, "Fuck Vietnam, can you still play ball? Not particularly sensitive, but honest."

He searched his pockets for enough change for another cup of lousy coffee. "I'm still healing some, but they gave me a clean bill of health. I hurt my left shoulder. Hasn't seemed to bother my throwing. I guess I wouldn't know until I went full contact."

"I can set up a meeting with Coach. You could maybe play Spring ball with the team. Damn, a year away, only a soph, you could play three seasons. We don't play the same brand of ball you did at Eastern, but our program is improving."

Sean winced at his second cup of machine coffee. "Sure, Mark, set it up. I'll be glad to talk to him. I hope to be ready by Spring. Not sure your coach would want an ex-Grunt as a signal-caller, though."

"An ex-Grunt? What's a Grunt?"

"Never mind, Mark. It was part of the heavy trip."

Mark's mouth opened again. He paused for a moment. "Here's my address and phone. I'm having a kegger at my house Friday. Come on by. Lots of kids from Denby will be there. Bring a lady, or come stag. The place will be packed. Hell, Sean, half of our senior class is here at Wayne."

Sean's stomach ached from the acid build-up of coffee on an empty stomach. He silently wondered about the other half of their senior class, those that couldn't go to college.

Mark stood to leave. "I gotta split. Got a class across campus. Try to stop by Friday, I'd really like to have you there. Lot of team guys will be there. Oh yea, speaking of team guys, you hear about Joe Bonner, our second-team guard?"

"Nope. Joe and I were tight in school. I lost track of him when I went to Eastern and my folks moved. Will he be there?"

"No, Sean, no way. Joe got drafted and sent to Nam. He got half his face shot off and is still in some V.A. hospital on the West Coast. A real bummer. Got to go. Hope to see you Friday."

Sean tossed the full cup of coffee into the waste basket. The wave of brief nausea passed but he suddenly felt if he didn't get outside, he wouldn't be able to breathe. Sean had seen young men with their faces shot away. It most certainly was a "bummer".

The cold damp air made him feel physically better. He had never considered how many of his old civilian friends might be hurt or killed in the war. He had only thought of his platoon. He prayed it would end before it threatened his own brothers.

He looked at the address of Mark's house. He stuck it in his psychology book like a book mark. He and Terri had made a non-commitment pact on her return to school. Maybe seeing his high school friends would help him force to readjust to being back in the world.

Sean walked along the Cass Avenue sidewalk toward his next class. A Detroit police recruiting van was at the curb. A handsome, well-groomed Black officer braved the wet snow and handed out brochures to anyone who would take one. Several students called out names and insults as they walked past. The officer seemed to ignore them.

Sean took a brochure. The officer seemed very friendly and offered to answer any questions. Even the officer was caught by surprise when Sean asked if he could apply there and then.

"If you're serious, young man, go to this address on W. Grand Blvd., near 14th St. You can fill out the application, the written exam is only 12 minutes, and the process will begin. They do a background check, oral board. You look like a jock; a college jock would have no problems making it if it's what you really want." He gave Sean another visual once over. "How old are you?"

"I'll be 21 in March."

"If all went smooth, you could start the acadamy right after your birthday." The officer had developed his own sixth sense. He felt something about Sean he did not feel with the other students he spoke with. "You been in the military yet, young man?"

"Yes, Sir, I got back last month. I'm having a rough time adjusting to the instructors and my fellow students. The school work is a cake walk. The fuc . . . darn atmosphere here really sucks."

The young policeman put his hand on Sean's shoulder and told him to sit inside the van with him, out of the wet snow. "You were in Nam, then, I assume?"

"Yes, Sir, with the Marine Corps. I didn't want to get drafted, so I joined for two. I got an early-out to go to school when my tour was done. My dad's the greatest. He was a Grunt in the Pacific and fought the Japs. He knows what's going down.

"But Dad's got the world by the nuts now. He owns two businesses and bought a big house in Grosse Pointe. He wants me to get my degree and step right into his shoes. It all seems like bullshit to me. School, these naive, liberal, asshole students, even my dad's job offer. I need a real job. I need a job where I feel like I'm really doing something more than making a living. Hell, I'd be a doctor, but I'd have to be with these wimps an extra four years."

The police officer smiled a knowing, friendly smile. "O.K., kid, let's talk man to man. I was in the Crotch. I was in Nam in '66. It was a mother then. I've heard it's only gotten worse. Unless you were wounded so badly you can't pass the physical, you'll stroll onto the department. You'll have to live in Detroit by academy time. But unless you got a family, and I don't see a wedding ring, you can find a place easy enough. Those streets out there are for real, Pal. Maybe too damn real. Don't expect too much from being a cop, going in. It won't make up for the frustrations of Nam. My man, this job has way enough frustrations of its own. Dead is dead, kid. It doesn't matter whether a Gook does you or some strung-out junkie with a Saturday Night Special."

"I appreciate the time, Officer. I'm not expecting some kind of Adam-12 B.S. But it's got to be better than this."

"Kid, 'better' is a relative term. Better than the bush in Nam? For sure it is. Better than a safe classroom or working for your Dad? You'll have to decide for yourself. Those are tough streets out there, kid. Tough mean streets."

Sean was quiet during the family dinner. As his youngest sister cleared the table, he asked to speak with his parents alone in the family room.

Sean sat close to his parents and spoke in low tones, so as not to be heard by his brothers and sisters.

His mother reached across the coffee table and firmly clutched him by both wrists. "Sean Dennis Cavanagh, I'm praying that you didn't bring us in here to tell us you've re-enlisted and you're going back to that God-forsaken war?"

"No, Mother. I'm done with the Marines. I wouldn't do that without talking to you and Dad first, even if I thought of it. And I swear to you, I haven't."

She released her grasp, "Oh, sweet Jesus, Mary and Joseph . . ."

"Don't celebrate too much yet, Mother. I don't think you'll be thrilled with what I did do. I joined the Detroit Police Department today. If all goes as scheduled, I'll start their academy right after my birthday. The quarter ends in March. Three of my instructors said I could finish their classes early, if necessary."

Sean's father's face was expressionless. He initially feared, as had his wife, that Sean had secretly re-enlisted. "Three instructors, Sean, what did the fourth say?"

"I'm only in three classes now, Dad. I'll get a full refund for the drop. Look, that's a whole different story."

"Son, you've told us about being unhappy with school. Maybe it's just too soon. Tough out the quarter, and I'll find a place for you in our Personnel Department. You can work for me until you're ready for school again."

"Come on, Dad. You've known all along that I didn't plan to take over your business. Back in high school, I wanted to be a teacher and a coach. You've got two other bright sons to carry on the Cavanagh name and the Cavanagh business."

Sean's mother's voice was concerned but uncommonly stern. "I would have thought you'd enough violence and suffering. My Lord, Sean Dennis, two Summers ago over 40 people were killed in that terrible riot."

Sean was privately amused. At least he was down to his first and middle name with his mother. He knew the conversation was totally rational when he was called by only his first name.

His mother displayed more anger than he could remember. "Damn it, Son, I didn't raise you — I'm sorry, Dennis — we didn't raise you to work in the filth of that city and be hurt or even killed by those people."

"With all due respect, Mother, you didn't raise me to go to war. You did raise me in a loving atmosphere. You did raise me to be my own person. Mother, it's 1969. The big cities of this country are in trouble and I believe you educated me and brought me up to be the kind of young man who can help the city. I don't expect to do it alone, overnight, the white-caped crusader. But I believe that a white ghetto cop who really cares can make an actual impact in Detroit, especially after that terrible riot in '67."

"Sean, I feel like you're too nice a boy to be a policeman."

"Ah, Mother, listen to yourself. Too nice a boy to be a cop? Maybe I was too nice a kid when I went to the prom in '66. But the government didn't think I was too nice a boy to go to war."

"Sean, I sat silently the night you told us you were quitting Eastern Michigan to join the Marines. I will not be silent tonight. I don't understand how a boy as bright and loving and sensitive as you insists on thrusting himself into life's worst horrors."

Sean did not speak for a moment. He felt the frustration of his parents' lack of support building. He had expected it, but he could not control the emotion.

"I'm going to be 21 soon. You both understand I don't need your permission to do anything. But I can't express the amount of love and respect I have for you two. I know what you have given me, done for me, offered me. I know how hard Dad has worked so that I could have every chance in life. Mother, I know how terrible it must have been for you while I was in combat, 12,000 miles away. I'm asking you to trust my feelings, to respect my decision, and to support me, as you always have. I know I can legally do as I choose. I will not lie to the people who have devoted their lives to me. If you insist I not become a Detroit policeman, I will withdraw my application tomorrow."

There was a full minute of silence. Sean's dad finally spoke.

"You'll need a place to live in Detroit. We own a duplex on Moross Road. A unit will be vacant next month. You can live there. We don't have to like it, Son, but we'll support you. All you owe us is to be the best damn cop in the department."

6

January, 1969—June, 1969

JANUARY, 1969
DETROIT, MICHIGAN

Sean decided to attend Mark's party. With Terri at school, his social life was non-existent. He and Terri had made a friendly, non-commitment agreement when she left for U of M after New Year's and he felt certain that she was taking much better advantage of that agreement than he was.

Sean followed Mark's directions and found the house. With the collection of assorted vehicles in the driveway and in the street, it was not difficult to guess where the party was.

The house was a well-kept, two-story frame bungalow not far from their old high school. An attractive blonde dressed in a mini-skirt answered the door and let him into the party. It was a typical college kegger. The house was filled with Wayne State students and a collection of former high school classmates. Loud rock music pounded out of a large stereo in the living room, which was dark except for the annoying flashes of a strobe light.

His impromptu hostess told him the beer keg was in the kitchen sink at the rear of the house. Sean slowly worked his way through the crowd. He saw that the pot smokers were gathered in a rear bedroom. The strong odor suggested that he could get a contact high by merely standing in the room for two minutes. The room was lit by a black light and the walls were covered with black light posters; "What if they gave a war and nobody came?" "Give peace a chance." "Peace and love." Sean had a cynical smirk on his face. "What if they gave a war and nobody came? Don't show, and they'll come looking for you."

The beer keg sat in the large ice-filled kitchen sink. Sean stuffed a $5 bill in the contribution jar and grabbed a plastic glass, filling it with beer. He considered going back into the crowd in an attempt to locate the cute blonde in the mini-skirt, but the strobe light bothered his eyes. He felt his heart beginning to pound in his chest from anxiety. The thumping beat of the loud music and the strobe light was taking his conscious mind to another place. It reminded him of the white-hot, dancing light from illumination flares. He took several swallows of beer and refilled the glass. He turned away from the light and concentrated on calming himself.

Mark entered the kitchen and shook Sean's hand. From the strong smell of marijuana smoke on Mark's body, it was obvious why he didn't see Mark when he came in.

"Cav, everybody here is either a student at Wayne State or from our senior class. Lots of unescorted chicks. Have a good time. If you want to do some blow, it's in the back bedroom."

Sean poured himself another beer. In the midst of all of those young adults and he still felt out of place, alone.

In the corner of the kitchen, Sean caught sight of a young man leaning his chair against the wall. He was sitting alone. He recognized him to be an ex-Denby teammate, Roger Greco.

It was obvious to Sean that ol' Rog was well on the way to a good drunk. He hadn't seen Roger since the night of their senior prom. Roger belched loudly and took several swallows of beer. He smiled when his eyes finally focused and he recognized Sean.

"Well, I'll be damned, if it ain't Mr. Q.B., the All American, cutest boy in the senior class. How the hell you doin', Cav?"

Sean moved over to talk with his high school friend. "I'm getting by, Roger. How's life treating you? What have you been doing with yourself since we graduated?"

Roger belched again. "Me? I've been proudly serving the cause of freedom, in the service of my country in Southeast Asia. I got to travel abroad for a year, courtesy of Uncle L.B.J. and my draft board. I spent 12 entertaining months in a place called Vietnam. You've heard of Vietnam, haven't you, Mr. Q.B.?"

Sean took Roger's near empty glass from the table and poured them both a fresh glass full from the the beer keg. Sean was somewhat aggravated by the sarcasm dripping from the tone in Roger's voice.

"Yea, I've heard of Vietnam, Rog. In fact, I just got back from a visit there myself."

Roger sat up in the chair as if hit by an electric shock. "Hey, Cav, I heard you went to Eastern Michigan on a full ride. Last I heard, you were doin' O.K., playin' on the freshman team. I just got back a few weeks ago. No one said you'd gone to Nam."

"I was a second-stringer at Eastern Michigan, so I figured I'd get the military thing over with. I got to play first string with the Marines up in I Corps for a few months. I got benched by them in the fourth quarter because of injuries."

Roger stared at his beer glass for a full minute. "No shit? The All American boy who moved to Grosse Pointe went to Nam. Were you an officer?"

"Nope, just another Grunt. I was an E-4 when I got out last month."

"I'm sorry I put that smart-ass bullshit on you about Nam. I've still got a chip on my shoulder, and you were one of the last guys I ever expected would have to go there. Hell, I thought you were a good enough player for college ball. You were a good student, an' your folks got money. I figured only guys like me went."

"I didn't like the draft hanging over my head, and I didn't plan on staying in college forever. I joined the Marines for two years. Where were you at in Vietnam, Roger?"

"I had a pretty good job. I was with the Military Police in Saigon. Our jeep got hit by an RPG during Tet of '68. It turned over and I broke my arm. I was still on light duty during the May '68 offensive."

Sean was now just sipping at his beer. "We were there about the same time. I was in Hue during Tet. We wasted a lot of Gooks, but they tore our ass up."

"So, Cav, how you like bein' home? It's one hell of a feelin', ain't it? A couple months ago we were fighting to stay alive, watching friends die. Come home and — poof — no more war."

"Let's face it, Roger, we're fucked. I went into the Marines because I was tired of the naive, idealistic crap they were running at us at Eastern Michigan. I get sent to Vietnam, and that place does a real tap dance on my head. Now I'm back home, back in the midst of this silly bullshit. I'm not certain I belong anywhere."

Roger felt comforted. It was the first time since his return home he had found a pre-Nam friend that shared his doubts and frustrations.

"Cav, I shit you not, sometimes I think I'm gonna freak. That's why I got an attitude with you before I knew you were there too. They find out you were in Nam and they treat you different, like maybe you're crazy or like you killed their little sister. All the posters and signs and anti-war slogans are bullshit. What do these wimps know about the war? All they know is what some college instructor tells them. As long as Daddy and Mommy pay their way, all they gotta worry about is their student draft status and jerking off at parties. There ain't two people in this whole house, even the real smart ones, can really tell you why they are against the war. They'll just rattle off some student slogan. Well, fuck them. I'm gonna go do some dope. They got some decent grass here. You want to join me, my treat?"

Sean sipped his beer. "No thanks, Rog. I'll pass. The beer is doing a job on me. If I mix them, I'll never make it home. Be cool Roger, they say it gets better with time. Keep your head down, Pal. See ya' around."

Roger was unsteady on his feet. He patted Sean on the back. "I think I'll do what I did in Nam; stay stoned all the time. It's the same now that I'm home. I'm either stoned, or I'm scared shitless. Ah, fuck it, Cav. It don't mean nothing."

Roger disappeared into the pot-smoking room. Now Sean sat alone at the kitchen table, staring at his beer glass. He thought he recognized the female voice behind him before he turned around.

"Excuse me, Sean Cavanagh?" It was an ex-Denby classmate, Lyn Denier. "I saw you come in but wasn't certain it was you with that darn strobe light. You were never known as being anti-social. What are you doing sitting in here alone?"

Sean stood to be polite. "I was talking with Roger Greco. He just went into the other room. Those strobes give me a headache, and I can hear the music fine from in here. It's so loud you couldn't talk to anyone in there anyway."

"Good point, I can only take it for a half hour at a time. When everyone starts looking like silent movie characters, I know it's time to leave for a while."

Sean and Lyn sat at the table. He watched the other party guests parade to the keg and forge back into the crowds. The men had long hair, some had beards. Most wore bell-bottom pants with a wide selection of shirts, from flowered tunics to patch-covered military shirts. Sean may have fit in perfectly the way he was dressed at a Grosse Pointe casual function, but he was far too preppie for this group. But no one seemed to notice his clothes, or shorter than average length hair.

Lyn's hair was much longer and straighter that it had been at high school. He was comforted that her attire was nearly as conservative as his.

Lyn sipped from a soft drink can. "So, fill me in on what my favorite Denby jock has been up to since graduation."

Sean smiled and sat down his beer. "Nope, ladies first. Let's see, I don't see a ring, so I can only guess you are not engaged or married. National Honor Society in school, so I'm sure you're going to college. And since you worked part-time even in high school, you also have a job. How did I do?"

"You should have been a detective. No steady guy. I work downtown for an insurance company and go to Wayne State part-time. Now, cutest boy in the senior class, how is it at Eastern Michigan?"

"I couldn't tell you, Lyn, I haven't been there since May of '67. I dropped out after my freshman year. I got the military obligation over with, and I'm going to Wayne State full-time this quarter."

They talked together for almost an hour. Their conversation flowed easily, and Sean sensed Lyn felt as out of place at the party as he did. He invited her to go with him to get something to eat. She accepted, and they left Mark's loud college kegger together.

They found a quiet Italian restaurant near their old high school. The atmosphere was in pleasant contrast to the party, and they chatted quietly over dinner.

Except for her hair, Lyn looked the same as the day they graduated from high school. Her soft, light brown hair seemed to perfectly match the shade of her brown eyes. She looked fit and filled out her burgandy monogramed sweater.

Lyn was from a strict French-Canadian, Catholic working-class family. Her father had worked at Chrysler his entire adult life. They lived in a bungalow not far from Mark's. Lyn was the oldest of three girls. Sean had shared several classes with Lyn at Denby and they had worked together in the student government. He liked her wit and sense of humor back in school, and he was warmed by it again that night. She was intelligent and could be serious, but she could laugh. He felt comfortable with her. They talked about their past unsuccessful romances and the differences between Eastern Michigan and Wayne State.

The waitress removed the empty plates, and their discussion continued over a cup of coffee. "You said you had been in the military. Which one, the Guard?"

"No, I joined the Marine Corps for two years. They gave me an early release so I could go back to school."

Lyn couldn't hide the wince. "Marines? Did you go to Vietnam, Sean?"

"Yes, I was there for a few months."

Lyn became very serious and looked down at her coffee cup. "I think I should tell you up front, Sean, I'm against the war."

Sean put down his coffee cup. "Oh really? Which parts in particular?"

"What do you mean?"

"Well, I'm against war in general. I'm against the terrible waste of human life and human suffering. I'm against having 19-year-old friends torn to pieces and die in my arms. I'm against physical conditions and discomfort you could not even imagine. I'm against safe, cowardly fellow students waving the same flag as the Army that tried to kill me. Like I said, Lyn, which parts are you against?"

"It's the politics of our involvement in Vietnam. We have no right to be there. It is an immoral war."

Sean took a thoughtful sip from the coffee cup. The gesture forced him to pause before he spoke. It was a move he had done on purpose.

"Ah, the politics of the immoral war. I see. It's been over a year since I could sit down and really consider the politics of the war. When you're there, you're kept too busy thinking about not getting your butt shot off to have time to debate the politics of it. Thing is that the people most qualified to debate the war are the ones trying to kill you."

"I don't understand, Sean. Why did you go to Vietnam? You didn't have to go."

"That's not exactly true. I could have tried to avoid or delay being drafted. I could have stayed a student forever, or moved to my uncle's cabin in Canada. But I didn't volunteer to go to Vietnam. Once I decided to get my military obligation out of the way, I was theirs. My destination was a moot point."

Sean took another sip of coffee. He felt his insides turning with frustration. He silently wished he could legally order a drink at the restaurant. He really liked Lyn. The discussion of Vietnam might as well run its course now.

"You make some good points, Sean. But the basic truth is that we are in the middle of their civil war."

"Civil war? Lyn, if England would have entered America's Civil War, would we still only call it a civil war? Since February of '68, nearly the entire war has been fought against troops from North Vietnam, an invading Army. I did almost all my fighting against the North Vietnamese."

"This is not the same as Korea in 1950."

"No, and Korea was not like World War II. Lyn, seven years ago President Kennedy had this planet on the brink of destruction because Russian rockets were in Cuba. We struggle to stop the spread of Communism throughout all of Southeast Asia, and that's immoral? The Russians told us that they would bury us, and you people want to give them the shovel."

"Sean, I think you have a biased opinion on this issue."

Sean finally grinned and shook his head. "Biased, but well informed. I spent a year at college hearing your side. I went there for a year. Now, I'm back in the classroom hearing your side again. Let's say I've been exposed to both sides of the Vietnam issue. I've decided in my own biased way that most of the people who talk about the war don't have any idea what they're talking about."

Lyn also had no intention of ruining the otherwise pleasant evening with a heated debate. "How about if we just agree to disagree and drop the whole topic for now?"

Sean dug for his wallet to pay the dinner check. "Kind of our own 'Peace with Honor.' I like the concept."

They stepped out into the biting January wind. "Would you like to go for a ride before I take you home?"

Lyn checked her watch. "Sure, no work or school tomorrow."

"We can take a drive down Lakeshore, and while we're there, I'll show you my folk's new home."

"I should warn you, Mr. Cavanagh, I am a sucker for rides down Lakeshore."

Sean's mind flashed to the thought of Terri Murphy. "Yea Lyn. Me too."

To Sean's surprise, Lyn was initially supportive of his decision to join the police department in Detroit. She had an uncle and a cousin on the force, so policemen were always popular in her family.

They began to date on a regular basis. The unique quality Sean identified in Lyn that made her special was her honesty. He could only be attracted to a very stable person at that stage in his life. Terri's betrayal the year before ironically played a role in Sean's growing attraction to Lyn.

The first time they made love, Sean felt a strange sense of guilt afterward. He actually felt as though he was cheating on Terri. The time with Lyn was as it should be, a mixture of young passion and love. Sean knew that when Terri came home for Easter break, he would have to completely close the chapter on that part of his life.

Lyn's family took an immediate liking to Sean. He felt comfortable with them. They were simple, honest, hard-working people with a strong religious background.

Lyn was an instant hit with the Cavanagh family, too. His mother was pleased that he had become interested in a nice Catholic girl. Now he would leave Terri Murphy out of his life. Sean's father saw in Lyn yet another loving, positive vehicle to help bring his eldest son some inner peace. Sean was keeping up a good facade, but his father knew Sean was still angry and frustrated inside. He didn't know how to get to that pain and he could only pray that it would pass with time.

FEBRUARY, 1969
CAMP PENDLETON, CALIFORNIA

T.J. walked back to the company office in long strides. He had a handful of mail which included that month's *Playboy, Leatherneck,* a letter from his mother and one from Sean.

He grinned broadly, "Ol' Irish. Boy writes least twice a month, no matter what. He's lucky if I send him a short letter every six weeks, but his keep comin' regular."

Sean had also sent along several pictures with the lengthy letter. He sent photos of downtown Detroit as it was decorated for Christmas. He sent a picture of his Triumph buried under six inches of snow to remind him what he was missing by being in southern California. He also sent a photo of Lyn and described his newest romantic interest on the first page of the letter.

T.J. studied the photo of the attractive young woman. He felt good about Sean's choice. She was pretty and didn't look anything like the girl that had Dear Johned his buddy when they were still in Vietnam. He studied the picture with all the Christmas lights on Woodward Avenue and the one with the car buried by a typical Michigan storm. The snow picture helped reduce the level of homesickness caused by the Christmas photo.

T.J.'s friend and co-troop handler, Hawk, was seated at his desk in the company office. "Say, Bro, let me check out your *Playboy* while you readin' the rest of your mail."

T.J. tossed the magazine onto Hawk's desk. "You can look at it, but I don't want none of the pages stuck together when I get it back."

Hawk was moaning over the magazine fold-out and T.J. went back to reading his friend's letter. T.J. suddenly pounded his fist on his desk and began shouting at the letter. "Oh no, Irish! Say it ain't so! You stupid, crazy, little mother fucker! Why you go do something like that?"

Hawk looked up from the fold-out. "What it is, Bro?"

"Damn Hawk Man, the dude from Motown I was with my first tour, me and him is real tight. He's gonna be a De-troit po-liceman. Boy's gotta have shit for brains. He been to college. His daddy owns a couple businesses, live in a big house, cabin on a lake, new car every year. Why in the hell do he want to go messin' around them streets for? Hawk, me an' him seen enough shit last tour to last a lifetime."

Hawk's eyes went back to the magazine. "Be cool, T.J., so the Chuck dude wanna be a pig, ain't no sweat offa yo' butt."

"I told you about this white dude, Hawk. Sure he's white, but he is number one, square business. The boy saved my Black hinny boo-coo times back at ol' Hue City. Fact, he got hisself shot runnin' to help me after I was hit."

Hawk put down the magazine.

"Yea, over in combat, we need each other and all that shit is cool. I seen white dudes risk their lives for Brothers and the other way. But back in the world, Bro, a honkie is a honkie. You can't trust no Chuck when he's back in the world. They forget that needin' stuff from Nam, an' we go back to bein' just niggers again."

T.J. picked up the letter again from his desk.

"Hawk Man, if you had been in our squad, you'd understand what I'm sayin'. Except for the fact we from the same city, we got nothin' in common, 'cept likin' sports and ladies. He's a rich college white boy from the suburbs. Fact, he's probably the whitest dude I ever met. Drives a British sports car an' plays golf at the country club an' shit like that. But the boy is a straight shooter. He really cares 'bout people, his friends. Somethin' special about that white boy, he got him some Soul."

Hawk laughed and turned his attention back to the magazine. "A honkie with Soul, T.J.! What you been smokin'?"

"Damn, Man, I'm tellin' you, he's different. We friends like brothers are friends. I ain't talkin' racial brothers, I mean like blood brothers. We lay dying in the same fuckin' bomb crater together, you don't get no closer to a man than that."

"Don't go talkin' no Brother shit to me about some honkie. I know there are righteous white Marines in combat. But in the world, they all the same. What white folks ever done for you?"

T.J. was getting angry. He grew tired of defending his friend to Hawk. "What white folks do for me? Mostly nothing. That's except for this white boy. He saved my life."

"Fuck it, T.J. It don't mean nothin'."

"Maybe not to you, Mr. Bad Black Ass Chicago Hawk Man. But when some dude gets shot savin' my life, it means everything, whether he's Black or white."

After reading his mother's letter, T.J. took his letter writing gear from his desk drawer. He started a letter to Sean several times, with the intent of talking him out of being a cop. His waste basket was half filled with crumpled attempts at the first page.

T.J. stared at a blank piece of paper for a moment, then returned the letter writing folder into the desk. He sipped from a warm soft-drink can and put his boots up on his desk, leaning way back in his chair. "What the hell," T.J. thought. "Better Irish become a cop than some crazy bigot honkie. At least Irish knows how to take care of hisself and still care about people." T.J. allowed himself a private chuckle, "That white boy better have his shit together. The dudes back in the neighborhood could tear off his head an' shit in the hole, if he ain't ready for them. Them Detroit streets maybe not as bad as ol' Hue City, but they ain't no Grosse Pointe neither. Got to worry 'bout Irish. He was wrapped too tight for all the bullshit of the Vietnam war. The bullshit of the ghetto could make him crazy."

MARCH, 1969
DETROIT

The day after Sean's 21st birthday, he stood at attention in the midst of 71 other student patrolmen. The group was gathered in the gymnasium of the old Detroit Police headquarters. The grey, nine-story building was across Clinton Street from the county jail at 1300 Beaubien Street.

The group was sworn in, and they filled out a mountain of forms and other documents. The following day they would report to the academy facility at 900 Merrill Pl. The building was at the south edge of Palmer Park, located near the northern central border of the city.

While attending the academy, the student patrolmen wore khaki uniforms. They would not be allowed to wear the Detroit Police blue uniform until their graduation, early in May. His class was designated Class 69-E. The class consisted entirely of men. More than one-third were Black. The department's aggressive minority recruiting efforts were finally paying off in the ranks.

———————

The recruiting officer Sean had spoken with in the van had been correct. With Sean's I.Q., educational background, physical condition, and military experience, getting accepted to the academy had been a cakewalk. Those same traits made the academy itself actually enjoyable for Sean.

As a member of Detroit Police Academy, Class 69-E, Sean waltzed through the weeks of classroom lectures and training. The level of discipline, physical training and mind games demanded by the para-military staff were mild compared to Marine boot camp. Sean understood that it was all part of their game to help ready the men for the street. There was nothing the academy staff could do to him that could rattle him in the slightest.

The weeks in the academy seemed to serve as a healthy emotional buffer for Sean. It served as a step from the choke-hold of Marine Corps life to the unnatural civilian world.

Sean was elected class vice-president. He got along well with his classmates, both Black and white. He could relate with his fellow Vets in the class and relate to the college boys, too. He took the instruction very seriously, but outside the classroom he soon took on the deserved reputation as one of the class clowns.

Discipline was second nature to Sean. He had good self-discipline with the bookwork. The years of football and his Marine experience gave him an attitude such that he never had a problem with any instructor.

Sean felt the classroom work was about first year junior college level. He studied hard and gave 100 percent, even though the paper and pencil portion of his training came very easy for him. He helped struggling classmates when he could. The weeks seemed to roar by. When it was graduation week in May, Sean had finished first in his class in academics. He would never say that the Detroit Academy had been easy, but he would tactfully say that it was not any problem for him.

The Sunday before the academy graduation ceremony, Sean was invited for dinner at his parent's home. He had been living in the duplex on Moross Road, owned by his father, since he started the academy. It was only a couple of miles from their home, and he stopped by several

times a week. He had invited his family and Lyn to the graduation
ceremony at Cobo Hall that Thursday.

After a pleasant dinner, Sean went into the backyard with his brothers to play some catch. Dennis and Maureen Cavanagh poured themselves another cup of coffee and remained seated at the dining room
table. They took pleasure watching their three sons rough-housing and
enjoying each other's company.

Maureen became pensive as she watched her oldest son still being a
boy, a boy playing in the safety and beauty of their backyard. "Dennis, no
matter how hard I try, I still to this day do not understand why Sean
insists on this police thing."

Dennis had a paternal grin. He was enjoying watching his three sons
playing a spirited game of backyard baseball "pickle." He poured himself more coffee.

"Maureen, we gave that lad our verbal support when he came to us in
January. We've got to have trust in him and his ability to think for
himself and take care of himself. Sean is a bright young man. He is
worldly and mature far beyond his 21 years. We don't like this, but we
can only silently hope he'll grow tired of being a policeman and come
and work with me and finish his college education. He asked for our
support. I share your concerns, but he damn well deserves our
support."

The assembled young men of Class 69-E restlessly moved about in
their four rank formation. The class' favorite instructor briskly walked
from the building holding the list of their precinct assignments. The
class was called to attention to quiet the nervous chatter, then put at
the position of at-ease.

Officer Anderson read out the student patrolman's name, then his
precinct assignment. Sean was headed for the 13th Precinct.

"Terrible 13" was literally in the heart of Detroit. No other precinct
offered such dramatic contrasts or variety. Number 13 contained
Wayne State University, the Cultural Center, General Motors' world
headquarters building, the Fisher Theatre and huge medical facilities.

It also covered some of the roughest ghetto neighborhoods in the
country. These neighborhoods were separated from each other by
man-made dividers, and each had a mood and culture of its own. The
oldest section of residential blocks across the Chrysler freeway had
once been the northern fringe of the city's old Black Bottom. The
southwest portion of the precinct contained the majority of the crime-
swept "Cass Corridor." The blocks of ghetto housing across Woodward
Avenue from the precinct station had the highest crime rate in the

United States. Certain streets in that area had street whores accosting motorists from the comfort of kitchen chairs set upon the sidewalk. The residential areas at the precinct's north end were hostile, combed with militant groups and dope houses. It was a tough, violent, yet exciting precinct.

Sean could not have been more pleased with the assignment. It had been the precinct he requested prior to graduation week. The staff attempted to match requests with assignments whenever possible. The streets of the 13th Precinct were filled with enough victims and criminals for any young rookie cop's fresh, idealistic enthusiasm.

There was a small family gathering at Sean's parents' home after the graduation ceremony. His mother's parents were back from their winter home in Florida.

Grampa Cavanagh put his arm around Sean's shoulder and they walked out into the yard. The May evening was mild and smelled of Spring. "Never figured you'd want to become a flat foot, Sean."

Sean was not even slightly surprised by the senior Cavanagh's disapproval. "Well, Grandfather, not a lot of walking beats anymore. I'm more apt to become a flat butt."

"Your father and I always expected that you would take over the businesses some day. Boy, you're never going to live like I do, or your Grandpa Kelly, or your dad, on a policeman's pay."

"I know that, Grandfather. You and dad brought me up to be my own man. Maybe this will seem silly to me in a year and I'll do what you planned, but I feel I have to do this now in my life. I'm really sorry if I'm letting the family down."

His grandfather took his arm from Sean's shoulder. "Boy, you are not becoming a gangster. We're proud of you. It's just that we worry and we want the best for you. You know what you're getting into. You just be careful out there so you still have that choice to make."

Lyn talked comfortably with the Kelly grandparents. It was the first time they had met.

Sean looked a bit young to be a policeman, but he otherwise looked like a recruiting poster in his tailored uniform.

Sean's dad bought him a new Colt Python .357 magnum revolver as a graduation present. The department-issued .38 Special was not thought to be enough weapon to afford proper fire and stopping power in an emergency. Many street officers carried personally-owned revolvers, approved by the department.

In contrast, Sean's mother gave him a gold Catholic medal to wear around his neck, as he had in Vietnam. Only this medal had a gold chain, rather than hanging on his dogtag chain.

Lyn had bought him a new shock-resistant wrist watch.

The mood at Sean's academy graduation party could be best described as less than festive. The day after graduation, the rookies were to report to their precincts for orientation. Their first full work day would be the following Monday.

Sean was the only member from his class to be assigned to the 13th Precinct. He reported in to the shift commander at the precinct desk. He was told to wait until the precinct commander had time for him. Sean nervously paced outside the C.O.'s office. He felt like a freshman waiting to see the school principal.

Robert Belloti had been the C.O. of 13 since before the riot of 1967. The veteran neared retirement, and was well-respected throughout the department. He had done some amateur boxing in the Navy during World War II, and the shape of his nose did not fairly reflect his level of success as a fighter. He was an old-breed copper who had grown up on the street and earned every police promotion. He was the type of tough old street boss one would expect at a precinct like the 13th.

Belloti brought Sean into his office and sat him in a straight-back institutional chair across the cluttered desk from his big reclining office chair.

While Belloti thumbed through Sean's personnel folder, he gave him the standard welcome-aboard, keep-your-nose-clean lecture. Sean sat at attention, only speaking to answer a question.

Sean thought his new C.O. was done with him. Belloti slipped off his reading glasses, lit up a big cigar and leaned back in his chair.

"Looks like we got us a prize here with you, Cavanagh. Finished number one in your class, college boy, war hero, family lives in Grosse Pointe. Yes sir, you've got quite a background."

The C.O. put his glasses back on but looked over them to give Sean another visual once-over.

"I see you've got your uniforms tailored, and bought yourself a nice new gun and holster. Tell you what, Son, your attitude better be as good as your background, or you won't last two months out there. Like the hippie poster says, 'Today is the first day of the rest of your life.' You are just another baby-face rookie to these men. Don't look down at those men out there because they're not as smart as you or they don't have the future you do. There are some real dinosaurs out there still working the shifts. You don't have to like what they say or how they act, but respect that they have survived 20-plus years of that insanity out there.

"The streets of this precinct are different from anything in your life experience. Keep your mouth shut and your eyes open and learn what these men have to teach you. Your academy fitness report says you have an outstanding attitude. Don't lose it. I'm going to let you finish out the month with the day shift, platoon two. They're short some people.

"Cavanagh, this city, this department is changing so damn fast, I thank God I'm near retirement. It will need people like you if it's going to survive. If you keep your head out of your ass, there is no reason why you can't sit in this chair one day, on your way up the command structure."

Belloti stood and shook Sean's hand firmly. "Good luck, Kid, and welcome aboard."

Sean thanked him and left the office. Belloti leaned back in his chair and puffed away at the good cigar. He was truly thankful he neared retirement. Hell, Cavanagh was younger than his own kids. In his day, a rookie walked a beat for a year before he pulled scout car duty. Now, with all the violence, the militants, the dopers, they took 21-year-old baby-face kids and threw them directly into the fray. The job had treated Belloti well, but he was thankful his two sons had chosen other careers. Young Mr. Cavanagh, bright, sharp, combat-experienced, likable, his whole career was ahead of him. If he survived.

Monday morning at 7:45 a.m., two ranks of uniform police officers stood at attention in the squad room. The impressive-looking shift lieutenant stood at the podium, in front of his assembled platoon.

The lieutenant read over a long list of pre-shift briefing items. He introduced Sean to the platoon, and Pete Mayer, Sean's partner for the day, waved when the lieutenant read off their assignment.

Briefing ended, and the platoon descended the stairs and walked out onto the concrete driveway ramp where the officers of the graveyard shift stood by their vehicles, waiting to be relieved.

Sean felt like an F.N.G. again. At least in the academy, everyone was new. Here, it was like when he joined up with his platoon in Vietnam. Everyone knew everyone else but him. Sean tried to blend in with the other officers, to make himself disappear.

Pete Mayer was a big, good-natured, seven-year veteran of the street. While they looked for their assigned vehicle, Mayer introduced himself warmly. They found their black 1969 Ford sedan, and Mayer drove away from the station.

"Kid, we're scout 13-13 today. It's a good idea to mark it in big letters on your clipboard. At first, you ride a different unit almost everyday. Picking up your own radio calls is tough at first, with all the radio chatter. It's even tougher if you forget your code for that day."

Sean nodded, then wrote 13-13 in bold numbers at the top of the clipboard.

"Kid, there's so much to learn out here it's better if your partners do all the driving. Next week, start to concentrate on the street names. By the end of the month, you should always know where you are, even if you're not driving. It could save your life some day. You get ambushed mid-block and your partner gets taken out, your only chance might be calling for help. You can't do that if you don't know where you are.

"I'm going to lay a whole lot of information on you. Absorb as much as you can, then when you've got some time under your belt and heard different techniques, use the one that fits you best. I'm not going to pull any of that old-timer, jerk-with-the-rookie shit on you. As long as we think you're trying, the guys on this shift won't fuck with you. It's too dangerous out here for frat house initiation games. You and I are partners. Ain't no asshole ever going to cut us a huss because you are a rookie. Day shift is a good place to start. It's slower, so we can talk. Only thing on days is, if we get a hot radio run, watch your butt. Not a lot of phony runs on day shift."

Sean and Pete Mayer discussed job-related topics for the first two hours of the shift. Sean decided he would continue to question the helpful veteran partner until he sensed Mayer grew tired of the questions. Mayer was patient, and even through their coffee break continued Sean's first day of lessons on the street itself.

They spoke briefly of their military service. Mayer was expressionless when Sean told him he had been with the Marine Corps in Vietnam. Mayer had been in the Corps in the early '60s, prior to Vietnam. He said the closest he came to combat was when the fleet waited off shore to invade Cuba in October of '62.

Shortly after 10 a.m., a unit in the north end of the precinct received a call that there was an alarm at the bank on the corner of Oakland Avenue and Woodland Avenue.

Sean and Mayer were at the opposite end of the precinct. Mayer increased the police car's speed and headed toward the bank.

"That's way the hell at the north end. We'll just head in that direction. Even if it's an in-progress alarm, we're too far away to do any good. But if they were to step in some shit, we'd get there in time to help out."

Sean nodded and tried not to grin from the excitement. Driving 80 miles an hour up Woodward Avenue at 10 a.m. was a new experience.

The old two-story bank building sat directly on the northeast corner of Oakland Avenue and Woodland Avenue. There was a customer door facing each street.

Officers Dickson and Brice in scout 13-9 had been the first to arrive at the scene. Brice carefully entered the lobby through the front door off Oakland, while Dickson entered the lobby through the Woodland side door.

The two officers realized they had walked into a real problem. The bank was empty. Their eyes met briefly and they shared a worried expression that silently told them both to retreat. They both began to back out. Brice made it to the sidewalk.

As Dickson reached the side door, two men emerged from the bank's back room. A tall middle-aged Black man held a sawed-off shotgun to the head of an elderly Black man in a banker's suit. The tall man was sweating freely. His hands shook and his excited voice cracked.

"Drop your gun and kneel down on the floor, pig, or this old fool gets wasted where he stands."

Dickson froze for a moment. He couldn't risk a shot, and if he turned to run, the gunman could shoot him and the bank employee.

"Drop it, honkie, and hit the floor. I ain't foolin'."

Dickson carefully put his gun on the tile floor and dropped to all fours. He cursed his own bad luck and thought of his wife and children. They were to leave for a cabin on Lake Huron when he got home from work that day. He was to start vacation, and they had rented the cabin for a week. Judy and the kids were probably packing and loading up their station wagon that very moment.

The gunman had not seen Brice. Outside, Brice was attempting to maintain his poise as he called into the portable radio carried on his belt.

"13-9 to radio, officer in trouble, Oakland and Woodland. We've got a hold-up in progress. Barricaded gunman. An officer is a hostage."

Sean was nearly tossed into the back seat by their vehicle's additional sudden acceleration. Mayer activated the blue overhead emergency light and the loud yelp of the electronic siren.

"Cavanagh, when we got there, stay close. I don't want to have to go looking for you. You be like my fucking shadow. First day on the street, two hours into the shift and we step in some deep shit. Welcome to crazy Number 13, Kid."

Within minutes, scores of police officers surrounded the bank. Lt. Max, the shift boss, and the precinct C.O. Belloti were at the scene. Belloti had let Lt. Max remain in command of the situation. The 13th Precinct's Cruiser crew was parked next to their vehicle, directly across from the front of the bank. The four veteran officers cooly took cover behind their vehicle.

Sean took cover behind the rear wheels of their car, as he had been taught in the academy. The veterans from the Cruiser crew concentrated on the bank. Sean felt as though they didn't know he and Mayer were next to them.

The Cruiser crew chief was a stout 15-year vet who was on the current sergeant's list. He had his arm around Officer Brice, and by their posture, it looked as though he was comforting his kid brother after he'd lost a tough ballgame.

Lt. Max ran over to check on Brice and obtain as much information as possible about conditions inside the bank.

Lefty Harris, the Cruiser crew chief, pulled the Lieutenant aside, within ear shot of Sean's position. He asked to make an immediate, quick attempt to get Officer Dickson out of the bank, before the actual hostage negotiations began. Only the Cruiser crew's driver was in uniform. Lefty's plan was to take two uniform shift officers with him and make a quick attempt at the side door, where Dickson might still be seen kneeling on the floor. Lefty's Cruiser driver had fallen from his grace. He liked Pete Mayer and saw he was positioned next to them. The other Cruiser crew members were in position to offer effective cover fire, if Lefty and his rescue plan ran amuck.

The Lieutenant rubbed his eyes. "Shit, if we don't get Dickson out of there before the Brass and the media gets here, we'll be jerking around for a week with those pricks, and Dickson will end up dead. O.K., Lefty, I agree. Dickson's best chance is now. For Christ's sake, be careful. We don't need four dead coppers."

Lefty picked up a department 12-gauge shotgun and ran to where Pete Mayer and Sean were positioned. "Pete, I'm going to take a try to get Dickson out of there. Will you and your partner come with me as backup?"

Pete Mayer knew that Lefty Harris had no idea it was Sean's first day. The Cruiser crew did not attend briefing with the shift, and their members had little contact with the new officers. The Cruiser crews worked different hours than the shifts. Lefty had glanced at Sean. He looked young, but he looked like he knew what he was doing. Sean carried himself with confidence and held his magnum revolver with two hands, like he knew how to use it.

Mayer hesitated for a moment, considered Sean's status, then got to his feet from his knees. "Lead the way, Lefty. My partner and I are right behind you."

Lefty carried the riot gun at port arms as he sprinted across Oakland Avenue to the bank building. Mayer and Sean ran close behind. They passed Cruiser crew member Cal Lindow, who cooly aimed an M-1 carbine at the front of the bank, covering their advance.

Lefty, Pete, and Sean moved to the side of the bank, then carefully walked along next to the wall, to the side door. Lefty briefly glanced inside and saw that Dickson was still on the floor near the side door. The robber's hesitation to move Dickson offered them a chance to get Dickson out.

Lefty spoke softly. "I'm going straight in and stand next to Dickson. You two follow me in and each take a side of the door. If I can get him out, cover our retreat. If the shit breaks loose, well, do the best you can to get your own ass back out onto the street."

Lefty strolled into the side door of the bank as if he was there to cash a check. He stood next to Dickson, who was still on all fours on the lobby floor. Sean and Pete stood to the rear and either side of Lefty.

Lefty's cool and unthreatening posture caught the robber by complete surprise.

"What? Are you crazy, Man? You and them pigs with you drop your guns now, or this old bank nigger dies. You gotta be crazy coming in here like this. I swear, drop your guns or this man is dead."

Lefty spoke calmly and slowly. "No, I'm sorry, we can't do that. Tell you what, we'll just back out of here and leave you alone. We don't want nobody to get hurt. You see, Mister, we can't leave a police officer in here. It's against the rules. I'm sure you understand."

"Bullshit, pig. You're fuckin' crazy, Man. I got a shotgun to this man's skull. The pig on the floor stays. You all can back out, but do it now or this old fool dies."

Lefty racked a 00 buckshot round into the riot gun's chamber and pointed it at the gunman. The metallic sound seemed extra loud in the bank lobby.

"Listen to me, Mister. This is how it is. All of the police officers are going to leave right now. We'll just back out of the door and you and the folks outside can talk about settling this problem, without anyone getting hurt."

The bank robber pulled the bank manager even closer to him, using him as a shield. "You won't shoot me, not with this old nigger in front of me."

Sean's eyes searched the other portions of the bank's interior for other robbers, other threats if the shooting started. He held his magnum with both hands and remembered to squeeze the trigger if he had to fire, not to jerk it. He had six shots in his revolver, not like the 20 rounds in his M-16. He was fully aware of the drama unfolding in front of him, but his eyes were everywhere.

"You ain't gonna shoot. The pig on the floor stays. Now get out."

Lefty clicked the riot gun off of safety and pressed the stock against his cheek. "Don't bet your life on it, Mister."

The robber felt himself losing control. "Anybody move and I swear . . ."

Lefty spoke calmly but with complete authority. "O.K., everybody back out of the door, let's give this man some room. We don't want anyone hurt. Pete, go ahead, get Dickson and the kid outa here."

In less than five seconds, Dickson, Pete, and Sean were outside of the bank and away from the side door. A moment later, Lefty backed out of the building and joined them. They ran along the side of the bank, then sprinted across Oakland Avenue, to the cover of their vehicles.

A collective cheer went up from the assembled officers when they saw that Dickson had been freed, unharmed. The mood of the confrontation changed, now that the robber did not hold a police officer. The robber had nearly made a serious tactical error by attempting to take advantage of Dickson's capture. The negotiation team could make many more concessions with civilian hostages. Policy dictated that there was little bargaining when a cop was the hostage.

Back behind the vehicles, the four policemen sat with their backs against the Cruiser, trying to catch their breath. Officer Brice and the Lieutenant came over to congratulate Dickson and Lefty Harris. Dickson wiped the sweat from his forehead with his own forearms.

"Damn, Lefty, was I ever glad to see you guys show up. I knew I'd really screwed up when I dropped my gun. I was certain I had bought it. I think the robber was so shocked I dropped my gun so he wouldn't waste the old man, that he didn't know exactly what to do with me."

Lefty patted Dickson on the back. "I'm just glad you're alright, Dickson. Hey Pete, you and your partner did great. Thanks a lot. Hey Kid, what's your name?"

"Cavanagh."

Lefty reached over Dickson and shook Sean's hand as he introduced himself. "How long you been on the street, Kid?"

Sean didn't answer. Dickson put his hand on the veteran cop's shoulder. "Lefty, I really don't think you want to know."

"What are you talking about? The kid handled himself just fine. How much road time you got, Kid?"

"About two and a half hours."

Lefty slammed his eyes shut and shook his head in disbelief.

"Sweet Jesus, we got a cop held hostage and I've got a kid doing his first day backing me up. Well, Cavanagh, first day or not, you did a hell of a job. Ain't nobody gonna tell you that you don't learn real quick at this precinct."

The Lieutenant moved back to the command vehicle. Except for Dickson, the other officers returned to their positions, watching the bank.

Officer Cal Lindow was still intently aiming his M-1 carbine at the building's front door. He spoke loud enough to be heard by the small rescue team.

"Word is that there's three of them. They're holding four bank employees, the old manager and three women. Everyone involved is Black. Sounds like they're older assholes, maybe three-time losers. They want a car, or they say they'll kill an employee every half hour."

Lefty had moved next to Sean.

"Yea," he said. "Guy holding the gun on the old man was no kid. If they were real pros they would have snatched up Dickson right away.

Probably three small timers decided to try their hand in the big league."

Cal Lindow looked down Oakland Avenue and moved back to aim at the bank's front door.

"They're bringing up a car now. Once those assholes come out of the bank, it's show time. The cop dropping off the car is going to switch keys. That way, even if they make it into the car, they're not going anywhere."

The unmarked Plymouth police car was parked at the corner. The officer driving put the car in park, turned off the engine and ran from the vehicle to the cover of the line of police cars.

A moment later, two figures appeared at the side door of the bank. They stepped out onto the sidewalk. A stocky Black man about 40 held a tall, female teller in a choke hold with his left arm. He held a revolver to her head with his right. The attractive bank teller was as tall as the robber and she served as a effective human shield.

Although Pete and Sean were covering the front of the bank, they could see down the side of the building from their position.

There was movement at the front door of the bank. The robber holding the bank manager inched his way out onto the sidewalk and slowly moved toward the get-away vehicle, using the bank manager as his shield. The two robbers could not see each other.

The Lieutenant called out to the robbers one last time to surrender. They both only shouted back obscenities.

Sean carefully aimed his handgun at the robber at the front of the bank. He was ready, but the robbers would have to attack their position before he intended to fire, considering all the fire power around him.

It was as though the next few seconds were taken from a slow motion segment of a violent movie. The teller somehow twisted and broke free from her captor's grasp. She ran toward the front of the bank. As she ran from his grip, the gunman hesitated for a second. He froze, not knowing whether to fire at his hostage, fire at the assembled police or try to make it back into the bank. As he was deciding, a dozen police gunshots bounced the man's body off the side wall of the bank. He fell to the sidewalk, dead. Two officers moved from behind their cover, grabbed the woman teller and ushered her to safety. She was not harmed.

In response to the volley of shots at the side of the bank, the robber in front stopped his advance toward the car and leaned back against the wall, pulling the elderly manager even closer to him. He began to shout a panicked warning to the assembled police officers that surrounded the bank.

The ordeal of the attempted robbery and the noise of the police gunfire had become much more than the frail bank manager could endure. He fainted dead away in the robber's arms. He was not a big man, but the limp body became dead weight and more than the robber could hold with one arm. The bank manager's body slipped to the sidewalk. He was no longer a shield.

The single shot from Cal Lindow's rifle struck the hapless robber in the center of the forehead. The bullet exited the rear of his skull and splashed some of its contents on the front wall of the bank. The lifeless body dropped the sawed-off shotgun and slid slowly against the wall until the body was in a macabre sitting position, the unconscious bank manager still at his feet.

Cal Lindow put his rifle on safety and said under his breath, "Bye-bye, asshole."

Sean looked over at the veteran officer. There was no expression on his face. "Hell of a shot, Officer."

Cal Lindow shrugged his shoulders and took aim at the front door again. There was still a robber in the bank with two hostages.

The Lieutenant called from his car several yards down Oakland Avenue. "Pete, you and Cavanagh go get the bank manager and drag him over here. We've got a wagon ready to get him to the hospital."

Pete and Sean holstered their revolvers so they could use both hands to carry the man to safety. Pete moved into position again to get to his feet and run. "You ready, Kid?" Sean merely nodded. "O.K., like the man said, it's showtime."

As Pete and Sean got to their feet, they heard Cal Lindow call to them. "You guys will be alright. The front door is covered. If the third asshole even peeks out of the door at you two, he's history."

They reached the unconscious bank manager. Each of them took an arm and grabbed him by the back of this belt with the other hand. They ran him to the police station wagon, with a stretcher waiting to rush him to the hospital.

Pete and Sean ran back to their vehicle. As they passed the shift lieutenant, he gave them the thumbs-up sign.

Back behind their car, Pete and Sean redrew their revolvers. Lefty Harris called over to Sean's partner. "Hey, Mayer, I ain't never seen you run so fast. You trying to impress the kid with your famous footwork?"

"No, I was trying not to get my ass shot off. You were moving pretty good for an old fat guy when we went and got Dickson."

"Naw, the legs are shot. I may have the legs of a 40-year-old, but I still got the prick of a 17-year-old."

Cal Lindow spoke without moving his rifle from the firing position. "Yea, and most the time you got the mind of a 17-year-old."

The third robber slowly walked out of the side door of the bank, his arms raised high above his head. The Lieutenant and two other officers quickly approached him. The Lieutenant called out to the assembled police officers, "Hold your fire, don't shoot, men. The whole world is watching."

His comment referred to the large gathering of local media representatives with T.V. mini-cams and newspaper photographers.

They handcuffed the third robber and gently took him to a marked police car and drove him Downtown to Homicide. Five officers rushed through the side door of the bank to make certain that there were no other members of the robbery team inside the bank. They found the remaining two employees unharmed in a rear office. The bank was secure.

Pete, Sean and the Cruiser crew slowly walked across the street, to the fallen robber.

Precinct C.O. Belloti walked up to the gathered group. "Damn fine job, men. Who shot this one?"

"Lindow did, Boss."

"Hell of a shot. Cavanagh, you guard the body until the morgue wagon gets here and the boys from Central Photo are done with their crime scene pictures."

Sean felt a bit silly standing over the body of the robber, still seated on the sidewalk, his back against the wall. He whispered under his breath.

"Guard the body? He sure as hell isn't going anywhere. Besides, nobody would pick it up and steal it with the back of the head gone."

When the corpse began to attract flies, Sean managed to locate a blanket so it could be covered. He carefully placed the blanket over the body so as not to disturb its position in any way.

Sean was amazed by the flurry of activity around him. Uniform and plain-clothes officers moved in and out of the bank. Media people interviewed police officers and civilian witnesses. There were cameras and microphones all around him.

He glanced at the ugly blood stain on the front wall of the bank. He had a morbid thought: who would clean up the mess? The thought had never crossed his mind before. He had seen a thousand people die on T.V. and at the movies, but who cleaned up the mess? Someone would have to wash down the wall and sidewalk after they took the body away. He imagined the manager giving instructions to the janitor.

"Be sure to dust, wash the floor, do the windows, and by the way, don't forget the blood and brains on the front wall."

Sean found Pete Mayer and they called the dispatcher to return to service. Pete drove slowly toward their own area of assignment at the opposite end of the precinct.

"You did good, kid. For a cherry on his very first day on the street, you handled yourself just fine. I thought I'd shit when I saw the expression of Lefty's face when he found out you were brand new."

"Pete, I hope you don't think I'm a head case, but I swear to you, I wasn't afraid. I knew I could get wasted, but unlike Vietnam, I knew I could say fuck it and walk away whenever I wanted. You couldn't quit the Marines. I think not feeling helpless eases the fear. I was excited as hell, really pumped up, but not the fear I felt in Nam."

"I know what you mean, kid. That's why some people are convinced all cops are fucking crazy. We do shit like this morning and we don't have to. If the average guy heard that there were three gunmen at a bank, he'd go the other direction. Not us. We drive 80 miles an hour toward the trouble.

"Just keep in mind, kid, this ain't Nam. There are no free fire zones or air strikes. The assholes get the first shot, and then anything you do will be analyzed and second guessed.

"We were real lucky today. If one of those employees would have got greased, the media would have our ass. Since the hostages were also Black, the media probably won't fuck us over for killing two Black suspects. You walk a fine edge out here, kid.

"Look at these streets. It's a nice Spring afternoon and they look mean. Wait until 1 a.m. on a hot July night. You'll feel the tension in your chest, maybe even a little of that fear will come back. If you let down, these assholes will take your head off at the waist. If you come on too strong, you end up getting bounced or riding a desk your whole career.

"Don't expect too much from these people. It took them a long time to get this fucked up, and one baby-faced white rookie cop isn't going to make much impact. Do the best you can. Care, but don't let it eat you up. The street people have been fucked up since long before you were born. They will still be fucked up long after you're gone.

"Last bit of the lecture: if you start waiting for these people to thank you, you'll grow old and bitter. Accept these people for what they are, all fucked up. Then do as much as you can for them."

Sean took in every one of Pete's words of advice.

"Get the radio, kid. We got a radio run. Third Street and Willis, a cutting. Tell dispatch we're on the way. Damn, Cavanagh, we're going to start calling you 'Black Cloud.' Luck of the Irish, my ass."

It was nearly 5 p.m. when Sean pulled his Triumph into the narrow driveway of his duplex on Moross Road, on Detroit's far Eastside.

The small two-bedroom duplex had been decorated with the remainder of his savings. It was neat and comfortable, but far from any bachelor's pad featured in *Playboy*.

Sean went to the kitchen and took a Pepsi can from the refrigerator.

He was still charged from the day's events, and the cold soft drink eased his thirst.

He moved into his bedroom and stood in front of the full length mirror on the closet door. He felt like a real bad ass. He looked young, but he looked sharp. He knew it, and he liked the feeling. He drew his magnum revolver and aimed at the reflection on the mirror with both hands. Twenty-one years old and he believed he had one of the most exciting jobs in the world.

His moments of self-indulgence were interrupted by the phone. It was his mother. She had heard of the shootings and was concerned. She was comforted when Sean told her he had seen the incident but did not fire his weapon, and that no innocent people or policemen were hurt. He promised to stop by their house that week and tell them all about his new job.

Later, Lyn called when she got home from work. She was going to drive over and make them dinner. "How was your first day?"

"Fine."

"Anything exciting happen?"

Sean paused for a moment. A terrible feeling rolled over him like a huge wave. He realized that as with Vietnam, he could not talk about his job with an outsider. What was he to say? How could he tell her that he saw two men shot to death and a stabbing homicide on his first day?

"It's a pretty active place, Lyn. I don't think I'll get bored. Don't you have school on Monday?"

"Yes, but I thought I'd make you a nice dinner and we'd have some wine to celebrate your first day."

Sean smiled as he hung up the phone. "She's trying. Got to give her credit. She wants me to be a cop about as much as my mom does, but she's trying."

In the weeks that followed, Sean was bled on, puked on, punched out, and knocked down enough times to take some of the glimmer from his very shiny badge.

He made enough typical rookie errors to cause him to be appropriately humble. He was a fast learner, and he was well accepted by the other officers of his shift. He got along well with the precinct supervision, and he followed the C.O.'s advice to the letter.

He was falling in love with the job as if it were a mistress. The uniform and gun had become a part of him. The inside of a police car seemed to fit like a comfortable pair of shoes. He was as much at home on those ghetto streets as he was in Grosse Pointe. At 21, Sean was not yet mature enough to realize that part of his initial fascination with the job was violence. Society gave him a gun and a badge and licensed him to enforce the law. In the Detroit ghetto, that was a sanctioned ticket to kick ass and take names. He was "The Man," and he damn well liked it.

JUNE, 1969
GROSSE POINTE

Sean sat at the kitchen table with his dad. They had been watching the Tiger game on the family room television and moved into the kitchen to finish their beers after the game ended.

His mother was busy at the kitchen sink preparing dinner. "What time is your friend coming for dinner tomorrow?"

Sean went to the refrigerator and took out another beer for his dad and himself.

"I told him any time after noon. Mom, you can have dinner any time you'd like. I want to be able to spend some time with him. That's why he's coming so early in the day."

She pondered over her grocery list. "What kind of food does your friend like?"

"Mom, T.J. is still in the Marines. I've seen him eat anything. Just don't have 'ham and moth . . .', ham and lima beans."

Sean's father winked at him from across the table.

"Well then, does he have some special favorites?"

"I'm certain he does, Mom. But since Soul food is not your strong suit, I bought some steaks on the way over. I thought dad could cook them on the grill and make a salad and baked potatoes"

"What about something to drink?"

"Mom, with beer in the 'frig and Dad's bar selection, there's no problem. Come on, relax. T.J. is very flexible. He's Black, but my friend, not the president of some African country."

"I know, Son. I just want him to feel welcome and have a nice dinner for him."

"I know, Mom, and I really appreciate it. I'm sure everything will be fine."

Sean's dad was amused. The Cavanaghs had never entertained a Black guest at their home. That had not been by design. They never had the occasion with their suburban circle of friends. His wife was a bit naive of the cultural differences. He detected that she was nervous but, as always, she was sincere.

On Sunday, T.J. drove in front of the Cavanagh home just after noon. He had borrowed his stepfather's car and successfully followed Sean's detailed directions. Sean had parked his red Triumph in the driveway as a marker.

Sean walked out to the street to greet his friend. They shook hands, and Sean gave T.J. a brief hug. "Well, there goes the neighborhood. Damn, T.J, you're looking fit. It's really good to see you."

T.J. grinned broadly as he looked around at the houses. "My, oh my. Sure is nice to see how the other half lives. You quit college and left this to go to Nam? Boy has got to have brain damage. Square business, Irish, you are lookin' good. You all tan, ain't got no Gook sores or jungle rot. You ain't got fat from the good life yet. Remember, though, I can still whip yo' ass, real po-lice or not. Speakin' of that, where's your piece? I thought you po-lice always had to carry your piece."

"They do allow us to leave it off some times. I wear it at work or out shopping. And, of course, I wear it to bed."

"No shit, you wear it to bed? It must be a snub nose."

"I can't lie to a man who's seen me in the shower. It may be snub-nose, but it's a magnum. Small, but powerful."

T.J. put his arm on Sean's shoulder as they walked up to the house. "Irish, you still more full of bullshit than a Christmas goose. You still a honkie, but I been missin' you, Brother."

Sean introduced T.J. to his family. His brothers went to play baseball until dinnertime, and his sisters helped his mother in the kitchen. Sean and T.J. joined his dad in the family room. The Tigers were on television again with an afternoon game against the Boston Red Sox.

The game served as a common denominator and helped ease T.J.'s natural tension in the very different environment of the beautiful Cavanagh home.

The three men sipped from beer cans and discussed the game and the Tigers' dim chance of repeating their 1968 Championship.

Boston's Yaz bounced a double off of Fenway Park's Green Monster in left field. Sean raised his beer can toward the television screen as if in gesture of a toast. "Ol' Logs would have really grooved on that. If he was still alive he'd probably be at Fenway, half shit-faced, cheering with his crazy Irish neighbors."

T.J. had seen Sean's gesture and did the same. "Mr. Cavanagh, your son and that boy Logs, from Boston, they were really somethin' when they were together. Talk about a couple of stone crazy Irish boys. Ah, no offense meant, Sir, but the two of them was always cuttin' up and could always say somethin' to get us to laughin'. I swear, if it wasn't for their bein' silly and joking those first couple weeks in the Hue City, all my people would have become head cases. It had been raining for days. We were wet and cold and tired and scared as hell. The clouds were so heavy they seemed to almost reach the ground. Your boy would walk up to our new brown bar, turn his face up into the rain for a minute and say, 'Look's like it's lettin' up, Lu-tenant.' He'd do that 'bout twice a day. Finally, the brown bar got so rattled, he ordered your boy to just stay away from him. We thought we'd bust a gut. We'd be walkin' down a street snoopin' for Gooks, and somebody'd yell, 'weather report.' Your boy'd turn his face to the rain and real cheerful like say, 'Looks like it's lettin' up.' "

Sean's dad opened another beer. "Son, wasn't Logs the buddy you lost the week before you two got hit?"

Suddenly, Sean's mood became sullen and he stared at the floor for a moment. "Yea, he's the one I told you about a couple of times. He got hit while we were clearing a house."

"Gentlemen, this old war horse lost a lot of buddies on those two stinking Pacific islands. I know about the sorrow and frustration. It can't bring your buddy back, but it helps if you know you got the guy that did it."

Sean and T.J. exchanged knowing glances. "You're right, Dad. The Gook that killed Logs didn't get away."

"When I was on Peleliu and we were trying to take that damn Bloody Nose Ridge, a Nip in a cave shot and killed my best buddy. I bet I killed that Jap about 12 times. They could have buried him in a juice can."

Sean left the room to go check on a time for dinner. Sean's dad could see the expression of surprise on T.J.'s face. It was as if T.J. didn't realize that veterans of other wars had similar experiences.

"T.J., after talking with Sean, I get the impression that you Nam Vets are too hard on yourselves. It's not your fault, all the media bullshit. We did things to the enemy and civilians in World War II that make you guys look like the Peace Corps. War is semi-organized madness. The actions that take place in combat must be judged by a different set of standards."

"I understand where you comin' from, Mr. Cavanagh. Your boy, he knows all about the other wars like Korea and World War II, even World War I. The boy usta get kidded for bein' a walkin' war history book. He knows all that, yet he was always feelin' bad and guilty 'bout things. Never seen a better man in a fire fight, but he was wrapped too tight not to have guilt."

Sean re-entered the family room with a fresh beer. "Mom says the grill is ready. Your presence is requested as soon as the game is over, Dad."

After the game, they ate the grilled steak dinner in the dining room. Sean's mother was silently pleased to see the only thing left on T.J.'s plate was the foil used to wrap his baked potato.

After dinner, the men went back into the family room. This time they were joined by Sean's younger brothers. Sean, his dad, and T.J. took turns sharing war stories of the lighter variety. Most of their stories were of funny boot camp and training experiences. The younger

Cavanagh boys were not quite ready for the real stories of combat.

In the early evening, T.J. thanked the Cavanagh family half a dozen times, and Sean walked him out to his car.

"You got you a fine family, Irish. You be certain to tell them how I appreciate gettin' to meet them and thank them again for the fine meal. I'm sorry I didn't get a chance to meet your new lady. By your letters, sounds like it's gettin' serious."

"She's up North at a family reunion. They plan them a year in advance. She's, of course, disappointed that it happens to be this weekend. She wanted to meet you, and she wanted me up there to meet her family."

"Ooooh, meet the family. Soundin' real serious. Jus' remember what I always been tellin' you: don't do your thinkin' with your dick. You 'spect she maybe won't like me cause I'm Black?"

"Shit T.J., Lyn is one of those liberal college types. Initially, she'll like you *because* you're Black."

"Well, least wise the lady's got good taste."

T.J. slipped into the car. They continued their conversation through the open window.

Sean put his hand on T.J.'s shoulder. "You want me to write you a pass to get home in case the Grosse Pointe Police stop you on the way?"

T.J. smiled and bobbed his head. "Naw, little Brother, it's cool. I got me a passport."

"How long before you figure they'll ship you out to Nam?"

"I gotta report to Staging Battalion on Wednesday. I figure I'll be back in Nam the beginning of next month. Hell, just in time for the Summer season."

Sean's voice changed tone slightly, and he became serious. "You keep that bubble butt of yours down. I've grown rather fond of you the last couple of years, damned if I know why. I won't be with you this time to keep you out of trouble."

"Listen, Cherry, I was already in Nam when you were here a couple Summers ago, eatin' steak, tryin' to get in your girlfriend's skivvies. I'll admit that I'd feel better if we was going together, but I can still take care of business on my own. You better be careful your own self. Pretty white preppie boy ridin' around in a po-lice car on them mean streets. Irish, ain't you heard? It's a jungle out there."

Sean smiled. They shook hands firmly. "I'll write and send you some goodies every month."

"Thanks, Irish. Man, they ain't ever gonna believe me. Wait till I tell them I was sittin' in a big house in Grosse Pointe, eatin' steaks. Damn, like I died and went to heaven. Be cool, little white Brother. You keep your head down, hear?"

A moment later, T.J.'s car drove out of view. The evening was as pleasant as a Michigan Summer dusk could be. With the setting sun, the air had cooled slightly. Sean stood at the curb of Birch Lane and stared after T.J.'s car. He heard the low rumble of an approaching thunderstorm from the West. He felt goose bumps rise on his arms and had a shiver. He wasn't certain whether the cool evening breeze had caused the physical response or the distant rumble of the approaching storm. It reminded him of a distant arc light air strike or far off heavy artillery. They were just a bad memory for Sean.

He realized that his friend would soon hear the roar of cannons and bombs and the countless other frightening sounds of war. He shook his head at his feeling of helplessness. T.J. faced 13 more months in the special hell that was Vietnam. A ghost inside Sean caused part of him to want to go back there with T.J. To go back and even up some imagined debts and close the books for all of his dead and maimed friends. He was mature enough to understand that it was an impossible task.

The driving portion of Sean's conscious mind thanked God in silent prayer that he would never again return to that insanity. He said a brief prayer for his friend and crossed himself. He was amused by a thought as he walked back to the house. The ghettos of Detroit were certainly enough insanity for anyone.

Huge rolling thunderstorm clouds now loomed overhead. A sharp bolt of lightening was quickly followed by a crack of loud thunder. Instinctively, Sean ducked his head. "Incoming!"

7

August, 1969—March, 1970

AUGUST, 1969
DETROIT, MICHIGAN

It was still hot and humid at 4 p.m. when Sean started his shift. He had been assigned to a regular crew as the third man. He worked with one partner while the other was off. On the days they both worked, he was teamed with someone else.

That night, Sean was working with Ron Henner, the younger of his two senior partners. Ron was 30 and solid as a linebacker.

Sean liked working with Ron, who didn't seem to mind Sean's steady stream of questions. Although he usually referred to Sean as "Kid," he treated Sean more like a partner than a rookie.

Ron also liked working with him. Some of Sean's natural rookie enthusiasm always seemed to give him a morale boost. Sean was a quick learner, and in a few weeks Ron felt he had seen enough to know he could trust the youngster when the shit really hit the fan. He only had to help Sean learn the ways of the street. Ron admitted that Sean already wrote much better reports than he did.

Sean was driving. He attempted to keep the black, marked, Ford sedan moving so the air would circulate inside the hot vehicle. Even with their portable "cool seats," the backs of their shirts were soon sticking to them.

Sean was quieter than usual. He was troubled by the obvious bad attitude and bitterness he had read in T.J.'s first letter since his return to Vietnam.

Now formally engaged to Lyn, the pressure for him to quit the department and join his dad's business had become less than subtle. He wasn't ready to quit. The job was exciting, and he still believed that he could do something really worthwhile as a cop.

Ron scanned the cluttered streets of their assigned area. He took a cigar from his shirt pocket and carefully unwrapped it. "Hey, Kid, you feeling alright?"

Sean's deep thought was broken and he was surprised by the question. "I'm fine, Ron, why do you ask?"

"Well, we're almost three hours into the shift, and you have hardly spoken. When you're not jacking your jaws, you're either feelin' punk or thinking about pussy. Since it's kind of early to be thinking of pussy, even for you, I thought maybe you didn't feel good."

"Damn, it's the same old bullshit, Ron. Now that I'm engaged, I guess the family thought I'd give up this job. They act like this is some post-teenage phase I'm going through. It's like all those rich little assholes who hitchhike around the country so they can find themselves."

"Well, you sure as shit are not going to find yourself down in here."

"Screw it. Is Tasty Bar-B-Q alright for our code?"

"With the limited choices in this precinct, it's as good as any. Despite the heat, I'm hungry as hell."

Sean drove north on Woodward Avenue, leaving their area, and headed for the restaurant near Grand Boulevard.

The calm, monotone voice of the male dispatcher seemed in direct contrast to the information he reported. "13-9, 13-11, and cars in 13: Woodward and Clairmont, at the drugstore, a hold-up in progress. Shots fired."

Ron turned on the overhead emergency light as Sean roared through the Grand Boulevard intersection. At their speed, they were less than a minute from the scene.

Ron drew his revolver. "O.K., Kid, that drugstore is on the southwest corner of the intersection. Don't stop too close to the front door, and watch your ass."

Sean intended to drive just past the store's front door and stop so they could use their car as cover. Another responding unit arriving from the north suddenly occupied that space. Sean brought their car to a squealing, smoking stop in the center of Woodward Avenue, just north of the front door.

"Get the hell out of the car, Kid. You're exposed." Ron was out of the car and aiming at the drugstore across the car hood. Only four empty traffic lanes and a narrow sidewalk separated Sean from the front door of the drugstore.

Sean drew his magnum as he sprang from the car. He noticed the two officers from the other vehicle had exited their car and stood with weapons in hand. They also were using their vehicle for cover. He recognized the other crew as being 13-9, Reggie Marlen and Walt Stockden.

Sean moved quickly to get to the other side of the car but stopped at the rear bumper when he heard two distinct gunshots from inside the drugstore.

He held his revolver with both hands and aimed at the drugstore's front door. Sean knew he was caught out in the open, but he decided his best chance to survive was to position himself to confront the danger immediately.

The front door of the drugstore burst open. A lean white man about 30 staggered out of the store and onto the narrow sidewalk. He held an old battered automatic pistol in one hand and a brown paper sack in the other. He wore khaki trousers and a pale yellow sport shirt. There was a large expanding blood stain on his left side. The man seemed dazed. He leaned hard against the front wall of the drugstore.

Ron and Sean called to the man to drop his weapon.

The man looked up toward their voices and was obviously surprised at their presence, despite their nearness and the rotating blue lights of both police cars. He stared at Sean for a moment and began to walk north, still leaning against the building.

Ron called out another warning and ordered the man to drop his weapon. As Ron was calling out, Sean realized the man was not dazed from his wound. He was so high he was numb.

The man reached the corner of the building and took a step toward Clairmont. In his drug-induced stupor, he decided to make an escape attempt west down Clairmont. He raised his automatic pistol, intent on shooting at Sean, who was still standing in the open.

The four police officers fired a brief but vicious volley. Some of the rounds struck the gunman, and their impact caused him to discharge the pistol into the street. He was knocked backward into the gutter.

Sean and the other officers slowly and cautiously approached the body of the fallen gunman. As Sean neared the man's body, he saw two uniformed private security guards exit the front door of the drugstore, their revolvers still in hand.

To the absolute astonishment of everyone witnessing the incident, the badly shot-up gunman somehow struggled to all fours. He had lost grip of the paper bag, but still held his pistol.

Sean and Reggie were closest to the man, who mumbled something to them and began to raise the pistol in their direction once again.

Sean quickly brought his .357 magnum up to firing position. He called out a command, his voice nearly cracked from excitement. "Give it up! Drop the gun, fool."

As the man moved the barrel of his pistol in their direction, Sean and Reggie each fired another two rounds at the gunman. Walt and Ron could not safely fire because of their position. At the sound of the gunfire, both security guards dove face down onto the sidewalk.

The second volley picked the gunman up and tossed him on the sidewalk against the building and onto his back. The officers could not believe what they were seeing. Despite his many severe wounds, the man was still conscious. He was swearing, and like a huge wounded turtle, he struggled to get off of his back and into an effective firing position.

Just as he raised the upper part of his body from the concrete and prepared to fire again, Sean and Reggie reached him. Reggie grabbed him hard at the throat. Sean grabbed his gun hand at the wrist. He could not pry the man's fingers from the pistol.

"Let go of me, you fuckin' pigs. I swear I'll kill you, I'll kill all of you." The man spat at Reggie.

Sean was kneeling on the man's arm but still could not free the pistol from his strong right hand. Sean jammed the barrel of his magnum hard into the man's ear.

"You're not going to kill anyone. Now asshole, let go of the gun or I'll spread your brains all over this sidewalk."

The gunman's eyes were red and glassed over. He glared in Sean's direction but it was as though he couldn't focus his eyes on the figures in blue. Sean was nearly as high on adrenaline as the wounded gunman was on heroin. Sean finally pulled the pistol from the gunman's tight grasp and unloaded it. He and Reggie struggled to handcuff the man's bleeding arms behind his back.

The two Black uniformed guards timidly got back to their feet and approached the officers. Sean and Ron moved to talk with them. Sean took out his small notebook from his uniform shirt pocket. "Was he alone?"

The older guard stepped forward. "Yep. He is one crazy white dude, Officer. No offense. He came strollin' into the store, walked right past me to the pharmacy. I seen he was higher than a 707. He pulls out his piece and orders the man at the pharmacy counter to load up a bag with all the drugs an' money he got. When me an' my partner here approached him, he opens up a firin' on us. I swear, it was an act o' God he didn't hit nobody. He shot up the place, reloaded, an' went to shootin' again. We finally fired a couple times as he was running out the front door. I think we hit him once."

Sean glanced at the two security guards. "Too bad you fell on the sidewalk and got your uniforms all dirty. The shooting wasn't anywhere near your direction."

The man smiled a knowing smile. "Well, Officer, I done growed up on these streets. When the po-lice start a shootin', best thing for a Black man to do is see how low he can go, if you get my drift."

Sean grinned and wrote down their names and addresses. "Sounds like good judgement to me. You can always wash your shirt."

"You got that right, Officer. Somebody put a hole in my Black ass, I can't jus' wash it away. Even if it's put there by accident."

Ron grabbed Sean firmly by the arm. Ron had the paper bag with the stolen money and drugs. "Kid, go get our car and drive it up onto the sidewalk, right next to the asshole's location."

"Christ, Ron. That guy is shot to shit. He should go to the hospital in a wagon. A ride in a sedan all that way could kill him."

"Fuck him! Look around, Cav. We've already got a crowd of a couple hundred. The nearest wagon is way the hell on the south end. The only reason we don't already have a riot is because the guy is white. We've got to get him out of here before the crowd gets bigger and their mood changes."

Sean inched the police car through the crowd. Walt and Reggie lifted the badly-wounded gunman and lay him across the Ford's back seat. Ron jumped in the front seat. A wire screen separated the front seat from the back seat, offering the officers some protection from their prisoner occupants.

"Come on, Cav. Let's get this car and that crazy asshole away from here."

Sean backed the vehicle through the crowd until he reached the center of Woodward. He turned south, put on the siren and headed for the city hospital with a tire-squealing start.

He maneuvered the speeding police car through the evening traffic. He worked his way to the Chrysler freeway and increased their speed. The hospital was now only minutes away.

During the rapid drive to the hospital, the wounded gunman continued to thrash about on the back seat. He kicked at the metal screen behind Sean's head and yelled threats and obscenities at both officers. He was bleeding severely, and soon his blood was all over the back seat and the floor, and had splattered on the side windows and the backs of Ron and Sean.

"Come on, you chickenshit pigs. Stop this car and take off these cuffs. I'll still kick both of your asses."

Ron turned around in his seat, "Shut the fuck up and sit still asshole, or we'll shut off the lights and siren and take you to the county hospital via the scenic route."

"Yea, yea, big tough cops. Remember, pig, it took four of you to take me down."

Sean was busy concentrating on driving. Ron shook his head and tried to wipe some of the blood splashed on his arm with a clean handkerchief. "I've been a street copper over seven years, and I've never seen anybody like this asshole. I know he's higher than a kite, but he's shot to hell and wants us to stop the car and go a couple of rounds with him. It kind of renews my faith in the white race. I mean, talk about your white power, I think we've arrested Superman. He must have gone bad and become a junkie. That's why he's not on television anymore."

Even as they pulled onto the Emergency Room ramp, the man was threatening them. He never once complained of pain.

Sean had radioed ahead, so the hospital staff would know they were coming in with a badly-wounded prisoner. Even they were surprised by the prisoner's strength and aggressive behavior. They had to tie him to a gurney with leather restraints so he could be wheeled into the primary trauma treatment room.

They started two I.V.s and probed the wounds. He still had not received any form of anesthetic and he had yet to say one word of complaint about pain or discomfort. In fact, he continued to threaten the officers and shout obscenities at them.

The doctor carefully probed and inspected each wound. "I don't like the looks of this gunshot just below the navel. Nurse Curtis, do a catheter to be certain his bladder isn't damaged."

The middle-aged nurse moved to the supply table and picked up a long, narrow rubber tube.

The doctor was bent over the victim's body, making certain he had not overlooked a wound. The efficient nurse's face was expressionless as she took hold of the man's flaccid penis and began to insert the tube of the catheter.

Suddenly, the gunman's behavior took a dramatic 180° turn from being the department's most recent legend. He began to complain and cry about the discomfort of the catheter's tube.

Sean walked over next to Ron. "Well, I guess we didn't meet up with Superman after all. I do believe they've located his Achilles' heel, in a manner of speaking."

The gunman was identified as Clay Hannon of New York. He had just been released from Attica prison after doing a couple of years for armed robbery. He had returned to the Bronx just long enough to get back his heroin habit. He was working his way to the West Coast, city by city. He'd do a few quick robberies and stay long enough to score some heroin, then move to the next city. He was wanted in three states, including New York for robbery and parole violation.

To save the Michigan taxpayers' money, as soon as Hammon could travel he would be turned over to the New York State authorities, and sent back to Attica.

Sean and Ron relaxed on the ride back to the precinct. The night air was cooler and felt refreshing against their faces. Ron unwrapped a new cigar and lit it. He spoke from the side of his mouth, the cigar held tight in his teeth.

"You know, Cav, some guys go their whole career without ever firing a shot, even some cops who work down here. You've been deflowered,

Cav. You dropped your hammer on somebody for the first time as a cop. Don't let it do a number on your mind. Remember, you only did what you had to do. You handled yourself just fine tonight. I was proud that we're partners. Hell, I'm still hungry. Can you stop for a burger and a beer on the way home?"

Sean was still silently enjoying the compliments. "A cold beer would taste real good about now. We never did eat. I better do all my staying out late before I get married."

"Bullshit, Kid. You just got to train them right from the beginning. Take it from me, I'm an expert. That's why I'm divorced."

Sean became serious for a moment. "You know, Ron, after I'd killed my first Gook in Vietnam, I was worried because I didn't feel anything. There was none of that guilt and remorse and trauma we all hear about and see in the movies. And now, tonight, well it's the same thing. I don't feel bad about shooting that asshole. Don't misunderstand, shooting people doesn't make my dick hard. There's just no emotion there."

Ron took a long thoughtful puff from the cigar. "Cav, we've worked together long enough for me to tell you that your lack of guilt about shooting people who deserve to be shot is a blessing. For a kid who's as concerned and angry about the injustice in the world around you, that useless guilt would probably put you over the edge. It's just too bad that your first police shooting had to be with Superman."

Years later, Sean would wonder about the fate of Clay Hammon during the bloody riot at New York's Attica Prison. Sean was confident that the super tough man would have survived the violent riot, as long as he kept his dick covered.

AUGUST, 1969
VIETNAM

T.J. was in a deep depression. He had been back in Vietnam for almost a full month and was again assigned to the First Marine Regiment. Now, the First was operating from Da Nang. They had a different firebase as their battalion's center of operation. The larger, better-constructed base was only about 50 miles inland from Da Nang.

Most of T.J.'s first tour was up in the mountains near the D.M.Z. He remembered it as being cooler up there. He didn't like the flat, sandy terrain around his new firebase. T.J. hated the ugly, long, hot patrols along rows of dried rice paddies lined by potentially deadly hedgerows and paddy dikes.

T.J. had been promoted to sergeant when he was shipped out. Even though he was only an E-5 "buck" sergeant, he was the platoon sergeant. That position was normally held by staff N.C.O.s, but in 1969, the Marine Corps was painfully short of experienced people.

As the platoon-sized patrol snaked down a worn dirt road with nothing but dried rice paddies on both sides, T.J. took a mental look at the platoon's members. It was all so very different from his first tour. So different, and all of the difference was to the negative. Now there was ugly, racial tension and somebody always was stoned on something. They all knew by then that the U.S. did not intend to win the war. They were going to de-escalate until they could get their people out without it looking like a massive cluster-fuck retreat.

T.J. knew that the platoon's bad morale and piss-poor attitude would cost lives. They didn't want to fight or help each other to stay alive. Most of them wanted to bitch at every order, skate in every way known to a Marine, and smoke their dope. T.J. was self-driven to keep as many of them alive as possible in spite of themselves.

The young white platoon commander was fresh from Officer Candidate School and still very proud of his second lieutenant brown bars. He arrived with the company one week before T.J. joined the outfit. Lt. Klause was a year younger than T.J. and initially seemed more threatened by T.J.'s experience than willing to used his knowledge. Lt. Klause was the type of white man T.J. most detested. He sensed that Klause felt superior to him because he was Black, and that reduced the credibility of anything T.J. suggested. A white squad leader shared with T.J. that once Klause had indicated concern about being "fragged" by a Black platoon member because they could not be trusted. T.J. laughed to himself.

"Brown bar peckerwood, he better stop worryin' 'bout us niggers and concentrate on the N.V.A. If he don't, he won't last long enough to get himself fragged."

The sandy, narrow road was scarred from past battles. Ugly holes on the sides and top of the road told of booby traps that had killed and maimed Marines since '65.

T.J. looked over the long single file of Marines. He snapped at them in a loud voice. "I been tellin' you people, don't bunch up. How many times I gotta tell you? Keep your proper interval. If one of you crybabies hits a booby trap, I don't want to lose a whole squad."

T.J.'s eyes scanned the thick tree line and hedgerow a little more than 100 yards to their right flank like a stalking cat. He silently wished the members of his old squad were with him. "Hell, with Irish, Logs, Yance, Mr. Cool, Fox, I wouldn't be afraid of no Gook-filled tree line," he thought. "Them boys would help me whip this herd into a good platoon. Help keep me alive."

T.J. smiled when he remembered the large C.A.R.E. package he had just received from Irish. The well-secured box contained gum, hard candy in a plastic bag, Tang, Kool-aid, a *Playboy* and a Supreme's cassette tape. "Little white Brother still remembers the creature comforts a Grunt needs while he's in the bush."

The terrible crunching sound of exploding 60mm mortar rounds on the road broke his train of thought. Automatic weapons and rifles opened up on them from the tree line.

Those not hit by the initial ambush fire took cover along the left side of the road which served as a paddy dike. T.J. cursed himself for not hearing the mortar rounds leave their tubes. They were probably set in a paddy bed behind the tree line, and the thick trees and bush broke their sound.

As one Marine dove off the road to cover, he hit the trigger device for a well-concealed booby trap. The N.V.A. had taken an unexploded U.S. 250-pound bomb and converted it into a huge killer mine. Even well buried into the side of the road, the powerful explosion launched soil and bodies in all directions. The roar of the explosion nearly deafened anyone it didn't kill or maim.

T.J. was unhurt. He ran in a low crouch looking for Krause, past the row of survivors.

"Come on, you'd better put out some fire into the tree line. You just lay here feelin' sorry for yourselves, they gonna pick you off one by one."

Most of those unhurt began to return fire. T.J. passed Ace, the first squad's M-79 grenadier. He sat with his legs folded and calmly lobbed the 40mm fragmentation grenades into the tree line. T.J. patted his helmet as he ran past him. "Good work, Ace, keep pouring them in there. I'll try to find you some more ammo if them other M-79 boys are hit."

T.J. found Lt. Krause. He had lost both legs above the knees. A near frantic corpman was attempting to tie off the ugly wounds. Krause was unconscious and out of the fight. What was left of the platoon was T.J.'s now. He moved to the body of the dead radioman. The PRC25 field radio was peppered with shrapnel, but somehow it still functioned. T.J. calmly radioed back to the firebase for help.

The young Lieutenant's map had been shredded along with his legs. T.J. couldn't call in an accurate artillery fire mission without a map. He gave the command post their approximate position. They were sending two helicopter gunships to help suppress enemy fire and identify the exact location for the 105 cannon battery at the firebase. The medevac choppers would be dispatched as soon as they could secure a L.Z. near the ambush site.

T.J. could hear the thud of the HUEY gunship rotors above the gunfire. The pilots radioed that they had a visual on the Marine's position and could see the tree line that was their target. The ships made several passes, spraying the enemy position with rocket and gunfire.

T.J. yelled out to the platoon. "What the hell you waitin' on? Put some LAW rockets into them trees. You savin' them so they can put them in the body bag with you?"

The two chopper gunships made a low pass over the platoon and left the area.

"O.K., get your heads down and your dicks in the dirt. Artillery is on the way. Let's hope them boys workin' the 105s know what they're doin'."

The tree line erupted in rumbling red and orange flashes. The chopper gunships had called the artillery strike right on the money. The savage barrage continued as the large explosions blew trees out of the ground.

The command post told T.J. by radio that a company-sized Reaction Force was en route by choppers. They'd land as soon as the shelling stopped and would join the remainder of his platoon in their move to check the tree line for a body count, weapons, and possible bunkers. His dead and wounded would be taken out by the same choppers that brought in the Reaction Force.

T.J. thanked the voice at the firebase command post. He let the radio handset drop into the bloody sand.

"Fuck all of this, Man. We keep chasing them little Gook cocksuckers until they catch us."

OCTOBER, 1969
DETROIT

The long-awaited transfers to the Motor Traffic Section came through for both of Sean's senior partners. He took some good-humored precinct house kidding about driving both of his partners from the precinct, but the truth was that both men had requested the transfer before Sean had considered being a cop, more than one year before, while Sean was still in Vietnam.

Lt. Max called Sean aside. He told him he was going to make him second man on a crew with Tom Miller. Miller, 22, had been on the job only six months longer than Sean. Lt. Max said he felt Miller and Sean had proven they had the knowledge and good sense enough to work the street together, despite their short time out of the academy.

In November, Tom Miller and Sean Cavanagh became the youngest regular scout-car crew in the entire department. They were fondly called the "kiddy car" by their shift. They were often teased about their obvious enthusiasm in responding to calls, but the men of the shift knew they could always depend on them for backup in the midst of any fray.

Any potential jealousy caused by their arrest statistics was set aside by their consistant willingness to assist other shift members in every way.

Tom and Sean kept their self-praise confined to their private conversations. They knew they were doing an outstanding job, but it was much more self-serving to accept the veterans' constant kidding with their baby-faced charm and any compliments with shy modesty.

Tom and Sean became friends as well as partners. They quickly learned to anticipate the other's actions in any situation.

Tom was a gifted driver. His skill behind the wheel of a speeding police car was unmatched by anything Sean would experience as a cop. Tom did not tire behind the wheel, even after driving an eight-hour shift. By design, he did most of the driving.

Sean was an excellent report writer, so it was a partnership made in police heaven. Their teamwork seemed to work that way with everything they did. The pilot and the author, as they referred to themselves tongue-in-cheek. They had developed something very special to a cop. They had become real partners.

DECEMBER, 1969
GROSSE POINTE

In all the years of attending St. Paul's Church, Sean could never remember it looking more beautiful.

A fresh blanket of snow covered the city and the early December evening was clear and crisp.

Rookie cops had to draw their vacations after the veterans, which normally meant they got what was left. Sean managed the first two weeks of December. He'd be back to work the last two weeks of the month, the prime Winter vacation selection.

Sean waited in the small room just off the altar. He chatted nervously with his brothers and hid a wince of anticipation when the organ music began. Father Pat stopped briefly, said a quick prayer and blessed him.

Sean had a roaring case of the eleventh-hour doubts. He couldn't help but feel he was playing out another predetermined role that someone else had selected for him. He and Lyn had become engaged that

Summer. Now it was the wedding and two weeks at Grampa Kelly's condo in Ft. Myers, Florida, for their honeymoon.

It was like some television rerun. The neat, three-bedroom brick bungalow on McKinney Street. The Olds Cutlass for her. It all seemed as it should be. Except for his refusal to quit the police job, he was doing all the right things. And only Sean himself didn't quite believe he'd see the light sooner or later and go to work for his father.

He tried to tell Father Pat that he had some real doubts and fears that he was not ready to marry. He had only been back from the war a year and he and Lyn often couldn't agree on the color of the sky. He shared with the long-time family priest that he was afraid he cared more about his new career than starting a family. But it was 1969, and despite the sexual revolution, in 1969 a good Catholic couple in love had the choice of only one lifestyle. They got married.

The organ music grew louder. Sean and the men in the wedding party were given the signal. They moved out into the church, next to the altar. Everyone stood, and Sean saw Lyn and her father approach the altar together. He wondered what T.J. would have given him for advice. He knew it wouldn't be a 300-guest wedding.

After the picture-perfect ceremony, the reception was held at the clubhouse of Sean's grandfather's country club.

The food was wedding-reception food, with wedding-reception music, photos, and awkward toasts.

Two days later, Sean and Lyn rested on a warm Ft. Myers beach. Lyn silently planned how she would redecorate the kitchen. Sean silently ached to get back to work, to get back on the streets.

DECEMBER, 1969
VIETNAM

T.J. smiled when he saw he had received a letter from Sean. Inside there were some pictures of the wedding and the reception. T.J. laughed aloud when he read that Sean was glad T.J. was away and couldn't be his best man. Sean told him they wouldn't have let T.J. into the reception at his grandparent's high-brow country club unless he'd have promised to help clear the tables. He laughed again when Sean wrote that T.J. would rather have pictures of the wedding night but would have to settle for the ones he sent him. Then Sean got serious and told T.J. how much he missed him and, as always, told him to keep his head down.

Just before Christmas, T.J. received a package from Sean. It contained everything from gum, hard candy, and music tapes to skin books. T.J. thumbed through one of the books and sucked on a piece of hard candy. He remembered that this was the third Christmas away from home. In '67, he had his favorite squad and his new friend from Motown, Irish. In '68, T.J. and Hawk Man had got drunk and laid in Long Beach. But this year was the worst. He had chosen to be a loner as the platoon sergeant, and he never felt more alone in his life.

T.J. slipped a new tape in his tape player. At least he'd be dry, get some hot chow, a couple of beers. Better than being out in the bush.

T.J. thought of his white preppie upper-crust friend.

"Ol' Irish, he'd have grooved at me bein' his best man an' showin' up at the wedding reception an' shit. Boy always did have balls. Too damn serious. But he always had stones."

MARCH, 1970
DETROIT

Traces of a late Winter snow storm still lingered in the gutters and patches near the buildings where there were permanent shadows.

Sean leaned against the long lobby precinct desk and sipped a cup of coffee. It had been made before the 4 p.m. shift had started. Now at nearly 11 p.m., it was barely drinkable. Tom was upstairs in the men's room. Nature had called him and the crew came into the precinct for a break from the cold damp night.

The veteran cop who was the regular shift desk clerk walked up and slapped Sean on the back. "So, ya had a birthday, hey Kid? Did you decide what you want to be when you grow up?"

The other officers at the desk smiled at Stan's good natured kidding.

Sean's facial expression did not change. "Come on, Stan. Who says I've got to grow up."

The big man pinched Sean on the cheek. "You can't stay a baby-faced boy forever, you know."

Sean grinned when Stan released his grip. "O.K., I want to be like my favorite policeman here. Stan, I want to be like you when I grow up. Old, crabby, and fat."

Stan made a playful grab for Sean, but he escaped. "Come over here, you little shit. I get my hands on you and I'll show you how old I am. I'll twist your little neck for you."

A citizen entered the precinct lobby. Lt. Max had been amused by the friendly exchange, but saw the visitor. "O.K., you two, knock off the horseplay. We've got a customer," he said. The tall Black man of about

40 said he was there to make a missing person report. They directed him to an officer seated at a table in the corner of the lobby who took all walk-in reports.

Tom appeared at the doorway leading to the second floor stairway. He walked up and stood next to Sean at the end of the desk. "Well, I see your eyes are blue again. Did everything come out alright?"

"What, Cav, you want a detailed report on my toilet habits? I promise I washed my hands when I finished."

"You want a cup of coffee before we go back out?"

"You know I don't drink coffee and if I did, I wouldn't drink that stuff. It looks like a cup of crude oil."

Sean took another sip, then tossed the cup in a large trash can. "Nope, crude oil doesn't taste quite as bitter."

"Come on, Partner, let's go back on the street and fight crime and evil. We've only got an hour left in the shift to make this precinct safe."

Sean recovered a breath mint from his pocket to erase the terrible taste left by the coffee. "The only way to make this precinct safe would be to call for a massive air strike and make a parking lot out of it."

"What's that, Marine Corps urban renewal?"

"It would be a lot more effective than any program they're using now."

"Let's go out and try to win their hearts and minds for now."

Tom drove their marked police car slowly along the curb. Sean scanned the shadows and gave the street people who braved the cold damp night the visual once-over.

"So, Cav, how's married life been treating you?"

Sean searched for another breath mint. "Three months, Tommy, what can I say in only three months? I had my own place before I bought the house, so regular sex had never been a problem. I don't know, I guess there are a lot of adjustments when you first start to live with anyone."

"I hear that. The ol' rabbit died a couple months before we graduated from high school. We got married that June and I worked two jobs until I turned 21 and became a cop. Talk about adjustment, we had to live with my folks for almost a year."

"That's a tough way to start a relationship. Hell, we've got a nice house, two cars, money is no real problem and it still isn't easy. I'm kind of a neat freak like you are, and little things like having her make-up all over the bathroom and pantyhose drying on the shower curtains takes adjustment. Tom, except for an occasional romp in the hay, I never slept with anyone on a regular basis my whole life. Hell, I never had to even share a bed with either of my brothers.

"And she's always bitchin' because she's lonely. I can't blame her. I'm taking a couple of part-time classes at Wayne State. I work this shift and she works during the day. We only see each other a few hours a week. I really don't think this marriage started out the way she expected. Even with cops in her family, she still can't believe I don't want to quit and work for my dad."

Their conversation was interrupted by the dispatcher. He sent them, the street sergeants, and two other units to a four-story apartment building on Brainard Street, near Second Avenue. There was a missing three-year-old child.

Sean looked at his watch. "Christ, after 11 p.m. and the parents get around to reporting a three-year-old baby missing. Oh Tommy, I've got a bad feeling about this one. We get missing kid calls every week, but not a three-year-old this late."

They pulled in front of the apartment building and climbed the battered stairs to the third-floor apartment. The man they had just seen in the precinct lobby was describing the child to the sergeants and a Black crew, 13-4, Ed Baines and John Thompson.

Three-year-old Tara Jefferson was last seen on her small, plastic tricycle riding down the apartment building halls at about 7 p.m. She was wearing her favorite bright red party dress and white shoes.

Tara's parents were both frantic. They had four other young children in the small apartment. Tara's father had become involved in a basketball game on their old black and white portable television. Tara's mother was busy with the baby and the family ironing.

Scout 13-13 arrived at the scene. Pete Mayer and Bob Pollock would aid in the search for the missing child.

Sean wondered if he could make such an oversight as a parent. The Jeffersons thought Tara was in her bed. She put herself to bed every night. There was no reason for them to check on her until they went to put their other children to bed and discovered that she was missing.

Sgt. Allard assigned the crews areas to search. The sergeants would stay in the Jefferson apartment to coordinate the search. Mayer and Pollock would check around the exterior of the old apartment building. Baines and Thompson were to check from the second floor to the roof. Sean and Tom searched the first floor and the basement.

Sean and Tom started down the stairs to the first floor. Tara's tricycle sat empty at the end of the hallway. Sean checked the light from his new metal flashlight.

"Oh my. I've got a real bad feeling about this one, Tommy."

Tom checked his light. "It sure as hell looks bad. Maybe we'll get lucky. Maybe she was playing and got tired and crawled into a corner and fell asleep."

They knocked on every apartment door on the first floor. The few people who answered their door had not seen the child that evening. It seemed that everyone in the building knew the "pretty little thing with the red dress," but no one had seen her that day.

Sean knocked on the last door on the first floor. He could hear someone inside unlocking a series of dead bolt and chain locks. The door finally opened and a frail, elderly Black woman stood in the doorway.

"Yes, sir, Mr. Po-lice. What can I do for you all?"

Sean could understand the woman but she reeked of cheap whiskey. "Ma'am, we're looking for a three-year-old little girl in a red dress with white shoes. Have you seen her this evening?"

The old woman leaned hard against the door frame. "Oh sweet Jesus, I see that pretty little thing playing in the halls on her little tricycle 'most every day. Tara, I think her name be. I ain't seen her tonight, Officer. Lord have mercy, how come that chile ain't wif her mama and daddy this hour?"

"They seem like nice folks, Ma'am. They thought she'd gone off to bed."

Tears began to roll down the old woman's weathered cheeks. "Officer, I fear somethin' terrible done happened to that poor little chile."

Sean patted the woman's hand. "Now don't you worry yourself. We'll find her alright. Now you get yourself back inside and rest. I tell you what, I'll stop by and tell you when we've found her, so you don't fret all night."

She removed a handkerchief from the belt of her house dress and wiped her eyes. "Bless you, Officer. I'll pray you find her and she's safe."

Sean felt a burning in the pit of his stomach as she closed the door. There was only one place left for he and Tom to check. The basement.

Sean moved toward the stairway leading down to the apartment building's dark, rat-infested basement. Tom was at the end of the hall talking with a first floor occupant.

Sean hesitated. Every part of his being, every sense, every conscious instinct was telling him not to descend the battered, filthy wooden stairs to the basement. He wanted to leave the building and wait in the relative freshness of the cold night air.

He took two tentative steps and located the light switch. Only a half dozen light bulbs were functioning throughout the large basement area.

For a moment, Sean was frozen at the top of the rotted staircase. His hands became moist, his throat dry. This was different from anything he had ever experienced. He was not fearful that something harmful might happen to him. He was terrified by the thought of what he might find.

He said a brief, silent prayer that the portable police radio on his hip would suddenly announce that the child had been found unharmed. But the radio was as silent as the shadows of the evil-looking basement. He crossed himself and moved down the stairs slowly, one cautious step at a time.

He held his flashlight firmly in his left hand and drew his magnum from its holster with his right. The poorly-placed basement ceiling lights created ugly, unnatural shadows. The only sounds in the basement were created by rats running for cover.

As he reached the concrete floor of the basement, he instinctively checked the area under the staircase. He found the surrealistic image of three-year-old Tara Jefferson. In the dull brown light, partially concealed by a dark shadow, the sight of the little body seemed as if it was from some fever-induced, terrible, screaming nightmare.

The lifeless body of Tara Jefferson hung four feet from the basement floor. An old electric cord was wrapped in a death grip around her throat, the other end tied to a cross beam on the basement ceiling. She was still wearing her red dress, but now it was soiled and blood stained. Her white shoes were nowhere in sight. Even from that distance, Sean could see the child had been brutally sexually molested.

The sight of the dead child was terrible but it neither startled or shocked him. It was if he had expected to find her in some manner of death. He leaned against the wall and fought off a wave of nausea. Sean felt very much alone and had an urgent need not to be the only person with the small corpse. He called out for Tom at full voice.

Tom appeared at the stairway. Halfway down the stairs he stopped. His eyes followed Sean's stare and he observed the dead child. "Oh Christ, just exactly what we were afraid we would find."

Ed Baines had also heard Sean's call for Tom. He camed down the stairs and stopped next to Tom. "Poor little baby, what kinda sick mother fucker would do something like this?"

John Thompson arrived at the doorway. He didn't need to descend the stairs. He could see by the expressions on the other three young officers that they had found the child's body. He called to the others. "I'll get Pete to seal off the basement. I'll go up and tell the sergeants so none of the family comes down here. I'll call it in so the photo and lab guys can come down with Homicide. You know, sometimes I really hate this fuckin' job."

John closed the door and hurried down the hall.

Sean was still leaning against the wall, staring at the child's body. Baines walked down the remainder of the stairs and stood next to Sean. "You find her, Cav?"

Sean merely nodded his head. His eyes never left the child's body.

"You gonna be alright, boy? You're lookin' kinda poorly."

He didn't answer, but continued to stare at the child. He took out a pocket knife from the space between his cartridge carrier and his belt. "Help me cut her down, Tommy."

Tom pushed his police uniform hat onto the back of his head in a gesture of consideration of the decision. In their months working together, they had yet to disagree. "Don't think we should do it, Sean. We leave everything the way it is. Let the lab boys and Homicide . . ."

"Fuck Homicide." Sean had raised his voice. "Let's cut the poor little kid down and cover her up."

"Sean, we'd better not touch her."

Sean walked toward the child's body. "Bullshit. Then I'll do it by myself."

Ed Baines firmly grabbed Sean by the upper arm as he passed, stopping him. "Leave her be, Cav. Do as Tommy says."

Sean glared up at the veteran Black officer. "It's not right letting her hang there like that."

Ed Baines maintained his grip on Sean's arm. "Listen up, boy. You'd better get your head outa your ass. What are you talkin' about, *it ain't right*? Don't be a fool. Was it right some crazy man did this to her? You are the Man, the REAL po-lice, remember? Ain't none of us like to see some poor baby abused and killed this way. But we've got a goddamn job to do, and we're going to do it the right way. This child ain't gonna know if she's left hangin' here until Christmas. Nobody can see her except us. Just maybe, if we don't touch nothin', they can get some evidence to help identify the sick fucker that did this."

Sean glared into Ed Baines' stern and determined face. He slowly closed his pocket knife and slid it back behind the carrier on his belt. By the tone in Big Ed's voice, the status of the little victim's body was not open for any debate. Ed made an effort to ease an awkward moment.

"Cav, why don't you and Tommy check out the rest of the basement. Probably ain't a million-to-one chance the killer is still here, but we better be certain."

Ed released Sean's arm. Sean and Tom made a complete check of the basement. From the disturbed dust on the floor and blood stains, it appeared the actual assault had taken place in an unlit boiler room near the stairway. A child's white shoe lay at the base of the aging boiler.

As Sean searched the empty basement, his mind was filled with a murderous prayer that the child's killer was still down there hiding. He wanted to take revenge on the man who had committed such a horrible injustice to the little girl and her family. The killer now represented all the injustice in his world, every dying, bleeding victim, every shattered, grief-stricken loved one.

The basement was empty. They found no one.

Tom and Sean joined Ed, who was "guarding" the crime scene. John Thompson had joined him.

Ed put his big arm around Sean's shoulder. "It will be your report, Cav. You found the body. We've got everything under control here. Why don't you and Tommy go down to Homicide and start your paperwork. I'll stay here with the child until the people from downtown take over."

Sean looked up at Ed and nodded. He took a brief glance at the child, then silently left the basement with Tom.

Once on the first floor, he had one last task at the old apartment building. He knocked on the door of the old woman. She opened the door. She wept openly and her eyes were red. "Oh Officer, they done told me that sweet little baby is dead. Please, tell me it ain't so."

Sean got a lump in his throat and fought the tearing of his eyes. He remembered Big Ed's words. He was the Man, the po-lice. "I'm so very sorry, Ma'am. I hate to bring you such terrible news, but I promised I'd come back and tell you when we found her."

"Did you find her body, Officer?"

"Yes, Ma'am."

"Lord Jesus. Did some crazy man touch that baby?"

"I'm sorry, Ma'am, I can't say. I must be going."

The elderly lady clutched Sean's hand. She reached into the wide pocket of her house dress and took out a nearly empty pint bottle of whiskey. "Here, boy, you take yourself a big swallow of this here, it'll make you feel a bit better."

Sean took two large gulps of the warm whiskey from the bottle. "Thank you, Ma'am. One thing for certain, it won't make me feel any worse."

As Tom increased the distance between them and the horror of the ugly apartment building, Sean began to feel gradually better. By the time they reached the Homicide offices, he felt like himself. He was still upset, but he had regained his self-control.

Sean's report complete, he stared out of the window at the county jail building across Clinton Street from police headquarters. He crushed his empty styrofoam coffee cup and lobbed it into an empty waste basket. Ed walked up to him and watched the activity in the street below.

"No matter how hard I try, it still doesn't make any sense. I saw terrible things in Vietnam, Ed. But what kind of God damn sick animal could do that to some little kid?"

Ed continued to stare out of the window. "The kind of animal we have to deal with every day in them streets, Cav. When we get back to the precinct and check out, let's talk for a spell, jus' you and me."

Less than an hour later, the officers involved were signed out and leaving the precinct station for their personal vehicles in the parking lot. Sean's Triumph was nearest the building. He started the engine and turned on the car's heater and radio.

A minute later, Ed Baines slid in the other side. He carried a six pack of canned beer. He gave one to Sean, kept one for himself, and left the other four outside the car to remain cold.

"I keep these in my trunk at all times for nights such as this. You have a day like this one, you know, a real mother fucker, and by the time you get done with the paperwork, ya can't buy a legal drink in the whole city."

Sean took a long series of swallows. "Thanks, Ed. Damn, it tastes good. Nectar from the gods."

Ed located the seat adjustment handle and carefully put the Triumph's seat all the way back. "Well, I ain't no detective yet but I can bet that your bride ain't no 6'4"."

They made small talk until mid-way through their second beer. Ed turned and half leaned against the door so he could look clearly at Sean as they spoke. A smaller man, Sean was able to lean between the seat back and the steering wheel to face Ed. "You ain't no two-beer lightweight drinker, are you, Cav?"

"Come on, Ed, I'm Irish. Would I insult you and ask if you had naturally curly hair?"

"O.K. Cav, here it is. We've worked the same shift since you got out of the academy. Truth is, you seem sincere, and with less than a year on the street, you're already a good cop, despite that baby face. Everybody on the shift knows they can depend on you, no matter what. You try to treat the citizens right. I seen you come down on some street Brothers, but you do the same to street Honkies, maybe even harder on them. Square business, Cavanagh, I think that you ain't no phony. You're a for-real guy. On the one hand, you ain't some crybaby liberal wimp, and on the other you're no sadistic bigot.

"What I'm saying is, you got it all, Boy. You are book-smart, street-smart, well-liked, and respected. You could go a long way with this outfit some day. Your only problem is that you gotta lighten up. Cav, you're trying too damn hard, you know, pushin'. You ain't never gonna be Black, you realize that? Hell, you wouldn't want to be. Next best thing down here is to just be a fair white cop. Just do your job, then let it go, Man.

"You've got the smarts and the guts, but too much heart will make you soft. Just don't care too much. Your only real problem is that you expect too much from these folks down here. You expect them to kiss your ring and say 'thank you, Mr. White Po-lice for giving a flying fuck!'"

"It ain't gonna happen, Boy. These people been this way long before you were born. And, most will be this way long after we're dead and buried. Remember though, we're all they got. We can't go crying for them, we've got to be strong. Let them liberal wimps do the crying. We've got to be strong and keep our heads and be there when they need us. But, remember, you're still different from them. You believe in somethin', believe you're helpin'. If you let carin' eat you up, they got the advantage. If it comes to that, go buy a farm.

"Last thing, you gotta stop thinkin' that everything that happens out here only happens to you personally. Be a cop, not some half-ass liberal Nam Vet lookin for all the goddamn answers to life. Son, you don't even know the fuckin' questions. Like that baby tonight, I got me one at home 'bout the same age. White boy ain't even got no babies yet you dare think you the only one hurtin', only one who cares?

"I really like you, Cav, but don't you ever again insult me the way you did tonight. Like you care more for that little dead Black darlin' than me. You really want to be the Man down here? Then start actin' like the po-lice all the time. Be as cool and professional at the scene of a baby murder as I've seen you at a gun fight. Gotta be strong all the mother-fuckin' time in this job. When the people need us, we gotta be there for them." Ed paused.

"I'm sorry, Cav. Got myself all wound up. Here, take the last beer for the ride home. I laid a ton of shit on you because I like you, and as a work friend, I want to help you. Sort it out. Use what you think is true and ignore the rest. Either way, we stay friends. I'm damn glad you and Tommy and guys like Bruce Munier are on the shift. Damn sight better than all them old funky bigots that were still on the street when I come on the job."

The men shook hands firmly and Ed quickly left for his own car. Sean wondered just how much of Ed's lecture had been meant for him, and how much had been meant for Ed.

MARCH, 1970
VIETNAM

T.J. stood alone in the center of his platoon's night defensive positions. He nodded to himself in approval. The fighting holes were well spaced. His people had an excellent field of fire down the steep slope of the barren hill. The platoon was supported by two M-60 machine gun crews and two 60mm mortar teams from the weapons platoon.

T.J. lit a cigarette and looked at his people, still busy putting the finishing touches on their positions for the night.

"Full moon tonight, real nice. Come on up the hill to get us, you Gook bastards. We got somethin' for ya."

He looked over the assorted faces of the young men in his platoon. He had just turned 22. He was the old man of the platoon. Everyone else was 18 or 19. Even their new boot lieutenant was only 21.

T.J.'s best squad leader approached him at a brisk pace. Frisco was a handsome white kid with a mat of short blond hair. He was from the Bay area and reminded T.J. of Yance.

"I'm sorry, T.J., I don't mean to bother you with this bullshit, but I've got a real problem."

T.J. took a long drag from his smoke. "Don't fret none, Frisco, problems come with the territory. Hell, that's why I make so much money as a platoon sergeant, so I can solve problems. Free food, tools, travel, get to meet the interesting natives. A man has to do something for all them benefits."

"It's that little Soul Brother in my squad, Bad News. He is constantly jerking with me and bitchin' and not doing his share. Most of the time I can work around it, but not now. We've been in the bush over two weeks now. We draw the listening post again tonight. Everyone in the squad has done it once, some twice. Shit, I've done it three times to avoid the hassle. He flat-ass refuses to go tonight. He dressed me down in front of the whole squad. He insists I'm picking on him because he's Black. T.J., I swear, no other Black dudes in my squad have ever bitched. I'm telling you, T.J., man to man, I never fucked with him because he's Black. I've never fucked with him."

T.J. chain lit another cigarette. "Frisco, you don't hafta explain yourself to me. You treat your people fair, all of them. I've about had enough of that little maggot myself. It's about time I had a long talk with the little turd. Bad enough he gives you some lip. When it's in front of the squad, that's going too far."

T.J. and Frisco walked together to the area on the hillside where the squad was assembled. T.J. thought back to the first time he had met the nasty little Black Marine. A small group of platoon members had been talking together back at the firebase. Someone noticed him strolling up the dirt path between the company's tents. He carried his gear in one hand, head cocked to the side, the other arm swung freely with each stride. He had reminded T.J. more of a street nigger on a stroll to some poolhall than a Marine replacement reporting to his new unit.

Someone had said, "Here comes bad news." The prediction was correct and had become his nickname as well as his reputation.

Willie Peoples of inner-city Cleveland, Ohio, became known as Bad News. Peoples grooved on his new, tough street name. It was far better than the street name he had secretly owned on the streets of Cleveland: Little Bit.

T.J. and Frisco found Bad News resting alone in a fighting hole. He had his flack jacket and jungle jacket off. Instead of his helmet or a bush hat, he wore a red, black and green striped Afro-American head band. He had a black carved wood fist strung around his neck with a boot lace. It nearly concealed his dogtags. He raised his right fist to T.J. in the Afro-American salute. "Say, Sar-gent, what's happenin'? I see ol' white meat went runnin' to tell on me."

"You are what's happenin', Bad News. Frisco says you outright refuse to go out on the listening post tonight. Refuse? I got a hot flash for you, mother fucker. Look around. You ain't back on the block in Cleveland. I understand that it's past your turn for an L.P., and I say you're going."

Bad News began to bob his head as he spoke. He had a sarcastic grin on his face. His contempt for everyone was obvious.

"Ah, that's a roust and jive bullshit, Sarge. The Chuck been shittin' on me since the day I got here 'cause I'm Black."

T.J.'s posture seemed threatening. "Bad News, you're the biggest skate artist I've ever known in the Corps. I'm tellin' you that you are going to start doin' your share. Your skatin' days are over."

T.J. looked at the members of the squad that had gathered. "O.K., men, since we started this here operation in the bush, how many L.P.s you all been on?"

The other squad members, both Black and white held up one, two or three fingers. All but Bad News had taken at least one turn at the dreaded, potentially-dangerous duty.

"Well, look it there, little Brother. It does seem that it's your time at bat. You're up tonight."

Bad News was still bobbing his head. "Ain't no way, Sarge. You can rap that lifer Uncle Tom shit at me all day. I ain't gonna risk my life any more than is absolute necessary for that peckerwood president and his racist war."

"Stow away the jive, Bad News. Don't need it out here. You make it back to the world, you lay that rap down to people dumb enough to believe you. You talk some heavy shit, Bad News, but I'm thinkin' you got yourself a paper asshole. I've seen you in fire fights. Everyone else is puttin' out rounds and you laying on your rifle covering your head like some old mamasan. Even when a Black Marine gets hit, you never move to help him. I do believe you usin' that militant jive rap to cover the fact that you ain't got the balls to be no real Marine."

Bad News clenched his fists. He had been insulted in front of the same men he'd been attempting to intimidate for months.

"You all wrong, Sar-gent Oreo. I know I shouldn't be here fightin' Nixon's war. The one and only reason I'm here is 'cause I got busted doin' a drug store, and it was the Marines or prison."

T.J. shook his head in disgust. "How you think I got here, nigger? Where you think I'm from, Cape fuckin' Cod? Detroit judge do the same to me back in '67. But when I come to Nam my first tour, it didn't take me no time to realize the Gooks was my enemy here, not white boys."

"That's all bullshit, Sarge. I oughta be back in Cleveland offin' the pigs, than here getting jerked over by a honkie squad leader."

T.J. moved even closer and now towered over the small young man. "Oh, I see how it is. We get in a fire fight and you are too scared to even shoot back, but back in Cleveland you'll have the balls to hide in the shadows and shoot unsuspecting po-lice. I've seen you on night ambush. Still didn't know it was your style."

"You tellin' me I ain't got the balls to kill pigs when I get back?"

"Maybe you do. It takes a real man to hide and shoot at two po-lice who might just be sittin' doing a report. One thing, Bad News, you might get you a surprise you fuck with the po-lice when you finish your tour. Word tell that most of them old fat bigoted honkie po-lice we seen growin' up are bein' replaced by a tough batch of new boys, Black and white. Lots of Nam Vets ridin' those streets in po-lice cars now. Ain't exactly like before."

"Well, well Sar-gent Uncle Tom. You an expert 'bout everything. How you know so much about big city po-lice?"

"My main man from my first tour is a Detroit Po-lice. I tell you what, little man, you ever try an' fuck with him, you'd wish you was back here with us, fightin' Gooks."

"Ain't a pig alive, white, Black, Vet, none, that worry me. I'm tired a talkin' 'bout it. I tol' you, I ain't going on no listening post, an' no way you can make me. You know, Sarge, you gotta be careful if you walkin' around, especially after dark. I hear some officers and N.C.O.s been havin' terrible accidents. You know, like walkin' up on live grenades."

T.J.'s body movement was so rapid that it even startled Frisco. T.J. had wheeled his M-16 from his shoulder and held it pointed menacingly in Bad News' face. "Listen up, you little lowlife cocksucker. You been nothing but trouble since the sorry day you joined the platoon. Everyone's had to walk extra point, do extra L.P.s and other shit details 'cause you won't do your share. You think you can threaten to frag me an' walk away? I'll blow your nappy head all over that fightin' hole. We'll fire some rounds into those trees at the bottom of the hill and say a sniper greased you. Sorry about that, Mr. Bad News."

Bad News was visually shaken. "You couldn't do that, Sarge. Not in front of all these witnesses you couldn't."

"You mean these men you been shittin' on for a month? I don't see no witnesses. Frisco, you see any witnesses?"

"Sure don't, T.J. Not a one in sight."

The squad members were silent. Some silently hoped T.J. would shoot him and give them one less worry in their lives.

T.J. broke into a sadistic grin. "You know, Bad News, the thing about fraggin', it can work either way on the chain of command. You want to waste me because I expect you to do your fair share. I'm way more motivated. I'll do you so I ain't got to worry about your nasty Black ass. I got that will to survive. You survive by laying on the ground like an old woman. I survive by makin' the threat disappear."

Bad News began to wave his hands in front of his face. "Hey, O.K., Man, I'll do the goddamn listening post like Frisco said. I don't need this shit, man. I didn't ask to be sent here. I don't need no rifle jammed in my face from some hard-ass sergeant."

T.J. lowered his rifle. "Man, look around you for once. How many of the rest of us do you think asked to be here?"

The full moon made it a very bright night. The cloudless sky made it possible to read by moonlight.

At about midnight, an M-60 machine gun position opened fire on a running figure on the hillside, above the line of trees where the four-man listening post was positioned at the base of the long hill.

The 60mm mortars put up some flares but nothing else was observed. The Lieutenant called in the listening post for their safety, in case the man shot at was the advance probe for an N.V.A. ground assault.

T.J. was sleeping in the make-shift platoon C.P. made of poncho liners. Frisco crawled next to T.J. and carefully awakened him. "T.J., you better come quick, I think we got some real trouble."

T.J. grabbed his helmet and rifle and followed Frisco. "What's the deal. Shit, it's too damn bright for a Gook assault. We could hold off a whole fuckin' N.V.A. battalion from up here. We've called in the listening post. What's the problem, Frisco?"

"Damn, T.J. It's the listening post I'm talking about. Little Ski took his fire team down into the treeline at dusk. They get set up, and sure as shit, Bad News tells Little Ski to take a hike and he skyed out. Last they saw him he was moving back up the hill. Little Ski and the other two lay chilly for a few hours and don't hear nothin' moving in the trees or up the hill. Then, around midnight the M-60 shoots something between them and the platoon."

T.J. carefully looked down the long, steep moonlit hill slope. "Well, I'm not about to compromise the entire platoon's position to go lookin' for one sandbagger. We'll look for him at first light. It's alright, Frisco, ain't nothin' you done wrong. Go on back to your people; 50 percent watch the rest of the night."

The following morning, the stained, lifeless body of Willie "Bad News" Peoples was located approximately halfway down the slope. The machine gun fire had caught him in the throat and the chest. By the amount of blood it appeared that he had lived for a while after being hit. The throat wound stopped him from calling for help.

The Lieutenant approached T.J. and the other men gathered around the body. "Damn it to hell, Sergeant. Is this the man from the listening post you told me about?"

"Yes, Sir, Lieutenant. This time the boy went skatin' on the wrong pond."

"What do I call this in my report? Is this listed as a 'killed by friendly fire' death?"

T.J. covered the body with a poncho liner. "Best to call him just another Marine K.I.A., Lieutenant. Wouldn't be fair to the platoon to call the killing of that little mother fucker 'from friendly fire,' even if it was our own."

T.J. walked back to the platoon C.P. alone. Now he felt he knew exactly how Irish had felt when the bully Spike had been wasted after their brief but violent confrontation. A confrontation which would have continued with unknown results if Spike had not been vaporized by a mortar round. He remembered what Irish had said about it, and it fit his feelings exactly. "Sorry about that, Bad News, but not too sorry."

8

August, 1970—December, 1970

AUGUST, 1970
DETROIT, MICHIGAN

It was one of those Summer days that Detroiters wished they could bottle up and use again in mid-February, when the Michigan Winter had their spirits and resistance down. The air felt mild and fresh. A pleasant breeze from the river and Lake St. Clair had removed any hint of smog, even from the heart of the city.

Sean and Tom moved up toward West Grand Boulevard for a change of pace. Two hours in their regular assigned area was more than enough at any one stretch.

The area designated for 13-5 was bordered by Mack Avenue to the south, Woodward Avenue to the west, the Ford Freeway to the north, and the Chrysler Freeway to the east. In 1970, it was still one of the toughest areas in the city.

Tom drove their new blue and white Ford sedan. The new police chief wanted to change the image from the black Fords with bold gold letters. The new cars were said to look "friendly." The officers couldn't help but wince when they saw "Protectors of Liberty" printed across each trunk. At least they were not forced to wear "Cab Driver" hats like their brother officers in Chicago.

Tom drove past the G.M. building with the specific intent of he and Sean doing some serious girl watching. There seemed to be hundreds of attractive young women working in the office buildings around West Grand Boulevard and Second Avenue.

Sean adjusted his aviator sunglasses. "Oh my, look at the legs on the lady in the blue dress. Tommy, take me to the precinct for a cold shower. They go all the way up and make an ass of themselves."

"Shame on you, boy. You're a newly-married man."

"Yea, well I may be on a diet, but I can still enjoy the hell out of the menu."

"You better cool down there, stud. It's a good thing those lusting blue eyes of yours are hidden by the sunglasses. That young lady might file charges against you for mopry and oogling with intent to grope."

Sean lowered his glasses to the bridge of his nose. "Come on now, Tommy, is this the face of someone who would misbehave?"

Tom merely shook his head and rolled his eyes.

The dispatcher dramatically changed their playful mood. "Thirteen-9 and cars in Thirteen, Second and Collingwood, at the market. Hold-up in progress."

Had they not been on their sight-seeing tour, they would have been too far from the scene to respond.

Sean turned on the blue overhead emergency light. "That's what I get. God is punishing me for driving up here to have immoral thoughts."

Tom skillfully moved through the traffic and raced north on Second Avenue.

At 80 mph they were only seconds away from the small ghetto market. They worked as a team. Sean watched the cross streets for approaching cars, not just a passenger but the co-pilot. Sean drew his .357 magnum with his right hand, and clutched the door handle across his body with his left. The instant the vehicle stopped, Sean would be out of the car, covering their few seconds of extreme vulnerability, while getting out of the car.

The emotions of the officers inside the speeding car would be nearly impossible to explain to someone who had not experienced them. Both young men realized they might launching themselves toward extreme danger. There was anticipation of the unknown. There was an addictive adrenaline rush. But there was no fear.

The small storefront market was mid-block, in a row of small shops. Tom pulled the police car to an abrupt stop approximately 100 feet south of the market's front door. Sean turned off the emergency light and the vehicle was out of view from inside the market.

Sean was out of the car and he aimed toward the market, covering Tom's exit from the car. They quickly moved up against an abandoned storefront, two doors south of the market.

Scout 13-9, with Bruce Munier and Stan Kaminski, pulled to a stop directly behind their vehicle. (The Fire Department's new Emergency Medical Service was still months away from being operational.) Thirteen-nine was a station wagon with two stretchers in the back for emergency medical transportation. Both men ran up next to where Tom and Sean were standing.

Revolvers drawn, the four men gracefully covered each other and advanced toward the front of the market like a skillfully-choreographed dance troupe.

Tom went to his hands and knees and carefully peeked into the inside of the small market through the bottom lower corner of the front window. A moment later, he moved and sat on the sidewalk, his back against the wall.

"It's a real hold-up. Looks bad. The robber is still in there with about half a dozen people. Looks like he's alone. He's got everyone face down on the floor. Big black dude in a red shirt. He's about 25, holding a big, long-barrel revolver; a .38, maybe larger. He's a real space cadet. He is slapping people around and looks stoned right out of his gourd. It looks like he's just staying in there to mess over the people. Everyone inside is Black. It doesn't figure."

Bruce quietly informed the dispatcher that they had an actual robbery in progress and 13-5 was with them. With afternoon traffic and the busy precinct crews, it might be minutes before additional help could reach the scene.

Tom crawled over for another quick look, then moved back. "That asshole is like a bomb about to go off. He may just stay in there beating on those people until he kills one or all of them. We can't wait. I know it's risky, but we've got to go in and take him down before he flips out."

There was no debate. The other three officers simply reacted.

Tom and Sean would quickly enter through the open door, unannounced. Bruce and Stan would do what they could to cover their entry from the sidewalk just outside the store.

Tom and Sean positioned themselves to run inside. "O.K., Cav, they're all at the rear of the market. Once inside the doorway, you move to the right, I'll go left. Be careful, Partner. This fucker is crazy. The only advantage we have will be surprise."

Sean nodded and gave Tom the "thumbs up" sign.

The two officers sprang to their feet and ran through the open doorway. Sean located the gunman with the red shirt at the rear of the store. Their eyes met for an instant. The gunman's black eyes were glassy but his expression was deadly cold. His crazed look drove a shudder of apprehension through Sean's body.

Tom and Sean were bringing their weapons into position to fire, while they shouted verbal commands to the man to surrender. He seemed neither startled nor surprised by their quick entry. He had calmly raised his large revolver and fired three shots at Sean and Tom as they entered.

Sean dove for cover, crashing into a display and rolling on the floor, concealed by some shelves. Tom managed to fire a single shot in the direction of the robber, then took cover behind the cash register counter to the left of the doorway.

Outside the market, Bruce and Stan hugged the sidewalk, keeping below the front windows. Sean mumbled to himself as he crawled to his knees and readied himself to return fire. He heard Tom's voice from behind the cash register. "So much for surprising him before he could really hurt someone. Now we're really fucked."

Sean firmly clutched his magnum with both hands and struggled to his feet. He located the man with the red shirt and swung his revolver to his target. He began to squeeze off a shot but stopped a millisecond before the revolver discharged. The gunman had picked up a four-year-old boy from the floor. He had been forced to lay face down with the other hostages. He had entered the store with his mother just before the robbery. The gunman held the little Black boy around the waist with his left arm, the gun in his right hand. The child's body shielded the majority of his torso.

Tom was bent over the cash register counter, using it like a shooting bench rest. Bruce moved into the doorway, his revolver pointed toward the gunman.

The gunman had been holding his gun to the child's head. He moved it and fired a shot at Bruce, still in the doorway. The shot narrowly missed, and Bruce retreated. The gunman quickly returned his gun barrel to the child's head.

"You leave that doorway open, man, 'cause me an' this little sucker is walkin' outa here," he shouted.

Sean cocked the hammer of his revolver and took careful aim at the gunman's head, just above the struggling, protesting child. "Give it up. There is still no one hurt. Put down the boy and the gun, and we'll all walk out of here alive. There is no need to make this any worse."

The gunman pushed the barrel of his gun even harder against the child's head. The little boy screamed in discomfort. "Fuck you, honkie. I ain't jivin' you pigs. Everybody get outa my way. I'm walkin' outa here or I swear I'll off this little nigger right now in front of his mama."

Sean carefully held his aim. He felt the frustration and apprehension building. They had lost control of the situation, at least for the moment.

"We're coming out. Every pig stay outa the way or the boy dies." The child cried and struggled. The officers worried that the little boy's natural resistance was about to cost him his life in the hands of the crazed junkie.

"This is it, pigs. We're outa here."

The gunman started to walk slowly toward the front of the market up the center aisle. With the child as his human shield, it was a very dangerous stand-off. The officers, including Bruce, who had entered the market and stood near Sean, were exposed to the gunman's fire but would not be able to return fire without great risk to the child. Sean had decided that he would not let the man leave the store with the boy. He would chance a well-aimed head shot as he neared the door.

As the gunman slowly inched his way up the aisle, the child reached out and took hold of a stationary support beam. The man's next careful step created a slight tug from the boy's grip on the vertical beam, causing him to lose his grip around the child's waist. The man lost his hold and the boy fell hard onto the floor. The gunman started to bend down to pick up the child again, raising his revolver to protect himself from the police.

There was a ear-splitting barrage of police gunfire. Sean, Bruce, and Tom let loose with a volley of gunshots at the same moment. Over the roar of the firing revolvers in the narrow confines of the small market, Sean could hear himself screaming at the gunman, "Sorry about that, you rotten son-of-a-bitch."

Most of the police gunfire struck the junkie. His posture was contorted as his body was twisted, lifted from the floor, then slammed into a metal potato-chip rack. The unconcious man and the metal rack crashed to the floor amidst the chorus of cursing policemen and screaming civilians, still face down on the market floor.

The gunman's motionless body lay twisted in the prongs of the metal rack in a macabre position. He seemed to be bleeding from everywhere.

Sean quickly moved to check on the condition of the little boy, who was still crying and near hysteria but otherwise not harmed. Sean holstered his revolver and gently carried the boy to his mother, who was also crying. He held the child until the young Black woman was in control enough to hold her child. The woman threw her other arm around Sean and hugged him tightly around the back of his neck. For a brief moment, he was afraid she might injure the boy pressed between them. "Mr. Police, you done saved all our lives. I swear, that crazy nigger would have killed us all. He was talkin' 'bout what he was gonna do to the womens 'fore he shot us dead. He was outa his fool head."

Despite the deadly exchange of gunfire, only the gunman had been injured. Bruce carefully inspected his motionless body. He reholstered his revolver and shook his head in disbelief.

"I'll be go to hell, you can't kill these damn junkies. He's still alive. Cut off his head and hide it until the sun goes down. Stan, get a stretcher. He's breathing. We'd better convey A.S.A.P."

They placed the gunman's body on a stretcher and began to wheel him out. Bruce spoke to Sean under his breath. "He is shot to pieces. Massive head wounds. If he does pull through, he'll be a veggie."

The store was now full of uniform and plain clothes officers. The ex-hostages called out insults and obscenities at the body as it was quickly wheeled by them. "You all can let that funky devil die. He ain't right in his head. Mother fucker do that-a-way to my poor little chil'. I hope he dies an' goes straight to hell."

They loaded the stretcher into the back of 13-9 and watched it speed off toward Detroit General Hospital. The street sergeants ordered Tom and Sean to go directly to the Homicide Section to fill out their statements.

On the way Downtown, Sean leaned far back in the seat and put his feet on the dashboard. He rubbed his eyes and then slid the brim of his police hat over his eyes. He was still coming down from his adrenaline high but wanted to appear as calm as Tom seemed to be. "You know, Tommy, I still can't get used to the way it works out here. This crazy junkie asshole is about to murder a store full of innocent people. We show up and he nearly shoots three cops and a little boy. We're forced to blow his ass all over the market, then we rush to put him on a stretcher and get him to the hospital to save his life. At least in Nam the Gooks had the good manners to take care of their own wounded after they tried to grease you."

Tom grinned, "You read the words on our trunk. Man, we're the 'Protectors of Liberty.' Blast them, then save them. That's what you do when you're protecting liberty. Besides, from what I hear, you Marines weren't much for taking prisoners, wounded or not."

"It cuts down on a lot of unnecessary bullshit. No prisoners. It's a philosophy we might want to consider out here in the street. I think it's an interesting concept."

"You and your interesting concepts. This one is almost as bad as your idea for air strike urban renewal."

"Think of it, Tommy, a B-52 arc-light mission on Third Street, south from Canfield. On that street, they wouldn't kill an innocent by-stander. There are none."

"Do us both a favor, Cav. I know you're just kidding, but don't mention your concepts to the Homicide dicks or Internal Affairs guys when we get Downtown. They might not realize you're being sarcastic and think you're some sort of crazy bigot."

"I'm no bigot. There are a lot of white assholes on Third Street too."

"Cute. Save the stand-up comic routine until we get back to the precinct."

"You know me, Tommy. Hell, my knees are still shaking. This whole Mr. Cool joking around is just bullshit. It's like whistling past the graveyard, Partner, and I've really become quite good at it."

The officers who had fired at the gunman were isolated and had to wait for the attorney furnished by the Detroit Police Officers' Association, the police union, prior to statements and any formal questioning.

The first call from the hospital emergency room listed the gunman in very critical condition. He was identified as William Ray Howes, 25, of Detroit. Howes had an extensive criminal record and he was out on parole.

After the attorney and the union representative arrived, the numerous statements and forms were started. With half a dozen supportive Black witnesses to verify the gunman's violent actions, there was no cause for concern about accusations of wrongdoing.

Bruce and Sean had finished their reports and drank coffee in an empty office while waiting for Tom. Bruce stared down at the black liquid in his cup. He frowned and was pensive. "Sean, do you feel it too?"

"What, is the Earth moving?"

"No, damn it. I'm serious. I'm afraid it's happening to us too. We're starting to change like the others. We're getting hateful and bitter. Back at that market, we weren't professional law officers, we were avenging angels. He forced us to fire, but I know in my heart that the three of us wanted to kill him. We are supposed to do our jobs out there in an objective manner."

Sean took a sip of coffee.

"For Christ's sake, Bruce, how objective can you be when a gunman tries to kill a little boy, two of your friends, and you? Don't be so tough on yourself. Don't be afraid to feel normal emotions. They expect us to control our anger and fear. *Control*, not eliminate."

"But Sean, I was actually disappointed when I realized he was still alive. If young white cops like you, Tommy, and I let the streets change us, we'll be no different than those old veteran coppers we all detest so because of their 'I don't give a shit' attitudes. Worse, the street slime will bring us down to their level. Then we'll be no better than they are. I'm not sorry we shot that gunman. We were forced to shoot him. I just don't like the way I felt about it."

"O.K., Bruce, you have a point. But I still believe our expectations of ourselves must be realistic. We spend our initial weeks after the academy learning to build emotional walls around our mind to keep our sanity amidst this madness. I use poor-taste humor, cynical cracks, and macho cliches. We've got to walk the line between being heartless killers or walking emotional time bombs. So, you got personally involved and angry at an asshole with a gun. Fuck it, Bruce. It don't mean nothin', as we use to say in Nam."

The Black Homicide Detective Sergeant seated nearest them answered the phone. He spoke for a few moments and hung up the receiver. "Hey, you men from 13, that was a call from the hospital. Your boy just passed into the other world. You know the drill, all three on suspension until after the review board. Hang by your home phones."

Bruce looked across the table at Sean. "Like in Nam, Cav? Fuck it, doesn't mean anything? Really?"

Sean finished his coffee and tossed the cup away. There was a long, awkward pause. "So the asshole died. What do you want from me, Bruce? Am I now supposed to say something profound or feel some remorse? Will you feel better about me as a man and a partner if I cry or puke or bang my head on the desk? I'll always put my life on the line for you, Pal, but don't hold your breath for some profound, professional statement. I know what's eating at you. I've been there, and I've learned to live with the paradox. You feel real guilty about not feeling guilty. Every bit of your conscious mind tells you that you should feel bad for greasing that asshole and you don't. You're one hell of a guy, Bruce, but you're only human. Save all that feeling-bad energy for when a copper or an innocent victim gets killed."

"You are probably right, Cav, thanks. It puts things in a different light."

"Bruce, a few months ago a cop I really liked gave me some advice. When he was finished, I realized everything he had said was as much for his benefit as for mine. I'm telling you, Bruce, is it was the same thing tonight. I only wish I took advice half as well as I give it."

AUGUST, 1970
VIETNAM

T.J. walked alone up the sandy road in the center of the ugly Marine firebase. He placed a brief letter he had just finished writing to Sean in the outgoing mail drop.

Somehow T.J. knew he would finish the last weeks of his second tour unharmed. He felt confident that he would walk up the ramp of the Freedom Bird without a scratch. Thirteen months of ambushes, booby traps, snipers, rocket attacks, and firefights would not injure him physically. He was certain that the Gooks couldn't hurt him this tour.

With no conscious fear, T.J. had time to concentrate on all that was wrong with his fellow Marines and their collective attitudes. He was frustrated and outraged by the futile waste from their fighting tactics, with meaningless operations out in the bush, and deadly, nonproductive patrols to nowhere for nothing. He had become cynical and bitter about the only thing that had ever given him purpose, the Marine Corps.

Frisco ran up to where T.J. was walking. T.J. was pensive. He walked with his hand down deep in the large trouser pockets of his jungle fatigues. Frisco was out of breath.

"Hey, T.J., I've been looking all over this stinkin' firebase for you. Top Sgt. Jimenez wants to talk to you. He wants you at the battalion Admin tent A.S.A.P."

"Thanks for huntin' me down, Frisco. Any idea what the Top wants? Think it's bad news from home?"

Frisco offered T.J. a cigarette. "Can't be sure, T.J. I didn't see any Red Cross people or a chaplain. I heard he's been doing the re-enlistment rap with everyone who's getting short. Watch out, T.J., ol' Top Jimenez is gonna try and make a lifer out of you."

T.J. lit the cigarette and took a couple of quick drags before his meeting with the Battalion's senior Staff N.C.O. "Square business, Frisco, if this lousy war was over, I would probably stay in the Corps. All the crybaby, racist dopers would then muster out, and the Corps ain't a bad alternative to them Detroit streets for a Black boy from the ghetto. But damn, I'm only 22 and this is my second tour already. I nearly lost my leg first tour. My whole platoon was wiped out, Tet of '68. If I re-up, they'll keep sending me back to this place until the fuckin' Gooks finally succeed in killin' me."

T.J. did the best he could to square away his uniform as he walked to the Admin tent. He buttoned all of his pockets, zipped up his flak jacket and stuffed his dogtags back inside his shirt. He knocked on the wooden tent pole at the large canvas tent's entrance.

"Enter."

The short, thick Mexican-American veteran Marine First Sergeant sat up straight in his chair behind the field desk. "Sgt. Johnson, it's good to see you again. Please, have a seat. The smoking lamp is lit. You'll find a butt can on the deck under the desk."

T.J. lit a cigartte from a fresh carton he had just received from Sean. He sat at attention in the small chair, the butt can held between his knees so that not so much as an ash fell onto the plywood floor.

He watched the first sergeant thumb through his thick personnel folder. Jimenez grinned and his head nodded slightly. He obviously enjoyed what he was seeing in the file. "Sgt. Johnson, as I'm certain you have already determined, I've called you here to discuss your career as a Marine. Your first enlistment is drawing to a close, and I'd like to take some time to discuss your options.

"Since this is your second tour, I would not recommend a tour extension unless you requested it. But with your outstanding service record, I do believe you should consider re-enlisting. I know with the terrible turnover in junior officers, you commanded your platoon a great deal of time over the past year. I'm certain that an officer's commission would not be an unrealistic consideration if you re-enlist. If you join for another six years, I am in a position to guarantee you a promotion to staff sergeant and a pick of any duty station for a year."

T.J. sat at attention. He stared directly at the veteran Marine seated across the field desk from him. "After my year at a choice duty station, then what happens, Top? Where do I go then?"

"What do you mean, Johnson?"

"It's cool, I make staff, jerk off for a year State-side or Japan, then bingo, back in the Nam for another 13 months as an 03 Grunt platoon sergeant."

"Johnson, there is no guarantee that you would draw another Vietnam tour."

"No? O.K., Top, then guarantee me that I won't. Write it as part of the re-enlistment contract that I don't get another tour in this shit hole and I'll sign it right now."

"Damn it, Johnson, this is the Marine Corps, and you are a damn fine Marine. I can't give you a written guarantee like that. We go where we're told. That's the tradition of the Corps."

"No disrespect to you or the Corps, Top. But as long as I'm an 03 M.O.S., I'm gonna keep comin' here until the thing is over, or the Gooks zap my Black ass."

The First Sergeant chain-lit another cigarette. "Sgt. Johnson, you can't decide your whole career, your future, on the chance of another Nam tour. The war is winding down for the U.S. We will start significant troop withdrawals soon, and turn the whole shootin' match over to the ARVNs."

"Withdrawal? I like that term, Top. It always reminds me of a lousy method of birth control, withdrawal. Trouble with withdrawal is, somebody's still gettin' fucked. We both know the ARVNs won't last two years against the North without us."

"The ARVNs have made giant strides in recent years. They will hold their own when we've gone."

"Come on, Top, don't bullshit a bullshitter. This ain't like Korea. Those little fuckers can fight. I had me a buddy up in Hue City in '68. He said given a choice, he'd rather fight with the N.V.A. than against them. Way I figure, we pull our people out, the N.V.A. will roar across the D.M.Z. like a big train, and we'll be sent back to bail out their sorry asses again. Only we'll have to fight to take back everything the ARVNs lose while we're gone.

"Top, I've watched damn fine staff N.C.O.s with over 10 years in this big green machine muster out because they feared a third or fourth tour in this stinkin' place. Ball is in your court, Top. You write the guarantee, and I'll sign for another six, right here and now."

There was a long moment of awkward silence in the shadows of the hot, smoke-filled tent. Jimenez slowly closed T.J.'s personnel folder. "Johnson, I'm really sorry. I can't give you your guarantee."

T.J. stood and shook the First Sergeant's hand. "I understand, Top. Thanks for your time and interest. Hey, Top, how many tours does this make for you?"

"This is my second; I've got five years before I've got my 20 years in."

"I really hope I'm wrong about the way things gonna be. You take care of yourself, Top. You know, there ain't a safe place in this whole fuckin' country."

T.J. was in a foul mood. He felt as though he was being consumed by the moist heat and driving rain. He had grown weary of being wet and uncomfortable for three days. The overall fatigue seemed to penetrate his entire body. He ached from the two weeks in the bush, with the last three days spent walking in a steady rain. The platoon was on another senseless operation, humping through wet rice paddies, hedgerows, and rural villages with 80 pounds of assorted gear on their bodies.

The rain was starting to let up as the long, slow file of tired Marines snaked along a road near a typical looking rural Vietnamese farming village.

Babble, an ugly farm kid from Ohio, was walking in front of T.J. He got his bush name because the irritating 18-year-old never seemed to shut up but never seemed to say anything worth listening to.

"Hey, T.J. Man, you're gettin' pretty short, ain't you? This'll probably be your last operation out in the bush. I figure I'm about halfway there myself."

T.J. was not in the mood for conversation that afternoon, especially with a numbnuts like Pvt. Babble.

"Just shut the fuck up and watch what you're doin'. We've been hit every time we even get close to that damn ville over there. If they don't do us with a booby trap or a sniper, it's an all-out ambush. Babble, you just watch where you're steppin' and keep an eye on those trees. Let me worry about how much time I got left in this piss hole they call a country."

"Sorry, T.J., I was just . . ."

"I know you're sorry, Babble. You're about the sorriest excuse for a Grunt I've seen in two tours. This whole platoon is nothing but a collection of the sorriest dudes I've ever come across. All these piss ants wanna do is bitch and smoke dope. If you all concentrated half as much on being Grunts as you do complaining, half the damn platoon wouldn't have got tore up on these bullshit operations. This sorry excuse for a Marine platoon wouldn't have lasted a full day back in Hue City in Tet of '68."

Babble stopped for a moment and turned toward T.J. "Ah come on. Now you are starting to sound like one of them old Corps lifers, rather than a short-timer about to go back to the world."

"Damn it, Babble. Just get your . . ." T.J. saw Babble's face explode the same instant he heard the crack from an AK47 rifle in the treeline to their right.

Before Babbles' body crumbled to the muddy road, the treeline erupted with N.V.A. rifle, light machine gun, and R.P.G. fire. T.J. carefully took cover on the side of the road. He called out to his platoon to take cover and return the enemy fire. He crouched low and changed magazines in his rifle.

"Damn, I'm so sick of this bullshit. Every month we waltz past that lousy ville, they tear our asses up at will, then go hide in their holes or disappear into the bush."

T.J. raised up and fired an entire magazine into the treeline. "Come on, people, how many times I gotta tell you? Put out some fire. Ol' Luke the Gook won't shoot so good when he's ducking his head."

T.J. crawled along the roadside ditch until he found his new platoon commander, Lt. Harrison. T.J. really liked Harrison. He was green, but he knew it. He always asked T.J.'s opinion when possible. He reminded T.J. of Lt. Fox.

Harrison had a field map in his lap. He calmly spoke into the handset of the PRC25 radio. He spoke with the artillery battery back at their firebase and requested an immediate fire mission on the enemy position in the treeline. He put down the handset and moved to talk with T.J.

"We'll get a 105 mission into the trees in about a minute. Have our people keep their dicks in the dirt until they finish. As soon as the 105's stop, we'll take the treeline. Then from there we'll sweep that ville. No doubt that the Gooks will sky out to the ville as soon as the 105s shit all over that treeline."

T.J. checked his equipment and again changed magazines. "What kind of ordinance the 105s gonna give the trees?"

Harrison smiled at his veteran platoon sergeant. "Don't worry, T.J., I didn't forget what you told me. I asked for some Willie Peter along with the high explosives. I remembered your lesson. The Gooks are afraid of it, and the big show is good for our people's morale. To tell you the truth, those rounds still impress the hell out of me when they go off."

"Lu-tenant, if it's alright with you, I'll put a squad with an M-60 to the rear of the ville before we sweep it. We know they'll sky out the treeline. It's my bet they'll sky from the ville too. I'll have them set up some claymores and give them the remaining LAWs. I heard tell that ville has been V.C. for at least 10 years. The squad can maybe return the Gooks surprise with a little ambush of their own."

"Damn fine idea, T.J. Do it."

The barrage of 105mm Marine cannon rounds tore into the treeline. T.J. shook his head, "Get some arty. Damn, Lu-tenant may be green, but he sure can call in an artillery mission. Right on the money. Get some."

As soon as the artillery barrage lifted, T.J. moved out the platoon on line toward the torn, smoking row of shattered trees that had stood halfway between the old village and the crude road.

"Come on, you bunch of raggedy-ass Marines. Advance on those trees. Keep your proper interval. Don't bunch up."

A corpman stayed with the four Marine casualties from the ambush back on the road, waiting for a chopper medevac.

The advance to the treeline was unopposed. The platoon took up position in the smoking debris, preparing for their advance across a muddy open rice paddy to the village.

Lt. Harrison joined T.J. in what was left of the treeline. The platoon made a quick survey for an N.V.A. body count. There were none. The only evidence that the Communists had ever been in the trees were several blood trails, a few shredded human limbs, and some destroyed weapons.

T.J. took off his helmet for a moment. He wiped his forehead with the sleeve of his jungle jacket and shook his head in disgust.

"I swear, Lu-tenant. Damn Gooks are like ghosts. They lay up in these trees and kick our asses while we're there on the road. You have the 105s shit all over them, and we don't even find one whole dead Gooner body. Those little fuckers are damn spooky. Those Marines back on the road waitin' for the medevac chopper didn't commit suicide. Somebody was in these trees. Sure glad it wasn't us in here when the 105s came."

T.J. found Frisco, and after giving him complete instructions dispatched his squad to the rear of the village. They were to move around the right flank and remain undetected by the ville occupants.

T.J. moved next to Lt. Harrison, who was looking carefully at the village through his field glasses. "Looks real quiet. I can't see anything moving."

"Naw, course not. They're in there waitin' on us to come strollin' across that open paddy. Lu-tenant, we all know that ville is V.C. We been hit every time we even come near it. Why don't you get a B-52 arc-light on that dump, and then the Seabees can come with their equipment and make a fuckin' playground out of it?"

Harrison grinned and put his hand on T.J.'s shoulder. "Why, Sergeant, you know that wouldn't be sporting. Besides, S-2 says that's a friendly ville, and it would be against the rules to bring any fire on a friendly ville."

"Yea, I got somethin' for S-2, and for all the stupid fuckin' rules in this war. The only thing I've seen these rules do is get our people killed. The only thing I hate worse than this stupid war are the useless people we are supposed to be fighting it for."

Harrison readied his own equipment and checked his rifle.

"Come on, T.J., hang in there a little while longer for me. I need you to help me keep these boys alive for one last operation, then you're outa here."

"Lu-tenant, couldn't they just drop a few 105 rounds into the ville to soften it up and keep their heads down before we bring the platoon across 200 yards of open rice paddy?"

"With all the crying about us killing innocent civilians, they'd never authorize a fire mission on a populated ville, unless we were pinned down."

"Well then, lie. 'Cause they got no trouble authorizing a whole Marine platoon to go walkin' in the open so we can get our young asses shot off. I don't mind tellin' you, Lu-tenant, this is some jive bullshit. I'm way too short for this. If Charlie ain't still in the ville waitin' on us to cross that paddy, I'll re-up for six months."

Harrison gave T.J. the resigned look of no choice he had seen so many times in Vietnam. T.J. grinned back at his young lieutenant and shrugged his shoulders. He moved into position.

T.J. moved to his feet and walked out of the treeline. "Alright, men. Move out. On line. Watch your interval. Bronx Man, set up your M-60 to give us cover fire if we need it."

"Can do, Brother. You all be cool. Gooners probably in there for sure."

T.J. waved at the expert Black machine gunner. He looked over to Harrison and rolled his eyes. "No shit, Bronx Man. Gooks in the ville? Why didn't I think of that?"

The re-enforced platoon, minus Frisco's squad, came out of the treeline and advanced across the open rice paddy on line. If they were to be hit, it would be past the halfway point, when they were in the center of the large empty rice paddy with no cover and nowhere to go.

It had finally stopped raining but the air was still moist and hot.

Approximately 75 yards from the village the men could hear Vietnamese voices and movement from the unseen rear of the village. T.J.'s initial thought was that the N.V.A. ambush survivors were grouping to escape. Suddenly, several AK-47 rifles opened fire on the Marines from the nearest row of hooches. The platoon fell to the ground and aggressively returned fire without T.J.'s coaching.

T.J. saw that Lt. Harrison had been hit. He and a corpman ran to his aid. The young officer had been shot in the right shoulder and upper right leg. The corpman skillfully applied combat bandages to the wounds. They had to hold Harrison down. He kept trying to get up to lead his platoon. He finally laid still after the corpman's second injection of morphine.

"It's your platoon now, T.J. Take them in."

They could hear Frisco's squad open up with savage fire, unseen at the rear of the village. "You were right again, T.J. I hope that squad tears their ass up."

"You'll be cool, Lu-tenant. I'm sure those boys are doin' a job on the Gooks. Frisco is a good man." They heard the claymore mines explode. "Get some, Frisco! You lay chilly with Doc until medevac comes. We gonna go get some for you, Lu-tenant."

"Be careful, T.J. Good luck."

"Lu-tenant, I'm too short to be careless."

T.J. was certain that it was only the escaping N.V.A.'s rear guard that had fired on their platoon. The men rushed the ville and reached the first row of hooches. The explosions and rifle fire from the rear flank sounded like they were from U.S. weapons. He could recognize the M-16 fire and L.A.W. explosions. Even the grenades sounded American. If the N.V.A. force was returning fire, it could not be heard over Frisco's squad's vicious ambush.

The main portion of the platoon entered the village and searched for the V.C. and N.V.A. rear guard members. The village occupants were herded into the muddy center street of the typical Vietnamese village.

They could hear medevac choppers that had arrived to take Lt. Harrison and the other dead and wounded Marines back to the firebase.

The platoon members were angry and frustrated. Some occupants of the village were struck or kicked when asked about the V.C. and N.V.A. T.J. and a new replacement, Abe, checked the interior of the hooches. They threw the contents around and broke everything breakable.

In the last hooch in a long row, they found a middle-aged couple hiding under some bamboo mats. T.J. pulled them roughly to their feet. They jabbered wildly in Vietnamese and bowed at the two Black Marines. T.J. struck them both with his rifle butt. "Save the bullshit, you Gook bastards. Where's V.C.? Where's N.V.A.? And don't give us this crybaby bullshit."

The man stepped forward. "V.C., N.V.A. go. No like V.C. V.C. number 10. Ma-leen number one, N.V.A. make plenty shoot. They go."

"Oh yea, Marine number one alright. Hey Abe, take a careful look at these two. They aren't farmers. He's got hands softer than yours, and her teeth are in better shape than mine. She's never chewed one of those red fuckin' nuts in her life. They belong here about as much as we belong in the suburbs."

"No lie, T.J. They gotta be N.V.A. agents. We turn them over to S-2?"

T.J. moved a floor mat and found a recently fired AK-47. "Well, look it here. I guess we haven't done a very good job of winning their hearts and minds."

T.J. couldn't help but enjoy the expressions on the faces of the two N.V.A. agents. They knew they were surely doomed when T.J. found the rifle. "Wait for me outside for a second, Abe."

T.J. motioned for the two people to back against the wall of the hooch. He slowly removed a hand grenade as they watched in terror. He backed to the doorway and stopped. "Marines still number one, mother fucker?"

T.J. pulled the pin and tossed the deadly grenade at their feet. He moved out of the hooch. "Fire in the hole."

He could hear them frantically move to pick up the grenade, before it exploded. They could not. After the explosion, T.J. re-entered the hooch and sprayed both bloodied bodies with rifle fire. He took out his Zippo lighter. "Abe, pass the word. Frag every hooch. Zippo it and kill every living thing in the ville except the people. Except for the villagers, I don't even want to see a chicken alive. Destroy the rice, the animals, every hooch."

Abe had a grin on his face as he watched T.J. set the inside of the hooch on fire using some lamp oil. "Yea, I can dig this man. Burn, baby, burn."

As T.J.'s last official act as a combat Marine, he decimated a V.C. ville that would never be rebuilt. They'd have to select a different road for the killing of Marines.

SEPTEMBER, 1970
DETROIT

The clock-radio alarm sounded and filled the bedroom with a song by the Jackson Brothers. It was 10:30 p.m., and Sean cursed as he struggled to locate the off switch. He winced. He had left the volume on the alarm too loud.

September, the graveyard shift. Days spent fighting for every minute of sleep and nights spent drinking countless cups of bad coffee while fighting to stay awake. Sean liked the street work of the midnight to 8 a.m. shift. He did not like what it did to his personal life and his body. If a tour in Vietnam could be best described as a mind assault, working the midnight shift could best be described as an assault on the body. The drastic change of working and sleeping hours had an effect on most officers. Sean jokingly had said he didn't trust anyone who wasn't bothered by midnights or didn't drink. He said he'd refuse to ride with anyone with neither of those traits.

Sean emerged from the dark bedroom, still half awake. He could hear

Lyn still watching television in the living room. He stumbled into the bathroom to shave and shower. He returned to their bedroom and dressed in his crisp, clean, tailored police uniform. He gave himself a quick inspection in the bedroom closet's full-length mirror. He walked out and quietly sat at the dining room table, still feeling somewhat in a daze. Not really hungry, he ate two pieces of toast with a glass of milk to put something in his stomach.

Just before Sean was to leave for work, Lyn sat down across the dining room table from him. "Sean, do you notice anything different about me?"

Still not fully awake, he focused his eyes on the cute 22-year-old brunette across the table from him. "You shaved your moustache?"

"Come on, Sean. I'm serious."

"I'm sorry, Lyn. But you know how working this shift kicks my butt, I can only sleep three hours at a time. I almost always have to take a nap after you get home from work or I wouldn't last the night. I don't mean to be insensitive but I kind of go in a shell when I work the shift all night. Your hair is the same. You look as cute as ever to me. What am I missing?"

"You know, Sean, you wouldn't have any of this shift work or violence like last month, if you'd just give up this police thing and go to work for your dad."

"Darn it, Lyn, not now, please. This is no way to go off to work. I'm not going off to sit behind some desk for eight hours. I don't need to be upset before I even get to work. We'll talk about this another time, but not tonight. Before I leave for work, I really don't need this."

"I'm sorry, I don't want to argue with you. I have something to tell you. Sean, I went to the doctor today. He's certain that I'm pregnant. The baby is due in the Spring."

Sean was struck speechless. He knew any lengthy pause might be identified as a negative response. He forced a smile and walked over and gently hugged his young wife. He leaned over and kissed her.

"It's a good thing we have a female letter carrier and no milkman or I might wonder about being the father. With these crazy hours, I guess I really am surprised. I wouldn't know if you missed a period if I don't even approach you for days at a time. I must admit, I never thought I'd be the type of husband that would be caught by complete surprise. Are you going to be alright?"

"Doctor said I'm doing great. No morning sickness yet, the weight is fine. He says I can work up to the seventh month."

"I'm really happy, Lyn. That's just great. It's a little sooner than we'd planned, but so long as you're alright. I'm really sorry to leave now, but I'll be late. We'll talk tomorrow."

"Sean, with a baby on the way, please at least think some more about the job with your father."

Sean sprinted to his Triumph. "I sure will, Lyn. Now take care. Go get some rest."

He raced west on the freeway toward the precinct. He popped a Simon and Garfunkel tape into the dashboard and turned up their melancholy song. His head was spinning with mixed emotions. He laughed at himself in sarcasm.

"Well, so much for the good old Catholic rhythm method. So much for waiting at least a year before we even try. I know it only takes one time, but we hardly make love enough times to keep in practice, much less make babies. If we'd ever made love without first looking at a calendar, I would have felt like I was making love to another woman and cheating on Lyn. The great rhythm method. What it probably really means is making love with the radio on. A baby. God knows I'm not ready to be a father. I started playing house sooner than I should have. This is a shit job to have when you've got kids, but I still love it. I'm not ready to quit yet, not even for a baby. The damn rhythm method, a crock of shit. She didn't want to take the pill because it made her put on weight. What the hell does she think having a baby is going to do? And the church is against the pill. Fine, let's all show our support for the church and have a baby for the Pope."

He leaned over and turned up the tape even louder. "I need this shit at this time in my life about as much as I need another scar on my ass."

Sgt. Del Greene had been appointed to be in charge of all of the 13th Precinct's special precinct level units. The new Black precinct commander wanted some dramatic change in those assignments. He realized that he would come under a great deal of criticism. He was identified as an affirmative action example, and he intended to silence his critics in a year with good performance and statistics. If it meant he would ruffle feathers by assigning young hard chargers to assignments traditionally given to the veteran street coppers, he'd take the chance.

The new C.O. had decided to expand the number of plain clothes, anti-street crime units known as the Booster Crews. He was also going to make changes in personnel in the Cruiser Crews and Precinct Vice Unit. He gave veteran police Sgt. Del Greene the assignment to select a quality bi-racial group and supervise them. Greene intended to select men that would require very little supervision.

Sean, Bruce Munier, and Tom Miller had been ordered to Sgt. Greene's office after off-duty roll call. He explained the Booster Crew's hours and responsibilities. When he was certain they really wanted the assignment, he allowed them to leave. They were to start their new assignment the following day.

At the announcement of their new assignment, several veteran street officers complained. The police union's representative reviewed a year's worth of monthly performance reports for Sean, Tom, and Bruce. The complaints never went formal.

Sean, Tom, and Bruce would work from 6 p.m. to 2 a.m. They would dress in plain clothes, but casual, rather than the detective's traditional suit and tie. Their regular vehicle was an unmarked Ford. Their only instruction was to help reduce the terrible rate of street crime that plagued the precinct.

In 1970, the street people were conditioned to easily identify the precinct's plain clothes cops. They either wore suits or very conservative casual clothes. Most of the plain-clothes cops were over 30.

Bruce was the oldest of the three at 26. Sean was still only 22. They let their hair grow a bit longer than regulation and dressed like the college kids at Wayne State. Sean wore an assortment of military jackets, jeans, and his old jungle boots. For weeks, it was like shooting fish in a barrel. The young crew could often walk right up to a suspect, while he was attempting to break into the car, because they didn't "look like cops".

Expecting his first child or not, with the new assignment, Sean was hooked. With only a year and a half on the street, he had a prime assignment. The young crew was filling the jail cells, and they were making good arrests. They were very enthusiastic. Despite their collective lack of experience, they were good. And they had the unspoken part of successful police work: they were charmed. Night after night, they were lucky enough to be at the right place at the right time.

Even with the constant pressure at home for Sean to quit, he had never felt that he was helping his city as much as he would the next several months. He would always fondly look back at this time as the best of his career. He was a 22-year-old cop who realized the danger around him and somehow drew strength from it.

In the Fall of 1970, the Detroit Police Department organized a 40-member semi-pro football team.

In a nationwide campaign to improve police public relations, scores of "Pig Bowls" were held. Some of these games featured local law enforcement agencies playing against one another, while some had any combination of opponents for the police teams. There were "Pigs vs. Freaks" games where the police squared off against local long hairs.

Detroit enjoyed financial success in their "Pig Bowl," unique from the others. It was decided at the end of the 1970 season, that the team would return in the following Fall.

Sean went out for the team in 1970 on a whim. It would have been his senior season if he would have opted to play for Wayne State after returning from Vietnam. At only 5'11", 175, and 22, Sean was certain there would be a talented, mature quarterback in the ranks of the nearly 6,000 police officers.

The Detroit Police maintained the team until the mid-70s, when, faced with budget cuts and big city political critics, the new Chief had to disband the team. The games made money for the Police Athletic League (P.A.L.) program. But faced with cutbacks and layoffs, a football team would be far too difficult to explain, even if it made money and was a worthwhile police-community program.

Sean enjoyed five full seasons as the team's starting quarterback. The spirited games with the quality, semi-professional players of the big police team doused the embers of football frustration and self-doubt that had smoldered since Sean's freshman year at Eastern Michigan.

In jest, Sean often identified himself as a semi-pro quarterback who worked as a police officer in the "off season."

DECEMBER, 1970
CALIFORNIA

It all seemed to be a dream to T.J. He woke up in a clean, safe barracks at Camp Pendleton, California. It seemed for a moment that he had fallen asleep under a wet poncho the night he and his angry platoon had destroyed the V.C. village. He had developed blood poisoning from open sores, and a high fever put him away. He was too drugged and sick to really appreciate leaving Vietnam, the Freedom Bird, or the actual arrival back to the world.

He skated back at Mainside for a few days. He received two more re-enlistment lectures and a complete physical. The corpmen were satisfied that the rest and the drugs had made him well enough to go home.

Although involving less time, T.J. was faced with the same situation that got Sean an early release. He was too short for a "real" assignment, so they released him a few weeks early.

T.J. flew military stand-by, and got stuck in the center seat of a 707. He uncomfortably tucked away his long legs during the long ride from L.A.X. to Detroit.

At Detroit Metro, T.J. was met by his mother, step-father, half-brothers, and half-sister. His mother hugged him lovingly, but there was nowhere near the emotional explosion Sean had experienced in 1968.

By late 1970, America was moving rapidly out of the war, and except for the protests, the people were tired of Vietnam. None of them more tired than T.J.

T.J. began to walk down the hall, from the gate to the terminal lobby. He suddenly felt more afraid than he had walking patrols in Vietnam. He had been gone almost four years, with only brief visits. He was coming back to a different city, as a different man. He had prayed for this moment for four years, and now he grew weak with fear.

What would he do? What kind of a job can a Black Nam Vet get, and a Grunt at that? He couldn't even be a policeman like Irish, with his pre-Marine arrest record. Maybe he could work in the factory with his step-daddy.

"Work on some mindless assembly line all my life," he thought. "Two years of gettin' my Black ass shot off to work on the line screwing on bolts."

T.J. felt better when they reached the large terminal lobby.

He had a private wish, a secret personal fantasy. He wished time could be frozen a few weeks before Tet of '68. He actually enjoyed those weeks. Lt. Fox, Yance, Mr. Cool, Logs, and their new boy, Irish. They went out on operations and beat up on the N.V.A. and he was respected and looked up to. He was their leader, their friend.

"Shit," he thought as he waited for his seabag to appear at baggage claim. "Ain't no fightin' outfit in the whole world was any better than that squad. None in the world."

In his private fantasy, he wished that special squad could travel the world, helping fight in all the little wars. They could be the mercenaries of the '70s. Even T.J., with little formal education, knew there would always be a war someplace in the world. Just a hopeless fantasy, half of his all-star squad was dead or maimed.

He stared out of the window at the snow-covered streets of Detroit, as his step-dad drove them home from the airport. He didn't feel any of the emotions or excitement Irish had described during his final homecoming.

T.J. knew he was much more flexible than Irish. Even before Vietnam, T.J. had developed the ability to take things just as they came, without explanation or understanding. He laughed at his own life paradox. The reason he didn't stay in the Marine Corps was because he didn't want to return to Vietnam for another tour, yet his life wish was to round up his Grunt buddies and become professional soldiers. But in his fantasy, they could fight *their* way, and no one would ever die or lose limbs.

When they reached the house, T.J.'s mother fed him and he retired to the small make-shift bedroom they had made for him in the old house's basement, so he wouldn't have to share the small bedroom with his two half-brothers.

He crawled under the covers. His old bed felt familiar. He planned out his next few days. First, he'd buy himself a nice used car with the money he'd saved. He'd spend a day with Irish. He would go Downtown to do his Christmas shopping and look at the light display. Then he'd get busy finding himself a job.

T.J. sat up in bed in the small dark bedroom. He was tired, but couldn't sleep. He walked over to the small chest of drawers in the corner of the room. He found the pint bottle of Old Crow whiskey he

"Four years away, two of them in combat, and this is the welcome home. Well, fuck it. It don't mean nothin'."

DECEMBER, 1970
DETROIT

It had been snowing all day. The temperature had been hovering around the freezing mark and approximately three inches of wet slush covered the inner-city landscape.

That night, Tom, Bruce, and Sean were working together. They hit the street at 6 p.m. and the streets were wet, but Tom had no trouble keeping their unmarked Ford under control.

It was Sean's informal turn to ride in the back seat and carry the extra protection of a long gun. Sean carried his privately-owned M-1 carbine and carefully placed it at his feet.

There was light conversation regarding their combined disbelief of how rapidly Christmas was approaching.

Bruce had mentioned that he found himself checking the work schedule to see which other officers were on duty each night. Sean ran the parody of checking to see which players were in the huddle before walking up to the line of scrimmage. There was an added sense of confidence when there was a good mix of cops on duty.

They were only on the street for an hour when the dispatcher interrupted their conversation with an all units call. He sent the cars of the 13th Precinct to an address on Collingwood Street, near Third. He said there was a man with a rifle, threatening people.

They were only a minute away from the location at their position at Seward Street and Second Avenue. Bruce picked up the radio mike. "13-33 to radio. We're near the scene. Plain clothes officers at the scene."

The dispatcher acknowledged. It was always a safe idea to remind responding units that some of the cops at the scene would not be in uniform.

Tom stopped their car several houses east of the trouble call's actual location. Another Booster crew pulled up behind them. Sean could see units responding several houses to the west of the radio run location. The responding officers quickly exited their vehicles. From the point where Tom had stopped their car, they were not in line of sight from the house in question.

Five officers began to slowly approach the house. They walked on line, as they felt they were still more than 50 yards from any real danger.

The houses were brick two-story single homes and two-story flats. They had long, covered porches and sat in a perfect line, about 60 feet from the street curb.

At the 13th Precinct, a "gun run" was a nightly occurrence. It didn't create an atmosphere of carelessness, but with the frequency of those types of calls, there wasn't a great deal of excitement.

Sean chatted with Bruce. He carried his rifle with his left hand. He looked up toward the house of the call, and mentioned to Bruce that he thought the house illuminated by a porch light was the one they wanted.

The metallic sound of a storm door slamming echoed up Collingwood Street. Under the bright porch light, Sean saw a middle-aged Black man, dressed in only work trousers and a sleeveless undershirt. He seemed to be moving very fast. Sean saw that the man was armed with a long-barrel 12-gauge. He shouldered the shotgun and fired in their direction.

The line of five policemen dissolved. Sean heard a second shotgun blast. In two seconds, Sean had moved from the sidewalk to the street's gutter. He had chambered a round into the M-1 and taken the safety off. The rifle was shouldered and he skillfully had found the only available cover, the cement curb. He located his target in the rifle sights. The gunman had turned after firing two poorly-aimed shots, and was darting back into the house.

Sean could have taken a shot at the retreating gunman. It was a decision an inner-city cop had to make all the time. His shot would be justified. Would he shoot the retreating gunman so he wouldn't remain a serious risk, or would he hold fire and pray the man surrendered without hurting anyone?

Sean had reconditioned himself for armed contact in his own city. This was Detroit, Michigan, U.S.A, not Vietnam. There were no free fire zones, no peace through fire superiority. In Detroit, it was much stricter fire descipline with every moment being second guessed.

Sean tried to remember he was performing police work and not in combat, as he did the low crawl through the slush to the additional cover of a parked car in front of the gunman's house. Sean lay prone on his stomach on the sloppy wet snow. His clothing became saturated by the ice cold water. His rifle was shouldered and aimed at the front of the house.

He had the best seat in the house. He could fully cover the entire front of the house. The catch was that he could not move from his position of cover without exposing himself totally to the gunman. The porch light of the house remained lit. Sean adjusted his position again and put the carbine back onto safe.

Sean could see Bruce hidden between the houses. "Hey, Cav. Are you alright?"

Sean gave him a thumbs up sign, not wanting to give away his location by calling out.

Bruce waved, "Just hang tight, Cav. No one has been hit. They're tryin' to reach him by phone."

Sean waited there in the wet cold slush of the gutter. He waited for the senior officers and the gunman to work out a solution to the standoff.

Sean's concentration on the front of the house was broken by the realization that his body was numb from his waist to his knees from the soaking cold water.

Despite the physical discomfort, Sean couldn't help but be pleased with himself. Damn, he had been well trained by the Marine Corps. He reacted to the gunshot blast like none of his peers. He had found the best cover, where he could be in position to return fire. He had readied his rifle and found his target. It had been all so automatic, so natural.

"Shit," Sean thought to himself. "I've found the only job in the world where being a Grunt was on-the-job training."

He thought about the difference between combat and street confrontations. In Vietnam, if a Gook had fired two shots at his people, he would have emptied his 30-round magazine at the gunman as he attempted to run back into the house. Just one frag grenade and Sean would end this standoff and warm his front side.

The minutes ticked away. The senior officer at the scene continued to call to the gunman on the bullhorn. Sean prayed that the man would either quickly surrender, or they'd be given the order to rush the house.

The gunman was given the guarantee of safety if he gave up. Sean thought it was one hell of a guarantee, considering the assembled group of cold cops.

The wet cold of the street actually began to cause pain to his lower body. He rolled onto one hip to try to get some relief, but it did little to ease the discomfort. The house was lit up with all the shades pulled down. Sean struggled to concentrate on the potential danger from inside the house. He didn't want the gunman to take his head off with the shotgun while he worried about being cold and wet.

The brick two-story house had a macabre look, with a dozen blue police car emergency lights dancing across its front.

After another few minutes of pleading over the bullhorn, another few minutes of agony on the sloppy cold street, the front door began to slowly open. The officer on the bullhorn was now shouting for the assembled officers surrounding the house to hold their fire.

The gunman slowly walked out onto the porch, his arms raised. He was still dressed only in a sleeveless undershirt and trousers.

The shift lieutenant approached the house.

"Cavanagh, come with me. Everyone else hold your position. Cavanagh, be easy with him, but be careful. Every mobile news team in the city is filming. Keep your cool."

Sean quickly helped handcuff the drunken gunman and slowly checked the house's interior with two uniform officers. The gunman's wife and neighbor were even more drunk than he was and unhurt. Sean realized how tense things inside the house must have been for the two women. They shared another bottle of whiskey. The gunman's wife grabbed Sean by the arm as he passed.

"Hey, Mr. Po-lice. What's all the fuss about?"

"An obvious misunderstanding, Ma'am."

"You all gonna take my James off to jail? He ain't done nothin'."

"We'll straighten it all out at the precinct. Seems that James did take a couple of shots at the officers."

"That for true? That's what I musta heard. He get him a temper on him, when he been drinkin'."

The gunman was quickly driven from the scene and the police units left the area as quickly as possible.

Sean went back to the car. He could hardly walk. Bruce and Tom casually talked with the other Booster crew near their car. Except for the two shots, neither of which hit anyone, it was little more than a routine "man with a gun" call.

Sean's physical condition seemed to worsen. He walked up to Tom. "Let's go, Partner. I've got to get to the precinct station right away."

Tom seemed slightly alarmed at the unusual urgency in Sean's voice. He moved behind the wheel of the car, started the engine and motioned for Bruce to get in.

Tom turned the police car around and they headed for the station. Tom reached over and put the car's heater at maximum. "I'll turn the furnace all the way up, partner. Christ, you've got to be chilled to the bone, laying in that slush for an hour."

Sean made certain his rifle was on safe and the round had been removed from the chamber. He put the rifle on the car floor. The entire front of his body ached from the extreme exposure. Tom and Bruce did a brief critique of the incident. Bruce became concerned by Sean's silence. His usually verbose partner had been silent since they got in the car.

"You alright, Sean? You didn't catch any bird shot from that guy, did you?"

"No, Bruce. I'm uncomfortable. I just want to get to the precinct right away."

"You sure you're not hurt? You hit the pavement pretty hard when that asshole opened fire on us. We can stop at Ford Hospital if . . ."

"Damn it, Bruce, I'm not shot, I'm not hurt. I'm just fucking wet and cold. I just want to get to the goddamn station so I can change. O.K.?"

The unusual snap response increased Tom's and Bruce's concern for their partner's welfare. They decided not to push any further. No one spoke again until they reached the precinct.

Bruce announced that he was going to get coffee and start their portion of the report. Sean asked Tom if he'd go to the second floor with him where the locker room and large men's room was. Tom put his arm on Sean's shoulder and quietly spoke under his breath.

"What's the matter, Cav? Are you sick?"

Sean looked around to make certain no one could hear them. "Listen, Tommy, I think I might be in real trouble. I can't feel my dick. It's numb."

"You what?

"You heard me. I can't even feel my pecker it's so numb. I'm afraid I may have frostbite."

Tom still could not tell if Sean was being serious. "You're shittin' me, right? You really think your pecker is frostbitten?"

"Listen, asshole, if you lay in the wet snow for an hour with your hand in the cold, your fingers would get frostbite. Go back out there and lay in the cold slop for an hour and see how well your dick bears the elements."

"What the hell you gonna do?"

"I've got a complete change of clothes in my locker. I need you to stand guard on the men's room for a couple of minutes and let me check things out."

Sean gathered the dry clothing from his locker and hurried into the second floor men's room. He quickly stripped off the wet clothing and redressed before he gathered the courage to even look at his manhood.

It did not show any of the obvious signs of advanced frostbite that he had been taught to identify in countless first aid classes. But they always talked about fingers and toes. He couldn't remember any class that discussed a frostbitten penis. Sean had never been the legend of the locker roon, but he had never seen his 22-year-old sex organ ever look greyer or smaller. It was still numb and felt cold to his careful touch.

He shook his head, "I had to go and play Marine in the slush. If they have to amputate this thing, I'll blow my own fucking brains out."

He walked to one of the sinks and filled it to the top with room-temperature water. Because of the height of the sink, Sean had to stand on his tip toes and put both hands on the mirror for balance, in order to soak the small flaccid part of his body in the water. He prayed his first aid technique would bring his lifeless penis back to the world of the living.

In less than a minute, his penis began to tingle and he felt a slight burning sensation. It looked like it was returning to its normal color. It was also returning to nearly normal size. Although not impressive, at least now someone could identify his true gender from across the room.

Tom walked into the men's room to check on his friend's condition. He saw Sean's awkward position, balanced on his toes, penis soaking in an over-filled sink of water. He stared at the vision before him for a moment, and then burst out laughing.

Sean may have got the normal color back in his penis, but he had not recovered his sense of humor. "What the hell are you laughing at?"

Tom shook his head. "I walk in here and find you standing on your tiptoes, soaking your pecker in the sink, and you've got the nerve to ask me what I'm laughin' at?"

"Well, it's not that damn funny!"

"Look, Sean, I may not be any comedy critic, but I know what's funny. Pal, you standing there soaking your dick in the sink is funny."

Sean was still concerned. "If this is frostbite and I have to go to the hospital with a frozen dick, I'll never live it down."

Tom controlled his laughter but could not conceal the sarcasm in his voice. "Hey Sean, I know. We'll go down on Third Street and find you a nice warm place to soak it."

"Man, I'm really glad you're having such a good time with my problem, buddy. My dick could fall off at any moment, and you're doing Henny Youngman one-liners."

"Lighten up, Sean. You'll be alright. Let me see it. If it looks bad we'll get you to the hospital."

"Fuck you. Just go stand guard by the door like I asked you. I'll decide if I need a doctor."

"Relax, Sean. I'm not queer for your gear. I just wanna look to see if you're alright. Besides, you're not my type."

"Damn it, Tom. Please go guard the door and just let me soak for a while more."

At that moment, Bruce briskly walked into the men's room.

"Cavanagh, what in the hell are you doing?"

Sean rolled his eyes in disgust. "Oh, this is great. Why don't you go down to the precinct desk in the lobby and have everyone come up here and watch me soak my pecker?"

Bruce immediately identified the treatment. It made perfect sense to him. With Sean face down in the wet slush for an hour, his penis could of course be exposed to the danger of frostbite. "How bad is it, Sean? Let me see it."

"I'm not sure how bad it is, and no you can't see it. Suddenly everyone wants to view my pecker."

"Listen, stupid shit. It so happens that your pecker is your current problem area. Personally, I'd rather check your arm. I promise, the mere sight of four inches of your frozen hooter will not excite me. You seen one, you seen 'em all, at least that's what I keep trying to convince my wife. Come on, if it's hurt, we've got to get you to the hospital."

Sean slowly removed his burning penis from the sink. "Bruce, I swear, you're such a ghoul that if it did drop off, you'd make a key chain out of it."

Bruce quickly bent over and gave the organ a brief visual inspection. "Nope."

Sean waited a full ten seconds, but Bruce said nothing else. "Nope what, Bruce?"

"Nope, there's no frostbite, and nope, I wouldn't make a key chain out of it. An ear ring, maybe, too small for a key chain."

"I'll tell you well-hung studs something. You lay your peckers in the snow for an hour and tell me how you'd look. My balls are so far up in my body I couldn't make a baby for two months if I wanted to." Sean finished getting dressed and put on his gun.

Bruce put his arm on Sean's shoulder. "Tell you what you've got to do. Go soak it in beans. Human-beans."

Sean looked in the mirror and made certain he had all his gear. "I don't believe you two; 10,000 out-of-work comics and I draw the Marx Brothers for partners. I've got to tell you how much I appreciate all of your heart-felt fucking sympathy."

Bruce led the way out of the restroom. "No big deal, Sean. It was just your pecker. If it did fall off, no one would notice."

"It may not be all that significant, but I'm havin' fun with it."

"That's not what you've been complaining to us about."

"Good point. Never could argue with the truth."

"Come on, Woodward Avenue Flasher. Let's get back out on the street. Do us all a favor to try and stay dry the rest of the night."

"Fuck you guys."

"See how he is. As soon as his dick gets to feeling better, he goes and gets romantic."

9

March, 1971—December, 1971

MARCH, 1971
DETROIT, MICHIGAN

Sean rubbed his tired eyes. He sipped a hot cup of vending machine coffee as he sat alone in the father's waiting room in the maternity wing of St. John Hospital. The big wall clock showed 4:30 a.m.

He had been at work when he received the call that Lyn's mother was taking her to the hospital. He spoke to Lyn briefly when he arrived, before they took her into the delivery room.

Sean had been alone since 3 a.m. He removed his coat, and his .357 was visible in its shoulder holster.

An elderly man entered the room, also sipping a hot cup of bad coffee. He saw the big revolver at Sean's side and stopped mid-stride. "You expecting some trouble, young man?"

Sean smiled and showed him his badge case with badge and I.D. card. "No, sir. I got the call from work. My wife is in there now. I took off my coat because I was alone. I didn't mean to make anyone uncomfortable."

The man made a gesture with his hand.

"A policeman with a gun doesn't bother me. You try and make yourself comfortable. The waitin' is the worst part. My daughter is havin' her first. Her mother is with her now. Poor girl, her husband is still over in Vietnam; he's a helicopter pilot in the Navy."

"I'm really sorry he can't be here for his first child. I was there in '67 and '68. The only things I missed were Christmas and the World Series."

"I was away in Korea when my youngest was born. You're right though, young man, I can't ever have that moment back. All we can do is pray he comes back home safe and in one piece. He flies rescue choppers off of a carrier, but you never know."

The notification telephone in the waiting room rang. Sean picked it up and began a brief, silent prayer. "Hello".

The voice on the other end was that of the nurse at the maternity ward desk.

"Mr. Cavanagh? Would you please walk down to the nursery and meet with Dr. Nicholos. Nothing to worry about, Mr. Cavanagh. Everyone is fine. The doctor just likes the thrill of telling the fathers the good news himself."

Sean hung up the phone and slipped his jacket on over his shoulder holster. "Showtime. The best of luck to your daughter and her husband."

"Thank you, young man. I hope your child is healthy." He raised his coffee cup as if proposing a toast. "Let's hope these children don't grow up to fight in a war."

"They'd be the first generation in a long time that didn't, but it's a good thought."

Dr. Nicholos was still in his surgical suit. His face mask still hung on his chest and he wore his surgical cap. "Mr. Cavanagh?"

"Yes, Doctor."

"Your wife is fine. You have a fine, healthy son, that child in bed number one. Would you please verify the name and other data on the crib so we're certain that it's correct?"

Sean was too busy giving his new son the visual once-over to even hear the doctor. He counted fingers and toes. The infant appeared a little larger than average, but otherwise he looked normal.

"Mr. Cavanagh, please. Is the data correct?"

"Yes, Doctor. When can I see my wife?"

"She's resting now. Come back this afternoon and you can spend time with both of them. Now, go get some sleep and buy your cigars."

"I don't know how to thank you, Doctor."

"You don't have to say a word, Mr. Cavanagh. This is what it's all about. Medical school, all the rest, it's all for this. I feel like I should thank you. A fine couple has a healthy child, and I get to be a part of their miracle. By the way, Mr. Cavanagh, it's easier talking this way when I know your insurance is paying all the hospital costs."

The tired doctor smiled, and he and Sean shook hands.

The boy was baptized Dennis Sean Cavanagh. Dennis, in honor of his grandfather. Sean, in honor of his paternal great-grandfather and his father.

The Cavanagh tradition was carried on for yet another generation. The generation's first male child was named after the child's grandfather and his great-grandfather.

Dennis Sean was baptized at the old St. Paul's Catholic church on Grosse Pointe Boulevard. The post-baptism gathering was held at Grampa Cavanagh's big house on Lochmoor Boulevard, in Grosse Pointe Woods.

The small party was catered with a full wet bar and bartender. Sean made certain his new son was resting peacefully in his portable crib. He looked over the small gathering of guests at his grandfather's large home.

He smiled, shook his head and thought, "Ol' Grampa Cavanagh, he sure knows how to do it up right. Not bad for an old Irish WWI Grunt. A catered baptism party. A long way from the proud family stories of hard work and suffering of the first Cavanaghs to come from Ireland."

Sean waved to Lyn who was talking with her family near the fireplace. He got himself a fresh drink and moved up to the hors d'oeuvres table. He was busy feeding his face and didn't notice T.J. had arrived until he felt a solid slap on the back. "So, how's the proud father holdin' up?"

Sean warmly greeted his friend. "I'm O.K. The baby and Lyn are doing great. Come on over, and I'll show you my boy. Did you have any trouble finding the house?"

"Man, I was impressed at your daddy's house, but this here place of your granddad's is bigger than most funeral homes I been in. This is outa sight, dude. Like right outa the movies. You know, a bartender, food servers, a maid to answer the door, too much."

"As you can see, there's not a lot of other Black guests. In fact, there are no other Black guests. I just hope no one steps on their tongue. If someone insults you, I'll be so embarrassed I'll shit."

"What you mean, embarrass or insult me? You mean like askin' me to get them a drink or fetch their car? Don't worry, Irish, that won't happen. The hired help is way better dressed than me. Only person that give me a second look, or any roust, was the Black maid that answered the door. I wasn't for sure she was gonna let me in without askin' you first if it was O.K. I had to show her my invitation." Both young men shared a laugh and walked over to the crib.

T.J. was noticably touched by the sight of the infant in the crib. Little Dennis was on his back. He kicked his legs and seemed content with watching the movement around him.

"Damn, Irish. That's one fine-lookin' child. You and Lyn did good, made you a fine lookin' boy."

"She did all the work, Pal. You told me since I've known you that ain't much in the world that's fair. Same with making babies. The only part I have in it is fun, poor woman does the rest."

"Been that way forever, son. You couldn't change that if you wanted to. Hey, Irish, I'll be damned, the boy's got brown eyes."

"No shit, T.J. Lyn and her whole family have brown eyes."

"Since all Black folks got brown eyes, I thought maybe we really had become blood brothers in Hue."

"Yea, well dogs and cows have brown eyes too. It doesn't mean a thing."

"Oh, my boy copped an attitude. You afraid he can't be a preppie and get into the country club with brown eyes?"

"Damn, T.J. An Irish kid with brown eyes."

"Remember, Brother, this lad is only half Irish. You said Lyn's family was French."

"Half Irish?" Sean looked to see if any of the other guests were nearby. "Well, since he's a boy at least we know which half." They laughed and slapped hands. "Come on, T.J., I want you to meet my grandfather."

They found Sean's father and grandfather in the large den at the rear of the house. Sean introduced T.J. to the elder Cavanagh. T.J. had not seen Sean's dad for some time and also greeted him.

"Sean and his father tell me that you and he served in combat together."

T.J. couldn't help but be impressed by the mere presence of Sean's grandfather.

"That's right, Sir. I had to do my second tour without his help. I hear you was in the Marines in World War I. Well, you'd have been proud of Sean. He was a damn fine combat Marine; kept gettin' hurt, but a good Marine in a fight."

Mr. Cavanagh smiled and appreciated the compliment. "Sean's father and I never served with any colored Marines. The military was as segregated as everything else."

T.J. really liked the senior Cavanagh. "I'm glad they did away with most of the segregation, but they could have kept me out of combat for two years."

Sean's grandfather smiled. "Well, from one old leatherneck to another, welcome to my home. Sean, make sure this man gets enough to drink and eat."

T.J. and Sean chatted at the bar. "Irish, your grandfather and father sure are nice men. Think of it, a couple of ex-Grunts come home and made all this for themselves. If you come to your senses and quit being a cop, you can live in a house like this."

"Not you too, T.J. Everybody's been on my case."

"Thanks for inviting me to your son's first party. I gotta be goin'. You know, graveyard shift at Jefferson assembly. I'll say 'bye to Lyn on my way out. I'll be in touch. You be careful on them streets, Brother. You're a daddy now."

"How's your job going, T.J.?

"Ah, Irish. That plant's got more bad shit going down than what's happening on the street."

"Say the word and I know my dad will find a decent job for you. It's a clean place, and he treats his people well."

"Hey, Bro, don't rag on me about workin' for your daddy an' I'll leave you alone about you being a po-lice."

"Take care, T.J."

"Yea, Buddy, you too. I'll keep in touch. Keep your Irish ass outa trouble."

APRIL, 1971
DETROIT

There was a hint of Spring on the mild Saturday evening. The full crew hit the street at a little after 6 p.m.

That evening, they drove the low-profile unmarked car that had become their regular vehicle. The white, full-sized Ford Galaxy sedan had white walls and a radio. It was not as Spartan looking as the average unmarked police car. With the crew's enthusiasm, it was as well known on the street as any marked police car. But at night, the civilian-looking vehicle allowed them to blend in with other traffic.

They worked the Cass Corridor for a while, then Tom drove to their northern-most area of saturation, Second Avenue and Seward Street. The crew had made a secret pact to make Seward Street a safe place to walk after dark. The occupants of the numerous apartment buildings had been prisoners once the sun went down.

Tom drove along the curb lane, north on Second Avenue. They scanned the alleys and shadows between the buildings. Sean saw a man in the shadows up against a building. "Hold on, Tommy. There's one in the doorway. Let Bruce and me talk to him. He's only 30 yards from the China Doll restaurant. He might be waiting for a stray customer to come out."

Tom stopped the car. Sean and Bruce walked up to the Black man in the doorway. They had their badges out. "We're police officers. We'd like to talk to you."

"I know who you is. What the fuck you want, honkies? I ain't done nothing."

Sean put his badge case away and improved his position to get to his magnum. "Lighten up, asshole. We're going to check you out and then you can be on your way."

The man stepped out of the doorway. He held his arms at his sides, fists clenched. "You pigs ain't puttin' yo' hands on me. I ain't done nothin'."

"Give us some I.D., Slick."

The man handed Sean a Social Security card. "You po-lice is always fucking wif me."

"Gee, a pleasant guy like you? I can't guess why. You have any better I.D.; something with your picture, a driver's license?"

"I ain't got to have no license. I ain't drivin'."

Sean reached to begin to pat down the man for weapons. He slapped Sean's hand away. Sean grabbed the front of the man's jacket with both hands and slammed him against the wall.

"You aren't going to be able to walk if you ever do that again, asshole. I'm going to check you for weapons, that's for certain. Whether you lighten up and let me do it the easy way, or I do it while you're on the way to the hospital, is up to you."

"Go ahead, pig. You put your hands on me. You hassle me. I ain't done nothin', mother fucker. You ain't got no right to be messing with me."

Sean pulled the man away from the wall and slammed him back against the wall, his head snapped back against the brick. "Are you some kind of a street-lawyer?"

"I know my rights, peckerwood. I gonna complain."

When Sean was satisfied the man was not armed, he released his grasp.

"Complain all you want, asshole. What are you doing in this dark doorway?"

"Ain't against the law to stand here."

Sean grabbed a hand full of the man's hair and looked at his Social Security card.

"Listen, Mr. Maurice Styles, these streets in your neighborhood are not safe. We have a legal right to check on a man standing in the shadows of a vacant building. Even if you're waiting for someone, it's warm enough to wait out on the sidewalk."

"You just fuckin' wif me 'cause I'm Black."

"Save that bullshit. Look around, asshole. Except for the cops, everyone is Black in the neighborhood. That means the victims of all this shit are Black too."

"If you didn't have that gun and your partners, you wouldn't be puttin' your hands on me."

"Wrong again, Ace. I'd take your sorry junkie ass out if I was sick with a headcold. The only thing that bothers me is that I would really enjoy it. The only thing that keeps me from pounding in your foul mouth is the law and the badge in my pocket."

"Man, I just standin' here waitin' for my ride. I was in the doorway to take a piss in private."

Sean released the man, and he and Bruce started back to the unmarked police car. "Man, you are one stupid shit. Does that doorway look like a urinal? You put us all through this shit, for what?. So you can run your mouth? We could have checked you for a piece, I.D.ed you.

You tell us your waiting for a ride, we're out of here. No insults, no abuse. But you want to jerk us off and joust with us. Well, Maurice, you have succeeded in pissing me off. I'm not going to forget you. If you so much as jaywalk, I'm going to be on you like stink on shit."

"Oh, Mr. Po-lice, you is scaring me to death."

"Listen hard, slick. If you're on the street in five minutes, I'll do more than frighten you."

They got back in the car, and Tom turned onto Seward Street. Bruce wrote the man's name, birth date and address in their bound notebook. Bruce shook his head as he wrote. "Half the people we encounter are assholes, but that shithead was a real hemorrhoid. Maurice Styles. We won't forget that scroat."

Around 11 p.m., Tom made another pass down Second Avenue, past the China Doll restaurant. The restaurant was about eight steps above the Second Avenue sidewalk. They saw a new Buick Electra 225 in front. There was a young Black behind the wheel, the motor was running. Bruce was about to say something about the youth of the driver of the new Buick, when three other young Black men darted out of the front door of.the China Doll and down the stairs to the waiting Buick. They were carrying paper bags. One carried a small automatic pistol.

Sean grabbed the radio mike as Tom managed to stop the car in the center of the Second Avenue, and Seward intersection. As soon as the driver pulled from the curb, he spotted the unmarked police car. He made a rapid, panic right turn east onto Seward. He nearly lost control of the Buick.

Tom skillfully turned onto Seward in pursuit. Bruce leaned toward the front seat so he could be heard. Sean turned on the speaker of the siren, hidden in the grill of the unmarked Ford. "Sean, did you recognize one of those three assholes that ran out of there?"

"I sure as hell did, our new friend Maurice Styles. That's what he was doing when we saw him, he was casing the China Doll. That little mother fucker, it's not that boy's lucky day."

Sean informed the dispatcher that 13-33 was in a chase, and described the vehicle. They crossed Woodward Avenue in excess of 60 mph. The dispatcher told them that they had just received a call from the restaurant. The three young men had robbed the restaurant, and pistol-whipped the owner and a Chinese cook.

The vehicles blew the stop signs at John R. Street, then Brush Street, still doing more than 60 mph.

Sean had drawn his .357. "Don't lose the assholes, Tommy. Stay close and he'll lose control, sure as shit. That's got to be a stolen car and he can't drive like you can."

Sean no more than finished the sentence, when the Buick went into a skid, jumped the curb and hit a tree at Marston and Beaubien. The occupants abandoned the Buick. Sean yelled into the radio mike that they were "bailing out" as he gave their location and he vaulted from the police car.

Without speaking, the three policemen each went after a different suspect.

The driver of the Buick had been stunned. Tom pounced on him and threw him on the ground, sticking his snub-nose magnum in his ear. Bruce chased another east on Marston, down the sidewalk. The suspect in the front of the Buick had run south, between the old houses, with Sean sprinting after him. He knew he wasn't chasing Maurice. He believed he was chasing the one with the gun in his hand. The man had a 40-yard lead, but Sean kept him in sight. He had maintained the Fall's football-team wind over the Winter and was in good physical condition. The distance between them was closing quickly. They half-climbed and half-vaulted over the rear yard fences at the alley of each block. Sean could hear scores of police sirens approaching. It was insane. Sean was chasing a Black robber with a gun through the yards of an all-Black neighborhood, and he had no radio communication with him. But there was not even a fleeting consideration of ending the foot chase. Sean had closed the distance between them to 10 yards.

He had repeatedly ordered the man to stop. Sean wasn't getting tired, he was getting pissed. They were in the back yard of an old, dark, two-story frame house. The robber could not believe that Sean was gaining on him. Suddenly, Sean stopped, he raised his magnum and aimed.

"Last call, you asshole. Freeze or you're dead."

Just as suddenly, the suspect stopped and raised his hands. Somehow, he sensed Sean intended to end the chase. "Man, what's the deal? I ain't done nothin'. I was out walkin' my dog. You come running out of your car and I got scared and run."

"Save it, mother fucker, I saw you leave the car, and I saw you leave the China Doll. You tell the bullshit story to your lawyer. If you even open your mouth again, I'll take you out where you stand."

The suspect shifted his weight. "Better look around, White Meat. This is my block, Man. Best you just turn around and go back to your car. We call it a draw."

"Get on your belly, spread-eagled, you fucking nigger. You don't threaten me, Boy. If someone even passes wind on the way back to the cars, it will be the last sound you'll ever hear. So get down, and keep your arms away from your body."

Sean quickly searched the robber and took an automatic pistol from his waistband. He handcuffed the man with his arms behind his back and hauled him to his feet.

The young Black was about 20. He glared at Sean when he was back on his feet. "Still a long way back to them cars, Mr. Po-lice."

Sean jammed the barrel of the magnum hard against the man's head.

"I swear to you, asshole, if anyone even thinks about fucking with me on our way back, I'll blow your brains out, take off your handcuffs and say you jumped me. I could have killed you a half dozen times since we ran from the cars. Don't think it's too late for that. Now shut the fuck up and move out. Like you said, it's a long walk."

Responding uniform units were roving the area, looking for Sean. Bruce had caught his suspect halfway to St. Antoine Street and was back at the vehicles. Only Sean was still out. The minutes seemed like hours when one of the partners was out of contact on foot after a suspect. Every minute he was gone increased the odds that something had gone wrong. After five minutes, the officer was often found dead.

Sean held the man at the handcuffs with his left hand, his magnum tightly in his right. He led the man back toward the police vehicles, through the deserted yards and streets.

As the pair passed close to the side door of a darkened house, a large dog inside the house suddenly slammed into the door, barking wildly. The loud noise at the door startled both Sean and the robber. Sean pushed the man to the ground and pressed the barrel of his magnum against the base of his skull.

"Let me up, Man. It was only a fuckin' dog. Be cool, Mr. Po-lice. I was jus' runnin' my mouth. Ain't nobody know we here."

"Get up real slow, asshole, or I'll turn you into dog food."

They walked out into another darkened side street. A marked uniform precinct car was rolling by. The occupants did not see Sean emerge from between the houses. He yelled at the car. He was about to fire a round into the air to get their attention when they saw him and stopped. The robber knew his chances for escape were gone.

"Hey, dude. When that dog jumped on the door, I thought you was gonna shoot me."

Sean was being overtaken by the adrenaline high of the dangerous chase. "I almost did, fuckhead. You threaten me, and then wonder why I almost wasted you when that dog scared the shit out of me?"

Sean pushed the suspect in the back seat of the marked car. Sean heard the passenger officer talking to the dispatcher. "13-9 to radio. We have the officer from 13-33 and one in custody. Both are fine. We'll return the officer to the scene."

Sean could feel his heart pounding in his chest. He was coming down, and was starting to feel the fear and anger. He looked at Walt Stockten and his rookie partner. They had worked the shift together before Sean and the others were assigned to the plain clothes unit.

"Guys, would you look out the front windshield for a second?" he asked. Both officers turned their backs to Sean and his prisoner in the rear seat of the police car. Sean reholstered his magnum. He grabbed the prisoner with his left hand at the front of his jacket. He punched the man in the mouth with a hard right jab from his right fist.

The prisoner was dazed for a moment, then he put his tongue on his bleeding lip. "Man, you ain't right. Why you gotta hit me now for?"

Sean sat next to the prisoner for the ride back to his own car at Marston.

"The officers here didn't see me hit you. Listen to me, you stupid fuck. You rob a restaurant, pistol-whip the victims. There's a high-speed car chase, then a foot chase. You've got a gun. You jerk me off, threaten me, and you wonder why I punch your big mouth? You should thank your God I didn't blow your brains all over one of those dark backyards. I hit you because you're too stupid to even realize how lucky you are to be alive. You pissed me off, asshole. You are going to prison, but you'll still be a young man when you get out. Way better than being dead meat. Tonight you learned not to fuck with the police."

The one-in-a-thousand bust had yet another ironic twist: the only robber to escape was Maurice Styles, the only man previously known to the officers. Sean and Bruce spent Monday morning at the Wayne County Prosecutor's office. By late morning, they held an arrest warrant for Styles for armed robbery and assault. None of the other members of the hold-up group had made bond.

Bruce was off work for grad school finals. Sean and Tom roved the streets around Second and Seward and Styles' home, with no success in finding the street-wise robber. On Thursday night, Sean suggested they check the area in his TR6 Triumph, not as recognizable as their unmarked police car.

After an hour of driving around the area, Sean spotted a familiar figure on the sidewalk at West Euclid Street and the Lodge Freeway service drive. Sean slipped the sports car to the curb. Tom was out and in front of Maurice before he could react. He had been on the tough Detroit streets his entire 21 years and had never seen cops pounce on someone from a British sports car.

Tom had his gun in one hand, his badge in the other. "What's your name, Slick?"

Maurice Styles realized his life was about to change. He was not packing a piece; no use trying any stupid shit and getting himself wasted. Maybe one of his partners ratted on him. Maybe the cops had recognized him. "You know me, po-lice. I'm Maurice."

By then Sean had gotten out of the driver's seat. He had his magnum in hand and threw Styles against his car so he could pat him down for weapons. "Yea, I know you, Maurice. Guess what, motor mouth. You're under arrest for armed robbery."

Maurice Styles bumped his mouth hard against the roof of Sean's car.

"Read him his rights, Tommy, I'll call for a uniform car. Bruce will cream his jeans when he hears. I hope you're going to like it at Jackson, you low-life fuck."

Styles plead to a lesser charge. The man Sean had chased chose to have a jury trial. He was found guilty. All four hold-up men were sentenced to 10 to 15 years at Michigan's Jackson State Prison.

Sean, Tom, and Bruce often talked of that arrest. It had been a perfect "television arrest," with no loose ends. They would just enjoy the blind-ass luck. Not outstanding police work or investigative prowess, just luck and simple, normal, young male courage. Again the crew displayed their growing ability. They only lacked the experience and veteran's knowledge; they had the common sense and the luck of the Irish.

To reward their "luck," the department awarded the three of them Departmental Citations. The Brass had read all of the reports and decided the arrest and conviction of four young dangerous armed robbers, without injury to anyone, represented bravery and uncommon self-restraint.

Everyone harassed Sean about the award. They said that he was charmed, that the very first time he used any self-restraint he received a Citation for it. Sean replied that if that was the new criteria, this Citation would be his last.

JULY, 1971
DETROIT

Sean, Bruce, and Tom were taking a coffee break at the Waffle House on Second Avenue, north of Grand Boulevard. They sat at a booth against the wall, and discussed how to make the rain-swept evening productive. Tom had placed their portable radio on the countertop, so they could clearly hear it and wouldn't forget it when they left.

They received a call to go to the Homicide Section at headquarters and talk with Lt. Karlinski. Sean finished his coffee. "I wonder what Homicide wants with us."

Tom handed the portable radio to Bruce, who stuffed it in a back pocket of his jeans.

"I looked at the roster for tonight," he said. "We're the only plain clothes unit on the street other than the Cruiser and they're busy on a radio run. Homicide may want a back up or have us check a place for someone they want."

"That doesn't make any sense," Bruce said. "If that was the deal, they'd either have us call, or they'd meet us at the precinct station. They wouldn't waste our time by making us go all the way downtown."

Within half an hour, the crew arrived at the Homicide Section's fifth floor offices. They reported to the Detective Sergeant at the Homicide Section's entrance desk. "We're 13-33. Dispatch sent us here to meet with a Lieutenant."

"One of you Cavanagh?"

"That's me, Sarge."

"Go see Lt. Karlinski in the back office. He's wearin' a brown suit. Your partners can go in the waiting area. The Lieutenant wants to see you alone."

Although even more confused by the Detective Sergeant's instructions, the young crew followed them.

Det. Lt. Karlinski pounded on an old typewriter. He was about 40 with a thick build and an ever thicker salt and pepper mustache that matched the crop of thick hair on his head.

"Excuse me, Lt. Karlinski?"

He gave Sean the long visual once-over. He thought to himself how much the street coppers had changed in a decade. Sean was wearing a Vietnam-era lightweight jungle jacket to conceal his magnum. He also wore jeans and his old Marine jungle boots. Baby-faced cops. Looked more like they belonged at a college frat party than on the streets. "You Officer Cavanagh, 13-33?"

"Yes, Sir."

"You know a Black guy, 23, about 6'2", Tyler Lee Johnson?"

Sean's heart began to pound and he felt something terrible had happened. "We served in Vietnam, in combat together. We became good friends. Christ, Lou, is he dead?"

"No, Kid. But you better sit down so we can talk. I'll run it by you. He's really in the jackpot. He was the wheelman for a warehouse break-in on the Eastside. It went bad and one of his buddies dropped the hammer on an old guard that happened up on them. The old man's dead. There's still one of the suspects out. He's been read his rights but asked for you first, before we get him a lawyer. If we're going to be able to do him any good, he better talk quick. If he gives up the name of the suspect still out, and makes a full written admission, we won't charge him with anything but being part of the break-in. He better talk fast, before one of his companions opens up first."

"Is he hurt?"

"No. He was packing. Damn if I know why. With his experience, he could have greased the rookie that arrested him. He offered no resistance. Go talk to him, Kid, or he'll fall hard on this with his rap sheet, despite the war hero stuff.

"It ain't like before. The courts could care less that the man spent two years in combat, if it was in ol' Vietnam. I was in Korea, Kid. I know about the special friendship you make with a combat buddy. I never had any Black friends in the Army. They had ended segregation in the military, but we didn't have the same percentage in fighting units that you did.

"Look, Kid, what I'm telling you is that I'm no nigger-lover or liberal. I've been on the job too long for that. But this is different; the kind of a friendship you develop in combat, it's just plain fucking different. So go in there and be his friend. He's already signed a waiver to prove he asked for you before his lawyer. That way, you can go in there as just a friend and not worry about screwing up the case. Cavanagh, he's got enough cops up here tonight. Go in the room there and be his friend."

T.J. sat alone in a small interview room, on a plain wooden chair. His hands were folded on the wooden table that separated the two chairs in the room. His head was hung. Sean had never seen his brave friend in such a defeated posture.

Sean entered the room, closed the door and took a seat in the other chair. T.J. did not realize it was Sean until he spoke. "Hey, big Brother. Are you alright?"

The expression on T.J.'s face showed obvious embarrassment, but he forced a weak smile. "Well, Irish, I sure stepped in some shit this time, didn't I? Sorry if I did wrong by askin' to see you. I just figured I'd better talk to you if I could, before some wet-nose public defender shows up and wants to play Perry Mason at my expense."

"Lay it out for me, T.J. What went down?"

"Same old bullshit, Bro. After I got layed off from Chrysler, I went back out on the street. I was looking for a job during the day. But after a few weeks, I really got down about not findin' one. I ran out of bucks and started to drive for a couple of dudes doing break-ins. Somehow it didn't seem as bad to me if I was only drivin'. Then we have this one boy's cousin join up with us. He's a punk. He's got him this revolver and really proud of it. I swear that revolver make his dick hard better than a good-lookin' woman. We do this place tonight, some old man guard walked up on us by mistake. Irish, any of us could have taken away the old dude's gun without hurtin' him. But that crazy nigger wants to shoot his big revolver, so he wasted the old dude."

"How come you were packing, T.J?"

"Square business, Irish, not to hurt the police, I swear. I had me a gun 'cause what I said, the fool is crazy. I was more afraid of him than any police. I coulda greased the po-lice that arrested me. I wouldn't do it, Irish."

"They said you could have done the rookie. It means a lot to me but it's not much of a defense in court. They won't reward you much for not shooting a cop."

"Bottom line, Bro. What should I do?"

"You could really be in the hurt locker. We both realize your being a Vet won't mean squat compared to your previous record. You're legally part of the murder, even though you were only the wheelman. Murder, breaking and entering, carrying a concealed weapon, you're probably going to do some hard time. What you want to do is reduce the charges, so you can reduce the time.

"Look, T.J., if you make a full written admission, names, previous jobs, the whole shooting match, you'll only take a hit on the breaking and entering charge. It won't be like you're rolling over on your partners or turning State's evidence. You make the full admission on your own. T.J., you know they've got you by the balls. They're giving you a chance to lighten the pop you take in court."

"Can I trust what they promise?"

"T.J., goddamn it. Would I . . ."

"I'm sorry, Irish. I didn't mean that."

"The only thing they can't promise is how much time the judge will give you for the burglary rap. They can only recommend. It will be the judge's call."

"This the best way, Brother?"

"T.J., I'm a cop, but I'm in here as your friend. If I saw you had any other way to go, I'd tell you keep your mouth shut until your lawyer gets here."

"You stickin' your neck out for me on this, Irish?"

"No. Lucky for us the Detective Lieutenant in charge of the case is a Vet from Korea. He's got no use for a Black guy, but he's got a feel for combat friendships. He knows being a Nam Vet doesn't cut any shit in court like other Vets had. I guess he doesn't think that's fair."

"Irish, I'm sorry I brought you into this."

"T.J., if you hadn't called me, I would feel that you really didn't think of me a real friend."

"Bring me a pad of paper and a pen. Let's get it over with. Irish, will you stay with me as long as they let you?"

"I'll get the paper and pen."

With T.J.'s full admission, his time in the criminal justice process was greatly reduced. He stood next to his court-appointed attorney and faced the judge. The visiting suburban judge was in a conservative mode. He reviewed T.J.'s pre-sentence report from the county's probation department. Even though he was a Vet who had helped the police case, T.J. was still an unemployed, repeat offender. He was sentenced to seven to 15 years at the State Prison at Jackson, Michigan. His address would be 500 Cooper Street, Jackson, Michigan, for at least the next five years, minimum.

T.J. accepted the judge's sentence without any expression of surprise on his face. He kissed his mother and shook Sean's hand, before they led him from the courtroom.

Out in the hall, Sean lead T.J.'s mother to the elevators. She had come to court alone. His step-father refused to take off the day from work.

Sean couldn't keep the tears in his eyes hidden from T.J.'s mother. The kind woman put her hand on his shoulder.

"Now, Irish, don't go blamin' the war, or yourself, or society, or none of that. T.J. is a man and he always been taught the difference between right and wrong. I love that boy, my first born and all, but he knows what is right. You didn't see no tears in his eyes. He knows.

"Irish, you wanna still be T.J.'s friend? If so, do as he asked when you seen him last. Write him and send him things like you did when he went to Vietnam the second time. Then, call me every few months to keep in touch. Irish, you the best friend T.J. ever had. You been more like a brother than his own half-brothers. And you're white. If being different races never came between you, don't let your badge and his prison number."

She gave Sean a hug and a motherly kiss on the cheek. "This will be worse for T.J. than Vietnam ever was. Irish, he'll need you the next few years even more than me. He'll probably expect you to disappear from his life. Don't let it be."

The wise, kind woman disappeared in the crowded elevator.

On the ride home, Sean pledged to himself that while T.J. was in prison, he would write at least twice a month, and send a C.A.R.E. package every month. For the time T.J. spent in prison, he never broke his pledge.

T.J.'s first letter rang of optimism. The prison had an extensive sports program to help T.J. pass the days. He was excited as football season approached. The prison had a semi-pro level football team and T.J. couldn't wait for a tryout.

Sean felt that T.J. had received the short end of life's giant stick since 1948.

DECEMBER, 1971
DETROIT

Tom and Sean patrolled the dark streets of the Cass Corridor on a mild, clear night. Bruce was off, recovering from his semi-annual Michigan headcold.

The street traffic seemed light for such a warm December evening.

The department football team's season had concluded two weeks before. Sean had mixed feelings. He missed the teammates and companionship of the football team and the boyish pleasure of simply playing football. But he found that after several weeks he missed his partners and working the streets.

Sean's body was still sore from the wrath of their final game of the season. They had played a very large, aggressive local semi-pro team. What the Chargers had lacked in coaching and finesse, they made up for with size and brutality. The department team, though much smaller, was in excellent condition. They were able to play four full quarters of quality, well-executed, well-coached football and prevailed 14-7. For all of his efforts, Sean was repeatedly pounced on by defensive players more than 100 pounds larger than he. He managed a broken nose, bruised ribs, a hip pointer, and the winning touchdown pass. Sean critiqued the game by saying, "They were bigger, but we were more afraid than they were. Fear makes you quicker."

Tom had complained all night about his marriage. Sean could tell that the status of his high school wedding was near its end when he talked about the apartment he had found.

Sean let himself think of divorce as an alternative to his often-stormy marriage. But with his new son, the thought was out of the question. He could not imagine himself ever leaving his son, no matter how bad the marriage became.

Tom spotted a known street mugger following an old man in the area of Seldon and Second Avenue. By then, their big white Ford sedan was well-known by every street slick in the precinct. Tom pulled the Ford to the curb. They decided to split up and follow the mugger and his target on foot.

Tom slipped their portable police radio into his leather coat pocket. Sean did not have a radio. He wore his old Marine field jacket and jeans. He carried his .357 magnum revolver in a shoulder holster under the field jacket.

Tom sprinted across the street so he could tail their mugger from the opposite side of the street.

"Try to keep me in sight," he said. "If we get separated down here, we could be in as much danger as that old man is. It's almost midnight, change of shift. There won't be scout cars on the street for almost a half hour. Be careful, Cav."

Sean spotted the mugger. He waved to Tom and began to follow him in the shadows.

They followed the suspect, who followed the old man, for about two blocks. The elderly man seemed to be walking in a circle. Just as it appeared that the mugger was about to move in, the old man briskly walked up the steps of an apartment building and stepped safely inside. The mugger looked obviously disgusted. He turned and walked toward the open businesses and people at Second Avenue and Seldon.

Sean had lost sight of Tom. He walked to Cass and Seldon looking for his partner. Tom was nowhere in sight, so Sean decided to walk to the car, parked at the curb two blocks north on Cass Avenue.

Sean happened to look east down the short block of Seldon between Cass Avenue and Woodward Avenue. There was a small restaurant at the corner of Woodward and Seldon. It was a hang-out for local street people, street whores, pimps, Murphy men and assorted Johns looking to pick up a girl. Mid-block, Sean saw three young Blacks in the doorway of a closed building. One of the three nervously looked up and down Seldon as if acting as the lookout. Sean figured the other two had a victim pushed into the doorway and they were in the process of robbing him. Sean gave a last frantic look for Tom with no success.

Convinced he was watching a street robbery in progress, Sean drew his revolver and quickly moved toward the three young men from the north side of Seldon. He used a row of parked cars as concealment. He reached a position directly across the street from the young Black men in the doorway. From that point, he could see that they were just using the doorway as a place to observe the people come and go from the restaurant.

Two water spots on the door and sidewalk explained why two of the three were so close to the building. They were also using the building's doorway as a urinal. The door was a different color than the building. That was why Sean's over-active imagination had seen a victim, despite his good eyesight, instead of two street slicks pissing in a doorway.

Sean was initially relieved, but he realized he'd better get out of there undetected, or he could be the robbery victim they were looking for.

Sean had just changed positions from behind the parked car, when they spotted him. He slipped the four-inch barrel revolver in the large pocket of the military field jacket, and kept his hand on the gun. The size of the jacket pocket allowed him to fit his hand and the gun into the pocket and keep both concealed.

He sensed that he was in real trouble, alone with the three youths. He decided to cut through the parking lot of the small office at 100 Seldon.

He hoped to make it to the alley and out on to Cass Avenue, before the three street punks could catch up to him. To Sean's dismay, he realized the eight-foot fence for the parking lot blocked off the alley. He heard footsteps running up behind him. He realized he had unintentionally trapped himself in the small parking lot. It was well lit, but there was no one to see what the expensive lights illuminated in the isolated, concealed parking lot. The footsteps followed him into the small, vacant parking lot.

Sean turned around. Three young Black men slowly approached him. They had spread out and blocked Sean's only route out of the parking lot.

He backed against the building wall, so at least no one could move behind him.

The man in the center was a step or two closer than the others.

"You got a match, Mister?"

Sean knew the question was a delaying action so they could get closer to Sean before he broke and ran.

All three young men produced knives, blades exposed. They were now within six feet. "O.K., mother fucker. Give us your money. We got knives."

Sean's rapid movement caught the three young street robbers by complete surprise. He had pulled his magnum from his jacket pocket and aimed it at the center of the tallest youth's middle. "That's good, because I have a gun."

The two smaller would-be robbers ran from the scene. Sean announced that he was a police officer, and they were under arrest. The announcement had no results. Both young men escaped toward Woodward. The third, the tallest and closest, was convinced not to try to escape by the magnum pointed at him. Sean displayed his badge and I.D. folder.

"So if you the po-lice, where's your partner?"

"Our car is a couple blocks north on Cass. We're going for a little walk to the police car."

The youth still held the knife. He grinned in an attempt to intimidate the young officer. "How about if I refuse to go?"

Sean cocked the hammer of his magnum and pointed it eye level at the young man's head.

"You'll go, or I'll blow your fucking brains all over this parking lot right now. Numb nuts, I'm not going to stand here and wait for your asshole friends to bring some other shitheads from the restaurant to help you. You have one second to drop the knife and start toward Cass at a nice casual walk, or I take your fucking head off. Did you ever see what a magnum does to the skull at this range? It would make you want to gag."

The robber dropped thc knife and began to walk west on the side-walk, toward Cass Avenue. "You ain't gonna make it, Man. That's a long walk with all the bad dudes around here. Better just let me slide."

"Save your breath, maggot. I heard the same bullshit before. I'll tell you what I told him. If someone messes with us on the way to the police car, I'm taking you out first. They may get me, but I swear, they'll never rescue you, because you'll be dead."

Sean did not want to take the time or the risk to handcuff the young man alone in the parking lot. The morbid thought crossed his mind that if he was forced to shoot the young street robber, there would be far less explaining if he was not handcuffed.

By the time the duo reached Cass, every street thief, pimp and junkie from a four-square-block area had surrounded them. A large, red Mer-cury followed their progress, driving slowly in the curb lane. The passenger window was open and an angry drunk shouted at Sean. "What the fuck you think you doin', White Meat? You better let the Brother be or you gonna get your dumb white ass killed."

Sean showed the car load of angry men his police I.D. "This man is a police prisoner. I don't have any beef with you, but don't mess with me. You interfere with a lawful arrest and I'll ruin your night."

"We don't care if you are the po-lice. Let that young Brother be, or you gonna get dead."

When they started the walk for the police car, Sean had safely lowered the revolver's hammer. He didn't need a hair trigger for a three-block walk. It had been the first time that he had cocked the revolver without firing it. The gesture had given Sean the desired results in the parking lot. As the man in the red Mercury stepped from the car, he turned the magnum at him. He cocked the weapon and spoke with an ice-cold calmness. "Another step and this white meat will turn you into dead meat. I'll blow your nappy hair all over that pretty car."

The prisoner turned around. "I tol' you, pig. A stroll through the streets down here weren't gonna be easy."

"Don't get too excited, fuckhead. As soon as I kill this stupid nigger, I'm going to take the back of your head off."

"Be cool, Mr. Po-lice. I'm way too young to get wasted."

The man in the Mercury climbed back inside the vehicle. They kept pace, but backed off.

Sean was relieved to see Tom standing at their parked car.

"Where the devil you been, Partner? I was going to call for help. What you got there? Did you join the Big Brother program?"

"Oh yea, me and this scroat are real tight. Him and two other little fuckers were going to rob me on Seldon."

"Little fucker is lucky he didn't hit on a cop from that Decoy unit. It seems those fellows are a bit more aggressive, shall we say, than us. The morgue boys would be filling three body bags right now."

"Get the cuffs on him and let's get out of here. I'm afraid I've drawn a following."

Tom grabbed one of the tall youth's arms, Sean the other. Sean put his revolver back in his holster and located his handcuffs. He secured a cuff on the young man's right wrist. Suddenly, the young man began to violently resist. He may have believed that members of the small crowd they had attracted were ready to join in, given an opportunity. He was not correct. With the exception of obscene verbal abuse, the crowd kept its distance.

The struggle moved to the sidewalk next to the car, in front of a two-story duplex with no front yard. Tom and Sean were having a difficult time controlling the strong young man.

Sean heard the slamming of the storm door to one of the duplexes. He caught a glimpse of a white man on the small duplex porch. The man was dressed only in work trousers. He was armed with a 9mm P-38 automatic pistol. Tom finally saw the man as he chambered a live round into his P-38, and shouted at them. "What the fuck is going on here?"

Tom managed to retrieve his badge. Sean redrew his magnum. Tom called to the man on the porch, "Don't shoot. We're the police. This man is our prisoner."

Sean was perplexed. He held the struggling prisoner in one hand, his magnum revolver in the other. He couldn't decide who posed the greatest threat, their prisoner, the man on the porch, or the verbally aggressive crowd.

The man on the porch aimed his pistol at their prisoner. He called to both Tom and Sean, "Get back. I'll shoot the nigger for you."

Tom raised his voice, "No, no please. Just go call for help. Give your address and tell them some officers need help."

Sean decided the very best way to defuse the situation was to reduce the prisoner's physical struggle. He spun the man by the one handcuff and struck the tall, lean young man squarely in the face with the side of his solid revolver. The man fell to his knees, bloodied and dazed.

The man on the porch was as convinced of the young officers' determination as the members of the small assembled crowd that still surrounded them. "O.K., officer. I'll go in and call right away."

Tom managed to get the prisoner's other hand secured behind his back with the handcuffs. The prisoner mumbled something they could not understand. He was still on his knees. Sean was out of breath from the struggle and his poise and fear was giving way to anger. He turned to the small crowd around them.

"You assholes had better get the fuck out of here. When the cop cars start to arrive, you don't want to be here and I know you don't want any of this." He held up his magnum.

Tom withdrew the portable radio from his pants pocket. By the time he radioed the dispatcher, they already heard sirens filling the night air. The man with the P-38 had obviously made the phone call Tom had requested.

As the sirens drew closer, most of the street people wisely disappeared.

Several police cars seemed to arrive at the same time. One of the first at the scene was the night crew of 13 Cruiser. The four veteran officers piled out of their vehicle. "What you got here, Kid?"

Sean reholstered his gun.

"Started simple enough, Ski, then turned to shit. We were trailing some asshole and Tommy and I got split up. Three scroats tried to rob me on Seldon, the other two got away. This one decided to put up a fight just when we started to handcuff him."

The big veteran cop roughly grabbed the prisoner by the back of the neck. "Do you know who the other two are?"

"No. They split up to the small restaurant at Woodward and Seldon."

Ski began to drag the tall, thin would-be robber toward the Cruiser. "You take your time and get the names of all of the witnesses. We'll take the asshole into the precinct for you."

Sean moved close to Ski and spoke quietly under his breath. "Ski, no offense. But please don't chat with him to the point I lose the court case."

Ski looked at the prisoner's face. He grinned at Sean, then smiled. "Looks like you've already dished out a little summary punishment of your own."

"No, that was righteous. Some crazy white citizen was going to shoot him; a crowd was moving in on us, and the asshole was still fighting."

Ski got a sly grin on his face. "Good story, Kid. Stick with it. Don't worry, we won't hurt him . . . where it will show."

Fifteen minutes later, Sean was busy typing his report in the small precinct report room.

Ski walked in and gave Sean a small piece of paper with two names and addresses written on it.

"Here, Kid. Do what you want with this. They're the other two. Your boy is 19, two felony priors. The other two are only 16. Nice catch, Kid, I'd have capped the little nigger in the parking lot, but you did a hell of a job."

"Thanks, Ski. And thanks for the quick response to the call for help."

Sean decided to indicate on his own report that he could not identify the other two subjects. Better to let the Cruiser's method of obtaining the information remain unknown.

After the report was completed, Sean and Tom sipped at their coffee and tried to unwind.

Big Ed and his new partner Rich Wiggins entered the report room and they exchanged salutations.

"Hey, Cav, we heard about your arrest. Nice catch. You could have got yourself greased being out there alone."

Sean put down his coffee. "That's what pisses me off the most about this thing. All I had to do was be on the street after dark to get robbed."

Wiggins sat down next to Sean. "You were in Nam, weren't you, Cav? Would you have gone walking outside the wire, by yourself, after dark? Of course not. The night was theirs, Cav. It belonged to Charlie. Here, the night belongs to the street people. We can ride around because we can radio for help. If they mess with a crew, they know within two minutes there'll be a dozen cops there to shit all over them. Like in Nam, Cav, tonight you got caught alone outside the wire."

"Come on, Wiggins, since I started the academy, everyone has insisted that this job is not like Vietnam."

Wiggins shook his head. "Oh yea, they been laying that rap on me too. Man, we've been bombed twice here at the precinct; we get sniped at once a month; cops killed and shot every month. I was with a unit that guarded Da Nang in '65. It's worse here than I had it in Nam."

"So what do we do, Wiggins?"

"They own the night, Cav. Ain't nothin' we can do about that. All you can do for now is not go out past the wire, alone, after dark.

Early in 1972, the 'attempted-armed-robbery' charge was plead down to 'robbery-not-armed.' He was sentenced to seven to 15 at the Michigan State Prison in Jackson, Michigan.

As they led the defendant from the courtroom, Sean wondered if he would meet T.J. at the prison and discuss the incident.

Sean had no idea at the time that he would visit them both for a day at the prison before the year ended.

10

April, 1972—December, 1972

APRIL, 1972
DETROIT, MICHIGAN

The radio was very busy for a rainy night. There had already been a shooting on East Palmer and a serious stabbing at a "blind pig" at the far north end of the precinct.

Early in their shift, the crew had arrested one Henry "Hank" Carlin. Hank was a long-haul truck driver, who had arrived home to his little apartment near Third Street two days early. He didn't call his wife so he could surprise her by his unscheduled arrival. Rose Ann Carlin *was* surprised. So was the lover she was with in Hank's bed.

When the crew arrived at the apartment house, they found Hank holding his old duck shotgun on Rose Ann and her boyfriend in the small lobby. Hank's tired, worn face looked as though it had as many miles on it as his semi-rig. The three young, well-armed policemen were able to convince Hank that it was in his best interest to surrender his shotgun, and deal with Rose Ann's conduct another day, in a different way.

After the arrest paperwork was completed, the crew went back on the street. Sean popped a Tums in his mouth. The coffee acid was starting to be felt in the pit of his empty stomach. "Shit, it's been so damn busy tonight we haven't had time for our code."

Tom worked on keeping the windshield from fogging. "Ask Bruce. He'll probably tell us about the effect of the full moon on the city's people. The Professor would blame almost everything on the full moon."

Sean put another Tums in his mouth. "Full moon, my Irish ass. Pull over, Tommy, and I'll show Bruce my full moon."

Bruce lit a cigarette and finally joined in to defend himself. "Save it, Cav; seen one, you've seen them all, like your dick."

Sean was in a playful mood. "Mine is different, it's got zippers. I better not drop trousers in front of an ex-swabby. I've heard of you guys playing drop the soap on those long cruises."

"Get bent, Mr. Macho Marine. You're jealous because we always slept in clean, dry beds and ate real, hot food, while you slept in the mud and ate out of cold cans."

"Jealous, my butt. You Navy guys are all alike. You'll never be able to deal with this Navy-Marine conflict until you admit that the Navy is, in fact, a department of the Marine Corps."

"You're right, Cav. I would have joined the Marines, but they wouldn't let me in; my parents were married when I was born."

Tom raised his hand in a gesture for silence. "O.K. Come on, you two. If I want to sit in the middle of some family trouble, I'll go back to Hank and Rose Ann."

Sean slapped Tom playfully on the head. "Well, Bruce, that's that. The draft-dodger has spoken."

"Right, Tommy. We know, give peace a chance. Tommy was away from home once, Cav. He went to Boy Scout camp."

Tom put his hand down. "I should have known better than to open my mouth when you two are on a roll. Just remember who was here taking care of the women while you were away protecting our country."

"With your reputation, it must have been the other draft-dodgers."

The rain was light, but steady. The streets seemed to shine from the countless artificial lights as they reflected off of the water on the pavement.

It had started no differently than countless other incidents and arrests. The city and the department were on the defense, after the almost-monthly incidents involving the very controversial special street Decoy police unit.

The crew felt that the controversy had nothing to do with their daily operations. All three crew members seemed to see the small group of men at the same time. The four men were laughing, shouting, and staggering west on Seldon, toward Second Avenue.

The group consisted of a very drunk middle-aged white man, surrounded by three younger Blacks. They were not only younger; they were also much less intoxicated.

Salt and pepper friendships were not unusual in the Cass Corridor. But street sense indicated that there was something wrong with the make-up of that group. The Black men appeared to be 15 years younger than their white companion. They also seemed concerned about who was around them. They all moved their heads back and forth, as if looking for witnesses, or the police.

Tom pulled the Ford to the curb. They got out and Bruce put the portable radio in his jacket pocket.

"Don't lose sight of each other. Remember what happened to Cav in December. Sure as shit, they're just waiting to find the right place to rip off that white guy. Stupid Hillbilly. If he wanted to be robbed so badly, he should just have handed them his wallet when they met. It would have probably saved him from getting hurt."

Sean wore his leather, waist-length flight jacket. The dark brown jacket and dark slacks made it easy for him to stay concealed in the shadows as they followed the noisy foursome. The acid burn in the pit of his stomach was replaced by a classic case of the butterflies. He kept an eye on Tom and Bruce, and still managed to watch the small group of loud men.

They crossed Second Avenue and began to loiter near the corner, on the sidewalk, just north of Seldon Street.

Tom, Bruce, and Sean took up positions on the east side of Second Avenue. Tom was positioned to cover the group if they moved south or west on Seldon. Bruce was in the center and Sean hid behind a parked car, in position to cover any movement north on Second Avenue. Sean watched the group through the closed windows of the parked cars. He didn't like the change in pitch of the group's shouting. Sean reached inside his leather jacket and drew his magnum.

The stocky white man took several long swallows from a bottle of cheap wine. He passed it among the three Black men and wiped the top briskly before he took another swallow. "Poor dumb white boy," thought Sean. "He wouldn't have passed ol' T.J.'s acid test."

The tallest of the Black men was wearing a light-brown vinyl, three-quarter-length coat. His actions became more aggressive. He began to push the white man against a parked car.

Bruce pulled his magnum, and quietly called over to Sean. "Here we go, Cav. Showtime."

Sean wiped the rain from his face with his left hand and swept the wet hair from his forehead.

All three began to push and hit the drunk. He tried to fight back, but he was no match for the three sober, younger men. He was pushed up against the car and they went through his pockets.

Bruce left his position and began to cross the street. "That's enough. Let's get over there before they hurt him."

The street robbers were so involved in the assault, they didn't notice the three young policemen approaching them, on line, across Second Avenue.

Sean stood in the center of Second Avenue for an instant, frozen by what he saw. The normally-busy street was without traffic that rainy early morning.

The tallest robber retrieved the man's wallet. Then, for no reason, he produced a "slim Jim" street knife. He drove the long blade of the knife into the helpless white man's back. His body slid down the car when they let go of him.

The stabbing was so meaningless that its vicious nature caught even the street-wise crew by complete surprise.

With their victim on the ground, presumed dead, the three street robbers looked up to see the line of plain clothes police officers.

One of the robbers froze and raised his hands in surrender. The two broke and ran north on the sidewalk. A chorus of orders to halt from Sean, Bruce, and Tom stopped another in front of an old three-story stone house at 3977 Second Ave. The cutter in the light-brown vinyl coat continued to run.

Sean ran north in the middle of Second Avenue, keeping pace with the robber, calling out his identification and ordering him repeatedly to stop.

Sean glanced at the corner of Second Avenue and West Alexandrine Street. If the robber made it to the small gas station at the northwest corner, he'd have a chance to escape through the parked cars into the alley.

No street cop can explain why one time an officer will expose himself to extreme danger without firing, then, when faced with similiar circumstances he will decide to use deadly force. Some call it a sixth sense. Others believe it to be a very complex issue with numerous variables that flash through the officer's mind the millisecond before the decision is made.

As the tall street robber reached the curb, Sean raised the magnum to eye level and stopped running. He called out one last time. "Give it up!"

Sean found the form of the sprinting robber in the front sight of his revolver. He fired two rapid shots; the second as soon as he could relocate his human target, his eyes partially blinded by the magnum's red-orange muzzle flash. The roar of the powerful revolver echoed down the empty, rainy ghetto streets.

The robber crashed to the pavement as if blind-sided by a huge invisible tackler. His body lay twisted in the filth of the gutter of West Alexandrine Street.

The body twitched but Sean recognized the movement as involuntary body movements caused by the man's nervous system, not as an attempt to get up.

Sean and Bruce carefully approached the robber's body. Tom covered both of the other men at gunpoint, both were handcuffed. Bruce had given Tom the portable radio and he stood over the badly-wounded victim's body and radioed for assistance.

The twitching continued. A massive head wound had killed the man before he hit the street. The remainder of his body was being notified by the brain and it caused the "death twitch," as they called it on the street. There was also an ugly hole in the upper back of the vinyl coat.

Bruce reholstered his magnum. "Cav, you sure as hell greased this asshole. The victim's still alive, but stabbed in the kidney."

The night air was filled with the sounds of numerous sirens approaching the scene.

The Fire Department had taken over the city's emergency medical needs with trained medical techs and ambulances from the Emergency Medical Service.

Soon, the area was filled with other officers and Fire Department personnel. Crews from the Crime Scene Section took photos. Sgt. Greene and the field duty officer, Cmdr. Danoff, arrived at nearly the same time.

Sean had remained standing over the body of the man he had shot. A large pool of blood had formed under the body but the steady rain was washing it away down the gutter into the storm drain.

The body had stopped twitching by the time the E.M.T.s lifted him onto a stretcher and placed him in a Fire Department E.M.S. van.

Jimmy Haller, the young Black officer from one of the other Booster crews, walked up to Sean. "Are you alright, Cav? Don't know why they're takin' him away in such a hurry. Anyone can see that asshole is D.O.S."

Haller inspected the victim's wallet that still lay next to the open "slim Jim" knife and morbid pool of blood.

"Crazy mother fucker, stab a man to death over $17. White dude ain't even got a credit card. He still has a Tennessee driver's license. Lives in an apartment on Myrtle Street. You know, Cav, I grew up on these streets and I still don't understand how some asshole can do another dude for fuckin' $17, even when there is a racial difference. These ain't boys. The white guy is about 45, and these three are all around 30; ain't like young Bloods out proving their manhood. It's just crazy shit."

Uniform officers placed the two other uninjured prisoners in a marked police car. They called to Officer Jimmy Haller. "Hey, Brother. These crazy racist police shot down our cousin for nothin'."

Haller followed them into the back seat of the police car. "You two mother fuckers can save that Brother shit, or I'll kick yo' ass myself. I got one brother, and he wouldn't rob and stab some ol' funky drunk white dude. If they was crazy racist police, you two would probably be dead too."

"Officer, they didn't have to shoot our cousin."

"And what about the white dude? Did he commit suicide by backing up on a knife a couple times? And what did they do, drag your cousin a full city block away and shoot him? Save all that jive bullshit for some-one who'll listen. Them boys that arrested you are good police. They ain't them Decoy police, and they ain't trigger-happy. If that scum-bag cousin of yours got shot, it's 'cause he deserved it."

Jimmy walked back to Sean. Sean was standing alone at the curb, staring at the pool of blood, magnum still in his right hand.

"Thanks, Jimmy. I really appreciate you standing by me. I swear, Jimmy, man to man, I'm not sure why I opened up on him before I chased him for a while. I thought if he made it to all those parked cars at the gas station, he could get away. I wasn't going to let that fuckin' animal get away. Jimmy, I swear, I didn't shoot him because he's Black."

"Whoa, Cav. Don't even get to start talkin' that shit to me. If I even imagined you wasted that fucker 'cause he was Black, whether he deserved it or not, I wouldn't be standing with you. Put your piece away, Cav. You'll be lookin' like a rookie after his first shooting. Let it go. You've been in a lot of shootings since you came on the street. And before that, you was in Nam. Come on, man. Get your shit together. The field duty officer is roaming around."

Sean watched the last of the robber's blood disappear in a ministream of rain water down the storm drain. "Jimmy, I got out of the academy in May of '69. I've been in so many shootings since then . . . shit, I have actually lost count."

Jimmy Haller put his arm around Sean's shoulder. "It ain't gonna get no better for a long while, Cav. You're a good copper. Brothers on the job need your kind of white cop. You are a bad mother fucker when you need to be, but you're fair."

Bruce and Tom joined them. Bruce offered Sean a smoke but he refused.

"Come on, Partner, we've got to go to Homicide. We love you, Cav, but you'll do almost anything to get some days off." Bruce saw that Sean was not amused. "Come on, Pal. Lighten up. You've been to this dance before. Let's go downtown."

They sat in an isolated office, waiting for the police union representative and attorney to arrive.

A stout middle-aged Homicide Detective walked into the room. Sean already had coffee. The tough old-time copper handed Sean a coffee mug and winked. "Here, Kid. Drink this down before your lawyer gets here. It will put hair on your chest.

Sean drank from the mug of cheap whiskey, flavored with bitter coffee.

It was still raining when he wheeled his Triumph into his driveway at dawn.

The media would decide to bury the story of the fatal shooting. A precinct cop shooting the street robber who had obviously stabbed an innocent victim did not fit the front page theme of police violence they had been feeding the public in massive doses at the expense of the department's Decoy unit and its members. The second page article in both papers simply stated that an officer from the 13th Precinct shot and killed an alleged street robber after the stabbing of a victim. In the articles, the officer remained unnamed.

Sean showered, shaved and redressed for his trip downtown, for the first day of the shooting review. He was on the way out the front door with his off-duty .357.

Lyn emerged from the bedroom, still half asleep. "Sean, what's the matter? Are you alright?"

Sean gave her a kiss on the forehead. "We had some trouble last night, Lyn. I'll be home this afternoon. Then I'll be off for a couple of days. Call my folks for me and tell them I'm alright, please."

"Sean, did you shoot someone last night?"

"Yes, Lyn, I shot someone. I saw a man rob and stab another man. He tried to escape and wouldn't stop."

"So you shot him?"

"Yes, Lyn, I killed him."

"No remorse, Sean? You take a human life and no remorse?"

"Of course there's remorse. For the victim of a $17 street robbery who was nearly stabbed to death."

"How much does human life really mean to you?"

"Lyn, a hell of a lot more than 17 lousy dollars."

"We'll talk when you get home."

"No promises, Lyn. If you want to talk we will. If you want to lecture, save it. Say a special good morning to Denny for me. "

"O.K., Sean. Good luck Downtown. You take care, O.K.?"

On the ride Downtown, Sean knew he could never really tell Lyn about what had really happened. He could never share the sight of seeing the man's skull explode with the impact of his magnum round. He couldn't share the combination of agony and excitement of the terrible incident.

Sean pushed the accelerator of his Triumph to the floor and weaved through the morning expressway traffic. "Fuck this shit. It don't mean nothin'."

SEPTEMBER, 1972
DETROIT

September, 1972, was Sean's third season as the department football team's quarterback. After another violent Summer on the streets of 13, Sean welcomed the complete change of playing football. He enjoyed the racial harmony the team experienced. He often shared with Black teammates the unrealistic wish that the team's spirit of companionship could be brought back to the precincts with them when each season ended. Racial tension within the department was on the increase due to countless internal changes.

Semi-pro level football for a 5'11", 175-pound quarterback might seem like a strange kind of relief from the violence of police work. Weeks of being pounded to the turf by men much larger than Sean would be considered less than a respite from the street by most people.

But to Sean, football was the perfect escape. He could lose himself in the sport, emotionally and physically.

After two weeks of two-a-day practices in just helmets and shoulder pads, the team started full contact practice. That week they received their season game schedule. The regular games had been originally slated to begin in mid-October, but they discovered that a game had been added for Oct. 7th. To their complete surprise, the police officers saw that they were going to play a game against the inmate football team of Jackson State Prison.

This was prior to the release of the popular movie about an inmate team playing a team of prison guards, and the idea of cops going inside the prison walls to play a football game surrounded by inmates met with mixed reviews. Only masculine pride prevented some of the men from refusing to play the inmates.

Sean was the closest thing the team had to a scouting report. He shared some of the information T.J. had told him in his letters. Sean knew T.J. was doing the same, including a complete report on Sean himself. Sean made certain his teammates did not underestimate the inmate squad. He explained some of the things T.J. had told him. If football was a welcome escape for the cops, it was a reason for living for the inmates. Whatever they lacked in talent, the inmate team would make up for in raw strength and tenacity.

After practice, Sean was pensive. His friend and offensive co-captain, Perry Mann, came up to him. "You told me last year about your Nam buddy being on the Jackson team. Are you feeling bad that we're going to play against him?"

"No, I guess not. It's just I never imagined that we'd ever play the inmate team. We played against each other in high school. I guess it is like we'd say, what goes around, comes around."

Perry was the team's center, and since he was 6'4" and 240 pounds, Sean often credited him with Sean's survival each season. Perry had played college ball and made it to a pro team for two years before being cut and returning to Detroit to become a cop. Sean knew Perry was on his way to the Third Floor. He was bright, good looking, and a good cop. He was a perfect vehicle for affirmative action; Perry was also Black.

"Cav, I know how thick you were with that buddy in Nam, but even brothers can play ball against each other with no hard feelings. We're going to play a football game. You're not going there to arrest him."

"Perry, it's just that the sports program means so much to those guys. To be the guys who put them there, then go there and beat them in a game seems like rubbing it in."

"They invited us, Cav. They have trouble getting teams willing to play them because of the potential danger and no gate money. Only a couple of colleges and some semi-pro teams will chance going behind those walls. I'm sure your friend would accept nothing less than a 100 percent effort from you and from our team."

That night, Sean went home and wrote T.J. a brief letter. He mailed it at once so T.J. would receive it before game day. Sean shared with T.J. his mixed emotions, his delight in being able to see T.J., his reservations about playing against him again. Somehow, Sean felt that he and T.J. would always be on the same team, the same side, for the rest of their lives.

Two days before the game, Sean received a short letter from T.J. He said to thank the team for accepting their offer but his inmate team planned a special "welcome." He playfully told Sean to bring along some extra ice packs for himself. He ended the letter with a promise not to bite him during the game, maybe afterward if they lost, but not during the game.

No one could have asked for a more perfect Michigan Fall day. The cloudless sky, the cool snap in the fresh breeze made for an ideal day for football.

The morning of Oct. 7, 1972, the players, assistants and coaches of the Detroit Police football team filed onto the department's new converted Blue Bird school bus. The bus had screens over the windows and was probably one of the few Blue Birds which was, in fact, blue. The school bus was used for numerous purposes, from transferring prisoners, to conveying the riot police to trouble spots, to taking the department team to the State Prison in Jackson, Michigan.

There was more than the normal amount of nervous chatter during the two hour bus ride on the Interstate. Somehow, the talented players of the police team felt they were in for a unique day.

Sean sat up front next to Coach Paltier. Roger Paltier was a Detroit Public Schools administrator. As an ex-football coach, he was recruited by the department to be the head coach.

Coach Paltier and Sean discussed their offensive game plan over a small chalkboard.

The ballplayers were dressed in sports jackets or sweaters with ties. Their equipment was carried in large white canvas bags with draw strings.

It was going to be some real-life dramatic material: a football game between the cons and the cops. However, none of the media seemed interested enough to run with the story.

The bus left the Interstate and drove along Cooper Street. A short time later, it pulled onto the circle drive to the huge red-brick prison's main entrance.

Sean couldn't help but be impressed at the sight of the prison. The chalkboard slipped off of his lap. "Holy Mary, Coach. Will you look at that place? Have you ever seen anything like it?"

"I sure as hell haven't, Cav. It's going to take everything we've got to keep their minds on the ball game, and try to ignore all this."

"That's going to be 'Mission Impossible', Coach. This prison would intimidate any team, much less a team made up of guys who work at filling the place."

A guard climbed onto the bus, greeted them and led the way to the visitor's locker room. They were welcomed by the few inmates they passed with playful cat calls and warnings about the football game.

The locker room was void of conversation and charged with static electricity. Ankles and wrists were taped. The men put on the layers of clothing and equipment, and the often-used analogy of modern gladiators preparing for battle was obvious.

Sean put an elbow pad on his left arm and cloth wrist bands over the tape on both wrists. Despite the bright day, Sean decided he'd pass on the grease pencil under his eyes, it was going to be tough enough out on their field, he didn't need to give them any additional ammunition.

After they were suited up, the same guard led the police team down empty halls to the exit and into the walled-in sports area.

Once out in the prison yard, the silent file of police players came under a steady barrage of verbal insults, threats, and warnings. The calm guards were overwhelmingly outnumbered, but seemed to have no problem keeping the inmates a safe distance from the police and maintaining control.

The inmate team warmed up at the opposite side of the field. Their uniforms and equipment were Spartan and worn next to the professionally-equipped police team. The Golden Lions football team of Jackson Prison had green helmets, green jerseys with gold numbers, and white pants.

Sean would have no problem identifying his receivers. The police team had white helmets with navy blue stripes and logos. They had navy blue jerseys with white numbers, and white football pants.

Sean thought of T.J. It was seven years since their high school days and his football uniform was once again green and gold. He spotted number 40 and the two men exchanged waves across the field.

The police team's pre-game warm-up was much more quiet and subdued than normal.

The actual playing surface of the field was in excellent condition. There were only two sets of bleachers on the inmate side of the field. The vast majority of other inmates who would watch the game would have to stand in rows along the sidelines and end zones, as if standing on the sidewalk watching a parade. Most of the inmates and the team members were Black, Sean guessed 80 percent.

Warm-ups completed, both teams restlessly paced the opposite side-lines. There were nervous comments and tentative glances at the other team across the field.

The referees gathered at the mid-field and finally called for the team captains for the coin toss. Sean, Perry and the two police defensive captains met the four inmate co-captains where the referees had gathered.

The men held their helmets under their arms. Sean moved over to talk with the tall Black inmate player with the familiar grin, number 40. As the referees went over the basic rules and went through the coin toss, Sean and T.J. chatted.

"Well, little white Brother. What do you think of my new home?"

"The place intimidates the shit out of me. T.J., I feel like I'm in a lion's den, and wearing a pork chop suit."

T.J. nodded his head as he looked at the large crowd of inmates gathering around the field to watch the game. "Yea, Irish. I can dig where you're comin' from. It's kind of like a Marine ball team playing a game in Hanoi. Trouble is Irish, we only get to play home games."

With the coin toss complete, the co-captains exchanged handshakes. The inmate Golden Lions would receive. As the men began to turn away, T.J. addressed the referee crew chief. "Excuse me, Ref. Before we start, can I tell the po-lice captains something?"

The referee was puzzled for a moment but gave the go-ahead. He hoped he hadn't made a mistake.

T.J. approached the four police co-captains. "Gentlemen, I've got to tell you how important our sports programs are to us. We're going to play real hard and we stick real hard, but we play clean. There'll be no name-callin' or cheap shots on the field. You all know you'll hear a whole lot of verbal B.S. from the crowd. They're going to be tough on you 'cause you are the po-lice. Just remember the rap on the sidelines will have nothing to do with the sportsmanship on the field."

The captains shook hands again and returned to their own side of the field.

Perry spoke to Sean as they trotted back to their teammates. "Number 40, that's the guy you were in Nam with?"

"Yea, he's a defensive back. T.J.'s a good player. I may have to play around him."

"Hey, Cav, you never said he was a Black."

"You never asked. Come on, Perry, you know me after three years. I'm no liberal or Black crusader. I'm a white, middle-class, conservative, Republican honkie. I just happen to have a few friends who just happen to be Black."

"Yea, O.K., Cav, but I just realized that you're not as white as I thought you were."

Sean would never forget the 60 minutes of football played that beautiful Saturday afternoon. For most people seriously involved in a sport there is a day on which their performance is far above the norm; a day when they had the "magic".

Sean turned in the best football game he'd ever played. And only his "charmed" performance and the solid play of the police team's defense kept them a step ahead of the hard-hitting inmate team. Playing a regular game a week early turned what would have been a tough contest into a struggle.

The police team was plagued with terrible field position on every possession and was unable to generate a running game. The cops' offense turned into the "Sean Cavanagh Air Show." Their defense was as vicious as ever and held the inmate team to nearly non-existent rushing or passing yardage.

T.J. was the Golden Lions left cornerback. They used a basic 4-3 formation. T.J.'s responsibility was the second receiver out. Normally that was the slotback. He had his hands full covering the two speedy slotbacks that alternated each down, bringing in the next play from Coach Paltier.

As the first half ended, Sean had completed 20 passes for more than 200 yards, including a perfectly-executed bootleg pass for an 18 yard touchdown. The extra point try failed. When the gun sounded, ending the half, the police held a slim 6-0 lead, despite Sean's passing statistics.

Sean had paid dearly for his impressive performance. During the first half, he had experienced the worst physical punishment of his football experience. T.J. did not exaggerate when he said his teammates hit hard. A combination of stunts, blitzes and large, talented inmate defensive linemen and linebackers, not only stopped their running game, but pounded Sean to the cool turf on nearly every play.

The last play of the half ended in a typical way; Sean was blind-sided as he released the ball. He lay motionless on the turf, not certain about the condition of his painful left shoulder. He could hear his teammates moving to the far end zone for the half time conference. The guards could easily secure their area at the far corner of the prison yard.

Sean could tell someone was standing over him. He rolled onto his back and saw T.J., helmet under his arm, grinning down at him.

"Damn, Son. Why do you always play way out of your league when you play against me?" He helped Sean to his feet.

"You just bring out the best in me, T.J."

"Look, Irish. I told the other guys on the team you had a good arm, but what's with all this scrambling Fran Tarkington shit?"

"It's called self-preservation, T.J. With the rush your people have been putting on, I've got to scramble to stay alive, and the jury's still out on that. You were right, T.J. Your people sure can stick, but they're the smallest and cleanest team we've played to date."

"You hurtin', Irish?"

"Hell yes, I'm hurting. T.J., tell your teammates they made a believer out of the cop team's number 7. They can beat on someone else the second half."

"Sorry, Irish. You know better than that. You're the one that's beatin' us, son. You know you'll be gettin' our full attention the second half. Take care, little Brother. We'll talk after the game."

"Yea, I look forward to it, if I'm still alive."

Sean nursed his left shoulder, and slowly walked to where his team was gathered in the bright mid-day sunshine. They rested in small groups, discussing what had happened during the first half.

The department's professional trainer saw that Sean was in distress. He helped Sean take off his helmet, and inspected his sore shoulder.

Coach Paltier had never raised his voice at the men of the police team. He had never really had to. He pulled hard on the brim of the light blue baseball hat covering his head. He nervously tugged on his mustache and wiped his wire-rimmed glasses with his handkerchief. It was obvious the coach was less than pleased with his team's performance in the first half.

"Gentlemen, I know this is the first game of the year, and it is a full week earlier than expected, but this is our third season together as a team. There is no more time for excuses. If it wasn't for our defense and Cavanagh's throwing, we'd be three scores down, instead of leading by a touchdown. The offense and special teams better play ball the second half, or it's going to be a hell of a long bus ride home. I know those men over there are really hitting hard. But, men, they don't belong on the same field as this team. They're playing inspired football. Number 72 is in our backfield as much as our fullback. The bottom line, offense, is that Cavanagh cannot take another 30 minutes of punishment and carry you like he did the first half. Either start playing football like you know how, or you can kiss your undefeated record goodbye."

The second half started with the police receiving the kickoff. It also started in the same fashion as the first half, the kickoff receiver recovered his own fumble at the police 12-yard line.

After two running plays, the police team faced a third down on their own 15, seven long yards from a first down.

The 20-minute rest of halftime seemed to give Sean his second wind. In the huddle, he tried to calm and encourage his teammates. "We're alright, gang. We've had our backs to the wall all game. Let's get out of here."

The coach had called for a roll-out pass to the short side of the field. Sean took the snap and rolled to his right. He never had a chance to even look for a receiver. Big number 72 was all over him. The big man literally was on his back. Sean managed to stumble to the 10 where the rest of the defensive pursuit pounded him to the chalk line.

Sean trotted back to his bench as the punter came in. The same interior linemen had protected Sean all three seasons. The five huge men, three Black, two white, had all played college ball. One other member of the line, other than Perry, had made it into the NFL for a couple of years. Sean remembered the previous games in which he was hardly even touched because of their fine blocking. He had struggled like any rookie quarterback his first year and they encouraged and supported him. Despite the beating being dealt by the inmate defense, Sean had no criticism for the talented linemen. He could read the frustration on their faces. He also realized that with no effective running game, the inmates could key on him.

After an exchange of punts, the police team retook possession at their own 4.

In the huddle, Sean called the first down play given to him by Coach Paltier. Paltier hoped that the Golden Lions would not anticipate a pass on first down, from their own 4, and he was correct. Sean took the snap and gave a good fake on the play-action pass. He moved into the far left corner of his own end zone. The good fake had slowed the rush. Sean set to throw. His speedy split end used the good play-action fake to slip behind the Golden Lion secondary. Sean released a perfect pass the moment the inmate defense reached him and drove him into the crowd, off the playing field, with a crushing tackle. The split end gathered in Sean's pass at the 35. He raced up the sideline and was finally forced out of bounds by a great effort from T.J. at the Golden Lion 45.

From there, the police team managed to move the ball up the field with a time-consuming, sustained drive, keeping the ball on the ground and using short passes over the center. The well-executed combination of plays ate up most of the third quarter.

At third and goal, from the Golden Lion 6, Sean brought his team up over the ball. He had displayed a calm poise that seemed to settle down the offense, so they were playing up to their ability. He called out the signals and looked out over the inmate defense. His eyes caught those of T.J. His friend had an expression of concentration and determination, but the hatred he had seen in '65 was gone.

Sean took the snap and rolled to his right. Everyone on the field moved right with him except for his fullback. After sliding off of a block, the fullback moved into the left corner of the end zone undetected. While running to his right, Sean managed to throw a pass all the way across the field to his fullback for another touchdown. The extra point try was successful, and as the third quarter drew to a close, the police led 13-0.

The police players received a moderate amount of verbal abuse from the hundreds of inmate spectators. A handful of overzealous inmates were removed from the yard by attentive guards. With the exception of the name calling, there were no incidents between the police and their unique hosts. It was not only a tribute to the spirited inmate team, but also the guards and the total inmate population of the prison.

Despite their 13-point lead, there remained nervous anticipation on the Detroit Police bench.

Sean had found a plastic water bottle and sat at the end of the bench resting. He was approached by Coach Paltier. "Cav, that was a damn fine drive. How are you holding up?"

"As long as I keep warm and loose, I'll be alright."

"Good. We can't sit on this lead with a full quarter left to play. If we change our game plan and try to eat up 15 minutes, they could catch us."

Coach Paltier moved back to the sideline to watch the police kickoff. Sean slowly got back to his feet. Not since combat, had Sean been in such physical discomfort. He hurt all over. He knew he had to keep moving. As soon as he fully cooled down, he feared his entire body would seize up.

The police defense stopped the Golden Lions and took over possession on their own 30, after the punt.

Sean trotted to his huddle to call the first play. He tried to hide his collective discomfort as he passed the inmates defensive huddle. He glanced at T.J. and just shook his head.

T.J. recognized that his friend was really hurting from the beating he had taken all game.

Their middle linebacker called the defensive huddle to order. "Here's the deal, dudes. We gotta make them keep the ball in the air. If we shut down their running, they gotta throw and we gotta get possession. Keep up the pressure on their Q.B. He's the one been hurtin' us all afternoon. It looks to me like he's playin' hurt. If we stop his passes, we've still got a chance."

T.J. knew for a fact that his friend was playing hurt, but said nothing. T.J. would give 100 percent to win, but he could not contribute in any way to his friend's physical agony.

T.J. was pleased with his own performance. He recognized the combined talent of the police team and knew that, had the inmate team's defense not played their best game to date, the score would not be as close.

T.J. was thankful he was not on the offense. He watched the punishment they were taking from the police defense. He was convinced that the police defense was as good as some NFL teams.

T.J. was not exactly untouched by the game. In addition to the constant down-field blocks, he was punished every time he tackled one of their sturdy running backs, particularly the fullback, Joel Cline. Tackling Cline at full speed was like an encounter with a fire plug. T.J. thought that at least the fire plug wasn't also moving.

After two unsuccessful running plays, Coach Paltier sent in a third downpass play. Sean wasn't losing his poise, but he was getting frustrated. He spoke to the offense in the huddle before calling the play.

"We can't expect our defense to hold them all day. Their quarterback has got a cannon arm and it's only a matter of time if we keep giving them the ball. We've got a whole quarter to play. We've got to keep the ball and eat up the clock."

He called the play and brought the team out over the ball. Everyone in the prison yard knew Sean was going to pass. The inmate defense deployed their "prevent" pass defense.

Sean took the snap and rolled to his right. He searched for an open receiver as the inmate's effective pursuit was merely a step behind his sprint into the right flat.

Joel Cline had rolled out with Sean and was blocking in front of him. Unable to locate a receiver, he called to Cline that he was going to run. Cline took out the outside linebacker and Sean evaded the middle linebacker by cutting to the sideline. Sean cut up the field. T.J. cut across the field, he had the angle to stop Sean. He reached Sean at mid-field, directly in front of the Golden Lion bench. Instead of stepping out of bounds, Sean lowered his head and shoulder as T.J. drove his shoulder into him, pushing him into the inmate players around the bench.

Across the field, at the police bench, Coach Paltier couldn't believe his eyes. He threw his clipboard to the ground angrily.

"Damn him! What the hell is he trying to prove? He already had a first down! He's played the best game of his life, and he goes one-on-one with their best defensive back! Tell Williams to warm up his arm. If Cavanagh keeps up that shit, he won't last the series."

Sean slowly got to his feet with the help of T.J.'s hand. "You've still got it, T.J. You sure as hell still can hit."

They both trotted back onto the field. "Irish, you stupid shit. I know you're hurtin'. Why didn't you step out of bounds? You got nothin' to prove here. You more than paid your dues today."

Even with the clock stopped by Sean stepping out of bounds, Coach Paltier used a time out so he could "chat" with his battered quarterback.

"Cav, this is the first game of the season. Don't use yourself up on one damn afternoon. This team needs you healthy. This isn't your first season, start acting like a mature semi-pro quarterback, instead of some damn 19-year-old macho Marine. Now, go back in there, and use your head, or I swear, Cav, I'll pull you out."

He received mixed reviews in the huddle. He got several slaps on the back and a threat from Perry to boot his ass.

The offense managed another first down, and the drive stalled again. On third down, Sean was forced to pass. They attempted to conceal the obvious with a good fake sweep on a bootleg pass. It gave him time to set, but all of his receivers were covered. He threw deep to his split end, running a crossing pattern. The pass was on target, but the receiver got turned around and the ball struck his shoulder pads. It bounced up, then into the alert hands of T.J., who was covering the receiver.

T.J. tucked the ball under his arm and skillfully evaded two would-be tacklers. He reached the sideline and cut up field, running past the police bench.

There was only one police player between T.J. and an 80-yard touch-down run, Sean.

Sean had played some defense from little league until his junior year in high school. He was not a semi-pro level defensive back, but he had not forgotten how to tackle a ball carrier.

T.J. was running upright, at full speed. He never saw where number 7 had come from. Sean hit T.J. at the 50 with a textbook-perfect shoulder tackle. The crisp tackle was nearly painless to both men as they rolled into the police players.

"Irish, you peckerwood. I'll never hear the end of it. Not only is my big chance for a T.D. ruined, but I get tackled by a damn quarterback."

"Quit your bitching. I threw it to you, I should get to tackle you."

As the police defense took the field, Sean's teammates playfully chided him as he searched for a plastic water bottle. "Hey, Cav, what you doing, looking for job security?"

"I bet he's tryin' to get named defensive and offensive MVP, with plays like that."

Coach Paltier walked up to Sean. He lightly tapped the side of Sean's helmet. "Not a bad pass. Sometimes plays like that just happen, the way the ol' ball bounces, and all that. That was no shabby tackle, Cav. I didn't know you could do that."

Sean squirted a long line of water into his mouth from the plastic bottle. "Luckily I haven't had to call on my old defensive basics until today. I'd much rather our guys catch my passes. I'm not supposed to be the tackler; I'm the tacklee."

Sean discussed the interception and possible open routes with his split end.

Perry Mann came up and placed his hand on his shoulder. "You're lucky, son. If I hadn't seen the ball bounce off of Lewis' pads, I'd have wondered whether you didn't pass the ball to that inmate buddy of yours."

"Bite my butt, Perry. Five minutes ago you were going to kick my ass because I was bumping heads with number 40, now you accuse me of tossing him a gift."

"The ass-whipping you've taken today, I thought you might have some brain damage."

The Golden Lions managed one first down, but were forced to punt. The ball took a classic Golden Lion bounce, and the police took possession on their own 5.

Sean had convinced Coach Paltier to use the slot I-formation. The belly series used fakes and misdirection. It was a variation of the much-used triple option of the '70s.

The entirely new offense caught the Golden Lions defense off balance. The fakes and misdirection opened holes for Cline and Ashford.

Sean continued to mix in the short pass. They sustained an excellent drive, keeping the ball in play to keep the clock moving.

Coach Paltier did not want to run up the score. He was satisfied with a 13-0 lead and running down the clock. The final gun sounded with the ball on the inmate 7 yard line.

Each team suffered one serious injury. The police team lost a defensive tackle with a broken ankle. The inmates lost a running back with a broken collar bone. With the unusually hard, clean hitting, both teams felt fortunate that they had only suffered one injury each.

At the gun, the police team was moved to the far end of the field, while the yard was cleared of inmates. The team was unusually sedate after the hard-fought victory. They exchanged handshakes and subdued conversation.

Once the yard was cleared, a guard guided the police team back to their locker room.

Perry helped Sean get his football jersey off over his head. His arms and shoulders hurt so badly he couldn't manage alone.

Sean slowly limped into the shower room, and stood under the hot water for more than 10 minutes. He told Perry that he had enough lactic acid in his body to charge a car battery.

As part of the prison P.R., the police team and the inmate team shared a late lunch in an isolated portion of the cafeteria.

The police team changed back into their ties, blazers and sweaters. Their guard guide led them to the cafeteria. Sean needed help to get his blazer on. He painfully moved down the halls with his teammates, trying to hide his discomfort.

In the cafeteria area, Sean found T.J. and set his tray down next to his. They shook hands and were oblivious to their own teammates.

"Well, Irish. What do you think of my home for the next few years?"

Sean carefully inspected the thick slice of lean beef on his tray. He was impressed by its taste. "T.J., at first glance, it scared the shit out of me. But, I'd say we've been in worse places."

"No way, Brother. Square business, I'd rather be back in Nam like it was my second tour than be in this place."

"I'm not making light of it, T.J. I know I can't even begin to know what it's really like behind the walls here. I saw a lot of all the queer shit you wrote me about in the yard during the game. Do they try and mess with you?"

T.J. emptied a carton of milk and opened another. "No way, Bro, I'm cool. I'm big enough to protect myself, and playin' ball, I got enough bad-ass friends to help me if I need it. Baby-faced, pretty white boy like you is what they like. You better stay outa here, Irish."

"Oh, yea. I got that idea from your fellow inmates during the game."

"Did them boys watchin' the game bother you?"

"Well, one big guy kept telling me he liked my ass and wanted me to go to his cell with him and be his housewife. And one other time some guy on the sidelines grabbed my ass."

T.J. stuffed a large piece of beef in his mouth and spoke between the chews. "Got to realize, Irish, ain't like the Corps in this place. We could all see the light, you know. Even a year wasn't too long to wait for a woman. Here, some dudes are here for what must seem forever. Here, they even hold hands and kiss in public. 'Bout makes me wanna puke."

They finished lunch and Sean introduced T.J. to some of his police teammates. T.J. then took Sean over to the inmate team's seats. The tension was so thick that T.J.'s introduction was awkward. Sean complimented the team and asked to be introduced to number 72. The large, sullen Black slowly stood. "I'm Number 72. What about it?"

Sean offered his hand. "I've had my ass whipped in the Marines, and on the street, but I'll never forget the clean, complete ass-whipping you gave me today."

There was a long pause of silence. Then, the big man shook Sean's hand, which disappeared inside the large black hand. "Say what, number 7. You played a good game. You can take a beatin'."

"Like I said, T.J. and I, we were both Marines."

Sean's conversation with the inmate team seemed to break the ice. The members of both teams talked together after lunch and during a brief tour.

An hour later, their equipment already loaded on the Blue Bird, the police players readied to leave the prison.

T.J. hugged Sean briefly.

"You be cool out there, little white Brother. I've heard your name. You ain't makin' no friends out there on the street. They say you're fair, but one hard-ass honkie. Try to come back with your boys, that was the best lunch we've had since I been here."

"Keep your head down, T.J. I'll write, Brother. Good luck the rest of the season. I won't walk the right way for a fucking month. I'll call your mother this month and tell her we got to see each other, so to speak."

"Take care of that baby boy of yours. If he grows up to be a Marine or a preppie, I swear I'll whip yo' ass my own self."

"I miss you, Brother."

"Well, you always know where to find me."

As the bus left the prison driveway, it was silent, still filled with tension. As the distance between the bus and the prison increased, the nervous tension decreased.

Still on Cooper Street, the bus pulled off the street into the parking lot of a liquor store, less than a mile from the Interstate. The coaches slipped off the bus. Minutes later, they returned, loaded with bags full of hard liquor and cases of cold beer. They were greeted by a chorus of cheers.

By the time the bus was headed east toward Detroit on the Interstate, the battered ballplayers had distributed the assorted alcoholic beverages.

Coach Paltier stood at the front of the bus and asked for the attention of his team.

"You men know I'm not into any of that Knute Rockne shit. I know you realize the kind of game you played today. We know the defense won the game. Other than Cavanagh's tackle, we might have to name the entire defense the game's defensive MVP. Now, offense, we all know who the MVP is. Mr. Cavanagh, our quarterback, had a day to be remembered. Cav had over 30 completed passes, for over 400 hundred yards and two T.D.s. Today, gentleman, we needed number 7, and he was there. I want to present the offensive and game MVP with a small token of our appreciation."

Coach Paltier handed Sean a pint bottle of Canadian Club whiskey from the brown paper bag in his hand.

The bus erupted with cheers and shouting. As the distance from the walled prison increased, the police players relaxed and began to really celebrate their toughest victory to date.

Sean blushed as he took the bottle from the coach. The good Canadian whiskey would help ease the pain and numb the aches.

He took a large swallow from the fresh bottle. The happy chatter of his teammates and the lukewarm whiskey warmed his insides.

Sean wiped a tear from his eye. He wished he could capture that moment forever. Teammates of both colors enjoying each other's company, needing one another, like in combat. No talk of politics or affirmative action, just pure friendship.

As the coach sat down, Sean stood, holding his pint bottle trophy. The chatter of the bus quieted.

"I'd like to propose three toasts . . . First, to our outstanding defense, the baddest defensive unit in football."

The team cheered.

"Secondly, Coach Paltier and his staff of professionals for their support and guidance."

Again, cheers and toasts.

"And lastly, men, I propose a toast to the inmate team. When somebody kicks my ass, like they kicked mine, they deserve my respect. For Christ's sake, let's really consider how significant today really was. We put those men in there, and it was the cleanest game we've ever had. They deserve a special respect and, by God, at least a toast."

There was a moment of silence, then the busload of police players toasted and cheered a tribute to the inmate team.

Sean sat on the floor of the bus, near the front, and drank from his bottle. Tears built up from the years of frustration and he wiped them away before anyone else could notice them.

It had been his day. That sunny October afternoon erased the lingering disappointment of Sean's college football experience. He had finally put to rest a part of his macho frustration that had existed since the Fall of '66.

Sean would never be able to describe how he felt on that bus ride home. He thanked God for the chance to close a chapter in his life. He felt a closeness to his team like he felt to his squad in Nam and his street partners.

He thought of T.J. They would celebrate in their own way, knowing they played their very best, and lost, 13-0.

Sean felt that he finally had his day in the sun, at least as it related to football. Except for the obvious financial reward, no player savored a Super Bowl victory any more than Sean enjoyed the victory bus ride back to the city.

The team had assembled their private cars at the building which housed the Police Athletic League office and facilities. Some of the members decided to carpool a few of their teammates home. They had celebrated a little too much.

Sean had consumed most of the contents of his MVP trophy, but with the dose of adrenaline in his body, the whiskey had little effect.

Sean began to get into his Triumph. Perry Mann and the four other members of the interior offensive line stood next to the open door. "You have any plans tonight, Cav?"

"No, not that I'm aware of."

"That's good, then you ain't got to cancel nothing. We'll be picking you up at your house at 7 p.m. That will give you time to shave, shower and get ready to party, our treat. We'll show your candy quarterback ass how real men party down. Tell your wife not to wait up."

Sean pulled his Triumph into the driveway of his neat little brick home a little after dusk. He let himself in the front door and concealed his slight limp and overall discomfort. Denny was playing with his toys on the living room floor. Lyn sat in the rocker reading a book. Sean leaned over to kiss and hug his son in greeting. Lyn looked up from her book for a moment. "Are you alright?"

Sean plopped down on the lounge chair. "I'm pretty sore, but I'm fine. Thanks for asking."

"How did the game go? Did you get to see T.J.?"

"We won. It was really a tough game. I saw T.J. throughout the game, and we got to eat lunch with the team from the prison."

"That's nice. Do whatever you have to and get ready. We're eating dinner at my folks' house in an hour."

Sean sat forward in his chair. "Your folks' house, for dinner; did you mention this to me?"

"No. My mom called today to invite us. We didn't have any plans, so I told her we'd be over."

"I'm sorry, Lyn. You'll have to take Denny and go without me. I've been invited to go out with some of the guys for kind of a celebration dinner."

"Oh, fine. Practice, games, now this. When are you going to spend some valuable time with Denny and me?"

"Come on, Lyn. Save it. We saw your folks last week. How do you figure going to your folks' house is spending so called 'valuable time' with you two? It works out better this way. You don't spend the night alone. You and Denny have dinner with your parents and I go out with the guys. Come on, be fair, Lyn. I never do this."

"I don't know how much longer I can put up with this macho crap."

"Let me know when you've had too much."

Sean saw Perry's big red Cadillac pull into his driveway. He gave Denny a quick kiss on the cheek and called out to Lyn that he was leaving.

He heard her voice over the sound of running water in the bathroom. Her tone had softened. She called to him to have a nice time and to be careful. He was thankful that he could begin the evening with his teammates in good spirits.

Sean trotted to the passenger side of the big car and got in the front seat.

Perry chuckled out loud.

"Look at this pretty boy. You all decked out like we're going to one of your daddy's country club dinners. Oxford button-down shirt, blue blazer, penny loafers. Man, the Brothers gonna love that outfit down on Linwood."

"Hey, I'm sorry, Perry. My Kelly green suit and wide brim hat are at the cleaners."

The car filled with good natured laughter. "I ain't saying you gotta dress Black, I'm just sayin' you didn't have to dress so white."

"You know what they say, Perry; 'you are what you wear.' "

Perry grinned as he backed out of the drive.

"The saying is 'you are what you eat.' In which case, we gonna have to have some Soul food tonight, so we can unpreppie your white ass a bit."

Sean felt as though he was in the company of giants. Sean and the two huge white interior linemen, Perry and the two other Black linemen were stuffed in the interior of Perry's large Cadillac.

"Say, Cav, what are all your white neighbors going to say about some Black dudes picking you up in a red Cadillac?"

"Well, if they don't burn my house to the ground tonight, I'll tell them its none of their damn business. No, on second thought, I'll tell them it was the new owners taking me out to dinner."

"Whoa, don't tell them that. They'll burn your house down for sure. There isn't a Black family within five miles of here. They'd be burning crosses in your front yard."

Sean savored the moment as he had the bus ride home. This was not the real world of Detroit. But that day had been special. If they could go to the State prison and share a unique experience with the inmates, six cops, fellow teammates, could go out and enjoy a night in their city together.

Perry's voice changed and he sounded serious.

"Cav, we've got tonight all planned out. After where we were today, what we all did, we've decided there is no place in this city where we shouldn't be able to go together. First we're going to some white redneck joint for a couple of drinks. Then we're going to an all-Black place, you know, kind of like a gesture. Then we'll relax, get dinner and party at some place Downtown where Black and white folks can be seen together without any trouble."

Sean adjusted the magnum in the shoulder holster inside his blazer. "Some people will say we went looking for trouble if we step in some shit while making our racial statement."

"Yea, I suppose you're right, Cav. We said this is your night. We're taking you out. If you don't want to fool with that shit, it's your call."

"Are you kidding? I want to see anyone fool enough to mess with you five at the same time. In fact, I know of a great place to start. There is an outlaw biker, redneck topless bar over on Whittier. They'll just love you three in there. Three Black guys and me dressed like Joe College. This will almost be as entertaining as this afternoon."

The topless bar sat alone at the corner. The assortment of chopper motorcycles and pick-up trucks in the parking lot suggested the mix of patrons they'd find inside.

The music was loud and lights flashed on the expressionless dancer on the stage and throughout the seating area.

The three dozen white male patrons turned from the topless dancer on the stage to watch Sean and his five teammates enter the lounge and sit down around a table near the rear. They filed past a greasy little man in a beige leisure suit standing at the bar with a dancer on each arm. Sean guessed him to be the owner. His shirt was open and a wide gold chain held the Italian horn around his neck. He didn't have any vacant body space for additional jewelry with his collection of rings, bracelets, and Rolex watch.

The dancers served as cocktail waitresses when not on stage. After two minutes, one of them approached Sean's table and took their drink order, while cracking her gum and staring at the six of them in utter disbelief.

Perry leaned over toward Sean. "I certainly am pleased to see that you white folks have some fine places for entertainment. This place has got style, Cav, kind of like your blazer."

The other patrons were all seated between the stage and their table. Even after they received their drinks, more of the patrons watched them than watched the topless dancer.

The attractive young dancer seemed to direct her nearly-naked bump and grind routine at their table, as if in an effort to provoke the regular patrons.

Russ playfully slapped Sean on the back. "Say, Cav. I think that sweet thing with the nice titties has got her eye on you."

"No thanks, Russ, I'll pass. My bet is that the sweet young thing has already been about worn out. I'd guess she's got about 20,000 males on her."

Suddenly, a huge outlaw biker, wearing his "colors," stood so quickly he knocked over his chair. He clenched his fists and walked toward their table.

Perry took a long swallow from his drink. "Oh my, I do think we are about to step in it."

The big biker was unkempt. He wore a full beard that was matted. He was balding and a huge beer gut hung over his belt. "What are you doing here with them?"

Sean was closest to the man. "Hey, buddy, we don't want any trouble. We came in for a couple of drinks, we're not bothering anyone. We'll be finished in a couple of minutes and be on our way."

"I ain't your 'buddy,' you little sissy college boy. And you are bothering us by having these stinkin' niggers in here. You ain't stayin'. Get the fuck out of here now, or you'll all be dead."

Sean put down his glass. "No, I think we'll stay for another round."

The man pulled a large Marine Ka-bar knife from his boot. "I'm going to like cutting you up, pretty boy."

Sean had drawn his magnum revolver and had it pointed at the big biker before any of the other men had even made a move for their guns.

The surprise sight of the gun pointed at his chest stopped the biker for a moment. "Well, look it here. Baby-face got him a gun. You think you're man enough to shoot me, sissy?"

"I know I am. Only the first time was a little tough. Greasing you won't be difficult at all. Take another step, and I'll really surprise you."

The big biker was not convinced. He readied the big combat knife in his hand and crouched, preparing to strike out at Sean.

Sean cocked the magnum for effect and raised the aim to his face. A flash of recognition raced through his mind. He saw a bulldog tattoo on the biker's forearm. The Marine logo tattoo and a Marine combat knife persuaded Sean to try to talk to the biker one more time.

"Damn shame, you forcing me to kill another former Marine."

"What, sissy?"

"You heard me. I said that killing you wouldn't bother me. If I find out you were a Marine, it might bother me after all."

The big biker hesitated for a moment and stood erect. "You tellin' me you were in the Corps, sissy boy?"

Sean's voice became stern, almost defensive. "I'm not wearing my dogtags, Pal, but I've got three Hearts and three Bronze Stars that say I was man enough to be a Marine back when I was 19."

"What makes you think I was in the Corps?"

"You don't seem the type of a guy who would get a Marine tattoo unless you had been a Marine. That big pig sticker is a Marine Ka-bar, that and the tattoo adds up to a fellow Marine."

The biker seemed to relax. "Was you in Nam?"

"No, shit. I didn't get three Hearts and the Stars in California."

"Yea, man. No shit. I was there too, in '68."

Sean uncocked his magnum and lowered it to his side. "I was there in '68 too. What unit were you in?"

"I was with the 1/26."

"The 1/26 was at Khe Sanh. You guys went through some real shit."

The big biker put his knife back into his boot. "Oh yea, you were in the Corps. Where were you, Mr. Three Heart Man?"

"I was with the 1/1 at Hue City during Tet. It was a bitch, too."

"I pegged you wrong, dude. I'll go back with my friends. You know I ain't backin' down. It's just that I won't kill a Marine Vet. It wouldn't be right. We kept each other alive in Nam. It would be fuckin' dumb to waste another Grunt after we survived."

"I understand, buddy. You're not backing down. You've just decided not to do battle. Go back with your friends and let one old tired Grunt buy the Khe Sanh Vet and his companions a drink."

The big man held out his hand for a handshake. "I'm sorry I insulted your friends. I had Soul Brother buddies in Nam. I got hit bad. I still got a metal plate in my head."

The little man in the beige leisure suit told his bartender to call the police.

Sean turned to the man still standing at the bar, flanked by dancers. Now Sean was certain the cocky little man covered in jewelry was the bar owner. Sean held up his badge and I.D. folder toward the bar owner.

"Hey, asswipe. The police are already here. The man was ready to cut us up and you stand there grinning like a big dog. We make peace and you want the blue suits? Go ahead, call the precinct cops. When they get here, I will cite you for every chicken-shit liquor law violation from the temperature of your wash water to the drain and tile in the men's room. Two of those ladies have dropped their drawers during their act. Need I continue? My friends and I are going to finish our drinks, then leave your fine establishment. If you want to fuck with us, go ahead and call. This toilet will have a padlock on the front door within an hour."

"Oh, big man, Mr. Po-lice."

"That's correct, Mr. Jerk Off. It's your move, either bring the blue suits, or put down the phone and we're out of here in a few minutes."

The big biker put his hands on his hips and enjoyed a long belly laugh. "Damn, Marine. I shoulda known you were the law. Only a crazy man or a cop would come in here with Soul Brothers."

Sean had put his badge and his revolver away. "You know, Khe Sanh, these men are my friends, my buddies. I depend on them like we depended on the Soul Brothers in Nam."

The big biker shook his head. "Detroit is a hell of a long way from Nam."

Sean put his hand on the big man's shoulder. "Yea, but it's all the same when somebody is trying to waste you. When you're under fire, it doesn't matter whether it's Nam or Woodward Avenue."

"I'm really glad I didn't cut you, dude. I seen you lookin' so clean-cut, with these Soul Brothers, I just assumed you were some liberal draft-dodging college puke."

"I may look that way, my man, but I'm an 0311 Grunt all the way."

Sean paid for their drinks and a round of drinks for the big ex-Marine biker and his table full of friends.

Perry spoke to Sean under his breath. "Damn, Cav, we told you that tonight was our treat."

"Perry, let's get out of here alive. We can worry about the finances outside."

The tab paid, and tip left on the table, the six men filed out of the lounge. The topless dancer seemed to wave good-bye with one particular part of her body.

The greasy little bar owner had his ego damaged in front of his people. He felt the need to save face in front of his girls. "You wouldn't be such a hard-ass if you didn't have that badge and gun."

Sean stopped and moved very close to the little jewelry-covered bar owner.

"You may be correct, asshole. But the truth of the matter is that I do have a badge and a gun. We're on our way out. If you piss me off, this could get personal. You may not want me as a regular patron, but I guarantee you that you don't want me pissed at you. I'll become your worse fucking nightmare: an honest cop with a personal chip on his shoulder. I'll close you down every week, so just let it go."

Sean called to the big biker, who was enjoying his free beers with his friends. Sean raised his fist in a salute. "Hey, Khe Sanh! Semper Fi. Keep your head down."

The biker raised his fist in a returned gesture. "Careful out there. Like in Nam, they say it's a mother."

Back in Perry's Cadillac, the six men nervously joked about the incident in the all-white bar.

Perry turned up the R & B song on his car stereo. "Say, Cav, if we have any trouble in one of the Black bars, you sit quiet and let us handle it. If somebody messes with us, he probably won't be an ex-Marine."

"No problem, Perry. I know when I'm out of my element."

Perry shook his head in disbelief. "Shit, Cav. I thought you were going to blow away that big sucker."

Sean just stared out of the window at the passing traffic. There was no emotion in his voice. He looked over at Perry without smiling. "I was. Another step and I'd have greased that big fat head case in his tracks."

Perry shook his head. "Cav, I feel like I learned more 'bout you in one day than the other two years put together. You are one unique dude. I'm really glad that we're on the same team, and I don't only mean football."

Sean readjusted the magnum in his shoulder holster. "You've got to admit, gentlemen, this has been quite a day."

Perry was grinning again. "If you think those redneck honkies didn't like us, wait 'till we go to the bar on Linwood and all them Brothers get a look at you. Boys, we've only just begun."

In fact, the remainder of their evening was pleasant, but uneventful. They closed a Downtown night club after dinner, where the sight of Black and white friends together did not turn heads or draw trouble.

The only ill effect of the night of drinking was a mild hangover. But with the aches and pains from the beating he took at the game, the dull headache went unnoticed.

Oct. 7 had been a day all the players involved would never forget. There had been a unique combination of conflicts and comradships. From Khe Sanh to Jackson, convicts and cops, Black and white, the day had created a spark of personal re-evaluations that could break down walls of hatred and mistrust greater than the impressive brick walls of Jackson Prison. The effects of that day may have been short-lived for most. Yet, everyone was personally touched by the events of a perfect Fall day, in a far from perfect place.

DECEMBER, 1972
DETROIT

The late 60s and early 70s were terrible, violent times for the Detroit Police Department.

Unprovoked ambushes of police became commonplace. Somehow, in the midst of the continuous stream of injury and death, December of 1972 would stand out as special to any Detroit cop who had experienced that time.

There was very little Christmas spirit for the troops that December. Seven Detroit officers were shot during that one month. Two men were killed, one was paralyzed from the waist down for life, three were hurt badly enough to force early retirement, and only one ever returned to full duty.

Aside from the personal loss felt by the men who knew these officers, the whole department somehow seemed affected by the shootings.

All seven were from the same special unit, but were wounded in three separate incidents, which spanned the month.

Going to a gut wrenching, emotional, paramilitary police funeral just before, then just after Christmas, did nothing to enhance the mood of the department.

Sean knew one of the murdered officers and had even played softball with the man who was paralyzed.

The individual impact caused by that one Winter month can never be measured. There was an extra frustration caused by the shootings. There would be no way for them to "get even." No number of retaliation shootings could even the score. Seven men from the same small unit also added to the trauma. Sean recognized their new mood. He and his Marine friends had experienced the feeling of doom in Hue City, when his platoon disappeared before his eyes.

They all felt more threatened, more vulnerable than ever before. The month would cause a few to be brutal and even cross the line to murder. It would cause others to quit, not from fear, but rather from a feeling of hopelessness.

No other single month had ever had the impact on the collective psyche of the department in all of its colorful history, as did December, 1972. For many officers it had a greater negative impact than the famous Summer riot in July of '67.

11

January, 1973—August, 1973

JANUARY, 1973
DETROIT

The original concept was sound and well thought through. Anyone over the age of 15 would point to Detroit's thousands of heroin junkies as the overwhelming reason for the city's staggering crime rate.

Rather than double the number of personnel in the Central Narcotics Section, it was decided to create a small, hand-picked Narcotics Unit at each of Detroit's police precincts. These units would concentrate on the local dope houses and heroin shooting galleries in their precinct.

Their primary tool would be the "No Knock" search warrant. Recent court rulings had allowed an unnamed civilian informant to make controlled narcotic buys with marked money. The drugs purchased by the informant were confiscated and sent Downtown to the police lab to be analyzed. After two such documented and controlled buys, a search warrant for the premises could be obtained from a Detroit judge. The officers executing the search warrant were only required to announce their identity and intent before entry, not giving those inside the time to dispose of any contraband. The dealer would be charged with possession, rather than sale. In that way, the police would not have to give up their informant's identity in court.

At Number 13, the new Narcotics Unit consisted of three Booster Crews, with Sgt. Del Greene as their supervisor. Initially, the precinct commander thought the Booster crews could work on their new Narcotics assignment and still have some time to work the streets.

During the previous month, the new members of each Precinct Narcotics Unit went to the academy for additional hours of classroom instruction. The formal training included an overview of the international problem presented by a Federal D.E.A. agent, and a complete run-down of the who's-who in Detroit's heroin trade.

Representatives from the County Prosecutor's office explained how the program was discussed at length with Detroit's judges. The judges had committed to give stiff prison terms to those charged with the possession felony. In addition, the junkies loitering in the dope houses would receive large fines and a month in Detroit's House of Correction. A junkie facing a month in the "House," going cold turkey from his heroin habit, might be a willing recruit to become an informant. Most junkies would do anything to stay on the street.

With the precincts hitting the small-time local dealers, Central Narcotics could concentrate on the medium-sized and big-time sellers, using their undercover agents, and working with the Federal Drug Enforcement Administration.

It had all looked promising on the drawing board. When the crews started their new assignments that January, there was optimistic talk that the new program would have a marked impact on Detroit's heroin trade by mid-Summer. Cynics also promised to have the troops home by Christmas.

If the Booster assignment was being part of the street, then the Narcotics assignment was being a part of the gutters.

During the weeks and months that followed, Sean's whole life became part of that terrible heroin underworld. He spent his hours with junkies, whores, Murphy men, informants and dealers. The filth and violence of the assignment began to wear him down emotionally. He wasn't a cop any longer; he'd become a mercenary.

The first month was easy. The new units caught the local dealers off guard. But soon, thinking of methods of gaining entry into the newly-fortified dope dens became as much of a challenge as obtaining the search warrant. Every crew had to get a battering ram and sledge hammers, which became standard equipment on every raid. Then, the level and frequency of violent shootings increased dramatically. Shoot-outs were becoming commonplace city-wide, and dealers were so paranoid that they were killing each other and any junkie they suspected might be a police informant.

At 13, Sean, Bruce, and Tom tried to make the best of their new assignments. The other unit members were Ed Baines, Jimmy Haller, Paul Hursch, and Rick Gillis. Sean concentrated on the unit's arsenal and body armor. The precinct C.O. and Sgt. Greene had arranged with the General Motors world headquarters motor pool to use any available vehicle in the pool for their undercover surveillance. The motor pool consisted of almost every vehicle made by G.M., from Cadillacs to Corvettes. The dope house surveillance was safer, effective and more pleasant when the men could use a different vehicle every night, especially if it was a new G.M. car.

The Narcotics assignment allowed them to purchase and carry weapons that were not authorized for any other department officers. The weapons only needed to pass the careful safety inspection by the department gunsmiths. Then, the men were issued "special weapons" permits.

Since single-action automatics were not authorized for use by other officers in the department, it was predictable that all three crew members bought single-action automatic pistols. Bruce and Tom each bought a 13-shot, Browning high-power 9mm. Sean bought a Colt Commander, nickel-plated, .45-caliber automatic.

The young crew was living in a terrible, violent adult world. Yet, they were still young enough to experience what other young men their age felt, that desire to get away with as much as their system could allow. Bruce summed it up while making fun of himself. "If they told us we could carry a friggin' bazooka, I'd probably go out and buy one, just because we could have one."

The Narcotics assignment put even more strain on Sean's relationship with Lyn. The hours got worse, with more overtime. Now, Sean was also going to court at least twice a week. He still managed to take two classes at Wayne State every quarter. He could never complain about his assignment to Lyn because she would pounce on the opportunity to use it as just another reason why he should resign and go to work for his father's business.

By late Spring, Sean often felt more comfortable in the Narcotic Unit's small office than he did in his own home.

As each day passed, Sean became less a professional police officer, and more and more just another survivor of the streets. The Narcotics assignment stripped Sean of whatever remaining innocence or idealism he had before.

Working the Booster assignment was living in the fast lane. The Narcotics Unit thrust him into the Indy 500. The narcotics world was life on the dark side. When pressed, the only positive things Sean could say about the assignment were that they worked in plain clothes, they could carry special weapons, and drove a fleet of brand new, expensive G.M. cars.

Despite his life experience, including combat and street work, there had been nothing to prepare Sean for the constant negative influence of the dark side of life in Detroit; the stark, ugly narcotic world with its violent, complex network. If Sean was a cynic before working Narcotics, afterward he became a sarcastic, disillusioned hardass with a giant chip on his shoulder. The Narcotics Unit didn't burn Sean out; it literally burned him up.

APRIL, 1973
DETROIT

The 13th Precinct's Narcotics crew led the way in making fun of themselves. They referred to their search-warrant execution raids as taking their "circus" on the road. The verbal signal to begin the raid had become "Showtime."

With the strange assortment of men, clothing, protective gear, weapons and vehicles, a circus was not a bad description of the Precinct Narcotics Unit, know as 13-P.N.U.

They hit the house named in the search warrant at 10 p.m. The officer who obtained the warrant in his name directed the raid with Sgt. Greene's approval, and was the first into the dope pad. The system took the "Let me go first" argument out of each raid.

It was Sean's warrant. The informant for the newly-opened dope house on the South End of the precinct was Gum Drop. Gum Drop represented the level of street scum they dealt with on a daily basis. He was a heroin junkie, a street thief and a homosexual. He made the money to buy his heroin by impersonating female prostitutes. Since he offered oral sex for money, he was usually not discovered as a male by his "customers." The common label for a person like Gum Drop on the street was a "he-she."

When Sean was satisfied everyone was in position, he drew his .45-automatic and yelled, "Showtime!"

Gum Drop had told Sean that the dope house was so new that the front door was still not well fortified.

Before they used the battering ram, Sean tried the front door with a strong kick from his jungle boot. The front door flew open and the officers poured in amidst the surprised junkies and the dope house resident dealer, Marvin "Mouse" Monroe.

The well-trained officers moved with purpose and coordination. Bruce gathered up the heroin and the paraphernalia. Tom and Jimmy Haller secured the junkie loiterers. Sean sought out Mouse, sat him down and handed him a copy of the search warrant.

The cocky little Black dealer leaned back in the kitchen chair. "Say, Officer Cavanagh, why you messin' with me? This is all jive bullshit an' you know it. Ain't gonna be no legal arrest. You're bustin' me for nothin'. You can't come breakin' in here, you know that."

"Read the paper, douche bag. It's called a search warrant. It says that a judge has given us the legal right to kick in your door, confiscate your dope and lock up your Black ass for possession."

Mouse skimmed over the wording on the search warrant. "It says here an informant come in my place a couple times. Who is it?"

"Oh, come on, Mouse. We can't tell you that."

"My lawyer will find out, and then he's deadmeat."

"Wrong again, low life. Read the warrant. We're busting you for possession, not sale. That means that you will never know who the informant was. We don't need him to testify and your attorney can't get him."

"You all can't get away with this. I'll walk on this beef and I'll get the snitch what did me."

Sean pressed the cocked .45 hard against Mouse's wide nose. "Say, Mouse. It seems to me you should be more concerned about pissing off John Wheston. We understand he is the fuck wad in charge of this neck of the ghetto."

Mouse laughed as if at a private joke. "Mr. Cavanagh, where you been? This here place *is* one of John Wheston's. I'm jus' runnin' it for him. It's his dope, his bread. John Wheston will have me out on bond before you are done with your report. Then he'll find out which no good nigger junkie snitched us off and have him wasted. John Wheston will deliver that no good informant's dead body on your door step."

Sean twisted the barrel of his .45 hard against the small Black man's face.

"Put a lid on that kind of talk, shithead. If I were you, Mouse, I'd worry about not doing hard time on this rap and forget about the snitch. If you think John Wheston is even going to lift a finger for you, you're having a wet dream. The way I figure it, Mouse, with your record, you'll be July's playmate of the month at Jackson prison."

"This is a roust, Cavanagh, and you know it!"

"No, Mouse, you little fuck. It's not a roust. It's legal and you're going to fall and fall hard. We'll really miss you here at Number 13, Mouse. Try to get time to write, you know, between lovers."

"This is some jive bullshit, Officer Cavanagh."

Sean grinned at the little small-time drug dealer. "Yea, Mouse. Ain't life beautiful. See you in a couple of years, asshole."

AUGUST, 1973
DETROIT

It was a hot Summer night in Detroit. Sean had grown very tired of the lousy working hours and the constant tension at home with Lyn. The precinct station was uncomfortable, the hot air was still and moist. It was 2 a.m., and the Precinct Narcotics Unit had just finished the paperwork from their midnight raid on a small dope house on the precinct's North End.

The small group of Narcotics officers walked out into the precinct parking lot together. The outside air felt fresher, but it was still warm and muggy.

Sean took down the top of his Triumph TR6. He concealed his .45 in its shoulder holster with an O.D. Vietnam-era, military jungle jacket. He reached over to the passenger seat and recovered his Tiger baseball hat. He was in a foul mood. He decided to take the longer scenic route home, in order to give himself some time to think things out and to unwind. He was going to drive Downtown to the river, then follow the river east to Lake St. Clair. He would then drive up Moross Road a couple of miles to his street.

Sean waved good-bye to the other Narcotics Unit members as he pulled onto Woodward Avenue. He mulled over the fact that it made no difference whether he got home at 2:30 or 3:30. When he went directly home, the house was quiet. Lyn and little Denny would be sleeping, it was like coming home to an empty house. To unwind, Sean would put on the headphones of his stereo and sit alone in his dark living room, sipping a beer.

Sean was very frustrated with the Narcotics assignment. When they worked the Booster assignment, he actually felt they were accomplishing something positive. The idea of using the precinct level Narcotics units to help battle the city's terrible heroin problem, along with the department's large Central Narcotics Section had been an excellent premise. But they were not getting the support they had been promised in court. The commitment that dealers would get stiff prison terms turned out to be a shallow one. After the arrests passed through the Detroit criminal justice system, the extreme, continuous violence of the dope-house raids did not seem to be worth the results.

Sean hoped that the lonely ride by the water might help take the edge off of his piss-poor attitude.

The cooler night air pushing against his face was refreshing. Sean enjoyed one of the few times in the year when he could use the Triumph's cloth top. He just wanted to be left alone with his thoughts and his car stereo.

Sean stopped his car for the red traffic signal at Mack Avenue. He turned up the mellow sounds of his Moody Blues tape and rested his head back against his seat. He tried to force himself to begin to unwind.

A full-sized, older-model Buick pulled to a rapid stop in the next lane. The big Buick was occupied by four aggressive, half-drunk, Black, teenage street kids. They were loud and charged up. They were out looking for trouble in any form. They were ready to harass anyone they encountered for their night's entertainment. Driving up next to a lone white boy in an open sports car was like a wish come true. They could not have known by first impression that they had chosen the wrong white boy to mess with that night.

By instinct, Sean realized the car and occupants were next to him, without turning his head. He briefly hoped that if he ignored them, they might choose to go fuck with someone else.

The signal light turned green and both vehicles resumed their drive south on Woodward Avenue, toward the Downtown loop, and the river. The Buick's occupants began to shout obscene names and threats at Sean. The driver swerved into Sean's lane twice, causing him to go into the center lane to avoid contact. The Black youth seated in the left rear seat threw an empty wine bottle at Sean's car. The poorly-aimed throw caused the glass missile to pass over Sean's head and smash into the street.

Sean was certain that they had no idea that he was an off-duty cop. He fit the stereotype of a preppie suburban boy who dared drive Downtown after midnight.

Both vehicles were forced to stop at another traffic signal. The verbal attack on Sean became ever more intense. With the nearness of the two cars, Sean felt exposed in the smaller, open Triumph. The occupants identified Sean's attempts to ignore them as fear. "Hey, White Meat. What you doin' down here so late? Did you take a wrong turn, or are you jus' slummin'?"

Sean finally looked over at his tormentors. "Hey, look, I don't want any trouble. Why don't you guys just drive on and I'll go about my business?"

The Buick's driver bobbed his head and laughed.

"You don't want no trouble? I bet you don't, honkie. Look around, peckerwood. You are Downtown, boy. Not in them pretty suburbs with all the other white folks. How 'bout we jump out, whip your sorry white ass, an' steal your money and that sissy car?"

They had managed to cause Sean to revert from a young, professional, off-duty police officer to an angry 25-year-old with a gun, and the ability and attitude to use it. It had only taken them a few city blocks on that hot, muggy August night. All that was wrong with Sean's world was suddenly emotionally transferred to the occupants of the old Buick.

They identified Sean's silence as total intimidation. It was their second error in judgement. The light was still red. The sound of the Buick's left rear door opening activated his response, which by now was instinctual and conditioned. He reached inside the light-weight jacket and drew his .45 from the shoulder holster. Sean aimed the impressive-looking nickel pistol at the Buick's driver.

"You guys are really getting on my nerves. I'm sick of hearing all those big lips flapping. You're fucking with the wrong honkie tonight, boys, so get the hell out of my face before somebody gets hurt."

The Buick occupants howled, mocking Sean's threat and the fact he was armed. "Oh my, the honkie got himself a big gun. How do you know we ain't got us some guns too, punk?"

"Because, shithead, if any of you had a gun, you'd have been so proud you'd have threatened me with it back at Mack Avenue."

"What you figure that big gun gonna do for you, White Meat?"

"I figure it allows me to drive down the main street of my own city at 2:15, without getting fucked over by a car load of assholes. Well, what's it going to be? Either come on over and get some, or just leave me alone."

The driver glared at Sean, the .45 still pointed at him. "You think you got the balls to take all four of us, honkie?"

The signal light was halfway through the green cycle, but both vehicles remained stopped at the intersection.

"I'm really getting fucking tired of this silly shit. Come on, damn it. If you're feelin' froggy, leap on over here. If you're not too drunk or too fucking stupid to really consider this, you'll just let it go."

As the Buick's occupants discussed their potential options, Sean drove off. He reholstered his .45, between changing gears.

If there had not been heavy cross traffic, he'd have driven through the red traffic signal at the Jefferies Freeway service drive. He was again forced to stop. Sean was not at all surprised when the Buick pulled up next to him again.

"O.K., peckerwood. We've decided. You got the gun, better get ready to really use it, or you gonna lose it." The young man in the left rear seat opened the door and one foot reached the pavement.

Sean's movement was so sudden, it seemed to freeze every muscle in all four young men. Sean had redrawn his .45. He fired one well-aimed round into the Buick's left side, about a foot from the exiting occupant. The roar of the powerful pistol made all of their ears ring. Even under the bright artificial street lights, the reddish-orange muzzle flash lit up the area. The .45's round put a hole in the side of the Buick the size of a dime.

The Buick's driver had the expression of absolute disbelief on his face. "Hey, mother fucker! You crazy? Look what you done to my ride."

Sean held the smoking .45 and moved it toward the driver again. "Last fucking chance, cocksuckers. Either come on and try to take this from me, or get the hell out of my sight. If that rolling hunk of shit pulls up next to me again, I'm going to empty this .45 into it."

The driver of the Buick still couldn't believe Sean had shot his car. The passenger had slipped back into the Buick and closed the door. "Man, you put a hole in my car! You've gotta be crazy. Big man with a big gun."

"That's right, you have a belly full of cheap wine and I've got a gun.

They both make us brave. It's your choice. Either drive away, or keep on fucking with me and die."

There was a brief exchange of words within the Buick's interior. Suddenly, the Buick made a rapid right turn onto the freeway service drive, through the red signal, nearly hitting a west-bound vehicle.

The traffic light finally turned green. Sean went on with his scheduled drive home.

He passed through the Downtown area and when he reached the river, he turned east onto East Jefferson. He decided to drive out onto Belle Isle Park, in the center of the Detroit River. His car was alone on the aging concrete bridge.

There were still hundreds of people at the island park. Most of them were inner city dwellers attempting to escape the terrible heat of their apartment buildings. There was a fresh breeze coming from Lake St. Clair. The air smelled fresh, even with the hint of grain from the large liquor distillery within view on the Canadian shore. Sean parked his car and sat on the hood, watching an ocean freighter pass between the island park and the Canadian shoreline.

The confrontation with the young men in the Buick was just another chapter in a growing book of conduct that caused him to be increasingly disappointed with himself. He had been so damn idealistic and dedicated when he started in '69. Now, the constant violence and frustrations had brought him down. He often put his badge and the law aside and reacted as violently as the assholes he dealt with every day on the streets. It was becoming easier by the day to decide to take the law into his own hands.

He remembered the brief conversation he and Bruce had at Homicide years before, the day they shot the robber holding the small boy at the grocery store. He was becoming just like the cops they had disliked then.

That night, if he had identified himself as a policeman, Sean believed the incident with the boys would have only been escalated. They would have pushed and pushed until someone got hurt. It really was better if they thought he was a crazy white suburban boy with a gun. Except for the big hole in the Buick, no one was hurt. It was another example of the non-stop madness. He remembered years before when Bruce had asked him what it would be like if the "good" young cops crossed over to the dark side. Now he knew. It would be like this. Something had to change, or it would only get worse.

Sean got back into his car and resumed his ride home. He put another Moody Blues tape into the dash stereo.

"What a fucking place to live. It's not safe to take a ride down the main street without a car load of assholes ready to grease you. What if I hadn't had the gun? What if I was an ordinary citizen of metro-Detroit and unarmed? What if, what if. Bullshit! Like the man said, what if frogs had wings? I've got to give up on all of life's 'what ifs'. There's nothing in this city that makes any sense. There's nothing that has any real order. In fact, I can't remember the last time anything made sense, sure as hell not in Detroit, not Grosse Pointe. God knows, not in Nam. Not anywhere. Ah, fuck it. Like I told Bruce three years ago when we greased that asshole at the grocery store, 'It don't mean nothing.' "

AUGUST, 1973
MICHIGAN STATE PRISON, JACKSON

Life in prison was far from easy for T.J. Even before his time in the Marine Corps, he was proud. There was little to make him proud as a prisoner. He was very grateful for the prison's sports programs. With baseball, basketball, and football, T.J. was kept occupied either by playing or preparing for each season.

T.J. was disappointed that the Detroit Police football squad was not on the 1973 fall schedule. He had enjoyed the previous year's game and the brief visit with his good friend, Irish.

He struggled with the junior college classes offered by the prison and took one at a time. He wrote Sean at least once a month. The letters were often short, but there was little to write about in the redundancy of prison life, especially in the off-season.

Sean wrote on a regular basis. He sent T.J. two sports magazines each month and often sent photos, especially pictures of his growing young son. In honor of T.J.'s last birthday back in March, Sean had found an infant-sized green and gold football jersey with the number 40 on the front and back. The photo of the little blond white boy in the football shirt was taped on the wall next to T.J.'s bunk in his cell. With several pictures of white friends from Vietnam also on the wall, no one ever questioned the little boy's photo.

T.J. had a realistic hope for parole in '78. He would take prison in the same fashion that he had survived the bush in Nam, one day at a time, just one day at a time.

Most recently, T.J was bothered by the tone of Sean's letters. Sean had not previously complained in any of the letters T.J. received while in Nam and in prison. He had told T.J. he never complained because he didn't have the right. Sean felt that nothing he experienced could match what T.J. was living through. But after almost five years, T.J. knew his friend well enough to read between the lines. T.J. didn't like what those mean Motown streets seemed to be doing to his idealistic, fair-minded white blood brother.

T.J's experience had taught him to mind his own business. He was big and tough enough not to be bothered physically by any other inmates. Being a member of the sports teams gave him some large and important inmate friends.

T.J. had lived for over a year at a time without female companionship in the Marines. But even after his time in prison mounted, he could not comprehend why so many of his fellow inmates diverted to homosexual activity. He had never been exposed to it before. While growing up, it was not out in the open in his neighborhood. And while in the Marines, the mere suggestion of homosexual feelings was tantamount to suicide. At Jackson Prison, homosexual activity was not merely present, it was a part of every inmate's life in some fashion. Even if it was just avoiding it.

A new white kid was added to their block. He was from a southern Michigan redneck county at the Indiana border.

The baby-faced 20-year-old had been sentenced to the state prison by the county's new hard-nosed judge for breaking into a rural gas station. Tommy Randle would have probably avoided any real "hard time" had he not attempted to part the arresting State Police Officer's hair with a wrench. The assault and burglary, on top of two other vehicle theft convictions as an adult, sent Tommy Randle to Jackson Prison for a minimum of four years.

Big Jake was the block's resident bully. The big white inmate refused to play sports. He was serving a life sentence for the murder of a Lansing Police Officer. Big Jake was in the fifth year of his prison term, and he spent his time with body building, fighting, and homosexual encounters. More often than not, his sexual partners were not willing.

The moment Big Jake first saw Tommy Randle, he was attracted to him.

Big Jake was over 6'4" and weighed 240 pounds. He was nearly 30 and lifted weights as if weight-lifting was a fanatical religion. He was open with his opinion on sex with other men. He often declared that sex with a young inmate was a poor substitute for a woman but it was much better than beating himself off.

It took Big Jake only three days to corner Tommy Randle in a secluded cell. Big Jake slammed Tommy against the wall. "Hey, pretty boy. You might as well relax and accept the fact that you're gonna be my punk until your term is up and they let you outa here."

Tommy Randle attempted to push the powerful man away. "No way, man. That ain't my style."

Big Jake slammed Tommy Randle up against the wall again.

"You try and resist me and I'll just have to hurt you. It don't matter to me none, feels the same to me no matter how fucked up you are. The simple fact is, baby face, you gonna suck my dick and take it up the ass whenever I choose. Don't matter whether you wanna or not. If I gotta beat you half to death first, don't matter none to me."

Tommy Randle struggled to resist the firm grasp of the big inmate. Big Jake firmly held the front of Tommy's shirt with his left hand. He reached down with his right hand and began to unzip his own trousers. Every time Tommy Randle attempted to struggle, Big Jake roughly bounced him off the cell wall.

T.J. appeared at the cell door. He spoke calmly but with determination.

"Hey, Big Jake. Say, man, why don't you leave the boy be? There are more than enough sissy boys here that be more than glad to take care of your needs. That boy says he's straight. You don't need to hurt him."

Big Jake did not release his grip and continued to undo his pants.

"Fuck off, nigger. Look around, boy. You ain't in the Marines now. You ain't no big deal combat sar-gent. This here baby-face boy just happens to make my dick hard. This is the way it is, nigger. It don't matter none if he wants to. I only know that I want to. And I get what I want in this joint 'cause I take it."

T.J. moved into the cell and put his hand on Big Jake's shoulder. "Come on, Big Jake, be cool. Let the boy alone."

Suddenly, Big Jake wheeled and struck T.J. in the face with the hand that had held Tommy Randle, who used the moment to escape from the cell.

Big Jake and T.J. squared off.

"You let the baby face get away this time. How 'bout you suck my dick, nigger?"

T.J. clenched his fists. "You think you bad enough to make me, honkie? Come on and give it your best shot."

Big Jake saw four of T.J.'s Black football teammates gathered just outside the cell door.

"You better mind your own business, boy."

T.J. touched his swollen lip. "Right, big man. Tell you what, honkie. You better start watchin' your back. You just fucked with the wrong nigger. If you even look in my direction, I'll make you go away like a bad toothache."

"You scare me to death, shadow."

"Go ahead and fuck with me again, chump, and I'll do more than scare you to death. You gonna need to do more than lift weights."

"I'm telling you what, Mr. Marine badass. Stay out of my way or you are a dead man." Big Jake stormed out of the cell, past T.J.'s friends in the hallway.

Ronnie Brown approached T.J. "Tell you what, Brother, you just might be messin' with the wrong honkie. That dude ain't right in his head. Don't know why you step in to save some young little honkie. Shit, over half of the young boys comin' in here end up gettin' passed around."

"I know that, Ronnie, but it don't make it right. I got tired of that big peckerwood pushin' people around. Brother, we ain't talkin' about shakin' some boy down for a pack of smokes. We're talkin' about takin' a normal boy and turning him into a punk."

Ronnie walked away. "Ain't none of my concern."

"That's cool, Ronnie. What if you see that big Chuck ready to do me in?"

"You know that's different, Brother. Man, we're teammates. You're a Soul Brother. I'd be there for you. T.J., you gotta remember all that Marine shit don't fit in this place."

T.J. considered Ronnie's advice. Maybe the Marine Corps code of conduct did not fit into prison life, but the Vietnam survival code certainly did. As in Nam, T.J. planned to eliminate an obvious severe danger to his life. He readied his own search-and-destroy mission. He considered Big Jake little more than a massive wild animal, an animal with a primitive unnatural urge that seemed to direct his behavior.

T.J. also recognized that the matter would not be settled until either young Tommy Randle was raped, T.J. was killed, or both. T.J. had decided on another solution. He would use the military solution: he would eliminate the threat with extreme prejudice. He planned his attack on Big Jake with the same forethought of a complex military operation.

T.J. studied Big Jake's daily routine from a distance. He selected the location, a small shower room just off the prison's weight room. He constructed a handmade garrote. If his initial attack went as planned, the thin, strong wire of the garrote would cut the big man's throat enough to cause a fatal injury, even if he didn't have time to suffocate the huge white man.

The Fall season's first Monday night football game was on the television in the prison recreation room. T.J. made certain that he was observed by others in the rec room, especially his football teammates.

In the middle of the first quarter, T.J. slipped out of the rec room and moved down to the weight room, unnoticed. Big Jake was always the last to leave. Other men were afraid to be alone with the huge, aggressive homosexual.

T.J. could hear a single shower running in the narrow, Spartan shower room:

He silently moved into the shower room. Big Jake was naked, his back turned toward T.J. He had soaped up his hair and face. Big Jake sang a country-western song to himself, and intently pulled on his soap-lathered penis.

T.J. moved nearer to Big Jake, without being detected. He struck like a big cat. In a brief flurry of motion, T.J. slipped the wire of the garrote over Big Jake's soap-blinded head. The instant the wire lowered to neck level, T.J. crossed his hands and snapped his strong arms in opposite directions. The big man's entire body violently jerked, as if struck by a powerful electric shock.

A moment later, the hulk of a man fell to his knees, breathless. T.J. had struck so quickly that Big Jake did not utter a sound or even move a hand toward his throat.

A full minute later, T.J. was certain Big Jake was dead. He carefully pulled the wire garrote from the dead man's throat so as not to get blood on his prison uniform. He quickly washed off the death tool and his hands in the running shower water. Big Jake's body fell hard onto the tile floor face first.

T.J. left the shower room and skillfully disassembled the garrote. Within 24 hours, the simple murder weapon would be moved out of the prison, free of any fingerprints.

T.J. moved back into the crowded recreation room. No one had noticed T.J.'s brief absence during the exciting game. Back inside the rec room, he made certain he was noticed by fellow teammates with the critique of the Lions' defensive play. No one in the entire room had noticed he was gone for even a moment.

It was nearly an hour before a guard found Big Jake's body. He lay face down in a pool of shower water and his own blood. The shower was still running. The sight of the big man's throat nearly cut in half caused the young guard to gag.

Shortly after the discovery of the murdered inmate, the prisoners were all ordered to their cells and the prison was secured.

After lights out, T.J. lay on his back in his bunk, staring at the dark ceiling. Even in Nam, he had never wasted anyone with his bare hands. They had trained him to do it. It had been easier than he thought it would be. He couldn't help but consider the irony of the actual murder.

"Big mean faggot, sure seems appropriate that he was pullin' on his dick the moment he died. Thinkin' with his dick is what got him into trouble in the first place."

When State Police Detectives investigated the homicide, they discovered the list of inmates and guards without a motive was smaller than the list of suspects. With Big Jake's constant spurts of violence, even some of the prison guards had to be considered as possible suspects. The detectives realized early in their investigation that Big Jake's death meant little more than a decrease in prison population.

Their investigation was not destined to develop well, when so many inmates actually hated the victim.

The official statement to the media said inmate Jacob Clyde Wiltz died under mysterious circumstances and the State Police were in the midst of a comprehensive investigation.

No one attended the short funeral service for the late Jacob Clyde Wiltz at the prison chapel. His remains were buried in the prison graveyard at minimal tax payer expense.

The State Police filed the case away as open, pending further information.

T.J. buried his thoughts and energy into the inmate football team. He managed to bury his guilt along with Big Jake's casket.

The inmate team finished its morning conditioning practice. T.J. pulled off his helmet and talked with other players as they headed for the showers.

Tommy Randle waited to talk to T.J. just outside the building.

"Excuse me, T.J. Can I talk to you?"

"Go ahead, boy. What's on your mind?"

"Well, that day in the cell, you know, with that Big Jake. You took a shot in the face for me. I mean, a white guy, and you risked trouble with that big crazy dude to save me. I really appreciate it."

"Thanks for the gesture, kid, but it don't mean nothin'. The big mother fucker had been havin' his way with people long enough."

"I was wondering who wasted him. Whoever it was did all of us a big favor. I was talking to a guard. He said it looked like a professional job, choked Big Jake out and nearly cut his head clean off."

"Well, don't wonder too hard, boy. Let it go. One thing for true, I got my mouth punched to keep you from being a punk. If I ever catch you doin' some faggot shit of your own will, I'll stomp your honkie ass to a pulp."

"Ain't got to worry about me, T.J. If I don't get in trouble in here, I'm gone in a year or two. I like pussy way too much to turn queer in only two years. I'd jerk off before I'd touch another guy, I swear."

"You play any football in school, Randle?"

"Yea. I played some defense in high school, until I got kicked out."

"You interested in a tryout with our team?"

"Hell yes, it would help the time pass."

"I'll have you talk to the coach."

"Thanks a lot, man. Say, T.J., one thing, how come you go out of your way to help some white guy you don't even know?"

T.J. moved into the building. "You might say you remind me of a white kid I knew a few years ago. That's all."

12
September, 1973

SEPTEMBER, 1973
DETROIT, MICHIGAN

A steady, cold rain fell on the city. When the rain began two days before, it had been a welcome break from a week of unseasonable heat. Day three of cold Fall rain caused the heat relief to become long forgotten. The dampness began to have a collective negative effect on the mood of the city.

Sean and his partners were in the Precinct Narcotics Unit's office, on the first floor. Bruce typed away at a report, while Tom struggled to keep their own narcotics "who's who" 3x5 card file up to date.

Sean took the incoming phone call. He glanced at his watch and logged it in. It was 8 p.m., and in the space beside the time, he wrote the caller's code number. With all the rumors of police narcotics corruption and the impending grand jury crack down, every unit was busy with the basics of C.Y.A., cover your ass.

The caller was Pee Wee, the crew's newest and least-tested informant. "Say, Officer Cavanagh, what it is?"

Sean doodled on a scratch pad near the phone log sheet. "It's your dime, Pee Wee. What do you want? I'm in no mood to fiddle-fuck around."

"O.K., dig this, I gotta talk to you all. I got the word some dudes are gettin' ready to move some serious shit."

"I'm all ears, Pee Wee. Talk to me."

"Ah . . . no way, Officer Cavanagh, not over the phone. Can you meet me at our regular spot at 8:30? I'll lay it all out for you then. This is big time, square business. I ain't doin' any serious rappin' over the phone. Dig?"

Sean looked out of the window at the rain and winced at the mere thought of going out into the weather. "Yea, Pee Wee, at least one of us will slide by and talk to you at 8:30, regular place."

There was a pause. "Say, Officer Cavanagh, probably be better if you was all there. That way, I can lay it out to all three of you in one rap. Besides, this action is goin' down soon. You're gonna want to move on it right away."

Sean felt his palms become moist. "You alright, Pee Wee?"

"Yea, Officer Cavanagh. I'm cool."

"O.K., we'll all be there at 8:30. Don't keep us waiting or it's your ass."

Sean heard a nervous cough. "Right, 8:30. Solid." The receiver clicked twice in Sean's ear.

Sean put down the phone and wiped his sweaty hands on his Levis. Pee Wee had sounded too cool, as if he was reading from a script. The little junkie usually spoke in rapid, fragmented sentences. Sean felt certain that Pee Wee had just done up and was unusually mellow, or he had been coached about what to say.

Their normal meeting spot for Pee Wee was an isolated vacant lot near Fourth Street and Prentis. The area was absent of street lights. A G.M. pool car or the unit's navy blue unmarked Plymouth went unnoticed, unless someone was looking for it specifically.

The hair on the back of Sean's neck stood on end and he had a shiver of anticipation. By now, his partners knew to respect when Sean had one of "those" feelings, as he did that night after his conversation with Pee Wee.

Sean explained the content of the call and conveyed his deep concern. "Gentlemen, if this isn't a set-up, I'll buy dinner for the rest of the year."

Bruce poured himself another cup of coffee. "Let's assume it's a set-up. What kind, a frame or an ambush?"

"I don't think Pee Wee has the stones for an ambush, but I can't be sure. I know Big Ed and Jimmy are on the street in a car pool Cadillac tonight. I think we should go meet Pee Wee at 8:30, and have Ed set up so they can eyeball us from the other side of Third Street. That way they can back us up, whether it's a frame or an ambush. If we call for the uniforms before anything goes down, they'll either blow it off or think we're calling wolf if nothing happens. If we don't show, they'll try to do us when we don't expect something."

After a little conversation, Bruce and Tom agreed with Sean's plan. Sean called for Big Ed on the radio and briefed Ed and Jimmy when they arrived at the office.

The crew was silent and pensive as they prepared for their 8:30 rendezvous with the unknown at the rain soaked vacant lot. Sean secured his .45 in its shoulder holster. His primary weapon would be his M-1 .30-caliber rifle. He rechecked the 30-round magazine and the two 15-round magazines in the O.D. canvas stock pouch. He put two extra 15-round magazines in the pockets of his military field jacket. Sean understood better than any of them that if the initial ambush was done correctly, they were, in fact, committing suicide. Their only hope would be if they survived the initial attack. They would have to turn the tables on the attackers with a heavy volume of unexpected return fire, putting any ambushers on the defense.

Bruce checked his magnum revolver and filled the pockets of his rain slicker with extra "00" shotgun rounds. He carefully loaded his personally owned 12-gauge with 3″ shotgun magnum rounds.

Tom put his 13-shot 9mm Browning automatic in a shoulder holster. He loaded his short, ugly High-Standard, Model 10 shotgun. The strange weapon got mixed reviews from the street cops because of its very hard trigger pull and strong recoil. As the driver, Tom's initial assignment would be to get them help via the radio if they were ambushed.

Big Ed and Jimmy each took a shotgun from the weapons wall locker. Even from their back-up crew's nearby position, if it was an ambush, the first few seconds would determine whether Sean, Tom, and Bruce were to survive.

They walked out into the weather to their car. The navy blue, 1972, unmarked Plymouth was used when an undercover car pool vehicle was not necessary. It was damp inside the vehicle and the blue vinyl seats were cool. Tom started the engine and waited until the vehicle's interior was warm so they'd be certain their windows wouldn't fog up.

Big Ed radioed that they were in position. He added that they saw nothing "unusual."

Tom started to drive to the meeting location. "I wonder what you'd have to see at the corner of Third Street and Prentis to have it qualify as *unusual?*"

Both Bruce and Sean chambered a round. Sean sat in the backseat and stared out of the back window. "Shit, Third Street and Prentis; a U.F.O. with little green men could land there, and no one would notice."

The vacant lot was only a little more than a mile from the precinct station. The nervous anticipation inside the car was almost electric. They quickly reviewed their defensive strategy if they were hit. Tom would drive into the vacant lot as usual, but turn in the lot and stop the car facing south. There was nothing but vacant lots and deserted streets north of the lot. South of Prentis sat rows of old two story houses and vehicles parked in the street. If they were going to be ambushed, it would probably be from the south. Facing south, the police car's engine block would offer some cover, and they would be facing any attackers that waited.

Tom slowly drove the Plymouth onto the soggy vacant lot, stopped the car and turned off the lights. "Cav, what do you think the chances are that this is an ambush, and not just an attempted frame job?"

Sean carefully stared out of both side windows. "Back at the precinct, I'd have said 50-50. Look around, Partner. I think we're about to step into some shit."

Bruce readied his shotgun and grabbed the door handle. "Pee Wee, that little fuck, if he set us up I'll . . ."

A rifle opened up on their car from their left front. At the same moment, a shotgun opened fire on them from their right flank. There was the sound of the car windows exploding and the terrible sound of metallic thuds as rounds struck their car.

Bruce rolled out of his door and opened fire on the ambusher with the shotgun, to their right. Sean rolled out of the left rear door into a muddy puddle and returned the other gunman's fire. Tom grabbed the radio mike and fell to the floor of the front seat. Sean could hear Tom's voice over the gunfire.

"Thirteen-33, Fourth and Prentis. Officers are under fire. Officers in trouble!"

The car took hit after hit. Sean finally spotted the gunman with the rifle by his muzzle flash. The man was taking cover behind an abandoned car on Prentis, just west of Third Street. Sean shouldered the carbine and began to fire well-aimed shots at the gunman's position. His accurate return fire neutralized the sniper's fire. The man dove for cover behind the abandoned car.

Bruce finally located the sniper with the shotgun. He had been temporarily blinded by the muzzle flash of his own shotgun, and had been shooting in the direction of the sound of the sniper's fire. Tom crawled out of the car on the right side and poured 9mm pistol fire at the shotgun sniper, while Bruce reloaded.

The sound of sirens filled the area and could be heard amidst the shooting.

Sean rolled onto his side and quickly changed magazines. During the brief pause of return fire, the sniper raised back up and fired at the dark police car and Sean. A rifle round smacked the water in the puddle next to Sean. Sean rolled in the mud several feet to his left, away from their car and shouldered his rifle again.

The big red Cadillac with Big Ed and Jimmy screeched to a stop in the center of Third Street. The car's headlights illuminated the rifle sniper's position. The sniper stood and fired a poorly-aimed shot at the Cadillac, as Big Ed and Jimmy were getting out of the vehicle.

Sean got to his knees in the mud and cut loose with a vicious 10-round volley at the sniper. Big Ed and Jimmy were also able to get off a few rounds in the hapless sniper's direction. The man was hit several times and crumbled to the wet street, his rifle falling to his side.

The ambush had fallen apart in majestic fashion. If more than two snipers were involved, they had chosen not to participate once the shooting started.

The sniper with the shotgun was no more skillful than his partner, but his tenacity and obvious courage kept Bruce and Tom busy. The sniper seemed more intent on hitting the car then shooting at the men lying in the mud, or one of them would have surely been hit by some of the No. 5 shot from the ambusher's shotgun.

Sean moved back to the car. He leaned across the hood and aimed his rifle at the other sniper's position. The gunman had used a parked car and a large tree as effective cover. Sean fired his remaining five rounds into the shotgun sniper's position. He then bent down behind the car and changed rifle magazines again.

The sniper was now totally convinced that the whole idea had been the worst decision of his life, a mistake that was about to cost him his life. He fired two quick shots toward the police car in hopes of forcing the policemen to duck. He stumbled to his feet and sprinted to the mouth of the alley that ran south from Prentis.

Bruce got off two shotgun blasts and Tom fired his 9mm. The sniper stumbled and jerked, but kept his feet and reached the entrance of the darkened alley.

Just as he reached the alley, Sean was back into firing position. He sprinted after the sniper at full speed, covering his own advance by firing his carbine from the hip. He collapsed behind the cover of a parked car, at the mouth of the alley. He caught sight of a figure limping away in the shadows, about 30 yards down the muddy alley. Sean fumbled with his empty rifle for a moment, attempting to reload a full magazine from his field jacket pocket. He put down the empty rifle in frustration. He left the cover of the parked car and ran a few yards into the alley. He drew his .45 and fired eight blinding rounds toward the escaping figure, into the darkness of the littered alley.

"Come on back and fight, mother fucker. Why you running, you gutless cocksucker? Come on! Come back and get some." Sean reloaded his .45 and started down the alley. He felt Bruce on one side of him, Tom on the other.

Bruce grabbed Sean firmly by the forearm and pulled him to the cover of the parked car, as a score of uniform cars arrived at the scene. "Come on, Cav. We've saved our butts so far. Let's not go and do something stupid and get shot. We've got a couple dozen coppers at the scene. Let them check the area the safe way. They're putting a chopper in the air despite the weather. Come on back to the car. We've got enough explaining to do already."

Sean put his .45 on safe and put it back in his shoulder holster. He picked up his carbine on their way back to their shot-up police car.

"I'm so sick of this bullshit. It's not bad enough that once a month some stupid dealer wants to have a shoot-out during a search warrant raid. Now we get fucking ambushed in an attempted hit. What's next, bombing our cars, our families? And for what? All this bullshit and violence and the fucking judges put them on probation, or they get a nickel-dime sentence. I don't need this bullshit, Bruce. I'm telling you, I've fucking had it."

Sean saw an Emergency Medical Service crew over at the location of the downed sniper with the rifle. The shift's street sergeants were looking over the shot up unmarked police car. Sgt. Davidson shined his flashlight over the hood and windshield. "I can't believe none of you three were hit. They shot the shit out of this car."

Three young officers were coming down from their adrenaline high. The scores of rotating emergency lights lit up the area like a disco light show. The rain made everything shine and increased the reflections. Sean sat on the hood of the car. His knees were beginning to shake, and he was afraid it might show if he remained standing. The three of them, especially Sean, were covered with mud and soaking wet.

Sgt. Davidson offered Sean a cigarette. Sean shook his head and looked at his police car in disbelief.

"Most of these hits came after we had got out of the car. I don't think they could locate us once we got out, so they kept shooting at our car, hoping someone was still inside. Stupid shits, these turds were minor league, probably their first attempt. If they had been pros, we'd have been lucky if even one of us had survived."

Sean explained for the first of many times that night what had led up to the ambush.

Big Ed walked over from where the fallen sniper was taken away to the hospital.

"Damn, Cavanagh. You sure as hell called that one. Jimmy and I will slide down Third Street to Pee Wee's crib, just in case he's dumb enough to go home. I'd never figure that little nigger'd have the guts to set you up for a hit. Fire Department E.M.T.s say the sniper is still alive, but he's all fucked up. He's hit at least four times, head shot." He shook hands with Sean. "Really glad you boys ain't hurt. I don't figure this shit. Don't make no sense."

The scores of officers checked the entire area around the alley with the assistance of the huge flood light on the department helicopter. The gunman had evaded the police net. A citizen reported seeing a man limping across Myrtle Street, into the housing project. A shotgun was found at the opposite mouth of the alley, at Myrtle. If he had made it into the projects, it would take a Marine Battalion to locate him. He had slipped away.

Officers from the Crime Scene Investigation Section were busy taking photos and collecting empty shell cases.

Sgt. Davidson escorted the field duty officer, code 2400, Cmdr.

Smith, to where Sean, Bruce, and Tom were talking together. They gave the Commander a brief run down of the night's events. He listened but could not take his eyes from their car.

"Damn, you men are lucky."

Sean still sat on the car hood, his head resting in his hands. He was soaked to the skin from rolling in the puddles and from the continuing rain. His clothing was covered with mud. "That's us, Commander, we're three charmed guys."

Cmdr. Smith studied the expression on the sarcastic young officer's face.

"Sergeant, take these men to the precinct so they can get some dry clothing. Then, get them a car so they can drive together to Homicide. I want their vehicle towed to the headquarter's garage. Let's clean up and get our people out of here. If it wasn't raining, we'd have a hell of a crowd."

He took another look at the bullet-riddled police vehicle. "This isn't police work anymore. I look forward to reading the report. I want to know how in the hell you three survived. And by the way, Sergeant, make certain these men get something to warm their insides before they go downtown to Homicide."

The Commander patted Sean on the back and returned to his vehicle.

Bruce started to walk toward Sgt. Davidson's car. "Come on, Sarge, you'd better get Cavanagh into some warm dry clothes. Certain portions of his body are very vulnerable to the cold."

"What are you talking about, Bruce?"

"Nothing, Sarge. Inside joke."

Sean slid off of the hood. "Fuck you, Munier."

Bruce lit up a cigarette. "See how those Marines are. Give them just a little taste of violence and they go and get romantic."

"Just remember that it was good ol' Marine fire superiority that saved your ass tonight."

Bruce took a long drag from his smoke. "I will also remember that it was Marine logic that convinced me to ride into the middle of an obvious ambush as the bait."

Still at Homicide, Sean and Bruce talked and drank coffee while waiting for Tom to complete his portion of their report.

Sean was very serious and stared at the inside of his styrofoam coffee cup as if watching a vision. "Bruce, a few years ago, you and I had a conversation in this very room about good cops and attitudes and crossing the line."

"I remember, pretty idealistic stuff. We were still kids working uniform."

"Yea, and now we're burned-out, mean kids working Narcotics. I say we're only a half a step better than the scum we deal with every day. I'm telling you, Partner, I've had enough. Either I get a change of pace or I'll cross that line to the dark side. I'd love to call them out, all of the low-lifes. Call them out and we'd just do one big O.K. Corral number, and they'd take away the bodies in a fucking dump truck. Let the best side win. One big fire fight, and be done with it."

"Sean, you need a major attitude adjustment."

"I sure as hell need something, Bruce."

An hour later, Sean, Bruce, and Tom were on their way back to the precinct station from the Homicide office at police headquarters. Bruce chain lit another cigarette. Sean balanced the contents of his styrofoam coffee cup. He had lost count of how many cups he had consumed that night. He had half a roll of Tums and coffee for dinner. Tom concentrated on driving, and his private thoughts seemed to take him a million miles away.

Bruce leaned back and put his feet on the padded vinyl dashboard. "O.K. Partners, who's got the money and nerve to try to hit three cops at once?"

Sean ate another Tums.

"I went over with Big Ed and eyeballed the sniper we wounded. I don't recognize him as an arrest but I'm certain we've seen him on the street, in the Cass Corridor. My bet is that whoever wants us is bankrolling the hit and these two assholes tonight were a couple of junkie drones looking to make some big bucks. If the asshole who is out to waste us decides he's willing to pay for a pro hit, we'll be filling a body bag if we don't find out who it is."

Bruce took a long drag from his cigarette. "Gents, we've made some righteous enemies on these streets the last few years."

"Yea, but Pee Wee was the vehicle for the hit set-up. That narrows it to the South End, and I think it's narcotics-related. No one else has the bread to bankroll a hit."

Tom's head turned from the road briefly. "Do you think another cop could be involved in this?"

"I don't think so, Tommy. The hit attempt was really bush league, amateur all the way. If a cop was even remotely connected, I think we'd have really been in the hurt locker. The sniper with the shotgun had some spirit, but other than that, my sweet Irish grandmothers could have planned a better ambush. Think about it. The guy was using No. 5 shot from across the street. I could understand No. 5 bird shot if he was going to get up next to us, but not from across the street."

Sean had called Lyn from Homicide, and let her know that he would be very late.

Back at the office, the other crew members paced nervously.

The senior crew, Paul Hursch and Rick Gillis, was still in the office. They were working with the P.N.U. of the Seventh Precinct on a special assignment, and didn't learn of the shoot-out until they returned to their precinct at 2 a.m. They figured their younger unit members might need a method to relax, despite the fact that the city's bars closed at 2 a.m.

Sean, Bruce, and Tom entered their office. Paul Hursch walked over and put one of his massive arms around Sean. "Now, what are we going to do with this here kiddy car? Me and Rick leave the precinct for one night, and you lads go out and get in trouble. If you boys don't behave, we won't leave you the keys to the car."

Rick put an arm around Sean's other shoulder. "Either that, or we'll have to set a curfew."

Paul's voice turned serious. "No kidding, guys, we saw photos of the car. Damn glad you boys are alright. We're sorry we weren't available to assist you. To make it up to you, we're going to take you to our afterhours watering hole."

Bruce grinned and shook his head. "You mean a blind pig?"

Paul laughed. "Blind pig? Now, Bruce, you know those are against the law. No, this is a place where you can buy a drink, play some craps, talk with some ladies and rub elbows with everybody from city councilmen to media and local sports figures."

"What if we're in there and Vice busts the place?"

"Kid, this is Murder City, U.S.A. Vice goes through the motions once a year. As long as no one is on the take, or shaking down anyone, Vice would let you walk, kind of like professional courtesy. There are a hell of a lot worse things a copper can do than have a drink in a blind pig, especially after he's been ambushed and nearly killed."

They drove to Theodore Street and entered the old house with Paul and Rick through the side door. The doorman recognized the two senior cops and welcomed them in.

Sean got home at 6:30 a.m. It was time enough to shave, shower, and change. He was due in court downtown at 8:30 a.m. for a trial on a previous drug bust.

Neither Lyn nor Denny were awake as he got ready and left. He wrote a brief note and left it on the kitchen table for Lyn. He told her he'd be home after court. He didn't even mention the ambush shooting.

While at court, Sean, Bruce, and Tom decided they would work that night. The badly-wounded suspect clung to life, so no one had been placed on automatic administrative suspension.

Sean drove home from court and arrived at around 3 p.m. The two hours gave him time to eat a real meal, shower again, then change into his work clothes. He normally left for the precinct at 5 p.m.

Sean could tell that Lyn had not watched the local mid-day news. The morning *Free Press* sat on the end table unopened. She had taken Denny to her mother's for a visit and missed the dozen phone calls about the incident Sean imagined came in from concerned friends and relatives.

Sean was stronger and refreshed after dinner. He felt as though he had his second wind, and even though he had been up all night, he could make it through another eight-hour shift. Department football started in two weeks, and he'd been working out daily to get ready. He was certain the work outs had improved his physical endurance.

The 13th Precinct Narcotics Unit's supervisor was still Sgt. Del Greene. Greene was off the night of the shoot-out. His recent hemorrhoid operation was still causing him a great deal of discomfort. The unit members privately kidded that Greene got hemorrhoids because half the time he had his head up his ass.

Greene was past his retirement time and he could leave whenever he chose. He had been a good street cop in his day, and had decided to keep working until his youngest child finished high school. She was a senior.

When they created the Precinct Narcotics Units, Greene's job and his life changed. Policy moved Greene from behind a desk and back on to the front lines for his final months with the department.

Greene wasn't a bad boss. Sean had a tough time finding much wrong with him. He had clearly saved Sean's life at a dope house shoot-out a few months prior. Compared to actually saving his life, the Sergeant's weaknesses were easy to overlook.

Greene sat at his desk and carefully read over the numerous reports of the previous night's shoot-out. By coincidence, Sean, Bruce, and Tom had arrived at the precinct parking lot at about the same time. After a brief conversation, they entered the small P.N.U. office together.

Sgt. Greene put the report he was reading down on the desk and said, "What the hell are you three doing here?"

Sean went directly to the coffee pot and poured himself a cup. "Yea, and we missed you too, Sarge. That's a hell of a welcome. It kind of sets the mood for the night."

"Don't be a smartass, Cavanagh. I didn't expect you guys to be at work tonight after what happened last night."

"Well, Sarge, you know how it is. You've got to get back in the saddle, and all that macho bullshit."

"You men should take tonight off."

"We can't, Sarge. We're not going to sit at home if someone has bank rolled a hit on us. If he decides to hire a pro, we'll come back to work next week to get greased."

"O.K., you men go out and beat the bushes. But get an undercover car from the car pool, and for Christ's sake, be careful. We have a search warrant to serve at about 10 p.m. It's Big Ed's and Jimmy's warrant. We'll have you three cover the rear and try to keep you out of trouble. You men are lucky the Old Man is out of town on vacation, or you'd ride a desk for a week. If you get in a jam after what happened last night, he'll have my ass."

"Come on, Sarge, have you ever known us to get in trouble? Besides, your concern for us is really touching."

Sgt. Greene took a large swallow from his bottle of Maalox. "Just be careful out there. If someone is trying to get you killed, don't make it easy for them."

Bruce called Homicide. The critically-wounded sniper was still in a coma. The other sniper was still at large, and they had not been able to locate their informant, Pee Wee.

They went to the G.M. car pool and found a dark grey Olds 98. Bruce and Tom reminded Sean he could own a big car like the Olds, if he'd quit the department and go to work for his father.

"Don't tempt me too much, Partners. The mood I've been in the past few months makes that very possible. I may quit some day, but I won't be forced out by something like what happened last night."

Bruce leaned back in the plush seat.

"I don't know, Cav. Being ambushed by two gunmen would be considered motive for serious career evaluation by most people. My wife and I talked for a couple of hours today when I got home from court. Now that I have my grad degree, I'm going to seriously look for a teaching job on the East Coast this Fall."

Sean frowned and stared out the car window.

"I don't know what it is with me. I get fucking crazy. I know I don't want to do what we did last night for the next 30 years. Maybe it's some damn ghost left over from Vietnam. I was forced out of there twice. No one and nothing will force me to quit the job. If I quit, it'll be because I've had enough and I'm ready to quit or they're putting me in a body bag."

They drove all over the South End of the precinct looking for their wayward informant, Pee Wee.

Bruce lit a cigarette as he scanned the people on the crowded sidewalks of Second Avenue and Seldon. "Hey, Cav, if we find Pee Wee, don't put him to sleep before he can tell us who's behind the set-up."

Sean grinned and unwrapped a breath mint. "I'd better put a bag over my head.   If that little maggot even sees me, he might drop dead of a heart attack. I won't have to touch him to intimidate him."

"That's because you've touched him with your fist once or twice before."

The search for Pee Wee was fruitless. They returned to the precinct in time to be briefed for Ed's search warrant dope house raid.

Their destination was an old two-story brick home on West Willis. Big Ed drew a crude chalk drawing of the house's interior, as described by their informant. He had reported that the house was being run by two cousins who were new to the precinct. The word was that it was a satellite dope pad of one of the large dealers on the precinct's South End.

The crew members put on the bulky navy blue armored vests over their clothing. Each vest had the words "Detroit Police" boldly printed in white paint across the front. Uniform officers from the shift would accompany the unit. Clear and immediate identification that the dope house intruders were the "real" police cut down the chance of violence from paranoid drug dealers fearing deadly rip-offs by rival dealers. It also made for a solid assault case if the officers were fired upon.

The uniform crew of Bob Jenson and Reggie Marlen was selected to join in the raid. Every month that Jenson and Marlen worked during the time of the raids, they were requested as the uniform support. They had already been along on so many search warrant raids that they were like part-time unit members.

The plan was simple. Big Ed, Jimmy, the Sergeant, Paul, Rick, and Reggie Marlen would use the battering ram and enter through the front door. Sean, Tom, Bruce, and Bob Jenson would cover the rear and sides of the house, until the interior was secured.

Big Ed said that the informant had never seen any guns and that the dope pad's atmosphere was described as being "laid back."

The group of heavily-armed officers received more than a curious glance from the civilians in the precinct lobby as they walked from their office to their vehicles.

Sean decided to carry his 12-gauge shotgun for the dope raid. He carried magnum rounds in the well-built, personally-owned shotgun. He filled his field jacket pockets with extra "00" magnum shotgun rounds, and carried his .45 on his hip. With the bulky armored vest, a shoulder holster made his .45 difficult to get to.

Bruce carried his shotgun. Tom was satisfied with just his Browning 9mm, while Jenson carried a .357 in his uniform rig.

The group going into the house through the front door had a collection of hardware from sawed-off double-barrelled shotguns, to a .45 caliber Eagle carbine that looked like the famous Thompson machine gun.

Sgt. Greene carried his "off duty" five shot .38 Special. It didn't matter to the unit. With their collective firepower, he could carry a squirt gun and not lessen the unit's overall ability to protect each other.

They drove to the scene in a motorcade of three vehicles. They moved with quickness and coordination when the vehicles stopped near the dope house.

Sean and Jenson stood on either side of the back door, which opened to the house's kitchen. Bruce covered one side of the house, Tom the other.

Even from the back of the house, they could hear Big Ed's verbal announcement. Then they heard the booming sound of the battering ram striking the solid, well-secured front door.

Then, the sound of the ram striking the door was joined by the crack of gunfire from inside the house. The group on the front porch was taking fire from someone in the front room of the house.

The gunfire cancelled all previous strategy. Their collective response to gunfire had always been the same. It was rapid, immediate and aggressive action to neutralize the assault, as if taken from a page of Marine combat tactics.

Without a word spoken, Bruce, Jenson, and Tom had joined Sean, as he managed to kick in a large back window to the small kitchen. The four officers climbed into the house and quickly moved toward the gunfire. Sean and Bruce racked rounds into their shotguns. Sean, Tom, Bruce, and Bob Jenson stopped for a moment in the dining room, at the center of the house. The room was without furniture and they began to spread out.

Suddenly, a dark, shirtless Black man charged at them from the front room. He wildly fired a P38, 9mm pistol as he ran. Bob Jenson was struck in the upper left leg and went down. As Tom moved for a safe shot, he tripped over Jenson and fell to the floor, unhurt.

Bruce and Sean each fired one shot from their shotguns. The shots were so close together, some of the officers at the scene thought only one shot had been fired. Bruce had fired from the hip, and his round tore into the gunman's lower body. Sean had shouldered his shotgun and his powerful magnum shot hit the drug dealer in the upper chest. The force of both shotgun blasts seemed to pick the man up and toss him against the wall like a stuffed doll.

They could hear the crew at the front porch resume their attack on the door with their battering ram.

Sean moved to open the front door for the men on the porch. There was no need to check on the condition of the gunman. He was obviously dead.

Bruce and Tom quickly went to the aid of Bob Jenson, who was conscious, but bleeding badly.

In their initial actions after the shooting, they made a deadly tactical error. The informant had never mentioned the house's second floor.

The men had focused all of their attention to any other potential physical threats only on the first floor. The stairway leading to the second floor was nearly concealed in the shadows of the corner of the dining room.

Sean heard the man on the stairway before he actually saw him. Sean turned back to the dining room and racked in another round into the shotgun's chamber.

The man had shouldered a double-barrelled shotgun. Bruce was still kneeling over Bob Jenson, attempting to tie off the badly-bleeding leg. The second gunman's initial shot struck Bruce squarely in the left shoulder, knocking him to the floor, unconscious. Tom raised his pistol, but the man's second shot struck Tom in the center of his chest. He was still kneeling and the force of the direct hit knocked him over backward, pounding the breath from his body.

In the brief, violent exchange of gunfire, Sean saw that Jenson, Bruce and Tom had been hit. He didn't know how badly they were hit, but he assumed that Bruce had been killed.

The gunman ran up the stairs to a large second-floor attic bedroom. Sean fired at him but the shot only blew up a section of wooden bannister. The gunman reached the second floor unharmed.

Sean sprinted to the stairway and vaulted up to the second floor two steps at a time. He chambered another live round into the shotgun as he ran. As he did, he heard the remainder of the unit still trying to gain entry into the house.

The decision to pursue the dangerous gunman alone, with half a dozen officers just outside the door would long be a point of debate. Sean believed despite the school of police training with the emphasis on immediate withdrawal, cover, and control of the scene, that from his own experience there were isolated incidents which called for reckless, all-out, blind-ass, vicious assaults on your attacker. The aggressive tactic had saved him in Vietnam and the night before, and he saw that it had worked again that night.

As Sean stood at the top of the stairs, he saw the gunman standing next to an old, soiled twin bed. The gunman's hands shook as he fumbled to reload the sawed-off shotgun. He was so startled by Sean's immediate arrival on the second floor, that he dropped two live shotgun shells. The man knew the police would be up after him, but he never anticipated Sean's immediate, aggressive pursuit.

The gunman looked to be about Sean's age. His dark, black skin seemed to shine from his cold sweat of fear. The naked ceiling light bulb reflected artificial light from the man's trembling body. He wore only a torn pair of dark blue work pants and a badly-soiled sleeveless undershirt.

Flustered, the gunman dropped the shotgun onto the bed. He grabbed the butt of a revolver, stuck in the front waistband of his pants.

Sean had shouldered the shotgun and taken it off safety. "Freeze, fuck wad! Unless you've got a death wish, don't even think about it."

The gunman kept his grip on the revolver's wooden grips, but he made no move to remove it from his waistband.

Sean kept his eyes carefully focused on the gunman's hands. He was aware of the man's overall movements but his focus never left his hands.

The gunman's hateful black eyes stared hard into Sean's cold blue ones, staring back over the sights of the carefully-aimed shotgun. The man knew he only had seconds if he was going to make a move.

Sean's eyes never moved. He spoke into the stock of the shotgun but he could be understood. "Why? Why in the hell is every asshole in the precinct trying to waste us? Who's behind all this? Man, we don't even know you or your partner."

The gunman seemed frozen, as if he had been captured in a still photograph. He maintained his grip on the revolver butt. His stare never left Sean's eyes. If his motive was meant to intimidate, he was failing in a grand manner.

"Fuck you, pig. I know my rights. I ain't sayin' shit without my attorney. I thought you all was gangsters. You broke into my home and killed my cousin. Elsewise, I got nothin' to say."

The gunman's attitude compounded the agony of seeing three of his friends go down in gunfire in the dining room.

"Who's the money behind all this crazy shit, asshole?"

The man smirked and bobbed his head as he spoke. "Like I tol' you, mother fucker, I ain't sayin' shit without my lawyer."

The gunman kept his grip on the revolver in his waistband.

Sean heard the remainder of the unit finally gain entry into the house. He heard Big Ed calling for him.

"Last chance, asshole. Who's bankrolling a hit?"

The man's posture relaxed as he heard another officer at the foot of the stairway.

"Screw you, pig. Like I been sayin', I don't say nothin' without my lawyer."

Sean lowered his voice slightly and shocked the gunman with a slight, evil looking grin. "Say good-bye, asshole. You're never going to see a lawyer."

The gunman experienced an instant of unexpected panic. "Say what, man?"

Sean's first shotgun blast hit the gunman's middle and pushed his body up and back against the wall. While the body was still on its feet, Sean racked in a second round and fired again. The second shot roughly bounced the body back against the wall in an ugly and violent convulsion. Finally, the gunman's lifeless body slid down the plaster wall to the bare hardwood floor. The two magnum shotgun shells had nearly cut him in two.

The shots brought two of the other P.N.U. members running up the stairs. Jimmy and Rick carefully checked over the remainder of the attic bedroom. They slowly walked next to Sean who was standing over the bloody remains of the dead gunman's body. Jimmy shook his head at the mess. "What in the hell happened, Cav? When we heard two shots, we thought you bought it."

Sean seemed calm as he stared at the shredded corpse of the small-time-doper-turned-attempted-hit-man. "No, both shots were mine. Don't touch him. He's still got his hand on the gun he had in his waistband. He couldn't get the shotgun reloaded so he went for the revolver."

"What was the delay?"

"Some conversation."

"Did you learn anything?"

"Yea, this guy wasn't very bright."

Sean went back downstairs to check on his friends. The team from the Emergency Medical Service worked on Bruce and Bob. The talented Emergency Medical Techs often reminded Sean of the corpmen of Vietnam.

They gently placed Bruce on a stretcher and rushed him to nearby Ford Hospital. An additional E.M.S. Unit took Bob Jenson to the Hospital with an ugly leg wound.

Sean was shocked to see Tom walk back into the house, unharmed. The full blast of the gunman's shotgun blast had been absorbed by the heavy, armored vest. It had knocked the wind out of him and given him a nasty bruise, but not a single pellet penetrated the body armor.

The two gunman were both obviously dead and left on the floor for crime scene photos.

The field duty officer arrived at the scene and he sent everyone involved in the raid down to Homicide for statements. Sgt. Greene said he would go to Ford Hospital and keep them up to date on Bruce's condition.

Greene put his arm around Sean. "You gonna be alright, Cav?"

"I'm alright, Sarge. How about Bruce, does he have a chance?"

"Hell yes, Cav. He'll make it. The E.M.T. said it looks worse than it is. The asshole was shooting bird shot. A slug or "00" buck would have killed him. He's lost a lot of blood and his shoulder is torn up real bad, but no doubt he'll pull through."

Tears filled Sean's eyes. He had been certain that Bruce had been killed. It was as though he was brought back from the dead. Bruce being alive gave his spirit the boost it needed for him to take another step.

Tom came out and Sean put his arm around his partner. "Listen, asswipe. Don't scare the shit out of me like that again. I thought that cocksucker cancelled your ticket."

Tom was pensive. "Damn it, Cav, all that and I didn't even get a shot off."

Sean had that evil grin on his face again. "Cheer up Partner. The night is still young."

Soon the old house was filled with assorted police officers, taking photos, physical evidence and statements.

When they all arrived at Homicide, Sean and Tom were seated in a large room with tables, chairs and a single typewriter. Sean would not be questioned by anyone until the police union's representative and their attorney were present. Sean had been through the whole routine before. He sipped at a coffee and talked with Tom until they arrived.

It was just at 3 a.m. when the crew finally made it back to their office at the precinct. Sgt. Greene was still in the office. He had been waiting for them since he left Bruce at the hospital.

Greene had gone into his desk and taken out a pint bottle of Kessler's whiskey. He poured everyone a half-of-a-styrofoam-cup portion. "Mixed news from the hospital men. Bruce and Bob will both pull through. Bruce took a tough hit in his left shoulder. The doctors doubt that he will ever regain full use of it."

Sean went to the weapons wall locker. They had confiscated his shotgun as per policy in a fatal shooting. "Exactly what does that mean, Sarge, *full use?*"

"It means he can lead a normal life, not look deformed or anything, but he'll never work the street again." Greene raised his whiskey-filled styrofoam cup in a toast. "To Bruce and Bob. Thank God they're alive and here's to their speedy recovery."

The six other men in the room raised their cups and drank down the warm whiskey.

Sean removed a Savage 12-gauge double-barrelled shotgun from the locker, and began to fill his pockets with regular "00" buck. He put his .45 in its shoulder holster and put it on.

Sgt. Greene poured himself another half-cup of whiskey. "Where the hell you think you're going, Cav, to war?"

"You might say that, Sarge."

"To hell you say, Cavanagh. You're going home. You know the policy. You are suspended until the shooting review board puts you back to duty."

"Yea, well that's just fucking beautiful, Sarge. They suspend me for a

week. Then, if that little fucker Pee Wee still is in town, he'll sky out of
here so fast when he hears what happened tonight, we'll never locate
him. Until we find out who's bank-rolling the attempted hits, it's going
to be like this every night. There is one last possible chance that little
shit is still in town. The welfare checks come tomorrow. If this thing
caught him a little light on cash, he might be waiting to get the check
before he leaves town. Remember, Pee Wee has a main squeeze, a little
whore with the street name of Peaches. She works Second Avenue and
Seldon. We busted her for loitering in that white doper's pad on West
Alexandrine last Spring. She's got a little apartment on Cass Avenue, just
north of Myrtle. There's a chance he's laying chilly at Peaches' crib until
they get enough money to rabbit out of here."

"Possible, but you are suspended. We can have some uniforms check
it out and they can . . ."

"No disrespect meant, Sarge, but no fuckin' way! Two nights in a row
some assholes have tried to kill us. Pee Wee is the one lead we have to
who's behind this. You can order me, suspend me, even fire me, but I'm
going to see if Pee Wee is at Peaches' apartment. Then, if he is, he's
going to tell me who's behind this."

Sgt. Del Greene poured another cup full of whiskey.

"We've never had this conversation, you hear me? I'm too goddamn
close to retirement for this kind of shit. The goddamn Grand Jury is just
waiting to piss all over some cops. Damn Internal Affairs is around every
corner, the Feds are involved, and you guys want to go on an unauthorized witch hunt, while on official suspension."

"Witch hunt? Come on, Sarge. We've had the shit shot out of us the
past two nights. By the end of the month at this rate, you'll be doing
dope house search warrant raids alone."

Greene put his bottle back in his desk and put on his coat.

"Men, like I said, we never even talked about this. I'm sorry, I still got
a kid in school and I'm too close to my pension to fuck up over 25 years.
I won't try to stop you, but I can't go with you on this."

He left the office without further conversation. No one in the room
could blame him. Besides, he would only have gotten in their way.

Sean finished the last of the whiskey in the bottom of his cup.

"Anyone else that wants to leave, I fully understand. It could really
get ugly. No matter what, there'll be a lot of explaining to do. Justified
or not, we'll get our asses in a sling."

The other five men in the room said nothing. They didn't move from
their casual positions throughout the office.

"O.K., here is my idea. Tommy and I slide over to Peaches' place.
We'll go there alone and take the carpool Olds. If we all go, it will look
like a cluster fuck, and we'll draw too much attention to ourselves.

Tommy and I can slide in the back unnoticed, in case someone is having Pee Wee watched. If we find out who the bank-roller is, we'll drop a dime and tell you where to meet us."

Paul went into his desk and took out his favorite skin magazine. "We'll be right here waiting on your call. Don't take too long, most of these pages are already stuck together."

It was nearly 4 a.m. when Sean and Tom quietly climbed the back stairs of the old ghetto apartment building on Cass Avenue.

Sean sensed he was nearly out of self-control. The tension had been building for months. The meaningless waste and constant frustration were coming to a head with the desperate search for the man responsible for the shootings. He was determined to see this thing through to the end, even if it cost him his career, or his life.

They reached Peaches' third-floor apartment. Sean readied his shotgun, Tom drew his 9mm. He turned the door knob. "It's locked. Think we should knock?"

Sean moved in front of the door. "Naw, we might disturb the sleeping neighbors. I'll use my size ten door key."

Sean kicked the old hollow-core door with such force, it burst out of the frame and landed on an old stuffed chair in the small living room of the apartment. They rushed in and raced to the tiny bedroom facing Cass Avenue.

There, in the bedroom's darkness, they saw the figure of a man sleeping in the center of a filthy double bed. Tom located a light bulb that hung down from the ceiling. He turned on the light as Sean put the barrels of his shotgun against the side of the man's head.

The light clearly revealed the sleeping form of their now-famous informant, Pee Wee.

Sean shook his head in absolute disgust. "Do you believe this little mother fucker? He's about to sleep through his own murder."

Sean struck Pee Wee hard on the bridge of his nose with the sawed-off shotgun's barrels. The sharp pain caused the little man to wake suddenly. Both hands held his bleeding nose as he tried to focus his vision. "What the fu . . ."

"Guess who, mother fucker? It's a couple of ghosts from your worst fucking nightmare."

Pee Wee's eyes finally focused through the deep sleep and sharp pain. When he recognized the occupants in the room with him, his eyes nearly bulged from his head. "Oh, my Lord."

Sean pushed the shotgun barrels hard against the side of Pee Wee's head. "Where's your main squeeze, asshole?"

"Peaches is out workin'."

"Mighty white of her to stay on the street all night doing tricks, while you're here sleeping."

Pee Wee studied the blood on his hands. "Well, we need all the bread we can get. After checks come tomorrow, we was gonna try our luck in the Windy City. Peaches gots family there."

"How come you're leaving town now? Any special reason for the timing?"

"Well, sure. I was afraid you all might figure I had something to do with the trouble you had after I called to meet you. I was walking over to meet you when I seen all that shootin'. I just got scared and run off. Me and Peaches decided it was time to get outa town. I sure don't want no trouble."

Sean jabbed him again with the shotgun barrels.

"I'm already pissed enough to kill you, Pee Wee. You lay a line of bullshit on me, and I'll make you regret the day you were born. In Vietnam I learned some real interesting things to do to people. We know you were never there last night. You called us to meet you as a set-up for a hit. You even insisted all three of us be there."

"I know it looks bad, but I swear fo' God, I wouldn't do nothin' to get you all hurt."

Sean smashed Pee Wee's cheek with the butt of the shotgun.

"Tonight Officer Bruce was seriously shot. Stop fucking with us or I swear I'll break every bone in your body before I kill you. Who's the money behind the hit attempts?"

"Please don't hurt me no more. I ain't done nothin', an' I don't know nothin'."

Sean struck Pee Wee's already broken nose. "You lying sack of dog shit. Someone had you set us up. Now, you'll tell me, or I'll have you begging for me to kill you to put you out of your misery. Or maybe I'll break every bone in your body, charge you with a couple major felony raps and the boys up in Jackson Prison will pass you from cell to cell as entertainment while your bones are healing. Let's see, conspiracy to murder, possesion of heroin, resisting arrest, violation of probation. By the time you get out, not only will Peaches have a new man, she'll be a grandmother."

Pee Wee tenderly touched his bleeding nose. "Oh man, I think you broke my nose. Why you doin' me this way, Officer Cavanagh? I done tol' you, I don't know nothing."

Sean drove the butt of the shotgun into Pee Wee's groin. His hands quickly moved from his nose to his testicles. Another shotgun butt stroke hit the little junkie informant in the mouth, chipping some teeth and cutting his lower lip. A blow to the side of his head rolled him off of the bed, onto the hardwood floor. Tom kicked the crying informant solidly in the side, lifting him from the floor.

Tom held his foot hard against Pee Wee's throat as he lay on his back on the floor.

"Pee Wee, my man, you'd better tell Mr. Cavanagh the truth. I've worked with him for about four years. I've never seen him like this. I think he really is going to break every bone in your body. I get the idea that he's kind of enjoying this. I don't know who's got you so scared, Pee Wee, but I gotta tell you he's no match for what we're going to do to you. The man learned some tricks in Vietnam, no shit. I'd have to leave the room, and I've got a strong stomach. You'd be no good to Peaches when he got through."

Pee Wee motioned to Tom to remove his shoe from his throat so he could talk. "O.K., I had more than enough of all this bullshit. I don't know what he could do to me more than kill me, and you two are doin' a good job at that. This is some crazy shit, man. I mean, you dudes are suppose to be the real po-lice. You supposed to enforce the law. This ain't no law."

Sean bent down and lifted Pee Wee from the floor by the front of his shirt with one hand and dropped him back on the bed.

"You listen to me, you little scroat. Don't you dare talk to us about the law. You set us up for an ambush. Munier gets hit tonight and you expect us to let you hide behind a row of books called the law. Fuck you and the law, Pee Wee. We're playing hard ball now. No rules tonight, no code of honor, no Marquis of Queensbury. Street justice is the order of business for tonight, Pee Wee. Someone wants us dead because we're honest cops, not on the take."

There was a moment of silence.

"If you only talk while you are in pain, Pee Wee, I'll be more than happy to motivate you."

"No, Officer C. I'm done. I'm a real believer. It was John Wheston, down on Brainard. He was just expanding his business last Winter, when you all started the raids. Every dope house you hit south of Forest is one of his pads. You really startin' to put the hurt on his business. One day he says he'll pay five grand to any dude who takes one of you out. Then he gets to laughin' and says he'll pay 20 thou' for all three of you. Man, you dudes know what five grand means out here. Some stupid narc from Central Narcotics Downtown left one of your reports on his desk when he went to get a coffee. One of Wheston's men was bein' booked and seen my name and knew I was workin' for you. He spilled his guts to Wheston. The dude went crazy. He threatened to O.D. me and do some terrible shit to Peaches before they killed her."

"Who were the triggermen the night you called."

"Sweet Jesus, I'm a dead man. I swear I don't know. I never seen them. John Wheston told me what to say. I never saw the shooters. I swear."

Sean gave Pee Wee another butt stroke to the side of his head.

"*Oh, I don't know anything, Officer Cavanagh.* You lying little fuck.

I'm going to go look in the mirror and see if I look that goddamn stupid. You'd better hear me, Pee Wee. We're going to let you leave town with Peaches. You'd better be gone tomorrow. I'm going to take down John Wheston and let him know you snitched him off. If I ever see you out on the street, I'll blow your fucking brains out, then make it right when they read the report. They'll find dope and a gun on your body and I've already named you in the conspiracy."

"Don't say no more, Officer Cavanagh. Me and Peaches are out of here. I swear."

A moment later, they were gone. Tom turned out the bedroom light as they walked out. Pee Wee lay back down on the bed. He hurt everywhere. He held his broken, bleeding face. He was thankful in retrospect that he had finally told them what they wanted. He had been certain that they were going to kill him anyway. "The people in this city is crazy. Even the po-lice is crazy. Shit, a nigger can get himself half beat to death down South. Might as well go home with Peaches to Alabama. If I get my face stomped by the po-lice down in Alabama, at least I'll be home."

Tom and Sean located a pay phone that was in operating condition. Most inner-city phone booths became an outdoor urinal once the receivers were torn from the phone and the coinbox shattered.

Sean reached Big Ed. He told Sean that while they were visiting with Pee Wee, Paul and Rick had received word that a badly-wounded man had turned himself in at Ford Hospital. The man was suffering from four day-old gunshot wounds. He had been arrested at once as the suspect sniper. In his weakened condition, he had freely admitted his shotgun attack on Sean, Tom, and Bruce. He confirmed that John Wheston was the bank-roll behind the hit attempts, and that, rather than a contract hit, Wheston had placed an open-offer bounty on the three policemen.

The P.N.U. members decided to meet at Third Street and Seldon, then drive to Wheston's house on Brainard Street together.

With the gathered information, the detectives would easily obtain a warrant against Wheston for conspiracy to murder. John Wheston could make even the highest bond, and by trial time, the witnesses and their case against him would be gone. If not, Wheston would leave the state.

The unit members decided to arrest John Wheston themselves. Collectively, they might convince John Wheston that he had been in error and any continued murder attempts would not be in his best interest. Sean was motivated by blind rage and a personal need for immediate and severe street justice.

The 70-year-old three-story ex-boardinghouse loomed over the 600 block of Brainard Street, near Third Street. It was the castle of the South End's prince of darkness.

The six remaining members of the P.N.U. stood on the littered porch of the old house. Sean pounded on the front door. On the cold, damp September morning, even the street people had deserted Third Street by 4:30 a.m. Void of people and vehicles, the streets still had looked evil. Combined ghetto filth, aging, poorly-kept buildings and a knowledge of those who spent their lives there, created a foul atmosphere any time of the day, any month of the year.

Sean pounded loudly on the door. After a full minute, there was finally a voice from the other side of the door.

"Who's there and what you want?"

Sean held up his badge case to the front of the door. "Look out the peep hole, dip shit. It's the real police. Open the fucking door. We've got a warrant and want to talk to Wheston. We're not here because we're lonely."

The big man behind the door was Rufus Jefferson, John Wheston's unofficial bodyguard and the dope dealer's number one "Lieutenant." He stood 6'4" and only Paul Hursch of the Precinct Narcotics Unit matched him in size and strength. Rufus was very loyal to Wheston, who treated him with more respect than anyone ever had. He was willing to die for John Wheston, if necessary. "Why you want me to open the door?"

"Just open the door, jerk off. We're not out here enjoying the night air. I told you that we've got official business with your man, John Wheston."

"It's in the middle of the night, man. He ain't gonna want to talk with you."

Sean held a neatly-folded piece of paper in front of the peep hole. "We've got a search warrant. Come on, Rufus, you've been to this dance before. If we're forced to break down the door, you get charged with interfering, then everybody goes to the hospital before they go to jail. Just open the fucking door."

Rufus was perplexed. If he went all the way up to John Wheston's third-floor bedroom, the officers might break down the door while he was getting Wheston's instructions. He could sense the anger in the young policeman's voice. He decided to have a look at the search warrant and buy some time, hoping Wheston had been awakened by the knocking at the door.

Rufus checked the large-caliber automatic in his back pocket. He locked a night chain, unlocked the other half dozen deadbolt locks and removed the drop bar. Rufus slowly opened the heavy door about three inches. "Let me see that search warrant."

"Sure, Rufus. Here you go. Take a good look at it. Take your time."

As the door opened as much as the chain lock would allow, Rufus reached out for the paper.

Sean squarely kicked the heavy door near the knob with all of his strength. The corner of the door hit Rufus in the center of the forehead. He fell backward and down to the floor, stunned. He grabbed for his bleeding forehead and for his pistol.

The officers moved inside from the porch.

Sean stood over Rufus. He pressed his .45 automatic against the bridge of Rufus' nose. "Don't take our that pistol, Rufus. We've got no beef with you. Lay still, or I'll take your head right off."

Rufus hesitated. Big Ed disarmed him and handcuffed the large Black man to the solid stair bannister.

Rufus began to call out to Wheston on the third floor. Big Ed punched him in the mouth with his fist.

"The boy told you, Rufus. Ain't got no beef with you. If you press us, we'll rip out your tongue and slap you silly with it. You've done all you can for that no good nigger upstairs. Now let it go."

Rufus wiped his swollen, bleeding lip on his shirt sleeve. He nodded his head in a gesture of surrender.

The six policemen quietly but quickly ran up the three flights of stairs to the Wheston's bedroom. They knew the layout of the house. They had been there twice before with search warrants. Both cases were awaiting trial.

Sean reached the room first. He kicked the unlocked door from its hinges. As he stepped into the room, Tom turned on the bedroom light.

Sean stood six feet away from Wheston, aiming his .45 at the dazed dope dealer with both hands. "Go ahead, John Wheston. Grab that gun, you fuck. Grab it, and and I'll make you a part of that stained mattress."

Wheston focused his sleepy eyes at the men in his bedroom. "Oh, it's you Officer Cavanagh. Don't shoot, man. Don't shoot. I for sure didn't know it was the po-lice. Thought it was a rip-off. What you all want this time of the night?"

Sean moved up to the prone figure. He held the .45 purposely up against Wheston's left shoulder, at the joint. If the weapon discharged at point blank range, Wheston would lose his whole arm.

"It's this way, John, my man. Since you managed to make certain Officer Bruce Munier will never work the street again, and I wasted the guy that did Munier, I figure I should be able to collect the bounty. Miller and I figured if we turned ourselves over to you, we might qualify for the bonus."

"Now, Officer Cavanagh, I don't know what in the world you talkin' 'bout."

The other members of the unit had never seen Sean act this way. They were watching a stranger, and it unsettled them. There was no racial motivation in Sean's rage. It was man against man. Not even young

Jimmy Haller believed Sean would act any differently if John Wheston was white.

"Say, Officer Cavanagh, that big .45 is cocked. If I even twitch, it'll blow my arm clean off."

"Yea? Then don't twitch. Officer Bruce Munier will not be able to fully use his left arm because of your reward. Maybe I should blow your right arm off instead, then I'd also ruin your sex life."

"Say, you talkin' the fool, man. I got no idea what you're rappin' on."

Sean felt himself begin to lose the last of the thin fibers of his self-control. Still holding the .45 in his right hand, he grabbed John Wheston by his Afro hair with his left hand. With a vicious thrust, he yanked Wheston out of bed and onto the floor.

"You scummy fucker, what do you think we're doing here? We know you've bank-rolled the hit attempts on us with your cash bounty. Now you dare act innocent and insult us? Wheston, I'm going to kick so much shit out of you, all they'll find is a soot stain."

John Wheston's voice took the tone of a whine and he began to plead. "Square business, I don't want no problem with you all."

Sean threw Wheston into the room's cheap kitchen set. The force of his body knocked over table and chairs. Sean holstered his .45. He grabbed Wheston with both hands and drove the upper portion of Wheston's body into the open oven of the old gas stove. He bounced Wheston's head around in the oven.

"No more bullshit, Wheston. You know why we're here. You better start to be straight with us, or I swear, I'll beat you to death with my bare hands. And guess what, you rotten, dope-dealing cocksucker? I'll enjoy every second of it."

Sean turned on one of the gas burners. He pulled Wheston's head close enough to the flame to singe his hair.

"Enough, Officer Cavanagh. Please, enough. O.K., I kind of offered sort of a reward for you three. First, it kind of started as a joke. Then, it got out of hand, out of control. You and Miller and Officer Bruce really put the hurt on my business. Everybody says you're too tight-ass for a bribe or a payoff. Well, seemed like I had only two choices, to get you all fucked up or go out of business. I decided no three young honkie cops was gonna ruin all I done."

Sean slammed Wheston's face hard against the stove top. "Why didn't you just shoot us yourself, or have that dumb fuck downstairs, Rufus, try to waste us?"

Wheston's mouth was swelling, "No way, Officer Cavanagh. I ain't a violent man myself."

Sean bounced Wheston's head against the stove again.

"Yea, that's what Pee Wee said. You don't like violence but you like to pay for it. Well, John Wheston, too bad you don't enjoy violence. You're going to be exposed to a great deal of violence in the next half hour. I'm going to help you collect some of what you paid for."

Big Ed found a large baggie of heroin in a dresser drawer. "Hey, Cav, look here, Mr. Wheston got him quite a stash. I figure 15, maybe 20 grand worth."

Jimmy carefully inspected the contents of the room's old refrigerator. He opened the freezer door and tossed the ice trays onto the floor. "Well, well, look it here, Cav. I figure the man got him about three grand in hundreds here. Cleaver Wheston, my man, you can say you got cold hard cash when you keep it in the freezer."

Tom recovered a .44-magnum from under the bed. "Oh my, look at this piece. You going elephant hunting, Wheston? What is a non-violent fellow like you doing with a great big nasty gun like this?"

"It's for protection. You dudes know how it is, rip-offs and murders. I seen one of these in a movie and paid $500 for it from a guy. It's clean, not stolen, never even been fired. You ain't got no warrant. Ain't none of this gonna make it to court."

Sean slammed Wheston's face into the stove again.

"Get ready to take notes, Mr. Street Lawyer. We came here to arrest you for conspiracy. Once inside, we found the heroin on your dresser along with the money. You resisted arrest and assaulted us with that big gun, so we were forced to defend ourselves."

Wheston touched his swollen face with his right hand. Sean had firm hold of his left arm and had it twisted painfully behind his back. Wheston's hand nearly touched the back of his own head.

Wheston cried from the pain. "Just take the shit and go. You know you ain't got no real court case. Ain't nobody gonna believe that jive by the time we go to trial. Let's talk some business 'bout the money. I can get you some more."

Sean dragged Wheston's limp body and pushed him hard against the old cast-iron steam register. "Don't even suggest a bribe, fucking scroat. You're probably correct about the money and drugs, even about the gun. I've got a better idea, we'll take care of the entire matter here tonight." He looked over his shoulder to the other crew members. They picked up on his cue.

Jimmy walked over to the gas stove with the stack of money. "These here $100 bills are too cold to hold. I think I will warm them up." Jimmy began to burn the one hundred dollar bills, a handful at a time.

Sean bounced Wheston's body off of the steam register again, then put him in the arm lock and dragged him over to the stove so he could watch his money burn.

Big Ed walked over to the sink and turned on the water. "I don't want to go to all the trouble of puttin' this shit into evidence and doing all the paperwork. Like you said, Wheston, we probably don't have a good court case." He opened the baggie and began to pour the thousands of dollars worth of heroin down the kitchen sink.

Wheston mustered all of his strength and tried to break Sean's grasp. Sean's counter move snapped Wheston's left arm and he screamed in pain. "You all are crazy, I tell you. We can talk business. You ain't gonna get away with this roust."

Sean dragged Wheston to the sink so he had a good view of his assets going down the drain.

Tom emptied Wheston's expensive revolver. "A lay-back, non-violent guy like you shouldn't have such a dangerous weapon in the house. You could hurt yourself with this big gun." He held the revolver by its long barrel and smashed it to pieces against the steam register.

Wheston moaned in pain. "You all are crazy. You can't do this."

For the next minute, the entire crew took out months of built up frustration on John Wheston's house, while Sean continued his physical punishment of Wheston. "Look, Wheston, we *are* crazy and we *can* do all this."

Wheston lay semi-conscious on the floor. His third-floor living area was gutted and in ruin.

Sean grabbed Wheston by the hair and the back of the shirt and lifted him to his feet.

For the first time in several minutes, Wheston felt that the group of angry young policemen was not going to beat him to death. If they were, in fact, going to arrest him, he would live long enough for his own revenge.

Sean spoke slowly to Wheston, who was very unsteady on his feet.

"We played this silly game by the rules for the first few months, John Wheston. Then you changed the game when you put a price on our heads. We all have families, and you pay to have us killed because we're bothering your profit margin. As of now, you are out of business in this precinct. When you get out of jail, if you try to set up again, we'll be back. We'll make this visit seem like a fucking cocktail party."

The officers began to file out of the room one at a time.

John Wheston's entire body screamed with the pain from the beating by Sean. He feared his left arm was broken, along with his nose. He limped toward the stairs. John Wheston had been a cocky street dealer too long to use common sense, even under these extreme circumstances. He touched his swollen face.

"You mother fuckers ain't gettin' away with all this. My attorney is gonna make certain you gonna pay for all this you done to me."

Sean's actions were so rapid that no one was in position to stop him, even if they would have anticipated his intention. Wheston was taller and heavier than Sean's 5′11″, 175 pound frame. Sean suddenly picked Wheston up from the floor by the front of his shirt. Wheston's mouth dropped open with shock, as the startled drug dealer felt himself being carried to the corner of the large third-story room by the smaller man. There were two, double pane, tall windows in the corner of the room, opposite the bed.

Tom was the first to realize what was about to happen. He muttered under his breath. "Holy shit, Cav, don't . . ."

Sean shoved Wheston backward with all of his strength. As Wheston's limp body smashed through the window glass, Sean shouted at the falling dope dealer, "Look out, he's going to jump."

After crashing out of the window, Wheston fell three stories and partially struck a metal fence before finally hitting the sidewalk. Wheston lay unconscious on the damp cement. The fall broke his collar bone and caused a minor skull fracture. His nose and left arm were broken prior to the fall. The trip through the window glass caused several deep lacerations.

Big Ed stood next to Sean as they looked down at John Wheston's body on the sidewalk.

"You better do the report on this one, Cav. You write it up, we'll all sign it. I'll go have a chat with Rufus and let him slide. I'm sure I can convince him that it's in his best interest not to stick around so anybody can find him. Rufus is a wise old dude, he'll know that his meal ticket has been cancelled and it's time to move on."

Ten minutes later, an E.M.S. van was taking the unconscious John Wheston to the city hospital as a police prisoner. He was charged with several felony counts.

Sean's official arrest report would always be considered a police literary masterpiece. Anyone at the scene that night knew it also qualified as a work of fiction.

The six silent men exchanged glances as each signed the report. It was not a question of justification for their brutal actions. They had decided as a group to personally take action. The lengthy incident report was merely a necessary formality.

———————————

The police shooting tribunal had called for Sean to report at the precinct at 10 a.m. By the time he had finished the reports on the Wheston arrest, Sean only had time to make it home to shower and change clothes.

He was shocked to find his home empty. There was a brief note on the kitchen table from Lyn. It said that she and Denny were at her parents. The note's tone was cool. It was not signed.

The three senior command officers of the shooting board utilized the vacationing precinct C.O.'s office.

Sean knocked and entered the office on their verbal command. He managed to shave and he decided to dress in a business manner. He wore dress pants, his navy blue blazer and tie. He had been awake for about 48 hours. As he sat down in front of the three command officers, he was thankful he had consumed more coffee than alcohol during those two days. He slipped another Tums in his mouth before the conversation formally began.

The review board consisted of two veteran white Commanders and a Black deputy chief. The Deputy Chief was in charge of the review of the shootings. He was seated behind the C.O.'s desk and flanked by a Commander on each side. "You don't look too much worse for the wear, Cavanagh, considering what you've been through the past two days. Do you want an attorney, or a union rep involved in this investigation?"

"Only if I'm about to be criminally charged. The Homicide people said there shouldn't be any problem with the Prosecutor's office. I had an attorney help me with the official report. As long as this is strictly an intra-department review, I believe an attorney, or union rep will only slow things down. This will be complex enough, Sir. I see no reason to make it worse."

The Deputy Chief made a brief note on a legal pad. "Cavanagh, I see by your record that you have been through all of this before. In addition to returning to the scene of the fatal shootings last night, I'd like you to show us the shooting scene of the ambush the night before. It would be a long day, Officer. Are you up to this?"

"I've never been very good at waiting. I'd rather get this over with as soon as possible."

All day, the three veteran command officers were sullen. They asked many questions and frowned at every answer. They drove to the old house on West Willis, the location of the shoot-out.

They gave the scene of the fatal shootings the once-over, as if they were Homicide dicks looking at the crime scene for the first time.

The Deputy Chief inspected the ugly blood stains and bullet holes on the second floor. He called Sean upstairs. They stood next to each other and stared at the blood stain. The two Commanders remained on the first floor.

"You shot him twice, Officer Cavanagh. Twice with a pump shotgun?"

"Yes, that's right, Sir."

"With your military background, other previous shootings, not exactly what I'd expect even under the extreme pressure."

Sean walked over to the wall and put his finger in one of his shotgun pellet holes in the wall.

"Deputy Chief, I've thought about it a great deal since last night. The suspect shot Miller and Munier. When I ran up the stairs after him, I thought Bruce was dead and that Tom might be. Sir, I was trained that when you are forced to use a weapon to save your life, you do it with gusto. That type of aggressive response saved our lives the night before. The suspect dropped his shotgun on the bed and went for the gun in his belt. I was trained to neutralize his threat. Today, it looks like I killed him twice. It seemed like the right thing to do at the time. We were set up and ambushed two nights ago, then attacked for no reason last night. I may not have used minimum force last night, but it all looks different as we safely stand here in the daylight."

"You're no idealistic rookie, Cavanagh. You realize that you are no longer in the Marines or in Vietnam. You know if you kill two men in one night, shoot two others the night before, you'll be second-guessed, no matter what the circumstances are around the shootings."

Sean stared down at the large blood stain on the floor and the blood smeared on the wall.

"You know, Sir, I became a cop so I could do something meaningful with my life after Vietnam. I didn't do anything to provoke what happened the past two nights. Once things started to happen, I did what I believed I needed to do to survive. I fell back on my training and my instincts."

The Deputy Chief slowly removed his glasses and placed them in his inside jacket pocket.

"I've really studied your file, Cavanagh. Even though each one of your shootings stands well on its own, you've been in too many in only five years if you want to advance through the ranks. You've taken the sergeant's exam. You have a transfer request in for the academy staff. You wanted off the street before all of this. Come to think of it, you didn't ask to work Narcotics.

"Listen carefully to me, Cavanagh. At the ambush, you fired 68 rounds. I'm not suggesting that your actions that night were not tactically sound and justified, but consider how that would sound if the media jumped on it. Then, by mere fate, you kill two men the following night. Our Public Information people did an outstanding job with these incidents. Nothing gets more photo coverage than a police car with scores of bullet holes in it. And nothing dilutes the killing of two suspects as much as two wounded police officers.

"It's a political battlefield out there, Officer. Don't curl your lip and get an attitude, or you're done as a copper in this town. If some cub reporter starts to notice your name too many times, and he finds out you are a Nam Vet, you'll be on the front page of the Sunday magazine. Then you'll get a reputation that could delay or even ruin your career."

Sean rubbed his tired eyes and sat down on the soiled bed near the blood stain.

"What can I do, Sir? As you saw in my file, I didn't ask to be transferred to the Narcotics assignment. We were really getting something done on the street, making an actual difference out there, in the Booster assignment. I went out the past two nights just doing my job. I'm forced to defend myself and my partners and I chance ruining my career."

The Deputy Chief took out a pipe from his pocket. He looked Sean in the eyes as he stuffed tobacco in the pipe's bowl.

"How about you step down off that soap box and you and I talk straight to each other? You're walking a fine line, my young friend. I know your shootings were righteous. I've got my doubts on what really happened up here, but the morgue results prove he had his hand on his revolver, just as you said. What you obviously don't know is that I know about what happened last night after you got back from Homicide, while you were on official suspension."

Sean didn't even attempt to conceal his expression of surprise and concern. "Has someone filed a formal complaint?"

The Deputy Chief lit his pipe and enjoyed a few puffs.

"No, and I don't expect there'll be one. I doubt whether your former informant will come back to Detroit to file a beef. And from what I understand, you made a real believer out of Mr. John Wheston. When he makes bond, he's history. You see, Officer Cavanagh, the D.E.A. has been working a case on Wheston for three months, and you men fucked it up for keeps last night. The only reason they're not screaming for your badges is because we found out that they knew about the price Wheston had put on your heads weeks ago. They didn't warn you because they didn't want to chance spoiling their case on Wheston. So, you men are nearly all killed two nights in a row, while they sit on the information."

Sean shook his head. "I'm really sorry we spoiled their case. Now, we were nearly killed for nothing."

"You boys may be good street cops, but you'd make crummy crooks. Internal Affairs has had a tail on you for a month. They followed you to your visit to the informant's apartment on Cass, and to Wheston's place. You boys pulled the kind of search and destroy mission last night that would have you riding a desk forever, if you didn't lose your job. But you lucked out again. An Internal Affairs crew was watching you when you were ambushed. Some tight-ass sergeant decided not to help you because it would have compromised their month-long surveillance. When his C.O. found out, he wouldn't let him take you down for last night's activity. The C.O. figured your trial board hearing might get pissy for I.A. when it came out that two of his men stood by and watched you get ambushed without acting."

Sean looked over at the blood stain on the wall.

"This is a real paradox. If the D.E.A. would have tipped us on the bounty on us, none of it would have happened in the first place. Internal Affairs could have followed us for the next year and not even seen us commit a traffic violation. They fuck up, we nearly get killed and go kicking ass, and they can't take us down for it because they fucked up."

"I worked the street enough to have an idea what went on here last night, Cavanagh. You men lost control and you became no better than the slugs you were dealing with. I know it was not a racial thing. Everything and everyone indicates you're honest cops, whose worst crimes are isolated sessions of street justice and an occasional visit to a local blind pig to unwind. But last night you crossed the line. You weren't cops. You were brutal men seeking revenge."

"Well, Sir, I've been given another chance by default. What do you suggest that I do with that chance? I'm a cop because I want to be. I don't need this job but I expect to make it my career."

"Cavanagh, I'm having your C.O. pull you and Miller off the street until after the holidays. You start football with the department team next week, and then you'll only ride a desk about a month. After promotions and transfers are over in January, re-evaluate where you are and where you want to go. Get off the street for a year or so. You need the change. Don't spoil a promising future."

"Thank you, Sir. If you know about what we did to the informant and Wheston, why aren't you charging us?"

"Like I told you, neither of them have complained. The D.E.A. and Internal Affairs have nothing to say, officially. And besides, I was ordered to investigate the shootings. There is no indication of misconduct at the actual shootings. The bottom line, Cavanagh, is that I think you and your crew are good young cops who deserve another chance."

The shooting review board and the Wayne County Prosecutor's office cleared Sean and the others of any misconduct in both shooting incidents.

That afternoon, after receiving the good news, Sean was sent home. He and Tom were given a five day special leave.

Before Sean left the precinct, he learned that Bruce and Jenson were doing well, that Pee Wee and Peaches had got on a bus headed south and that Wheston made bond and left the city hospital by private ambulance. It was last seen headed for the airport.

Sean sat for a moment in the precinct parking lot behind the wheel of his Triumph. He decided to stay off of the freeway. He was exhausted and decided to take the pre-rush-hour surface streets home.

A third of the way home, a wave of breath-taking anxiety crashed over him like a huge ocean breaker. He couldn't catch his breath. It felt as though his entire life was falling to pieces around him. He knew the terrible truth about the gunman in the attic bedroom and he could share it with no one. The circumstances and physical evidence verified his official version, but Sean alone knew that he had murdered the man in cold blood. Then, he tortured information from Pee Wee and finally, he gave John Wheston a near-fatal beating as street punishment for trying to have them killed.

Sean's disgust with his own actions sickened his stomach. He pulled to the curb, in front of an old, inner-city church. He stepped from the car and put a stick of gum in his mouth.

He was so tired it was as though he was in a daze. He realized he was in the Seventh Precinct. He finally was breathing normally and his stomach settled. He intended to step inside the old church for a moment but the huge wooden doors were locked. He sat down on the church steps and rested his head in his hands.

An old Black woman walked past on the sidewalk, pulling a grocery handcart. She approached Sean. "Say, boy, you alright? Did yo' car break down or is you sick?"

Sean raised his head and forced a grin. "No, Ma'am, the car is fine. I just needed a couple of minutes to pull myself together."

The woman walked back to her grocery cart. "You better have yourself a look around, white boy. You ain't in the kinda neighborhood that's safe for somebody like you to sit there sortin' out your problems. You not careful, some local home boys gonna come by and really give you something to fret about."

Sean nodded his head. "I understand, thank you for your concern. I'll be out of here in a minute."

The old woman shrugged her shoulders and continued on her way.

Sean was feeling better. The scenes of the night before raced through his mind again, but he knew the old woman had been right and he got back into his car and drove home.

Sean parked his Triumph in the driveway. He sat in the car for a moment, collecting his thoughts, clearing his mind and forcing himself to relax from the frightening anxiety attack. He had lost track of how many hours he had been awake without a hint of sleep; it was well over 50.

He slowly walked to his front door and let himself in. His father sat alone in the living room on the Colonial-style stuffed couch. He sipped a can of beer and watched the end of the the national news on Sean's television.

"Hello, Son. Are you alright?"

Sean plopped himself down in the recliner. "I'm not hurt, Dad, but I feel like I've been hit by a truck. Then it backed over me."

Sean's father moved and turned off the television. "There's a pot of soup on the stove your mother sent over. She also sent a loaf of French bread. If you haven't eaten much during the past couple of days, she said to put something in your stomach, but not too much or anything heavy."

"Thank her for me. I guess she'll always be Mom. I'm going to make myself a drink, Dad. You want another beer?"

"No, Son, I'm fine. I spoke with Lyn for some time today. She's still with her folks. She and Denny are fine. She's very worried about you. I called your precinct. They said you were tied up all day with that shooting review board. I'm certain you have been to busy to see the papers or watch the news. You and your people made front page and lead story on the television news. My God, Son; four gunman shot, three officers, in only two nights. Sean, all those shootings and the others, what kind of a job is this? You're not a policeman, you're an urban combat Marine."

"So, Dad, what does Lyn want? Is there a list of conditions before she'll move back into our house and bring my boy back?"

"Be fair, Sean. You two are in trouble. You're really scaring the shit out of everyone who cares about you. It's got to be a constant pain in the ass, Son. I know how much bitchin' your mother does about your job. You must be in the doghouse every day here at home."

"That's right, Dad. You brought me up to be my own man. Not Lyn or anyone else is going to brow-beat me out of this career."

"Sean, you're married and have a son. You can't take that lightly . . . I'm sorry, Son, I know you don't. That isn't fair. But, are you willing to lose your family for the sake of this job?"

Sean took a long swallow of his drink. "If she's demanding a choice today, Dad, she'd better not ask the question if she doesn't want the answer."

"Sean, you've never been unreasonable. At least meet her halfway. She's been through a great deal since you started this job."

Sean shook his head in frustration and broke into a slight sarcastic grin.

"Yea, Dad. No disrespect, Sir, but she's breaking my heart. I was a cop when we got engaged and married. I've never said I was going to quit being a cop. Dad, I've been through as much violence and emotional stress the past couple of days as I was in combat. I come home after three days of hell and my loving wife has taken my son and run home to Mommy. Dad, I'm too tired. What's her idea of halfway?"

"You get off the street for a while, and you two get some professional help. After six months, you take a hard look at where you are and make a decision. She stops pushing you to quit; you show some interest in your relationship and family."

"I don't mean to act like a spoiled kid, but here it is, Dad. I'm going to eat some of Mother's soup, have a couple of drinks, and go to bed for two days. I'm going to take the phone off the hook when I go to bed. Next week, I go see the department shrink as part of the administrative suspension for any fatal shooting. I should be cleared for duty at the end of next week. Next week is when the department's football practice starts. They made it clear that Tom Miller and I will ride a desk at least until the middle of January. After promotions, I've got a chance for a non-street assignment. I'm not going to call her, Dad, I'm too damn tired. If you or Mother want to call and pave the way, I'd really appreciate it. But I'll only talk to her here, in our home."

"What about some professional help, you know, a marriage counselor?"

"Sure, Dad, a psychologist, a priest, anyone with an I.Q. larger than their hat size."

"I'm going to leave now, Son. You go ahead and eat. Get some rest. I'm certain that Lyn will be here tomorrow to talk to you. You just give it a chance, Son, that's all anyone of us who love you will ask of you. If you really try, well, think of Denny. That's all we could have the right to ask. Do you want to talk about the shootings, Sean?"

"Not now, Dad. I'm far too tired to discuss it now. The bottom line is I nearly got my rump shot off three times. Then we put our code of ethics in the closet for several hours. It was butt ugly, Dad."

A week later Sean read over the official report from the Prosecutor's office, the psychiatrist and several intra-departmental sections. He and the other officers were fully cleared of any wrongdoing. Tom, Bruce, and Sean were awarded Departmental Citations. Bruce and Bob Jenson also received the Wounded In Action Medal.

The same week that two-a-day football practice sessions began, Sean and Lyn had their first hour session with a marriage counselor. They had not even begun to solve their marriage problems, but once again there was Peace with Honor.

The exciting 1973 department football season may have literally saved Sean's career. It gave him a break from the street, regular hours, and even more importantly, a complete change of pace.

In early December, when the season came to an end, Tom and Sean continued to work the day shift and remained off the street, away from even potential trouble, while Bruce continued to recover.

Sean spent time with little Denny, and nervously waited for January, for the long-awaited promotions and transfers.

13

January, 1974—June, 1975

JANUARY, 1974
DETROIT

A week after the holidays, Sean and Tom were still riding their desks at the Precinct Narcotics Unit, on the day shift. Bruce had been released from the hospital and he was recovering at home. They visited Bruce every other day.

Sean and Lyn were still going through their trial period. His "normal" hours, since the terrible incidents of the previous August, did not have the positive effect of their relationship he had hoped for. He had asked Lyn to give him until the semi-annual burst of departmental promotions and transfers.

Sean and Tom had spent the morning in court on a year-old case, so they were well dressed. They had a comfortable lunch at the Normandy, a favorite New Center-area lounge.

When they returned to their office, Sean had a phone message to call the C.O. of the police academy, Commander MacMurry.

The academy had moved to a building donated to the city at 6000 Cass Avenue, a few blocks from the precinct station. Sean called and briefly spoke to Cmdr. MacMurry's secretary. She said that the commander wanted Sean at his office for an interview at 2 p.m.

MacMurry was a lieutenant when Sean was at the academy as a student officer. The veteran cop was razor sharp. He was intimidating without even speaking. He had the deserved reputation of being tough but fair. MacMurry was very well respected. It was well known that he was a highly-decorated Marine veteran of Korea. He fit the stereotype of a senior Marine officer, with a hard, lean build, short hair, well-tailored uniforms and steel-blue eyes.

At 2 p.m., Sean stood tall outside Cmdr. MacMurry's office. He was glad he had a fresh haircut and that he was wearing a suit because of their morning court appearance.

The door opened and MacMurry appeared. "Nice to see you again, Officer Cavanagh. Fix yourself a coffee. It's over there on the table. Then, come on into my office so we can talk together for a while."

Sean poured himself a cup of coffee and followed MacMurry back into his office. He closed the door and sat on an ugly green institutional straight-back chair. MacMurry seated himself in his office chair behind his desk. He paged through Sean's personnel folder and sucked on an empty pipe. He took the pipe from his mouth and put it in the top desk drawer. "I stopped smoking two weeks ago. A friend said a pipe will help, even if I don't light it. Tell you the truth, the jury's still out on that advice."

Sean sat at attention, holding his styrofoam coffee cup with both hands.

MacMurry continued to review the numerous documents in Sean's file, including his request for transfer to the academy staff. "How have you been, Cavanagh? You and your partners really had a terrible time of it back in August."

"Football season started for me right after we were returned to duty. They have had us riding a desk through the holidays. Football really helped me get over the incidents emotionally. It was a great escape."

"How is your wounded partner, Bruce Munier?"

"He's been home recovering. He'll never work the street again. Bruce has his grad degree. He's going to take a couple weeks and tour some Eastern colleges, do some interviews for a teaching position."

"Cavanagh, you indicate that you've been going to college part-time since the academy. What's your present status?"

"I have enough hours to be a senior. My major is political science, with a minor in social science."

"When could you graduate?"

"If I could go full-time, this Summer. Part-time, it would be next year some time."

Sean could tell MacMurry was looking at one of the fatal shooting reports. "In a thousand words or less, Cavanagh, why do you want to teach at the academy?"

"Teaching always interested me, but it was a poor career choice when I started college. Now I have enough experience to share with student officers and I'm still young enough for them to relate to me."

MacMurry frowned at Sean. "Other than your tactical experience to help them in violent situations, what could you offer them from your rather brief experience?"

"Before they graduated, they'd know that there are only victims on the streets. The people ripped off are victims; the criminals are victims; the witnesses; the coppers: everyone out there becomes a victim in one way or another."

"That's pretty pessimistic stuff for a class of enthusiastic rookies, Cavanagh."

"Not if presented properly, Sir. It might stop some of those kids from going out there with unrealistic goals. Then, they're destined to fail and become disenchanted and unhappy poor performers."

"Like anyone you know, Cavanagh?"

Sean allowed himself a sip of coffee. "Yes, Sir. All except for the poor performer part. That hasn't happened yet. I'd damn well quit before I'll ever become a poor performer."

"Do you want off the street?"

"Yes, Sir, for a while."

"Why, Cavanagh? You losing your nerve or looking for a good place to retire?"

If Sean had thought MacMurry's insulting question was sincere, instead of a routine test of his attitude, he would have been angry.

"Neither, Commander. You have my record in front of you. I'm ready for a break, that's all. I came back from Vietnam, came on the job and saw two suspects killed my first day on the street. It's been like that ever since. I've been in more shootings in five years than some suburban police departments. I've had a belly full, but my only transfer is here to the academy. If I don't get it, I'll reconsider my career and my options."

MacMurry leaned back in his chair, moving away from the personnel folder. "What are your feelings about our aggressive affirmative action program?"

There was a long pause, as Sean collected his thoughts. This answer could do it either way for him, and Sean knew it. "It's a great solution to all racial injustice of the past in theory, at a cocktail party, or in a social science classroom. The real truth of it out in the precincts is not nearly as simple or pleasant. As long as I work for the city, I'll support its programs 100 percent, while I'm on duty. With the affirmative-action candidates I've seen of late, you'll need a street-qualified staff to get them ready for the precincts."

"And what makes you believe you are more qualified than any other transfer request? I detect a bit of vanity in your voice when you identified yourself as street-qualified."

"I've never been called vain. But I'm proud that I earned my rites of passage on the street, not riding some desk. I obtained my formal education at the same time I got my practical education. Vanity? No Sir. But I'm confident enough to sit in this room with you."

MacMurry had the posture and expression of a man who knew an inside joke. "What about the sergeant's examination you took a few months ago?"

"I write a good test, Commander, but I don't have much hope with only five year's seniority and it was my first sergeant's exam."

MacMurry leaned forward and wrote on a form, then placed it in Sean's file.

"Well, Cavanagh, I've got some good news and bad news. The bad news is that we don't have an opening for any officer instructors on our staff. The good news is we have an immediate opening for a sergeant. I received the new sergeant's list this morning. You'll make it on the first draw, you're in the first five. You'll be the talk of your precinct, a wonder boy. If you still want it, you can start here as a sergeant on Feb. 1. I was told the next staff member here would be Black, until the sergeant's list was published. Deputy Chief Wellington called and said I could take whoever I wanted, and just happened to mention your name. Do you know Deputy Chief Wellington?"

"He was in charge of the shooting review board back in September. He was really straight with us."

"Cavanagh, he's calling you in off the street. So Sgt. Cavanagh, what's your pleasure?"

"My request for transfer stands pat, Commander. Either as an officer or a sergeant."

"Outstanding. Be here at 7 a.m. on the First. You only have two weeks to get your uniforms squared away. You were a Marine, you know what I expect in your appearance. And get a haircut."

Sean stood to leave. "Thank you, Sir."

AUGUST, 1974
DETROIT

Sean and Lyn had been seeing the young marriage counselor since the week after the shooting, the previous August.

It was in the midst of their regular Monday night session, Sean wasn't fully paying attention to the conversation between Lyn and the 30-year-old counselor, Clay Greenway. Sean's mind wandered. He considered the approaching football season. He had worked extra hard that year to remain in good physical condition. He was intent on setting the very best example possible for the student officers in his classes.

"We don't seem to have your attention tonight, Sean. We asked you a question. Why would you say you are intent on remaining a policeman?"

"That's simple, Clay, I'm intent on getting a paycheck on a regular basis."

"Why are you a cop?"

"Because I'm not a bus driver. What do you want, Clay? We've been at this for almost a year. If you have a specific point to make, don't dance around, ask the damn question."

"Why are you a cop? What do you enjoy about the job?"

"In a thousand words, or less? How would you briefly answer the same question, Clay? I believe I'm doing something worthwhile. God damn it, I'm really tired of this attitude. I'm not a crazed hit man, I'm a police sergeant. I don't work the street, and I work normal hours. For a year, I've sat here while she talks about how my police job is bothering our marriage. That's bullshit, Lyn. It wouldn't matter if I worked for dad or shovelled shit, you'd be jealous of my job. Just like when I'm playing football; great hours, no danger, lots of time at home, and you complain about that."

"You know, Sean. You come here every week and sit there looking out the window. If you tried half as hard to make our marriage work as you do at everything else in your life, we'd have the best relationship anyone could ever want. You gave 100 percent of yourself in the Marines, the academy, on the streets, everywhere at work, the damn football team. What about your family?"

"Look, you bitched about the hours, so I got a transfer. I come to these sessions, and I've spent more time at home with you and Denny than I ever have."

"Listen to yourself, Sean. Damn it. You are home more, but it's not quality time. You spend a little time playing with Denny, then you lock yourself in your den with your stereo and work on lesson plans and paperwork from the academy. You don't spend your free time with us. You're either playing football or softball, or getting into condition for either season. I can't remember the last time you went to Mass with Denny and I. Don't you understand, Sean? I'm jealous of everything you do because you make me feel like you care more about everything else in your life than Denny and me."

"Look, Lyn, you won't change who I am, nor will you run my life. You are my wife, not my mother. My mother didn't attempt to overpower me like you do."

Clay leaned forward, "Well, tell her, Sean. Is your police career more important to you than Lyn?"

Sean's unintentional hesitation revealed his true answer. He changed position in his chair and cleared his throat. "No, of course not."

"Well, Mr. Macho, maybe we shouldn't have married in the first place."

Sean's attitude was still more verbally combative than softened by the frank discussion. "So, we won't renew the contract when it expires."

"You are a sarcastic bastard. I'm talking about our lives, and you'd rather be a smart ass than work it out."

Sean slouched down in his chair and looked bored. "Like I told you both last year when we started this, I'll give it my best shot. Now if you believe I'd try harder at something else, I can't change that. I'm not going to quit my career and all my personal activities because you can't deal with your feeling of having to take the back seat to my personal life. You have certainly covered the negative very well. How about our physical relationship? You've never complained."

"I've spoken to Clay about that in our private session. You've always been a gentle, considerate, good lover. You always make an all-out effort to satisfy me. But Sean, even with our sex life, if you put in that much effort throughout the marriage, we'd be fine. It's got so, I doubt your true motive in bed. I'm not certain whether we're making love, or you're merely giving 100 percent in another of your male physical activities, where you must be the best you can possibly be, like playing in a ballgame."

"You say I'm a good lover, but you don't know what really motivates me?"

"Something like that."

"It seems to me that you're really trying hard to ruin even the positive things we still have together."

"And it seems to me you've just stopped trying."

Their ride home was devoid of conversation. Usually, they would either continue the discussions, or critique the session.

This ride home was different because the session had been different. When Lyn said it, it snapped true in his conscious mind like a tightly-coiled spring.

She had said that Sean had stopped trying, and he had no rebuttal. He didn't mind a verbal joust, but he also couldn't argue with the obvious truth.

Sean felt an ache inside. He didn't like the feeling that had swept over him. He somehow felt as if he was out of control. It was as if he was watching himself falling down a mine shaft, with a destroyed marriage at the bottom.

Lyn had given him a son, and she had attempted to be supportive. What made Sean feel out of control wasn't the new knowledge that he had stopped trying in their relationship. What really bothered him was that he didn't care.

Not unlike the time in his life when he had married Lyn, Sean felt that he was outside himself emotionally; watching his marriage fall apart, helpless.

In reality, Sean was in total control, if he would have chosen to take it. There was still time to save the marriage Lyn was working overtime to hold together.

Sean was a natural for the academy staff. He worked very hard to fit in with the other staff members and their program. He was a well-prepared and interesting instructor. He spoke candidly with the student officers when the class work allowed for an open forum. He enjoyed the personal interaction with the student officers, who found the young, squared-away Sergeant officially tough and unyielding but fair and sensitive to their personal problems.

The morning formal inspections were a perfect vehicle for the staff to exercise verbal para-military harassment on the student officers to test their poise and maturity. With Sean's perfect appearance, there was little surprise that his harassment tool was the appearance of his academy class of student officers.

Monday morning roll calls were the worst, followed closely by Friday. Monday was uniform inspection day, Fridays the staff moved up and down the ranks of the nervous student officers asking verbal test questions.

Moving down the first rank, Sean stopped in front of Student Officer Virgil Randolph. Sean read Randolph the riot act for his unsatisfactory appearance.

"Randolph, you'd better get with the program. Those things covering your feet, I assume you would call them shoes? It looks to me that if you have ever shined them, you did so with Hershey bars."

Randolph's verbal response caught Sean off guard. He attempted not to show his shock. He stared at Randolph as the angry, excited student officer snapped back. "Get offa my back, Sgt. Cavanagh. I'm gettin' tired of you pickin' on me 'cause I'm Black. Us affirmative action niggers are darkening up your nice white police department. You figure if you come down on us we'll just drop out."

"You are out of line, Mr. Randolph. You do not address me unless I ask you a question. Then, you will not speak to me in that manner. I don't care what your personal opinion is, Mr. Randolph. If you have a complaint regarding your treatment, you may request to see me in my office, or make a formal complaint to Cmdr. MacMurray."

"This is a roust. I got rights, I..."

"As you were, Mr. Randolph. Save all these jive, street talk cliches' for someone else, it will not cut it here."

"Man gotta act like a robot to cut it here?"

"No, but you will follow orders if you are to cut it here. I'm giving you a direct order to be quiet in the ranks. I've offered you two options. Either follow them and keep quiet in the ranks, or you're out of here."

"You think you got the horsepower to kick me outa here, Sar-gent?"

"I *know* I do. If you want to test my horsepower, open your mouth just once more."

Randolph's fists were clenched at his sides. He looked as though he was about to speak, but said nothing.

Sean finished the inspection and dismissed student officer class 74-D to their first period of classroom instruction.

Sean had an hour before his first class presentation of the day. He poured himself a mug of coffee and moved toward his small office. The obviously tense Student Officer Randolph waited just outside his office at the closed door.

"I wanna talk to you, Sar-gent."

Sean took a sip of coffee. "Certainly, Student Officer Randolph. Come inside and close the door."

Sean heard the door close soundly as he sat down behind his desk. Randolph stood inside his office. "I ain't here for no damn social call. I'm here on business."

Sean took a sip of coffee. "You may take a seat, or will that compromise your intentions?"

Randolph sat down, nervously holding his knees with his hands. He was obviously tense and upset. "I want to talk to you man-to-man, off the record."

Sean leaned forward in his chair and sat down his coffee mug. "Alright, Mr. Randolph. Go ahead, off the record."

"The way I figure, you and the rest of the honkies on the academy staff been riding me and fuckin' me over since the first minute I got here. First, I don't look good enough. Then I'm a bad speller. You say I don't study enough and ain't gettin' with your program. Then, you embarrass me in front of the class all the time. You mother fuckers have been doin' everything to ..."

"Knock it off, Randolph. At ease. If you really want to talk man-to-man, then talk to me like a man, not a street punk. If you want to go off the record so you can insult me and call the staff obscene names, forget it."

"Fine then, Sar-gent. We're back on the record. Well here it is. I ain't gonna quit, and no matter what you do, you'll never make me."

Sean held his coffee mug with both hands to hide his building anger. "I have a news flash for you, Mr. Randolph. You may not have a choice. If you don't get your act in gear, I'm going to blow you right out of here."

"Young Mister White Sergeant, you figure you got the horsepower to boot my Black ass outa here, with all this affirmative action and the new Black Mayor and City Council?"

"Randolph, I know I do. I've read your file. If you figure that because your mother goes to the same church as the new Black councilwoman, that I'm going to let you slide through with substandard overall performance, you have a terrible surprise in store for you."

"If I wasn't Black, you'd..."

"Enough of that bull too, Randolph. I don't pick on you because you're Black, but what you don't seem to understand is that I will not accept anything less of you because you are Black. Randolph, my duty is to send you people out to the precincts as well prepared as possible. We teach proper appearance habits so you start to feel good about yourself. We give you the classroom basic knowledge and firearms training so you can build on it."

Randolph's fists were balled tight on his knees. "You try and fire me and I'll have you in court, even if you could get it through the department without being stopped."

"I've been to court before, Randolph. If you want to take proofs into court, you will waste your money and be embarrassed. I have documented every time you even passed wind in ranks. You have not passed a spelling test since you've been here, and your weekly test average is well under the minimum of 70 percent. If you can't meet the very basic performance standards, I won't send you to the precinct."

"I can be a po-lice officer."

"Then prove it, Mr. Randolph. So far, all you've proven is that you have a poor attitude and you're an underachiever. What I see is a young man with a giant chip on his shoulder. A man who's not willing to take any responsibility for his own actions or shortcomings. I see a man with no respect for authority and damn little respect for himself."

Randolph stood quickly. "And I see a bigoted young white sergeant who is full of shit."

"You are entitled to express your opinion, Randolph, but not in my face and not in my office. I'm writing you up for insubordination. I'm also placing you on formal, written one-week special probation. A week from today, if you don't show me you want to really be a good cop, you're outa here, Mister."

"You figure 'cause you got three stripes on your starched shirt sleeve, you're some kind of awesome dude?"

Sean stood, still holding his coffee mug with both hands. "I don't have to explain myself to you, Mr. Randolph. Do you really think that because you're an inner-city product you have all the street wisdom necessary to be a police officer? You've got to know the law to be The Man. Randolph, you'll see more shit go down in one month as a cop as you did your whole life growing up on the block."

"What would you know about growing up in the ghetto."

"I worked those streets long enough to thank God I didn't grow up there, and my son will not grow up there. Mr. Randolph, if I was Black and from the ghetto, I'd probably be a militant or in jail. I can't tolerate injustice and I'd be wired with hate every day. Randolph, I respect your attempt to change your city. I know you must work twice as hard as your classmates from good schools and good neighborhoods. Despite that respect and realization, I will not lower the standards for performance I expect from you. I can't, Randolph. The coppers at the precincts deserve qualified rookies and more importantly, the people on the street won't cut you a huss because you're a Black young man who grew up in the ghetto."

"Sounds like you are talking out of both sides of your mouth. You say you respect me, then you treat me like shit, write me up and threaten to boot me outa here."

"Randolph, you were never in the military. I'm certain there was no discipline in your high school, so unless you had formal discipline in the home, it is still something you must learn. If you meet me half way, Randolph, you have a good chance to make it. If you insist on this street-kid attitude, you're out of here. Last point, Randolph. Even if you can't respect me as a man, you've got to learn to respect the rank. It's the only way a street cop can stay sane with some of the recent promotions. If you still hate the police more than you want to be a cop, get out now, before the inner-conflict ties you in knots. Out there, Randolph, all the cops have are each other."

"Can I be excused now, Sergeant?"

"Certainly, Mr. Randolph. Your first hour is first aid. Why don't you go to the men's room and get yourself settled down before you join your class?"

Randolph nodded, left the office, and firmly closed the door behind him.

Once Randolph was out of view, Sean walked to the coffee pot to refill his mug.

One of Sean's staff was already at the coffee maker. Officer Leon Ashford leaned against the wall near the coffee, waiting for a fresh pot to finish. The stocky Black officer was a fine, well-liked academy instructor. Sean had known Leon since the fall of '70; they played on the department football team together.

"That boy is short on good sense. I thought you were going to be forced to fire him at roll call. He wouldn't stop his mouth from flapping. Did he give you a ration of shit in your office?"

"Same old tired rap, Leon. He can't realize that he's doing himself in. Everything is our fault, from spelling tests to poor inspections. His mother goes to church with a city councilwoman and he may actually believe we can't bounce him out. He's really riding the Black issue all the way, Leon."

Leon leaned over and checked the progress of the coffee. "So, other than the famous Cavanagh lecture, what did you tell him?"

"I wrote him up for insubordination, and put him on formal one-week suspension."

"Don't let him get to you with that racial bullshit, Cav. If he goes to the Old Man, I want to go in with you. He's a pain in my ass too, and he can't cry that racial shit with me."

"Thanks, Leon. It's the same problem we've discussed before. This is the part of affirmative action that frosts me the most. They hire kids that can't quite cut it and we start to condition both Black and white officers about the unconfirmed truth of a double standard. If that kid puts out some effort and he still can't compete with his classmates, who's fault is it? Damn it, Leon, they should either give these people pre-academy schooling, or quit insulting everyone by pretending we don't have two departmental standards."

"Be cool, Cav. Talk like that will not do you or your career any good. We've known each other long enough for me to know where you are coming from in your heart. I know you're fair to these people, even when you don't like what you see in the ranks. Cav, you know how strongly I feel for affirmative action. But I will agree with you on one point, I wouldn't want to work with a shit bird like Randolph if I was still on the street."

"Well, my friend, we certainly agree on that one. We owe it to the good officers at the precincts to give them the best people we can out of what they give us. I'm really dedicated to that, Leon. When they won't allow me to do my job, even with affirmative action, I'm outa here."

"Come on, Cav, this place is no different than your Marine Corps; we need a few good men."

The following Monday morning, Officer Leon Ashford called class 74-D to the position of attention for their weekly inspection. Leon would follow Sgt. Sean Cavanagh down the ranks of nervous, intimidated student officers.

Just prior to the inspection, Sean gave Leon a copy of Student Officer Virgil Randolph's first-aid examination, taken the previous Friday. Randolph had received a 90 percent on the easiest written test of the 10 examinations taken during the length of the academy. It was no indication of a significant turnaround, but it was a positive sign. Leon Ashford raised his eyebrows.

"Well, well, Sarge. It would appear that the lad finally studied for an exam. I talked to Neil. He said that Randolph had passed every morning spelling exam since your talk last week."

Sean moved down the straight rank of student officers. He stopped twice to verbally insult student officers before he reached Randolph. He stopped in front of Student Officer Virgil Randolph. He carefully gave the young man the visual once-over. His khacki uniform was clean and pressed. His shoes and leather gear were highly shined. He also sported a fresh haircut.

Sean looked sternly at the student officer. "Mr. Randolph, concerning radio codes, who is the 60 series? For example, who would be 13-6-0?"

There was a slight pause. For a brief moment, he thought he had expected to much, too soon, from Student Officer Randolph.

"Sir, the 60 series is the unit or the shift lieutenant."

"Correct. Mr. Randolph, your appearance today is outstanding. Your classmates can look to you today and see what I expect in overall appearance for inspections. Looking good, Mr. Randolph, keep up the good work."

"Thank you, Sergeant."

It was still lunch hour for class 74-D. Sean ate a sandwich at his desk with another mug of coffee. There was a knock at Sean's office door. He could see Randolph through the window in the door. "Enter," he said.

"You wanted to see me, Sgt. Cavanagh?"

"Please come in, close the door and be seated. Mr. Randolph, I was very impressed with you today. You have made such an obvious attempt to get with the program. I want you to know you are off of special probation. The formal insubordination write-up will stay in my desk. I will give it to you to rip up as a graduation gift, if you keep this attitude and behavior."

"Sgt. Cavanagh, what I said last week was out of line. I talked with... Well, I know I had you all wrong. You know, I figured you were just another tight-ass white cop."

"That's fair, Mr. Randolph. I am another tight-ass white cop. I'd have put my money on you forcing me to boot you out of here. Mr. Randolph, you now have me convinced that if you put your mind to it, you'll be a damn good cop."

Randolph stood and shook Sean's hand. "I'll make you proud, Sergeant."

"I know you will, Virgil. Criminal law exam this Friday: toughest one of the academy, hit those books this week. If you have any trouble, talk to Officer Ashford or myself."

Randolph left his office in long confident strides, wearing a wide grin.

Minutes later, Sean saw Officer Leon Ashford pass his office, toward the coffee maker.

"Excuse me, Leon. Would you get your ass in my office for a moment, please."

"Say, Cav, how's it going?"

"Alright, Leon, no bullshit. Did you talk with Randolph? What turned him around like that?"

"Come on, Cav, you know me. I just told him you were related to Abe Lincoln."

"Please, Leon. We seem to have gotten through to that kid. I've got to know what did it."

"Well, after class last week, he stopped me outside. He wanted to talk to me before he went to MacMurry. He lays all that Brother shit on me and says he can't figure you. He had never really known any white dudes. On one hand you are all over his ass, but you still seem like you really care about him."

"What did you tell him, Leon?"

"The truth, of course, Cav. I told him you were riding his Black ass out so he didn't darken up your white department."

"Come on Leon, stop fucking with me, or you won't carry the ball twice all season."

"Ain't that the way it is? Can never mess with the coach, or the quarterback. I layed some general shit on him. I said you were fair but you would never accept less than the established minimum. I said your sincere goal was to make him a good cop."

"Come on, Leon, what else?"

"O.K. I mentioned some of the shit you did while out on the street. I merely told him you are a sergeant because of a lot of things other than a written test. You've seen some real shit. I assured him you ain't got a paper asshole."

"Leon, you know how I feel about that shit. I don't want to encourage the gunfighter syndrome. Some of the best cops I know have never even fired a shot in anger."

"Cav, it's not much different than when we played football our first season together. You look even younger than you are. You may deserve their respect because of your stripes. But in your case, you've really earned the respect."

"Leon, I never want them to think the way to a speedy promotion is to grease some asshole."

"No, but you are living proof that you can still get promoted, even if you do grease some asshole."

"How come I still feel like we're still losing the war?"

"One battle at a time, Sarge."

"Maybe my wife was right, Leon. Our marriage is on the ropes. She said I don't try as hard at home as I do here. I can't remember giving her the effort I gave Randolph."

"Maybe if she joined the department . . . "

"Leon, I'm serious, I'm about to destroy my marriage and I can't stop it."

"No offense, Cav. I've just never seen you fail at something that you've really wanted to do. I've got to believe that if you want this marriage to work, it will."

"Leon, maybe that's the bottom line truth. I challenged Randolph not to blame others, maybe I should do the same. Maybe I must decide if I really want to save the marriage."

APRIL, 1975
DETROIT

Still dressed in his police sergeant uniform, Sean glared at the image on the television as he watched the evening news.

The national news reports showed HUEY choppers getting the last Americans out of Saigon. Then, Navy crewmen were forced to push undamaged choppers from the decks of Seventh Fleet aircraft carriers to make room for other choppers.

The rage built up inside of Sean as he watched the images on the screen. He feared he would explode.

When a South Vietnamese chopper pilot jumped from his craft, just before it crashed into the sea, nearly hitting him in the water, Sean stood in protest.

"You gutless Gook bastard. I could buy three houses with what it cost for that HUEY. I hope you at least brought someone out with you. One gutless Gook for one perfect chopper is not much of a return on investment. Too fucking bad that bird didn't crash right on your sorry ass."

He went into the kitchen and poured himself a glass full of Canadian Club over ice.

Sean watched as a large N.V.A. tank knocked down the gate of the South Vietnam Imperial Palace in Saigon. A huge North Vietnamese flag flew from the tank.

Sean emptied his glass and went and poured himself another glass full of whiskey.

"Well, boys, that sure as hell wraps it up. We pull out, and those poor damn A.R.V.N. don't last two years. For God's sake, if we were going to just let them walk in, why didn't we do it in '65 and save all those people. 58,000 Americans killed, and for what? What a bunch of bullshit. What about 'Peace with Honor'? How about the fucking domino theory? How about Logs, and Yance's leg, and Stoney and Mr. Cool? Congress! What a fucking joke. Congress lets those good men die and suffer ten years for nothing. Wonderful! Back to isolationism. Maybe Congress will get off their butts when the Communists take Canada."

Sean was thankful Lyn and his son, Denny, were visiting family that evening. He wanted to be alone. He knew he would be very poor company.

Sean watched the city of Saigon filled with N.V.A. troops. He threw the empty glass against a wall, smashing it. He buried his face in his hands and wept. He wept so hard that he could hardly catch his breath between the sobs. He got up and got himself another drink in a new glass, "What a fucking waste!"

The recreation room at Jackson Prison was filled with two dozen Vietnam Vet inmates. Some stared at the screen of the television as if dazed. Others wiped tears from their eyes. Still others wept openly and unashamed.

T.J. sat next to a large prison guard who had been a Nam Vet with the 101st. T.J. and the big Black guard, Mr. Justin, had often talked about Vietnam together.

T.J. shook his head, "I swear, Mr. Justin. I usta say the A.R.V.N. wouldn't last two years without us, but I never really thought I'd live to see this."

"Well, T.J., we know we done the best we could. We served our country and we should be proud."

"Come on, Mr. Justin, proud of what? All them boys died for nothing. Look at the television screen. How can we explain that to the boys that lost limbs, or to families that lost their sons? I told you about my white Nam buddy, you know, the Detroit Po-liceman that came here to play football in '72. He's wrapped way too tight for this shit. Ol' Irish, he's gotta have a reason for everything. He don't handle injustice for shit. He would have made a lousy Brother; he'd of ended up in here with me."

By the time Lyn and Denny arrived home, the news had been over for an hour. Sean still drank from his whiskey glass, but he had cleaned up the broken glass.

She briefly greeted Sean and began to prepare dinner. Denny crawled up on Sean's lap and they watched television.

Sean picked at his dinner, and he was able to conceal his level of intoxication.

Lyn asked what had happened to the large cocktail glass that had been broken against the wall. She did not comment when he coldly said that it had committed suicide.

With Denny put to bed hours prior, Lyn and Sean watched the 11 p.m. news together. Sean had renewed his drinking in preparation to the telecast.

Lyn watched the N.V.A. tanks on the streets of Saigon, from over the book she was reading. "Now I understand why you're this way. It's this Vietnam thing, isn't it?"

"Yes, Lyn, you might say that. The Vietnam thing is bothering me. I lost some damn fine friends there, and it was all for nothing. God damn Congress."

"Well, I say, 'thank God it's over.' We should have never been there to begin with. It was an immoral war, a civil war. And now, those people are one nation."

"Stow it, Lyn. I've never wanted to talk about Vietnam with you, and especially not tonight."

"It's more than Vietnam, Sean. We can't seem to talk about anything. I really think we need some time apart to sort things out. Your day job and the counseling haven't seemed to help. I really believe if you live without Denny and me for a while, you'll realize how good you really have it."

Sean walked from their bedroom with an athletic bag filled with enough items for overnight. "I'll stay with Tom for a while. I'll be back Saturday afternoon to get some things, so why don't you take Denny away. No use upsetting him until we're certain how this is going to go."

"You never gave this a try, did you Sean? I mean 100 percent?"

Sean stepped from the front door. "I always thought I was a person who gave 100 percent at everything I did. But you may be right, Lyn. Maybe I never really got on track."

"Do you love me, Sean?"

"I'll always love you, Lyn. You had our child. We've grown up together. I'm not certain that we love each other enough to live together. Let's see what the separation tells us."

April, 1975 marked the end of the long and terrible conflict in Vietnam. It also marked the end of what might have been a long-term, loving marriage. Both events were caused by countless variables.

Sean sat at his parents' kitchen table. He stared into his cup of coffee, considering his words carefully.

Sean's father took a sip from his cup and broke the ice, as he placed the cup back in its saucer. "Well, Sean, you've called this meeting. I don't believe you need to play 20 questions with your Mother and I. We know what the topic is."

Sean could not lift his head up to face his parents. "I was served the papers at work yesterday. Lyn has filed for a divorce."

There was a strain in his mother's voice. "You walked out almost a month ago. Are you surprised?"

"I didn't walk out, Mother, we agreed to separate. Look, Dad helped us hold this thing together this long. She walked out on me September '73, remember? Mother, I'm not here to blame Lyn, I'm here to inform you of what's going on."

"Are you certain that there's no hope?"

"We've been trying for two years with our counseling. This isn't like breaking up over an argument, or a single issue. It just isn't there for us."

Sean's father was obviously tense.

"You and Lyn are adults now. If you have decided that more than five years of marriage that created a fine little boy are over, there's nothing anyone can say. You've gone to a marriage counselor every week; you changed your work hours. There was only one thing lacking. Sean, I just don't understand your absence of what I would identify as an all-out effort to make your marriage work. You went through all of the motions, but I've seen you put more of yourself in a sandlot softball game than you did to salvage your marriage. Am I off base with this, Son?"

"No, Dad. I've given it a great deal of thought. Since the shootings, since you helped Lyn and I make another try of it, I realized I was just going through the motions for everyone else. I've been a coward, Dad. I agreed to give it another attempt with Lyn and do all of those things because I was afraid of what everyone would say and judge me."

Sean's mother was pensive. She folded her hands. "It's your life, Sean. Of course, we would rather you and Lyn work it out, especially for little Denny's sake. But you're our son, and nothing you do, or don't do, will change that. We're always here if you need us."

Sean's father handed him a set of door keys. "Here, the duplex on Moross has been vacant for two months. Have your brothers help you paint the inside. It really needs it. I'll have the carpet cleaned when you're done. If nothing else, we'll get you back on the Eastside where you belong. I'm sure you don't want to impose on your friend Tom any longer than necessary."

The divorce process was like a snowball rolling down hill. It seemed almost too simple. Sean was able to pay child support and maintenance until the divorce became final, and still have money in his pocket. With his parents subtle assistance, and a lack of other bills, Sean did not suffer the financial trauma experienced by most divorced fathers of young children.

There was some bitterness in both directions, and occasionally harsh words. But soon after the divorce became formal, Lyn got a full-time job. Her mother helped by watching Denny while she worked.

Sean had put in for a formal transfer to the Homicide Section. They would grant the move when his current class graduated.

Sean began to live the life of a single young man. At 27, being single seemed rather strange at first. Initially, he saw Denny at least twice a week. As time passed, the visits became less frequent. He paid his financial obligation on time, but often the visits were more painful than rewarding.

Sean sat in the dark living room of the duplex. He sipped Canadian Club and listened to his old Moody Blues albums. He recognized the sensation he had that night. It was the same private feeling he had the night he and Lyn were married. He felt like a spectator. It was as though he was being swept through the process of the dissolution of his marriage, and he could do little to stop it, even if he had wanted to.

Sean privately realized that he thought more about his impending transfer to Homicide than he did his impending divorce. And a private shame went with that realization.

MAY, 1975
DETROIT

Sean read the intra-department memo. His old football buddy Perry Mann had been promoted to commander, in command of Special Operations.

Sean leaned back in his chair and smiled. He always knew Perry had bigger and better things in his future. He had heard that Perry was a well-respected shift lieutenant at Number 10 before the Mayor had him transferred to the Public Information Section to be the department's official spokesman.

Sean wrote a brief note of congratulations. He told Perry it was one hell of a feat for an interior lineman to learn how to read, much less be promoted to commmander.

Perry cornered him at his promotion party. The big man grabbed Sean in a playful bear hug and threatened him because of his note. Sean attempted to deny sending the note.

Perry lifted Sean from the floor. "Don't give me none of that innocent crap. When I first saw that neat, pretty handwriting, I knew it was from you. Hell, only school teachers and sissy quarterbacks write that nice."

"Easy now, Commander. If you abuse me, I'll be forced to file a grievance."

"Oh yea, Sergeant? You won't file anything in a body cast."

14

June 1975—December, 1976

JUNE, 1975
DETROIT

The area occupied by the Detroit Police Homicide Section consisted of several large rooms and adjoining offices. There were rows of grey metal, institutional desks and office chairs in the larger rooms. The conditions of the numerous desk tops ranged from those that were neat and well-kept, to those that resembled landfills.

Det. Sgt. Gary Burger was 37 years old. It took him 14 years on the job to make detective sergeant and two years as a precinct detective to get transerred to the coveted Homicide Section.

Gary was one of the last of the old breed of white copper. He was nearly a legend on the tough streets of the Fifth Precinct. But a tough veteran white cop, with no college degree, was lucky to make sergeant under the new administration.

Gary Burger was under the old retirement plan. He could retire after 25 years of service, and he fully realized he would retire as a detective sergeant.

Gary knew he was fortunate to even make detective sergeant, he had no unrealistic career aspirations. He could be satisfied being a productive Homicide dick, until it was time for the gold retirement badge and being put out to pasture. Gary had already been a well-respected street cop by the time Detroit experienced its terrible riot of '67.

Gary Burger was from a proud German-American family who'd lived in metro-Detroit for several generations. He stood just under six feet tall, but was thick and broad at the shoulders. With his full handsome face and constant battle with his waistline, Gary always appeared to be bigger than he actually was. Sixteen years as a Detroit cop had made Gary sarcastic and cynical. He was born with natural wit and a dry sense of humor.

Gary was less than tactful regarding his opinion of affirmative action and female officers working the streets in uniform. In fact, Gary was less than shy when it came to expressing his opinion on any department-related topic.

Gary's first Homicide partner had recently retired and it was his first day back from a three-week Summer vacation. When he returned from the men's room, *Free Press* sports section in hand, there was no deep mystery about the reason he had been summoned to the C.O.'s office.

Gary emptied the remains of his coffee cup and headed for Cmdr. Hail's office. Hail was a long-term Homicide dick and one of the most respected Black cops on the force, by both races.

Since Gary had been summoned, he knocked on the closed door and let himself in.

Cmdr. Hail sat comfortably behind his desk, smoking and sipping from a coffee mug. Seated in the corner of the office was a neat young man that looked to be 25. He held a styrofoam cup of coffee.

Gary was impressed by the younger man's mode of dress. His Summer suit was crisp, and Gary thought he was about to be introduced to a cub reporter from the *Detroit Free Press* or *Detroit News* for a story.

Cmdr. Hail offered Gary a fresh coffee. He accepted, and carefully sipped at the hot liquid, then took a seat at Hail's non-verbal direction.

"Gary, I'd like you to meet Det. Sgt. Sean Cavanagh. He will be joining us from the police academy staff. His transfer is effective as of today."

Gary's facial expression could not conceal his obvious displeasure. Sean had stood to shake Gary's hand. The handshake was firm, but Gary couldn't help but recognize that Hail intended the new kid to be his replacement partner.

Cmdr. Hail wanted to talk to Gary alone, before there was any opportunity for their first meeting to damage a potential partnership.

"Sgt. Cavanagh, why don't you go out and find Lt. Harris. Harris will get you settled at your new desk and show you around. I know you were here a lot as an officer, but Harris will show you our secret goodies. Go ahead, Sergeant, go get settled in. I need to discuss a few matters with Gary. I'll be back with you shortly."

Sean excused himself and left Hail's office. He smiled at Gary as he left, knowing that Gary was giving him another visual once-over. The young man was dressed in a light-blue Summer suit, white shirt, with navy tie and penny-loafer shoes.

Once Sean was out of earshot, Gary put his hot styrofoam cup on the Commander's desk. "Come on, Boss. Who did I piss off?"

Cmdr. Hail grinned as he chain-lit a cigarette and sipped from his coffee mug. "What are you talking about, Gary?"

"They've got to be kidding us, Boss. That pretty baby-faced boy is as much a Homicide dick as I am a fucking Harlem Globetrotter. The way he dresses, he should be going to some damn yachting event, rather than investigating a homicide. How old is that kid, anyway?"

Hail smiled and puffed on his fresh cigarette. "The lad is 27. He has been a sergeant for over a full year."

Gary buried his face in his hands. "Twenty seven. Come on, Commander. This damn sports jacket I'm wearing is older than he is. Christ, 27. When I was at the precinct, you couldn't get a decent precinct assignment until 30. This boy lands the best assignment in the department, and he's too white and too male to have it be an affirmative-action assignment."

Hail leaned back in his office chair. "Lots of changes in this department over the past five years, Gary."

Gary shook his head. "Yea, Commander, tell me about all the changes. Boss, this is still Homicide, hardball. I can't be expected to perform good police work while I'm baby-sitting some kid who's still wet behind the ears."

Cmdr. Hail leaned forward across his desk. "Damn, Gary. I know the way you feel about things, but I've never known you to be totally unfair. This young man taught at the academy as a sergeant. He didn't just graduate from it. The man has one hell of a street record."

Gary was not convinced. He sipped from his coffee cup and winced. "Straight business, Boss. What's this kid's sugar on the Third Floor? Is he related to the ex-mayor or does his old man rank a favor from the present mayor?"

"Ex-mayor? Come on, Gary. Would that help with this administration? His dad is well-heeled, but a registered Grosse Pointe Republican. This mayor isn't tied to this kid in any way I can tell. Come on, Gary, you remember, academy staff has almost an open transfer within the department. A look at this kid's file shows he could make it on his own previous work record.

"Gary, you just came off vacation. I see you've got your usual deer-hunting furlough in mid-November. Partner up with the kid until then. Give him a real chance. If you're not satisfied by then, give me the word, and when you get back from the woods, you get a new partner, no questions asked. You know, Gary, for an old corps German, you could do a hell of a lot worse than a street smart kid like Cavanagh, if you get my point?"

"November? This is June. What do I do until then?"

"You do your damn job, Burger. You and the kid work the Robbery-Homicide Squad until further notice. How about you give the kid a chance to fuck up before you become so sure you dislike him?"

Sean had been assigned the empty desk facing Gary Burger's cluttered desk. He was silently putting some of his personal items in and on his desk.

Gary came out of the C.O.'s office and plopped down in his chair. He didn't say a word. He just watched Sean turn the empty desk into a piece of furniture with his own personal items.

Sean carefully put his .45-automatic and shoulder holster in the largest desk drawer and locked it.

Gary leaned cross his desk. "What is that for?"

Sean folded his hands on his desk top and leaned toward Gary. "Well, Sgt. Burger. Unless things have changed in a drastic way during the year I've been off of the street, that's for shooting at bad guys."

Gary glared across the desks at his new partner. "I don't know where you worked prior to the academy, kid, but this is the big leagues. You taught at the academy. You know the department doesn't allow us to carry single-action automatics. You won't carry an unauthorized piece if you work with me."

Sean dug out a card from behind his photo I.D. card in his leather badge carrier. Sean tossed the card across the desks to Gary.

"Department-approved, Sergeant. It's been tested, and as you see by the authorization card, there's no expiration date on it. I don't intend to carry it all the time. If we think we might go step in some shit, the extra firepower wouldn't hurt."

"Can you handle all that hardware?"

"I heard you've won the departmental shooting contest a couple of times. I'm not in your league, but I'm a decent shot out on the street."

"We'll see. The street shooting is what counts. The department trophy is nice, but punching holes in paper has nothing to do with how you shoot on the street. What do you carry under that pretty tailored suit for everyday use?"

Sean opened his suit coat to display his .357 magnum, with a two-and-a-half-inch barrel.

Gary leaned back in his chair and shook his head in sarcasm.

"Magnum revolver. Big auto pistol. That's a lot of firepower for a baby-faced kid, Sergeant."

Sean had lost his sense of humor. "What are you busting my chops for, Burger? With a snub-nose barrel, you know the muzzle velocity is little more than a .38 Special. If the shit hit the fan, I'd want more than this pretty little revolver. The .45 ammo I carry pushes a 250-grain round at over a thousand-feet-a-second."

"Well, the lad is a fucking gunsmith. I hope you know as much about being a detective as you do about muzzle velocity."

"Look, since we're going to be working together for at least a little while, what do you want me to call you?"

Gary searched his desk top for his coffee mug. "I really don't care."

Sean leaned even farther across his desk. "You don't care? How about asshole?"

Gary's expression did not change. "Asshole might turn out to be a little awkward when we're in public."

"No problem. In public I'll refer to you as Det. Sgt. Asshole."

"Well kid, the sharpness of your tongue matches your mode of dress.

My bet is that you are all show and no go, Sgt. Cavanagh."

Sean sat the cardboard box containing his personal things on the floor. "O.K. Burger, bottom line. Why are you jerking me around? We never met prior to this morning, and you don't like me. You didn't like me even before we started talking."

Gary found his coffee mug and frowned as he inspected its contents.

"You're one of those up-front, bottom-line kind of guys, are you? Well, I don't like anything about you; not your candy-ass clothes, your baby-face good looks, or your accelerated promotion and choice assignment. I've half-accepted all those bullshit affirmative-action promotions and assignments. Then here comes the All-American Boy, and he's white and he gets the same rank and assignment I've got, in half the time."

Sean got to his feet. He put both hands on his desk blotter and spoke sternly at his senior partner.

"Jealousy? You've got a wild hair up your ass because you're jealous? I expected that I would have to prove myself to you. But I must admit, I thought you'd give me a chance. You don't want to partner with me, fine. I thought you could teach me a lot. I know about your reputation as a copper at Number Five. You don't want to even give me a chance to partner with you, then you tell the Boss. And Sgt. Big-Fucking-Deal Burger, get bent."

Sean quickly moved away from his desk. He decided he needed a walk to dilute his disappointment with Gary Burger's initial response to his assignment.

"Cool your jets, Sgt. G.Q. Let's talk again after lunch, before I go in to see the Old Man."

"What the hell difference will it make after lunch?"

"Just oblige an old cop, O.K., Kid?"

Sean slammed down a framed photo of him and his son on his newly-assigned desk and walked out without another word.

Gary smiled to himself as he poured a fresh mug of coffee. "Boy's got spirit."

Gary rushed down to the Personnel Section on the second floor of police headquarters. He grinned as he located his veteran partner from Number Five. Officer Art Barnwell had been Gary's partner and broke him in on the street. As Barnwell reached retirement age, he was put to pasture at the Personnel Section to ride out his time.

Gary eased up behind his ex-partner and slapped the balding, middle-aged man on the back. "Well, Art, you old war-horse, are you keeping yourself out of trouble in this hot spot?"

Art rubbed his large belly. "Listen, Kid, I earned this soft job just like I earned this beer gut. They're both bought and paid for, so don't jack my jaws. So how the hell is my favorite Homicide detective doing these days?"

"The day started shitty, but it's so nice to have somebody still call me 'kid,' you made my day. Art, I see these kids coming on the job, getting promoted, I feel as old as history. I just got partnered up with a new boy wonder today, white kid, 27-years-old. He's dressed like he's going to a fucking lawn party."

Art poured himself a mug of coffee. "I should have figured you had a reason to be here at lunch time to visit your old partner, who just happens to work in Personnel."

"Come on, Art, give me a break with this. The Old Man stone-walled me when I tried to find out about him. All I know is he got promoted last year and transferred from the academy staff."

Art quickly looked around the office. "I've got Cavanagh's folder on my desk. I was working on it this morning. Let's be quick about it. If the Lieutenant catches me, I'll be back working midnights with a Black female rookie partner."

"Just a quick run-down, Art. If I've got to trust my butt to this kid for a while, I need some info."

Art thumbed through the contents of Sean's personnel jacket. He shook his head as he glanced over the documents inside.

"He may be a kid, Gary, but that Cavanagh is no feather-weight. He graduated first in his academy class; he worked at 13, Boosters, Precinct Narcotics; wrote in the top five for sergeant. Let's see, Departmental Citation, 'at-a-boys' up the ass while an officer at 13. Holy shit, Gary, the kid has a fist full of officer-involved shootings. Look at this one, he greased two dopers himself at the same search-warrant raid. Gary, you remember this kid. A couple of years ago him and his partners got ambushed one night. Next night they got in a gun battle at a dope pad. His one partner got hit. Partner had to retire, screwed up his shoulder."

Gary looked stunned. He sat down next to Art and read over his shoulder.

"I'll be damned. I remember hearing about this kid and his partners. They had already capped a couple assholes before all that went down. They were all squeaky clean, righteous shootings. They took him off the street for a while, so he wouldn't get a reputation. No shit, Art. You should see this kid, pretty-boy looks like he's never seen the streets, much less worked them."

Art dug out his application and the initial background check done on Sean in '69.

"There's more, the kid was a combat Marine in Vietnam. He's got a list of medals and citations. He was wounded three times. It says his

father is a businessman and lives in Grosse Pointe. What the hell is he
doing being a cop? Gary, this kid ain't tied into nobody. With his work
history, he probably would have been considered for Homicide even if
he wasn't coming from the academy staff. It looks to me as though you
got lucky with your new partner. Hell, give the lad a chance.
Remember, you weren't much when I broke you in."

Gary took Art over to Greek Town and bought him lunch. Sean was
already seated at his desk when Gary came back to the office. Gary was
not at all surprised that Sean's desk top was very neat, not so much as a
pencil out of place.

Gary sat down and stared across the desks at Sean, who pretended to
be busy in a desk drawer and not notice. "So Kid, where'd you work
before you got promoted and went to the academy?"

"Thirteen. I started early '69."

"Did you work any special assignments?"

Sean slammed the desk drawer closed and glared across the desks at
Gary. "Now what, 20 questions? O.K., Sergeant. I worked Boosters and
Precinct Narcotics."

Gary had decided in the Personnel office that he had, in fact, been
lucky to draw Sean as his partner, baby-faced or not. He also decided to
have some fun at his new young partners expense. "Narcotics? Oh, yea.
Didn't your partner get shot a couple of years ago?"

Sean became very serious and pensive. The tone of his voice lowered
and it was as though he was telling the story as an apology. "We had a
brief let-down. Some asshole came running at us from the front room
and we wasted him. We focused all of our attention to him. An asshole
suddenly appeared on the stairway to our left flank. We saw him too
late."

"What did you do after he shot your partner?"

Sean's voice did not change. "I chased him up the stairs and killed
him."

"What did you do before you came on the job?"

Sean stared off at nothing, obviously still thinking of the dope house
shootout. He paused for a moment, then answered Gary's question, his
mind seemingly elsewhere. "I went to college for a year, then went in
the service, Marines."

"You go to Vietnam?"

"Yea."

"How was it?"

"Sgt. Burger, you wouldn't be jealous of the time I spent in Vietnam."

Gary walked over and poured himself a fresh mug of coffee. He held
up the pot in an offering gesture to Sean, who handed Gary his coffee
mug with the Detroit Lion's logo on the side.

Gary carefully set the two mugs of hot coffee on their desks.

"Cavanagh, I came on like some old-time dinosaur this morning. You deserve a hell of a lot more respect and better treatment than I gave you. I'd like to work with you, if you're willing to give it a try."

Sean's expression changed and he broke into a wide grin.

"Hell yes, I want to work with you. You think I'd put up with all that bullshit if you weren't reported to be a good copper? Hell, Gary, you're still a legend in your own time at Number Five. You caught me off-guard. I was sure you'd come back from lunch and tell me how you've got more time in the shitter than I have on the job."

"I would have said that this morning if I would have thought of it."

"So when do we start, Partner?"

"Cavanagh, I've got good news and bad news. The good news is that we've pulled assignment with the Robbery-Homicide squad. They are a good bunch of detectives, and you'll learn quick. The bad news is that we pulled morgue detail tomorrow morning because the Section is running light due to Summer vacations. How do you hold up watching autopsies?"

Sean winced, "I had to walk out when my academy class went on the morgue tour and watched a post."

"Eat some breakfast. No kidding, better than an empty stomach for a couple of reasons. And Cavanagh, you can bring your nice big .45 if you want."

"Uh, the fucking morgue. You may need my .45 just to get me there tomorrow. By the way, Gary, all this pulling my chain about my .45 and snub-nose magnum. I see you carry your four-inch .44-magnum."

"Yea, but remember, Kid, I'm the one with the shooting trophy."

———————————

In the weeks that followed, Gary not only became his partner and mentor, but also his friend. Gary had given him his chance.

With the exception of Sean's well-fitted, extensive clothing selection, the new Homicide Sergeant kept a low profile. He went back to the advice given to him by Cmdr. Belloti when he came out of the academy as a rookie; he kept his eyes and ears open, and his mouth shut.

The other senior men on the squad also rode Sean about his preppie wardrobe, but it was good-natured kidding. Freshly separated, and going through his divorce, the squad members steered away from that topic for a while. In a few months, they would ride him about a situation more than half of them had personally experienced.

At first, Gary's wife was concerned. A younger, single partner was not her first choice. After they met, she felt better. Sean hardly gave the outward appearance of being a bad influence.

Sean was not insulted by the constant barrage of kidding and harassment from the senior officers. They called him Prince Valiant and the All-American Boy, while they taught him everything they knew about being a good Homicide detective.

Affirmative action had affected the ranks of the Homicide Section too. But the women and Blacks assigned to the Section to fill number quotas were hard-working detectives, and everyone tried to get along. The C.O., Cmdr. Hail, had a feel for his people and seemed to have a gift of putting the right people together.

Sean slammed away at the aging typewriter with his four-digit technique, finishing an update report on a nowhere case.

Gary had been down the hall in the Armed Robbery-Major Theft Section. He sat down at his desk with a fresh mug of coffee. "Excuse me, Sgt. G.Q. We got a tip from a Robbery snitch that the assholes we've been looking for, who've been doing the robbery/shootings at the gas stations on Seven and Eight Mile roads, are held up at some half-abandoned apartment building on the near Eastside off of Gratiot, in the Seventh Precinct. If you can tear yourself away from that exciting report, we'll go make the apartment house with the rest of the squad and some uniforms from the precinct."

Sean attempted to hide the grin of excitement and anticipation, as he took out his .45 shoulder holster and extra magazines from his desk drawer.

Gary smiled and shook his head. "Hey, Clint Eastwood. Just remember, we're Homicide dicks now, not like on television. We make the scene, but we utilize the uniform coppers as much as possible, and try not to get in their way during the actual arrest. Just keep one thing in mind, Kid. You've got nothing to prove out there. We've already partnered together long enough for me to know what kind of a street cop you were."

Sean secured his .45 and put on his light-beige Summer suit jacket. "Your call, Partner. I'm just along for the ride."

"The Boss wants us at the scene of the arrest so the blue suits don't screw up any of the legal case by mistake."

"Shit, I'm sure glad that when I worked the street, they let us make arrests without all this help."

"Don't be a smartass. These killers we're after are real bad news. They're wanted in three states for over two dozen stick-ups and a handful of murders. We back up the arrest in case it goes sour, then protect the legality of the search and interviews, so we don't lose the whole thing in court on some nickle-and-dime technicality."

"O.K., I'm convinced. Let's go catch bad guys."

Gary drove their unmarked Plymouth police car to the address of the ugly, half-vacant apartment building. The four-story building was at the corner of a crowded residential intersection. Gary pulled their car to a stop in the midst of a line of police cars.

The outside of the building was surrounded by uniform officers. Gary left his sports jacket in the car. His .44-magnum revolver was no longer concealed. He wore it secured firmly to his waist in a belt holster. "Hey, Kid. If we've gotta check that whole damn building, you might want to leave that suit coat in the car."

Sean grinned and pretended to tug on the end of one sleeve. "What, and ruin my image? Remember what I've been telling you, Gary, style before comfort."

"I think working Narcotics all that time gave you brain damage. It's almost 90° and muggy as hell. If those turds are not in room 333, like the snitch said, we'll have to search the whole place."

"Don't worry. I'll keep up."

Other officers took positions throughout the building. Gary and Sean followed half a dozen officers up the stairs to the third floor. They quietly moved down the hall to the room mentioned by the informant.

The officers flanked both sides of the door. Gary was down the hall covering them, and Sean stood a few feet from Gary, guarding the small group's rear flank.

The officers drew their weapons and prepared to enter. Sean leaned back against the wall and held his .45 with both hands.

A uniform officer kicked open the door to room 333. Several officers entered the apartment in a flurry of movement, shouting commands at the occupants as soon as they entered.

The apartment door directly across the hallway from Sean's position began to slowly open. Gary and a uniform officer stood in the doorway of the room they'd entered, covering the inside. Sean watched the door open up a bit more. He began to raise his .45. He didn't know if it was a curious neighbor, or a threat. Because of their position, the room's occupants could not see Sean, and Sean could not see the room's occupants through the partially opened door.

Suddenly, the long barrel of a shotgun appeared through the opening in the door, pointed toward Gary and the other officer.

Sean lunged across the hall and managed to push the barrel against the wall with his left hand. The shotgun discharged with an ear-splitting roar but the shot tore harmlessly into the old plaster ceiling above Gary. Sean was startled by the blast, but unhurt. He raised his .45, still grasping the shotgun barrel near the front grip with his left hand. The door burst open. A man had let go of the gun and bolted, running down the hallway at a full sprint.

The gunman's unexpected move startled Sean as much as the shot itself. He hesitated for an instant, the shotgun still in his hand. He dropped the shotgun and sprinted after the man at full speed, his .45 still clutched in his right hand.

Gary and the uniform officer, still in the doorway, did not realize what had happened behind them. Both men fell to the floor as the plaster exploded above them. By the time they got to their feet, they saw Sean disappear down the stairway in pursuit of the gunman.

The man Sean was chasing was part of the stick-up/murder group. By chance, he had spent the night in the apartment across the hall because he had found a street whore and wanted the privacy. When he heard the police go in after his friends, he opened the door wide enough to see Gary and the uniform cop, but not enough to notice Sean, who was positioned directly across the hall.

The gunman had been startled and panicked after his shotgun barrel was diverted.

The hapless gunman experienced his second surprise as he reached the first floor. The reason the young, well-dressed cop he had passed in the doorway had not fired at him was that he decided on a foot pursuit and was only a few steps behind him on the stairway.

The gunman pushed open the old building's door and sprinted up the street, past unsuspecting uniform officers on the sidewalk. By the time they responded, it was not safe to fire, with Sean so near.

The 25-year-old Black man had sprinted an entire city block. To his utter disbelief, the cop was still only ten feet behind him, easily keeping pace.

The gunman's lungs burned. The hot moist air seemed to become too thick to breathe. He was thankful he had done a hit of heroin with the whore that morning or he would have already dropped. He turned up a filthy, litter-covered alley lined with overfilled dumpsters.

Sean had maintained his good physical condition even though the football team had been eliminated. He jogged, lifted weights and played softball and racketball. He was nearly as high on an adrenaline rush as the gunman was on the heroin.

Mid-way up the alley, Sean called out at the gunman. "O.K., asshole, enough of this bullshit. As soon as I get tired of chasing you, I'm going to blow your fucking head off."

As a last resort, the gunman tried to lose Sean by going over the fences. They both cleared an old six-foot fence surrounding a large vacant lot, filled with trash and garbage. The gunman fell in the center of the huge pile of loose trash. He stumbled getting back on his feet. Sean could not stop in time and he crashed into the man, knocking them both down into the assorted rubbish. Before the gunman could consider renewing his flight, Sean punched him squarely in the nose with a solid left jab. The man fell back into the garbage. Sean grabbed the man by the throat with his left hand holding him to the ground and pointed his .45-auto between the gunman's crossed eyes. "What, have you got some kind of a death wish, cocksucker? I could have greased you back in the hallway. I'm all done fucking with you, jerk. You're under arrest. We're done playing. If you even twitch, I'll blow your brains all over this vacant lot."

Sean could feel the man's body go limp as if a signal of surrender. "O.K. Officer, I hear you. I don't want to go to prison, but I ain't ready to die in no garbage pile. I'm cool."

Moments later, Sean was joined by the officers who had followed the foot chase. They easily handcuffed and searched the prisoner. He was not armed.

Sean loaded the man into the backseat of a marked car and they drove him back to the apartment building.

The entire hold-up gang had been arrested. The diverted shotgun blast had been the only incident.

Gary was standing in front of the apartment building, his hands on his hips.

Sean stepped from the police car, still trying to brush the dirt from his suit.

"You stupid shit, where the hell do you think you are, Disney World? If you hadn't saved my ass, I'd kick yours all the way back to headquarters. A damn foot chase after a homicide suspect who tried to waste two cops with a shotgun. Why the hell didn't you drop the hammer on him in the hallway? What are you trying to prove?"

"Come on, Gary. I'm not proving anything to anyone. I reacted the same way I did when I worked the street. He dropped the shotgun and seemed to be unarmed. The moment I'd have started to lose him, or detected a weapon, I would have cancelled his ticket."

"Thanks for saving our butts in the hallway."

"Pure luck. I was out of his line of sight. If I'd have been two feet closer to you guys, he'd have smoked me. He didn't even know I was there."

"Well, Prince Valiant, I warned you. Take a look at yourself. You're a mess. You've gone and dirtied up your pretty suit and tassel loafers. Well, you did prove a couple of things today, kid. You're certainly not afraid to get your nice clothes fucked up, and you run as fast as any white guy I've ever seen. What's your secret?"

"All preppie shoes have rubber soles. Makes you quicker."

"Rubber soles, my ass. It would have taken me a half hour to run that far in jogging shoes."

The plain wooden desk was empty. There was an ugly wooden chair on each side of the desk. Sean sat across from his prisoner in the small interrogation room. He had been able to wash up, and wore a clean shirt and slacks from his locker.

The prisoner was still filthy from their roll in the garbage. He was still sweating freely, but he sat with his arms folded and an expression of defiance on his face.

He had been informed of his rights three times and would only agree to sign the form indicating he had been advised.

Sean didn't speak. He played with a ballpoint pen and stared at the prisoner. "You're really in the hurt locker, my man. Maybe you didn't get greased, but you're the one who'll lose by jerking us off and refusing to cooperate."

"I told them other po-lice, I ain't got nothin' to say until I talk to my attorney."

"Hey, you know your rights. You don't have to talk, but you can listen. I'm going to tell you what I told a Nam buddy of mine who fucked up a couple of years ago when we talked in this very room. We've got you and your friends by the nuts. According to the descriptions, you've been the wheelman. That shotgun attack today was the worst thing you've done to date. Statistically, the wheelman gets the least amount of hard time. But with today's attempted murder rap, you'll be at Jackson Prison until about year 2001. Fool, let some shave-tail public defender tell you to keep a tight lip. He'll plead you down and you'll still do so much hard time, you'll wish I had greased you today. So, you wait for your lawyer. Maybe one of your friends will roll over before you do and the Prosecutor's office will refuse to plead down, then you get even more hard time."

"So if I roll over, what's my sugar?"

"We drop the shotgun incident and all charges with the robbery murders. You only fall for the stick-ups."

"Why you do all that for me?"

"I want the robbery shooters. You'll do hard time, but you won't be an old man when you get out."

The man paused for a moment. "O.K. Sar-gent, I'll make a complete statement. You could have killed me today and didn't. It would be stupid to survive then spend the rest of my life in prison trying not to be somebody's punk. Tell me though, why didn't you kill me today?"

"If I killed people anytime that it wasn't 100 percent necessary, I wouldn't be any different than those scum boys you've been running with. The instant you became a threat again, I'd have put you down. I was carrying a .45. You would have gone down real hard."

The prisoner just looked back at Sean with a puzzled expression on his face.

Sean stood to get someone to take the man's admission statement. "Hey, forget it. It's way too complicated to explain. The bottom line is that I didn't take you out and I could have."

The man nodded his head, "Yea, well I can dig that."

Sean sat down at his desk with a full mug of coffee. Gary was busy typing their portion of the report on the arrests. Gary stopped to drink from his own mug. "I told you that you should have waxed that little fucker. They say he's being an asshole and is screaming for his lawyer."

"Nope, they're in with him now getting his full admission. He's going to roll over on the whole bunch."

"What did you do, Wonder Boy? Use a rubber hose on him?"

"Nope, I just convinced him that I had his best interest at heart. I told him that, as the wheelman, we'd drop the murder and assault charges, if he talked to us before any of his friends."

"Mighty white of you. They would have probably done that anyway."

"I didn't promise anything I couldn't deliver. Besides, he thinks trying to kill two cops is still against the law."

"You're pretty fucking pleased with yourself about all this, aren't you, Kid?"

"Yea, I've got to admit I really like it here. When I look at the condition of my new suit, it brings me back to earth."

"You made good arrests while on the street, so don't let this go to your head or I'll slap you down to size. Thanks again, Cav, for saving my ass."

"I told you, Partner, it was all luck."

"Yea, well at 4 o'clock, the whole shift is going to a bar in Greek Town. Lucky or not, you saved my life, and I'm buying until you need a ride home."

Sean sipped his coffee and grinned. "Until I need a ride home? I hope you brought your checkbook, Partner."

The back of the Greek Town bar was filled with off-duty cops. The release of the collective nervous energy could be felt. It had been a dangerous day and once again they had cheated the odds and walked away. Each cop, Black, white, female or male, had their own reasons for purposely flirting with death on a regular basis. Now, together and safe, the alcohol released the tensions that had been carefully concealed at work. They were not unlike a bunch of kids just coming off a frightening rollercoaster ride. They had all been wound very tight.

Sean was keeping pace with the alcohol consumption with the same ease he had kept pace with the fleeing suspect. Gary realized his young partner's cavalier attitude about the events at the apartment building was his defense, his method of "whistling past the graveyard." Gary decided he would use the opportunity to get deeper inside his new partner's head.

"Well, Cav, now that you've had time to think about the arrests, would you have done anything differently?"

Sean thought for a moment and grinned, "Yea, I'd have worn a cheaper suit."

"Cut the standup routine with me, Cav. We both could have been killed today. You don't have to pretend to be that cold and uneffected by it with me, I'm your partner."

Sean motioned to the waitress for another round of drinks. "Gary, no macho bullshit with you. I've been under fire every year since '67. Today was exciting, but nothing more. We were damn lucky. No coppers hurt. I wouldn't be like this if anyone of our people had been hurt."

Gary believed that Sean actually wasn't afraid at the apartment building. "What would you have done if that asshole with the shotgun had hit one of us?"

"I'd have taken his fucking head off."

"What if he would have dropped the gun and surrendered?"

"Same answer. Some asshole shoots a cop, he does not surrender. I'd take his unarmed head off."

"You act like a man possessed, Cav. You're only 27-years-old. You don't have to cram a career's worth of experiences into every single year on the job."

Sean emptied his glass, then half emptied the fresh drink. He became pensive and looked down at the table. It was as if he couldn't look at Gary because he was about to tell him something that was very embarrassing.

"You couldn't understand how I feel, Gary. Everything has always come easy to me. I've had to be the best at everything I've done. Well, I screwed up my marriage and lost my wife and son. I cared more about this job than my marriage. If I gave up so much for it, I've got to give it my best. It's all I've got left. I was pleased with myself today because it went well. I have fucked up my personal life. I need to be a complete success in my carreer."

Gary tapped his empty glass on the table top. "Lighten up on yourself, Cav. You're not the first copper to have this job screw up their marriage."

"That's a copout, Gary. The job didn't ruin my marriage. I ruined my marriage. So at 27, my whole existance is this crazy fucking job."

"Kid, if we had five bucks for every cop divorce, we could both retire rich men. So now you're single, make the most of it. Go re-establish some social life. Find some groupie who wants to suck all the poison from your body. Just don't drive too hard for that perfection. It'll only frustrate you, and could end up killing you."

While Sean's organized sports activity was reduced to a slow-pitch, sandlot, softball team, consisting mostly of cops from Detroit's northeast suburbs, T.J. played semi-pro level football and baseball. He played basketball and lifted weights all Winter to stay in condition for the prison teams.

T.J. and the prison baseball players had a new identity since one of their members had made it into the major leagues upon his release. Neither T.J. nor the others had visions of following their teammate into the big time.

T.J. was a good hitter. He played first base. He took throws well, but even T.J. would admit that every ground ball was an adventure.

T.J. was disturbed about the letter from Sean. He was still concerned about his good friend's split from Lyn and his son. Sean's transfer to Homicide meant he was back on the street. T.J. knew how emotionally packed his friend was. He didn't believe Sean was ready for the bullshit of the street so soon after the emotional fall of South Vietnam and his marriage break-up in April.

T.J.'s letter concerned baseball and sports. He never once mentioned his pending divorce or transfer.

T.J. carefully marked the days off of his large wall calendar. With "good time," he hoped he only had three more seasons with his prison team. He could be satisfied playing sandlot softball, outside the prison walls.

Sean was oblivious to the conversation at the small table. He sipped at his beer and stared out at the assorted people in the crowded suburban lounge, deep in thought.

Little Tony's was a nice neighborhood lounge with a small grill. It was a favorite meeting place for suburban cops and it was the kind of lounge where you could bring your date or family for a burger and a drink.

Sean had stopped for a beer after practice with some of his metro-police teammates. The players were preparing for the National Police Softball Tournament on the first weekend in August, in Dayton, Ohio.

They had a talented softball team. Detroit's municipal cuts included the end of the department football team. With his football "career" ended, Sean enjoyed the change of pace of playing softball with the suburban cops. To his teammates, he was just another cop, not a Homicide Detective Sergeant. There were no racial or city political issues to dance around with his suburban cop friends.

He thought of T.J.'s letter about the prison's semi-pro baseball team. Sean let himself daydream about his own baseball experience. There were very few semi-pro baseball teams in metro-Detroit. If you didn't play for a minor league pro-team, you were destined to play softball. There were enough softball teams in metro-Detroit to accommodate men and women with skills that varied from marginal to those who had just missed the big time.

Sean's father had intercepted a copy of a pro scouting report completed after Sean's college freshman season in '67. The first portion of the report made him sound like a promising young prospect. Sean had good speed, excellent range, a good glove, an arm like a cannon, could hit all over the field. But Sean couldn't hit a curve to save his life. A pitcher with a big "hook" could either back him out of the box or have him swinging at a shadow. If he could have only been able to hit a curve, his whole life might have been different.

The friendly, familiar waitress brought the table another round. Sean joined in the conversation with his teammates. He talked with Brian Donner, a suburban cop who was the team's right fielder. Brian well deserved his reputation as the team's Don Juan. He paid the price. He was in the midst of his second divorce and was forced to live with another divorced cop because child support and other divorce expenses took most of his paycheck.

Brian leaned forward so Sean could hear him clearly. "So, Cav, how do you like being a single man again?"

Sean took a sip of beer. "I miss my son. Can't say I miss the constant tension between my wife and I. I've spent most of my time and energy with my transfer to Homicide and playing ball."

"You been dating, getting back into action?"

Sean motioned to the waitress for another beer. "Not really, I was seeing this nurse I knew, but she finished her training and went back home to Marquette. I've kept busy, but I can honestly say my social calendar is not filled."

Brian got a broad grin on his face. "When was the last time you were with an 18-year-old girl?"

Sean looked at Brian as if the beers had pickled his brains. "You mean really with an 18-year-old? I think when I was 19."

"Listen, Cav. I've been dating a 19-year-old fox for a couple months. Her best friend is 18. I'm taking my girl down to Dayton with us for the tournament. If you and her friend hit it off, she can come along and keep my girl company during the games. Needless to say, the wives that go along probably won't be very friendly."

Sean frowned and began to take swallows of beer. "I don't know, Brian, 18 years old. What in the hell do I have in common with a kid."

"You'd be surprised how much you might have in common. Come on, I'm 31 and the age difference hasn't hurt us yet. It's made a new man out of me, if you get my drift. When you take a look at her, you won't call her a kid."

Sean shook his head in doubt. "Eighteen is 18, Brian. I don't care how mature she looks, she's a kid."

"Yea? Well, at 19 they sent your young ass to Vietnam. They thought you were man enough to fight and even to die. Women mature quicker. At 18, she's old enough to date. Come on, Cav, she's of legal age. She's got a sense of humor. She's bright, and has the looks and figure of a photo model. We've got a regular season game tomorrow evening. Meet her after the game and we'll double for a pizza. If you two hit it off, you can both give serious consideration to going to Dayton together. It sure would make my trip with my lady easier."

"I've got to be the one with the brain damage. 18 years old. A date for a pizza and a beer won't kill me."

"Cav, you've got to learn to unwind, come down a notch. You don't have to be Mr. Perfect all the time. Think of it Cav, an 18-year-old star, a real change of pace."

Sean finished his beer. He thought of the advice Gary had given him the week before. "O.K., Brian. Your young friend might be just what the doctor ordered."

The July evening was clear, hot and muggy. The lights flooded the sandlot softball diamond with mid-day brightness. The metro-police team had jumped all over their evening's opponents in the first two innings and the outcome was never in doubt. The last batter set a soft pop-up into shallow left field. Sean carefully moved back, calling off his teammates. The ball fell solidly into his glove for the final out.

The players exchanged handshakes and filed to their bench to move their equipment for the team scheduled to play the next game. Sean changed shoes and loaded his spikes, batting glove and baseball glove into his blue athletic bag.

He had spotted the young woman in the first inning. Brian had not exaggerated about her physical appearance. She was sitting in the bleachers with Brian's girlfriend. She wore a peach-colored skirt and white blouse. The two attractive young women were a little over-dressed to watch a softball game, and had become the center of attention at the small softball complex. Sean had found it difficult to keep his concentration on the game after his first glimpse.

Sean felt like an adolescent at a junior high school dance. His eyes caught Brian's. He smiled and whistled, "You sure didn't lie about the package."

Brian grabbed his athletic bag and patted Sean on the back.

"Come on, boy, it's intro time. Let's see some of that Irish charm. Son, you played that game as if it was the World Series!"

"You know the importance of the first impression. Since her friend is dating the team's leading home-run hitter, I thought I'd better play well or she wouldn't want to be seen with a mere singles hitter."

Brian introduced Sean to Miss Holly Callahan. Holly still lived with her parents in a large house in Grosse Pointe Shores. He gently shook her hand. She was tanned, with pale blue eyes and auburn hair that fell softly onto her shoulders. His insides turned with an immediate attraction and they both smiled nervously in anticipation.

Sean fully enjoyed Holly's company and their first date. He only winced once, when Holly casually mentioned her recent high school graduation.

They were both attracted to each other enough to continue to see each other until the Dayton trip. The night before the drive to Dayton, Sean asked Holly to join them, and Holly accepted without hesitation.

The five-hour drive to Dayton from Detroit gave them a chance to get to know each other on a one-to-one basis.

Holly was fresh, young and represented the opposite of the serious life he had experienced since he was 19. Holly's youth seemed to somehow let him capture some of the youth taken from him by Vietnam and the ghetto streets.

Sean was like an adult adventure experience to Holly. The young-looking man was nine years her senior, but she found him very attractive and entertaining. It was high adventure being a woman with a real Homicide Detective Sergeant.

The tournament started on Friday evening with a single game. They managed to squeak past the Cleveland Police team 8-6.

After the game and a bite to eat, Sean and Holly found themselves alone in their motel room. The most intimate they had been to date was a good-night kiss. The atmosphere was awkward at best.

They turned on the radio and Sean took out a pint bottle of Canadian Club from his suitcase. He poured them both an ice-filled glass, hoping that if the alcohol didn't really help them to relax, it might serve as a placebo. They sipped at the whiskey and attempted to break the tension with small talk and humor.

Sean had showered after the game and wore only some loose-fitting gym shorts and a designer tennis shirt.

Holly had showered and had on a rather-conservative Summer robe.

The talking seemed to chip away at the tension more than the whiskey.

Sean refilled his motel room glass with ice from the ice bucket and poured some Canadian Club over the fresh cubes.

"Look, Holly, I'm starting to feel like this is one of those old-country arranged marriages. Somehow, this has become anything but spontaneous. We don't have to play between the sheets tonight, or this weekend, or any specific time or place. I don't know what you think I expect, but there are no obligations."

"You mean you are not going to ravish my body?"

"Only upon request. There are two beds in the room. I won't feel like less of a man sleeping in the other if you're not ready."

"And what if I am ready?"

"I may attempt to be noble, but I'm not crazy."

"Sean, I'm not pretending to be an innocent, naive virgin. I guess I am a bit embarrassed because I'm no sophisticated woman of the world, either."

"Holly, somewhere between a Susie Cream-cheese and a jet setter is all any man my age could hope for."

"Man your age? I read where 27 was approaching your prime."

"The jury is still out."

Holly got up and turned out the lights. She moved to the nearest bed and slid under the covers, after slipping off her robe. "Come over here and give me a hug, Sean. I'm nervous as hell."

Sean emptied his glass. He moved toward the bed, slipping off his shirt and shorts. "I never could turn down a request from a lady in distress. One small step for Man; one giant leap for my libido."

Life had just thrown Sean a big, wide curve ball, and he was too far out of the batter's box to notice.

Possibly, if the beginning of their physical relationship had been even slightly disappointing, it would have at least slowed their whirlwind affair. But by Saturday morning, they were well on their way to "falling in lust," if not also falling in love. Sean had not merely jumped from the frying pan into the fire, he was launched.

It was Holly's first encounter with a gentle, concerned, experienced lover. She had physical beauty and a willingness to learn that did more than just fascinate Sean.

It was a unique, learning year for them both. Holly was coming of age as a woman, and Sean seemed like the perfect vehicle to help her become an adult. Sean had an exciting new assignment at Homicide and spending his off-duty hours with the beautiful young woman and her wealthy family and friends seemed to fit his new self-image perfectly.

If he and Lyn could have ever made another try at it, the chance was destroyed by Sean's new romance with Holly. The divorce would now surely run its course.

JANUARY, 1976
DETROIT

The two rows of desks were empty except for Gary Burger and Sean. The Sergeant on the phones called into their room. "Cavanagh, call on line two. For you."

Sean sat down his coffee mug and rubbed his tired eyes with his left hand as he answered the phone with the other, "Det. Sgt. Cavanagh."

"Sean, it's me, Lyn."

"Lyn? Is Denny alright?"

"You're a real treat, you know that, Sean? Denny is fine, Mr. Hot-Shot Homicide cop. Tear yourself away from your mirror and look at your desk calendar. Does the day ring a bell at all? Our divorce was final today. You were not expected to show, but at least I thought you would remember the day. We did have a child and live together for five years. You'll get a copy of the papers in the mail, with a copy for your lawyer. You really want to know how your son is? How about you break yourself away from Miss Bubble Gum more than once a month and spend some real time with him."

"I didn't need it before. Now that we're divorced, Lyn, I don't need your bullshit advice."

"You need something, Mister. I hope this really makes you happy. Tell you the truth, Sean, I don't think you'll ever be happy."

"Like I give a shit what you think."

"Fuck off, Sean, and I really mean it."

JUNE, 1976
DETROIT

By early Summer, Sean had somewhat settled down to his new life-style. He and Holly were still in the middle of their romance. Their relationship was still in the infatuation stage. Sean's own family background in the old money of Grosse Pointe, and his extensive wardrobe helped him easily fit into Holly's upper-class lifestyle, despite the fact he was a Homicide detective in one of America's most violent cities.

Sean seemed to be comfortable at the fancy lawn parties and at home on the 30-foot Cruisers and sailboats. He enjoyed his Saturday afternoons with Holly and her brother, roaring across Lake St. Clair to an isolated beach in his new, powerful cigarette boat.

He had struck a compromise with Lyn regarding his visits with Denny. He spent one evening a week with his boy, and it eliminated the conflict that existed when they tried to arrange weekend visits.

Even with the age difference and Sean's recent divorce, Holly's parents couldn't help but like him. Sean was polite, witty and charming for a young man with such an extensive, violent background. There was an added sense of credibility to the new young man in Holly's life. He automatically inherited the combined success of his father and both grandfathers.

Sean's family was privately less than thrilled about Sean and Holly's relationship. They liked Holly and understood why Sean was attracted to her. But the difference in their ages and actual life experiences loomed like storm clouds on the horizon. Secretly, both of Sean's parents hoped that his exposure to the "good life" with Holly might motivate him to change careers and go work for his father, once he finally obtained his grad degree. Then, something good would have come from the relationship.

It was the kind of year Sean should have had at 18, not at 28. He lived in his father's duplex and drove a four-year-old Triumph. Except for his twice-monthly child support payments, he had no real obligations. He privately felt as though he had the world by the butt. For the first time in his life, Sean let himself unwind and take the Summer one exciting day at a time. Holly, his job, softball, and weekly visits with his son and his parents made him feel as though his life would settle down, at last. The possibility of that even amused Sean. He was not optimistic. For once, he was shallow enough to be satisfied with the superficial, at least for a few months.

Holly was the exciting free spirit Sean should have met when he came back from Vietnam. She would have exposed him to the "good life" in an exciting manner, without the pressure to settle down and save Mankind.

Even he had to admit that if they had met prior to his commitment to the Police Department, the lifestyle he could enjoy by working for his father would have been much more appealing. Like an addictive drug, the adrenaline high of working the Detroit streets would not have the same hold on him if he had not developed the need for it.

Sean enjoyed the fast boats and expensive cars and high-ticket parties. He blended right in with Grosse Pointe's social set. Yet somehow, he also fit in the scene of the crowded, Spartan Homicide squad room, working on a report behind his grey desk. He was an enigma, as at home at the yacht club as he was in some dangerous, dark, littered alley.

DECEMBER, 1976
DETROIT

Sean drove his car into the large circular driveway of the huge home of his Kelly grandparents. He sat in the car for a moment. In his entire life, he could never remember ever being summoned to the Kelly home by his kind, loving grandparents.

Grandmother Kelly answered the door. After a warm hug and kiss on the cheek in greeting, she directed him to the den, where his grandfather was waiting for him.

"Come in and sit down, Lad. Your grandmother is getting us a pot of tea. Come sit next to me here near the fireplace."

Sean sat by the roaring fire, sipping tea and eating his grandmother's famous Christmas cookies.

Grampa Kelly carefully held his china teacup and leaned back in his leather, winged-back reading chair. "How have you been doing since your divorce, Sean?"

Sean was naturally puzzled. He had dinner with his grandparents at his own parents home the previous Sunday. He had brought little Denny and they had enjoyed a very pleasant afternoon. "I'm doing just fine, Grampa Kelly. Sir, do you detect something wrong?"

"I mean financially, Sean. How are you doing in the money department?"

Sean became instantly embarrassed and stared down at his china teacup.

"Well, Sir, with the lawyer fees and child support, I've just got back on my feet. My car is getting in pretty bad shape and I have a grand in the bank toward a new car. Dad has really kept me out of hot water by letting me rent his duplex for next to nothing. Keeping up with Holly's family and circle of friends is a financial challenge, but I have kept my charges under control."

Sean's grandfather sat his teacup in its saucer on the endtable. He leaned forward and patted Sean on the knee.

"Lad, when you were born, we bought you a life insurance policy. We did the same for all the grandchildren when they were born. We invested the money after it matured in 20 years. When we're both gone, that was to be the major portion of our gift to each of our grandchildren. You're nearly 30, Sean. We feel that you can best use the money now, to get back on your feet. On Monday, before we go down to Florida for the rest of the Winter, go see our attorney, Armond. He'll best advise you as to how to purchase a house and new car in our names in cash, then transfer ownership to you for tax purposes."

Sean took his grandfather's hand. "Sir, you and Grandma Kelly have always been wonderful to me. But I can't take your money."

"Sean, have you been listening to me? This money has always been intended for you. We feel that you need it more now than ever. Go see Armond, he will explain the best way to use it. Since you must live in Detroit as a Detroit employee, you can find an excellent little house with this amount, buy a new car, and still have a little left to invest."

Tears filled Sean's eyes. "I've accepted help before, but nothing like this, Grampa Kelly."

"You've worked hard since you got back from the war, Sean. We all wanted you to work somewhere safe, but we respect your decision to be a policeman. We give you this now on one condition, you'll work it out with our attorney. We have nothing against your relationship with Holly, but you must protect this money so you do not lose everything you've worked for and we've saved for you, as you did when you split up with Lyn. Holly's family has money. She will never need yours."

Sean stood and hugged both of his grandparents. "I've learned my lesson. I may only be a police sergeant, but now I'll at least live the lifestyle of a police sergeant. Now that Lyn is engaged to an executive with a national investment firm, she doesn't need my money. I don't know how I could ever thank you."

Sean's grandfather smiled and lit his pipe. "Hold on to it. As long as you insist on being a cop, be a financially-comfortable cop."

————————

By the end of 1976, Sean had purchased a neat two-story Colonial brick home on Linville Street near Mack, a new Triumph, and invested the remainder of the money. Only his parents knew of the source of Sean's windfall. And his parents had nothing negative to say.

On New Year's Eve, Sean attended a large party at Holly's parent's expensive home. Sean sipped champagne and watched the snow storm through the French doors in the crowded dining room. It had been a good year. Only T.J.'s parole delay had taken the edge off his year-end enjoyment. Somehow, as Sean stood amidst the happy atmosphere of the party, sipping the expensive champagne, he had the feeling sweep over him like a muggy breeze of hot air. Not unlike the muggy stench of Vietnam. Standing there, Sean somehow knew that 1977 would not be as uneventful, or as pleasant, as 1976 had been.

15

June, 1977—November, 1978

JUNE, 1977
DETROIT, MICHIGAN

It was little surprise to anyone when Holly moved into Sean's new house in April. Neither family was thrilled about the concept of their unmarried children living with someone. But both sets of parents privately preferred that to marriage at that point. Holly was just about to turn 20.

Holly went to junior college part-time and worked Downtown. Sean continued his quest to get his grad degree, and they tried to schedule their schooling for the same nights.

With the infatuation stage of their relationship over, Holly and Sean somewhat struggled at having a "normal" day-to-day relationship. With the pressures of their jobs, school, and age difference, they were already beginning to detect some trouble.

That June evening was clear and cool. School had ended, so Sean had taken his son Denny to a night Tiger ballgame. The youngster already had a keen knowledge and interest in sports.

It was nearly midnight when Sean drove his son to the large new house of his new step-father, in the suburb of Harrison Township.

Sean walked Denny to the door and gave him a hug and kiss as Lyn let him inside. She tenderly instructed him to go upstairs and get ready for bed. She unexpectedly asked Sean to step in for a minute so they could talk. Sean stepped inside and refused Lyn's polite offer for something to drink.

Sean took a seat in the living room. He sat awkwardly waiting for Lyn to discuss the unknown topic. "You really have a nice house here, Lyn. It seems you've found a real winner with Howard. He's given you and Denny a great place to live and Denny really likes him. I'm honestly glad for you."

"I know you are, Sean, and I really appreciate that. Most real fathers are jealous of step-fathers, or vice versa. I'm glad for Denny's sake we don't have that."

"I have no right to be jealous. We're the ones that resolved our relationship. I'm just thankful he treats you well. If anything, I respect that he recognizes what he has and I didn't."

"Sean, I asked you in to tell you that we'll be leaving Michigan. Howard received a promotion to Regional Vice President in Houston. We'll try to get settled before Denny starts back to school in the Fall."

Sean was thankful he was tanned. His face flushed with anger. "Look, Lyn, I understand you have full legal custody. Even so, you have no right to take Denny completely away from me."

"I never meant for this to get ugly, Sean. We've already spoken to our attorney and we're on solid legal ground here."

"You're going to need more than solid ground to take my son out of state. You may need a combat platoon."

"Do you still use your Grampa Kelly's attorney, Armond what's his name?"

"That's correct, Lyn."

"Our attorney will be in touch with him as soon as possible. We really don't want this to get ugly. I'm really sorry, Sean. We never meant for this to happen. Maybe a complete change of living place could be the best for all of us."

"What is this move really worth, other than a vehicle for your revenge?"

"Revenge? Is that what you think? No, Sean. How about a promotion and over six figures a year to start?"

"I'll get back with you, Lyn, after I've talked with Armond. It's really strange the way things work out. What goes around . . ."

The following Thursday, Sean sat across the large antique desk from his attorney. First introduced to him by Grampa Kelly, the middle-aged lawyer had become one of the best-known and most-respected attorneys on Detroit's Eastside. Sean's grandfather had recognized Armond's talent right out of law school and was one of his oldest clients. He, in turn, enjoyed watching the senior Kelly's grandson's fine courtroom testimony as a police officer. He had handled Sean's divorce solely as a favor to the senior Kelly.

Sean had taken off an hour early from work to reach the Eastside law office before it closed. He was still dressed in his Summer business suit. "Armond, how do Lyn and her new husband propose to take my son a thousand miles away, without a fight?"

The well-dressed attorney leaned back in his antique chair and sipped hot coffee from his mug.

"Sean, I respect you and your family far too much, so I'll be right up front with you. I won't take you into court with a no-win situation. If this was a criminal case, Sean, I wouldn't attempt to plea bargain, I'd throw you on the mercy of the court."

"There's got to be some angle, Armond."

"Look at the individual issues of your case. She is the custodial parent. New hubby will make six figures as a V.P. if they move. On the other hand, although improved, your visitation record is not consistent and believe me, Kid, she documented the dates over the past two years. You are a Homicide detective in Murder City, U.S.A., playing house with a girl that just turned 20. Michigan law says child support is an obligation, while visitation is a privilege. So, with the exception of me telling them you're a good policeman who loves his son, to a judge who was a lawyer, and probably doesn't like cops all that much, can you suggest a more solid approach?"

Sean leaned forward, putting his elbows on his knees. He looked down at the floor and went pale. "I get the point, Armond. Is there anything I can do?"

Armond put his mug on the desk and leaned forward. "Listen, they really don't want the delay that going to court would create. If it wasn't for their wish to hurry the process, they'd be holding all of the cards. Obviously, they don't need your money. You put $150 a month in a trust for your son, they'll forgo other support, due to transportation costs you absorb during yearly or bi-yearly visits."

"That's my choice?"

"Sean, on what you make, most men would offer their left nut for only $150 a month payment. The option is having the judge let them go at the same or even increased child support payments."

"They'll go for that $150 trust fund thing?"

"It was their idea. Their attorney already drew it up for my review."

"So, Counselor, what do you advise?"

Armond slid some documents across his desk. "Sign, Sean. Denny will always be your son. When he's 18, he can live wherever he wants."

Sean stood and removed a gold Cross pen from an inside suit pocket. He signed the documents as indicated.

Armond took out a bottle of expensive Scotch from his desk drawer.

"You look like shit, Kid. Get a fresh cup and let's have a glass of this. It may not help, but it can't hurt."

He dumped his coffee in his waste basket and poured a mug full of Scotch.

"Sean, you've been a cop long enough to know that there is damn little justice in this world. Don't go looking for what's fair in this. Divorce is like the rest of life. It's a bitch, not idealistic justice. Sometimes the good guy doesn't win. Sometimes we don't even know who the good guy is."

Sean grinned and held out his clean emptied cup for another portion of Scotch.

"Armond, just give me another drink. You are a far better lawyer than you are a philosopher. If I want to hear about all of the injustice in life, I would have stayed at work. Tell me how much money you're making me with Grampa Kelly's investments."

———————

Sean's last day with his son was as painful as any in his life. They spent the day together at the Cavanagh cottage on Lake Huron.

No matter how hard they tried, they couldn't help but let their tension keep a wedge between them. That wedge did not allow father and son to fully enjoy their last day together before Denny left for Houston.

It was an emotional good-bye. Sean and Denny stood alone on the dock, locked in a tearful father-son embrace.

Denny was sobbing as he crawled into the back seat of Sean's father's car. His grandfather would drop him off at his home. It would be easier for all involved.

Sean locked the buckle on his son's seatbelt and gave him a last tearful hug.

"I don't want to leave, Dad."

"I know, Son. You'll be fine. Give it a chance. You make me proud of you. And remember, Denny, no matter what, I'll always be here for you. I love you, Son."

"I love you too, Dad."

———————

With his son gone and Holly living a somewhat separate life, Sean lost himself in his job, in grad school, and in a Canadian whiskey bottle.

Sean was turning his feelings inward. His life was now more complex, but the way he dealt with his personal problems was similar to his return from Vietnam. He kept everything inside.

He often felt guilty about complaining about his personal problems when he considered T.J.'s terrible life in prison.

It was as though his Homicide partner was the only person he could really open up to. Gary Burger had become the most important person in Sean's life. They spent a lot of time in cop bars, so Sean could blow off steam.

Sean walked the edge of becoming an alcoholic for the next year. Gary kept him from going over that edge.

JANUARY, 1978
DETROIT

It was Sean and Gary's turn to work the graveyard shift as the Homicide crew on all-night duty.

Sean had always hated the all-night shift. With grad school classes two nights a week, he dreaded their tour on the overnight shift as much as he hated the Morgue detail.

The Detective Sergeant at the front desk yelled back into the half-darkened squad room full of empty desks. "Cavanagh, call on line one. Sounds like a cit-i-zen, he asked for you by name."

Sean glanced at his wristwatch, it was after 1 a.m. He punched the flashing button on his desk phone, wondering what "citizen" would be calling him at that time of night. "Homicide, Sgt. Cavanagh."

"Say, Sar-gent Cavanagh, this is your number one, main man from when you was at 13th Narcotics. You know, Gum Drop."

"Hey, Gum Drop, what's shaking? You've got to be in a serious trick bag. I haven't heard from you in almost a year. Not nice for a snitch to stay away so long, Gum Drop. You might make me think you only call when you get yourself in the jackpot."

"Naw, it ain't that way, Sar-gent. I was busy an' keepin' my ear to the ground like you always tol' me to. Say, dig this. I done heard some shit about that dude that been offin' cabbies."

"I'm listening, Gum Drop."

"Well, I got this here problem with Central Narcotics. They did a raid and got me holdin'. I wasn't sellin', square business. It's a roust bust by some new narc, but with my rap sheet, I'll do some hard time for certain."

"You're breaking my heart. Come on, Gum Drop, it's late. Tell me what you've got and I'll see what I can do."

"Will you help me from doin' some hard time?"

"No promises. Look, asshole, we've worked together for over five years. I've never gone back on my word. So quit jerking me around and tell me what you've got. My coffee is getting cold."

"O.K., O.K. Dig this, Sar-gent. I heard who's doin' all the cabbies in them robberies. Dude's street name is Mad Dog. Word is that he ain't right in his head. He come into De-troit from Philly about three months ago."

"Mad Dog? From Philly? Listen, if you are trying to sell me a wolf ticket, I'll help that narc put you in Jackson. In fact, I'll personally kick your ass there myself."

"No way, Mr. Cavanagh. I've worked with you enough times for me to know not to mess with you all."

Sean found an empty legal pad and took out his pen. "Start talking to me, Gum Drop. I'm hanging on your every word."

Gum Drop gave Sean the man's reported address, where he copped his dope, and other specifics.

"No jive, Sar-gent, the man is stone crazy. He's got himself a bad Jones and it seems like he gets off on shootin' people. Black, white, makes him no never mind. It's like shootin' them cabbies makes ol' Mad Dog's dick hard, dig it?"

"Yea, Gum Drop. I've got his address, description, and apartment number. If this pans out, I'll take care of business with the narc."

"Solid. Just be cool with this dude. Like I been sayin', he ain't right."

After Sean finished talking with Gum Drop, he called his own home. Holly had gone out with her single sister and best friend. He went through the all-night shift a bit easier when he knew she was home safe. There was no answer. She wasn't home from the bars yet, and he felt his stomach turn in anger. It was an issue that had been argued a hundred times, and they were still no closer to settling it. He slammed the unanswered receiver down on his phone. He put his pen back in his suitcoat and bit his lip in frustration.

Gary dropped into his own desk chair, behind his cluttered desk. "Cav, you have any Maalox? My gut is killing me."

Sean searched his desk. "Hey, Partner, just ease up on the damn coffee. That's got to be your third cup already tonight."

"Kid, I've already got a mother, but thank you for looking after me. Just give me the fucking Maalox, then I can drink the coffee and not fall asleep on my desk. Trust me, I don't nag you about the booze, leave me alone about the damn coffee."

Gary took two large swallows from the Maalox bottle. He made a face "I wonder how many police careers have been saved by this stuff. Who makes this stuff? We should buy stock."

Sean went over and took his London Fog trench coat from the coat rack. "Do you remember that faggot-junkie-snitch I had at 13? We used him a couple of times. Gum Drop?"

Gary frowned and poured himself a fresh mug of coffee. "Yea, another one of those high-quality individuals you met while working 13 Narcotics."

"Come on, Gary, just because he is a fruit, Black, junkie, snitch, doesn't make him a bad guy. Besides, he called with info on the douche bag who is smoking the cabbies during the hack robberies. He says the shooter's handle is Mad Dog. I've got his address, some shithole hotel near the bus station and old city hall. Let's take a ride by and see if Mr. Dog is home."

"Mad Dog? I've heard some stupid street names for real bad asses, but Mad Dog? Come on, Cav, you're shitting me."

"O.K., so it's a stupid fucking nigger street name for a shooter. But that fruit snitch has always been right, even when he's got his balls in a vice, like he does now. Some new narc from Central Narcotics wants him to take a big fall for possession because he was holding while loitering at a search warrant raid. Despite his sexual preference, he doesn't want to do hard time because of his heroin habit. I still think he won't fuck with me, even with the hard-time sword hanging over his head. I think he's more afraid of me than hard time."

Gary took another swig of Maalox. "So, write it up and the day crews can take the blue suiters over there with a warrant tomorrow morning."

"No good, Gary. Come on, a junkie shooter named Mad Dog, from out of town? We've got to move while the information from the street is still warm."

"How the hell do we get an arrest warrant to do his apartment?"

"At 1 a.m., on a rainy, damp, pissy, January night, on information from a faggot, junkie snitch? I'm not waking a judge or an assistant prosecutor for that."

Gary tried his coffee again. He half grinned. The Maalox had worked. He could put more acid in his stomach without physical discomfort. "O.K., Justice Douglas. How do we bust this asshole and keep it legal, without a warrant?"

Sean finished his coffee and winced when he saw the collection of grounds at the bottom of his mug.

"Man, have you ever become a tight-ass in your old age. We've got probable cause to at least go to this address. We've got a real good description from the hack drivers that survived. We eyeball this guy, arrest him on his physical description and get a search warrant in the morning, while they do a live showup on this turd on the Ninth Floor. That way, he doesn't sky out on us while the day shift is going through the process."

Gary looked through the empty Homicide offices. "There is no other Homicide crew to go with us. God, I hate it when you're right."

Sean took his .45 and shoulder holster from his desk.

"We can pick up a couple uniform crews from the First Precinct. The snitch says the best time to call on him is before 3 a.m. The M.O. sheet indicates he hits the cabs between 4 a.m. and 6 a.m. Then he goes to some toilet shooting gallery near John R. and Erskine to cop his dope. He's home by dawn and stays in his room all day. He changes hotels about once a week."

Sean put on his shoulder holster under his suitcoat, then his trench coat over his suitcoat. His .45 was totally concealed under his light-grey three-piece suit. He gave himself the visual once-over in the small mirror next to the coat rack.

Gary belched, "You look as beautiful as always, Mr. G.Q. man. My partner, the fashion plate. I wish you were as concerned about the trouble this Mad Dog-asshole could give us as you are about making the department's 10 best-dressed list."

"Gary, all I have to do is not wear polyester leisure suits from Sears and I'm in the running. I don't know what you're bitching about. That ratty-ass trench coat you wear is so old it's got dinosaur shit stains on it.

"You know, we're starting to sound like an *Odd Couple* routine. We can take this guy, Gary. He works alone. We slide in on him when he doesn't expect us, just us and a couple uniform back-ups. Piece of cake."

Gary called the dispatcher to have a uniform crew meet them near the hotel. Sean tried calling his house again. There was still no answer.

Sean slammed down the receiver. "Damn her! 1:45 in the morning and she's still not home yet. This is really bullshit, Partner. I don't blame her for being bored, especially the month we pull night rotation. But when I'm home, she's too tired for fooling around at 11 because she's had a tough day at work. She's never too tired to close the bars with her sister and friend when given the chance. I don't mind her going out. I just don't understand this need to stay at some bar until closing. She's got all the privacy she'd ever want. Hell, my house certainly is big enough for them to party in."

Sean punched the "down" button for the elevator hard with his fist. "Fuck this shit. I'm really getting sick of it."

Gary put his hand on Sean's shoulder.

"Sean, we've been partners and friends since you met Holly. Maybe I'm out of line with my opinion here, but you'd better not seriously consider marriage until this thing is settled. You two have got to work this out some way. It's been an issue since before she moved in. Kid, think about it. Holly has no married friends. She's only 20 years old. You're gone all the time. I'm not saying I wouldn't have the same feelings you do, it's not a simple problem. If her closing the bars makes you crazy, you'd better think about how much you really trust her. Then you should consider her real motives for staying out that late and closing the bars."

They found their beige unmarked Plymouth police car. Pissy was a good description for the weather. It was mild for January, but it was very damp, and a light mist rolled in off of Lake St. Clair.

Sean slammed his door. "I really need this bullshit with Holly like I need a case of hemorrhoids. I've got grad school, trying to find time to study for the lieutenant's exam, my son a thousand miles away in Texas, and my so-called live-in fiancee is goddamn belle of the ball of the Eastside singles bars."

"Let it go, Cav. We'll talk about it when we get back to the Fifth Floor. I'll let you buy me a coffee and bitch about how I drink too much of it."

"That's really white of you."

They waited in a vacant parking lot. Five minutes later, a marked unit pulled up behind them. Sean opened his door. "Stay warm, Gary, I'll go back and run over it with them. They can follow us to the scene. Dispatch said he's only got one car in service to back us up. It should be enough. We really only need the rear covered."

The uniform crew consisted of veteran Officer Tracy Stopeck and Tim Reynolds, a rookie. The concealed truth was that of Officer Tracy Stopeck's five years on the job, she had spent less than one year on the street. Sean explained the situation to them. He instructed Reynolds to cover the rear of the hotel room from the alley and Stopeck to cover their backs in the hallway, as he and Gary entered the apartment and attempted the arrest.

Sean dreaded telling Gary about their back-up. He got back in their car and fought off a damp chill.

Gary began to drive to the old hotel near the city's bus station. It stood within sight of the old city hall landmark. "Is the uniform crew anybody we know?"

Sean forced himself to look out the window. "I doubt it. Woman's name is Stopeck, the kid's name is Reynolds."

Gary gave Sean one of his famous looks of absolute disgust. "You've got to be shitting me, Cavanagh! We're going to try to arrest the most dangerous nigger shooter in Detroit with Mutt and Jeff as a back-up? Let's shut this thing down while we still can."

"Come on, Gary. Where's you spirit of adventure?"

"I left it back on my desk. I haven't needed it since I made sergeant."

"All these two do is cover our backs and keep out of the way. Come on, they haven't made a stick-up man that you and I can't take down. Hell, the legend of the Eastside and an ex-academy instructor. If things get rough, you can show him a shooting trophy."

Gary pulled in front of the hotel. Sean popped the trunk lock button under the dashboard so he could get a shotgun from the wooden gun box in the trunk.

Gary shook his head and popped a Rolaids in his mouth. "A shotgun, since when do you carry a shotgun on an initial investigation, when we've got my .44 magnum and your .45?"

"You know, like a variation of the umbrella cliché, 'if you take it, you won't need it.' "

"Cavanagh, you've got one of those damn premonitions, don't you?"

"No. Relax, Gary. I've just got the feeling the shooter is in there. I really think Gum Drop came through this time."

They sent Reynolds to the alley, with instructions to find cover and stay out of sight. Officer Tracy Stopeck followed them up the stairs to the second-floor hotel room, reported to be the killer's current home.

"Cavanagh, I've got to be going senile letting you talk me into this." He drew his .44 magnum as they reached the second floor.

Sean racked a round into the shotgun while they were still in the stairway, out of earshot of any hotel room. "Not to worry. Have I ever lied to you? This will be a piece of cake."

They quietly moved down the deserted hallway. Sean pointed to the spot where he wanted Officer Stopeck positioned. She stopped about half-way in the hall, between the stairway and the hotel room in question.

Gary and Sean flanked the door to the apartment. Faded numbers identified the single hotel room. There was no peep hole in the door. Sean and Gary leaned back against the wall, at least a foot from each side of the wooden door. Sean knocked on the door.

An irritated voice answered. "Who's there? What do you want?"

"I'm sorry to bother you, Sir. It's the gas company. We have a serious leak on the first floor, and we need to make certain none has leaked up here."

"Go away. I don't smell nothin'"

"Sorry, Sir, with a severe leak, you might not notice an odor until it's too late. There might be an extreme danger of explosion. We have the instruments to check. It'll only take a second."

"Yea, well, just a second."

Gary shook his head. They knew it hadn't worked by the tone in the man's voice. Gary looked across the doorway to Sean. "Piece of cake, eh, Kid?"

The gunman's first shotgun blast blew through the center of the old wooden hotel room door. Moments later, the second shot tore through the wall next to Gary. Gary was hit in the back of his upper left leg by the buckshot round. He collapsed to the floor of the hallway. Sean moved another step away from the doorway, as the third shot blew a large circle of plaster from the wall, a few inches from his head. There was a fourth shot at the rear of the room. It sounded as though it was from the window to the alley.

Sean turned back to see Gary. Gary had managed to crawl several feet down the hall, away from the shooting. Sean could see that Gary's leg was bleeding badly, but he was conscious and sitting up, revolver held expertly with both hands. He merely nodded to Sean that he was in position and in the condition to protect himself.

Sean turned to Officer Tracy Stopeck. She was laying face down on the hallway floor, covering her head with both hands. Sean yelled at her,

"For Christ's sake, Officer, at least get on your radio and get us some help here. Tell them we have officers down."

Sean's movements seemed fluid to Gary, who was nearly blinded by the pain in his leg. Sean moved in front of the hotel room door, firing the shotgun into the room through the wall and closed door as he moved. He dropped the empty shotgun and drew his .45 as he kicked open the door with one thrust of his foot.

The door burst open. Sean saw a Black man climbing out the rear window. The man was trying to reload a shotgun and get out onto the fire escape at the same time.

The man turned and fired a badly-aimed blast in Sean's direction. The shot tore into the plaster ceiling above Sean's head.

Sean leaned up against the wall and opened fire at the window with four quick rounds. The gunman was hit once in the right shoulder and in the forearm. He still managed to roll out onto the fire escape, then onto a dumpster. From the dumpster he jumped to the alley and ran toward the street.

As Sean began to crawl out of the window in pursuit, the man stopped at the mouth of the alley. He drew a 9mm automatic from his waistband. As Sean made it out onto the fire escape, the gunman opened up on him with his pistol. Sean dove off the second-story metal stairway and hit hard on the paved alley, next to the motionless body of Officer Reynolds. Reynolds was on his back. He had been hit in the chest by the gunman's fourth shotgun blast. The gunman had caught him standing in the center of the alley, out in the open.

The fall had knocked the wind out of Sean. He struggled to catch his breath.

The gunman hesitated for a moment, then fired twice more at Sean.

Sean managed to roll onto his stomach and empty the .45's magazine at the gunman. He missed, but the shots discouraged the gunman from returning to the alley to finish off Sean and the wounded uniform officer. The gunman broke and ran toward the bus station.

Sean painfully struggled to his feet. Initially, he thought he'd broken his left shoulder in the dive from the fire escape. He was catching his breath and the terrible pain in his shoulder was subsiding. He put in a full magazine in his .45 and chambered a round. He took off his light-colored trench coat and covered the badly-wounded officer with it. The light bone color would make him easier for the responding units to find in the dark alley.

Sean could hear half a dozen police and E.M.S. sirens in the damp night air as he ran toward the bus station.

The gunman was wearing black trousers and a dark green silk shirt. Sean was certain he could identify the man in the crowded bus station.

Even with Afro hair and a full beard, Sean would recognize the man's eyes. His eyes were as insane as the gunman he had faced in the little grocery several years before. He had not seen the same expression since then.

Sean sprinted through the cold Winter mist. He passed a bum in a doorway, wearing only a flannel shirt. He called out to Sean, "Hey Mister, hep' me out, will you? Some crazy nigger come runnin' by here with a gun, his arm a bleedin' to beat hell. He stole my coat. Believe that, young man with a gun gotta rob an ol' nigger man of his coat."

Sean showed him his badge. "Listen, Pops. I'm the real police. If you see a police car, you tell them I chased that man into the bus station. You get me some help and I'll buy you a new coat."

"Don't want a new coat, want that coat."

"What color's your coat?"

"It's light gray, about the color of that suit you all is wearin'."

"You've got good taste. Just tell the police where I went and you can have any coat you want."

Sean slowly entered the old bus station's lobby which faced East Lafayette Street. The lobby was always filled with an assortment of people; travelers, families, friends, street people. It was patroled by uniformed, armed, contracted private guards.

Sean realized that it was he who was out of place at the Downtown bus station at 2 a.m. A well-dressed white man with a gun was in more danger from the overzealous armed guards than he was from the gunman.

Just after the holidays, the bus depot lobby was more crowded than usual for that late hour.

Sean stood just inside the lobby doors for a moment, he held his .45 down next to his right leg, observing the assorted people in the busy depot lobby and ticket area.

Sean slowly moved to the center of the lobby. He didn't see the gunman, but blood spots on the tile floor told him he was in the right place.

He leaned against a cement support post and scanned the depot area. He saw a uniform guard walking briskly in his direction. The guard spotted Sean's .45 in his right hand. The guard stopped and went for his holstered .38 revolver. Sean held up his badge and I.D. folder. The guard slowly approached to speaking distance. "I'm a Detroit Police Detective Sergeant. Call 911 and tell them I'm here and I need help."

The guard began to nervously scan the people in the lobby for the unknown threat. "What's the deal, Officer? I can help."

"Please call, then come on back. That will be the most help."

The guard nodded and ran off toward the ticketing area.

The modest depot gift and magazine shop was still open due to extended holiday hours of operation. The shop's walls were made of glass. It was located on the East Lafayette side of the depot lobby.

Suddenly, Sean saw his man. He was inside the small gift shop. He was trying to conceal himself behind a tall paperback book rack. He had slung the bum's coat over his wounded shoulder and arm. The man had obviously not yet seen Sean.

Sean slipped his badge folder in his pocket so he could use both hands with his .45. He moved toward the shop, concealed by a small group of travelers walking out of the lobby. He made it to the doorway of the small shop undetected. He slowly entered the shop, moving to place the gunman in the best possible position, if he had to fire.

The gunman spotted Sean, and their eyes met for an instant. The flash of insane anger had not left the gunman's dark eyes. He let the coat drop to the floor, and he raised his 9mm to firing position. Sean brought up the .45 to fire, but an elderly Black woman looking at magazines had moved behind the gunman. Sean held his fire.

Sean heard the words, "Holy Mary", emit from his own mouth as the gunman opened fire with a five round barrage at him. Sean was blessed by the strong recoil of the gunman's 9mm pistol. The recoil made the gunman's aim poor and the weapon hard to handle because of his wounds.

One of the 9mm rounds struck Sean in the left side, just above the hip. The impact spun him around into a magazine rack, and knocked him to the dirty tile floor. There was a chorus of screams from by-standers and people dove for cover.

Sean rolled onto his back and clutched his .45 with both hands. Sean expected the gunman to move into position to finish him off. The gunman greatly over-estimated the damage created by his vicious volley of 9mm pistol fire. It was his fatal mistake.

The gunman moved out from the rear of the shop and from behind the book rack, looking for Sean's body. He looked down into the barrel of Sean's well-aimed .45. Sean fired five rapid shots from his automatic pistol. The five powerful, large-caliber rounds hit the gunman at the waist and walked in a line up his torso, with the last striking him in the throat. The force of the rounds picked up the man's body and drove it crashing through the glass counter. His 9mm discharged once into the floor. The gunman was dead before the second chorus of screams had ceased.

There were a few seconds of silence. Then, terrified people cautiously stepped out of the shop and away from the scene of the gore.

Sean didn't know how badly he was hurt, so he stayed on his back on the floor. He realized the guard had returned and was standing over him. "Be cool, Officer. I called E.M.S., and other police are on the way. You hurt bad? Got to tell you, Officer, you offed that other dude for certain."

"I think I'll just lay here until E.M.S. comes. Could you get a blanket and cover him. No use making people sick."

Yea, if you are alright, I'll go fetch a blanket."

"I'll be fine. I'm not going anywhere."

The guard raised his voice and spoke to the small group of gathered by-standers. "You folks be about your business. This is a police matter. There's no more danger. There's lots more police on the way, so stand clear." He ran off to get a blanket.

An elderly Black woman appeared over Sean. "Are you a police officer, young man?"

"Yes, Ma'am."

"What that man do?"

Sean rested his head back on the cool tile. "Well, in addition to shooting a half-dozen cab drivers, he shot two other officers tonight."

She kneeled next to him. "I read about the cab drivers. Don't fret none, Son, I'm a nurse. I've been one for 40 years. I saw what you did. You couldn't fire because of that old Black woman standing behind that there crazy man. That old woman is my sister. We're waitin' on our cousin to come visit from Mississippi."

She took out a beautiful white lace-edged handkerchief. She carefully and gently undid his suit vest and removed the shirt tail to inspect the wound. "No, it don't look bad at all. I'm sure it didn't hit any vital organs." She held the handkerchief to the wound to suppress the bleeding. "How do you feel, Son?"

"Pretty punk, Ma'am. You'd think I'd be better at this by now. This isn't the first time. I feel faint, dizzy. . ."

"Lots of folks go into shock, Boy. Ain't no disgrace on that. You rest easy, I hear the sirens. I'll stay with you until they all get here. And don't you worry your head none about the T.V. and the papers saying this is just another time a white po-lice shot and killed a Black man. I'm going to tell everyone who'll listen that you were nearly killed in order to save an old Black woman."

Sean felt himself slipping into unconsciousness. "No one wants to hear that, Ma'am. It ruins our reputation. No one cares."

"Well, Son. You could have died because of my sweet old sister. I sure as hell care. And I'm going to tell them until they listen."

An hour later, Sean was resting on a gurney in the hallway, just outside one of the city hospital's emergency treatment rooms. His gunshot wound was, in fact, superficial, as the old nurse had diagnosed at the bus depot. He had been probed, poked, sutured, and very well drugged before being placed in the hallway as they readied his room. He was on his back and he tried to focus his eyes on the suspended I.V. bottle through his drug-induced stupor.

He noticed the figure of a Black man in a trench coat standing next to him. It was Cmdr. Hail. Sean's eyes focused and he forced a grin, for show.

"How are you doing, Cavanagh? Do you need anything?"

"I'm doing fine, Boss. How are Gary and the uniform kid?"

"They had to dig some buck shot out of Gary's leg. He lost a lot of blood but they didn't hit the bone. The kid, Reynolds, he's in rough shape. He's in intensive care. He lost a lung but he's young and strong. They expect him to pull through. Your wound isn't bad. The bullet was stopped by the back of your belt. It almost fell out when they undressed you. No doubt the 9mm slugs match those of the hack driver-killer. You lost some blood, went into shock pretty bad. I'd have you room with Burger, but I need you back to work. He'd bitch at you 24 hours a day and you two would never rest enough to recover."

"Are they going to make me pay for a new gift shop at the bus station?"

"Don't laugh, Lad. You two destroyed that place. You're lucky some old Black woman thinks you're the Great White Hope. We got great statements about the bus depot shooting. After you are better, we're going to discuss the 2 a.m. visit to a possible shooter's pad with such soft back-up. I've never known you two to act like damn cowboys or take unnecessary chances. You know I don't usually second-guess my people, Cavanagh, but *damn*, Son."

"Boss, all I can say is that I talked Gary into it. It really seemed like the right thing to do at the time. It was a routine check on a snitch's tip until the shooting started."

"It's O.K., Cav. I'm not having your ass. I just never get used to seeing my people like this. I know it can happen every time we go out. You did one hell of a job, Cav. It took balls to go after that crazy fucker with the determination you displayed. Once a Marine and all that, I guess, hey Cav? Well, see you tomorrow. Get some good rest. There is someone here very anxious to see you. Take care, Son."

"Thanks for coming down, Boss."

Sean could smell Holly's expensive perfume before he actually saw her. She stood next to the gurney and clutched the hand not attached to the I.V. She leaned over and kissed him tenderly on the lips.

"Are you alright, Sean?"

"Yea, you should see the other guy."

"They told me Gary will be fine and that the young uniform officer will pull through. I'm sorry you were hurt and forced to kill that man at the bus station."

Sean stared up at the ceiling. "Yea, I'm glad we waited until the bars closed to do all this. Otherwise, they might not have found you home and you would have had to wait to hear about it on the radio tomorrow like everyone else."

"This is not the time or place for this, Sean."

"You're still dressed up and all made up. What were you doing when they came to get you, getting an early jump on tomorrow morning?"

"My sister and I built a fire and we were at home talking and having a beer."

"I must have dialed the wrong number when I called at 1:30."

"No, you probably just missed me. We'll buy a time clock so I can be more exact. Be fair, Sean. Look, I was terrified when they came and got me. You've told me the story about the ride to the hospital. I didn't even know if you were still alive. I called your folks. They're on their way down. Your dad ordered you a private room. I'll stay with you until you want me to leave."

"Well, at least you're sober."

"I wasn't. A 20-minute ride in a police car to find out whether your fiance is still alive has a sobering effect on anyone."

He smiled and squeezed her hand. He looked back at the ceiling and felt his eyes fill with tears. He was coming down from the adrenaline high, but the drugs still warmed him and protected him from the pain of his wound.

Crazy Mad Dog had been overmatched when he came up against the tough young Homicide Detective Sergeant. Sean could handle any killer, deal with any street violence, but Sean privately cried as he realized that only 21-year-old Holly Callahan could render him helpless.

The week of Sean's birthday in March, there was a small ceremony at Detroit's new City Hall. The timing was coincidental to his birthday; it was based on Officer Reynolds being strong enough to leave the hospital to personally accept his awards.

Sean was presented with the Medal of Valor, the department's highest award.

Gary, Reynolds, and Tracy Stopeck received Departmental Citations, and Sean, Gary, and Reynolds received the Wounded in Service Medal. It was the department's version of the Purple Heart.

Police Chief Hunter read the official account of the incident and personally presented the medals and documented citations.

The Cavanagh and Callahan families were well represented at the ceremony, and they stopped for dinner at Joe Muier's Seafood Restaurant at Gratiot and Verner to celebrate.

Before dinner, Sean spotted Cmdr. Hail in the restaurant's lounge bar. He briefly excused himself and took the stool next to the respected Black command officer. "Excuse me, Boss. Can I buy you a drink?"

Hail smiled and patted Sean on the back. "Well, it's my young Irish hero. You did us proud today, Kid. You looked sharp. Are you here with your family? They're a nice bunch of folks. I talked with your dad. Straight shooter. He'd have been a good cop."

"Boss, be a straight shooter with me. Why in the hell did Officer Stopeck get a Departmental Citation? Was it because she didn't run away?"

Hail took two swallows from his drink. "Come on now, Cavanagh, You damn well know why. How would it look if the three white male officers got awards and she didn't?"

"Screw how it would look, Boss. The truth sometimes hurts and the truth is, she froze."

"Did she freeze because she's a female?"

"I don't know. I really don't give a shit. I've seen men freeze. I think it was because it was her first shooting. Her lack of experience, not her gender."

"They gave Reynolds a Departmental for screwing up."

"O.K., I know that too, but it cost the kid a lung. He deserved it for nothing else than not dying. I didn't see her in a hurry to get a Wounded in Service Medal."

"Sgt. Cavanagh, you said it best. Sometimes the truth hurts. The truth is, she got it because of affirmative action politics. Now that she's a hero, she'll probably made sergeant next exam."

"You're right, Commander, I know the answers. The questions are stupid. It just takes the edge off of the whole thing. Cheapens it a bit."

"Climb off your high horse, Cavanagh. If you hadn't had those very supportive witnesses at the bus station, who wanted you crowned a saint, they might have had your ass for blowing up the gift shop, rather than giving you a medal."

"Then what is the real difference, Commander?"

"The medal won't buy you your dinner here tonight, Kid. But you'll know the difference when you test for lieutenant later this year. You have 25 years to go, if you stay, Cav. You've got to learn to just go with the flow. Get back to your family. Thanks for the drink. You don't have to like it, you just have to do it. When your insides tell you that you can't do it any longer, get out. As long as you carry that badge, stay off your soap box, and you may wind up on the Third Floor before you retire."

SEPTEMBER, 1978
DETROIT

Sean nervously paced the narrow aisleway between the rows of metal desks in the crowded Homicide squad room. He was pensive and stared down at the tile floor as he paced, occasionally taking a sip from his coffee mug.

Gary turned from the report he was typing.

"For Christ's sake, Cavanagh, sit the fuck down. You're putting the whole squad on edge with this damn expectant father routine of yours over the damn Lieutenant's list. Listen, asshole, you're only 30. I'm certain you'll get another crack at it by the time you retire."

Sean dropped into his chair and began to nervously tap a pencil on his desk top.

"I'm sorry, Gary. I don't know what's bugging me about this time. It's as if I am obsessed with making lieutenant this list. It's not that I don't want to keep working with you and that ever-pleasant personality of yours. Since the shooting last January, you've been about as much fun to be with as a live-in mother-in-law."

Gary frowned and leaned across his desk.

"I'm still pissed that I let you talk me into going to the hotel in the first place. We needed the fucking National Guard going up against that crazy, and we bring along two of the Mayor's finest as back-up. I swear, if you ever get another tip like that from a snitch, you go it alone. I'm leaving for Harbor Springs for a week."

Sean got up and poured himself a fresh mug of coffee. "Nine months and you're still on my case about that night. You are getting crabby in your old age. What do you want? Hell, it went fine. We stopped a dangerous killer and everyone got an award."

"Went fine, did it? Cavanagh, you silver-tongued devil. You should go into politics. You blow the shit out of the bus station, three cops get shot, and you make it sound like it was all in a day's work."

Sean sat back down and grinned at his partner. "You're a hell of a guy, Gary. You are insulting me just so I'll get my mind off of the lieutenant's list. That's why you call me names, to make me feel better."

"Hey, Kid. What are friends for? But I still say you're full of shit. I'll warn you again. If you ever pull a hero stunt like chasing that fucker into the bus depot alone again, I'll personally boot your ass all the way to your daddy's house in Grosse Pointe."

"If I had five bucks for every time you warned me since that night, I could retire now."

"Listen, you hard-headed Irishman. I want it etched in your little brain."

Sean sat back in his chair and a serious expression came on his face. "You know, Gary, the truth is that I really haven't accepted that if I get promoted, we won't be partners."

"Me neither, Kid. I'll miss that cute little baby face and your ever-exciting wardrobe. Be careful though, Cav. If you do get promoted, you might break precedent. They might actually promote someone who's qualified."

Sean's facial expression changed again. "Shit, Burger, don't be nice to me. I wouldn't know how to act. I might start crying or something."

"Cav, after three years together, I know what kind of a cop you are, but you might get a reputation as a Golden Boy, a hot dog. Medal of Valor in March, lieutenant in September. Remember how much shit I gave you when you got here in '75?"

"Yea, but you gave me a chance. If I get a chance, it's up to me."

The Detective Sergeant working the front desk called back into their room. "Hey, Cavanagh, Cmdr. Hail wants you in his office."

Sean took his suitcoat from the clothing rack and looked in the mirror to be certain his tie was straight and his hair was neat.

Gary raised his coffee mug. "Good luck, Partner."

Sean walked to Hail's office, and the squad members shared brief words of encouragement as he passed.

As he approached Hail's office, the Commander saw him through the window in the door and waved him in. "Close the door behind you and have a seat, Cav."

Hail leaned back in his office chair and savored his expensive cigar. "I'm not going to have you pace with anticipation about the list all morning. It's not going out until this afternoon, but I need for you people to do some work.

"You've been promoted to lieutenant, Cavanagh. Congratulations. It is effective the first of next month. The other good news is that you're merely moving down the hall to Armed Robbery-Major Theft Section. You'll head up the A.R.M.T.S. team that works with our people on robbery murders. You know all the people you'll be working with already. You even get to work with Gary on a regular basis, so he can keep an eye on you."

Sean stood and shook Hail's hand briskly. "Thank you, Boss. I guess I was pretty tense and it was driving everyone nuts."

Cmdr. Hail leaned back in his chair.

"I'm going to give you a lecture before you leave here, Cav. I think you need it. You're a good copper, and it seems that most everyone takes to you. You came here in '75 with six years on the job as a detective sergeant. You had a lot to prove, and I think you've done just that.

"Cav, don't cop the attitude that you've earned the right to be a detective lieutenant, at a choice assignment, at 30 years old. I know you've seen a lot of shit in a short time, but there are coppers out there with 20 years on the job who are just as good as you are, and they're still pushing a marked car around a precinct every day as a patrol officer. You've been in the right place at the right time, and you've been goddamn lucky. You write one hell of a promotional examination, but you know every promotion from now on is appointed."

Sean was confused by Hail's point. "Boss, are you saying that I come across as if I think I'm Super Cop?"

"No, Cav, but I hear you when you crawl on your soap box. You bitch about affirmative action standards and other policies. In the old days, before all this affirmative action shit, you'd never have been a lieutenant at 30. Even though you're white, they'd have passed you over to get to senior men."

Sean was still bothered by Hail's description of his career progress. "Sir, how do you figure I'm lucky? I don't consider it lucky to be involved in as many shootings as I have. My arrest and conviction numbers have squat to do with luck."

Hail could see his lecture had lost its intended direction.

"Cav, I said you were a good copper. I'm not talking about your arrests as an officer or while here at Homicide. Hell, if anything, you are a natural out on the street. For a suburban white boy, you get more out of the street slicks than most Black coppers. But you've been damn lucky at some of those shootings. You made yourself bait at an obvious ambush and survived. You could have been killed when your partner was shot at the dope house raid. Christ, the shoot-out at the bus depot nearly cancelled your ticket. You are obviously good under fire, Cav. But you were in combat. You know that you can do everything right and still buy it."

Sean felt better. Hail wasn't having his ass. He was just trying to keep Sean's head out of the clouds.

"O.K., Boss, I'll stay off my soap box and stay humble. I do feel very lucky. But you're right, I was starting to be pretty impressed with myself."

"Cav, you're a boss now. Just try to remember that every time you change your assignment, you start from scratch. Remember when you first got here, how you had to prove yourself to Gary? It will be no different now that you have a gold badge.

"Your first assignment will be easy. Those people in Robbery know you and know you're a good copper. If you leave there some day, it's back to square one.

"One other thing, stop thinking that everything going down is only happening to you. It can get in your way as a detective or street copper. It can destroy you as a boss. Don't take every pissy administration decision as a personal attack. Remember, when the shit hits the fan, everybody gets splashed.

"If you stay down to earth, you'll be a damn fine boss. If I see that you start to be some preppie, tight-ass who's become impressed with himself, I'm coming down the hall and boot you in the ass myself. Now go on, Lieutenant, report to the Robbery Section and make us proud of you."

Sean briskly strode out of Hail's office and returned to his own desk in the Homicide squad room. He sat behind his desk in a daze. A small group of detectives from their squad had gathered around his desk.

Gary stopped typing his report and he leaned across his desk toward Sean. "Hey, Partner, are you going to tell us what's going on, or do we have to read about it in some fucking department memo like everyone else?"

Sean took a sip from his cold coffee. "I made it. I move down the hall to the Armed Robbery-Major Theft Section. I'll be in charge of the squad that works with Homicide teams on robbery murders."

Sean stood and checked his tie knot again in the small mirror at the coat rack. "I've got to go meet my new Boss. I'll be back before lunch. I guess it's my treat, guys."

Gary extended his hand to Sean. "The Greek Town lounge after work, Partner. It's celebration time. I'll borrow a phrase from you, Cav. I hope you brought your checkbook."

Hail walked into the squad room after he saw that Sean had left. The men greeted their Section commander and offered him a coffee. Gary poured himself a fresh mug of coffee. "I hate to admit it, Boss, but I'm going to miss that preppie little shit."

Hail grinned and put his hand on Gary's shoulder. "We'll all miss him, Gary. Cav's a good detective already. You keep an eye on him. He'll be a commander in a few years, if he doesn't get himself in the jackpot. The department badly needs bright, street-wise, white command officers to help hold this mess altogether. And even this administration knows it."

It was just after 8 p.m. The majority of the well-wishers had gone, leaving Sean and Gary alone amidst the cluttered table at the rear of the Greek Town bar.

Gary emptied his glass and waved at the waitress. "Oh, Partner, I do believe that I'm shitfaced."

Sean looked down into the empty glass. "I'm on the way. With the excitement and the tolerance I've built up because of the way I've hit the bottle the last year, I'm still pretty straight."

"Listen, Cav, I might be way out of line, but I gotta get something off my chest while I'm drunk enough. Besides, once you're out from under my wing, who knows what you might do?"

"So, speak, old wise one."

"Holly is a beautiful young woman, Partner, and I'm sure she's a nice enough kid, but if you keep up this relationship with her, you're going to get hurt and hurt badly. You'll end up finally getting married, or you'll get her pregnant, then everybody suffers."

"Gary, inside I know you're right. The trouble is that I still love her too much to break if off, despite the nearly-continuous conflict. I don't have the courage to end it."

"Partner, this girl has got nothing to do with your son moving to Texas. Staying with Holly won't bring your son back. Let it go, and at least your friends won't have to watch you beat your head against the wall every day."

"Thanks, Gary, but I'm going to hang in there as long as I can."

"I figured, Kid. Well, now that you're a lieutenant, and you'll be leavin' Homicide, who's going to keep you out of trouble?"

"You mean like you did?"

"Don't be a smartass. You may be a lieutenant now, but I can still take you out back and whip your butt."

"Yes, Sir. Never any doubt about that, if we fought fair."

"A fair fight? Kid, I taught you never to use those words in the same sentence."

OCTOBER, 1978
JACKSON, MICHIGAN

T.J. stared out of the back window of his step-father's car. His parole finally granted, he was a free man for the first time since 1971. His mother and sisters had driven to the prison to get him. They chatted continuously during the drive to the family home on the near Eastside.

The thing that amazed T.J. the most was the way things hadn't changed. The cars were different, but with the exception of a few more vacant houses and vacant lots, the neighborhood didn't change.

There was a small welcome-home party. T.J. was not surprised by his step-father's coolness. The stern man shook T.J.'s hand and welcomed him home, but otherwise ignored him.

After the family gathering, T.J. retired to his basement bedroom. He couldn't believe he had been away so long. It felt as though every piece of modest furniture was an old friend. He went to the bottom drawer of his chest of drawers. He moved some clothing and took out a nearly-full bottle of Old Crow whiskey and a tattered cigar box. He sat on his bed. He took a swallow of the whiskey. He smiled and shook his head, "One hell of a way to age your whiskey; go to prison so you can't drink it up."

He opened the cigar box. Inside were numerous items that represented his life before prison. He took out his Marine dog tags. The chain still had a small C-ration can opener on it. He dug deep to the bottom and pulled out a photo taken with an Instamatic camera in December, 1967. He took another drink and grinned as he carefully studied the faces in the photo. There was the handsome, confident face of Lt. Fox. Kneeling in front of Fox was Yance. His little Soul Brother buddy, Mr. Cool, was standing next to T.J. Mr. Cool held his grenade launcher in his left hand and his right fist was raised in the air. Logs kneeled in front of Irish. Logs flashed the peace sign at the camera, while Irish pretended to be pulling the pin on a frag grenade behind him.

The whiskey warmed his insides as he stared at the photo. T.J. had never been happier with his life than he was when the photo was taken. He was very good at what he did. He helped his people, and they respected him. He had friends, Black and white, that he could trust his life to.

T.J. drifted off to sleep, holding the photo of his glory days and the nearly-empty bottle of seven-year-old whiskey.

T.J. didn't know that there was a copy of that photo in places of honor in homes and businesses across the country. Back in '75, Sean had come across the photo's negative. On a whim, he framed six 5x7 prints. After some research and help from a cop still in the Marine Reserve, he located the address of each member of the platoon in the photo.

In Portland, Oregon, the photo sat on the desk of corporate attorney Wayne "Yance" Yancy. In an Irish pub in Boston, the photo was displayed next to an oil portrait of a 19-year-old Marine, killed in Vietnam. The Logsdin family knew their son had grown up in the pub and loved it as much as they did. On the living room wall of a small frame home in Biloxi, Mississippi, the family of a proud young Black man, known to his friends as Mr. Cool, had placed the photo next to the collection of photos and medals dedicated to the son they'd lost. In the Miami, Florida office of James Fox, he displayed the photo on the wall next to the windows with a view of the ocean. Sean placed his copy on the wall of his den. He saved T.J.'s framed copy for his prison release. T.J. had often complained that it was difficult to secure personal items in prison. Few items were more personal to those involved than that 11-year-old picture.

———————

A month later, T.J. met Sean at a Downtown lounge. Sean came straight from his office at police headquarters. He spotted T.J. seated at a table with a view of the Detroit River. They exchanged a brisk "Brother" handshake and patted each other on the back.

"Oh my, Irish, look at you! Got you a fancy Dior trench coat. Son, you look like that dude Inspector Clouseau, in them *Pink Panther* movies. Now you're a lu-tenant and everything. Lu-tenant, my butt, you still always going to be a baby-face lance corporal to me."

Sean ordered a drink and slipped off his trench coat. "Tell you the truth, T.J., being called lieutenant still seems strange. I always think of Fox and it sounds too military. Someone will say 'Lieutenant,' and I wait around for someone else to answer up.

"You're looking fit, T.J. What are you up to?"

"I got me a job workin' nights at Chrysler's Jefferson assembly. They're bustin' my balls, but it's a job. I'm living with a lady friend over in that new development off of Mt. Elliot, near Lafayette."

Sean broke into a broad grin. "No shit, you're living with a lady? You didn't waste any time, did you Brother? Is it serious?"

T.J. grinned and ordered them both another drink. "Irish, I swear, you are one hopeless romantic dude. It ain't serious. It's kind of a business relationship. The lady is a whore. She works as an independent and don't want no pimp. So, she lets me live at her crib for free, like I'm her old man. She don't do no tricks at her own pad, so I got privacy. She lets me take care of business, whenever, and it don't cost me. Every small-time pimp on the Eastside was after her 'cause she's still pretty and ain't got to walk the streets yet. I act like a bad-ass gangster, you know, right outa prison. Since I moved in with her, ain't nobody bothered her. The lady is grateful and certainly knows how to show it in a most righteous manner."

Sean shook his head, but grinned broadly. "That sounds like one hell of a deal. Just be careful one of those asshole pimps doesn't decide to eliminate the competition."

"Hey, little Brother, you know I can take care of business out on the street. So how are things with you and your lady?"

Sean's expression changed, and he looked out the window at the river for a moment before he spoke. "We're still living together, but it's pretty fucked up."

"Irish, what you expect? You gonna have to learn not to fall in love every time you get your dick wet. The girl is only 21. You said that's why you and Lyn didn't make it, 'cause you got married too young. Well, you've had this girl wrapped up since she just finished high school. Brother, she's gonna break free, it's only a matter of time. I seen the lady's pictures. I understand why you're attracted to her but you met her five years too soon."

"Break free, my ass. I'm not holding her prisoner."

"No, but you ain't ready to let her go yet either. Irish, I'm sure the girl still loves you and don't want no one hurt. It probably ain't no easier for her to go, than for you to tell her to go."

"I love her, T.J."

T.J. leaned across the small table. "Yea, I'm sure you do, Irish. But we've had this lovin' bullshit conversation before, 'bout 10 years ago in a Da Nang hospital. Your son is in Texas. You're 30, a police lu-tenant and ready to settle down and be a man. She's 21 and never had the chance to be a kid. Like I told you when you got Dear Johned, you need her way more than she needs you."

"Brother, I do a hell of a job getting myself into those no-win situations, don't I?"

"Irish, you just gotta quit thinking with your dick. If you weren't such a tight-ass, I'd fix you up in a situation like I've got."

"Oh great, T.J. I can just picture me with a live-in whore as a roommate."

"Don't knock it 'til you tried it, Bro. Besides, I'd make sure she was white, so it didn't ruin your reputation."

"Well, don't go to any trouble on my account. When it comes to women, I am obviously capable of getting myself in enough trouble."

"You know, Irish, you so uptight. Why don't you stop over my new pad on your way home and have my lady take care of business and relieve some of that built-up pressure."

Sean smirked and looked across the table at his friend with a broad smile on his face. "I think I'll pass on that, T.J. I had no problem sharing canteens or C-rations or bomb craters with you, but this is a whole new ballgame."

"I never thought it of you, Irish: no balls. You gettin' conservative in your old age. I know what it is, like you not smokin' no cigarettes 'cause you were afraid you might like them and get hooked. You're afraid that once you had Black, you'd never go back. You're intimidated by that brown sugar, ain't you?"

"Now what makes you so damn certain I've never been with a Black chick?"

" 'Cause you've never been in love with one. And we both know you fall in love with every chick you ever screwed."

Sean slapped T.J.'s hand. "Well, I can't sue for the truth, Brother."

16
January, 1979

JANUARY, 1979
DETROIT, MICHIGAN

Being the lieutenant in charge of a squad of professionals from the Robbery Section was not unlike flying a plane on autopilot. Sean's squad was assigned to investigate robberies which involved a murder. They normally worked with a squad from the Homicide Section.

Sean's style of supervision was low-key with the experienced detective sergeants. Most of them called him "Lou," the semi-formal police abbreviation for lieutenant. When the Squad worked a case with Homicide's Sgt. Gary Burger, Gary still called him Cav, or just as often, Kid. It was not a gesture of disrespect, but rather a traditional priviledge extended to veteran ex-partners.

Sean's squad was established to work on serial robbery-homicides. They were often called on to assist Homicide or the Sex Crimes Section with other serious serial crimes.

Sean's squad was a unique mix of dedicated, experienced detective sergeants. The two female members had extensive investigative experience while they had worked at the Sex Crimes Section before their transfers. The male members, Black and white, had varied backgrounds, but they worked well together. There was very little friction, and they used each individual's strengths to improve the squad's effectiveness.

It seemed that whatever pleasure Sean enjoyed from his job was matched with conflict in his personal life. His relationship with Holly seemed to worsen by the week. Sean still held on to the hope that the problems would pass and their situation would improve. Nearly 31, Sean was finally ready for a life-long commitment. At least he thought he was.

At 21, Holly was feeling more trapped by the minute. She still loved Sean, but with their relationship starting the month after her graduation from high school, she couldn't help but feel that she had missed out on an important stage of growth. Their love affair was like a sled racing down a steep hill out of control, and neither of them could muster the courage to be the first to jump off.

A pair of vicious hold-up men had been making a twice-weekly sweep of Detroit's near Westside supermarkets. The two white men, both in their late 20s, had shot nine people in 12 robberies, two fatally. All of their shooting victims had been Black.

The squad's investigation was one dead end after another. Everyone hit on every informant they'd ever known, but there was no word of the two killers on the street. The department computers checked their M.O. against their description and came up blank.

Sean believed all that meant the robbers were from out-of-town. They would need a break, a real solid lead, if they were going to bust the killers before they tired of killing Black Detroiters and moved on to another city.

The squad brainstormed in their small squad room until after 7 p.m. Every bit of information they had covered a large chalkboard. The textbook exercise only served to increase their frustration. The collection of information drew them a large circle on the green slate.

Sean had called his house twice to let Holly know that he'd be late. He was mildly concerned when there was no answer.

Sean drove into his driveway just after 8 p.m. Holly's car was parked in its usual place near the garage, but the house was in total darkness.

There was a hand-written note propped upon the kitchen table. The brief message explained Holly's absence. Unannounced, Holly and her sister had decided to fly to Florida. She explained that she needed two weeks away to think over the future and to find herself. She hadn't informed him in advance because she didn't want him to try to talk her out of leaving, and she wanted no conflict that might influence her thoughts before the trip. She said she would call near the end of the two weeks and she hoped he would understand.

Sean didn't understand. He respected her need to sort things out, but an unannounced flight to Florida was nothing more than an act of cowardice as far as he was concerned. He had never even grabbed her in the heat of an argument. She had no reason to fear him and sneak away.

Sean crumpled the note into a ball and threw it into the sink. "I deserve more from her than a fucking note on the kitchen table," he said to himself.

Holly had gone to Florida *to find herself*. Sean decided to drive to his favorite local watering hole, Little Tony's, and try to find himself in the bottom of a whiskey bottle. He set out to do in one night with alcohol, what Holly planned to do in two weeks in Florida.

The following morning, Sean sat at his desk, staring out the window at the snowy January morning. Det. Sgt. Maggie O'Brien was walking past his desk, then stopped. "You look like your thoughts are a million miles away, Boss."

Sean looked up at the attractive female member of his squad. "Nope, Maggie, only about a thousand. On top of that, I've got the headache that devoured Cleveland."

"Do you have a cold, or is the headache self-induced?"

"I tried to drink up all of the Canadian Club on the Eastside last night."

"Did you succeed?"

"I only put a small dent in their inventory. This morning, my hair even hurts."

"I'm going for coffee. I'll bring you a fresh cup and a couple of aspirin."

"Maggie, you're a true Irish angel of mercy."

"Save the blarney, Lou. It doesn't appear you're up to it this morning. Are you problem-solving?"

"Problem-solving would not be correct . . . more like problem-forgetting."

She smiled and picked up Sean's empty coffee mug. "Well remember, Sister Maggie is always available for a shoulder to cry on. Lord knows, the past couple months you've heard about my divorce enough times. If you've got personal problems, I'm a good listener."

"Thanks, Maggie, it probably wouldn't hurt. Besides, I'm certain I'd feel better after talking to you than I do this morning. I know drinking doesn't solve any problems, but it helps numb you to the point that you don't give a darn."

Maggie smiled down at Sean. The tone in her voice was sympathetic, not condescending. "And this morning, you not only still have the problem, but you've also got a killer headache."

"You're right. Another year or two like this and I can leave my liver to the Wayne State medical school to use as a bad example. I tell you what, Maggie, if we get any lead on these two crazy supermarket killers, I'll take you up on your shoulder to cry on. Maybe I need some objective advice from a woman's point of view."

Maggie turned toward the coffee pots. "I've got a great deal of advice, Lou, but I'm not certain how objective it will be."

Sean wasn't certain what Maggie had meant. Except for Gary Burger, Sean had kept his private life just that, private. His squad knew he was engaged and living with a young woman. He suspected that most of them knew that there was now trouble in paradise. He wondered if they knew a lot more about him than he realized.

Clem and Ned Oley were brothers. Both in their late 20s, they were born and raised in some jerk-water town in West Texas.

The two sadistic young men gave new meaning to the term redneck. From the constant pinch of tobacco between their cheek and their gum, to their soiled yellow "Cat" tractor hats, they were a couple of good ol' boys. There was nothing they liked better than to turn up some shit-kicking tune on their favorite country-western radio station and sing along in a loud, off-key voice. Their second favorite thing was committing armed robberies and killing any Black citizens unfortunate enough to be at the scene at the time.

No one would ever know what motivated the Oley brothers to move their robberies on the road to the Midwest. Some would later surmise it was the lure of big city money. Others guessed their motivation was the easy opportunity to kill more Blacks, something they enjoyed more than armed robbery.

They had graduated to robbery-murder in Lubbock, Texas in October of '78. By January of '79, they had worked their way to Detroit, and were working on their grad degree in terror.

———————

The day after Sean's hangover, the squad finally received their first real lead. The Oley brothers hit that morning. During the robbery, they shot two Black store employees, one fatally. A witness recorded a license number of the get-away car.

Although the car had been stolen, the location from where it had been stolen and the vacant lot where it was later recovered, were only two blocks away from each other.

Sean held the entire squad overtime. Several blocks of the near Westside neighborhood were canvased, using expert composite drawings by the police artists.

At midnight, Sean and squad member Det. Sgt. Willie Henderson, entered a liquor store on the western edge of the Downtown Loop. The neighborhood consisted of dying old apartment buildings and vacant dwellings. The occupants remaining in the neighborhood made the liquor store a success.

In his Dior trench coat and three-piece suit, accompanied by a well-dressed Black man in a trench coat, Sean really didn't need to display his badge to the Black middle-aged liquor store owner.

"Sir, do you know either of these men or have you ever seen them?"

The man studied the photo-like police drawings over his glasses. "Yep."

Sean winced. He was in no mood to play games. "Yep, what?"

"Yep, I seen them and I knows where they stay. They're a couple of smartass honkies. They come in 'bout every night to buy cheap redneck whiskey and lots of chips and snacks an' shit. They always refer to me as a nig-ro, like I'm too stupid to realize they insulting me. Don't know their names, but one night they called and axed for a delivery to apartment four, in that ol' red brick building 'cross the street. They had some ladies wif them and didn't wanna come out in the cold. I had my nephew helpin' me that night, so I figure, what's the harm. Anyway, he brings over a box full of booze and snacks. Then the chumps stiffed him on the tip. Told him, his old nig-ro uncle already charged too much for the stuff."

Willie Henderson wrote in his small notebook. "How come you remember the apartment number?"

"It was four, sure enough. Four is my lucky number. It stuck in my mind."

Sean grinned over at Willie Henderson as if he'd won the Michigan lottery. "Can you describe what they wear?"

"Well, both about six-foot, kind of pale and skinny. They got a real thick Down-South accent, not like the Brothers or Michigan hillbillies. They talk kinda slow with a twang in their voice, like they fresh from some place else. One wears one of them yellow baseball type hats with 'Cat' on the front, you know, like them long-haul truck drivers wear. He's the one that also wears a wool red hunting jacket. He's always telling the other one in front of me that it's his coon-huntin' coat. Peckerwood mother fucker, like I'm so stupid I don't know what he means when he's sayin' coon. The other one, he mostly don't wear no hat. He wears one of them real dark blue double-breasted Navy coats, you know like the sailors wear."

"Have they been in tonight?"

"Yea, 'bout 9:30. If you all are going after them boys, I'd wait a spell, if I was you."

Willie put his notebook away in his coat pocket. "Why's that?"

"I figure they ain't right in the head. They act like they naturally mean. They bought a bunch of whiskey, as if they was celebrating somethin'. In a few hours, they'll be too fucked up to put up much of a fight."

Sean asked to use the phone in the rear of the store. Henderson stayed out front on the sales floor with the owner.

"Say, Officer, if you do tangle with them two honkies, you watch your hiney. They got a thing against the Brothers it seems."

Henderson lit a cigarette. "Thanks, Man. We already know that about them. I got a feeling that the white Lieutenant using your phone is going to give them a reason not to like white folks either. I think you just made four his lucky number."

Sean's phone call initiated a search warrant for the apartment and two John Doe arrest warrants.

Sean decided to raid the apartment with an arrest team at 5 a.m. The Robbery-Homicide Squad and uniform officer support would meet in a Robbery Section squad room at 4:15 for a quick briefing.

Sean and Henderson would stake-out the apartment building until they were relieved by another crew at 2 a.m.

Sean parked their unmarked car so they could observe both exits of the apartment building. He kept the motor running so they could keep the   heater on. The dry, warm air kept out the January chill.

Sean and Willie talked baseball for over an hour. Willie Henderson was in his early 30s and knew more about baseball than anyone Sean had ever known. Willie gave Sean a month-by-month account of the '68 Detroit Tiger season; the season Sean had missed while in Vietnam and the year the Tigers won the World Series against St. Louis in seven games.

Sean put a Tums in his mouth and grinned. "Willie, how did you get to know so much about baseball?"

The lean Black officer peered at the apartment building through powerful field glasses and spoke as he observed. "I grew up in the shadow of the stadium. We didn't have much money when I was a kid. But somehow my daddy always had enough to give me for bleacher seats. I don't think I missed a home game from when I was nine until I was out of high school. We had a small black and white T.V. I either listened to every away game, or watched those that were on T.V. I would keep the box scores and track each player's average."

Sean smiled at his junior partner for that night. "Who's your favorite Tiger, since you've been a baseball fan?"

Willie brought the glasses down from his eyes and rubbed away the temporary eye strain.

"I've always been a little guy, kind of short and skinny. I didn't start to grow until I was about 15. Up until then, I was one of the runts in my class. Willie Horton was my main man. I had the same first name as him and he was big and strong. When Willie got a hold of one, he could drive it into the cheap seats. Him playin' left field, I could see him pretty good, even from the bleachers. How about you, Boss? I hear you played ball in college and play some decent shortstop on some suburban softball team. Who was your favorite?"

Sean took his turn staring through the field glasses. "Willie, I've never played anything but short or second. But my favorite player has got to be Al Kaline. The man was a class act, a gentleman all the way."

Willie nodded his head. "I would have guessed Kaline would be your man."

Sean lowered the field glasses and glanced over at Willie. "How come you would have guessed Kaline?"

Willie took the glasses from Sean. "Lots of reasons. Most of them would sound like I was blowin' smoke."

Sean didn't push the question. He had a brief thought of Holly, but tried to concentrate on the important stake-out and force her from his mind.

"You seem like you got something heavy duty on your mind, Lou. These two dudes got you worried?"

"No, no more than any other assholes that go around killing people for the thrill of it. You know how it is, Willie. Hell, woman problems can make a confrontation with killers seem like a walk in the park."

"Oh my, I know where you're comin' from. I got divorced a couple years ago. We didn't have no babies, thank the Lord. I thought about gettin' married again. With this job it's a real bitch, even if you work good hours. It demands so much concentration. Then, you really can't talk about your work at home. Women can do a real number on your head. Like they say though, 'can't live with them, can't live without them.'"

Sean tried to rub the nervous tension from the back of his neck. "Yea, well, Willie, sometimes it's not our choice. The lady I've been living with for a couple of years just skyed out to Florida for a couple of weeks to be alone and find herself. I came home from work Monday evening to find a note on the kitchen table. Now, I've got to decide whether I want her back, if she decides she wants to come back."

Willie shook his head and lit a fresh cigarette. "You didn't know she was goin' until you come home and found the note?"

"Affirmative."

"Ouch. Man, you're hiding the shit real well, Boss. It's got to be a real bitch comin' to work with all that on your mind."

Sean tried to hide his flush of embarrassment by holding the field glasses back up to his eyes. "No, being this busy really helps me keep my mind off of it. If I went home, I'd just crawl into a bottle and feel sorry for myself."

They were relieved at 2 a.m. Sean drove to an all-night Coney Island restaurant on West Lafayette St., and they both ate a couple of chili dogs while they read over the early edition of the *Detroit Free Press*.

They went back to the Robbery Section offices. Both shaved and washed up in the Fifth Floor men's room. They always kept clean shirts and skivvies in their lockers.

As the squad began to file into their squad room at 4 a.m., Sean and Willie felt refreshed and charged with a sense of excitement and anticipation. Neither seemed the worse from the lack of sleep during the overnight assignment.

The restless but sleepy group was gathered in full by 4:15. Sean stood next to a chalkboard and went over each individual's assignment and the overall plan for their arrest raid.

Willie Henderson sat in the front row and studied his squad commander. He considered Cavanagh a unique dude. Pretty white Lieutenant with his expensive wardrobe and styled hair, grad school education. Would have figured him to be a real tight-ass boss, but Henderson found Sean easy to talk with, and even easier to work for. For a white guy, he found Sean to have street smarts and he was intense without having the squad's ass all the time.

After the briefing, the group broke for their vehicles. Gary caught up with Sean in the hall. "Say, Cav, all this shit with Holly's unannounced sabbatical, are you up to this?"

Sean patted Gary on the back. "Be fair, Gary. Have I ever let my personal life interfere with my performance on the street?"

Gary became unusually serious. "That's just the point, Cav, I'm not certain. The night of the bus station shoot-out, was any of that even remotely connected with those phone calls home while Holly was out?"

There was a brief pause. "I swear, Gary, if I thought it might interfere in any manner, I'd step aside. I know I talked you into going that night, but this morning, we're holding arrest and search warrants. We've got over a dozen well-armed, veteran plain clothes and uniform coppers who are going to make the arrest. It's been organized like a damn military operation. Be honest, Partner, would you do anything differently if this was your show?"

Gary half grinned. "Yea, I'd lead the group going in and have you with the people covering an alley escape attempt."

"No way, Partner. If you agree that all of the elements of our arrest attempt are sound, I go in the front door. You know that's the way it works. The one who's named in the search warrants leads the way. Like you taught me, it's tradition."

"Yea, well, watch your ass in there, Kid. I've grown rather fond of you. If anything ever happened to you, I'd have no one to fuck with."

"It warms my heart that someone cares."

Gary finished the coffee in his styrofoam cup. "Who's going in with you on the first wave again. I forgot the names."

Sean rubbed his tired eyes and combed his hair. "Two uniforms, Henderson, Van and O'Brien."

Gary frowned and gave Sean a serious stare. "O'Brien? Cav, are you sure?"

"Yea, Maggie has covered every back door since I took over the squad last Fall. She's a good detective, she shoots well at the range. It's about time she got off the bench and started with the first team on a real ass-kicker. There will be 12 of us going in the front, in two waves. She should be alright. Gary, they put these women here. They seem ready and willing to do the job. I'm not going to carry them forever."

Gary frowned. Sean had not convinced him. "If you ask me, it's like starting a rookie quarterback against the Steeler defense. If you're wrong, it's your ass."

"That's right and that's why she's coming on this one. You just keep those people in the alley behind some solid cover. I don't want any sort of repeat of our bus station experience. I sure as hell don't want back-up people hurt. This thing is already bad enough."

The 5 a.m. arrest raid was tactically a sound decision. The liquor store owner suggested that the two Oley brothers would still be sleeping off their drunk. With the apartment house located on the western fringe of the Downtown Loop, in a tough ghetto area, even those streets would be deserted at 5 a.m. in mid-Winter. In January, even the street people were in bed at that hour. It was also about an hour before the morning traffic started filling the streets.

The old six-story apartment building had long since lost her pride. The stained and soiled red brick walls stood against the bite of the cold wind that swept off of the river, but they revealed her decay and the years of standing in the midst of the city's polution. The once-handsome apartment building now waited its turn with those around her to become the next victim of the wrecking ball of urban renewal. While it waited, it had become the home of an assortment of human parasites. Apartments that had been home to proud ethnic families now housed small-time pimps, whores, dopers and most recently, two good ol' boys from West Texas who killed people.

The four police cars full of assorted officers drove to an empty parking lot a half block from the apartment house, but out of its sight.

The officers stepped from their vehicles and moved to their pre-determined assignments with little discussion. There was an obvious lack of conversation or gallows humor. As the officers moved toward the building, there seemed to be an unusual, collective, unspoken concern.

The entry plan was simple. The entry personnel were divided into two, six-member units. Unlike television police raids, real raids resembled a cluster fuck much more than a planned, well-organized para-military operation. It would be difficult enough getting six officers into the apartment at once, 12 would be impossible. The second wave would enter as soon as the first had cleared the doorway.

Sean waited with his people outside, waiting for Gary to secure the alley. Gary signaled that they were in position.

Sean put his search warrants into the inside pocket of his suitcoat. He removed his small portable radio from his trench coat and acknowledged Gary's report.

Sean's mind wandered a thousand miles away for an instant. He became fascinated by the steam of his own breath in the cold, January, early morning air. He knew that Holly would not be seeing her breath down in Florida that same morning. He ached inside when he thought of her that far from him. He considered what she might be doing a thousand miles away from that cold Detroit sidewalk at that exact moment. She was probably still sleeping. Sean felt helpless, standing on the cold, wind-swept sidewalk, where he could only pray that she was sleeping alone.

Willie Henderson nervously wiped his sweaty palms on his trousers. His mouth was dry. He made a curious visual study of his young Lieutenant. Cavanagh seemed detached from the tension around him. His voice was unnaturally calm. His face did not express the stress of the moment. Willie was unsettled. Cavanagh, dressed in his expensive wardrobe, looked more like a bored male model waiting for a location catalog photo session to begin than the senior officer of a dangerous arrest attempt. Willie wiped his damp hands again. "Ain't right. The dude is just too cool," he thought.

Sean carried his .45 in a shoulder holster. He wanted the added firepower against this pair of crazies. He had left his revolver back in his desk.

The officers quietly entered the old apartment building and moved in a silent file down the halls to apartment number four, on the ground floor. Then they formed into two smaller groups, huddled on either side of the apartment door.

Sean drew his weapon. He spoke into the small portable police radio as he stepped in front of the door. "Robbery-six-oh to all units. Showtime." He slipped the radio back into his coat pocket and held his .45 with both hands.

Sean's first kick at the door broke the lock from the frame. His second kick tore the night chain from the door and the door burst fully open.

The first wave poured in. Two uniform officers followed Sean. They went to the small living room in the middle of the apartment.

The second wave of six officers followed. There was a chorus of shouts of identification and warnings to surrender.

Sean pointed to a door down a small hall, just past the bathroom. It appeared to be a bedroom door. A uniform officer and Maggie O'Brien moved to the closed, frail, wood door, as Sean moved to cover their advance.

The uniform officer, armed with a shotgun, kicked open the door. He and Maggie rushed in, as Sean covered their entry from the doorway.

Ned Oley was somehow still asleep on a filthy twin bed. A Luger 9mm pistol sat on the nightstand next to the bed. An empty bottle of Wild Turkey whiskey was next to the pistol.

Maggie took a step toward the sleeping suspect, hand cuffs in hand. Sean raised his .45 to eye level. "Stop Maggie! You can't see both of his hands. His right hand is under his pillow. He's either sleeping off a drunk or playing possum, with a gun under that pillow."

Maggie stopped as if she were about to step on a snake.

Sean quickly and carefully moved next to the gunman, never losing sight of the suspect's hands. At the same instant, Sean jammed his .45 in the man's ear and grabbed the wrist of the hand concealed by the pillow.

Ned Oley had been, in fact, still sleeping. He was also holding a .41-magnum revolver in his right hand, under the pillow. He never got a chance to use it.

The uniform officer and Maggie handcuffed Ned Oley before he completely woke up. He shook his head as if to clear it from the daze of his severe hangover. "Hey, what the fuck is this?"

"This is you going to jail for robbery and murder. I have a search warrant for this lovely apartment and an arrest warrant for you and your partner."

"Fuckin' pigs, you're lucky you come in here while I was sleeping."

"Yea, with all the unarmed, helpless people you two have greased, you heroes strike fear in the hearts of brave cops across the country."

"Take these cuffs off, pig, and I'll show you how . . ."

"Save the motor-mouth routine, asshole. Officer, read him his rights. Take him out into the living room until the whole apartment is secured."

On the way out of the bedroom, Maggie carefully checked under the bed and Sean checked the closet. A complete search would come after they located the second suspect.

They entered the living room with the suspect. He was flanked by the uniform officer and Maggie. Sean was the last out of the hall and he stood behind the dazed, handcuffed Ned Oley.

Clem Oley had never gone to bed that night. He got drunk with his brother, but he was too excited about their new lethal purchase to sleep. He had cleaned and admired their new 9mm MAC-10 submachine gun all night. He had alcohol-induced visions of shooting scores of Blacks with a simple long burst from the small but deadly automatic weapon.

As the officers began to enter the apartment, Clem was in the kitchen, out of view from the door to the outside hall. He managed to squeeze himself into the narrow broom closet. Hidden there, he was passed by during their initial entry search.

Sean was about to call out a warning to the officers in the apartment that the second suspect could be hidden anywhere. He never got the chance.

Clem Oley's near panic of being trapped in the narrow closet was balanced by the feeling of power the new MAC-10 gave him.

Dressed only in his underwear, Clem Oley burst from the small closet. A blind spray of 9mm rounds into the kitchen hit Van in the arm and sent Willie Henderson diving to the cover of the refrigerator.

Clem ran toward the door to the outside hall.

Sean heard himself say "Shit," as Clem ran into the living room and turned the MAC-10 at them. Sean raised his .45 with his right hand and pushed Maggie to the floor with his left.

The long vicious burst of 9mm fire from the MAC-10 tore up the opposite wall of the living room. The uniform officer fired his shot gun once, but he was hit by 9mm fire and went down. Sean fired over the right shoulder of their prisoner, Ned Oley, until he fell to the floor in a jerking motion.

Sean hit brother Clem with his .45, and some of the shotgun buckshot had entered Oley's left leg. Clem still managed to take cover behind a couch and reload the MAC-10 with a full 30-round magazine.

Sean quickly changed magazines in his .45. The arrest attempt had turned to shit. There were bodies everywhere.

The moment that Sean was reloaded, he advanced on the hidden gunman's position behind the old couch. Every second that passed increased the risk.

Sean fired three shots into the couch, hitting Clem once in the stomach. Clem left his position, barely able to hold onto the MAC-10. He struggled to his fet. As his torso came into view from behind the couch, Sean and Maggie opened fire. Maggie was still on the floor but had moved into position to fire while the gunman reloaded.

As Sean's powerful .45 rounds hit Clem Oley, Clem sprayed 30 rounds of unaimed 9mm rounds around the apartment.

Sean's last shot caused a massive head wound and the lifeless body of the young killer from West Texas bounced off the wall and crumbled to the floor. Willie Henderson and the other uniform officer ran into the living room a moment later.

Sean's position remained frozen, aimed at the body of the gunman. He had instinctively reloaded the .45. Not moving his stance, Sean spoke.

"Maggie, are you hurt?"

There was a brief pause. Maggie's voice was not normal, but it did not sound as if she was in pain. "I'm alright."

"Willie, what have we got?"

"Van is in the kitchen. He's been hit in the arm. He's bleedin' bad. I don't know how bad it is. He's conscious."

Sean finally lowered his .45. He looked down at the handcuffed body of Ned Oley. He had taken several hits and he appeared to be dead. Clem Oley was obviously dead. The uniform officer that had been with Sean was hit in the legs, but he remained conscious.

Sean spoke calmly and barely raised his voice. "Willie, go back and help Van until E.M.S. gets here. Try to stop the bleeding, but watch for broken bones. Maggie, help this uniform officer. Just use direct pressure. We don't want to make it worse until we're certain he didn't get a femur broken. Webster, seal off this apartment. No one under the rank of lieutenant comes in until E.M.S. and Code 2400 get here, except for Sgt. Burger."

Sean held his radio to his face and calmly spoke to the dispatcher. He identified himself, gave their location to the dispatcher again and made his request for assistance.

"Notify the Medical Examiner. We will have two to go, not police personnel."

Sean looked over to Maggie, who stood next to him staring at the gore of the mangled corpse of Clem Oley. "Are you hurt, Maggie?"

"No, Sir."

"Then either go help the wounded officer or I'll ask someone else. Damn it, move or let me know you can't."

She started to tear up an old sheet for compresses and kneeled at the wounded officer's side. Sean looked down at the uniform officer, who looked up and forced a smile.

"No sweat, Lou. My ballistics vest took a couple hits, probably saved my bacon. Now I have a pretty Detective Sergeant looking after me, I'll be fine."

Sean bent down and shook his hand. "I know you will. You did a hell of a job, Officer. Just relax. E.M.S. will be here any minute."

Sean moved toward the kitchen to check on Van and ordered Clem Oley's body covered. The sight of the dead man did nothing for his own chances of keeping the early morning chili dogs where they belonged.

Gary Burger joined him. He put his hand on Sean's shoulder. "You were right, you should have led the arrest team while I covered the back. I'm way too old for this shit. I swear to Christ, Cav, you are a shit magnet. You plan a textbook arrest raid and one of the assholes buys a machine gun the night before and decides to stay up all night. You may have the looks and the money, but you don't have squat for luck."

"You know what they say, Gary, lucky in love . . ."

They checked on Van, who was still in the kitchen with Willie Henderson. Sean carefully inspected Van's wound. The wound was a through-and-through to his upper left arm. Van seemed to be more upset about the damage to his suitcoat and trench coat than the wound to his arm. Sean took Willie aside and assured him that his buddy Van would be fine and not to worry.

Minutes later, Fire Department personnel took the wounded uniform officer and Van to the neary-by city hospital. The bodies of the Oley brothers would be removed when the Crime Scene personnel were through with the apartment, and taken directly to the Morgue.

Sean and Maggie had helped lift the wounded uniform officer onto a stretcher. When they had finished, Sean noticed the expression on Sgt. O'Brien's face. He firmly grabbed her by the forearm. "Maggie, the bathroom is in that little hall we passed through to get to the bedroom."

She meekly nodded and quickly walked to the bathroom where she closed and locked the door.

The field duty officer, Code 2400, arrived at the scene and Sean explained the arrest attempt in detail.

The veteran commander carefully inspected the body of the dead, handcuffed prisoner.

"Let the evidence people do their thing with photos and physical evidence. I'll request an immediate post on this one here. When a handcuffed suspect gets killed, the media drools on itself. It's obvious to me he was killed in the cross fire. We must determine by whom, as soon as possible. Lt. Cavanagh, we'll talk after you and your people have made their statements at Homicide. What do we know about these two assholes?"

Sean handed the commander a pair of Texas driver's licenses.

"Brothers, from a town near Lubbock. The hand guns and descriptions are right on. We found some checks from three of the stick-ups and a couple of grand in cash. They are running an N.C.I.C. check on them now. The information will be waiting for us at Homicide."

The commander looked at the MAC-10 next to the bloodied body and then at the countless bullet holes in the walls. "You know, Cavanagh, when I worked the street, a couple of hick cowboys like this would blow into town armed with single-action revolvers. Now, they're armed with magnums and fucking machine guns. Damn, two rednecks from Po-dunk, Texas with a fucking machine gun."

———————

Maggie O'Brien was leaning up against an unmarked police car in the small parking lot where they had left their vehicles. She was pale and stared at the pavement, deep in thought.

Sean walked up and offered her a stick of chewing gum. "Here, Kiddo. This will freshen your mouth and help to settle your stomach."

She did not lift her head, but she nodded a silent thank you as she put the gum in her mouth. "I've seen a lot of homicides. How did you know I was going to be sick?"

"Come on, Maggie, we're Irish. I recognized the shade of green."

"I'm so damn embarrassed, I don't know if I can face the rest of the squad. First, I freeze, then I got sick like some damn rookie at my first sight of blood."

Sean put his hand on her shoulder. "Knock it off, Sgt. O'Brien. First of all, you didn't freeze. You had the self-control to help the wounded officer before you became ill. I'm the only one that knows you lost your breakfast. Secondly, I've read your file. This was your first shoot-out. It's not the same as driving up and looking at a dead body. Having someone shoot at you with a sub-machine gun would ruin anyone's morning. You had the courage to return fire. So you hesitated for a moment when it was over, that's not the same as freezing."

Tears rolled down her cheeks. "You pushed me out of the way and saved my life. You just stood there and . . ."

"Knock it off, Maggie, I didn't save anyone. I'm the one who took you all in there, remember? I only responded to previous training and experience. The shooter was still half drunk and he didn't know his new weapon yet. Had he been sober, he probably would have realized how badly he was initially hurt and given it up. With that kind of firepower, he could have shot half the squad by mistake if we hadn't taken him out right away."

Maggie held her hand out. It was obviously shaking. She put the hand on Sean's arm. "Look at me, I'm a wreck."

Sean gave her a clean handkerchief. "Come on, wipe you eyes, blow your nose, and drive with me to Homicide. We've got a hell of a report to write. We'll talk later. I heard the squad talking already. When they're done with us at Homicide, we're meeting for a drink at the lounge in Greek Town."

Sean started the car's engine. He offered Maggie the use of the rear view mirror so she could freshen up her make-up. "Boss, I know I gave you a temperance lecture a day ago, but I could really use a drink."

Sean smiled and adjusted the mirror when she was finished using it. "You, me, and everyone else at the scene this morning. It's frightening enough out here, Maggie. Shoot-outs are a whole different ball game. Machine guns are the Super Bowl."

Maggie O'Brien took a deep breath and concentrated on at least appearing to be more relaxed. "Lieutenant, you are so calm. You seem so unaffected by all of this."

"It's all a mental defense mechanism. I'm just whistling past the graveyard."

––––––––––––

It was lunch hour for most of the citizens of Detroit. For the small group of cops who had been on the 5 a.m. arrest attempt, it was the end of what had been an unique 28-hour work day.

Their first round of drinks initiated nervous chatter.

Sean was still closing out his reports at the Homicide Section offices. He surrendered his .45 and recovered his .357 from his desk. The group kept a chair in the center of their table vacant, awaiting his arrival.

The group gave a standing ovation to Det. Sgt. Mark Van, as he entered the bar. His arm was in a sling, he had been released from the hospital after treatment for the superficial gunshot wound.

Willie Henderson found a chair for his partner. "Say, Dude, if they let you out of the hospital, shouldn't you be home resting?"

Van poured himself a glass of beer from the pitcher. "Hell no, Willie. Since my divorce, I go home to an empty house. Why should I go and drink alone and buy my own beer, when I can come here, and get lots of sympathy from my friends, while they buy beers for their wounded partner?"

Gary signaled to the waitress that the group had an additional member. "Hey, Van, did you see Lt. Cavanagh? Do you know how long before he'll be here?"

Van took a couple swallows of his beer. "Yea, we talked. He'll be right over. The man needs a drink. I think he's got a case of the ass with a couple of new sergeants from Internal Affairs. He goes through the whole routine, lawyer, L & S representative, reports, statements, interviews, the whole nine yards. It's all wrapped up and in walk the two tight-asses from Internal Affairs. I guess they heard that a handcuffed prisoner got greased and rushed to Homicide without doing their homework. Well, ol' Cavanagh is not in the mood to play. This one I.A. guy asks Cavanagh why he fired 15 shots. The Lieutenant gets up in his face and says, 'Because I ran out of fucking rounds.' The I.A. Sergeant says it seems like a lack of firearms discipline. Cavanagh asks him if he knows how many shots the asshole fired. He didn't. When Cavanagh finds out the two I.A. guys don't even know about two coppers being wounded, Cmdr. Hail had to stop the Lieutenant from going over the desk after those two. Cmdr. Hail gets a call from the Morgue and orders the two I.A. guys off the Fifth Floor."

"Van, what did the goddamn Morgue have to say?"

"Oh, no doubt, the handcuffed prisoner was greased by his own brother, not even scratched by any copper's gun."

There was another loud ovation from the small group.

Willie Henderson downed a shooter of Kessler's whiskey and chased it with a sip of beer. He bobbed his head and patted Van on the back, obviously pleased his wounded partner was well enough to join them.

"Hey, did you all check out the Lu-tenant this morning? I spent most the night working with him. We found the liquor store owner that I.D.ed the shooters, did a couple hours stake-out, ate chili dogs, rapped for a long time. The man doesn't lay out any bullshit. He seems to be down to earth and a stand up dude. We've all worked for him since last September. Some of you worked with him when he partnered with Burger. I've never seen him chew a copper's butt. Hell, I've never heard him raise his voice. Then, this morning, our baby-faced Lieutenant pulls this big .45 pistol out of his designer trench coat and stands tall against some fool with a mother-fuckin' machine gun. He blows the guy all over the wall and the expression on his face doesn't even change. He pulls out his radio and calls for assistance in a calmer voice than I use to order a pizza, and there's bodies everywhere. It's suddenly like I don't know the man. He was so damn calm and cool, he was down right cold. It's kind of spooky. I mean, at 2 a.m. we're talking baseball and personal man talk. At 5 a.m. he blows up a guy and doesn't even wince."

Gary finished his first drink. "Just let it alone, Henderson. Would you feel more confident following his orders at another shooting if he would have pissed himself or cried or thrown himself on the floor."

"No, it's not that, Gary. I guess it's that he showed nothing. Shit, I'd follow that man anywhere. I sense that he felt responsible for all of us in there. I do know one thing for certain. I'm goddamn glad the man decided to be a cop instead of a crook. I'm glad he's on our side."

Sean entered the bar and gave his drink order to the waitress as he passed her station at the bar.

He seated himself at the vacant chair of honor. He greeted everyone and changed the subject when they asked about his confrontation with Internal Affairs.

"They were just doing their job. I'm overtired and got a little short with them."

Van laughed out loud.

Sean leaned across the table. He smiled at his slightly-wounded subordinate squad member. "That arm in a sling just might keep you on the light-duty desk until 1980."

"My lips are sealed, Lou."

"Somehow I doubt that, Van. Let that story die a natural death. We sure don't need an on-going pissing contest with I.A."

They ordered lunch. The alcohol and the increased time since the shoot-out began to ease the tension.

Maggie was pensive and quieter than normal. Every time Sean looked in her direction, he caught her staring at him.

After lunch, Sean stood to propose a toast.

"By the way, N.C.I.C. says our boys were from Hockley, Texas. They did some hard time for robbery and they were out on parole. As most of you know, the dipshit with the MAC-10 greased his own brother. The uniform copper that was wounded is stable and he will make a full recovery. Obviously our man Van is alright, if he doesn't piss off his Lieutenant. The asshole with the MAC-10 was hit by the uniform officer's buckshot in the legs. Maggie, you hit him once with your .38 and I've been suspended until the shooting board and the Prosecutor's office makes their decision. We all know that's procedure. O.K., salute to Maggie and Willie for not getting shot, to Van and Officer Warner's full and speedy recovery and to the asshole who was the worst shot with a MAC-10, east of Texas."

The group raised their glasses and toasted.

Gary stood and held Sean in a strong grasp hug across his shoulders. "I toast Lt. Cavanagh, who made working 28 hours straight and the shootout possible. As always, when it comes to stepping into shit, we couldn't do it without him."

They all laughed and raised their drinks.

The alcohol and lack of sleep began to take its toll on the group, as they began to come down from their adrenaline high. The only one of the group who did not seem affected by the alcohol was the only member that wanted it to, Sean.

They broke up their informal meeting so they could still drive home before the afternoon traffic rush began.

Sean walked from Greek Town to the parking structure near police headquarters. He was surprised to find Maggie waiting at his car.

"Are you going to be alright, Lou?"

"I'm fine, Maggie. How about you? We didn't get a chance to talk back at the bar."

"What are you going to do now, tonight?"

"I'm still wound up pretty tight. When I finally relax, I'll probably put on some sad records, get numb and feel sorry for myself."

She looked down at the pavement floor of the garage.

"My son stays with my parents in Roseville, since the divorce. I have a two-bedroom condo on East Jefferson, with a great view of the river. I was wondering... I really need to talk to someone about this and if you didn't have plans..."

"Sure, Maggie, but would you prefer a neutral location?"

"How about you stop by your place for a change of clothes? Like I said, I have a guest room. When you do unwind, you may be in no condition to drive home. Unless, of course, you're afraid it would compromise you in some way, if you spent the night?"

Sean smiled and put his arms around Maggie. "Sgt. O'Brien, we'd really have to misbehave in order to compromise me. I accept your offer and I'll be over with a fresh suit for tomorrow and my overnight gear. You're trembling, Kiddo. Are you alright?"

Maggie O'Brien rested her head up against Sean's chest. She softly cried. "I'm so damn scared and confused."

Sean gently patted her on the back. "Leave your car here. Come with me while I get my things and we'll talk on the way to your place. Maybe that way, we'll be relaxed enough to get drunk by the time we get to your place. You're just overtired. Your resistance is down."

She looked up at Sean. "I've got a stereo and a stack of sad records. We can feel sorry for ourselves together."

Sean looked down into Maggie O'Brien's soft green eyes. For the first time he let himself see her as only an attractive young woman, not a police detective subordinate. Her soft, pale green eyes were still filled with tears.

"I'm sorry. I'm making a fool of myself."

"No, Maggie. Don't worry about that silly police crap. We're alone, we're friends. Don't be embarrassed with me. If we are really going to be friends and help each other, you can't hold anything back. If you're really going to work through what happened today, you've got to let it go."

She put her head back against his chest. "Do you let it go?"

"A few more drinks, the sad records, a view of the river. Hell, once I get started, I may not quit for a week."

"That's fine with me. I've got the time off coming to me."

"Wouldn't be much of a way to spend a week's vacation."

Maggie wiped her eyes and got into Sean's car, "Let me be the judge of that."

They watched the Winter sunset from Maggie's tenth-floor river-front condo porch.

Sean had taken a long, hot shower and changed into his Adidas warm-up suit and jogging shoes.

Maggie had showered and wore a long, thick burgundy designer robe. She had opened the large glass doorwall and the brisk Winter air smelled clean coming off the ice of the river.

They stood together in silence, watching the sun disappear behind the Downtown skyline. The cold air made Maggie shiver. Sean put his arm around her shoulders and held her close for warmth.

Maggie sipped white wine from a long-stemmed glass. She closed the doorwall and they sat on huge pillows on her living room floor.

"I really appreciate you coming over tonight, Lieutenant. I don't know what I'd have done if I had to face tonight alone."

"Maggie, I'm sitting in your living room, drinking your whiskey, after using your shower. I don't think you will damage. my professional integrity by calling me Sean. And you don't have to thank me for coming over. I didn't enjoy the idea of being alone. I should be thanking you. I've been asked to do worse things than spend the evening with an attractive young woman in a great place like yours."

Maggie smiled and moved her pillows so she was seated next to him. "It's still early. We'd better clear the air so we know if there are to be ground rules."

Sean couldn't prevent the involuntary grin. "Ground rules?"

"I asked you here because of the shooting. I asked you here because I knew that, as my boss and my friend, you would help me. Well, that's only part of it, Sean. I was attracted to you when you were still working Homicide with Gary, even before my divorce. When I transferred to Robbery and you were promoted and took over the squad, the attraction turned into a school-girl crush. I've known your personal relationship has been on the rocks. The whole truth is that I have a transfer back to the Sex Crimes Section on hold, waiting for the outcome of your personal situation. If you broke up, I'd have been a great deal more subtle. But with your fiancee running off to Florida, then this morning's shooting, all subtle plans seemed very childish."

Sean could not conceal his surprise. He stared into Maggie's eyes and took her hand. "Look, for once I don't know what to say. Maggie, I couldn't help but to be attracted to you. As your Lieutenant, I couldn't even hint I thought of you as anything but another cop."

"And now, Sean, what does all that mean here and now?"

Sean paused to gather his thoughts. He took a sip of his drink and looked back into her eyes. "Maggie, two people could not be more vulnerable than we are tonight. We both have personal problems, the trauma of the shooting, our mutual attraction, I feel like a couple of characters in some dramatic World War II movie."

Maggie stared back, her expression sincere.

"I really need to talk about today. I want you to know up front that I would like there to be more to the next couple of days than just conversation. When all this is over, in a few days, each of us can make some kind of a decision. Maybe I'll realize it just won't work out. You can decide to go back with your fiancee. No promises from either of us, no expectations. We merely help each other get through the next couple of days and go back to the reality of everyday life when it's over. If nothing else, it will be one hell of a great adventure."

"Maggie, we'e setting ourselves up to get hurt. We shared an experience today that most friends, lovers, or even married couples never face together in a lifetime. We literally faced death together. We risked our own safety to protect each other while we took another human life. Those extreme emotions leave a greater impression than any physical attraction. If I'm a bum lay, you'll forget about that in six months. You'll never forget what we did this morning. We've got to go into this thing with our eyes wide open. It could be very easy to fall in love. We're both very tired, confused, lonely, and still damn frightened."

Maggie held Sean's right hand in both of hers. "We've worked together every day for nearly four months. We've done everything but sleep together. I already love you, Lieutenant."

Sean took another thoughtful sip from his glass. "I respect you too much to treat you like some school kid with stars in her eyes. I'm really whipped and not strong enough to set any ground rules, even if I wanted to."

They ate a light dinner, then sipped wine and talked until after midnight.

Maggie covered them with a warm, hand-made afghan, when the slight draft from the glass doorwall gave them a chill.

Their first kiss was brief and innocent, as if a good-night gesture. What followed was passion charged by the extreme emotions of the day and their individual building need for comfort.

They made love into the early morning hours.

Sean was gently awakened by Maggie, who was standing over him, a mug of fresh coffee in her hand.

"Good morning, Lieutenant. You'd better get in gear, Mister. It's bad form to be late for a fatal shooting investigation."

Sean squinted as he focused his eyes on the clock radio.

He sat up in bed and sipped the hot coffee, trying to force himself to fully awaken. "Call the Motor Traffic Section, I feel like I've been run over by a truck."

"Well, Don Juan, you could have slept instead of . . ."

"Whoa, on second thought, I don't feel that tired. A shower and a clean suit, and I'll be good as new."

"I'll ride in with you and pick up my car from the parking garage. If you'd like, I'll stop by your place and pick up some more things. I understand these shooting boards can be pretty hairy. This way, you can come directly here and crash, if you still intend to spend a few days here."

Sean savored each sip of coffee. "That would be thoughtful, Maggie. By the way, after last night, I'd like to add a few adjectives to you being bright, sensitive and . . ."

"I accept the compliment, Sean, you need not be specific. And while we're on the topic, remember your analogy last night? Well, for the record, I'll remember last night for much longer than six months."

"I bet you say that to all your lieutenants."

"Come on, smart guy, or you'll be late."

Unlike the television cops, it was not the norm for detective sergeants and lieutenants to be involved in fatal shootings of suspects. Uniform and plain clothes street officers faced the brunt of the daily danger and extreme violence.

Sean felt he had been treated with kid gloves during the bus station shooting board while a detective sergeant. As a lieutenant, he was given the V.I.P. treatment. The physical evidence, half a dozen eye witnesses, and two wounded cops made the killing of two white suspects anything but political fodder for the Detroit media. The unique twist of fate that one suspect killed his own brother in the crossfire was more of a news story than the young Detective Lieutenant with a familiar name. Except for his run-in with I.A., it was uneventful.

Sean identified himself to the security guard in the lobby of Maggie's condo. He called up to get her approval to let Sean in. Sean considered getting a blank search warrant to carry with him if he ever arrived when Maggie was out of the building.

She greeted him with a hug. "Well, how was it?"

"It was a hell of a lot different than when I was still a patrolman. They walked me through it once, bought me lunch in Greek Town and gave me the rest of the week off. They waived my visit to the shrink, and the prosecutor has already cleared me. I even got a call from the C.O. of Internal Affairs about yesterday."

"Well, we don't go back to work until Monday. What do you want to do until then?"

Sean eased out of his trench coat and suit jacket. "We'll think of something, I'm sure."

The following week back at work was uneventful.   Sean and Maggie concealed their new relationship from the squad. They would arrive and leave in their own vehicles, but ended their day at the same place, Maggie's well-furnished, river-front condo.

That Saturday evening, they again stood together and watched the sunset from her small porch. They both knew that their adventure was about to end.

"Maggie, Holly's coming back tomorrow evening. She called me at work and asked to speak to me at my house when she gets in."

"You know I love you, Sean, but it's too close to the excitement for me to know how much. I know you care for me. What do you feel you have to do?"

"I have to be there to talk to her. I guess you know that, too. I suppose I won't know how I really feel about her until she and I speak face to face. I'm asking a lot, but I'm asking you to let me talk with her and sort it out. I've got to know for certain, or it will always hang over our heads. I won't leave you up in the air. I'll be up front with you as soon as it's sorted out."

"Sean, I want to give our relationship every chance possible. You go sort it out tomorrow. If you two split, I'll transfer back to Sex Crimes Section next week and we'll let it run its course."

"Maggie, we've got a lot of stuff in our way: we're both on the rebound; we're both dedicated cops; I haven't even met your son yet; your ex-husband is a copper at the 15th Precinct; we can't match the emotions of our first nights together. That's a bunch of pot holes in the yellow brick road."

"I understand that. I won't mind if we never even come close to the excitement of our first night. As for the rest, let's take it one problem at a time. As I see it, the first problem to tackle fly-ins from Florida tomorrow."

She took him by the hand and started to walk toward the bedroom.

"Did I ever show you my etchings? Follow me, Lieutenant, I want to give you something to think about while you're waiting for the flight tomorrow."

The bleak Sunday afternoon matched Sean's mood. He sat in his favorite winged-back, reading chair and stared at the dying fire in the fireplace. He got up to make himself another drink and threw another log on the fire.

Holly's phone call from Florida on Friday had been brief. She had tried to sound calm and in complete control. He had tried not to sound angry or frustrated. The call was as tense as it was brief. Their meeting that night was destined to be more of a showdown than a problem-solving conversation.

Sean sat down and sipped his drink. The emotions rolled around inside him and he felt as though he might explode. He looked at the mantle clock. Holly was already 20 minutes late, which was fully expected. If anyone would be late for her own funeral, as the cliché suggested, it would be Holly.

Sean stared out of the window at the darkening sky. It was snowing lightly. The cold, brisk wind pushed traces of the white powder along the icy pavement.

Sean couldn't get Maggie out of his mind. He wanted a clear head to properly deal with Holly. Maggie had given him unforgetable emotional and physical comfort in a time of need. But he had been with Holly for more than three years and somehow that didn't evenly compare with the weeks with Maggie.

He loved what he and Holly once shared. He loved a dream of what they could have shared in the future. His present time with Holly was based on a personal commitment and tenacity.

The thought crossed his conscious mind that he had stayed with Maggie to somehow punish Holly. He forced the thought from his head. What he had shared with Maggie was special and separate. His unconscious mind may have wanted to hurt Holly, like she had hurt him. Even after constant consideration, Sean was certain his affair with Maggie was not the vehicle for an emotional payback.

It was dark when a car stopped in the driveway. Through the glare of the headlights he saw a figure step from the passenger side and recover a large suitcase from the back seat. The figure walked briskly toward the rear of his home, carrying a large suitcase and a large carry-on bag.

Holly let herself in through the back door. She dropped her bags at the stairs and tentatively walked into the living room. The only light in the room was from the fire in the fireplace. The fire light made strangely-shaped shadows dance throughout the room.

Holly attempted to adjust her vision to the strange light. She finally spotted Sean sitting silently in his chair, holding the large crystal glass of whiskey.

The tone in Sean's voice was not normal, but it was warmer than she had anticipated. "How was your flight?"

"The flight was fine. The ride home from the airport was no fun. The roads are really getting bad."

The silence was long and very awkward. Small talk about the weather was not the order of business for that night.

"Well, did you find what you were looking for in Florida?"

Holly paused for a moment. "What do you mean?"

"You went down there to find yourself, to sort out your life, to put things in order. Well, what did you find? Have you made an important decision? If so, I'll contact the media."

Holly became defensive. "I'm not on some damn witness stand. You being facetious will not make this whole process any easier."

"What process is that? The ol' *it's been grand, this is harder on me than it is on you* routine?"

"I've never wanted to hurt you, Sean."

"No? Well, you've done one hell of a good job of it without really trying."

"Sean, I need to be my own person, have my own identity. When we fell in love, the ink wasn't dry on my high school diploma. You have been very good to me, but I'm merely an abstract reflection of you."

Sean leaned forward in his chair, "An abstract reflection? Nice phrase, is that something you picked up in Florida or junior college? Look, Holly, let's cut through all the bullshit, O.K.? I want you back. I want you to unpack, get some rest and we give it another try. So, what is it that you want?"

Holly stood up straight, her voice now calm and confident, rather than defensive. "I'm sure you know I've given this a great deal of thought. I can't stay here with you, Sean. I need to move out on my own."

Sean had known by her posture and tone of voice that she was leaving since she had walked in the room. He turned to the fire to conceal the tears in his eyes. Waiting for her to actually say she was leaving had been like waiting for the explosion after you'd heard the mortar round leave the tube. He knew it was on the way but all he could do was wait.

"Holly, the words in the song say that love has no pride. I agree with that. I would beg or cry or throw myself at your feet if I thought it would make any difference. Love has no pride, but I still have some. There will be no emotional scenes outside of this house to embarrass you. I won't bother you or call you. I've never yet given you an ultimatum, but if you move out, we're history. You close the door behind you and it closes this chapter in your life. I won't spend another second waiting for you to find yourself if you're not willing to try to work it out together."

"It may make no sense to you, Sean, but I've got to leave. I'm certain that there's no other way."

Sean leaned back in his chair and took a drink from his glass. "There will come a day, Holly, when you will regret this."

"That may be, Sean, but I wouldn't hold my breath if I were you."

"No, I won't, I'm pale enough already. It may be a year, it may take five years, but some night you'll lay in bed staring at the ceiling, and you'll know that this was your greatest mistake. We shared something very special during a unique time in both of our lives. We're not apt to find that again."

"Sean, I can't expect you to accept and understand how I feel when I'm not certain I understand myself."

"I wish I was patient enough to put my life on hold and wait for you to come around. But I'm nearly 31, Holly. That's not old, but it's too old to watch important months and years pass by. I know it shouldn't matter, but it somehow does. Is there someone else?"

"No, Sean, no one. I swear. I need a change of life style, not a change in men."

Sean wiped a tear from the corner of his eye. He looked down at the light from the fireplace dancing inside his crystal drink glass.

"Why don't you take enough things now to get you through the week. I'll be sure to be gone on Saturday. You can get your brother to help you come and get the rest. You can take whatever you think is yours. You are welcome to use the old furniture in the basement until you buy some. On your last trip out next Saturday, leave your key on the kitchen table. After that, don't ever come here without calling first."

She turned and went to their bedroom. Sean sat for a moment, then joined her and actually helped her pack her car. They did not speak. They both seemed to be in an emotional daze, and it was if each was with a total stranger.

After Holly's car was filled to capacity with clothes and personal items, they stood silently facing each other at the back door.

Sean knew that Holly had consumed some in-flight liquid courage on the way home from Florida.

Holly recognized Sean's other self. She was dealing with the cool, controlled police lieutenant, not the sensitive, sometimes vulnerable and emotional man she had loved since '75. She envied his ability to throw up his emotional barrier.

They embraced for a long moment. He felt the warmth of her tears against his cheek.

"I'm so very sorry that it has to be this way, Sean."

"Yea, Holly. I'm sorry too."

There was a tender kiss that could only mean good-bye. Moments later, Holly was gone from his driveway and gone from his life.

He had watched her car's tail lights disappear toward Mack Avenue.

Another log on the fire, another drink. He sat back in the chair and watched the snow fall past the light from the street lamp. Stereo music and the cracking wood in the fireplace were the only sounds. His thoughts changed from a recap of Holly's departure to the voices of the Commodore's on the stereo. He wiped the tears from his eyes with the sleeve of his warm-up jacket. He closed his eyes and concentrated on the singing voices, "And I do love you . . . still."

He finally fell asleep in the chair around 3 a.m. He awoke in time to clean up and get to work on time, despite the layer of fresh snow and Monday morning traffic.

Sean would later say that if their relationship had gone as well as their separation, they would have had a romance worthy of historical documentation.

Sean missed Holly much more than he had expected but he

rebounded from the normal pain of a break-up much quicker than anyone anticipated. Sean suspected that he had been preparing himself for Holly's departure for months. And when he considered Holly's unique spirit, he realized he could not mourn the loss of something he'd never had.

Sean sat at his desk, silently staring into his half-empty mug of coffee.

Maggie O'Brien had been delayed by the snow and traffic. She entered the squad room brushing snow from her dark grey trench coat. She poured herself a coffee and sat at the chair next to Sean's desk.

"Are you alright, Sean? You look like hell."

"Ah, come on, Maggie, quit trying to cheer me up."

"I'm serious, Sean."

"I'm just wacked out, Maggie. Holly moved out last night. I didn't get much sleep. It's not that we didn't talk about it, or that I didn't expect it. You know how the last real good-bye is. You said that you and your ex had the same trauma your last time together."

Maggie spoke quietly so as not to be heard by the others. "Do you still love her?"

"I love who she was. I love what we had. I don't still love the stranger who walked out forever last night, but I'll miss her."

"I have a transfer request in my desk that I need to give to the C.O. if everything is the same between you and I."

Sean looked up at Maggie and warmly smiled. "I don't mean to sound corny, but I will really miss not working together. I agree, though, if we have any chance at a successful personal relationship, we can't continue to work together. Your husband couldn't handle the fact you out-ranked him. Working the same squad could create some real roadblocks, especially when everyone else finds out."

"Are you going to be alright this week, Sean?"

"Yea, thanks. I need a couple days by myself to get my head on straight."

"How about dinner at my place on Friday night, 7 sharp?"

Sean couldn't get the image of Holly out of his mind. "That would be very nice, Maggie. Yes, thank you."

Maggie walked to her desk and spoke to Sean over her shoulder, "Bring a nice bottle of red wine, that's mandatory. Bringing your toothbrush is optional." She smiled and winked a knowing wink.

Sean smiled back at Maggie, but his insides were still in a knot. The forced expression had been a gesture to be polite, not a true reflection of his feelings. He watched Maggie prepare her transfer request. She knew he was hurting and needed some time. He felt very fortunate that she was willing to offer him that time.

17

February, 1979—December, 1979

DECEMBER, 1979
DETROIT, MICHIGAN

1979 would not be fondly remembered as a banner year. Despite their efforts, Sean's relationship with Maggie faltered just out of the starting gate. Even with her transfer back to Sex Crimes, their conflicting work schedules and her numerous responsibilities as a single parent kept them apart. The embers of their initial passion seemed to cool in the routine of a normal lifestyle.

By Summer, they had developed a unique friendship. They were able to become dependable, close friends while remaining occasional lovers. It was a special relationship both needed more than a rebound love affair.

Grandfather Cavanagh passed away in June of a heart attack. The patriarch's sudden death was accepted with a quiet dignity and resolution by his proud Irish Catholic family.

The senior Cavanagh had enjoyed a long, healthy, productive life. He spent his last minutes on earth on the golf course, doing what he enjoyed most in his later years. Given his choice, Sean was certain he would have wanted to be buried near his favorite fairway.

He had started his business when he got back from World War I, with nothing more than cocky Marine tenacity, $200, and a prayer.

When Grandfather Cavanagh died, he left assets in seven figures.

The terrible economic climate in the Midwest made Detroit's future bleak. Recession elsewhere meant near-depression in metro-Detroit. The mass exodus to the Sun Belt was in full swing. The proud city that had drawn people from around the country and the world, the nation's melting pot, pride of the World War II production machine, was dying. The often-seen bumper sticker was "Last one out of Detroit turn out the lights." It was a grim example of the metro area's gallows humor.

Grandfather Cavanagh left all of his business interests to Sean's father. Each of the grandchildren inherited a significant sum. He had, of course, set up funds so that his wife would live out her life in financial comfort. Secretly, Sean's amount was the largest, as the oldest grandchild and his grandfather's favorite.

Sean set up a healthy trust for his own son, Denny, which eliminated his monthly obligation. He made several tax-sheltered investments and purchased a fine old house with the remainder of the money.

The 50-year-old, two-story, red brick, English Tudor home was a Detroit classic. It had been custom-built on Chandler Park Drive before World War II, and was within sight of the cross on top of St. John Hospital, not far from Balduck Park. It had natural wood floors, marble sills, wet plaster walls, two fireplaces, a two-car garage and a year-round sun porch built onto the rear.

Sean made a retired couple very happy with his cash purchase. They had the home on the market for two years, but with the poor state of the economy and high interest rates, the classic house with a Detroit address seemed almost impossible to sell.

Sean then rented his house on Linville Street to a young policeman and his family. He kept the rent lower than the house payment so he could show a loss at year's end for tax purposes.

Sean set out to renovate his new house, one room at a time. The garage, roof, furnace and electrical systems had all been recently updated. With no serious romantic interest in his life, remodeling the house helped fill a void.

Sean's only romantic encounters were brief, casual, sexual affairs. The shallow nature of those relationships seemed to reflect what he had become — emotionally shallow, guarded, and non-committed.

T.J. became a victim of the poor economy when he lost his job at Chrysler in a mass layoff. He had tried for months to find another, with no success. However, the live-in relationship with his whore roommate allowed him to get by on his unemployment checks.

Out of work, the proud young man avoided any social contacts with his long-time white friend. He had attended Sean's grandfather's funeral, but not seen him since.

On a hot Summer night, T.J. strolled down to the neighborhood pool hall to see if he could add to his pocket change. Between the time spent at the old pool hall on Mt. Elliot Street, when he was growing up, and the hours of pool played in prison, T.J. had become an excellent player.

The pool hall was filled with smoke. The hot humid day caused it to assume the odor of a locker room.

T.J. was running the table, a cigarette bouncing in his mouth.

The laughter and chatter inside the building suddenly stopped as a big red Cadillac pulled to a stop in front of the open door.

The vehicle was owned by Eastside Slim, the area's number one pimp.

The vehicle had all of the qualifications to make it a "Class A pimp-mobile." It sported extra-wide whitewall tires, tinted windows, spoked wheels, rear wheel skirts, air horns mounted on the hood, a T.V. antenna and a Continental kit mounted on the trunk.

The tall man dressed in a red jumpsuit and red wide-brimmed hat eased out of the front seat and strutted into the pool hall.

He shook his head in disgust as he stood in the center of the pool tables, with his hands on his hips, looking over the numerous patrons. "Say, is the nigger called T.J. in this dump?"

T.J. moved away from the table and stood facing the tall thin Black man, about his own age. "Ain't no niggers in here, Mr. Pimp Man. But if you lookin' for T.J., you found him."

The two men seemed to automatically square off. "So you're the bad-ass ex-con, ex-Marine who took over one of my ladies."

"My understanding was that she never was one of your ladies."

"Well, if she told you that, she's a lying bitch. Don't matter none, I'm takin' her back. So get your funky shit out of her place and be gone by midnight or be dead."

T.J. stood his ground and spoke calmly. "Don't think so, Mr. Pimp Man. The lady ain't gonna be part of your stable and I ain't moving out of no place until I'm ready."

Eastside Slim reached for a small automatic pistol concealed in his rear waistband. "I'm gonna make you ready now, nigger."

As the gun cleared the waistband, T.J. swung his pool stick like a baseball bat. There was a sickening sound of impact, as the thickest part of the stick slid under Eastside Slim's hat and struck him on the left temple. The stick broke and Eastside Slim slid to the floor, the gun falling from his hand.

T.J. picked up another pool stick from a table and stood over the motionless man in the bright red jumpsuit. "Come on up, Mr. Pimp Man. I got some more for you where that came from. Got lots more. Let's see how tough you are, mother fucker, without your little gun. Come on, get up."

The pool hall owner strode through a knot of on-lookers. He bent down over the motionless form of Eastside Slim, prostrate on the filthy pool hall floor. "Put down the pool cue, T.J. Ol' Slim ain't gonna get back up. He's dead."

T.J. threw down the pool stick. "Dead? Mr. Pimp Man takes a single whop on his thick melon with a skinny stick of wood and dies? Man, I got all the fuckin' luck. I'm in here mindin' my business, shooting some stick. This fool comes in, gonna kill me and I end up doin' him with one wack of a pool cue. Oh Lord, my parole officer is gonna love this."

The patrons began to file out as the police were called.

The owner moved to block the door. "Hey, y'all. Unless you are wanted by the po-lice or got warrants, everybody's staying. You all seen Slim go for his gun. We can't let T.J. take no murder rap on a self-defense."

T.J. spent the night in jail, but was released the next day when the Prosecutor's office decided that the killing of Eastside Slim was indeed self-defense.

T.J.'s parole officer was a brand new graduate from Michigan State University's criminal justice program. The 23-year-old had been raised in rural Michigan. The State's Parole system had recently come under fire for being too soft. It seemed to be on a five-year cycle. Every five years or so, a prisoner out on parole would commit a newsworthy crime. The conservatives and the media would take shots at the entire parole system. T.J.'s new parole officer had no intentions of letting T.J. embarrass him. Cleared of the murder or not, T.J. found himself on a bus on the way back to Jackson to finish his term.

The bad times were not over for T.J., but he arrived in time to be a welcomed returning veteran of their football team.

In mid-season, T.J. broke his leg in a brutal game against a tough semi-pro team from Pontiac. It was the same leg that had been shattered by an N.V.A. rifle bullet in '68.

By Christmas, T.J. was discouraged. His leg was not healing properly. The prison doctors seemed to do a fine job, but he realized he was no longer 19. Far from being an old man, T.J. still had to accept that he had become less indestructable in his 30s.

The year ended on a cold, clear Winter night.

Sean had volunteered to work the night shift at the Robbery Section on New Year's Eve. He did not have a date so the schedule change was like putting a favor in the bank.

He read over a departmental directive from Perry Mann, promoted to deputy chief just after the shooting in January. Sean disliked almost every aspect of affirmative action. He found comfort when a man of Perry's caliber was promoted to an administrative position.

Sean leaned back in his chair and stared out of the fifth-story window down at deserted Clinton Street.

It seemed to Sean that New Year's Eve had always been a night of self-evaluation and reflection for him. While in Vietnam, his concerns were simple, just to survive the next year. As the years passed, the issues became more and more complex. He thought of what had happened in '79. He took another life, lost his fiancee, a promising relationship fell apart and his grandfather passed away. He was on a roll. He winced when he considered what might be in store for him in 1980.

In reality, Sean was closing out the year with a stacked deck. He was healthy, he was financially set for life and he enjoyed his career. The positive aspects of his life were masked by his own self-pity that night. He knew he had a wonderful family, but he was a very lonely man that night.

Sean's thought's were sharply interrupted by the excited voice of a detective sergeant from another squad. "Hey, Lou. We've got a hold-up with a double shooting up on Linwood. The Homicide crews are all busy and they're asking us to make the scene."

Sean grabbed his trench coat from the rack and took a last quick sip of coffee. "A double shooting. Happy fucking New Year."

Ninety miles away, at Jackson State Prison, T.J. walked alone in the prison yard. He had convinced his favorite guard that the nightly walks were helpful for the proper healing of his broken leg.

T.J. considered his situation on the night most appropriate for reflection. In a year, he had lost his job, his freedom, and he still limped on his painful left leg. He realized he had lost yet another portion of his youth. T.J swore an oath to himself that he would learn from the events of the past year. He'd do the rest of his time but when he got out things would be different. He'd never be sent back behind those walls again.

If Sean had thought of T.J. that night, he might not have indulged himself in the same degree of self-pity.

The underlying difference between the two friends had remained the same through the years. No matter what Sean did or what happened to him, he came away somehow better for it. After all the pain and trauma, Sean remained in complete control of his own life.

In T.J.'s case, no matter what he did or didn't do, he couldn't seem to even buy a break. If life was a card game, T.J. kept getting all deuces.

Their lives continued to be a vivid paradox. T.J. never got a break in his entire life, and yet he refused to give in to self-pity. Sean had always had the world by the ass and he was still not a happy man.

MAY, 1980
DETROIT

Sean wrote to T.J. faithfully and sent him C.A.R.E. packages on a regular basis.

Sean had grown weary of the singles bars and one-night stands. He knew he was not ready to open up emotionally for a long-term, loving relationship but he moved out of the casual sex stage of his life, at least for a while. Gary kidded him that Sean had turned over a new leaf regarding his sexual conduct. Now, Sean had to know the woman's last name before he'd go to bed with her.

In fact, Sean began a series of brief but intense romances. Staying clear of female department personnel, he had successive relationships with a nurse, a bank loan executive, and finally an attractive divorced mother.

Nancy worked at a blood lab and she and her daughter had moved back in with her parents after a painful divorce.

Sean's family felt Nancy was good for Sean. She was mature and she seemed to settle him down. She was his mother's favorite because she somehow got him going back to mass on a regular basis.

Sean had the ability to do and say all the right things. He was easy to love, but not easy to get close to. After the trauma of her divorce, Nancy needed mature stability in her life, too. But Sean had not changed enough to be what Nancy needed.

In 1980, the Republican National Convention came to Detroit. Sean and his squad spent the week working with the Secret Service.

It was an exciting time and Sean often got lost in his work, not seeing Nancy for days at a time if he was on a case.

After the Convention, Sean was informed that he was to attend the National Police Academy in Quantico, Virginia. The selection to attend the National Academy was a sure sign that the Third Floor had additional promotional plans for him.

Before he left for Quantico, he and Nancy decided to use the time he was away to decide on the future of their relationship. They felt that being apart for several weeks would help them get in touch with their true feelings.

Sean returned from the National Academy no more certain of his feelings than before he left. Nancy made his decision a moot point. She told Sean that she was indeed falling deeply in love with him. But she felt she needed more emotional support for her and her daughter than Sean was capable of giving. She gave him a sisterly kiss on the cheek and sent him out of her life.

On the drive home, Sean realized their relationship was over and he had not exactly left kicking and scratching. Maybe Nancy just had the courage to identify what he had chosen to ignore.

During that drive, he decided that it was time to talk with a psychologist. He would be 33 in a few months and in his personal life he resembled a wealthy, college freshman. He decided he'd better grow up before he grew old.

18

January, 1981—August, 1981

JANUARY, 1981
DETROIT, MICHIGAN

S ean read over the robbery reports from the weekend. He received a call to report to Deputy Chief Mann's office.

After a half hour of casual conversation, Perry Mann told his long-term friend he was being transferred to the uniform division. Sean was to serve as a shift lieutenant on the Eastside's Fifth Precinct, to round out his supervision experience.

There was a commander's position opening within the year, and Sean had already been selected as one of the leading candidates for the position. Perry was lining up the ducks for him. The graduate degree, service record, National Police Academy, and now combined supervision experience would make Sean the front runner, despite affirmative action.

Sean was reluctant to leave his current assignment as detective lieutenant, to go back to working the shifts in uniform. But to make commander in a year, it would be well worth the sacrifice of returning to the trenches and the physical torture of shift work.

Sean explained the transfer to his Robbery squad. He was to report to the Fifth Precinct to command the graveyard shift on Feb. 1, 1981.

Sean had not been in uniform since he left the police academy staff in the Summer of '75. It took time and money to bring his uniforms up to date. When he was done, he looked as sharp in his uniform as he had when he was an instructor at the academy. But he still would rather work in a suit and tie.

Sean looked over the fleet of marked cars before he entered the precinct house rear door. He considered the changes since he came out of the academy in '69. Then, the fleet consisted of Ford sedans and wagons. They were black with gold letters and had blue rotating emergency lights.

The wagons had transported the city's sick and injured in the days before the Fire Department formed the Emergency Medical Service.

The early 70s saw the fleet return to Plymouths and a new Chief had made the cars blue and white, with gold lettering and blue lights, as in the 60s.

In the mid-1970s, Plymouths were still in use, but they received a whole new look. They were painted a solid dark blue, and sported a new identification panel on the doors. The white panel had a logo of the locally-famous statue of the Spirit of Detroit and 'Detroit Police' printed in the white panel. For reasons unknown, the overhead emergency light was changed from blue to red. The State Police was the only other Michigan police agency to use the single red rotating light on their cars. No one would have ever accused the Detroit Department of trying to be like the State Police.

The new look, with the new logo, of course, came under fire from the street coppers. Alternate logos were unofficially recommended. Sean had suggested the logo be an asshole. He reasoned that everyone even remotely connected with the Detroit city government had a shitty attitude, thus the asshole was more appropriate than a statue.

But the most significant change had been the influx of female officers into all areas of the department. Sean was already a sergeant by the time women became commonplace on the precinct shifts. He'd taught them at the academy, worked with women detective sergeants at Homicide and Robbery, and now he would supervise them as working members of his precinct platoon.

At 11:45 p.m., Sean stood at the squad room podium. The assortment of police officers that comprised the majority of his shift stood before him in two ranks.

Sean's reputation preceeded him. Everyone knew the young Lieutenant was a mover and a shaker. He had not given up his choice job as a Robbery Section lieutenant because he missed wearing a uniform. The Brass was obviously grooming Sean for bigger and better things. A couple of officers remembered him from the academy.

Fifth Precinct Cmdr. Clarence Hayden was only 18 months from retirement. He decided to stay clear of Cavanagh and ride out his remaining time from the safety of his office desk chair, with his door always closed.

Sean stood straight behind the podium, looking over the curious faces of his platoon. His poster-perfect uniform appearance made him appear taller than his 5'11" frame.

"I'm Lt. Cavanagh, your new shift commander. I'm looking forward to working with you and getting to know each of you. I understand that I have been fortunate enough to inherit the best shift on the Eastside. I'll spare you the typical you-play-ball-with-me speech. In return, share my message with the officers not on duty tonight. I recognize that it's the middle of Winter, and we're on the graveyard shift. When the weather improves, I expect a noticeable improvement in your overall appearance. I worked uniform at 13 and I managed to keep my appearance up. The department issues those uniforms. If they're not in good condition, survey them.

"Any time you want to talk off the record, I give you my word it *is* off the record. The most important rule is that you never lie to me. I know I need to earn your respect and your trust. Bottom line, ladies and gentlemen, if I ask you if it's raining, I'd better not have to look out the window to see if I need an umbrella. I'm not going to run this shift like some college fraternity, but I won't be the kind of boss who judges his success by the number of reprimands he writes. While behind closed doors, we can debate any of my decisions and directions. If we're out there on the street, there will be no debate. If I say 'jump,' you jump, and we can discuss it when we're back at the precinct. The street is no place for debate, and I won't allow it. End of my mini-speech. Are there any questions?"

A tall, young, white officer in the front slowly raised his hand. Sean nodded to him.

"If it's not too personal, Lieutenant, I think the shift's question is why you'd leave a choice position in the Robbery Section to go back into uniform and work the shifts in an inner-city precinct?"

There was a long moment of awkward silence.

Sean grinned and read the officer's name badge. "Officer Donahue, is it? Well, Officer Donahue, I really miss riding around ugly, empty ghetto streets all night, drinking terrible coffee, and fighting to stay awake."

There was some scattered, polite laughter which seemed to break the tension.

"Fair question, Donahue," Sean continued. "It is personal, but I believe you all have a right to know. It was strongly suggested that I round out my supervision background by returning to uniform duty for a while. I went to the National Police Academy last Fall. It is accurate to say this is a positive transfer for possible promotion in the future, not punishment for getting in the Third Floor's dog house."

Even the two shift sergeants were caught off guard by his candid, direct answer. Everyone in the squad room expected the standard, ambiguous answer like every formal departmental press release. Instead, Sean had delivered a frank, honest answer. Sean made his first gesture for an honest relationship with his shift.

Sean began the pre-shift roll call with briefing information and assignments. After roll call, the shift moved to their vehicles and Sean went to his post behind the long, elevated wooden desk in the precinct's lobby.

The afternoon shift lieutenant, Rufus Jefferson, was 40 and built like a defensive lineman. He stood and firmly shook Sean's hand. Jefferson signed himself off of the precinct's daily diary. "Welcome aboard,

Cavanagh. From what I heard of you, you gonna like it here at Number Five. This is one crazy place. You oughta fit right in."

Eddie Donahue and Willie Washington were assigned to their regular area, 5-4. Donahue gave their vehicle the visual once-over as Washington checked the weapons in the trunk. Washington settled behind the wheel and Donahue watched the passing ghetto-scape. Donahue sat his hat down on the seat between them.

"Say, Willie. What do you think of the new Lieutenant? The man looks like he could be a real tight-ass if he wanted to be. He looks young for a non-affirmative action white dude."

Willie Washington chewed on an unlit cigar. "Be cool, Donahue. The dude is almost 33-years-old. That puts him almost 10 big ones ahead of us. I heard the man has seen some shit. He's some kind of a Nam hero, and he greased some assholes while working the streets. Did you check it out, Donahue? The man is packin' a four inch .357, instead of the normal lieutenant's .38 snub nose. It ain't like he's hot-doggin'. I think he's for real"

Donahue checked a license number on their stolen car sheet. "Yea, Willie, he may know his shit, but I still say that he could be a real ball buster. I guess we'll just have to wait and see what the new Golden Boy does when the shit hits the fan."

Willie Washington finally lit his cigar. "Well, knowing this place, we oughta know by the end of the month."

Sean sat behind the elevated desk and became familiar with the equipment and the regular inside precinct shift personnel; the clerk, the switchboard operator, the turnkey and the report officer. He recognized that his predecessor had filled the precinct station assignments with senior officers and some people that could serve their department and city better in the relative warmth and safety of the precinct station, rather than out on the streets.

Their radio speaker was mounted in the desk near Sean's position. He adjusted the volume so he could hear the radio traffic and still talk with citizens in the lobby and hear the voices on his phone.

Around 2:30 a.m., Sean heard the dispatcher send two of his units to an apartment building on Kercheval Street, near Chalmers. There was a report of a domestic disturbance and a fight at the location.

Sean stopped writing in the precinct's large diary book for a moment. The call reminded him of old times. He smiled as he thought of the 13th Precinct's infamous "Kiddy Car" racing around with Tommy driving and Sean still idealistic and believing they could actually make a difference.

A few minutes later, Scout 5-4 radioed that they were on the way to the station with a prisoner.

Sean was having difficulty understanding the extremely drunk man standing in front of him in the lobby. Sean only knew the drunk had been mistreated by someone and he wanted to complain. Sean could not determine whether the man's slurred complaint was against one of his officers or another citizen.

Suddenly, the sounds of a violent physical struggle and shouting came from the tiled processing room behind the precinct desk. Sean, a veteran shift clerk and a young Black female report officer ran through the narrow doorway into the processing room to help.

Willie Washington had removed one handcuff from the prisoner's wrist, and the big drunken Black man went wild. He swung the handcuffs like a weapon, breaking the officer's grasp and hitting Washington on the head with his own handcuffs.

As the group closed in, the man bounced them off the walls with his powerful arms and shoulders. The prisoner drove his right shoulder into the petite female report clerk. She was sent to the floor stunned, with the breath knocked out of her.

Sean quickly got into position. He approached the man from behind and slid his right arm around the big man's throat in a choke hold. At first, the man lifted Sean off of his feet and tried to flip him over. Sean increased the pressure with a solid jerk of his forearm. The sudden lack of oxygen caused the prisoner to stumble and lose balance. Sean planted his feet and turned so that the man fell hard onto the tile floor, Sean on top of him, never losing the choke hold.

Once on the floor with Sean on top of him, the other officers handcuffed the man's arms behind him. The turnkey found some leg restraints. The man continued to struggle, but was finally under control.

Donahue held his four-cell flash light and moved into position to strike the prisoner on the head.

Sean looked up from his firm hold on top of the prisoner. "Hold off, Donahue. No need to send this asshole to the hospital if he's under control."

"He hurt Willie and Linda. He's still struggling."

Sean bit his lower lip and increased the pressure on the prisoner's neck. "Put it away, Donahue. No goddamn debate."

Donahue briefly looked at the expression on his new Lieutenant's face. He turned away to check on his partner's head wound.

A moment later, they dragged the prisoner into a holding cell.

The group of officers gathered together in the processing room to check on the wounded and catch their breath.

The turnkey lit up a cigarette. "You choked him out real good, Lou. Except for his pissing himself, he ain't hurt or bleedin'. If you hadn't got a hold of him, we would have had to crush his melon, or he'd have hurt everyone. That was one strong dude."

Sean made a fruitless attempt to brush the dirt and grey dust from his navy-blue uniform trousers.

The post-fight release of tension caused joking and conversation about the prisoner's strength. Everyone involved in the struggle had their uniform soiled or torn.

Donahue held a wet paper towel to the small laceration on Willie Washington's forehead. "Hey, Lou. You give us a lecture on the importance of appearance and look at your pants."

Sean gave up trying to brush off the dirt. "Donahue, you and Washington have some strange ideas about a 'welcome aboard' party. You could have let me be here long enough to find the restroom before you get me rolling around on the floor."

The laughter came easily and it was an important part of the emotional release process.

"Book that asshole for resisting and obstructing. Let the detectives jerk with the Prosecutor's office about it tomorrow. We'll take him for a high misdemeanor and he at least won't be out on bond before we're all in bed. I'll have Sgt. Hendricks take Linda and Willie to the hospital so they can be checked over. Don't milk it to death, but don't be noble. Your actual injuries will play a part as to whether we get a resisting warrant or a simple assault and battery. Donahue, you get started on the report while they check out Willie. Let dispatch know you guys are out of service for a while."

Sean walked into the small room where the officers made out their reports. Donahue was working on his report. Sean closed the door. "Can I talk to you for a minute, Ed?"

The expression on the young officer's face showed his actual concern but he tried to sound poised. "Sure, Lou. Have a seat."

Sean pulled up a stool and sat near Donahue. "Ed, back in '69, when I came on the job, if a prisoner acted like that we'd have pounded the asshole until he looked like a bowl of chili. Bottom line, this is 1981, and you've even got other coppers second-guessing any use of force. If I let you split his skull after he was subdued, because he hurt Willie, we weaken our court case, open everyone in the room to serious complaints, maybe you get a bad reputation.

"Donahue, if you've got to bust some asshole's gourd to protect yourself or your partner, don't ever hesitate. The days of street justice, especially with a crowd, are over. Once a prisoner is subdued, I blow the whistle and the play is over. Do I make myself clear?"

"I read you five-by-five, Sir. I understand where you're coming from. Thanks for jumping into the middle of all that. Sorry you got all dirty your first day."

"No problem. I've got a clean uniform in my locker."

Donahue smiled. "Somehow I'm not surprised."

Sean stood to leave, then stopped.

"Officer Donahue, I'd like to think I can take a joke and not lose your respect. I really appreciate coppers with spirit and a good sense of humor. We don't know each other yet. I hope you're not testing me. There's a fine line between wit and being a smartass. I know, because I've walked it my whole adult life. If the day comes that I think you cross the line from kidding to jerking me off, I'll blow your oars out of the water."

"No offense, Lou, honest. I was just . . ."

"None taken, Ed. Like I said, we don't know each other yet. I suggest that we keep aware of that so there are no misunderstandings."

"Thanks, Lou. You'll have no problem with me."

Sean cleaned up and changed into a fresh uniform.

At 4 a.m., Sean took the street supervisor's marked police car for a tour of the precinct. Sgt. Hendricks was back from the hospital and took the desk.

They put a butterfly bandage on Willie's head wound, and he insisted on finishing his shift. He and Ed Donahue were back on patrol.

Officer Linda Oliver had received three cracked ribs. She was taped up and driven home. She'd be off for a week.

As Sean pulled out of the drive of the precinct, he called the dispatcher. "Five-Six-Oh to Radio, 5-60 is in service, one officer."

There was a short pause, then the familiar radio squelch. "O.K. on that, 5-60."

Often, a very simple gesture can have a significant response. The crews in the Fifth Precinct that cold January night were even more comfortable with their new shift lieutenant. He made the simple gesture by letting them all know he was out on the road, out on their turf. He might turn out to be a picky tight-ass, but he was not sneaky. In a few hours, he had convinced most of them that he was a stand-up kind of boss. Now if they screwed up, shame on them. The ground rules had been set.

Sean had always hated the graveyard shift. He struggled to keep his eyes open. When change of shifts finally arrived at 8 a.m., he gladly signed the daily diary over to the day-shift lieutenant.

The middle-aged man put his massive hand on Sean's shoulder. "Well, Cavanagh, how was your first night back at a precinct?"

Sean rubbed his eyes. "I had two officers injured subduing a prisoner, a fatal shooting up on Mack Avenue, and we banged up a scout car in a chase. I'm glad things haven't changed on the street."

"Only the faces and the names change, Cavanagh. The street always stays the same. Welcome aboard, you've got a good reputation from working Robbery and Homicide. These kids need some shift bosses that earned their bars in the trenches, instead of behind a desk."

It was 9:30 a.m. before Sean finally crawled into his bed and slid between the crisp, fresh sheets. The room-darkening shades and drab, overcast sky helped make the bedroom very dark.

The graveyard shift. It meant restless, poor-sleep days, bone-tired nights, countless cups of bad coffee, Maalox, eating Rolaids like breath mints, and damn little social life. It was one hell of a way to spend a month, just working, eating and trying to sleep enough to do it all again the next night.

Sean adjusted his pillow to get comfortable and pulled the covers up over his shoulder. "Hell, just 22 years of this and I can retire. It's all downhill from here."

MAY, 1981
JACKSON, MICHIGAN

The prison team finished baseball practice, and T.J. limped over to the bench from his first base position. He sat next to his friend and teammate, Jerome Johnson.

"Say, Jerome, this leg of mine ain't ever gonna get better. When I got shot in Nam, doctors said it would be good as ever. Then when I broke it playin' football in '79, prison docs told me the same shit. Well, guess what! It ain't good as new. It hurts all the time. Damp days like this, I can hardly run."

"Go on back to the doctors, T.J. Let them have another look at it."

"No fuckin' way, Brother. With my luck, they can't find what's wrong and get worried about being sued, and then they pink slip my Black ass so I can't play no more sports. Jerome, I don't much like it here as it is. Without sports, I'd turn into one crazy nigger."

T.J. opened his latest letter from Sean. A photo of Sean in full uniform fell out of the envelope onto the ground. T.J. carefully picked up the photo, cleaned it off and studied it. He broke into a wide grin.

"Got a letter from your Chuck buddy?"

"Yep. Ol' Irish, he writes and sends goodies 'bout as regular as my Mama."

"Don't figure, T.J., you being close friends with some white cop from a rich family."

"Yea, we know that too. Don't know what it is. Maybe the only good thing about Nam is that it made all of us that went there exactly the same for long enough to become real friends."

Jerome studied the photo. "The boy looks too pretty to be the po-lice."

T.J. laughed and bobbed his head.

"Yea, that baby face has fooled lots of dudes, 'cept they ain't around anymore to rap about it. He ain't all that strong, you know, like a big bad-ass bully from growing up on the block. But he's got street smarts and in a fight the boy is down right vicious. When I was out on parole, before I violated and got sent back, I heard shit from other po-lice and some street people. He's not one of them liberal dudes. He can cop him an attitude and call a nigger a nigger. Got to say, though, Jerome, if Irish is as good a cop as he was a Marine, he deserves them lieutenant's bars."

T.J. rubbed his leg, and headed for the showers with Jerome. T.J. worried about Sean's safety out on the streets but could never properly express his brotherly concern. Sean's letters were so clear and well-written. Sean could easily describe an emotion or an event. Somehow, T.J. sensed that his white blood brother knew exactly how he felt, and appreciated T.J.'s concern.

AUGUST, 1981
DETROIT

Sean had worked hard to earn his shift's respect. He started by riding one full day with each regular shift officer. He didn't ride as the lieutenant, he rode as a partner. While working in the beat cars, Sean did routine reports, wrote traffic citations, babysat dead bodies, helped recover "floaters" from the river, and helped make all types of arrests.

The "ride along" idea helped him get to know each of his people. Almost as importantly, it helped them feel as they were getting to know their new shift commander.

Sean brought back shift-initiated crew match-up requests and crew-requested days off. He encouraged off-duty time together to break down the racial and sexual blockades caused by aggressive affirmative action.

Sean and his people were working the 4 p.m. to midnight shift. The Wednesday afternoon was hot and muggy. There was not so much as a hint of a breeze. The sun appeared to be twice its normal size as it descended into the smog-choked western skyline.

Sean stood in front of his shift in the squad room at on-duty roll call. The two ranks of officers stood at ease as Sean read department memos and information from the precinct detectives. His people already looked physically drained from the wet heat of the afternoon.

Sean finished the formal portion of the roll call and walked out from behind the small podium.

"Listen up, people. Not only are we in the midst of the dog days of August, but Sgt. Hendricks informs me that there's a full moon tonight. You know the mood of the people on the street. A simple traffic stop could turn ugly. Under these circumstances, I feel justified in using the words of our favorite T.V. roll call sergeant. 'Hey, and remember, let's be careful out there.' "

There was a brisk chorus of cheers and some hand clapping. Sean tried to send them out with a smile on their faces, even if it was at the playful expense of himself or his sergeants.

After eight months, Sean felt it was finally his shift. He knew their strengths and weaknesses. He cared about them, and he felt responsible for their welfare.

They knew him to be a demanding supervisor who accepted nothing less than their personal best. They believed he was fair, and recognized that he genuinely cared about them.

Three hours into the shift, Sean had asked a crew to bring him in a sandwich. Several cups of coffee were burning a hole in his stomach. He took a big swallow of Maalox from the bottle and hoped the crew would hurry with his sandwich so it would work with the Maalox to soak up the combination of acids in his empty stomach.

Sean went back to writing in the daily diary, but was stopped mid-word.

A voice on the desk radio monitor cried out to the dispatcher. "Five-five, Drexel at Kercheval. Officer down, shots fired. Officer in trouble."

Sean ran to the rear of the station to see if any crew happened to be at the precinct. Ed Donahue and his partner for the night were at the gas pump.

"Ed, I've got to get to the scene. I'll drive. Freeman, get in the back seat and hold on."

The dispatcher calmly dispatched the units in the Fifth Precinct to Drexel and Kercheval and said E.M.S. had a van en route.

The nearly-panicked voice came over the radio again, "Five-five has an officer shot. God, we need help here."

The dispatcher assured the excited young officer that help would be there at any moment.

Sean drove the short distance to Drexel and Kercheval at a frightening speed, emergency light and siren activated.

When Sean slammed to a stop, there were already four marked vehicles at the scene.

A small market was at the corner. Sean could see two officers at the market entrance and the others gathered near a marked unit stopped at the stop sign in front of the market. Sean moved over to the group. They silently stood in a circle around the body of Officer Henry Rubin. He had obviously been shot in the head with a large-caliber weapon. He lay on his back in the street, next to the open car door, his head resting in a large pool of blood.

Sean eased his way through the small circle of paralyzed young officers. He kneeled next to Rubin's motionless body. He gently lifted the young Black officer's head from the pavement and checked for any sign of life. By the look of the wound, Henry Rubin was dead before his body fell to the street.

The E.M.S. van arrived, and Sean moved aside so the medical techs could inspect Rubin's body.

Sean turned and quietly spoke to the group, "Come on, people, there are things that must be done. We're not helping Henry by standing here."

Donahue walked up to Sean, "Lou, store owner is shot dead inside. Homicide and code 2400 are en route. Ski was Rubin's partner tonight. He says they stopped at the stop sign just as two Black hold-up men capped the store owner. Rubin and Ski were getting out of their car when the two of them came out the front door. They got Rubin with the first couple shots. They shot the hell out of the car, but missed Ski. I took him into the market to sit down where he can't see Henry or the dead store owner. Lou, Ski is pretty fucked up. You'd better settle him down before code 2400 gets here, or they'll yank him off the street."

"Damn fine job, Ed. Get a full description out on the air right away."

"Will do, Boss. Same M.O. and description as the two assholes that have been doing Eastside markets all Summer."

A tall thin medical tech approached Sean, "I'm sorry, Lieutenant, your officer is obviously dead. We will cover him until . . ."

"Like hell you will! I won't have one of our people laying on the street collecting flies while we gather a fucking crowd. Put him on a stretcher and get him to St. John Hospital, now!"

"I'm sorry, Lieutenant. With his massive head wound, he is obviously dead. We have strict orders concerning dead homicide victims."

"Look, Pal. I respect that you're only trying to follow orders and do your job. Look around. I'm in charge here, and I'm ordering you to take that kid's body off the street and get it to the hospital."

"Sir, I'm sorry, but my orders..."

"Either you take him, or my men will confiscate your van and we'll do it ourselves."

"What about the man inside the market?"

"He's worse, but at least he's inside where the people can't stare at him. Now go on. Take our officer out of here."

"Alright, Lieutenant. I'm sorry, but I'll have to report this."

"I know. It's your job and you're dedicated and good at it. I respect that. Well, taking care of these people is my job. Even when they're dead."

The medical techs carefully lifted the lifeless body of Henry Rubin onto a stretcher. They loaded the stretcher into the E.M.S. van and drove off toward St. John Hospital.

Sean watched the van disappear going east on Kercheval. He then sought out Ed Donahue. He found him finishing his conversation with the dispatcher about the description of the two wanted men. "Ed, where is Willie Washington? I just remembered that Willie and Henry were close friends off the job."

Ed Donahue's facial expression changed, "I had to take Willie inside. Lou, Willie is as fucked up as Ski and I didn't let him get a look at Henry's body. Henry and Willie go way back. Henry talked Willie out of the old neighborhood and into joining the department. Christ, Lou, Henry was Willie's son's godfather."

Sean entered the market. The officers inside had found something to cover the gruesome corpse of the market owner.

Sean went to where Ski was seated, staring out at nothing. "Ski, come on, pal. I'll have Donahue take you down to Homicide."

"Lieutenant, Henry never had a chance. We heard the shots, I went for the radio, and they shot him as he was getting out of the car. I swear to God, Lieutenant, I didn't let Henry down. They hit us so quick, we never knew what happened. Until it was over."

Sean moved close to the young officer so no one else could hear, "Ski, I know first-hand what you've been through. For what it's worth, I believe you. I can't take away the guilt I know you feel, even if it's not your fault. But suck up your guts and be a fucking cop, the kind of a cop Henry Rubin was and would expect you to be. Ski, nobody ever gets over having a partner shot out from under him. By God, if you did, you'd be a head case for sure. There will be a time and place for tears, but not here. Now, go out of here like you cared about Henry, your shift, and the precinct. We'll talk before you go back on the street."

Sean walked over to Willie Washington. Willie sat in the small back office of the market, his face buried in his hands. Sean gently placed his hand on Willie's back. "Willie, it's me. Cavanagh. I'm sorry about Henry. I know you're hurting."

The young, proud Black officer stood. He put his face against Sean's shoulder and wept. Sean put his arms around him and gently patted the back of Willie's head, like he was comforting his kid brother. "I know, Kid. I know."

"Lou, Henry has been like a big brother to me."

"I know, Willie. If you're up to it, I want you to come with me to Henry's house to inform Henry's wife he's been hurt. We'll get her to St. John Hospital so when they tell her he's dead, she can get immediate medical attention if she needs it."

Willie stood erect and wiped his eyes. "Rather than a female police officer, we can get my wife to watch Henry's children while we take Henry's wife, Phillis, to where Henry is." Willie paused for a moment. "Say, Lieutenant, who's gonna be the one to tell Henry's wife?"

Sean put his hand firmly on Willie's shoulder. "Unless she has a problem with white people, I'll tell her. I sent Henry out onto the street tonight, I'll be the one to tell his widow."

"Ain't you supposed to stay here, in charge of the scene until Code 2400 and Homicide get here?"

"Come on, Willie, we owe it to get to Henry's wife before the media does. There's nothing more important now than Henry's wife and children."

The next hour would always be partially blocked from Sean's memory. They picked up Willie's wife and drove to the Rubin home.

All of the police supervisor's classes told him to never tell the family that the officer was dead until they reached the hospital. Phillis Rubin was far too bright and brave for Sean to lie to her even for a few minutes. Sean would have wanted Lyn or Holly told immediately.

Willie and his wife held Phillis as she wept in sorrow. She regained her poise and sat silently in the back seat of Sean's police car during the ride to Henry's body at St. John Hospital.

Willie walked toward the emergency entrance, with Phillis Rubin leaning against his shoulder. She turned back to Sean and spoke softly to him.

"Henry always told me what you were supposed to tell me if he ever got himself killed. Bless you for not making me wait all this time not knowing. I know you care for your people, Lieutenant. I'll never forget that you had the courage and respect for me to tell me the truth back there at the house."

Sean's eyes filled with tears and he couldn't control them. He turned away and spoke as he drove away from the hospital emergency entrance. "I'm so very sorry, Mrs. Rubin, so very sorry."

Less than an hour after Sean and Willie had left for the Rubin home, Sean returned to the murder scene. He chewed at a mouthful of chewing gum.

The Homicide crew sent to the scene happened to be Gary Burger and his newest partner, Stan Dombrowski. Code 2400, the field duty officer that night was Cmdr. Nelson. He walked around the shot-up police car with a half-a-dozen evidence techs.

A dozen assorted news media people converged on Sean as he stepped from his vehicle. He refused to make a statement and referred them all to Cmdr. Nelson, as he tried to find Gary, who was inside the small market.

Once inside, he saw other evidence techs moving about, taking photos and latent prints. The bloodied body of the elderly market owner still lay in a large pool of blood behind the counter, next to the empty cash register.

Gary approached Sean and put his arm around his shoulder. "I'm sorry about your man, Partner. It's a damn shame. They never had a chance."

Sean stared at the body of the dead market owner. "You have any idea who the shooters are?"

Gary moved Sean away from the gory sight of the dead man. "Looks like the same two turds that have been doing markets and liquor stores all over the Eastside. We're starting to work with your old squad because these two have started to take a liking to dropping the hammer on people for no reason. They are either real bad dopers or just head cases."

Sean and Gary walked outside together. Sean looked at the large spot of blood and brain matter where they had taken Rubin's body from the street.

Gary studied an uncommon expression on his ex-partner's face. "Hey, Kid, you're lookin' a little punk under that tan. Are you doing alright?"

Sean rubbed his burning eyes. "No, Partner. I'm not even a little alright. I've seen this carnage a thousand times, but I'm afraid this time I may get sick."

Gary walked away from the scene with Sean. "Come on, Kid. Let's go for a little walk down the block. You do look a bit green around the gills. I won't let you get sick in front of your shift and the media like you did when we viewed our first post mortem at Homicide together."

"Christ, Gary, don't remind me of that now!"

"What's the matter with you, Sean? Do you have a touch of the 'flu?"

Sean stopped and leaned against an abandoned storefront. He put his head back and took several deep breaths. He searched his pockets and found another piece of chewing gum. T.J.'s lesson from a bunker in Vietnam in 1967 helped settle his upset stomach and relieve the severe nausea. "Gary, I'm so fucking tired of this bullshit. The stress, emotions, fear, grief, all on a dozen cups of bad coffee and an empty stomach. There's enough acid in my gut for an acid rain storm."

Gary gently patted Sean's back. "Cmdr. Nelson is a good street boss. He's the field duty officer and he's here at the scene. You couldn't have a better man in charge for something shitty like this. Go fill Nelson in on the status of Rubin's wife. I hear that your Precinct Commander is out-of-state on vacation. This entire funeral thing will be your ballgame. Go get something other than coffee on your stomach and settle down. Partner, you're in for a tough few days."

The old Baptist church was filled to capacity with the friends and family of Henry Rubin and hundreds of police officers. There were officers from as far away as Toronto, Canada, and Chicago. They didn't attend Rubin's funeral because they knew him; they came to pay their respect for a fellow cop who had fallen in the line of duty.

The minister conducted a brisk, touching service. Willie Washington was scheduled to present a brief eulogy in the middle of the service.

Willie walked over to where Sean was seated with the shift, in a front pew. "Say, Lieutenant, you gotta do the eulogy for me. I'll go up there and make a fool of myself. I ain't never been a public speaker and I'd never make it through without falling to pieces. Henry deserves a first-rate eulogy, not some fool stuttering and crying."

Sean looked at Willie as though he had lost his senses. "Willie, you were Henry's best friend. I was only his shift lieutenant. Take another look, Willie. You want me to do Henry's eulogy in this church? How would his family react to a white man doing it? They'd be bitter. It would be like some stranger from the department butting into a very private thing."

Tears rolled down Willie's face. "No, Lou. It ain't like that with Henry's family. Henry grew up with white folks, got a lot a white friends. Fact is, when I told Phillis I was havin' trouble and couldn't do it, she asked for you to do it instead."

Sean leaned forward in the pew and his eyes met those of Phillis Rubin. She wiped away a tear from the corner of her eye, smiled and nodded.

Sean winced and nodded back in reply.

Rev. Samuel Lee Cross carefully stepped from the pulpit as Sean stepped in position to offer the brief, ad lib eulogy. The large Black minister moved very gracefully in his black robes. "May God bless your words, and may they bring comfort to those which hear them."

Sean automatically crossed himself. "Thank you, Reverend. Please be ready to help me if I get myself in trouble up there."

Sean stood at attention behind the pulpit and stared out at the sea of faces that filled the church to capacity.

Sean's own shift recognized that he held on to the top of the carved wood pulpit in the same manner he held the top of the squad room podium every day at roll call.

The front pews across the center aisle from the Rubin family were occupied by city government and police officials, including the Mayor, the Council, state and federal legislators, the Police Chief and every Deputy Chief.

Sean waited a moment for the buzzing in the church to subside. The large gathering was as surprised at the sight of a white man at the pulpit as Sean had been at the request. He took a small sip of water from Rev. Cross' water glass and cleared his throat, away from the pulpit microphone. He owed it to Henry and his people to maintain his poise and deliver a brief eulogy that Henry would be proud to be remembered by.

Sean's voice was clear and controlled. The church was silent except for the sound of his calm voice. He looked out at the sea of faces but most of his eye contact was with Henry's widow, Phillis Rubin.

"The mere fact that a white man offers Henry's eulogy speaks of the kind of a man and the kind of cop Henry was. I can offer little comfort to the Rubin family. That is the task of Rev. Cross and their friends and loved ones. I can only point to the hundreds of fellow police officers who are here today as a gesture of their respect. As Rev. Cross stated, no amount of hatred, revenge or street justice will bring Henry back to his family. There is no lesson to be learned from Henry's death. He made no tactical or judgement error. It may have been fate or God's will. But there is a critical lesson to be learned by the way Henry Rubin lived. Henry treated all people with dignity and fairness. He was a good and decent man who proved his views with deeds, as well as words. There is no way to measure the void that Henry's death will leave in his family. But in a city and a department still wracked with bitterness and mistrust, an officer such as Henry Rubin will be sorrowfully missed."

There was a long moment of silence as Sean stepped from the pulpit.

Rev. Cross gave Sean a solid pat on the back. "Bless you, Lu-tenant. You did just fine. I knew Henry since he was just a boy. He'd have been proud."

Sean felt his knees shake and he felt weak for a moment. "Thank you, Reverend, but I shouldn't have been up there in the first place."

"Hush that kind of talk, Son. You did just fine. If those things came from your heart, like I think, there was no better policeman in the church to say them."

The Reverend stepped back into the pulpit and raised his arms. "Let us stand together and pray . . ."

There were six long columns containing hundreds of solicitous police officers standing at attention. They had been formed across from the tent-covered gravesite. The narrow cemetery road separated the officers from the family, who were huddled under the canvas tent protected from the threatening sky.

The August morning was cool and overcast. A light rain had been stop-and-go since dawn. It was not presently raining, but the dark, rolling clouds promised another shower within minutes.

Sean stood in front of Henry Rubin's own precinct platoon. They were dressed in long-sleeve shirts, with ties and white dress gloves. They held the position of honor, at the front of the huge formation of uniform and plain clothes officers.

Sean had attended more than a dozen funerals at Mt. Olivet Cemetery, including his own family members'. It was a sad place, yet it seemed familiar and somehow comforting.

There was the special Honor Guard that fired a 21-gun rifle salute. Then, two talented members of the police band played "Taps," with its echo.

The assembled officers rendered their best hand salute during the playing of taps.

The Rubin family's sobs were muffled under the green canvas gravesite canopy.

Deputy Chief Perry Mann stood in the small cemetery road, centered in front of the entire formation. He looked over to Sean and signaled to him with a simple nod of his head. Sean smartly marched across the road to the inside of the canvas tent. He approached the Honor Guard and stood at attention. They handed Sean the folded flag that had covered Henry Lee Rubin's bronze casket. Sean rendered a perfect hand salute and took the folded flag. He briskly walked across the tent to where Phillis Rubin was seated with her family. She cried softly and was flanked by her eldest children and her brothers.

Sean presented the neatly-folded flag to Henry's widow. He leaned over and softly spoke to her. "Mrs. Rubin, I know there's nothing I can say that would offer any comfort to you. Phillis, please believe me, we're so very sorry. If there's anything you need . . ."

She took the flag and clutched Sean's hand. "The things you said at the church, all these police here, what everyone has done, even the Mayor coming . . . my Henry would be proud. You let them know, Lt. Cavanagh, let them know I appreciate what you've all done since my Henry was killed."

Sean smartly marched back to his position on the large formation. Tears filled his eyes, and rolled freely down his cheeks.

Minutes later, the silver hearse and the long line of limos had taken the Rubin family away from the gravesite. The vehicles had removed the family just a few moments before the Summer rain shower resumed.

Sean stood frozen, with the shift, staring across the narrow, paved cemetery road at the empty canvas tent containing only the lonely casket.

Sean remained at attention at his position in the formation. Most of the officers had been chased to their waiting vehicles by the light shower.

Henry Rubin's own shift began to cross the road to his casket in pairs, or alone. Some of Rubin's friends kneeled next to the casket and prayed. Some merely touched the impressive metal coffin softly, in a farewell gesture. Willie Washington put his hands and forehead on his good friend's casket and wept. They all cried, some privately, silently, others shamelessly wept aloud.

Now Sean stood alone in the rain. It was the kind of rain that had fallen for three weeks in Hue City, back in '68. He flashed back to Vietnam. He closed his eyes. He pictured a vicious fire fight that had occurred in an old Catholic cemetery in Hue. He thought of Logs. Sean had spoken to his psychologist often of the grief he still felt for the friends he had lost in Vietnam.

Sean had a sudden thought. He wondered if he could have said good-bye to Logs in this way. The cemetery, Taps, rifle salute, tears, casket. Maybe he could have left some of the awful grief at the ceremony. Sean believed at that moment that if he could have said good-bye properly to Logs, the terrible pain and guilt might be eased.

Sean opened his eyes to the reality of Henry Rubin's casket. He walked to the kneeler next to the casket. Sean kneeled next to Officer Ed Donahue. Ed wiped the tears from his eyes.

Sean crossed himself and said a "Hail Mary" and an "Our Father."

Donahue didn't try to control the emotions of the moment. "Why, Lou? Why does a good family man like Henry get wasted? He had everything to live for. I don't understand. It doesn't make any sense."

"Like my friends in Vietnam told me, Ed, when it makes sense, get the hell out of here."

Sean crossed himself and got back to his feet. He left the cover of the tent and walked back out into the rain.

He was surprised when he looked up and saw Maggie O'Brien standing before him. "Are you alright, Sean?"

Sean moved and hugged Maggie, holding her very close to him. Their faces touched. She felt the warm moisture of his tears mix with the cool rain. "I'm having a tough time with this, Maggie."

She softly patted Sean on the back. "Come on home with me, Sean. I'll make some dinner and we can look out over the river and get numb."

Sean held Maggie even tighter. "I accept. You're a good friend, Sgt. O'Brien, and I really need a good friend tonight. Maggie, I'm so tired of this, I don't know what I'm going to do."

————————

Sean glanced through a current edition of *Psychology Today,* while seated in the small, well-furnished waiting room.

He had learned in college that any emotional problem had a slow healing process, even with professional help. It seemed that the talented young psychologist and Sean had spent the first year just trying identify whether Sean really had a deep-seated problem.

He was finally called into Dr. Ireland's office. The office fit the stereotype. It had earth tone colors. Dr. Ireland sat in a high-backed leather chair and played with his pipe. The small, wooden coffee table had a box of facial tissue within reach of either the couch or the chair, depending on the patient's method of treatment. In Sean's case, he faced Dr. Ireland in the chair.

Dr. Ireland put down his pipe and picked up his notebook and pencil. "Well, Sean, since our last meeting, has anything happened that you'd like to discuss?"

Sean paused, deep in thought, staring at a picture of gulls in flight on the wall near Dr. Ireland's head. He thought of the emotional trauma of Henry Rubin's funeral.

"I cried."

"You cried? What happened to make you cry?"

"That was one of my people that was shot to death. You had to have heard about it. I was at his funeral and I cried."

"That seems perfectly normal, Sean. Those things can be very emotional and crying is a good release."

"Oh yea, I know, Dr. Ireland. You see, the problem is that my grandfather died last summer. I loved him dearly, but I never once shed a tear."

"Why not, Sean? Why can't you cry for him and for missing your son and for your friends lost in the war? Why not, Sean?"

Sean closed his eyes and he felt a single tear form in the corner of his right eye. His chest felt heavy as he struggled to maintain self-control.

"Because I'm afraid."

"Afraid of what, Sean?"

"I'm afraid that if I ever really let myself feel, really let it go, let it all out, I might never stop."

Dr. Ireland leaned forward in his chair. "And I'm afraid if you don't let yourself feel and hurt and cry, these sessions may never stop. You're in your thirties, Sean. Either open up and let go, or you'll ruin the rest of your life."

A full week after Henry Rubin's funeral, the shift remained stunned. They were very quiet at roll call and a few, including Willie Washington and Ed Donahue, walked around in a daze.

Since the night of the shooting, Sean spent most of each shift in a car, out on the street. He'd put his senior sergeant behind the desk. Sean felt he needed to be out with his people on the street to lend his support at the scene of trouble spots. With all of the tension, Sean did not want his people going out as avenging angels. Rubin's killers were still at large, and the entire precinct was like a powder keg. Sean felt that by being on the street, driving around, he could put out the fuse.

The two brothers had come to Detroit together from Greece just after World War II, during which they had fought against the Nazis with the Greek resistance.

They had purchased a small liquor store on Mack Avenue, near Alter. The neighborhood around their store had gone through a dramatic change since 1946, but their little store had done well enough to support both of their families as their children grew.

They did not intend to pass the store down to any of their children. Armed robbery had become a way of life, part of doing business in the city, especially in a liquor store.

The brothers kept a .38 Special near the cash register and a M-1 carbine in the back storage room. They had no desire to get into a shoot-out. In fact, they had been robbed twice in two years, and chose to surrender the money without even attempting to go for their hidden weapons. The weapons prevented the feeling of total helplessness.

The brothers enjoyed good relations with the people of the neighborhood. They decided that when they retired in a couple of years, they'd just close the business when they locked the door for the last time.

The brothers had also maintained a good relationship with the cops at the Fifth Precinct through the years. The old foot-beat cops of the 40s and 50s used their store to get warm on cold Winter nights. At Christmas time, the cops assigned to their area always got a free bottle of whiskey. They also supplied free bottles of booze for special occasions, such as retirement parties.

The brothers often spoke to each other about how the local police had changed. The sight of so many female and Black officers was a stark contrast to the large, nearly all-white male force of 1946.

The Greek brothers ran an honest business, never selling to minors or raising prices like other local businesses because the ghetto had caught up with the liquor store's location.

At dusk, two young Black men entered their liquor store. Nick was behind the counter. The two armed young men did not know George was busy doing inventory in the small back storage room.

Nick smiled and leaned forward across the counter. "Good evening, Gentlemen. What can I do for you?"

The shorter of the two men fired a revolver shot into the ceiling to announce their intentions. "You can give me the money out of the register and cash box in a paper bag, or I'll blow your funky old honkie brains all over this store."

Nick did as instructed. He stood frozen, his hands held in the air. The two young robbers turned as if to leave with no further trouble. Suddenly, the shorter man wheeled and struck Nick on the side of the head with his revolver. Nick fell to the floor, stunnned.

The robber moved back to the counter, cocked his revolver and pointed it at Nick's fallen body.

George had picked up the M-1 carbine. He had no intention of using it, as long as the robbers left with no one being hurt.

After fighting the Nazis 40 years before, he did not intend to stand by and watch his brother murdered by the little Black man.

George shouldered his rifle. The first three shots hit the robber pointing the revolver at his brother, Nick. The rounds bounced him off the counter like a tennis ball. The next five shots sent him crashing to the floor, dead.

The other robber was near the front door. He fired a poorly-aimed shot toward George.

George turned the carbine toward the second, taller robber and opened fire. The man escaped, but George was very certain he had hit him at least once.

Sean was driving alone. He was at Mack Avenue and Conner when the dispatcher put out the call. He sped to the scene with the red overhead light spinning and the siren screaming. The dispatcher indicated that there had been a robbery at the liquor store with shots fired and people shot. As his vehicle neared the scene, Sean silently prayed that another one of his people had not been the shooting victim.

Minutes later, Sean was inside the store. He carefully studied the body of the dead robber.

Nick was conscious. He allowed the medical techs from E.M.S. to put him on a stretcher to check his head.

George had gathered a small group of officers around him as he explained what had happened. George drank from a warm bottle of Ouzo as he spoke, still with a thick, Greek accent. "Me an' Nickie, we never want to hurt nobody. That son-of-a-bitch there on the floor, he hit brother Nickie for nothing. Then, he gonna shoot my Nickie like a dog. Dat is some kind of bullshit. I no stand-by and watch that little bastard kill my brother for nothing. Nickie, he no argue or fight or nothing. He give them money, then they gonna shoot him. I say not while I breathe."

Willie Washington and Ed Donahue arrived at the scene. Willie approached Sean. "What you got here, Lou?"

"Willie, take a long look at the dead asshole on the floor. Then look at the piece he was carrying. Willie, I'd bet a couple of paychecks that this is the shooter that capped Henry Rubin."

A knowing grin spread slowly over Willie's face as he studied the robber's mutilated body. "Little mother fucker never looked better. Where's his partner at?"

Sean stared hard into Willie's eyes. "We've got a good clothing description and he was probably wounded. We've got the word out to all local hospitals. He's probably still in the area. There's a lot of blood at the door and out on the sidewalk. I don't think he's gone far."

When the specialists arrived from Downtown, most of the shift went back on the street.

Sean felt a sense of urgency. It was as though he felt he had to be everywhere in the precinct at once.

One of his patrol units found an abandoned stolen car at a signal light at Alter Road and Charlevoix Street. There was still fresh blood on the front seat. The engine was dead. It appeared that the robber hadn't bothered to check the stolen vehicle's gas gauge.

The dispatcher was heard from again, informing the units in the Fifth Precinct that an unidentified citizen had called and reported seeing a wounded man limping into an abandoned house on Manistique Street, near Charlevoix.

Sean drove at a dangerous speed in order to be the second unit at the scene. He took immediate command. He sent four officers to cover the rear of the house. He gave them strict instructions to hold their positions and protect themselves from potential fire from the house.

Sean selected two veteran officers and had them both arm themselves with a shotgun. They were going in the front door. He did not intend to let the precinct's time bomb explode with the crowd that would gather in a barracaded-gunman situation. In fact, he was as worried about the mood of his own people as he was the people on the street.

Ed Donahue and Willie Washington arrived at the scene, their car screaming to a stop in front of the house. They ran up to Sean as he prepared to enter the old dark house. "We're going in with you, Lieutenant."

"Hold on, Donahue. Look around. I'm still in fucking charge here. You and Willie are too involved in this. You might fuck up and get one of us or yourself shot. You two cover us from the porch. You stay out until I call for you."

"But, Lou . . ."

"God damn it, Donahue. I told you our first night together, I don't fucking debate out here on the street. Watch my lips, Officer. Cover us from the porch until I call for you."

Washington and Donahue glared at Sean for a brief moment, then took up positions to cover their entry.

Sean and the two veteran officers with shotguns rushed into the old, abandoned house using cover-and-advance tactics.

Once inside, the three men stood frozen in the small living room of the two-story frame house. Sean wanted to wait a moment so their eyes could adjust to the darkness. He had always had excellent night vision, but just needed time for his eyes to recover from the flashes of bright emergency lights and spot lights from outside.

Sean held his .357 firmly in his right hand, a four-cell metal flashlight in his left. With both other entry officers carrying shotguns, Sean would be the primary light source. They'd have to depend on him to light the target and he'd have to depend on them to protect him.

Sean had not turned on his flashlight. He could make out furniture and the archway to the dining room and the rear of the old house.

Their eyes finally focused in the near absence of light. Sean gestured for both officers to aim at the archway. He had decided to give the wounded fugitive one chance to surrender. He got back an old familiar feeling from deep inside. He hoped the robber wouldn't accept his offer.

"Listen up, asshole. This is the Detroit Police. We have the house surrounded. Identify your location, then walk slowly into the living room with your hands over your head. If you give yourself up, I guarantee your safety. If we have to come looking for you, we'll consider you an extreme life threat and fire on sight."

There was a moment of silence, then the muffled sound of someone moving at the rear of the house.

"Mr. Po-lice, don't shoot. I give up. I'm comin' out."

It sounded as if he was dragging one leg as he slowly approached the living room through the dark house.

Sean heard both support officers take the safety off their shotguns. "Careful, you two. I won't stand for an assassination. I chose you two to come in with me because you're good, veteran street coppers. Don't make me regret my decision."

Sean could hear the man stop in the dining room, just out of their line of sight.

"Come on, asshole, out where we can see you. Move smooth and slow and put your hands in the air."

"I've been shot up, Mr. Po-lice. I'm bleedin' bad and in some terrible pain."

"You're breaking my heart. Now get your sorry ass out here and we'll get you to a hospital. I'm telling you, slick, you don't want me to come and get you."

Sean caught sight of the man moving into the living room from the dining room arch. He turned on his flashlight and lit up the figure of the second robber.

The Black man was about 25, tall and thin. His trousers and shirt were soaked with his own blood. He stood in the center of the living room meekly raising both hands, squinting at the light from Sean's flashlight. The man's revolver was still in the front waist band of his pants.

Sean carefully moved toward the wounded gunman. Suddenly, he caught sight of Willie Washington and Ed Donahue. They had silently entered the house. Willie had his revolver raised to eye level, pointed at the surrendering robber.

Sean took another step toward the robber. "It's all over now, Willie. Let it go. We'll take care of it in here. You and Ed go back outside and get some air."

"Fuck this low-life, Lieutenant. He killed Henry and now I'm going to do him."

Sean recognized the expression on Washington's face. "Come on, Willie, don't be a fool. You and I both know that the punk that shot Henry is the one ol' George greased back at the liquor store. This fool is his partner, but nothing says he's been a shooter."

"He was with the guy. That's enough for me."

"Well, not for me. I'm not going to let you murder this prisoner because of some bullshit street revenge and ruin your career, when he's not even the one who wasted Rubin."

"He's still got a gun in his belt, Lou. Go ahead, big man, go for your shit."

Sean took another step toward the man.

Sweat poured from the man's face. He trembled from fear and loss of blood. He was blinded by Sean's flashlight but understood enough of the heated debate to know his own murder was being discussed.

"How about you, Lieutenant? What if Henry had been your best friend? You was in Nam, you worked the street. I've heard of some of the shit you pulled a few years ago. You capped the fucker who had shot your partner."

"Willie, for the last time, get your ass out of here. What I did has got nothing to do with this tonight. If you off this mother fucker, I'll take you down all the way, Willie, I swear to Christ. Henry would not want you to lose your job over this."

Sean had grown very tired of the strange stand-off. He moved quickly and backhanded the prisoner across the side of the head with his metal flashlight. The man fell to the floor, dazed. Sean took the handgun from his waistband. "Fuck all this shit, Washington. O.K., shoot him now, go ahead, murder him. Any first-year medical examiner will know he was unconscious when you shot him. Now you face criminal charges, in addition to losing your job. Willie, this won't bring Henry back. Put down your weapon and get on out of here. If you shoot this scum, I swear to God, I'll lock your ass up for murder."

Willie Washington was shaken. Tears rolled down his cheeks. "And what if Henry had been a white cop and your best friend, Lieutenant?"

"Willie, go on outside. I'm going to forget you asked me that. If you still don't know the answer in an hour, you hunt me down and ask me again."

Ed Donahue gently guided Willie back outside. "Come on, Partner. Won't do no good taking verbal shots at the Lieutenant. That cock-sucker on the floor is fouling up the air in here. Let's go outside. By the time that turd gets out of prison, we'll be telling war stories to our grandchildren."

Sean's eyes met Willie's as he left. Willie's expression was a mixture of an outraged frustration with a hint of new understanding.

After Washington and Donahue were outside, Sean rolled the robber onto his belly and handcuffed him. "As I approached this man, I thought he was making a move for his gun, so I hit him. Either of you two have a problem with that?"

The veteran Black officer smiled as he cleared his shotgun. "Lou, compared to what we'd have had to say if Willie had capped that mother fucker, your story is like a kiss on the lips from Donna Sommers. Truth is, you hit him to save his life, not ours. You write it up, Boss, I'll sign anything. You saved Willie and the rest of us a whole lot of trouble. By now, the whole damn city is probably gathered outside this house."

The two officers, shotguns cleared, each took an arm and dragged the robber outside and turned him over to the waiting medical techs.

Sean reholstered his .357 and put his flashlight in a rear trouser pocket. He stepped outside of the small dark house and into the glaring lights of camera strobe flashes, the bright beams of T.V. mini-cams and police spotlights.

The collection of lights made Sean wince. Sean refused to talk to media people until he had briefed the field duty officer who had just arrived at the scene.

After talking with Cmdr. Jackson, Sean made a brief statement to the media. He related the connection between their arrest and the shooting at the liquor store. He stated that although they believed they had captured officer Rubin's killers, final results would not be available until the following day.

Sean silently sat behind the wheel of his marked vehicle, deep in thought. Willie Washington walked up to Sean's window. "You saved my job and even more tonight, Lou. I owe you a lot. I didn't mean that crack about the white cop. Donahue was right, you deserve more from me than a cheap shot like that. Anyway, I want you to know I really do appreciate what you did."

Sean rested his head on the car steering wheel. The anxiety swept over him like a huge wave. He fought to control his breathing so he would not hyperventilate but he couldn't seem to catch his breath.

Willie became concerned. He leaned into the car and put his hand on Sean's shoulder. "Are you alright, Lou?"

Sean sat up and rubbed his stiff neck with his left hand. "Yea, I'm fine, Willie. Thanks. I guess I'm just a little stressed out. Why don't you give Phillis Rubin a call and tell her about the shooting and the arrest. She should hear about Henry's killers from a friend."

On the ride back to the precinct, Sean thought over the many things Willie had said in the house. The professional young police lieutenant; it was all bullshit and he knew it better than anyone. Sean had cared deeply about Henry Rubin, but Willie had hit a nerve when he asked the question in the old house. What if it had been Gary or Tom or even T.J. he had buried a week ago? He knew he had first entered the house with the hope that the injured gunman would offer any form of resistance, any excuse so they could blow him to pieces.

He thought of all that separated him from that night when he was alone with the doper who had shot Bruce. There were the years, two relationships, two promotions, a handful of different assignments and a year of professional counseling since the night he had killed the man with the revolver still stuck in his belt.

The hot August air pushed against his face. It dried the tear in the corner of his eye. He realized that he was no different than he was that night years before. What made him act differently were the gold lieutenant's bars on his uniform shirt. He was responsible for the welfare of his people now. He couldn't allow Willie to play the avenging angel he had been, not in front of a crowd.

He ached inside and he wanted to stop the car and cry. So this was what Dr. Ireland was talking about, letting go, letting himself feel. After all the years since Vietnam, he was finally letting himself feel, and he felt like shit.

19

January, 1982—October, 1982

The city had grown weary of the lengthy bitter cold spell. The second week of sub-zero temperatures made something as simple as getting in your car and driving home an uncomfortable adventure.

Sean made notes as he prepared for the shift's on-duty roll call briefing. He read over the previous day's significant incidents. At least the terrible cold weather had one positive affect, crime had dropped below normal along with the temperature.

Sean felt as much at home standing in front of his shift after a year as he did standing in front of the fireplace of his new house. He knew each man and woman on his shift and over the past year, they had been through a great deal together. They had all managed to work through Henry Rubin's shooting together as a group. Henry would have been pleased that his death had somehow brought them much closer together.

Sean still hated the monthly alternating shift work, and working the weekends and holidays. It did little to help him with his sagging social life. He never had a problem finding a groupie or a companion for a few quick rolls in the hay. He couldn't find anyone he enjoyed spending time with, outside of the bedroom.

The remodeling of his house was complete. He had spent a great deal of time and money getting the custom-built house just the way he wanted it. The hardwood floors and fine woodwork were all redone. He had added stained glass where possible. There was a mixture of antique and replica furniture to match the natural earth tones of his furniture.

It had become a standing joke with his close friends that the only reason any young woman would agree to date Sean a second time was because she liked his house.

Sean divided his social time between the friends in the suburbs he had made while playing on the Metro softball team, and varied friends in the department.

The mixed race and gender friendships of his Detroit friends kept him in touch with the city and the department as a whole. Then he could escape into the traditional male-dominated, all-white domain of the suburbs. There he was neither "white" or a "Lieutenant," he was just another off-duty cop.

After roll call, Sean took his seat behind the long, elevated desk in the lobby. He signed himself into the daily diary and began to record the shift's assignments into the large book. He sipped from his mug of coffee and glanced up at the busy precinct lobby, already filled with assorted civilians, detectives and officers.

His desk personnel busy, Sean answered the phone. "Fifth Precinct, Lt. Cavanagh. May I help you?"

"Got Lieutenants answering the phone now, do they?"

Sean rolled his eyes and shook his head. He thought there was no way to please the public. Over half the callers wanted to speak to the officer in charge, and this guy was jerking him around because the officer in charge answered the phone.

"Well, Sir, we're a bit busy this morning, and we don't like to keep the citizens waiting. How can I help you?"

There was a deep chuckle on the other end of the line. "You can stow the bullshit for starters, Cavanagh. This is Deputy Chief Bowman. With thousands of unanswered radio calls each month, I doubt whether John Q. Citizen gives much stock in how fast you answer the phone. Well, at least you people show good intentions. That's something."

Sean cursed his luck for having answered Bowman's call. "Deputy Chief, the Commander is not in his office yet. I'll have him call you the moment he arrives."

"Cavanagh, I didn't call for the Precinct Commander, I called for you. I'd like to see you in my office as soon as you can get here."

"I'm on my way, Sir."

The phone buzzed in Sean's ear, but Sean sat paralyzed for a full minute.

Sean called in his street sergeants and took their marked car Downtown to police headquarters. The Brass still had their offices on the Third Floor of the old, grey nine-story building.

Sean pushed his way into a crowded elevator to the Third Floor. He stopped at the men's room to give himself one last visual inspection before entering Bowman's office. He looked very well-groomed but he cursed the length of his styled haircut. Hair length stardards had drastically changed since he joined in 1969, but Bowman was in charge of the department's precincts and was known to be a hard-ass from the old school. If you didn't have a brush cut, you were a hippie.

Sean introduced himself to Bowman's secretary. She notified the Deputy Chief and led Sean into Bowman's office.

The broad, middle-aged man was seated behind a handsome antique desk. It was obviously a personally-owned piece of furniture. Bowman, an old corps copper, was past the age for retirement. He had come to absolutely believe that the precinct cops, especially the white cops, needed Francis Bowman on the department's famous Third Floor to represent them in policy. He felt that he was their last true representative.

Bowman chewed on the end of an unlit cigar and spoke out of the side of his mouth. "Cavanagh, nice to see you again. Help yourself to a cup of coffee, there, on top of the file cabinet."

Sean attempted to conceal his natural apprehension. He poured himself a cup of coffee and took a seat across the fine antique desk from the tough-talking Deputy Chief.

Bowman leaned back in his chair and studied Sean for an awkward moment. Sean's mouth went dry from nerves and he burnt his mouth with a gulp of hot coffee. He still couldn't figure what the hell he was doing there.

Bowman continued to bite on the cigar and speak in his gruff voice out of the side of his mouth.

"Cavanagh, with all my time on the job, all these goddamn changes, I figure I've got a feel for the things that happen in this department. There's affirmative action, major cut-backs, layoffs, social programs, the whole nine yards and I still can predict things before they happen. At the very least, I know the *why* behind what happens. Then, out of nowhere, there is this thing with you. I've watched you since you worked at the police academy. You're the All-American rich white boy from Grosse Pointe. Outstanding street and service record; you've got your graduate degree, been to the National Police Academy. It just doesn't figure. I can't see where you are plugged in to this city's administration in any fashion. It don't goddamn figure."

Sean leaned forward in his chair. "With all due respect, Sir, I have no idea what you are talking about. What doesn't figure?"

"Lt. Cavanagh, effective the first of next month, you have been promoted to the rank of commander."

Sean nearly dropped his coffee cup and sat back in his chair, speechless.

Bowman shook his head and finally lit the soggy cigar. "The few token white staff promotions made by this administration are usually old, over-the-hill bastards like me, or else those brown nose, liberal, boot-licking college boys with no street experience."

Sean took another gulp of coffee. "Promoted to commander, Sir?"

"Yep, I have the distinct feeling that I've got you by default. My gut feeling is that they had other plans for you. But the C.O. of the 13th

Precinct has been out sick for months. He's finally going to retire, and we have an unexpected opening. Do you have any idea how you're tied in? It's not that you don't deserve the promotion, Kid. I'm damn glad to have you, but you don't fit their stereotype."

For a moment, Sean stared at the floor in deep thought. He thought of his mutual respect and long-term friendship with Perry Mann. "Maybe I'm just a favorite of someone who's really plugged in. Perry Mann and I go way back. I understand that if the Chief sits at the right hand of His Honor, Perry is at the left hand."

Bowman smirked at Sean's candor. "You and I will get along just fine, Cavanagh. Are you always this candid with your boss?"

"Yes, Sir, unless he screws me for it."

"Well, I'll be candid. The 13th Precinct has not had a C.O. for a long time. It's gone to hell in a hand-basket. She's like an old tramp freighter that's been sailing without a captain. The place is a fucking mess. Morale stinks. Performance level's the worst in the department. It is a real shitty first assignment for a new commander and it will be even rougher for you. You worked with some of those people when you were still a street copper. I'll be straight with you, Cavanagh, I'll dump on a new guy before I'll transfer one of my good commanders there just because they're doing a good job where they are. Not much of a reward, if you see what I mean."

Sean's mind flashed back to the day he first reported to Cmdr. Bellotti's office in '69. He had been correct. Sean would occupy that office after all.

"Thirteen will be fine with me, Boss. I'd rather work there in a shit storm than drive all the way to a Westside precinct everyday."

"Yea? Well, we'll see if you feel the same in a couple months. Take some advice from an old warhorse. You're not yet 34 and you look even younger. If you try that laid-back supervisor's approach at 13 that you use with your shift, they'll have you for lunch. I respect your command style. You get the job done. You knew how to be a hard-ass when you were an instructor at the academy. You may need to be one again at first. If you're fair and know the book inside and out, you can get away with jumping square in their shit to straighten that place out.

"You've got your work cut out for you, Cavanagh. This will be no cakewalk. If you need some help the first month or two, I can still pull a few strings."

Sean finished his coffee and stood to leave. "Thank you, Deputy Chief Bowman, I'll give you a good precinct."

Bowman stood and shook Sean's hand. "I believe you will, Cavanagh. But you be damn careful. You watch out for your young white butt. They may be grooming you for bigger things. You may, in fact, be moving up that political ladder. If you ever do screw up, they'll use you as the scapegoat in a heartbeat. If you get on the Mayor's shit list, you might as well sell red hots at the ballpark. When you put those gold commander's oak leaves on your uniform, it's a whole new ballgame, and it's hardball. And by the way, get your hair cut. You look like a goddamn hippie."

As is often the case, the accounts of the going-away party thrown by the shift were even more exciting than the party itself. Though in this case, neither was dull nor boring.

Sean had been given the several days off still owed to him on the books for vacation. It gave him time to do some homework on the personnel files of the people at what had become his precinct. It also gave his predecessor time for an orderly removal of his personal items from the precinct commander's office and the city painters time to cover the office walls with a fresh coat of institutional white paint.

Sean entered the lobby of the 13th Precinct at 2 a.m., two-and-a-half days before he was scheduled to report. He had parked his Triumph TR7 in front of the station. He was dressed in a suit and wore a trench coat.

Sean walked up to the precinct desk through the deserted lobby. He stood there for a long moment. The three officers behind the desk did not acknowledge his presence. They continued doing whatever they were doing when he entered the lobby.

Sean cleared his throat, but they continued to ignore his presence.

The clerk looked up briefly, then went back to his arrest cards. The operator at the switchboard was concentrating on the contents of a skin magazine.

After a full minute, Sean decided to break the silence. "May I speak to the officer in charge?"

The officer seated in the shift commander's seat directly in front of Sean finally looked up and spoke. "What can we do for you?"

"I'd like to speak to the officer in charge."

"I'm the officer in charge. What do you want?"

"Since when does this department place patrol officers in charge of a shift? I want the officer in charge. That normally means a sergeant or a lieutenant."

"Look, Mister, I don't know what your problem is, but you'd . . ."

Sean slammed his new commander's badge and I.D. card on the top of the desk. "I'm Cmdr. Cavanagh, your new Precinct Commander. I want to see the man in charge of the shift."

The officer sprang to his feet. He went pale and began to stutter. "I'm sorry, Sir. I didn't know, Commander. The Sarge is in the back having coffee. I'll go get him."

Sean was silent during the hour-long, unscheduled inspection of his new command. He saw very little that satisfied him. He knew the midnight shift developed its own culture, but there were too many things he would not accept on his command for any shift.

Sean shook the Sergeant's hand and cooly thanked him for the tour. He left the precinct with a clearer idea of the task ahead.

On Monday, the sergeants and lieutenants of the precinct gathered in the squad room for their first staff meeting with their new commander. They nervously chatted and drank coffee.

The room went quiet as Sean entered and walked to the podium. His uniform was poster perfect.

"Ladies and Gentlemen, I'm Cmdr. Cavanagh. I am giving you advance notice. Two weeks from today, if the people, the vehicles, and the building look as they do today, it will be the beginning of a very unpleasant relationship.

"Your patrol officers look like hell, the vehicle fleet should be scrapped, and a building only 34-years-old should be condemned. I've made an assignment roster. Each one of you has been given a special task to perform and maintain.

"For example. Sgt. Kennedy, as the Precinct's Executive Sergeant, you will be responsible to make certain we get these walls painted. Then you'll inform the janitorial staff that they had better start cleaning this place instead of pushing dirty water around the floors for eight hours. Tell your people on the shifts they have two weeks to get ready.

"This isn't the precinct station on the T.V. show. We will not wear unauthorized uniforms, except under extreme weather conditions. Have everyone review the police manual. Anyone not in proper uniform in two weeks will be sent home and written up.

"I have also scheduled an individual interview with each of you over the next two weeks. If the time conflicts with your personal schedule, please contact Sgt. Kennedy. I will answer any questions and discuss any transfer requests at those meetings. Thank you all for coming. This meeting is over."

Sgt. Kennedy and Lt. Ward were the senior white male supervisors at the precinct. They stood in the garage talking, as they sipped hot coffee.

"I tell you what, Sarge, I need some new tight-ass kid commander bustin' my chops about as much as I need another child-support payment."

Sgt. Kennedy stared down at his coffee. "I think it's way too early to tell yet, Lou. A classmate of mine from the academy worked for him at

Number Five. He said he was a damn fine shift boss. That hard-ass routine might just be for show. Hell, Lou, we've both seen this place go to hell. The kid was a rookie here in the late 60s. He was a good street copper; he worked Robbery, Homicide, Narcotics. He's no cherry, even if he is still wet behind the ears. We can both retire at any time. I think I'll give the Boy Wonder a chance. I wouldn't cross him, though. If these people don't take him seriously, in two weeks the shit's gonna hit the fan in a royal fashion."

The Lieutenant shook his head. "It must grind you some, Ben. You were a street sergeant when that kid came here out of the academy."

"Not a bit, Lou. I don't have an hour of college, I write a terrible test, and if it hadn't been for that huge sergeant's list after the riot, when all the war vets retired, I wouldn't have these three stripes. Lou, the only friends we old corps dinosaur cops have at the top are these sharp white kids. They still respect us as veteran cops. I'd much rather work for a kid like this Cavanagh, than some affirmative action, 90-day wonder who can't find his way to the precinct without a map. Those folks not only don't respect our experience, they don't even trust us."

"I hope you're right, Ben. Let's see now, he's got me responsible for the marked vehicles. He wants a list with mileage, needed repairs, appearance, and overall condition. What do you think, Ben?"

"If I were you, Lieutenant, I'd have an accurate list ready for him in two weeks."

Later in the morning, Sgt. Ben Kennedy knocked on Sean's office door. Sean saw him through the window in the door and waved him in.

"Am I disturbing you, Boss?"

"No, Sarge. Come in and sit down. I brought in a couple of boxes of personal items, you know, to make the place feel more like home. Well, have I got things buzzing out there?"

Kennedy sat down and grinned, taking a sip of coffee.

"That would be the understatement of the month. You're going to have a tough haul for a while, Boss. The minority supervisors and street troops will be ready to run Downtown with every complaint, and a whole lot of the white coppers see you as a token white for the Mayor and the Brass on the Third Floor. There are only a handful of people who were here when you left in '75. Even if they remember that you were a good street copper, they'll be jealous."

Sean took out several framed documents and pictures. "Sarge, I appreciate the inside scoop. I don't expect you to be my spy. You were a damn fine sergeant when I came here as a rookie in '69, and you helped me a great deal. I hope that part won't change. The bottom line is that we're going to turn this place around.

"We can do it the hard way or as easily as possible. I'm going to let you in on some information that shouldn't leave this room. I didn't walk in here with a paper asshole. I already have my ducks lined up. I've got a guarantee for a full interior paint job just waiting for your call. There are five new prototype police cars waiting for us at the M.O.G. All we need do is request them, after Lt. Ward submits his report on the vehicle fleet. The C.O. of the uniform store promised full cooperation when our people go there. I know it's all just frosting, Sarge, but it is a start."

Kennedy walked up to Sean's desk and started to pick up a framed 5 x 7 photo. "May I?"

Sean smiled and stopped what he was doing. "I keep it around to remind me of tougher times. Compared to then, Sarge, all this sometimes seems a little silly."

Kennedy studied the faces of the young Marines, posing, hamming for the camera. "Babies. The whole bunch of you were just kids. You should have been home sneaking beers and chasing girls."

Sean took the photo back and looked at his friends from December, 1967. He was silent for a moment, then set the photo on his desk, face down.

"Sarge, I'm really glad you're still at 13. I'm going to need your help. We'll talk more later. I'm going to come across like a tight-ass at first, but something has got to turn this place around."

"Boss, if I should ever come down with a case of the stupids, remind me never to underestimate you. I'll go call and get your precinct painted."

———

During the following two weeks, Sean had the opportunity to interview each of the precinct's supervisors. They were a mixed group with varied experiences and backgrounds. They ranged from veteran, white, male, old corps cops, to young, inexperienced, Black, female, affirmative-action promotion selections. They all seemed to have two common traits. They were frustrated with the condition of the precinct and defensive about taking any responsibility for that condition.

After clearly defining the ground rules and his expectations, Sean kept a very low profile for two weeks. He spent most of the time either in meetings Downtown or alone in his office with the blinds covering the window in the door.

During those two weeks, the precinct's interior was repainted a clean institutional light blue.

At 7:45 a.m. Monday of his third week in command, Sean stood in front of the podium in the second-story squad room. He waited for the two ranks of sleepy patrol officers to get settled, the precinct's second platoon, the day shift.

"As all of you know, I'm Cmdr. Cavanagh, your new Precinct Commander. As the months pass, I'd like to develop the same kind of relationship with the people of this precinct that I enjoyed with my shift when I was a lieutenant at Number Five. Unfortunately, that will be totally up to you. I realize it takes time to develop loyalty and trust. If I tell you something, people, you can take it to the bank. I expect the same from you. I will accept no less than 100 percent from you. In return, I'll do everything I can to protect you if you make an honest mistake out there. I'm not going to allow this precinct to be a dumping ground for every misfit in the department. Number 13 will not turn into a leper colony. Now are there any questions?"

An overweight white cop about Sean's age, raised his hand from his position in the first rank. "Excuse me, Commander," he said, sarcasm dripping from his voice. "Hope you don't mind if some of us don't get too excited about your pep talk. The way I figure, I was here when you got here, and I'll be here long after you leave, so we've heard lots of these talks the last few years."

There were some chuckles through the ranks.

Sean stared at the officer for a long moment, a smirk on his face. The silence created an awkward discomfort in the two ranks.

"Officer Kowalski, if I would have expected anyone would have become excited by my little pep talk, we'd have prepared cold showers or I'd have suggested you all go out and sit in the snow before starting the shift. So, please don't take this as a threat. You may have been here when I arrived, but there is no guarantee you'll be here when I leave. I've been sent here by Deputy Chief Bowman to straighten out this precinct. If any of you doubt my ability to have you transferred in a heartbeat, test me. Oh, and Kowalski, show up in ranks again with a mouth full of chew and I promise you it will be very unpleasant. Lt. Ward, prepare your shift for inspection."

There was a nervous chatter in the ranks as Ward moved them into inspection position and had them draw their weapons. Sean slowly moved down both ranks. He stopped at every officer, inspected some handguns, but did not speak.

He began to leave the squad room, but stopped at the door. "Lt. Ward, I want you in my office after roll call is complete. Your people had better read their department manuals in the areas concerning proper uniforms, condition of sidearms, and proper ammunition. I've given them two weeks to do it on their own. Now, they'll do it my way. You look like this tomorrow, Kowalski, and we'll see if I can excite you."

Sean poured himself a mug of coffee and waited in his office for the anticipated fallout from his morning's performance. There was a knock on his door as he heard the day shift decend the stairs and head for their vehicles. Sean could see a white, male officer of about 30, outside the door. He recognized him as the day shift's D.P.O.A. Steward. Sean motioned him to enter.

"Commander, can I speak with you a couple of minutes before you see Lt. Ward?"

"Come in and close the door, Peterson. What can I do for you?"

"As shift steward, it's my duty to inform you, Commander, if you continue to harass our people, I will be forced to file a grievance."

Sean leaned forward, both elbows on his desk, holding his coffee mug with both hands. "File a grievance, Peterson? May I ask on what premise?"

Peterson sat down and shifted to get comfortable in his chair. "Can I speak off the record, Sir?"

Sean remained perfectly still, staring at Peterson as he wiggled to find a position of comfort. "You want it off the record, man-to-man and all that? Do you want to take off our badges and step outside, too? Have your say, Peterson, off the record."

"O.K., if you keep up this chicken-shit stuff about the uniforms and guns and dirty cars, I'll have your ass Downtown with a harassment grievance so fast your head will spin."

Sean took a slow deliberate sip from his mug. He kept his stare on Peterson and got that look on his face that warned Peterson that his threat did not have the desired effect.

"Are we still off the record? Fine, listen up, Peterson. Don't you ever come in here again and threaten me, either on or off the record. If you want to discuss a potential grievance, the door is always open. That's your job. You want to play grievance hardball with me, Peterson, you'd better memorize the manual. I am attempting to create a precinct in which the officers follow established policies when possible, a precinct they can be proud of. I know that manual, Peterson. I'm not threatened by you or the grievance, or the D.P.O.A., because I'm acting within regulations spelled out in the manual and the union contract. If you ever threaten me with a grievance over a non-grievance issue again, I'll stuff that manual so far up your ass you'll limp for a year. How many people were late this morning, Peterson?"

"It's snowing and the traffic was terrible."

"Read the manual. It says you get here on time. Now, we're not going to write up the officers that were late, that would be chicken-shit harassment. But that manual works both ways, Peterson. Does this precinct look and feel better since the new paint job?"

Peterson paused for a moment. He was still stunned by Sean's verbal barrage and he didn't understand the question.

"Yea, it makes everything cleaner and brighter. So what?"

"It's the same premise with proper uniform appearance. When you show pride in the way you dress, it says you have pride in yourself. It's the same with the condition of our marked cars. I'm not trying to turn this place into the police academy. I just want to build some pride, even if I initially have to do it by being a real hard-ass. Peterson, go think on what we've talked about. Stop by after your shift and let me know what you've decided to do."

Peterson, seemingly in a deep thoughtful daze, walked out of Sean's office without another word.

Lt. Ward slowly walked into Sean's office as Peterson left. "About this morning's inspection, Commander. I'm really sorry. I thought that the . . ."

"Sit down, Vince. They weren't that bad. I didn't really expect you to turn them around in two weeks. See, this way I can be the asshole and they'll be pissed at me. You have to work with those people every day. They only see me once every three months. I'll play the heavy. Just support my programs on the official basis is all I ask."

"You've got it, Boss. Here is the report on the condition of our marked vehicles."

Sean carefully looked over the report. He handed it back to Lt. Ward.

"Vince, you know those cars much better than I do. Pick the worst five. Take them down to the M.O.G. on Jefferson and see a Mr. McCollough. He will give us five new prototype marked Plymouths. I'd like two assigned to the North End, two to the South End and the fifth in the middle of the precinct. The street supervisor's car looks to be in good shape. It will be better for morale if we give all five to the street troops. Tell your people, if these new cars look like hell in five months, they won't even see a new police car until '86."

Lt. Ward sat with his mouth open. "Five new cars. How in the hell did you pull that off?"

"It's all done with bullshit. It's no state secret, Vince. The new kid on the block gets some sugar when they send him to a precinct to fix it. We've got to take all we can get before my honeymoon phase is over."

Sean addressed, then inspected the other two shifts that day. The results were about the same as the morning's confrontation with platoon two.

By mid-week, some of the sting was gone. There was new equipment showing up, five new cars, the precinct had been painted. The officers found no problems getting uniforms exchanged or weapons repaired. No doubt that the kid Commander was most certainly a hard-ass. But they had to admit that he has improved life at 13 more in three weeks than anyone had in the past five years combined.

As the weeks passed, most officers decided it was easier doing it
Cavanagh's way. The loyalty and trust began to grow, and the precinct's
performance improved.

As Precinct Commander, Sean was assigned an unmarked police car
for personal use within the city. It saved wear and tear on his own
vehicle from the daily drive to and from his home on the far eastern
edge of Detroit.

When the new models came out, Sean treated himself to a new BMW,
to celebrate his promotion. The silver two-door had a great sound
system, and was a pleasure to drive. He had a police radio mounted in
the glove compartment for the numerous occasions when he didn't
want to drive the unmarked police car.

Sean's family teased him that he had waited until Grandfather Cavanagh's death before buying a German-made car, so he wouldn't be
removed from the will. His brother Brian had repeatedly said Sean
would probably buy a Honda as soon as their own father passed away.

Sean said he wasn't worried about his own son ever buying a car built
in Vietnam. He said if the Vietnamese sold a car, it would have to have
been built in Russia.

OCTOBER, 1982
DETROIT

Sean glanced out of his office window. The steady rain had been
falling all day and gave no indication of letting up. He rubbed his tired,
burning eyes and leaned back in his office chair, away from the stack of
paperwork on his desk.

It was already dark at 5:15 p.m., and northbound Woodward Avenue
was locked in bumper to bumper rush hour traffic. Sean had decided to
stay at his office and try to make a dent in the building pile of paperwork
until 6:00, when rush hour traffic would finally thin.

Sean looked at the time on his Seiko wristwatch. He had learned not
to trust the desk clock. He was to pick up his date at her far Eastside
home at 8 p.m. He estimated that if he left the precinct at 6, he'd have
time to shower, change and still arrive on time.

The intercom button flashed on his phone and it buzzed. When he
answered, the shift lieutenant sounded very excited and asked Sean to
pick up line one. There was an emergency concerning one of their own
people.

A Lt. Jeff David from the 15th Precinct was on the line.

"Commander, we're at the home of your Officer Walter Stockden, on
Novara Street, just off Kelly Road."

Sean shot up straight in his chair. "Christ, Lieutenant, what do you have? Walt and I go back to '69. He was still a rookie when I came here out of the academy. Hell, we've worked together. I know he's been into the sauce pretty heavy due to a family beef, but he wasn't bringing his problems to work. God damn it, is Walt dead, Lieutenant?"

Lieutenant David could recognize the concern in Sean's voice.

"Commander, we received a radio run to this address about an hour ago. Stockden's divorce became final today. He's been staying in some cold water flat with another divorced male cop over in Number Eleven. He got himself real drunked up tonight and came over here to where his kids and ex-wife still live. He and the wife argued for a while, then he chased them out of the house at gun point. He now has himself barricaded in the first floor bathroom. He's holding a cocked .357 to his own head and sitting in the bathtub. We can't get near him. He says he only has the job to live for and now he believes he's lost that. He won't believe me, Sir. He says the only person he'd believe that told him he still had a job is you, because he trusts you to tell the truth."

Sean looked back out the window at the traffic and the rain. "God damn it, Lieutenant. In this weather and traffic, it will take me over an hour to get there."

"Commander, I've got Deputy Chief Bowman's approval to put up a chopper despite the weather. They'll land on East Hancock Street, just west of Woodward, so have them blocked off. The chopper is en route from city airport, E.T.A. is five minutes from now."

Sean took his coat and police hat from the coat tree and still held the receiver to his ear. "Damn outstanding job, Lieutenant. I'm on my way. Tell Walt that I'm en route and . . .."

"I know, Commander. We'll do everything we can."

By the time Sean put on his gear and walked out of the garage door into the weather, a department Bell Ranger helicopter touched down on Hancock Street. They had cleared the wide concrete ramp of vehicles so the chopper blades could keep clear of the building across Hancock.

Sean ran to the rear door of the chopper, through the swirling wind and stinging rain. He held onto his hat as he ran. He dropped into the seat, closed the chopper door and they were airborne the moment he buckled his seatbelt.

Sean knew he could not be heard over the engine noise, with the pilot and observer wearing helmets. He gave them both the thumbs up sign.

The observer motioned to a helmet on the rear seat next to Sean. It was attached to the aircraft's inner-communications system. Sean carefully slid the helmet over his ears.

He clearly heard the pilot's voice in the helmet ear piece. "Commander, we'll be at the scene in less than 10 minutes. Have you ever been in a chopper before, Sir?"

Sean grinned and nodded. "I sure as hell have, Sergeant. Lots of times, but they were all green."

The pilot smiled. "Nam? That's where I learned my trade. On-the-job training, you know. Join the Army and learn a career."

Sean stared out of the rain covered window, "Yea, I also learned a trade. I was a Grunt. I really appreciate you guys going up in this weather."

The pilot gestured with his free hand. "Thanks, Commander, but it's really no big deal. These things can fly in this stuff with no problem. We can't see shit for any crime prevention because of the rain, so we don't waste fuel and flight hours."

They followed the bright red and white line of bumper-to-bumper traffic on the Ford freeway, east to Moross Road, then he turned north. The pilot spotted his make-shift landing zone in the center of a half-dozen police car emergency lights.

Sean thanked the crew and they wished him luck as he removed the helmet. He ran back out into the rotor wash created by the chopper as it lifted off without him.

Sean was greeted by Lt. David. He was updated on the situation as they entered the neat little frame bungalow, within sight of Kelly Road, near the eastern city limits.

The bathroom was at the rear of the first floor, at the end of a short hallway. The door was fully opened.

Sean could see Walt Stockden sitting in the bathtub, facing them, a cocked .357 held to his own head.

He took off his hat and handed it to David. He whispered under his breath. "If this doesn't work out, make certain my son gets this. He lives in Texas with his mother."

David nodded. The request needed no discussion. It wasn't gallows humor. Cops often made brief, last requests at life-threatening situations.

Sean slowly approached the bathroom.

"Don't you come no closer, Boss, or I swear I'll blow my brains all over this bathroom."

"Easy, Walt. I was told you asked to talk to me. I'm just getting close enough that our talk is private and we don't have to shout."

"That's close enough. Not another step, I mean it."

Sean stopped and raised the palms of his hands. "Can I take off this heavy coat and sit down here, so we can talk?"

"Yea, but no closer, and don't try nothin'."

"Walt, I'm not here to try anything. You asked for me, remember? You wanted to talk to me, so I'm here to talk, that's all."

"I got your word on that, Boss?"

"I swear. Just do me one favor. Uncock the revolver and rest your arm for a while. With me sitting here like this, I'm blocking the hall anyway. Your arm must be tired. With that thing cocked, you could shoot yourself by accident. Come on, Walt, if you are going to shoot yourself we can't stop you. But for Christ's sake, don't kill yourself by accident."

The drunken 40-year-old veteran cop skillfully lowered the hammer and rested his right arm on the top rim of the bathtub. "I've really gone and done it this time, Cav ol' buddy. First I lose my wife, my kids, everything I ever owned. Now, I fuck up and lose my job."

Sean tried to look relaxed and leaned back. "I'm afraid I don't know about your family matters, Walt. But let this thing end and I promise you that you've still got a job."

There was frustration in Walt's voice, not anger. "Don't you bullshit me, Cavanagh. I trusted you. They'll never let no head case like me back on the street."

"Hey, Walt. You asked me here so you'd get the truth. I'm not saying they'll thank you for an interesting night and you'll be back on the shift on Monday. I'm saying you won't be fired, and you won't ride a desk until your retirement. Lots of coppers have been down this road. It took you a few months to get your life this screwed up, it'll take a few months to get back on the right track."

"What if some department shrink decides I'm really a fruitcake?"

"Come on, Walt. Over half of this fucking department has gone through a divorce, and all of the bullshit that goes with it. Lots of cops have taken it this far, some even farther. How many names have we heard at roll call? So a guy loses his poise the day his divorce is final. How many times you been to a radio run like that? Walt, this shit is not front page news. It's no big fucking deal."

"It is when it's a cop."

"Now you're the one with the bullshit, my friend. If you do decide to blow your brains all over the bathroom, it won't make section A. You're not the first divorced man to lose his cool the day the papers become final, and you won't be the last."

"Cavanagh, I respected you as a street cop, and now as a fair boss. But what the hell do you know about this?"

"What do I know about it? I'm divorced and my wife split to Texas with my son. A few years later my fiancee walked out on me one night to go find herself. After I fucked up my third relationship, I went to a psychologist. I've been seeing him for two years.

"I've thought about eating my gun a couple of times too, Walt. But the thing that stopped me is pride. I'm too damn proud to let anything push me into that. We're survivors, Pal. They couldn't kill us on the street. I'll be go to hell if someone, anyone, will push me to take myself out."

Walt began to cry. Sean could not understand what he was trying to say through his heavy drunken sobbing.

Suddenly Walt stopped crying. He raised the .357 and aimed it at the center of Sean's chest.

Sean heard the officers behind him drawing their weapons. Sean merely raised his hand to the unseen officers, stopping their movement.

"They're going to have to shoot me, Cavanagh, or I'm going to take you out."

Sean displayed no emotions. He leaned his head against the hallway wall. He cursed his own fate. He thought of all the times he had faced possible death. Now, he sat in a clean little home in a nice neighborhood. He had rushed to help one of his people and now that man, a fellow officer, was aiming a gun at his chest.

"Walt, you've always been a good cop. Consider two points. Do you want to be remembered as the guy who asked to talk to another copper for help, and then killed him when he got there? Secondly, how about these people behind me? They get dispatched to a routine family trouble run and then are forced to kill a cop because he shoots another cop. Do they ever forget that? I won't shit you, Walt. I don't want to die. But if it's my time, I'd pray to God another police officer isn't the one who cancels my ticket. I'd rather be hit by a fucking bus."

"Cavanagh, I've got nothing left, without my family."

"It may be corny, Walt, but you've got this department. Not just me coming here, but Lt. David and his people. Deputy Chief Bowman put a chopper up in the rain to get me here. There are guys outside, praying you'll walk out the front door. Walt, we've seen a lot of changes, but we still take care of our own. The people at the precinct, they're family."

"I'm real confused, Cav."

"I know. Walt, listen to me. I'm going to offer you a trade. I'll have the Lieutenant pour you four fingers of whiskey in trade for your piece. We shut this thing down now and all promises stand. The longer you jerk us around, the tougher it will be getting you back on the street. After we trade, the E.M.S. people will take you to the hospital. I'll be there first thing on Monday to help schedule a timetable for your return to duty."

Without being asked directly, David had located a whiskey bottle and poured a tall glass, half full. He handed it to Sean, who was still seated on the floor.

It was a unique scene. Walt pointed his gun at Sean, who appeared to be pointing the glass of whiskey at Walt.

Walt lowered his arm. He held his face with his left hand and cried.

Sean slowly got to his feet and walked into the bathroom. He easily took the revolver from Walt's hand and replaced it with the whiskey glass.

"You really do care about me, don't you, Cav?"

"Hell, yes. Why else would the Boy Wonder come out in the rain?" Sean made no effort to conceal the tears in his eyes.

Walt raised his glass. "Salute, to ol' terrible Number Thirteen, the best damn precinct in the whole damn department." He quickly gulped down the contents.

The officers and E.M.S. people gently escorted Walt to a waiting van.

Walt's estranged wife gave David and Sean a hug and assured them she did not indend to prosecute, as long as he got professional help.

Lt. David and Sean moved into the kitchen. "Can I offer you a cigarette, Commander? That was a hairy one. I thought we'd lost the both of you a couple of times. It scared the shit right out of me. I'd have never forgiven myself for calling you here to be shot by a fellow cop."

"Lieutenant, I don't need a cigarette. Where's the bottle you found for Walt?"

David went to a kitchen cabinet.

Sean poured himself a healthy amount in a coffee cup. He tried to keep his hands from shaking. He made a face after a large swallow of the lukewarm whiskey. "My car is still at Thirteen. I live near St. John Hospital, if you can give me a lift home."

"It would be a pleasure, Sir."

Sean glanced at his watch. "Shit, let me make a call first. I've got a date, and I'm going to be late. Hell hath no fury and all that, you know."

Lt. David was a couple of years Sean's junior and the thought of the smooth young command officer dating like a teenager somehow amused him. It seemed contrary to that night's life-and-death confrontation.

Sean finished his coffee cup full of whiskey. "Come on, Lieutenant. Better get me home so I can change. I'm getting too old for this dating game bullshit, especially with this job. A fucking date. What the hell do I say if she asks in small talk about what I did today?"

David lit another cigarette. "You do the honorable thing; lie. Tell her it was a normal day and talk about the weather. If you tried to tell her the truth, you could forget any after-dinner drink and a goodnight kiss. Chopper ride in a blinding rain to risk your life for a suicidal officer. Only a copper would believe it."

"You know, Lieutenant, I've got a great family. Normal people don't ever go through all this bullshit. Everyone has family problems, but no one else lives it every day like us."

The Lieutenant took a long drag from his cigarette. "Yep, but normal people don't get to ride in a police chopper in the rain and have guns pointed at them."

"Come to think of it, David, the only non-cop people I really know is my family. How about you?"

"Commander, my dad, brother, uncle, in-laws, all are or were cops. I've been married to my wife since we were 20. I guess in my case, I don't know any normal people. Even my family isn't *normal* in that sense."

Sean put his arm around David's shoulder. "I'll follow your advice about conversation tonight. If I get lucky, I'll buy you a drink. Something better than that snake poison Walt drinks. Christ, that shit would take the paint off of your car. You and your people did a hell of a job here tonight, Lieutenant. You saved a decent cop's life and probably his career. It scares the shit out of me, David, when I wonder how close I've come to having been the guy in the bathtub."

Lieutenant David lead Sean to his police car for his drive home. "I find that tough to believe, Commander. You were sure as hell cool and controlled in there."

"Yea, but it wasn't my divorce that became final today."

20

November—December, 1982

NOVEMBER, 1982

In Portland, Oregon, Attorney Wayne Yancey had become a man possessed with the idea of a small reunion at the dedication of the Vietnam Memorial. The ceremony was scheduled for mid-November in Washington D.C., and Yancey had planned and orchestrated the reunion for months.

T.J. had recently been released from prison. He had family in D.C., and he was as excited as Yancey about getting together for the Memorial.

Yancey had been in contact with Jim Fox in Florida, and their former Lieutenant had also agreed to attend.

Yancey and Sean had corresponded at least twice a year since Vietnam. Yancey was a bit troubled. Sean had been the only Vietnam buddy he had kept in touch with, and now Sean was the only one who had not confirmed the four-member reunion.

T.J. spoke to Yancey on the phone. T.J. said he hadn't visited Sean since his release from prison. He promised he'd see their mutual friend, and assured Yancey that Sean would be there for the reunion.

———————

Sean worked on October's monthly report at his desk at the 13th Precinct. It was only a week after Officer Walt Stockden's suicide threat.

He was pleased with October's report. His people at the precinct had really displayed an effort and their numbers showed it. He was gloating over the report when the intercom buzzed. "Yes, what is it?"

The desk officer's voice was nervous and uncertain. "I'm sorry to bother you, Commander. There is a Mr. Tyler Johnson here in the lobby. He says he has an appointment to see you."

Sean broke into a wide smile. "You tell Mr. Johnson I'll be right there."

Sean opened the door to his office and saw T.J. standing in the lobby, wearing a suit and carrying a folder under his arm. "This way, Mr. Johnson. Thank you for coming." Sean turned to the officers at the desk. "Please hold all calls unless it's an emergency . . . or the Third Floor."

Sean closed his office door and closed the door's window blinds.

Once inside Sean's office, both men broke up with laughter. After much back-slapping and hand-shaking, they finally sat down. Sean poured T.J. a mug of coffee.

"Look at you, T.J., in a suit. Have you been to a funeral?"

"No, smart ass. I just figured if I'm gonna visit my big-shot friend, I should look more like a Black attorney than a nigger ex-con."

"Come on, T.J. I've never been ashamed of our friendship. You've never embarrassed me. You didn't have to dress up so you could come to see me. By the way, big Brother, it took you fucking long enough to get around to it."

"Well, I wanted to make a good impression, because we got some serious shit to discuss. I talked to Yance. He says you ain't told him yet you'd be at our little reunion in D.C. for the Memorial."

Sean's facial expression changed in a heartbeat. "That's because I'm not going."

"Say what?"

"Watch my fucking lips, T.J. I said, I'm not going."

"Why not, Bro?"

"Why not? I think a better question is why should I? No need to dig up all that grief and excess baggage again. I'd like to see Yance and the Lieutenant, but not there. They are finally going to let us vets out of the closet, T.J. In '77, President Carter welcomed back all of those gutless assholes that had skyed out to Canada. Now, five fucking years later the nation is going to dedicate a Memorial we vets had to pay for ourselves. So they finally forgive us for fighting, suffering, and dying for our country? Well, fuck them and their dedication ceremony. I'm over it now, T.J. I saw a shrink for a couple of years, and I'm over it."

T.J. could feel Sean's intensity of emotions. He sat silently for a few seconds. "Brother, that picture on the wall behind you, take it off and look at it for a minute."

Determined to prove his point, Sean removed the framed photo from the wall and looked at the young faces, holding the frame with both hands.

"Listen, white Blood, you owe them boys, and a whole lot of others, to go to that dedication."

"Bullshit, T.J.! I owe nothing. I paid my debts back, in spades. I have scars from head to toe, physical and emotional. I still have nightmares. Who knows how many of my personal problems were caused by the war? I don't owe jack shit."

"Look at the picture, Brother. Look at it, Goddamn it! See Mr. Cool and your man, Logs? If your name was carved in that Memorial, do you think they'd come to the dedication if they were still alive? We're going to pay our own respect to those boys that didn't come home. We'll be doing our own personal thing for those boys."

Sean stared at the photo. Tears filled his eyes and rolled down his cheeks. "Don't you understand, T.J.? I'm fucking scared."

T.J. was puzzled. "Scared? Irish, what you got to be scared of?"

"Ghosts, T.J. All of those ghosts."

T.J. reached across Sean's desk and clutched Sean's forearm. "Hey, Bro, think about it. You, me, Yance, and the Lu-tenant. Who could mess with the four of us? Ain't no home boys or no ghosts could take the four of us when we're back together. Besides, most them ghosts were our buddies, buddies who'd want us there."

Sean put the photo back on the wall. "O.K. T.J., if we're really going to pay tribute to our fallen buddies, I still have one condition. After D.C., we drive up to Boston to see some people before we come home."

"You mean see Logs' folks?"

"If I'm going to put this thing behind me, I've got to go all the way."

"Irish, it ain't never gonna be behind us 100 percent."

"I know, T.J. But if I'm really going to get on with my life, I've got to let most of it go. You were right, it's still dragging me down. I'm not really over it, and I know it."

"I'm going to stay at my Uncle William's house while we're in D.C. I been thinking about movin' to D.C. I got a cousin who owns an auto body shop there. It would be better than being out on the streets here. I ain't goin' back to no prison, Irish."

"I read the letter from Yance. He's got rooms for Fox and me already reserved. I'll tell him I'll be there."

"You don't have to, I'll tell him. By the way, you still ain't drivin' one of them sissy little Triumphs, are you?"

"No, I just bought a BMW. It's got a great sound system. I'll bring all my R&B and Donna Sommers tapes. You do still like Donna Sommers, don't you?"

"Like Donna Sommers? Man, like does a bear shit in the woods? You say a BMW? One of them high-class German cars, right? Oh, the Brothers in Uncle William's neighborhood gonna love your preppie white ass in your fancy car. Never mind no R&B tapes. Be sure you bring your piece."

"I don't know, T.J. I thought if the shit got bad, I could roll down the windows and play the Commodores for them."

"Like I said, bring your piece."

———

It was a full day's drive from Detroit to Washington D.C. T.J. told Sean that his BMW was no Cadillac, but it was pretty nice for a preppie car.

The two friends talked, laughed, and sang away the hours of the drive. They covered every topic, from their families, to the play-by-play description of the football game they had played against each other 10 years before at Jackson Prison. They never mentioned Vietnam or the boys they'd known there. In the solemn days that were to follow, there would be time to remember, time to relive their Vietnam experience.

The plan was to drop off T.J. at his Uncle William's house on the way to the hotel. Then at 9 p.m., T.J. would join them all in the hotel lounge for drinks.

Following T.J.'s less-than-perfect directions, Sean drove into the driveway of T.J.'s uncle's house before dusk.

T.J. had purposely misrepresented his description of the neighborhood. It was nearly all Black, but middle-class, with clean brick, two-story homes, not the rough ghetto T.J. had suggested.

Sean felt uneasy, out of his element. "If you can manage your bags, I'll split and see you at 9."

"No way, Irish. I wouldn't do that. If you leave without meeting Uncle William an' his family, then they'll think you're some kinda white tight-ass, like I already know you are. They treat white folks pretty good. Remember, my cousin Jessie was with the 101st. He got hisself killed in '69. He had some white buddies too. Just don't tell them you a po-lice an' you'll do fine. Leastwise say 'hi,' or they'll be insulted."

Sean was reluctant, but he helped T.J. carry his luggage onto the porch.

T.J. rang the door bell. Suddenly, the door burst open, and a middle-aged couple pounced on T.J. with hugs and kisses.

Uncle William was a huge man with a very deep voice. Sean's initial impression was that of a Black Santa, without a beard. His aunt was an attractive, well-dressed, well-spoken woman.

"Lord have mercy, look at this boy, William! He's looking fine. We're proud of you, T.J. I see that you took good care of yourself in that place."

Sean would rather have said a brief hello and make a break for the car. But they led him inside the home to meet the entire family.

After each family member hugged and greeted T.J., they were introduced to Sean. There was Uncle William, Aunt Virginia, cousins Billy, James, Kathleen, and Diane. The Preston family greeting was far warmer than Sean had anticipated or was led to expect from what T.J. had said.

Amidst the noise and confusion of the greetings and introductions, Sean was instantly attracted to T.J.'s cousin Diane. She was 24 and in her last year at the city college. Her features were soft. She had beautiful skin and a rather light complexion. Her dark eyes sparkled with a look of charm and obvious intelligence.

With everyone else huddled around T.J., Sean moved to where Diane was standing.

"Your dad said you're a senior at the city college. What's your major?"

For a moment, Diane seemed somewhat surprised at Sean's interest. She then decided he merely wanted to make conversation. Diane would help Sean's discomfort with small talk. "My major is social science, with a psych minor. I'd like to get a government job in the social services area when I graduate."

Sean politely nodded. He tried not to sound condescending. "I majored poly sci for my undergrad degree. My grad degree is in public administration."

Diane smiled. "Do you work for a government branch?"

Sean remembered T.J.'s warning about his job. He cleared his throat with a nervous cough. "Ah, yes, I work for the City of Detroit. If you have a choice, go federal. More security and better pay."

T.J. walked up to Diane and gave her a hug and a kiss. "Look at you, girl! You grown up to be a fine-lookin' woman. I bet you gotta chase the men away with a club. Pretty soon, you get your degree like your mama and Billy."

Now Sean was totally confused. T.J. had painted this image of a Black family in the center of the D.C. ghetto. Instead, he stood in the attractive living room of a middle-class home, with college graduates. Then, T.J. blew his oars out of the water.

"Diane, I heard my friend Irish here say he works for the city. He's just being modest. Why ol' Irish, he's a po-lice commander, in charge of a whole precinct. He figures 'cause he's white and a po-lice, you all won't like him."

The entire house went silent for a moment, the longest moment Sean could recently remember. No one spoke, coughed, or even moved. Sean could feel his face flush and he started to plan his quickest exit from the Preston home.

Suddenly, everyone in the house was falling over in laughter, obviously at Sean's expense.

T.J.'s Uncle William put his massive arm around Sean and gave him a hug. "Irish, T.J. called us and said he was going to set you up for some funnin'. My son Billy is a Washington D.C. police officer, and James is with the National Parks police, waiting to get on the D.C. force. T.J. knew you'd be nervous, not wanting to offend us. So, he set you up and we had to play along, at least for a while."

They all began to laugh again. This time Sean laughed too, laughing at himself. His own preconceived ideas made T.J.'s set-up painfully easy.

Sean apologized to Diane. "I guess I put my foot in my mouth mid-stereotype. After what T.J. had said, I didn't want to offend anyone."

"Would you have offered the information without T.J.'s warning?"

Sean paused and smiled. "Probably not, at least not until I knew you better."

Uncle William put his arm around T.J. "You know, Irish, having this man with us is like having a bit of my oldest boy Jessie back in the house. They were a great deal alike, even looked alike; both of them full of the dickens."

William Preston walked T.J. and Sean into the dining room. He sat them down and placed a full bottle of expensive whiskey on the table with three shot glasses. "Time for a few manly toasts. Billy, you and James get a glass and sit with us. We've got to welcome our boy T.J. and his friend Irish to D.C. the proper way. You do drink, don't you, Irish?"

"Yes, sir, Mr. Preston. I've been known to raise a glass or two on a regular basis."

"Irish, you call me William. The only Mr. Preston in this house was my daddy, and he's been long dead."

Diane sat in the chair next to Sean. She sipped from a glass of white wine. "Let yourself off of the hook, Sean. Black folks can stereotype too. Such as assuming you drink because you're Irish."

Sean watched her father fill a shot glass with whiskey. "Good point, Diane, but in this instance his stereotype was far more accurate than mine."

They toasted everyone from their beloved lost son Jessie to Pope John Paul.

Mrs. Preston wouldn't allow Sean to leave until he had eaten dinner, to help soak up their alcohol intake.

Sean checked into his hotel room, shaved, showered and changed. As 9 p.m. approached, with the combination of the pure excitement and the balanced, solid dinner at the Preston home, Sean was, in fact, sober.

Sean checked himself one last time in the room's full-length mirror. Fourteen years ago they had known him as a baby-faced Grosse Pointe preppie. That night, he wouldn't let them down. He still had a baby face and didn't look his age. For their initial reunion, Sean dressed in a navy blue blazer, buttondown light-blue Oxford shirt, grey slacks, a red tie, and black penny loafers. He stuck his snub nose .357 in his side waistband.

Sean's palms were sweating on the elevator ride to the lobby. He strode across the lobby to the hotel lounge. He entered the darkened lounge and stood for a moment, his eyes adjusting to the dim light.

A once-familiar voice came from a candle-lit booth to his left. "Look at that guy. He looks like a FNG to me. He'll probably go and get himself a medal his first night here, too."

Sean walked toward the sound of Yance's voice. "You fucking attorneys are all alike. Always distorting the facts. If you recall, Counselor, it was my third night in-country that I got the medal!"

Sean stood in front of the booth. Yance, looking every bit the successful corporate lawyer, was wearing an expensive three-piece suit. He stood effortlessly, despite one artificial leg. He leaned across the table and gave Sean a hug.

"Irish, this older gentleman flew all the way from the Sunshine State to join us. Allow me to reintroduce Lt. James A. Fox."

The Lieutenant stood and he and Sean exchanged a masculine hug. Fox, nearly 40, was still trim although starting to grey at the temples. He looked tanned and healthy. His expensive suit was custom-made and perfectly fit the successful Jewish businessman from Florida.

"It's been a long time, Irish. This night is better than the one when we said good-bye at the firebase LZ."

"So far, Lieutenant. But if we hang around with these two guys for a few days, we're bound to step in some shit."

T.J. was wearing his new suit, and he looked fit and well-groomed. No one would take him for a man out of prison less than a month.

T.J. held out his palm and Sean slapped it as he sat down.

Yance shook his head. "Look at that, Lieutenant. Irish has been with T.J. for a few hours and he's already got him acting like a Soul Brother."

Sean waved to their waitress. "Yance, if you're going to survive in Detroit these days, you've got to have Soul."

"Damn, Irish, you look more like you've just come from the country club than like a cop."

"Bite my ass, Counselor. When we're not on duty, they let us dress like normal people."

T.J. grinned and sipped from his drink.

"Yance, you know how preppie this boy is? Why, I seen that he's even got them little alligators on his po-lice uniform. You remember how he was out in the bush and in Hue City? Everybody else, all they talked about is gettin' some pussy. Irish, he talked about his preppie sports car and taking a shower. Cleanest boy I ever known, I swear."

An hour later, the four men took the elevator to Yance's penthouse suite. They had broken the ice in the lounge with small talk. They were all comfortable.

The suite was equipped with a fully-stocked wet bar and it looked like a well-furnished apartment.

T.J. walked in and gave the suite a quick inspection. "Oooh, my man Yance, does he know how to go first cabin, or what?"

Yance had a pitcher of martinis for himself, a bottle of Canadian Club and ice for Sean, vodka, tonic and limes for Fox, and T.J. drank his Jack Daniels directly from the bottle.

The men sat in an informal circle. Coats and ties came off as they laughed and talked together, recalling both funny and tragic events from 14 years in their past.

For a while, they split into twos. Yance and T.J. talked of their time together in Vietnam before they were joined by Sean and the Lieutenant. Sean and Fox talked about their experiences after Yance and T.J. had left Vietnam. Later, they had T.J. explain how it was in Vietnam during his second tour.

The men were getting drunk, but their conversation remained orderly and they seemed to make sense, in spite of their alcohol intake.

T.J. got to his feet. "I want you men to know I appreciate my being here with you three. You are all successful an' all, and I just got out of prison."

Yance spoke before the others could.

"Sit your ass down, T.J. The difference between us is only in this world. Over there, over in Vietnam, we were all the same. You came back here after two tours and didn't have shit going for you. Me, the Lieutenant, Irish, we had families with money, connections and the will to babysit our sorry asses until we got our heads back on straight.

"I lose my leg, get home in '68, I feel so sorry for myself I don't leave my room for five whole fucking months. Then, my folks finally got me to go back to college again. I was so fried on grass most of the time, I almost flunked out. The campus cops busted me with a dime bag of grass. Back then, a dime bag was a felony.

"My father did his legal magic act and bingo, case dismissed. It's not even on my record. In my junior year, I met this professor, he's got no legs and only one arm. The man gave me religion. I got my act together, and with my father's help and money, I became a lawyer.

"What I'm saying, T.J., is that without my dad's horsepower, I'd be a one-legged vet ex-con selling pencils on some Portland sidewalk."

Jim Fox stood and went to the bar for another drink. "T.J., when I got out, my family had just moved from New York to Florida. I went to grad school, let my hair grow, had a beard, smoked dope, screwed every co-ed in Florida, and joined some Vietnam Veterans Against the War group on campus. My family put up with my silly shit for two years. Finally, I cut my hair, shaved, and decided to grow up again and be a man, like I was when I was with you people."

T.J. shook his head and took a big swallow of Jack Daniels. "Lu-tenant, you really went and joined one of them hippie, anti-war groups?"

"Yea, after Irish and I were wounded again, I was feeling some real fear. I didn't want to ever go back. I heard all the anti-war lectures in the classrooms and read the papers. They threw me out after I attended my first rally. Some 4-F college puke was waving this big N.V.A. flag in my face. I tore up the flag and broke his nose."

The men broke into loud laughter. "Yea, get some Lu-tenant, that's tight."

Yance studied his martini. "Ol' Irish, he seems to have been the only one of us who could come back to the world and be normal."

Sean joined Fox at the bar to get himself a fresh drink. "Normal? Yance, I haven't been normal since that first night we got hit at the firebase. I came back to the world and did all the expected things that seemed normal. You know how I became a cop? I had just been kicked out of class for calling some 4-F professor an asshole in front of his students and I walked past a recruiting van. Shit, it's a good thing it wasn't a fucking Marine recruiting van."

T.J. watched his friend. Some of Sean's excess baggage was already on its way off. "You know, you're a damn fine po-lice, Irish."

"Tight, so I'm a good cop. I was a good Marine and I didn't stay in the Corps. I've been going to see a shrink for over two years and I still don't know why I have a job that can get me wasted any day, instead of working for my dad's business making four times the salary. Maybe if I would have jerked off a year or so, I wouldn't be divorced and still feeling fucked up. Not me, Brother, the All-American boy had to do the right things. I'm 34-fucking-years-old. Do you know the last time some-one pointed a gun at me and was going to kill me? Last month. Not in '68 or '78. Last fucking month. Fifteen Decembers ago, T.J., sitting in a stinking open bunker during a rocket attack, we identified the differ-ence. We've all had the silver spoon and we've all needed it. You needed it, and it was never there. The only break you've ever received in life was being blessed with as fine a mother that ever lived. "

"No, Irish, I got one other break in life. I served in Vietnam with some damn fine boys. Those boys that survived and turned out to be damn fine men."

Yance raised his glass. "Here's to no more of this serious talk. I want war stories. Stories from the days when my belly was as hard as my dick and I didn't have to work on either to get them that way."

Fox sat back down. "O.K. Yance, around the room. One Nam story and one civilian story. You go first, Counselor."

Yance thought for a minute. "When we had been in Hue City about two weeks, after you were hit, we just finished one hell storm of a fire fight. Both sides are taking five. The N.V.A. are in this church yard about 50 yards to our front, behind a four-foot-wall. Our squad is spread out along a five-foot field stone wall, down the street from the courtyard. We know where they are, they know where we are. We've got a 81 mortar forward observer with us and we're waiting our turn for a fire mission. We're all crapped out. We're satisfied just laying chilly until we get some fire support. Some guys start to cop some Zs, others get a smoke or some chow.

"One of the N.V.A. in the courtyard starts yelling shit at us in pigeon English, but we can understand him. I swear, it was like those old war movies with the Japs. We hear this, 'Ma-leens eat shit', coming from behind their wall. We insult his mother and his sister and Uncle Ho. We're just yelling back and forth. Then, he says President Johnson is full of shit. The Gooks must have freaked, because we start cheering and slapping hands and yelling how we agree.

"Then, the Gook makes a tactical error. He says something about the Black Marines fighting white America's war. Now, T.J. is not laughing. He grabs Irish and orders him to frag the N.V.A. behind the wall, 50 yards away. Irish thinks he's kidding and starts to crap out again. T.J. boots him in the ass and hands him a frag grenade. Irish sees the look on his face and realizes T.J. is serious.

"So, Irish peeks over the wall to get his range and kind of rolls his shoulders to loosen up his throwing arm. The forward observer thinks we're jerking him off because he's watching the N.V.A. position through field glasses, and he thinks it's about 60 yards away. Irish gets into position and lets the frag grenade fly.

"The forward observer can't believe his eyes when he sees the frag clear the wall and land in the Gook's lap. When the grenade goes off, all hell breaks loose. The frag really pisses off the N.V.A. They figure we're at the Paris peace talks or something. We're all bunched up and real lucky they don't have a Vietnamese quarterback who can throw grenades 50 yards or any mortars, or we'd be in a world of hurt. But they do lay down so much rifle-, machine gun-, and R.P.G.-fire, that we're pinned down.

"Irish and his arm is all we've got to surpress their fire, so T.J. starts collecting everyone's frags for Irish to throw. After a half dozen, ol' Irish about has thrown his arm out. The forward observer gets so scared he nearly skyed out on us. He calls for priority fire mission, and the mortars make the whole church courtyard, N.V.A. and all, just disappear."

The four intoxicated men laughed and slapped hands.

T.J. took the Jack Daniels bottle from his lips. "Little cocksuckers could say what they want 'bout ol' L.B.J., but when he start talkin' that racial shit to me, it really pissed me off. It might have been white men that sent me to Nam, but it had been them same Gooks tryin' to kill me for the past year, not no white dudes."

Sean stirred his ice-filled glass of Canadian Club whiskey with his index finger. "If you were the one angry at him, why didn't you frag his ass? I was minding my own business, trying to cop some Zs."

T.J. took a long pull from his bottle. "'Cause you know I can't throw that far. Besides, that's the only reason we let your cherry, young, preppie ass in the squad in the first place. Hell, if you couldn't throw like you do, we'd have traded you for a clerk or a tight-ass lifer."

The men laughed together again.

"O.K. Yance, now tell us a Portland attorney story."

Yance thought for a moment, then a wide grin came across his face.

"When I first got out of law school, I was the junior lawyer at my father's firm. You know, initially I got drunk drivers, shoplifters, simple divorce cases, wills, shit like that. Well, I do this simple divorce case. This 30-year-old-lady finds out her hubby is dicking this secretary and taking her on business trips. She files, and she's my last appointment of the day, to sign the final documents. The meter is running, so I don't think much of it when she wants all sorts of bullshit advice.

"She's wearing a silk blouse with no bra. It's cool in my office and I'm trying not to stare at her nips. About the time all the office help leaves for the day, she starts to move around in her chair and her shirt is moving up. Well, guess what? No stockings, no panty hose, no panties. Ten minutes later, the lady is giving me a full view of the beaver, telling me how lonely she is while taking my picture. I got a lump in my throat and pants and I don't know what to do."

Sean's voice oozed with sarcasm. "So what did you do, Counselor, as an officer of the court and all?"

"Irish, you'll be proud to know I did the right thing . . . I gave her the high, hard one right there on my desk. Ruined the desk blotter. Had to buy a new one."

The small group of friends howled with laughter.

"Yea, gave the old blotter to a fish market."

"Outstanding!"

"My man, get some Yance."

They went around the room, each telling two stories. Sean told of the L.A.X. confrontation, then of his nearly frost-bitten pecker. Their conversation and laughter went on for hours.

Daylight filled the large suite. Yance, unsteady on his feet, staggered to the window on his way back from the bathroom.

"Shit, it's daytime. I'll be damned, it's 9 in the morning. I'm sure as hell glad the dedication ceremony is tomorrow. Today, they'd have to medevac us to the Memorial. Let's go down and eat something and hit the sack or the dedication will be for us."

The four men marched up Pennsylvania Avenue with a large group of other Marine Veterans in the unique, solemn parade. Most of the Veterans in the parade and along the parade route wore some part of their Vietnam-era uniform.

The spirited crowds that lined the parade route cheered, held up signs and waved small American flags.

The country had finally, formally recognized its Vietnam Veterans. Today, it was a tribute to those who had died. In 1984, when their statue was to be complete, it would be for all who had served. Some Vets were still bitter, feeling as though it was like throwing a birthday party for yourself. But the bands, crowds, and speeches helped ease that bitterness. They were all there to pay tribute to friends they had lost while in the very prime of their youth.

The Memorial itself was a wide "V-" shaped trench, cut deep into the soft slope of a green, grass-covered hill. The ebony walls of the Memorial were a sharp contrast to the soft greens of the hillside.

The ceremony complete, Sean, T.J., Yance, and Fox waited about 100 yards from the Memorial for the crowd to disperse. Even from that distance, they could see that the names of each of the men killed in Vietnam were cut deep into the slabs of solid black stone.

The four of them huddled together, as if drawing strength from each other, not unlike they had done in combat.

As darkness approached, the large crowd thinned.

The four of them had traveled many miles to be in D.C. during that special week. But somehow, that last 100 yards to the Memorial itself would be by far the most emotional and the most difficult.

Every man who passed them after leaving the Memorial site was in tears. They walked together down the brick and slab path, toward the center of the "V" trench.

There were assorted flags, flowers, photos and personal items at the base of each section of stone. Each represented something private from a living person to a name engraved in that section of stone.

Some visitors gently touched the engraved names. Others traced the names with paper and a soft pencil. Everyone in that trench was touched by the common bond of the huge, impressive, black stone wall.

Sean felt like an emotional time bomb. Not since Christmas Eve of '68, not since Henry Rubin's funeral, had he felt this way. The lump in his throat and heavy pressure in his chest made it difficult for him to breath normally. He couldn't stop his eyes from watering, and he was touched as he sensed the collective sorrow from the people around him.

Sean moved away from the others and found Brian Logsdin's name in the directory. He slowly walked along the memorial walls to the appropriate section of stone.

Sean could see the top of the towering Washington Monument off to his right.

He found Logsdin's name in the stone and touched the engraved letters with his fingers. The realism of seeing the name in stone sent Sean over the emotional edge. He could no longer maintain his self-control. He leaned against the cool black slab and wept. He silently sobbed and his chest heaved with sorrow, tears flowing freely, burning his face. It was as if he was finally at Logs' funeral.

Sean felt a large, but gentle hand clutch his right shoulder. He turned and focused through a tearful haze to see that it was T.J.

T.J.'s eyes were red and teared. His nose was running. "I see you've already found Logs' name. You go on ahead and have a good cry for Logs and all our friends, Irish. I know you didn't want to come to this, but I think Logs and the others would groove on us all bein' here together, paying our respects. There's a whole lot of good men with their names carved on this here wall."

"Why, T.J.? If we were going to pull out and let the N.V.A. take it, why did they have to die?"

"I got no answer for that, Irish. You know that better than me. You always been the smart one. Cold truth is that Logs would still be gone, even if we'd have invaded North Vietnam and won the whole war. If Vietnam was now our 51st state, Logs would still be dead. There ain't nothin' could bring him back."

"But Logs wouldn't have died for nothing."

"You're right, Irish. But 20-year-old causes don't take up a seat at the family dining room table, or satisfy a woman, or have a beer with a buddy. Don't mix up your grief for Logs' death with your frustrations about the way the war turned out. Think of one more thing, little Brother. If we'd have fought to win, this here Memorial would be over twice as big. None of these boys would be brought back and it makes no never mind now, when you're driving your new BMW and gettin' trim on a regular basis."

"Goddamn it, T.J. Don't you insult me."

"Bullshit! It only matters 'cause you let it matter. Have you a good cry and let it go. Never could figure how you could be a ghetto cop. So you care, so the fuck what? It's still eatin' you up, Bro. Let it go, before you do to yourself what the Gooks couldn't do in '68. Destroy your life."

Later, they sat together, looking at the Memorial in silence. They watched as hundreds of people continued to file down into the "V-" shaped trench, past the thousands of names engraved in stone.

Sean wiped a single tear from the corner of his eye. "What busts my balls the most is when they say we lost the war. Hell, our people were out of there over two years before the N.V.A. invaded. U.S. troops never lost a major contact. We killed more Gooks during Tet of '68 than we lost in 10 years. I know about the politics and how they say they wore us down and we pulled out. Bullshit. They didn't wear us down. They wore down all those lard-ass wimps in the Congress. The next time some asshole comes up to me and asks me how I feel about fighting in the only war America ever lost, he's going to the fucking emergency room."

T.J. reached into a large pocket of the O.D. green Vietnam-era jungle jacket he was wearing and removed a large plastic flask full of whiskey.

"Here, Irish. Since you're up on you soap box, have a drink. I don't suppose anybody else thought to bring along a taste. I figured we'd need it after today. Shit, I gotta take care of you same as I did when we was in Nam."

The three other men laughed and each took out a flask of his own. Yance unscrewed the cap of his silver flask and took a large swallow of the contents. "Oh yea, T.J., you took great care of us in Vietnam. That's why we've all got Purple Hearts."

T.J. took three swallows of his Jack Daniels. "You all got Purple Hearts, but ain't none of our names engraved in that big wall over there."

Yance raised his flask toward T.J. in a gesture of agreement. "You have a point there, my friend."

The Canadian Club in Sean's flask was as refreshing as the drink of T.J.'s Kool-aid had been in the bunker his first night under attack at the firebase. He turned toward the Memorial. "I propose a toast, a toast to every man and woman who went to that fucking place for their country, under any conditions. For those who died, are still missing, and those of us who made it back."

"Hear, hear."

There was a second of silence as each man drank. "Now a special toast. I toast the South Vietnamese Army. Poor little bastards, they really did lose the war. They don't have a Memorial. They either had to sky out, or have the N.V.A. shit all over them. Their dead are treated like traitors by the new government."

T.J. pretended to choke on a swallow from his flask. "I got to be hearin' things. Is Irish really saying something good about the A.R.V.N.?"

"Come on, T.J. We've all learned a hell of a lot since we were over there as kids. Almost all of their people were poorly-trained, poorly-led conscripts."

"Conscripts?"

"Drafted, and for longer than two years. I admit that while I was there, I didn't think much of them. But hell, we taught them to fight the way we fought, then Congress pulled the plug and the N.V.A. poured across the D.M.Z. and rolled right over them. We whipped up their little guerilla war into a full-blown conflict then bailed out on them. The government didn't really fuck us up that bad. T.J. was right when we were talking today in the trench. I get my tubes cleaned on a regular basis, drive a nice car, live in a nice house. The war really is over for me. What about the average ARVN grunts? I wonder what life is like for them now?"

Sean raised his flask in the direction of the Memorial. "To the ARVN, our brothers in arms, the real losers of all that bullshit."

The three other men raised their flasks and took a swallow.

Sean emptied his flask. "In honor of our fallen buddies, let's go get properly shit-faced. It is the very least we can do for them. I know my fellow Irishman Logs would expect nothing less."

Yance put his arm around Sean and emptied his own flask. "Yea, and they'd want us to get laid, too. We should get drunk and laid."

T.J. put his empty flask back in his jungle jacket pocket. "Just as long as we don't eat us no ham and lima beans. All them poor boys, they'd be turnin' over in their graves."

Sean pretended to straighten his clothing. "Clams. Clams, a lady, and a good buzz. They would make my buddy Logs proud of me."

A while later, the four men silently walked away from the Memorial toward their car. As they passed the American flag, Sean turned toward it and offered his best Marine hand salute. Without speaking, the others did the same as they walked past. None of them ever mentioned their mutual gesture of parting respect to the Memorial and all that it represented.

They left D.C. on Monday. Yance and the Lieutenant left by air, Sean and T.J. drove up to Boston. It had been time together the four friends would never forget.

They drove up to the well-kept corner pub in the heart of Boston's Irish neighborhood. It was late afternoon and the pub was still nearly empty in anticipation of the after-work rush.

T.J. looked around. "Don't look like this is a real popular place for the Brothers."

Sean adjusted his off-duty revolver in his pants' waistband. "More importantly, the Brothers probably are not real popular anywhere around here, so stay close."

"You mean like your shadow?"

"You said it, smartass, not me. I don't expect any trouble, but parts of Boston are like parts of Detroit. If you go walking into the wrong neighborhood, somebody may decide to use you as a door stop."

They walked past the long bar and sat on stools, across from the small informal memorial the Logsdin family had made for the son they had lost in 1968.

T.J.'s presence drew the attention of everyone in the pub.

A thick, middle-aged man in a clean, white apron approached them from behind the bar. "What will you boys be havin'?"

T.J. politely requested a draft beer.

Sean studied the chalkboard menu behind the bar. "I'd like a Guinness and an order of fried fresh clams. I had a good friend in the Marines that said you had the best clams of any pub in Boston."

"That we do, Lad."

Sean recognized the man's facial features. He was certain it was Logs' father.

The man called out the clam order to the woman at the grill area of the pub. He sat their drinks down in front of them on the top of the bar. Suddenly, his head snapped to look at the picture taken in 1967 of his son with his friends in Vietnam. It sat next to an oil portrait of Brian in his dress blue uniform.

"Mother, come here quick. I do believe we have two very important visitors."

The woman came from the grill, wiping her hands on her apron. "Now what's got your tail feathers in an uproar, Patrick?"

She glanced at the two young men at the bar and froze mid-step. "Sweet Mother Mary, if it's not T.J. and Irish come to see us. We've been thinking of nothing but Brian all week, because of the dedication. I recognized you both straight away, from that fine photo that you sent us, Irish, some years back." She leaned across the bar and hugged them both. Sean had placed a $20 bill on the bar. She pushed it back at him. "Your money is no good here, Lads. You two go set yourselves down at that table in the corner. I'll call in some help and Patrick and I will join you in a bit. Bless you for stopping to see us. We've got so much to ask you about our son and how his friends are doing now."

They talked and drank and sometimes cried together, early into the next morning. If the Memorial dedication had been Logs' personal funeral for Sean, the visit to his parents' pub was the wake.

After the alcohol consumption of that night at the pub, they decided to take a room and leave for home early on Wednesday.

Sean couldn't explain the relief he experienced on the ride back to Detroit. The two friends talked and sang along with the tapes, and for a few hours they were 20 again.

By December, Sean was busy with his duties, commanding the greatly-improved 13th Precinct.

T.J. had moved to D.C. and was busy dating and learning a new trade.

Cousin Billy had introduced T.J. to a "nice girl," and he thought this relationship was something special.

———————

Sean sat across from the young psychologist. He was relaxed and he made no effort to hide the tears in his eyes when he described the emotions he had felt during his trip to the Vietnam Memorial in D.C., and to the little pub in Boston.

Dr. Ireland rubbed his mustache with his index finger and relit his pipe.

"Well, Sean, we've been seeing each other for some time now. You've come a long way from that hard-ass, macho cop who first walked into my office. If you had to sum up all that we've learned in the past two years, how would you describe it?"

Sean leaned back in his chair and smiled. "Damn Doctor, if I'd have known we were going to have a test, I would've studied."

The doctor grinned and shook his head. They had made giant strides, but Sean still blocked uncomfortable moments with his wise-ass humor. He had learned to use Sean's sarcastic comments to get to the truth. He had enjoyed his sessions with Sean. The once-troubled police officer had made considerable improvement and he obviously had tried to work with him to solve his own problems. "Come on, Sean, in a thousand words or less."

Sean's expression changed to serious.

"O.K. Most important is the identification of my dual life. There is the professional, successful 'me' and the personal, insecure 'me.' At work, I don't believe there is any task I can't master. In inter-personal relationships, I believe they will fail so I live out the self-fulfilling prophecy. I'm self-driven to be the best at everything because of my desire for my father's approval, which by paradox I have always had. I've got to separate my appropriate emotional control while on-duty from my appropriate emotional feeling of things when I'm away from the job. I've learned that it's no crime to feel sorrow, and to cry, and it's not too dangerous to feel good and to be happy."

Dr. Ireland rubbed his mustache again and made no effort to conceal his satisfaction. "Very astute, Sean. Are you certain you didn't study?"

"Well, maybe I did read over my notes."

"All kidding aside, Sean. I think we've come full circle. It's time to cut the cord and send you back out there alone. Is there still an unresolved issue that you believe necessitates more sessions?"

Sean thought for a moment. "Doctor, the violence thing, it still doesn't make any sense. Everyone tells me what a sensitive, gentle person I am, yet I can blow up some street punk and not even lose any sleep over it."

"You've said it yourself. You only feel bad about not feeling bad. Sean, I wouldn't worry about it. Considering your background, and as long as you carry a badge and a gun, I think it's a blessing. If you had terrible guilt about shooting people you believed should have been shot, you'd have gone mad or got yourself killed 15 years ago. If you ever get to the point where you feel nothing again, come right back to see me. Otherwise, just go out there and take each day as it comes, like the rest of us. And quit being so damn hard on yourself. If you want to be the best cop in the department, that's fine to a point. Just don't expect too much from yourself."

21

January, 1983—December, 1984

The intra-departmental memo announcing Sean's transfer as the Commander of the Armed Robbery-Major Theft Section was sent out the first work day of the new year.

Sean had a backlog of vacation time on the books. He decided to spend a week at the large Kelly condo in Ft. Myers, Florida to celebrate his transfer. Homicide and Robbery were the assignment plums in the department's pudding. They were usually a stepping stone to a desk on the Third Floor. Sean had secretly declined Perry's offer to command the Narcotics Section the previous Fall. He gambled on a better offer and the gamble had paid off when the Robbery C.O. decided to retire.

Sean dried himself with a beach towel. He had cooled himself with a dip in the ocean after a five-mile jog along the hard sand of Ft. Myers Beach.

He dropped into a lounge chair and leaned back to soak up the warm sunshine. He glanced through the newspaper and read that Detroit was getting clobbered by a mid-Winter snow storm. He put down the paper and turned his face back toward the sun in appreciation.

Despite the onslought of home cooking from Grama Kelly, Sean maintained his weight with a daily jog on the beach and by swimming laps in the condo's heated pool each night.

Sean tested the Ft. Myers night life but had trouble finding the right night spot for a 34-year-old man. He either felt like a chaperone at a place full of young adults or a visitor to Menopause Manor.

After 10 days of self-indulgence, Sean thanked his grandparents and drove his rented Firebird up to Tampa for his flight back to Detroit. On a last minute whim, Sean upgraded his ticket home to fly first class. He forced himself not to grin when he received his boarding pass. It was an appropriate way to conclude a trip on which he had totally spoiled himself from the onset.

Sean wore a three-piece business suit and carried his Dior trench coat over an arm. He didn't need the coat in Tampa's mild 70 degrees. He damn well expected he would need it when they arrived in Detroit.

Sean found his seat on the new wide bodied L1011 and settled in for the takeoff. The first class section was nearly deserted. Sean stared out of his window at the colorful Florida sunset, as the big jet began to taxi. He would miss the beautiful weather, but he was anxious to get back to Detroit so he could start his new assignment. He tugged on his suit vest. It still fit well. It would be a pleasant change to work in a suit everyday again, instead of the police uniform.

The friendly flight attendant had to repeat herself to get Sean's attention. "Excuse me, sir. May I get you something to drink as soon as we're airborne?"

Sean turned and looked up at the tall, attractive blonde. "Sorry about that. Yes, a Canadian Club and water, please. I'll need something to take the edge off of the culture shock of leaving this weather for Detroit's."

She smiled and wrote down the request. "It'll be worse than jet lag. I was in the storm last week. You show up there with your tan and you could get tarred and feathered."

Sean was facinated by the brightness of her large blue eyes. "You can't leave my grandparent's place without a tan, another five pounds, or both. If you do, they think you didn't enjoy yourself. So, the tan is simply a gesture of respect."

She made certain his seat was forward and his seatbelt was buckled. "Good excuse. I like it. Just don't try it on a couple of local boys with their car stuck in the snow. The cute explanation could be more dangerous than any threat of skin cancer." She turned and walked to her seat for the take-off.

Sean looked back out of the window. The jet roared down the runway and lifted off the concrete. The pilot pointed the plane to the north and it smoothly gained altitude. As the jet climbed into darkness, Sean turned away from the window and searched for his place in his paperback book.

The attractive flight attendant returned with his drink on a tray.

"If you really want to take the edge off, you'll need a couple of these. The pilot says we'll land on schedule, but they expect a couple more inches of snow tonight in Detroit."

Sean smiled and shook his head in mild disgust. "Typical welcome home for me in the Winter. Could it be punishment for the tan?"

She smiled. She felt comfortable with the man in the three-piece suit. He had a sense of humor and seemed to be more intent on being friendly than flirting. "That's alright. Wind burn helps the color last."

After the in-flight dinner, she brought Sean an after-dinner drink.

With the first-class section nearly deserted, she had a few free minutes and sat next to him.

Sean put down his book and turned toward her. He read her name plate on her suit jacket. "So tell me, Cheri, which exciting place do you call your home port?"

She grinned, "The same exciting place that you do. My father taught at U of M for 30 years. He's semi-retired and my folks live in Rochester, Michigan, where he's a part-time professor at Oakland University. I have a condo in Dearborn."

Sean felt strangely comfortable with the attractive flight attendant. There was not the normal barrier which seemed to exist between a man and a woman when they first begin to talk together. "Do you like being an attendant?"

The young woman pretended to look around to see if anyone was close enough to hear her answer. "Well, let's say the thrill wore off after about six months. I received my teaching certificate from U of M, but I couldn't find a teaching job anywhere that paid enough to pay the bills. My folks are getting up there in age and I really didn't want to leave Michigan. So, I joined the airlines a couple of years ago. Now I feel like an over-qualified, over-educated waitress in the sky. The travel and hours can get real old, but it beats working in some lounge."

Sean extended his hand in an introduction. "My name is Sean Cavanagh. I live on the far Eastside."

She smiled and shook his hand. "Cheri Remington. I'd better check and make certain everyone up here is all set. We've got to keep you first-class folks happy, you know."

Sean looked back at his book. "I'm here by default. I'm sort of celebrating something at work so I decided on first cabin for a change."

Ms. Remington was somehow impressed by the simple comment. Sean looked as though he fit the first-class section, yet he made no effort to impress her by admitting he would be in the coach section under normal circumstances.

After another quick check, Ms. Remington sat next to Sean again.

"The captain says we're on time but it's snowing like crazy. I brought you another drink. Considering the weather you've just left, I thought you might need a bracer for the long ride in the snow to the Eastside."

Sean put his book down and thanked her for the drink. "Ms. Remington, since we both have metro-Detroit as a home port, maybe we could have dinner sometime while you have a few days in town?" The wedding ring inspections had been made during the first conversation.

"I'm sorry, Mr. Cavanagh. I have a personal policy to never date crew members or passengers. I have this recurring fear that the guy's family will show up at the gate to surprise him, like in the movie."

Sean took out one of his new business cards and wrote his home phone number on the back. "I've been divorced since '76. If you change your mind and want to take a chance that I'm not Mr. Goodbar, give me a call. I'll bring my divorce papers and even a note from my Mom. I'm sure that you ladies get hit on all the time. I respect your caution. I'm not usually this bold, but it's only a three-hour flight."

Cheri Remington inspected his business card with an expression of disbelief on her face. "You're a Detroit Policeman?"

Sean couldn't help but to roll his eyes. "Yes, but my parents were married when I was born and they let me through the front door of most public places."

"I'm sorry. I didn't mean it that way. I've had such little personal contact with the police. You just don't fit my stereotype, I guess."

Sean smiled at her obvious shock. "With shorter hair and a mustache, I'd look just like two-thirds of the cops in the U.S., if I was in uniform."

She tucked his business card in her jacket pocket. "Commander? How does that compare with the guys you see riding in the cars?"

"How does the pilot compare with a flight attendant?"

"I get the idea. I've got to scoot. We'll be in initial approach soon. Enjoy your drink."

It was still snowing as the big jet touched down for a routine landing. The plane taxied slowly to the passenger tunnel leading to the terminal gate.

Sean put on his suit coat and trench coat. He filed down the aisle with the other passsengers toward the hatchway, past the smiling crew of flight attendants. He leaned close to Cheri as he passed. "Thank you for the pleasant flight, Ms. Remington."

She put her hand in the pocket where she had placed his business card.

"You're welcome, Mr. Cavanagh. I'll be in touch."

As Sean disappeared down the tunnel, Cheri's fellow flight attendant spoke to her under her breath. "He seemed nice and he's cute. Do you know him?"

Cheri continued to nod and smile at the departing passengers. "Not yet, but I think that I'm going to."

———————

Sean's first day as the Commanding Officer of the Robbery Section was more of a reunion than an introduction. There was little turnover within the coveted unit. The majority of the veteran corps of detectives had remained the same.

Sean spent the first few hours of the morning personalizing his small office. They had given the walls a fresh coat of institutional white paint for the changing of the guard. Sean had his own high-back office chair moved from his office at the 13th Precinct.

Sean locked the stack of the Section's personnel files in a file cabinet. He would review each of them at length to get to better know each member of his new Section. He knew he'd make some changes, but unlike his assignment at the precinct, he would wait a few weeks. He wanted the dedicated veteran cops of the Robbery Section to become accustomed to having him in the C.O.'s office before he made any changes. Sean was one of the youngest members of the Section, even though he was the C.O.

Just before noon, there was a loud knock at his office door. Homicide Cmdr. Hail and Gary Burger entered. He exchanged brisk handshakes with both men and there was some back-slapping.

"Look at the kid, will you, Boss? Still a goddamn fashion plate. Navy blue, three-piece, pin-striped suit, the boy still looks more like a rich, smartass lawyer than a copper. Well, pretty boy, the Boss and I are taking you to lunch to welcome you back to the Fifth Floor, if you can tear yourself away from the rigors of command for an hour."

"You know I'd never turn down lunch when you're buying."

Gary placed his arm around Sean's shoulder. "No, no, listen carefully. I said that Cmdr. Hail and I are taking you to lunch. You're buying. Besides, dressed like that, you should be embarrassed not to pick up the check."

Sean patted Gary's thick middle. "You've been on the rag ever since you lost most of your wardrobe when polyester went out of style. There's so much old polyester in your closet, it qualifies as a toxic waste site."

The following Saturday, Sean spent the afternoon at home reviewing the stack of personnel files and making notes. He had some ideas about partner realignment to improve efficiency. He still intended to wait a few weeks before he introduced any changes, to reduce the trauma. He had been lucky with his immediate changes at Number Thirteen. He wouldn't press that luck.

Sean answered the phone in his first floor den on the second ring. He recognized the voice on the line.

"Hello, is this Sean Cavanagh?"

"Yes. Is this my favorite over-educated flight attendant?"

"This is Cheri Remington calling from cloudy downtown Dearborn.

Now that your feet are on the ground, if you haven't changed your mind, I'd like to accept your dinner offer. I'll be in town all of next weekend."

Sean was pleased. He had not expected to hear from the attractive young woman. "I'm very honored that you'd break precedent by accepting my offer. Next weekend, can you hold a minute? Let me go check with the wife and kids to see if they've got any plans."

Cheri let the ribbing pass with a polite laugh. "I like your wit, Sean. But have you ever been considered to be just a wise-ass?"

"Daily. Let's see, how about Friday night at 7? I'll already be Downtown."

"How about making it 6, and I'll meet you somewhere, since Downtown is sort of halfway."

"You are sharp, Ms. Remington. Separate cars on the first date. That way if it turns into a bomb, either one of us can make a quick escape."

"I hope you don't take this personally, or think that I'm paranoid."

"Paranoid? No, Cheri. The only people more paranoid than single cops are married cops. The lounge on the top of the Plaza at 6. Alright?"

"I'll be there. I'll be standing at the doorway smiling and welcoming everyone onto the elevator. Old habits are tough to break."

The following Friday evening, Sean arrived at the lounge early to assure them a table. He wore the same suit he had worn his first day in command of the Robbery Section. He hoped that if it looked good enough to impress his old partner, that it would satisfy the interesting, attractive flight attendant.

He didn't recognize her at first. Her hair was different. She wore a light grey dress which complemented her tall, slender figure. She held her trench coat over her arm and searched the crowded lounge for the one familiar face. She located Sean and joined him at the small table. She ordered a white wine and they broke the ice with typical first-date small talk. Their conversation was naturally spiced with an on-going exchange of wit. Sean felt challenged. He'd have to stay on his toes with Ms Remington. The witty exchanges were not in the form of a joust, they made their conversation entertaining and comfortable from the onset.

After dinner, they returned to the lounge to a table with a view of the river.

Neither of them privately could remember feeling as interested, yet so naturally at ease with someone on the first date.

Sean found Cheri to be intelligent, with a unique, worldly sense of humor. She seemed to have been exposed to a great deal of life experience, both good and bad, but she still seemed to be a sincerely warm and sensitive individual.

Cheri was impressed with Sean's candor and down-to-earth approach. The well-groomed man was an enigma. He was obviously well-educated and well-mannered. Yet, every element of Sean's occupation and past created different images. Those images were a stark contrast to the nicely-dressed man who sat across from her, with the witty smile and the spark of mischief in his blue eyes. A Marine combat veteran, all those years on the Detroit Police force, a divorce, broken relationships; it didn't add up. Despite all of the red flags, she was really at ease with Sean.

Sean looked out over the ice-clogged river and the Canadian shoreline on the far side. "Well, since I've bored you to death with my past, how about you? You explained why you fly the friendly skies. Are you a single parent, divorced, all of the above?"

Cheri stared at her wine glass. She smiled. "I'm sorry I made you ask. No, in fact, none of the above. I'm 27 and I've never been married. A hundred years ago they'd have called me an old maid. Now, I'm either a late bloomer or a free spirit, depending upon who you ask."

"Not even engaged?"

"Well, I was, but I don't think he ever was. I wouldn't qualify for the sacrifice of a virgin, but I've never lived with a man. At 27, I'm not certain whether that's self-control or a lack of choice."

Sean took a long thoughtful sip of his drink. "Well, with my track record, I'm not the one to pass judgement."

She smiled and touched his hand. "Come on, Sean, you know what they say, 'better to have loved and lost . . .' "

"That's a crock and you know it, Ms. Remington."

The couple continued their pleasant conversation and closed the lounge.

Sean escorted Cheri into the parking structure to her car. The navy blue Fiero was as clean and sharp as its owner. "Thank you for the escort, Mr. Cavanagh. Get in and I'll drive you to your car."

Sean pointed to his silver BMW down the next parking aisle. "Thanks, but I'm right there."

Cheri raised her eyebrows. "That's a bit high-ticket even on a commander's pay, isn't it?"

Sean dug in his trench coat pockets for his keys. "Like I said, I came into some money, and living in Detroit, my expenses are minimal. Every boy has his toys. That's mine."

"Are you rich?"

"Nope. Just comfortable."

"Good. Every rich guy I've ever gone out with turned out to be a jerk.

Here's my phone number and next month's work schedule. If you enjoyed this evening as much as I did, please give me a call and we'll try it again."

Sean smiled as he took the papers. "I was almost too afraid to ask for the verdict. Thank you. I will call. Is tomorrow too soon?"

Cheri smiled from behind the wheel of her new Pontiac. "I'm spending the weekend at my folks. How about Sunday night for the call?"

Sean leaned into the car and gave her a quick kiss. "Take care going home. Lock your doors. You know what they say. 'It's a jungle out there.' "

He watched the Fiero disappear.

Sean took the long route home and drove out onto Belle Isle park. He filled the BMW's interior with the sound of his favorite old Billy Joel tape.

He felt something special inside after spending the evening with Ms. Cheri Remington. The young woman was something more than just bright and attractive. He couldn't identify it yet, couldn't put his finger on the mark. But he was very thankful that he had chosen that specific flight to return from his vacation in Florida.

In the months that followed, the relationship between Sean and Cheri developed at all levels. There was something special about their friendship, their romance, and their physical relationship. It had not exactly been love at first sight, but their love had started as a mutual attraction and bloomed into a deep love and respect.

A divorced, Irish Catholic cop may not have been the Remington's first choice for their youngest daughter, but they accepted Sean and treated him well. The old English Protestant family was very conservative and rich with tradition. Sean felt that his grad degree helped him more in his communication with Cheri's parents than it had ever helped his career.

Although naturally shy at first, Cheri was immediately liked by the Cavanagh clan.

By Summer, Sean and Cheri were spending all of their free time together. Her out-of-town flights gave them more than enough time apart to do the personal things they had done before they had fallen in love. While she was away, Sean had time for sports and time to spend with his police friends. When she was home and Sean was on duty, she had time for her private activities.

On Christmas Eve, Sean and Cheri became engaged for a May wedding. The five months would give Cheri time to give Sean's handsome home the one thing it had always lacked, the subtle comfort of a woman's touch.

They attended the New Year's Eve party at his parents' home on Lochmoor. Sean found a full glass of champagne on a waiter's silver tray. He was amused by the knot of young women gathered around Cheri, inspecting her new engagement ring. He went into his father's deserted first-floor den at the rear of the huge home. He sat in his father's overstuffed leather desk chair and leaned back, taking a sip of champagne, savoring the liquid and the private moment.

Sean stood and walked to the rear French doors. He unlocked the doors and stepped outside into the cold night. The biting Winter wind soon penetrated his three-piece suit and gave him a chill. He looked up at the clear sky and the moonless night's dome of stars. He fought off a feeling of uneasiness. He could not remember any other time in his adult life when all was going so well. There had been brief periods of happiness with Lyn and Holly, but it had never been like this. He had Cheri, his career looked bright, T.J. was happy in D.C., and all seemed right in his world. Everything was going just fine and it frightened him. It was as though he did not know how to just relax and enjoy life, how to let himself be happy. He remembered what Lyn had warned him of almost a decade before.

Cheri's voice startled him. "Sweetheart, are you alright?"

Sean put his arm around her waist and gave her a gentle kiss. "Sure, Hon, I just stepped out for a breath of fresh air, started thinking and lost track of time."

Cheri held her warm palm against his cool cheek. "What could you be thinking about that is important enough to have you stand out here and catch your death?"

He gave her another kiss and led her back into the warmth of the den. "I was just thinking about how much I love you, Ms. Remington."

JANUARY, 1984
DETROIT

The Section's reception desk officer informed Sean that he had a long-distance call holding on line one.

Sean carefully sipped at his mug of hot coffee and pushed the flashing button on his desk phone. "Cmdr. Cavanagh."

There was a moment of silence. Sean could hear the familiar sound of long-distance static on the line. Engaged to a flight attendant, he heard it often.

"Commander, my black ass. Like I always tol' you, ain't never gonna be nothin' but a baby-faced lance corporal to me."

Sean smiled and put down his coffee mug. "T.J., you old Grunt! How in the hell are you?"

"I'm cool, Bro. That's why I'm callin'. Me and Shirley are gettin' married next month and I wanted you to know."

"Whoa. I don't know about that, Buddy. I think in good conscience that you better let me talk with her first, out of decency, and tell her all about you."

He heard T.J. laugh on the other end of the phone. "That's cool, an' bring your pretty lady so I can fill her in on all your shit. It would be a real interesting four-way conversation."

Sean took another sip of coffee. "Alright. I get the message. Well, am I invited, or is this one of those all-Black things?"

There was a pause. "For real, Irish? You'd come all the way to D.C. just for the wedding?"

"Of course I would. I can fly in, rent a car, and fly back in time to be back to work on Monday."

"Irish, Cousin Billy is the best man. He introduced us an' all . . ."

"Come on, T.J. I don't expect to be in the wedding party. You know that I've got the funds. Besides, I can't miss watching Shirley finally nailing down your wild ass."

"Ain't no woman alive gonna put a ring through my nose."

Sean laughed a knowing laugh. "Yea? Well, we'll talk again in a year."

There was an obvious tone of excitement in T.J.'s voice. "Damn, Irish, it'll be great havin' you here. You gonna be uncomfortable bein' around Cousin Diane?"

Sean's mind briefly pictured the image of T.J.'s attractive cousin. "No, T.J., I think that we're still friends and there should be no problem."

"Irish . . . I really love this girl. She really makes me happy."

"Chill out, T.J. That's the way it is supposed to be."

"I know. That's what scares me."

JUNE, 1984
DETROIT

After Sean returned from his honeymoon in the Virgin Islands, he suggested they be renamed for truth in advertising. Cheri received a transfer to work at the airline's office on Washington Boulevard. She was ready for a land-locked position.

Sean initially was not impressed by being included to the invitation list to city social functions and parties at the Mayor's mansion. He thought it came with the position as Robbery Section Commander.

When he found that the Black commander who had proceeded him had never been invited, he called for an off-the-record meeting with his old friend, Deputy Chief Perry Mann.

Perry was as candid as possible. He told Sean that even though the Mayor was fully aware of Sean's background and views, he liked the young white Commander's style.

The Mayor had heard of Cavanagh as he had moved up through the ranks, but took a keen personal interest in him since he had seen him at Officer Henry Rubin's funeral. The old-time politician was impressed with Cavanagh because he felt Sean possessed the unique toughness of a politician and yet he sincerely cared about his people, Black and white. The Mayor could live with Cavanagh's conservative, Republican views, and felt it was healthy to have Cavanagh in his camp. He had enough "yes men" of both races. With Sean, he could get the views from the opposite wing without having to leave the comfort of his own mansion.

It was big city politics, to use and be used. Sean knew that he'd never be a Deputy Chief without the Mayor's approval. He also had to admit that he and Cheri enjoyed rubbing elbows with Detroit's social register. If Sean was the Mayor's token conservative honkie, that was fine with Sean. Sean remembered what old Deputy Chief Bowman had told him; he would never be the street copper's voice on the department's Third Floor unless he played their game.

———————

For both Sean and T.J., the Summer of '84 was a special time. T.J. and Shirley were married at the Preston family church. Then they set up a pleasant little home in the same neighborhood. T.J. and Shirley wasted no time and they were expecting their first child the following Spring.

T.J. was a good worker. He had quickly learned his trade, and for the first time in his life, he had spending money in his pockets and pride in his work.

Sean and Cheri traveled from coast to coast during that Summer. Using her airline discounts and his accumulated time off, they traveled to San Francisco, San Diego, the Cape, and Boston, and spent several weekends at the Cavanagh cottage on Lake Huron.

The Summer of '84 was also very special because of the Detroit Tigers' championship season. The Cavanagh business owned season box seats which were used more by family members than customers that season. The Tigers had last won the World Series in 1968. Sean and T.J. made up for the championship year they had missed as youngsters while they were both away from Detroit with the Marine Corps.

In November, Sean and Cheri drove to D.C. for an extended visit, complete with a tour of the city, to spend time with T.J. and Shirley.

The solemn "V" trench dedicated in 1982 paid tribute to those who had died in Vietnam. The haunting bronze statue of three men frozen in combat, frozen in time, paid tribute to those who had served and survived. It was dedicatd in November.

T.J. and Sean attended the dedication of the Vietnam Memorial statue. So many good things had happened to each of them since they were there with Yance and their Lieutenant in '82. There were still the tears and the feeling of grief while walking down the trench, but it was much different. They felt better about the completed Memorial; they felt better about themselves and their lives.

For the first time since his return home, Sean felt he was finally beginning to cope with his feelings about Vietnam, his feelings about himself as a person. Life settled down to a level of comfort and normalcy that Sean had not enjoyed in adult life.

22

March, 1985—May, 1986

MARCH, 1985
WASHINGTON, D.C.

The day T.J. and Shirley's son was born, Sean received an excited phone call. T.J. had named his boy Tyler Lee Johnson, Jr. He told Sean that they were beginning a family tradition, one like Sean always had been so proud of.

While they had wasted no time starting their family, T.J. made certain that his own son came into the world with married parents.

T.J. had big plans for his son. He vowed to be a good example for his boy. The child would be proud of T.J., even though he had gone to prison. He would show his son that a man could overcome the worst things in life and still make a good life himself. T.J. had gone to war, then gone to jail. But now he could hold a good job and care for his family.

T.J. would show his son his pride in his own family and the importance of a special friend, such as Sean.

T.J. had become a deacon at his Uncle William's church and he played softball on a local bar team with Cousins Billy and James. He spent every day making up for the hundreds of days he had spent behind the tall brick walls of Jackson Prison.

DECEMBER, 1985
DETROIT

Sean had just cleared the front walk of the fresh snowfall when the familiar letter carrier passed. She handed him several envelopes and they exchanged polite conversation about the weather.

He was pleased to find a letter from T.J. amongst the stack of bills, junk mail, and Christmas cards.

T.J. and Shirley were bringing their son for a lengthy holiday visit to Detroit to spend time with his mother. It would be good to see his friend again and to see how much Tyler Jr. had grown.

Sean hoped that T.J. would be able to attend his father's annual New

Year's Eve party. He sensed that T.J. would be much more comfortable about himself now, than he was the first night he entered the mansion on Lochmoor, 15 years before, after his own son's baptism.

Sean laughed to himself. He'd make a Black preppie out of T.J. yet. He had bought him an Izod shirt and sweater for Christmas. Top Siders were next. His birthday was in March. At that rate, Sean thought, T.J. would have a Volvo and a sheep dog by the end of the decade. T.J., a preppie. The thought made Sean laugh aloud to himself. He was thankful no one had seen him or they'd be measuring him for a padded room.

JANUARY, 1986

T.J., Shirley, and Tyler Jr. were ending their holiday visit to Detroit and planned to drive back to D.C. the following day.

Shirley dropped T.J. at police headquarters. He met Sean at his office. They planned an early dinner, a few drinks, some conversation and Sean could still get T.J. back to his mother's house early enough for him to spend some time with her on their last night in town.

Sean drove his unmarked Plymouth police car to a riverfront restaurant. A wet, sloppy snow fell on the city. The weatherman predicted a warming trend and the snow was to turn to rain.

Sean's and T.J.'s friendship had matured along with them. There was no longer a sense of urgency during their time together. It was relaxed and comfortable now. No matter how long it was between their visits together, there was a natural ease between them. They had learned to let themselves enjoy their unique friendship, in the same way they had learned to enjoy the rest of their lives.

At the restaurant, they ate steaks, laughed and enjoyed the river view and each other's company.

T.J. managed to speak over a mouthful of baked potato. "Say, Irish, you heard from your boy in Texas?"

Sean took a photo from his wallet. "We talk over the phone about once a month. He's coming to visit for a few weeks this Summer."

T.J. inspected the picture. He broke out into a wide grin. The teenage boy in the photo looked like a young version of Sean. "He playin' any sports?"

Sean replaced the picture in his wallet. "He's playing J.V. ball. He's a good-sized kid for his age. He plays cornerback and strong safety."

T.J. laughed and slapped his knee. "Oh my, ain't that something! Your boy a defensive back. That would never have happened if he hadn't moved to Texas."

Sean grinned and stared out of the window at the river. "No, I wouldn't push him to play quarterback or even to play. Football is an ass-kicking sport once you get to high school. A kid can only play at that level if he really wants to."

"You warning me about not pushing Tyler Jr. if he don't wanna play?"

Sean smiled and took a sip from his drink. "Sorry, I'm not the one who should be handing out fatherly advice."

"Bullshit, Irish. It's damn fine advice. Chill out, Bro, don't start to get down on yourself. Besides, ain't nothin' says you can't have you a baby now. Me and Shirley gonna do it again. Hell, you an' me ain't too old. The way I figure, we're finally grown up enough in our heads to have kids."

"Yea, I know, T.J. Cheri and I talk about it all the time. I think my being a cop is what stands in the way. The violence of the job really does a number on her mind."

T.J. cut into his steak again. "Well, what do you expect from the girl? You've been in some terrible shit since you pinned on that badge. Even a big wheel in the department, being a cop is a damn violent way to make a living. You and Cheri will decide to do what's best. She's a damn fine woman, Irish."

Sean watched the light reflect off of the ice in his drink glass. "Listen to us, T.J. We certainly have come a long way from the way we talked about girls when we were 19 and our dicks were hard all the time."

"Brother, my opinions may have changed, but my dick is still hard all the time."

Both men laughed and slapped hands.

"T.J., when Denny is visiting this Summer, if you could visit your mom and spend some time helping him develop his defensive back skills, I'd really appreciate it."

T.J.'s expression became very serious. "Irish, for real? You'd want me to teach your boy?"

"Sure. He's heard so much about you, and he knows I think you are one of the best defensive backs I've known in-person."

"Damn, Irish, I'd be proud to work with your boy. Don't start talkin' too nice to me or I won't recognize you. Deal is, when Tyler Jr. gets big enough, you show him how to pass as pretty as you do."

"Wouldn't you be afraid he might turn into a sissy quarterback?"

T.J. grinned as he filled his mouth with his last piece of steak. "If he can throw like you did when he grows up, I'll take my chances. Wouldn't that be the shits, though, Irish! If my boy turned out to be a quarterback while your son is a defensive back?"

"Not too unnatural, T.J. We are blood brothers, remember?"

When the waitress placed the check on the table, T.J. reached for it and paid for their dinner and drinks. Sean didn't protest. He sensed that picking up the tab was important to T.J. He recognized that for the first time since he had met T.J., he was in a financial position to easily pay for their dinner.

It neared 8 p.m. as Sean drove on East Forest Street, taking T.J. to his mother's home.

They discussed that Sean and Cheri would visit T.J. and Shirley in Washington, D.C. in the Spring. Then, T.J. would time his Summer visit to Detroit with Sean's son's visit.

T.J. leaned back in his seat. "Say, Irish, no offense, but this here po-lice car sure ain't as nice as your BMW."

"No shit! It comes with the rank and it saves wear and tear on my BMW driving back and forth to work, especially in sloppy weather like this crap."

T.J. stared out of the side window at the passing ghetto streets.

"Brother, there are times that I still miss this tough ol' city. But most of the time I thank the Lord I got my black ass outa here."

Sean turned down the volume on the unmarked police car's police radio. "This old town has had more than its share of hard times. T.J., I really believe these old Midwestern, industrial cities are on the ropes. What happens to them in the next 15 years will determine whether they survive or turn into huge fucking ghosttowns."

T.J. wiggled in the seat. "Listen to me, Irish. You've paid your dues a hundred times over. You owe this city nothin'. If the ol' girl bites the dust, don't let her take you down with her."

Sean smiled and shook his head. "After all these years, you're still looking after me like when we were in Nam."

"Like they say, Irish, some things don't never change. Say, find me a dark spot. I gotta take me a wizz real bad."

Sean pretended to be surpised. "What, again? You've got to piss? I swear, T.J., you've got the bladder of an old woman."

"Naw, ain't true. I'm only like this when I've been drinkin'."

"Oh yea. Well, you're always drinking."

"Good point, but I still gotta go."

"We're 10 minutes from your mom's house. Can you wait?"

"Irish, I gotta go like 10 minutes ago. Get my drift? Now unless you want me to pee all over the front seat of your new po-lice car, you find me a place to take a leak. There, that alley up ahead, that will do just fine."

Sean also felt the need to urinate, but he didn't dare after his verbal abuse of T.J. "Be careful, T.J. This is the Seventh Precinct. I understand they consider public urination a serious offense."

T.J. bobbed his head and chuckled. "Dig it. Look at this neighbor-hood. I figure your po-lice got more to worry about down here than a man relieving himself in a dark alley."

Sean cut the car lights as they entered the mouth of the alley. "It's real dark in here, T.J. Don't get lost."

"Not to worry, Bro. I'll jus' follow back the drag marks my pecker leaves in the snow."

Sean suddenly became very serious and he grabbed T.J.'s arm, stopping him from leaving the car. "Look down the alley, T.J. That car about mid-block, do you see people around it?"

T.J. leaned forward in his seat and strained his eyes. "Get a little closer. It's hard to say from here, in the dark. Shit, check it out. Looks like they carrying rifles."

Sean grabbed the police radio mike and called for a marked car to investigate. He turned to T.J. "No, we'd better get out of here. I don't want to step in any shit with you in the car."

"Come on, I ain't no cherry. You're the po-lice, ain't you? So, go on ahead and po-lice."

Sean moved the Plymouth slowly toward the figures near the vehicle, mid-block down the dark alley. "There are two shot guns and a bandoleer of extra shells in a box in the trunk if this turns to shit."

T.J. had an excited grin on his face. "If you make a bust, do I get to be your deputy or somethin'?"

"Sure, I'll get you a fucking badge and uniform . . . Holy shit, T.J.! They all have fucking rifles."

Sean slammed the car into reverse and yelled into the police radio mike that they were in trouble. The rear tires spun in the slush on the paved alley and the vehicle barely moved.

The first volley of automatic-rifle fire exploded the windshield and blew off the mounted rear view mirror. The flying mirror struck Sean on the side of the head.

Instinctively, Sean fell across the front seat, drawing his .357-magnum and opening the trunk with the dashboard-mounted release button. T.J. rolled out of the car and crawled toward the trunk. After a three-second pause, their car was the target of a murderous barrage of assorted fire from the area around the vehicle in front of them and the rear yards to their left.

A bullet tore through Sean's upper left arm. Another round ripped through the car door and smashed into his left ankle. Glass from the shattered windshield rained on Sean as he radioed that they were under savage fire and an officer was down.

Sean heard T.J. fire one of the shotguns and he decided to use the cover fire as an opportunity to leave the riddled police car.

Sean received another superficial wound in the left shoulder. In a burst of anger-induced strength, Sean managed to turn on the vehicle's head lights and lunge out of the front seat onto the alley's concrete pavement.

The lights illuminated the dark alley, revealing four men armed with automatic rifles advancing down the center of the alley toward their disabled police car.

Sean sat in the cold slush. T.J. readied the second shotgun and they both opened fire on the startled gunmen that had been caught in the open by the police car's lights. All four men dropped in the barrrage of return fire.

Sean and T.J. crawled to the partial cover of an old garage and an alley trash dumpster. T.J. had been hit in the shoulder and the side. Both frantically struggled to reload their weapons. The gunmen had renewed their fire on the car, shooting out both headlights.

"Irish, what in the fuck is this all about? You got some strange ideas on how to show a friend from out of town a good time."

Sean raised up again and fired his magnum at the approaching muzzle flashes. "You're the one who had to take a piss in the first place, remember? I wanted to rabbit out of here. We must have driven up on one hell of a drug and weapons deal by mistake. How do you like being my deputy so far?"

T.J. painfully fired the shotgun toward the gunmen at the other vehicle in the alley. "Irish, no bullshit, promise me that if we make it out of here, you'll quit this po-lice job, go work for your daddy and get the fuck out of this city. Promise me."

A figure suddenly appeared at the rear of the police car. He fired, hitting T.J. once in the left leg before Sean's return magnum fire downed him. "I promise, T.J., brother to brother. Do you hear all those sirens? If we can hold out a little longer . . ."

A rifle shot hit Sean in the right side of his chest and the impact blew him back against the rusted garage door. The savage fire continued.

"Irish, Irish! You hurt bad?"

Sean struggled to stay conscious. He screamed as he sat up so he could still return fire. "Well, I'm not hurt good."

"Don't cop no attitude with me. I finally buy me a real leather coat and some fools shoot holes in it while I'm wearin' it. You know, Irish, we're getting way too old for this kind of shit."

"T.J., I'm really sorry about this."

"Hush, Brother. Kind of ironic, though. Spent most my adult life in prison and end up gettin' wasted 'cause I'm mistaken for a cop."

Two men reached the front of the police car. They fired into the dark confine of their cover and both Sean and T.J. were hit again before they could return fire and down the brash gunmen.

Sean was out of .357 rounds and he was wounded too badly to use a shotgun. He rolled over onto his side.

"Damn this, T.J. We finally got our shit together. I don't want us to die."

T.J. inched close to his dying friend. "Looks like we ain't got a lot to say about it now. You know, Irish, I love you like a brother. Hey, we gave 'em hell, though, didn't we? Not too shabby for a couple of ol' Grunts. We always gave 'em the best we had."

A man stood at the rear of the police car with a shotgun. The last sounds Sean heard were approaching police sirens and the roar of the firing shotgun. He felt T.J take hold of his hand and move to cover Sean's body with his own.

The first police car to arrive in the alley caught the man with the shotgun in its headlights. He made the fatal mistake of aiming the empty gun at the responding officers. The officers killed him while he fumbled to reload the gun he had emptied into the helpless bodies of T.J. and Sean.

Police vehicles soon filled the alley and adjoining streets.

The young crew stepped from their car and carefully approached the gunman they had shot. They began to inspect the battered, unmarked police car, nearly shredded by bullet holes.

The young Black uniform officer tightly clutched his flash light and made the gruesome find, up against the old garage, several feet to the right of the police car. The two bodies were entangled together, laying in a pool of blood and slush. He gently inspected the motionless bodies.

He nearly dropped his light from surprise. He called out to his partner.

"Mark, for God's sake! Get us some medical help right away. I can't fucking believe it, one of them is still alive."

After the radio call, the officer joined his partner. They stood together, looking down at the bodies, their hands still clenched together in a final gesture of mutual support.

Mark pushed his hat onto the back of his head. "I don't know about you, Marcus," his partner said. "But I've never seen anything like this in my life. I guess when it comes down to being real partners, it comes down to this, doesn't it?"

———————

Subsequent investigations revealed that Sean had unknowingly driven up on the largest narcotics and illegal weapons sale in Detroit in a decade. The Eastside's deadliest dealer had been warned of a possible "hit" during the transaction by persons posing as police. Although the tip was incorrect, it explained the savage attack on Sean's unmarked police car before either occupant even stepped from the vehicle.

The dealer had meant to make an example of the intended hit men, to have it serve as a warning to the rest of Detroit's underworld. The dealer himself, and eight of his men, died while attempting to prove his point. In fact, T.J. and Sean had not done badly for a couple of old Grunts. Against terrible odds, they came within a minute of being rescued.

MAY, 1986
DETROIT

It was abnormally bleak for a Spring morning. The sky loomed dark and overcast. It had been raining since before dawn. It was the kind of rain which promised to last all day.

The new, steel-grey BMW drove alone through the large, deserted cemetery. It slowly moved along the black asphalt roadway that snaked over soft rolling green mounds of the well-kept cemetery. The vehicle's deeply-tinted windows created the eerie illusion that it had no occupants.

The vehicle stopped. Then its engine was turned off. Then the windshield wipers. It sat silently alone at the side of the narrow road. The only audible sound in the solemn place was that of the steady May rain falling on the BMW.

Finally, the driver's door opened. Cheri slid out from behind the wheel. She stepped out and quickly opened a black umbrella. She reached back inside the car for a single rose. She checked her purse for her clean handkerchief, then slowly walked up the side of the gentle grassy slope toward the headstone.

The passenger door opened. Sean awkwardly lifted himself out of the car and balanced himself on his crutches. He had made it very clear when she picked him up at the hospital that morning that he wanted no help getting around. In the hospital since January, Cheri sensed Sean desperately needed to do things for himself, even if he risked falling.

Still not accustomed to walking with the crutches, Sean slowly followed Cheri up the slope.

They stood together, looking at the handsome, light-grey headstone. T.J.'s full name and his familiar initials were clearly carved into the smooth face of the stone.

Sean turned up the collar of his new trench coat in an effort to stop the rain from dripping down his back. He reached into the right trench coat pocket and removed a small American flag attached to a thin pointed rod.

Without speaking, Cheri took one of the crutches and Sean carefully and slowly bent over and placed the small flag in the soft soil in front of the headstone. When Sean was secure on both crutches again, Cheri leaned over and placed the rose next to the flag.

Sean had not covered his head. The rain mixed with the tears that freely rolled down his cheeks. He spoke to Cheri, but his stare never left the headstone. "I wish I could have been at his funeral. The man was like a brother since '67. God, Cheri, he died saving my life."

Cheri straightened his trench coat collar and gently patted his back. "Those were horrible days, Sean. The day they buried T.J., the doctors were still not certain that you would survive. Your father and the department made certain that he had a hero's funeral. The Marines even sent an honor guard. I know you would have been proud of the way it was done. I don't believe you'd have changed a thing."

Sean moved a step closer and ran his hand slowly across the top of the cool grey stone. "You and Dad picked out a beautiful headstone for him. I hope none of his family was insulted because I bought him this. They lose T.J. saving my life and all I can offer them is this in return."

Cheri put her arm around Sean's waist and gave him a gentle hug. "I talked a great deal with T.J.'s mother and the Preston family. They all know how close you and T.J. have been since Vietnam, despite all the circumstances. They could have never afforded a tribute like this, and they fully understand that it was your personal gesture to your friend."

Sean fought back a sob and struggled to speak clearly. "It's been almost 20 years that we became friends. Most of that time we've been apart, but this will be so different. I'm really going to miss him."

Cheri leaned over and kissed his wet cheek. "It sounds trite now, but I'm certain a part of T.J. will always be with you. The priority now is that you get fully recovered. You know that's what T.J. would want for you."

Sean was still very weak. His first day out of the hospital since the shooting, Sean was pale, with large dark circles around his eyes. His arms ached from the extended time on crutches on the uneven ground.

Sean leaned heavily on Cheri. "I have decided for certain. I am going to take the disability retirement and go to work for Dad's business as soon as I get the doctor's approval. With a couple of years of experience under my belt, he can decide what role I'll play when he retires in '88."

Cheri wiped the tears from her eyes. She also struggled to maintain her self-control. "You know how I feel about this, Sean, but I want you to be happy with your decision. All of the doctors have said that you should be 100 percent by the end of the year. The Mayor and Perry assured you that they are promoting you as planned. I love you and I want you to be satisfied with your decision. It will affect the rest of our lives."

Sean couldn't help but smile at his attractive, loving wife. No one wanted him away from Detroit more than Cheri. She could somehow stay objective so Sean would make his decision for all the right reasons.

"I've had a hell of a lot of time the past weeks to decide this, Kiddo. No, I'm all done being a cop in this town. Like Dylan's old song says, 'I've got to put my guns in the ground, I'm knocking on Heaven's door.' There are a lot of reasons; our relationship, Dad's approaching retirement, and last January, in a sloppy, dirty old alley, I made someone a promise."

They hugged one another and Cheri rested her head on his shoulder, covering them both with the umbrella. "If this is what you want, Sean. If you're certain."

"I'm certain."

"Your father has loaned us the Lake Huron cottage for the Summer. He thinks staying there will help speed your recovery. The lake, sun, sand, and my tender loving care is just what the doctor ordered. With his library, stereo, T.V., V.C.R. and my cheerful company, you shouldn't get bored. I've taken a leave of absence from work. If you do get restless, we can make a baby."

Sean could not hide his expression of pleasant surprise. "Make a baby, Cheri? Are you sure?"

"Yes, Sean, I'm very sure."

"What made you finally decide?"

She looked up at him and smiled. "You're not the only one who made a promise over the past few months. I'm going back to the car. We will visit here again before we go up North for the Summer. You stay for a minute and say goodbye to your friend. Then, I'll get you out of this rain and we'll go have a nice lunch."

Sean kissed Cheri on the cheek. "God, no more hospital food. If I even see a bowl of Jello I'll have a flashback. I remember how I hated ham and limas. Now Jello has taken over first place on my hate-list."

Left alone at the headstone, Sean crossed himself and said a brief prayer for his friend. He ran his hand slowly across the long top of the headstone. It was cool and wet to the touch. "We saw some shit together, didn't we, T.J.? You never have to worry about Tyler, Jr. being in need of anything. He'll go to college if that's what he wants. I'll make certain of that. I'll miss you, T.J., but you'll always be my brother."

Sean slowly made his way back toward the car. He stopped half way and looked back at the headstone. He was somehow comforted by the inscription carved in the stone below T.J.'s name.

A courageous man . . . who always gave the best he had.

THE END

GLOSSARY

Adam-12 — Jack Webb production of a 30-minute television series in the late 1960's. Featured idealistic view of duties of L.A.P.D. uniform police.

AK47 — Standard Communist assault rifle, 7.62 mm.

Arty, abr., slang — Artillery, 105mm cannons, etc.

A.R.V.N., abr. — Army of Republic of Vietnam, South Vietnamese Army, U.S. ally against Communist forces.

BITS, abr. — Basic Infantry Training Section, four-week phase of combat training after bootcamp and I.T.R.

Blind Pig, local slang — Non-licensed, illegal drinking and gambling establishment. Most frequented after hours of legal establishments.

Bug Juice, slang — Small plastic bottle of military issue insect repellant.

Charlie, slang — Derogatory term for enemy Communist personnel.

Chuck, slang — Derogatory term for white males, used in conversations between Black males.

Code, local slang — Originated from old police term Code 30, the 30-minute meal break during the eight-hour shift.

Crotch, slang — Term for the Marine Corps, only used between Marines in conversation.

Cruiser — Detroit Police assignment, four veteran officers, three plain clothes with uniform driver in large black marked sedan. Called "The Big Four" on the street.

D.M.Z., abr. — De-militarized zone, border and "buffer zone" between the countries of North Vietnam and South Vietnam.

Doggies, slang — Marine term for U.S. Army personnel.

D.O.S., abr., slang — Dead On Street.

Early-out — Early release from active service to attend college or start civil service job.

E-3, abr. — Enlisted pay grade E-1 through E-9. Marine Corps, E-3 is a lance corporal.

E-tool, abr. — Entrenching tool, small field shovel with hinge at the handle and blade.

F.N.G., abr., slang — Fucking New Guy.

Frag, abr. — Fragmentation hand grenade (M-26 or M-79) round. Verb, to frag, is to throw a hand grenade at a target. Later in the war, to frag meant to wound one's own officers or senior enlisted personnel.

Freedom Bird, slang — The commercial plane which takes troops back to the U.S. after Vietnam tour is complete.

Garrote — Lethal weapon consisting of a strong wire with a handle at each end. Designed to strangle victim to death from behind.

Gooks, slang — Derogatory term for enemy Asian personnel.

Gooner, slang — Derogatory term for enemy Asian personnel.

Heart, abr. — Purple Heart, medal awarded to personnel wounded or killed in combat area.

Hooch, slang — A Vietnamese house or small village dwelling.

I Corps — Pronounced "eye corps." Northern military sector of responsibility for South Vietnam.

In-country, slang — The time actually spent in Vietnam.

ITR, abr. — Infantry Training Regiment, four weeks of basic infantry training following bootcamp.

Jar Head, slang — A term for a Marine.

Jones, slang — A severe addiction, usually associated with heroin addiction.

Kegger, slang — A party where a keg of draft beer is the primary refreshment.

LAW, abr. — Light Anti-tank Weapon, U.S. disposable rocket launcher, single-shot, max. range 325 meters, 15-meter casualty radius. Shoulder-fired, primary use against enemy bunkers.

Lay Chilly, slang — To stop, freeze in your tracks, remain perfectly still.

L.P., abr. — Listening Post, overnight position of four personnel set out to protect the main force. Placed in enemy's expected route of approach. A very dangerous assignment.

L.Z., abr. — Landing Zone, for helicopters.

M-16 — Standard U.S. military assault rifle, 5.56mm.

M-26 Fragmentation Hand Grenade — 1.5 lb. hand grenade. More effective than old WWII "Pineapple" grenade. Fifteen-meter casualty radius.

M-60 Machine Gun — U.S. military, Vietnam-era, light machine gun, 7.62mm.

M-79 — 40mm grenade launcher, single-shot, 300-meter max. range, 15-meter casualty radius, varied type round. Known as the "Blooper".

M.A.C.V., abr. — Military Advisory Commmand Vietnam, U.S. advisors and liaison with South Vietnamese armed forces.

M.O.G., abr. — Municipally-owned Garage, a large building where city-owned vehicles are stored and repaired.

Motown, slang — Nickname for Detroit in 60's. Originated because R&B record company was based in Detroit. Also known as "Motor-City" due to concentration of auto industry headquarters.

Mule — U.S. small motorized wheeled vehicle. A platform on wheels, used to transport equipment and weapons. Sometimes mounted with a 106mm recoiless rifle.

Murphy Man, local slang — Street thief, mugger, often using a street whore to decoy a victim.

Mustanger, slang — A commissioned officer who has come from the enlisted ranks.

N.C.O., abr. — Non-Commissioned Officer, enlisted ranks from corporal through sergeant major. Pay grades E-4 through E-9.

N.V.A., abr. — North Vietnamese Army, regular army Communist troops sent down from North Vietnam.

106mm Recoiless Rifle — Breech-loaded, single-shot, direct-fire weapon, 460 lb., 1000-meter range, 25-meter casualty radius.

Ops, abr. — Operation, a military mission or assignment carried out by a unit.

Pogues, slang — Derogatory term for support personnel with non-combat assignments, clerks, etc.

Point — The lead position in a column. A very dangerous assignment in a combat area.

Puff, also Spooky — Prop plane gunship armed with several deadly, rapid-rate-of-fire weapons, 7.62mm mini-guns, 20mm guns, etc.

Reaction Force, React Force — Quickly organized force to respond to a crisis situation. A rescue or relief unit created to respond to an unexpected event.

R.P.G., abr. — Communist weapon, Rocket Propelled Grenade, single-shot, shoulder-fired, anti-tank, anti-bunker weapon. When used against personnel, approximately same effect as U.S. LAW rocket.

S.A.M., abr. — Communist anti-aircraft, surface to air missile.

Salt, Salty, slang — A veteran Marine or sailor. Also actions or equipment deplicting a long term veteran.

Salt Peter — A chemical rumored to be placed in military food and drink to prevent erections and reduce sex drive.

Satchel Charges — Backpack-sized explosive charge used to blow holes in protective wire barriers and fortified positions. Carried by enemy "sappers".

Saturday Night Special, slang — An inexpensive handgun, easily purchased at a dope pad or from a fence.

Skate, slang — To relax, rest, to have no duties or assignments. Also to goof off, avoid one's share of workload.

Skinny, slang — Correct and accurate information, the word. An update on the current situation.

Stand Down — To come out of the field for rest and resupply in a rear area, firebase.

Stars and Stripes — Small newspaper published and distributed by the U.S. military to its personnel.

3.5 Rocket Launcher — U.S. weapon, single-shot, shoulder-fired weapon. Like the WWII bazooka. Used most against bunkers and fortified positions.

Three-Heart Rule — Stipulation that any Marine receiving three Purple Heart medals in a single tour was rotated out of Vietnam.

V.C., Victor Charlie, abr. — Communist enemy personnel living in South Vietnam, local guerilla forces.

Wolf Ticket, local slang — A complex scam, con game, or lie.

Willie Peter, W.P., slang — A white phosphorus shell. When it exploded it created white smoke and burning phosphorus shrapnel.

X.O., abr. — Executive Officer, the second in command of a unit or a vessel.